Dear Reader:

Hemlock Bay is the sixth novel in the FBI series, and I'm hoping it will make your hair stand on end. Meet Tammy Tuttle and start praying. She becomes the nemesis of FBI agent Dillon Savich. If this isn't enough, Savich learns that his sister, Lily, has crashed her Explorer in an apparent suicide attempt. Or is it really a murder conspiracy by her husband and his family to gain Lily's very valuable paintings?

Enter Simon Russo, art expert, and longtime friend of Savich's. Together, Russo and Lily are thrust into ever-widening circles of danger that radiate from a notorious collector's locked room.

Savich and Sherlock are in top form. I hope you like Hemlock Bay. I further hope that it will make you want to hide under your bed.

Do let me know at P.O. Box 17, Mill Valley, CA 94942 or e-mail me at ReadMoi@aol.com. My website is www.CatherineCoulter.com.

Catherine Coulter

"I am really enjoying the FBI series (love to read about the Savich duo). I really enjoyed *The Edge*, *The Target*, and *Riptide*. BUT—*Hemlock Bay* is definitely my favorite."

—Merle Carter

"[*Hemlock Bay*] was FANTASTIC and I loved it. You are a WONDERFUL author. I hope that we can possibly see another FBI book."   —Janet Posey

"UTTERLY . . . TOTALLY . . . COMPLETELY . . . WONDERFULLY FAB-U-LOUS!!!! I finished reading *Hemlock Bay* in less than two days. I can't wait to read your next book."   —Phyllis Schumacker

"You are coming between my husband and me!! Recently he has been snuggling every night with *Riptide* and I have been snuggling with *Hemlock Bay*. Seriously, we love these books. You are a great author and our favorite."

—Alice Friebel

"*Riptide* was great. *Hemlock Bay* even better. Don't let Dillon and Sherlock ever retire."   —Frank Stone

"Once I started reading [*Hemlock Bay*] I was unable to put it down. If I had socks on, it would've scared my socks off. You sure kept me guessing throughout the entire book. It's a wonder I didn't chew my nails off."   —Ina le Roux

continued on next page . . .

"Vivid . . . titilating . . . a cliff-hanger to the end . . . blending charm, wit, and intrigue. The result is a fast-paced melodrama that is sure to keep readers turning the pages."

—*Naples Daily News*

THE TARGET

"You've done it again . . . Even more exciting. I've just read *The Target* in one day. I skipped lunch and could barely put it aside for even five minutes." —L. J. Gerstemeier

"I purchased and read *The Target*. Wow! Loved it! I gave the copy to my wife, who is not the avid reader that I am, and she could not put it down. It's the first time in thirty years of marriage I have seen her sit up late at night reading, unable to sleep over a book." —Bob Spense

"[Coulter's] central figures—wary, quietly resilient Molly; musically gifted Emma; and tough, decent Ramsey—make this an absorbing read." —*Publishers Weekly*

"Anyone who starts this book will immediately come under the spell of Ramsey and Emma . . . Coulter's biggest bestseller yet . . . [*The Target*] makes reading fun."

—*Fort Worth Daily Sun*

THE EDGE

"You've done it again! Another winner with *The Edge*! It was a late night until I finished but you kept me guessing until the end. I love your books. Keep it up."

—H. Tomlinson

"Wow. It took about twenty-one hours, of which four hours I slept, to read *The Edge* cover to cover. What will you do for encores? And to think I have to wait." —T. Johnson

continued on next page . . .

RIPTIDE

HEMLOCK BAY

CATHERINE COULTER

JOVE BOOKS, NEW YORK

This is a work of fiction. Names, characters, places, and incidents either are the product of the author's imagination or are used fictitiously, and any resemblance to actual persons, living or dead, business establishments, events, or locales is entirely coincidental.

HEMLOCK BAY

A Jove Book / published by arrangement with
G. P. Putnam's Sons

PRINTING HISTORY
G. P. Putnam's Sons hardcover edition / August 2001
Jove edition / July 2002

Copyright © 2001 by Catherine Coulter
Excerpt from *Eleventh Hour* copyright © 2002 by Catherine Coulter
Cover design and art by Marc Cohen
Book design by Julie Rogers

Visit our website at
www.penguinputnam.com

ISBN: 0-515-13330-2

A JOVE BOOK®
Jove Books are published by The Berkley Publishing Group,
a division of Penguin Putnam Inc.,
375 Hudson Street, New York, New York 10014.
JOVE and the "J" design
are trademarks belonging to Penguin Putnam Inc.

PRINTED IN THE UNITED STATES OF AMERICA

10 9 8 7 6 5 4 3 2 1

I wish to thank the following people at FBI Headquarters and at Quantico for their generosity and enthusiasm.

William Hayden Matens, *Special Agent, retired*
Thomas B. Locke, *Deputy Assistant Director, Inspection Division*
David R. Knowlton, *Assistant Director, Inspection Division*
Wade M. Jackson, *Unit Chief, Firearms Training Unit*
Gary J. Hutchison, *Agent Instructor*
Alan H. Marshall, *Special Agent, Indoor Range*
Jeffrey Higginbotham, *Assistant Director, Training Division*
Douglas W. Deedrick, *Unit Chief, Information and Evidence Management Unit*
Lester "wingtips" Davis, *Officer, National Academy Association*
Ruben Garcia, Jr., *Assistant Director, Criminal Investigative Division*
Kenneth McCabe, *Section Chief, Laboratory Division*
Michael J. Perry, *Firearms Instructor*
Sheri A. Farrar, *Deputy Assistant Director, Administrative Services Division*
Royce Curtin, *Special Agent, Hostage Rescue Team*
Stephen R. Band, *Unit Chief, Behavior Sciences Unit*

Lew Elliott, who teaches cops how to fight

I wish to thank my husband, Dr. Anton Pogany, yet again, for his excellent instincts and his eagle eye that never misses a thing—he remains the Editor from Hell.

To Ildiko DeAngelis, Director of George Washington University Museum Studies Program. She is very smart, very experienced in both law and art history, and has extensive knowledge of museum procedures both in the United States and abroad. She's answered every question I could come up with and provided me valuable insights into a very esoteric world.

She's also the best sister-in-law a body could have. Thank you, Ildi, for your time and sharing your magnificent brain with me.

Catherine Coulter

1

It was a chilly day in late October. A stiff wind whipped the last colorful leaves off the trees. The sun was shining down hard and bright on the dilapidated red barn that hadn't been painted in forty years. Streaks of washed-out red were all that was left of the last paint job. There was no charm left, at all.

FBI Special Agent Dillon Savich eased around the side of the barn, his SIG Sauer in his right hand. It had taken discipline and practice, but he'd learned to move so quietly that he could sneak up on a mouse. Three agents, one of them his wife, were some twenty feet behind him, covering him, ready to fan out in any direction necessary, all of them wearing Kevlar vests. A dozen more agents were slowly working their way up the other side of the barn, their orders to wait for a signal from Savich. Sheriff Dade of Jedbrough County and three deputies were stationed in the thick stand of maple trees just thirty feet behind them. One of the deputies, a sharpshooter, had his sights trained on the barn.

So far the operation was going smoothly, which, Savich

supposed, surprised everyone, although no one spoke of it. He just hoped it would continue the way it had been planned, but chances were things would get screwed up. He'd deal with it; there was no choice.

The barn was bigger than Savich liked—there was a big hayloft, and too many shadowy corners for this sort of operation. Too many nooks and crannies for an ambush, just plain too many places from which to fire a storm of bullets.

A perfect place for Tommy and Timmy Tuttle, dubbed "the Warlocks" by the media, to hole up. They'd hopscotched across the country, but had dropped out of sight here, in Maryland, with their two latest young teenage boys taken right out of the gym where they'd been playing basketball after school, in Stewartville, some forty miles away. Savich had believed that Maryland was their destination, no sound reason really, but in his gut he just felt it. The profilers hadn't said much about that, just that Maryland was, after all, on the Atlantic coast, so they really couldn't go much farther east.

Then MAX, Savich's laptop, had dived into land registry files in Maryland and found that Marilyn Warluski, a first cousin to the Tuttle brothers, and who, MAX had also discovered, had had a baby at the age of seventeen fathered by Tommy Tuttle, just happened to own a narrow strip of land near a good-sized maple forest that wasn't far from the serpentine Plum River. And on that sliver of property was a barn, a big ancient barn that had been abandoned for years. Savich had nearly clicked his heels together in excitement.

And now, four hours later, here they were. There'd been no sign of a car, but Savich wasn't worried. The old Honda was probably stashed in the barn. He quieted his breathing and listened. The birds had gone still. The silence was heavy, oppressive, as if even the animals were expecting something to happen and knew instinctively that it wouldn't be good.

Savich was afraid the Tuttle brothers were long gone. All they would find, despite the silence, would be their victims: teenage boys—Donny and Rob Arthur—dead, horribly mutilated, their bodies circumscribed by a large, black circle.

Savich didn't want to smell any more blood. He didn't want to see any more death. Not today. Not ever.

He looked down at his Mickey Mouse watch. It was time to see if the bad guys were in the barn. It was time to go into harm's way. It was time to get the show on the road.

MAX had found a crude interior plan of the barn, drawn some fifty years before, documented in a computerized county record as having been physically saved and filed. Kept where? was the question. They'd finally turned up the drawing in an old file cabinet in the basement of the county planning building. But the drawing was clear enough. There was a small, narrow entry, down low, here on the west side. He found it behind a straggly naked bush. It was cracked open, wide enough for him to squeeze through.

He looked back, waved his SIG Sauer at the three agents peering around the corner of the barn, a signal to hold their positions, and went in on his belly. He pushed the narrow door open an inch at a time. Filth everywhere, some rat carcasses strewn around. He nudged his way in on his elbows, feeling bones crunch beneath him, his SIG Sauer steady in his hand.

There was a strange half-light in the barn. Dust motes floated in the narrow spears of light coming through the upper windows, only shards of glass sticking up in some of the frames. He lay there quietly a moment, his eyes adjusting. He saw bales of hay so old they looked petrified, stacked haphazardly, rusted machinery—mainly odd parts—and two ancient wooden troughs.

Then he noticed it. In the far corner was another door not more than twenty feet to the right of the front double barn doors. A tack room, he thought, and it hadn't been shown on the drawing. Then he made out the outline of the Honda, tucked in the shadows at the far end of the barn. The two brothers were in the tack room, no doubt about it. And Donny and Rob Arthur? Please, God, let them still be alive.

He had to know exactly who was where before he called in the other agents. It was still, very still. He got to his feet and ran hunched over toward the tack room door, his gun fanning continuously, his breathing low and steady, his steps silent. He pressed his ear against the rotted wooden door of the tack room.

He heard a male voice, clear and strong, and angry, suddenly louder.

"Listen, you Little Bloods, it's time for you to get in the middle of the circle. The Ghouls want you; they told me to hurry it up. They want to carve you up with their axes and knives—they really like to do that—but this time they want to tuck you away in their carryalls and fly away with you. Hey, maybe you'll end up in Tahiti. Who knows? They haven't wanted to do this before. But it doesn't make any difference to us. Here come the Ghouls!" And he laughed, a young man's laugh, not all that deep, and it sounded quite happily mad. It made Savich's blood run icy.

Then another man's voice, this one deeper. "Yep, almost ready for the Ghouls. We don't want to disappoint them now, do we? Move it, Little Bloods."

He heard them coming toward the door, heard the scuffling of feet, heard the boys' crying, probably beyond reason now, heard curses and prods from the Tuttle brothers. It was then that he saw the huge, crude circle painted with thick, black paint on a cleared-out part of the rotting wooden barn floor.

Zero hour. No time, simply no time now to bring the others in.

Savich barely made it down behind a rotted hay bale before one of them opened the tack room door and shoved a slight, pale boy in front of him. The boy's filthy pants were nearly falling off his butt. It was Donny Arthur. He'd been beaten, probably starved as well. He was terrified. Then a second terrified youth was shoved out of the small tack room next to him. Rob Arthur, only fourteen years old. Savich had never seen such fear on two such young faces in his life.

If Savich ordered the Tuttles to stop now, they could use the boys for shields. No, better to wait. What was all that crazy talk about ghouls? He watched the two men shove the boys forward until they actually kicked them into the center of the circle.

"Don't either of you move or I'll take my knife and shove it right through your arm into the floor, pin you good. Tammy here will do the other with her knife. You got that, Little Bloods?"

Tammy? Her knife? No, it was two brothers—Tommy and Timmy Tuttle, more than enough alliteration, even for the media. No, he couldn't have heard right. He was looking at two young men, both in black, long and lean, big, chunky black boots laced up the front to the knees like combat boots. They carried knives and guns.

The boys were huddled together on their knees, crying, clutching each other. Blood caked their faces, but they could move, and that meant no bones were broken.

"Where are the Ghouls?" Tammy Tuttle shouted, and Savich realized in that instant that he hadn't misheard; it wasn't the Tuttle brothers, it was one brother and one sister.

What was all this about the ghouls coming to murder the boys?

"Ghouls," Tammy yelled, her head thrown back, her voice reverberating throughout the ancient barn, "where are you? We've got your two treats for you, just what you like—two really sweet boys! Little Bloods, both of them. Bring your knives and axes! Come here, Ghouls."

It was a chant, growing louder as she repeated herself once, twice, then three times. Each time, her voice was louder, more vicious, the words ridiculous, really, except for the underlying terror they carried.

Tammy Tuttle kicked one of the boys, hard, when he tried to crawl out of the circle. Savich knew he had to act soon. Where were these ghouls?

He heard something, something that was different from the mad human voices, like a high whine, sort of a hissing sound that didn't belong here, maybe didn't belong anywhere. He felt gooseflesh rise on his arms. He felt a shock of cold. He was on the point of leaping out when, to his utter astonishment, the huge front barn doors whooshed inward, blinding light flooded in, and in the middle of that light were dust devils that looked like small tornadoes. The white light faded away, and the dust devils looked more like two whirling, white cones, distinct from each other, spinning and twisting, riding up then dipping down, blending together, then separating—no, no, they were just dust devils, still white because they hadn't sucked up the dirt yet from the barn floor. But what was that sound he heard? Something strange, something he couldn't identify. Laughter? No, that was crazy, but that was what registered in his brain.

The boys saw the dust devils, whirling and spinning far above them, and started screaming. Donny jumped up, grabbed his older brother, and managed to jerk him out of the circle.

Tammy Tuttle, who'd been looking up, turned suddenly, raised her knife, and yelled, "Get back down, Little Bloods! Don't you dare anger the Ghouls. Get back in the circle, now! GET BACK DOWN!"

The boys scrabbled farther away from the circle. Tommy Tuttle was on them in an instant, jerking them back. Tammy Tuttle drew the knife back, aiming toward

Donny Arthur, as Savich leaped up from behind the bale of hay and fired. The bullet ripped into her arm at her shoulder. She screamed and fell onto her side, the knife flying out of her hand.

Tommy Tuttle whipped about, no knife in his hand now but a gun, and that gun was aimed not at Savich but at the boys. The boys were screaming as Savich shot Tommy through the center of his forehead.

Tammy Tuttle was moaning on the floor, holding her arm. The boys stood, clutched together, silent now, and all three of them looked up toward those whirling, white cones that danced up and down in the clear light coming through the barn doors. No, not dust devils, two separate things.

One of the boys whispered, "What are they?"

"I don't know, Rob," Savich said and pulled the boys toward him, protecting them as best he could. "Just some sort of weird tornado, that's all."

Tammy was yelling curses at Savich as she tried to pull herself up. She fell back. There was a shriek, loud and hollow. One of the cones seemed to leap forward, directly at them. Savich didn't think, just shot it, clean through. It was like shooting through fog. The cone danced upward, then twisted back toward the other cone. They hovered an instant, spinning madly, and in the next instant, they were gone. Simply gone.

Savich grabbed both boys against him again. "It's all right now, Donny, Rob. You're both all right. I'm very proud of you, and your parents will be, too. Yes, it's okay to be afraid; I know I'm scared out of my mind, too. Just stay nice and safe against me. That's it. You're safe now."

The boys were pressed so tightly against him that Savich could feel their hearts pounding as they sobbed, deep, ragged sobs, and he knew there was blessed relief in their sobs, that they finally believed they were going to survive. They clutched at him and he held them as tightly as he could, whispering, "It will be all right. You're going to be home in no time at all. It's okay, Rob, Donny."

He kept them both shielded from Tammy Tuttle, who was no longer moaning. He made no move to see what shape she was in.

"The Ghouls," one of the boys kept saying over and over, his young voice cracking. "They told us all about what the Ghouls did to all the other boys—ate them up whole or if they were already full, then they just tore them up, chewed on their bones—"

"I know, I know," Savich said, but he had no idea what his eyes had seen, not really. Whirling dust devils, that was all. There were no hidden axes or knives. Unless they somehow morphed into something more substantial? No, that was crazy. He felt something catch inside him. It was a sense of what was real, what had to be real. It demanded he reject what he'd seen, bury it under a hundred tons of earth, make the Ghouls gone forever, make it so they had never existed. It must have been some kind of natural phenomenon, easily explained, or some kind of an illusion, a waking nightmare, a mad invention of a pair of psychopaths' minds. But whatever they were that the Tuttles had called the Ghouls, he'd seen them, even shot at one of them, and they were embedded in his brain.

Maybe they had been dust devils, playing tricks on his eyes. Maybe.

As he stood holding the two thin bodies to him, talking to them, he was aware that agents, followed by the sheriff and his deputies, were inside the barn now, that one of them was bending over Tammy Tuttle. Soon there were agents everywhere, searching the barn, corner to corner, searching every inch of the tack room.

Everyone was high, excited. They'd gotten the boys back safely. They'd taken down two psychopaths.

Tammy Tuttle was conscious again, screaming, no way

to keep the boys from hearing her, though he tried. They held her down on the floor. She was yelling and cursing at Savich as she cradled her arm, yelling that the Ghouls would get him, she would lead them to him, that he was dead meat, and so were those Little Bloods. Savich felt the boys nearly dissolve against him, their terror palpable.

Then one of the agents slammed his fist into her jaw. He looked up, grinning. "Took her out of her pain. Didn't like to see such a fine, upstanding young lady in such misery."

"Thank you," Savich said. "Rob, Donny, she's not going to hurt anyone ever again. I swear it to you." Sherlock came to him, and she looked angry enough to spit nails. She didn't say anything, just put her arms around the two boys.

The paramedics came through with stretchers. Big Bob, the lead, who had a twenty-two-inch neck, looked at the two agents comforting the boys and just held up his hand. He said to the three men behind him, "Let's just wait here a moment. I think these boys are getting the medicine they need right now. See to that woman. The guy is gone."

Three hours later, the old barn was finally empty again, all evidence, mainly food refuse, pizza boxes, some chains and shackles, a good four dozen candy bar wrappers, carted away. Both Tuttles had been removed, Tammy still alive. The boys were taken immediately to their parents, who were waiting at the sheriff's office in Stewartville, Maryland. From there they'd go on to the local hospital to be checked out. The FBI wouldn't need to speak to them again for at least a couple of days, giving them time to calm down before being questioned.

All the agents drove back to FBI headquarters, to the Criminal Apprehension Unit on the fifth floor, to write up their reports.

Everyone was bouncing off the walls. They'd won. High

fives, slaps on the back. No screwups, no false leads. They
hadn't been too late to save the boys. "Just look at all the
testosterone flying around," Sherlock said as she walked
into the office. Then she laughed. No one could talk about
anything but how Savich had brought them down.

Savich called all the agents who had participated in the
raid together.

"When the barn doors swung in, did anyone see anything?"

No one had seen a thing.

"Did anyone see anything strange coming out of the
barn, anything at all?"

There wasn't a word spoken around the big conference
table. Then Sherlock said, "We didn't see anything, Dillon.
The barn doors flew inward; there was some thick dust in
the air, but that was it." She looked around at the other
agents. No one had seen any more than that. "We didn't see
anything coming out of the barn either."

"The Tuttles called them Ghouls," Savich said slowly.
"They looked so real I actually shot at one of them. It was
then that they seemed to dissipate, to disappear. I'm being as objective as I can. Understand, I didn't want to see
anything out of the ordinary. But I did see something. I
want to believe that it was some sort of dust devil that
broke into two parts, but I don't know, I just don't know.
If anyone can come up with an explanation, I'd like to
hear it."

There were more questions, more endless speculation,
until everyone sat silent. Savich said to Jimmy Maitland,
"The boys saw them. They're telling everyone about them.
You can bet that Rob and Donny won't call them natural
phenomena or dust devils."

Jimmy Maitland said, "No one will believe them. Now,
we've got to keep this Ghoul business under wraps. The
FBI has enough problems without announcing that we've

seen two supernatural cones, for God's sake, in a rampaging partnership with two psychopaths."

Later, Savich realized while he was typing his report to Jimmy Maitland that he'd spelled "Ghouls" with a capital G. They weren't just general entities to the Tuttles; they were specific.

Sherlock followed Savich into the men's room some thirty minutes later. Ollie Hamish, Savich's second in command, was at the sink washing his hands when they came in.

"Oh, hi, guys. Congratulations again, Savich. Great work. I just wish I could have been with you."

"I'm glad to see a man washing his hands," Sherlock said, and poked him in the arm. "In a few minutes I'm going to be washing my hands, too. After I've beaten some sense into my husband here, the jerk. Go away, Ollie, I know you'll want to protect him from me, and I don't want to have to hurt both of you."

"Ah, Sherlock, he's a hero. Why do you want to hurt the hero? He saved those little boys from the Warlocks and the Ghouls."

Savich said, "After what I told you about them, do you spell 'Ghouls' with a capital G in your head?"

"Yeah, sure, you said there were two of them. It's one of those strange things that will stay with you. You sure you weren't smoking something, Savich? Inhaling too much stale hay?"

"I wish I could say yes to that."

"Out, Ollie."

Once they were alone, she didn't take a strip off him, just stepped against him and wrapped her arms around his back. "I can't say that I've never been more frightened in my life, since you and I have managed to get into some bad situations." She kissed his neck and squeezed him even tighter. "But today, at that damned barn, you were a hot dog, and I was scared spitless, as were your friends."

"There was no time," he said against her curly hair. "No time to bring you in. Jesus, I scared myself, but I had no choice. And then those howling wind things were there. I honestly can't say which scared me more—Tammy Tuttle or whatever it was she called the Ghouls."

She pulled back a bit. "I really don't understand any of that. You described it all so clearly I could almost see them whirling through those barn doors. But Ghouls?"

"That's what the Tuttles called them. It was like they were acolytes to these things. I'd really like to say it was some sort of hallucination, that I was the only one who freaked out, but the boys saw them, too. I know it sounds off the wall, Sherlock, particularly since none of you guys saw a thing."

Because he needed to speak of it more, she just held him while he again described what had burst through the barn doors. Then he said, "I don't think there's anything more to do about this, but it was scary, Sherlock, really."

Jimmy Maitland walked into the men's room.

"Hey, where's a man to piddle?"

"Oh, sir, I just wanted to check Dillon out, make sure he was okay."

"And is he?"

"Oh, yes."

"Ollie caught me in the hall on my way to the unit, Savich, said you were getting the bejesus whaled out of you in the men's room. We've got a media frenzy cranking up." Jimmy Maitland gave them a big grin. "Guess what? No one's going to pound on us this time—only good news, thank the Lord. Great news. Since you were the one in the middle of it, Savich, we want you front and center. Of course, Director Mueller will be there and do all the talking. They just want you to stand there and look like a hero."

"No mention of what we saw?"

"No, not a word about the Ghouls, not even speculation

about whirling dust. The last thing we need is to have the media go after us because we claim we were attacked by some weird balls of dust called into the barn by a couple of psychopaths. As for the boys, it doesn't matter what they say. If the media asks us about it, we'll just shake our heads, look distressed and sympathetic. It will be a twenty-four-hour wonder, then it'll be over. And the FBI will be heroes. That sure feels good."

Savich said as he rubbed his hands up and down his wife's back, "But there was something very strange in there, sir, something that made the hair stand up on my head."

"Get a grip, Savich. We've got the Tuttle brothers, or rather we've got one brother dead and one sister whose arm was just amputated at the shoulder. The last thing we need is a dose of the supernatural."

"You could maybe call me Mulder?"

"Yeah, right. Hey, I just realized that Sherlock here has red hair, just like Scully."

Savich and Sherlock rolled their eyes and followed their boss from the men's room.

The boys claimed they'd seen the Ghouls, could speak of nothing else but how Agent Savich had put a bullet right in the middle of one and made them whirl out of the barn. But the boys were so tattered and pathetic, very nearly incoherent, that indeed, they weren't believed, even by their parents.

One reporter asked Savich if he'd seen any ghouls and Savich just said, "Excuse me, what did you say?"

Jimmy Maitland was right. That was the end of it.

Savich and Sherlock played with Sean for so long that evening that he finally fell asleep in the middle of his favorite finger game, Hide the Camel, a graham cracker smashed in his hand. That night at two o'clock in the morning, the phone rang. Savich picked it up, listened, and said, "We'll be there as soon as we can."

He slowly hung up the phone and looked over at his wife, who'd managed to prop herself up on her elbow.

"It's my sister, Lily. She's in the hospital. It doesn't look good."

2

HEMLOCK BAY, CALIFORNIA

Bright sunlight poured through narrow windows. Her bedroom windows were wider, weren't they? Surely they were cleaner than this. No, wait, she wasn't in her bedroom. A vague sort of panic jumped her, then fell away. She didn't feel much of anything now, just a bit of confusion that surely wasn't all that important, just a slight ache in her left arm at the IV line.

IV line?

That meant she was in a hospital. She was breathing; she could feel the oxygen tickling her nose, the tubes irritating her. But it was reassuring. She was alive. But why shouldn't she be alive? Why was she surprised?

Her brain felt numb and empty, and even the emptiness was hazy. Maybe she was dying and that's why they'd left her alone. Where was Tennyson? Oh, yes, he'd gone to Chicago two days before, some sort of medical thing. She'd been glad to see him go, relieved, just plain solidly relieved that she wouldn't have to hear his calm, soothing voice that drove her nuts.

A white-coated man with a bald head, a stethoscope

around his neck, came into the room. He leaned down right into her face. "Mrs. Frasier, can you hear me?"

"Oh, yes. I can even see the hairs in your nose."

He straightened, laughed. "Oh, that's too close then. Now that my nose hairs aren't in the way, how do you feel? Any pain?"

"No, I can barely feel my brain. I feel vague and stupid."

"That's because of the morphine. You could be shot in the belly, get enough morphine, and you wouldn't even be pissed at your mother-in-law. I'm your surgeon, Dr. Ted Larch. Since I had to remove your spleen—and that's major abdominal surgery— we'll keep you on a nice, steady dose of morphine until this evening. We'll begin to lighten up on it after that. Then we'll get you up to see how you're doing, get your innards working again."

"What else is wrong with me?"

"Let me give you the short version. First, let me promise you that you'll be all right. As for having no spleen, nothing bad should happen in the long run because of that. An adult doesn't really need his spleen. However, you will have all the discomfort of surgery—pain for several days. You'll have to be careful about when and what you eat, and as I said, we'll have to get your system working again.

"You have a concussion, two bruised ribs, some cuts and abrasions, but you'll live. Nothing that should cause any scarring. You're doing splendidly, given what happened."

"What did happen?"

Dr. Larch was silent for a moment, his head tilted a bit to one side. Sun was pouring in through the window and gave his bald head a bright shine. He said slowly, studying her face, "You don't remember?"

She thought and thought until he lightly touched his fingers to her forearm. "No, don't try to force it. You'll just give yourself a headache. What is the last thing you do remember, Mrs. Frasier?"

Again she thought, and finally she said slowly, "I remember leaving my house in Hemlock Bay. That's where I live, on Crocodile Bayou Avenue. I remember I was going to drive to Ferndale to deliver some medical slides to a Dr. Baker. I remember I didn't like driving on 211 when it was nearly dark. That road is scary and those redwoods tower over you and surround you and you start feeling like you're being buried alive." She stopped, and he saw frustration building and interrupted her.

"No, that's all right. An interesting metaphor with those redwoods. Now, everything will probably all come back to you in time. You were in an accident, Mrs. Frasier. Your Explorer hit a redwood dead on. Now, I'm going to call in another doctor."

"What is his specialty?"

"He's a psychiatrist."

"Why do I need..." Now she frowned. "I don't understand. A psychiatrist? Why?"

"Well, it seems that you possibly could have driven into that redwood on purpose. No, don't panic, don't worry about a thing. Just rest and build up your strength. I'll see you later, Mrs. Frasier. If you begin to feel any pain in the next couple of hours, just hit your button and a nurse will pump some more morphine into your IV."

"I thought the patient could administer the morphine when needed."

He was stumped for a moment, she saw it clearly. He said, "I'm sorry, but we can't give you that."

"Why?" Her voice was very soft.

"Because there is a question of attempted suicide. We can't take the chance that you'd pump yourself full of morphine and we couldn't bring you back."

She looked away from him, toward the window, where the sun was shining in so brightly.

"All I remember is last evening. What day is it? What time of day?"

"It's late Thursday morning. You've been going in and out for a while now. Your accident was last evening."

"So much missing time."

"It will be all right, Mrs. Frasier."

"I wonder about that," she said, nothing more, and closed her eyes.

Dr. Russell Rossetti stopped for a moment just inside the doorway and looked at the young woman who lay so still on the narrow hospital bed. She looked like a princess who'd kissed the wrong frog and been beaten up, major league. Her blond hair was mixed with flecks of blood and tangled around bandages. She was thin, too thin, and he wondered what she was thinking right now, right this minute.

Dr. Ted Larch, the surgeon who'd removed her spleen, had told him she didn't remember a thing about the accident. He'd also said he didn't think she'd tried to kill herself. She was just too "there," he'd said. The meathead.

Ted was a romantic, something weird for a surgeon to be. Of course she'd tried to kill herself. Again. No question. It was classic.

"Mrs. Frasier."

Lily slowly turned her head at the sound of a rather high voice she imagined could whine when he didn't get his way, a voice that was right now trying to sound soothing, all sorts of inviting, but not succeeding.

She said nothing, just looked at the overweight man— on the tall side, very well dressed in a dark, gray suit, with lots of curly black hair, a double chin, and fat, very white fingers—who walked into the room. He came to stand too close to the bed.

"Who are you?"

"I'm Dr. Rossetti. Dr. Larch told you I would be coming to see you?"

"You're the psychiatrist?"

"Yes."

"He told me, but I don't want to see you. There is no reason."

Denial, he thought, just splendid. He was bored with the stream of depressed patients who simply started crying and became quickly incoherent and self-pitying, their hands held out for pills to numb them. Although Tennyson had told him that Lily wasn't like that, he hadn't been convinced.

He said, all calm and smooth, "Evidently you do need me. You drove your car into a redwood."

Had she? No, it just didn't seem right. She said, "The road to Ferndale is very dangerous. Have you ever driven it at dusk, when it's nearly dark?"

"Yes."

"You didn't find you had to be very careful?"

"Of course. However, I never wrapped my car around a redwood. The Forestry Service is looking at the tree now, to see how badly it's hurt."

"Well, if I'm missing some bark, I'm sure it is, too. I would like you to leave now, Dr. Rossetti."

Instead of leaving, he pulled a chair close to the bed and sat down. He crossed his legs. He weaved his plump, white fingers together. She hated his hands, soft, puffy hands, but she couldn't stop looking at them.

"If you'll give me just a minute, Mrs. Frasier. Do you mind if I call you Lily?"

"Yes, I mind. I don't know you. Go away."

He leaned toward her and tried to take her hand, but she pulled it away and stuck it beneath her covers.

"You really should cooperate with me, Lily—"

"My name is Mrs. Frasier."

He frowned. Usually women—any and all women—liked to be called by their first name. It made them feel that he was more of a confidant, someone they could trust. It also made them more vulnerable, more open to him.

He said, "You tried to kill yourself the first time after the death of your child seven months ago."

"She didn't just die. A speeding car hit her and knocked her twenty feet into a ditch. Someone murdered her."

"And you blamed yourself."

"Are you a parent?"

"Yes."

"Wouldn't you blame yourself if your child died and you weren't with her?"

"No, not if I wasn't driving the car that hit her."

"Would your wife blame herself?"

Elaine's face passed before his mind's eye, and he frowned. "Probably not. All she would do is cry. She is a very weak woman, very dependent. But that isn't the point, Mrs. Frasier." It wasn't. He would be free of Elaine very soon now, thank God.

"What is the point?"

"You did blame yourself, blamed yourself so much you stuffed a bottle of sleeping pills down your throat. If your housekeeper hadn't found you in time, you would have died."

"That's what I was told," she said, and she swore in that moment that she could taste the same taste in her mouth now as she had then when she'd awakened in the hospital that first time when she'd been so bewildered, so weak she couldn't even raise her hand.

"You don't remember taking the pills?"

"No, not really."

"And now you don't remember driving your car into a redwood. Your speed, it was estimated by the sheriff, was about sixty miles per hour, maybe faster. You were very lucky, Mrs. Frasier. A guy just happened to come around a bend to see you drive into the tree, and called an ambulance."

"Do you happen to know his name? I would like to thank him."

"That isn't what's important here, Mrs. Frasier."

"What is important here? Oh, yes, do you happen to have a first name?"

"My name is Russell. Dr. Russell Rossetti."

"Nice alliteration, Russell."

"It would be better if you called me Dr. Rossetti," he said. She saw those plump, white fingers twisting, and she knew he was angry. He thought she was out of line. She was, but she just didn't care. She was tired, so very tired, and she just wanted to close her eyes and let the morphine mask the pain for a while longer.

"Go away, Dr. Rossetti."

He didn't move for some time.

Lily turned her head away and sought oblivion. She didn't even hear when he finally left the room. She did, however, hear the door close.

When Dr. Larch walked in five minutes later, his very high forehead flushed, she managed to cock an eye open and say, "Dr. Rossetti is a patronizing ass. He has fat hands. Please, I don't want to see him again."

"He doesn't think you're in very good shape."

"On the contrary, I'm in splendid shape, something I can't say about him. He needs to go to the gym very badly."

Dr. Larch laughed, couldn't help himself. "He also said your defensiveness and your rudeness to him were sure signs that you're highly overwrought and in desperate need of help."

"Yeah, right. I'm so overwrought—what with all this painkiller—that I'm ready to nap."

"Ah, your husband is here to see you."

She didn't want to see Tennyson. His voice, so resonant, so confident—it was too much like Dr. Rossetti's voice, as if they'd taken the same Voice Lessons 101 course in shrink school. If she never saw another one of them again, she could leave this earth a happy woman.

She looked past Dr. Larch to see her husband of eleven months standing in the doorway, looking rather pale, his thick eyebrows drawn together, his arms crossed over his chest. Such a nice-looking man he was, all big and solid, his hair light and wavy, lots of hair, not bald like Dr. Larch. He wore aviator glasses, which looked really cool, and now she watched him push them back up, an endearing habit—at least that's what she'd thought when she'd first met him.

"Lily?"

"Yes," she said and wished he'd stay in the doorway. Dr. Larch straightened and turned to him. "Dr. Frasier, as I told you, your wife will be fine, once she recovers from the surgery. However, she does need to rest. I suggest that you visit for only a few minutes."

"I am very tired, Tennyson," she said and hated the small shudder in her voice. "Perhaps we could speak later?"

"Oh, no," he said. And then he waited, saying nothing more until Dr. Larch left the room, fingering his stethoscope. He looked nervous. Lily wondered why. Tennyson closed the door, paused yet again, studying her, then, finally, he walked to stand beside her bed. He gently eased her hand out from under the covers, something she wished he wouldn't do, rubbed his fingers over her palm for several moments before saying in a sad, soft voice, "Why did you do it, Lily? Why?"

He made it sound like it was all over for her. No, she was being ridiculous. She said, "I don't know that I did anything, Tennyson. You see, I have no memory at all of the accident."

He waved away her words. He had strong hands, confident hands. "I know and I'm sorry about that. Look, Lily, maybe it was an accident, maybe somehow you lost control and drove the Explorer into the redwood. One of the nurses told me that the Forest Service has someone on the spot to see how badly the tree is injured."

"Dr. Rossetti already told me. Poor tree."

"It isn't funny, Lily. Now, you're going to be here for at least another two or three days, until they're sure your body is functioning well again. I would like you to speak with Dr. Rossetti. He's a new man with quite an excellent reputation."

"I've already seen him. I don't wish to see him again, Tennyson."

His voice changed now, became even softer, more gentle, and she knew she would normally have wanted to cry, to fold into herself, to have him reassure her, tell her the bogeyman wouldn't come back, but not now. It was probably the morphine making her feel slightly euphoric, slightly disconnected. But she also felt rather strong, perhaps even on the arrogant side, and that, of course, was an illusion to beat all illusions.

"Since you don't remember anything, Lily, you've got to admit that it wouldn't hurt to cover all the bases. I really want you to see him."

"I don't like him, Tennyson. How can I speak to someone I don't like?"

"You will see him, Lily, or I'm afraid we'll have to consider an institution."

"Oh? *We* will consider an institution? What sort of institution?" Why wasn't she afraid of that word that brought a wealth of dreadful images with it? But she wasn't afraid. She was looking at him positively bright-eyed. She loved morphine. She was tiring; she could feel the vagueness trying to close her down, eating away at the focus in her brain, but for this moment, maybe even the next, too, she could deal with anything.

He squeezed her hand. "I'm a doctor, Lily, a psychiatrist, as is Dr. Rossetti. You know it isn't ethical for me to treat you myself."

"You prescribed the Elavil."

"That's different. That's a very common drug for depression. No, I couldn't speak with you like Dr. Rossetti can. But you must know that I want what is best for you. I love you and I've prayed you were getting better. One day at a time, I kept telling myself. And there were some days when I knew you were healing, but I was wrong. Yes, you really must see Dr. Rossetti or I'm afraid I will have no choice but to admit you for evaluation."

"Forgive me for pointing this out, Tennyson, but I don't believe that you can do that. I'm here—I can see, I can talk, I can reason—I do have a say in what happens to me."

"That remains to be seen. Lily, just speak to Dr. Rossetti. Talk to him about your pain, your confusion, your guilt, the fact that you're beginning to accept what your ambition wrought."

Ambition? She had such great ambition that her daughter was killed because of it?

She suddenly wanted to be perfectly clear about this. She said, "What do you mean exactly, Tennyson?"

"You know—Beth's death."

That hit her right between the eyes. Instant guilt, overwhelming her. No, wait, she wasn't going to let that happen. She wouldn't let it happen, not now. Beneath the morphine, beneath all of it, she was still there, hanging on, wanting to be whole, wanting to draw her cartoon strips of No Wrinkles Remus shafting another colleague, wanting... Was that the great ambition that had killed her daughter? "I can't deal with this right now, Tennyson. Please go away. I'll be better in the morning."

No, she'd feel like hell when they lessened her pain dosage, she thought, but she wouldn't worry about that now. Now she would sleep; she'd get better, both her brain and her body. She turned her head away from him on the pillow. She had no more words. She knew if she tried to speak more, she wouldn't make sense. She was falling, falling ever so gently into the whale's soft belly, and it would be warm, comforting. Move over, Jonah. She wouldn't have nightmares, not with the morphine lulling her.

She stared at the IV in her arm, upward to the plastic bag filled with fluid above her. Her vision blurred into the lazy flow of liquid that didn't seem to go anywhere, just flowed and flowed. She closed her eyes even as he said, "I will see you later this evening, Lily. Rest well." He leaned down and kissed her cheek. How she used to love his hands on her, his kissing her, but not now. She simply hadn't felt anything for such a very long time.

When she was alone again, she thought, *What am I going to do?* But then she knew, of course. She forced back the haziness, the numbing effect of the morphine. She picked up the phone and dialed her brother's number in Washington, D.C. She heard a series of clicks and then the sound of a person breathing, but nothing happened. She dialed a nine, then the number again. She tried yet again, but didn't get through. Then, suddenly, the line went dead.

She realized vaguely as she let herself be drawn into the ether that there was fear licking at her, from the deepest part of her, fear that she couldn't quite grasp, and it wasn't fear that she'd be institutionalized against her will.

3

Lily awoke to feel the touch of fingers on her eyebrows, stroking as light as a butterfly's wing. She heard a man's voice, a voice she'd loved all her life, deep and low, wonderfully sweet, and she opened to it eagerly.

"Lily, I want you to open your eyes now and look at me and smile. Can you do that, sweetheart? Open your eyes."

And she opened her eyes and looked up at her brother. She smiled. "My big Fed brother. I've worshiped you from the time you showed me how to kick Billy Clapper in the crotch so he wouldn't try to feel me up again. Do you remember that?"

"Yes, I remember. You were twelve and this little jerk, who was all of fourteen at the time, had put his hand up your skirt."

"I really hurt him bad, Dillon. He never tried anything again."

He was smiling, such a beautiful smile, white teeth. "I remember."

"I should have kept kicking guys in the crotch. Then

none of this would have happened. I'm so glad you're here."

"I'm here, Lily, so is Sherlock. We left Sean with Mom, who was grinning and singing the 'Hallelujah Chorus' as we drove out of the driveway. We told her you'd been in an accident and that you were okay, that we just wanted to see you. You can call and reassure her later. As for the rest of the family, let Mom do the telling."

"I don't want her to worry. It's true, Dillon, I'll be okay. I miss Sean. It's been so long. I really like all the photos you e-mail me."

"Yes, but it's not the same as being in the room with him, having him gum your fingers, rub his crackers into your sweater, and drool on your neck."

Sherlock said, "You touch any surface in the house and come away with graham cracker crumbs."

Lily smiled, and it was real because she could see that precious little boy dropping wet graham cracker crumbs everywhere, and it pleased her to her very soul. "Mom must be so happy to have her hands on him."

Savich said, "Yes. She always spoils him so rotten that when he comes home, he's a real pain for a good two days."

"He's the cutest little button, Dillon. I miss him."

A tear leaked out of her eye.

Savich wiped the tear away. "I know, so do Sherlock and I and we've only been apart from him for less than a day. How do you feel, Lily?"

"It's dark again."

"Yes. Nearly seven o'clock Thursday evening. Now, sweetheart, talk to me. How do you feel?"

"Like they've already lightened the morphine."

"Yeah, Dr. Larch said he was just beginning to ease up on it now. You're gonna feel rotten for a while, a day or two, but then it'll be less and less pain each day."

"When did you get here?"

"Sherlock and I just got into town. The puddle jumper from San Francisco to Arcata-Eureka was late." He saw her eyes go vague and added, "Sherlock bought Sean a Golden Gate oven mitt at the San Francisco airport."

"I'll show it to you later, Lily," Sherlock said. She was standing on the other side of Lily's bed, smiling down at her, so scared for this lovely young woman who was her sister-in-law that she would have bitten her fingernails if she hadn't stopped some three years before. "It was be-tween an oven mitt with Alcatraz on it and the Golden Gate. Since Sean gums everything, Dillon thought gum-ming the Golden Gate was healthier than gumming a Fed-eral prison."

Lily laughed. She didn't know where it had come from, but she even laughed again. Pain seared through her side and her ribs, and she gasped.

"No more humor," Sherlock said and lightly kissed her cheek. "We're here and everything's going to be all right now, I promise."

"Who called you?"

"Your father-in-law, about two in the morning, last night."

"I wonder why he called," she said slowly, thinking about the pain that was now coming through and how she would deal with it.

"You wouldn't expect him to?"

"I see now," Lily said, her eyes suddenly narrow and fierce. "He was afraid Mrs. Scruggins would call you and then you would wonder why the family hadn't called. I think he's afraid of you, Dillon. He's always asking me how you're doing and where you are. When you were here before, I think you scared him really good."

"Why would I scare him?"

"Because you're big and you're smart and you're a spe-cial agent with the FBI."

Sherlock laughed. "Lots of people don't relax around

FBI agents. But Mr. Elcott Frasier? I took one look at him and thought he probably chewed nails for breakfast."

"He could, you know. Everyone thinks that, particularly his son, my husband."

"Maybe he called because he knew we'd want to come here to see you," Savich said. "Maybe he isn't all that much of an iron fist."

"Yes, he is. Tennyson was here earlier." She sighed, tightened a bit from a jab of pain in her bruised ribs, the pulling in her side. "Thank goodness he finally left."

Savich looked over at Sherlock. "What happened, Lily? Talk to us."

"Everyone thinks I tried to kill myself again."

"Fine, let them. It doesn't matter. Talk, Lily."

"I don't know, Dillon, I swear I don't. I remember that I had to drive that gnarly road to Ferndale, you know, 211? And that's all. Everything else is just lost."

Sherlock said, "All right, then. Everyone thinks you tried to kill yourself because of the pills you took right after Beth's death?"

"Yes, I guess so."

"But why?"

"I suppose I haven't been exactly honest with you guys, but I just didn't want you to worry. Fact is, I have been depressed. I'll feel lots better and then it's back down again. It's gotten progressively worse the past couple of weeks. Why? I don't know, but it has. And then last night happened."

Savich pulled up a chair and sat down. He took her hand again. "You know, Lily, even when you were a little girl, you'd hit a problem, and I swear you'd worry and work and chew on that problem, never giving up until you had it solved. Dad used to say that if he was slow telling you something you really wanted to know, he could just see you gnawing on his trouser leg until you ripped it right off or he talked, whichever came first."

"I miss Dad."

"I do, too. Now, I still don't understand that first time you wanted to die. That wasn't the Lily I knew. But Beth's death—that would knock any parent on his or her butt. But now seven months have passed. You're smart, you're talented, you're not one to be in denial. This depression—that doesn't make a lot of sense to me. What's been happening, Lily?"

She sobered, frowning now. "Nothing's been happening, just more of the same. Like I said, over the past months sometimes I'd feel better, feel like I could conquer the world again, but then it would go away and I'd want to stay in bed all day.

"For whatever reason, yesterday it got really bad. Tennyson called me from Chicago and told me to take two of the antidepressant pills. I did. I'll tell you something, the pills sure don't seem to help. And then, when I was driving on that road to Ferndale—well, maybe something did happen. Maybe I did drive into that redwood. I just don't remember."

"It's okay. Now, how does your brain feel right now?" Sherlock asked, scooting in a little closer to Lily on the hospital bed.

"Not quite as vague as before. I guess since there's less morphine swimming around up in there, I'm coming back."

"Are you feeling depressed?"

"No. I'm mainly just mad because of that idiot shrink they sent by. A dreadful man, trying to be so comforting, so understanding, when really he was a condescending jerk."

"You smart-mouthed him, babe?"

"Maybe. A little bit."

"I'm glad," Sherlock said. "Not enough back-mouthing from you lately, Lily."

"Oh, dear."

"Oh, dear what?"

But Lily didn't say anything, just kept looking toward the door.

Savich and Sherlock both turned to see their brother-in-law, Tennyson Frasier, come into the room.

Savich thought, Lily doesn't want to see her husband?

What was going on here? Seven months ago, Lily had come back to Maryland to stay with their mother for several weeks after Beth's funeral. While she'd been there, Savich had done everything he could, turned over every rock he could find, called in every favor, to discover who had struck Beth and driven off. No luck. Not a clue. But then Lily had wanted to go back to Hemlock Bay, to be with her husband, who loved her and needed her, and yes, she was all right now.

A big mistake to let her come back here, Savich thought, and knew he wouldn't leave her here this time. Not again.

Savich straightened as Tennyson came striding toward him, his hand outstretched. As he pumped Savich's hand, he said, "Boy, am I ever glad to see you guys. Dad told me he called you, in the middle of the night." Then he stopped. He looked at Lily.

Sherlock never moved from her perch on Lily's bed. She said, "Good to see you, Tennyson." Such a handsome man he was, big and in pretty good shape, and at the moment he looked terrified for his wife. Why didn't Lily want to see him?

"Lily, are you all right?" Tennyson walked to her bed, his hand out.

Lily slipped her hand beneath the covers as she said, "I'm fine, Tennyson. Do you know that I tried to call Dillon and Sherlock earlier? And my line went dead. Is it still dead now?"

Sherlock picked up the phone. There was a dial tone. "It's fine now."

"Isn't that strange?"

"Maybe," Tennyson said, leaning down to caress Lily's

pale face, kiss her lightly, "with all that morphine in you, you didn't do it right."

"There was a dial tone, then a person's breathing, some clicking sounds, and then nothing."

"Hmmm. I'll check on that, but it's working now, so no harm done." He turned back to Savich. "You and Sherlock got here very quickly."

"She's my sister," Savich said, looking at his brother-in-law closely. "What would you expect?" He'd always liked Tennyson, believed he'd been a solid man, one who was trustworthy, unlike Lily's first husband, Jack Crane. He'd believed Tennyson had been as distraught as Lily when Beth was killed. He had worked with Savich trying to find out who the driver was who'd killed Beth. As for the sheriff, he'd been next to useless. What was wrong? Why didn't Lily want to see him?

Tennyson merely nodded, then kissed Lily again. He said, his voice as soft as a swatch of Bengali silk, "I can't wait to get you out of this place, get you home. You'll be safe with me, Lily, always."

But she hadn't been safe, Sherlock thought. That was the bottom line. She'd run her Explorer into a redwood. Hardly safe. What was wrong with this picture?

"What about that psychiatrist, Tennyson?"

"Dr. Rossetti? I would really like you to see him, Lily. He can help you."

"You said you would institutionalize me if I didn't see him."

Savich nearly went *en pointe*.

Sherlock laughed. "Institutionalize Lily? Come on, Tennyson."

"No, no, all of you misunderstood. Listen, Lily very probably drove into that redwood last night. This is the second time she's tried to end her life. You were both here after the first time. You saw how she was. Her mother saw as well. She's been on medication, but obviously it hasn't helped. I want her to speak to a very excellent psychiatrist, a man I respect very much."

"I don't like him, Tennyson. I don't want to see him again."

Tennyson sighed deeply. "All right, Lily. If you don't like Dr. Rossetti, then I'll find another man who could possibly help you."

"I would prefer a woman."

"Whatever. I don't know of any female psychiatrists who do anything other than family counseling."

Savich said, "I'll have some names for you by tomorrow, Lily. No problem. But we're a bit off the subject here. I want to know the name of the antidepressants Lily's been taking and I want to know why they seem to have the opposite effect on her."

Tennyson said patiently, "It's a very popular drug, Dillon. Elavil. You can ask any doctor."

"I'm sure it is. I suppose there are a certain number of people who simply don't respond appropriately?"

"Unfortunately, yes. I was considering whether or not we should try another drug—Prozac, for example."

Savich said, "Why don't you just wait on all the drugs until Lily has seen a new psychiatrist. What happened to Dr. McGill? Weren't you with him for a while, Lily?"

"He died, Dillon, not two weeks after I began seeing him. He was such a sweet man, but he was old and his heart was rotten. He had a heart attack."

Tennyson shrugged. "It happens. Hey, I saw you on TV, Savich, there with all the FBI brass. You got the Warlocks."

"Turns out there was only one warlock, the other was a witch."

"Yes, a brother and a sister. How did everyone miss that?"

"Good question." Savich saw that Lily was listening closely now. She loved hearing about their cases, so he kept talking about it. "Turns out one of them wasn't really a guy, just dressed like one—Timmy was really a she. She even lowered her voice, cropped off her hair, the whole deal. The profilers never saw it and neither did any of my unit. Instead of Tammy, to the world she was Timmy."

"Did the brother and sister sleep together?" Tennyson said.

"Not that we know of."

Lily said, "It was MAX who managed to track down that barn?"

"That's right. Once we knew the Tuttles were back in Maryland, I knew in my gut that this was their final destination, that they'd come home, even though they'd been born and raised in Utah. They kidnapped the boys in Maryland. So where were they? MAX always checks out any and every relative when we know who the suspect is. He dug deep enough to find Marilyn Warluski, a cousin who owned this property. And on the property was this old abandoned barn."

Thank God no one had mentioned anything about the Ghouls.

Lily said, "How many boys did the two of them kill, Sherlock?"

"A dozen, maybe more. All across the country. We'll probably never know unless Tammy decides to tell us, and that's not likely. Her arm was amputated thanks to Dillon's shot. She's not a happy camper. Thank God it's over and the last two boys are all right."

Tennyson asked, "You shot her? Did you kill the brother too?"

"The brother's dead, yes. It was a team effort," Savich said, and nothing more.

"Those poor little boys," Lily said. "Their parents must have been torn apart when they were taken."

"They were, but as I said, everything turned out okay for them."

Nurse Carla Brunswick said from the doorway, "We

don't have to worry about crooks while you guys are in town. Now, I get to order the FBI out. Time for Mrs. Frasier's sleeping pills. Say good night—even you, Dr. Frasier. Dr. Larch's orders."

It wasn't until they were in the hospital parking lot that Tennyson said, "I apologize for not realizing sooner that you'd only just arrived. You will stay with me, won't you?"

"Yes," Savich said. "Thank you, Tennyson. We want to be close."

An hour later, after Savich had called his mother and told her not to worry and had spoken to his son, he climbed into the king-size bed beneath the sloped-ceiling guest room, kissed his wife, tucked her against his side, and said, "Why do you really think Mr. Elcott Frasier called us?"

"The obvious: he was worried about his daughter-in-law and wanted us to know right away. Very thoughtful. He thought it through and didn't just call your mom and scare the daylights out of her."

"All right, just maybe you're right. After that heavy dose of craziness with the Tuttles, I guess my mind went automatically to the worst possible motive."

Sherlock kissed his neck, then settled back in, her leg over his belly. "I've heard so much psychobabble about Lily. She tries to kill herself because it's the only thing to do if she wants to gain peace. She has to drive her Explorer into a redwood to expiate her guilt. It just doesn't sound right. It doesn't sound like Lily. Yes, yes, I remember the first time. But that was then."

"And this is now."

"Yes. Seven months. Lily isn't neurotic, Dillon. I've always thought she was strong, stable. And now I feel guilty because we didn't make an effort to see her over the last months."

"You had a baby, Sherlock, not a week after Beth's funeral."

"And Lily was there for me."

"She wasn't there with you—not like I was. My God, Sherlock, that was the longest day of my life." He squeezed her so hard, she squeaked.

"Yeah, yeah," she said.

"You never curse, but toward the end there you called me more names than I'd ever been called, even by linebackers during football games in college."

She laughed, kissed his shoulder again, and said, "Look, I know Lily's been through a very hard time. She's been understandably depressed. But we've talked to her a lot since Beth died. I just don't believe she was in a frame of mind to try to kill herself again."

"I don't know," he said. He frowned and turned off the lamp on the bedside table. He pulled Sherlock against him again and held her tight. "It really shakes me up, Sherlock, this happening to Lily. It's so hard to know what to do."

She held him harder than she had in her life. And she was thinking how fragile Lily had been seven months before, so hurt and so very broken, and then she'd taken those pills and nearly died. Savich and their mother had flown out to California for the second time, not more than a week after Beth's funeral, to see Lily lying in that narrow hospital bed, a tube in her nose, an IV line in her arm. But Lily had survived. And she'd been so sorry, so very sorry that she'd frightened everyone. And she'd come back with them to Washington, D.C., to rest and get her bearings. But after three weeks, she'd decided to go back to her husband in Hemlock Bay.

And seven months later, she'd driven her Explorer into a redwood.

She squeezed more tightly against him. "I just don't know how I'd handle it if anything happened to Sean. I couldn't bear that, Dillon. I just couldn't. No wonder Lily didn't."

After a long time, he said, "No, I couldn't bear it either, but you know what? You and I would survive it together. Somehow we would. But I think your instincts on this were right. You said something doesn't feel right. What did you mean?"

She nuzzled her nose into his shoulder, hummed a bit, a sure sign she was thinking hard, and said, "Well, just last week, Lily sent us a *No Wrinkles Remus* strip she'd just finished, her first one since Beth was killed, and she sounded excited. So what happened over the past four days to make her want to try to kill herself again?"

4

"I stole the bottle of pills," Savich said, as he walked into the kitchen.

Sherlock grinned at her husband, gave him a thumbs-up, and said, "How do we check them out?"

"I called Clark Hoyt in the Eureka field office. I'll messenger them up to him today. He'll get back to me tomorrow. Then we'll know, one way or the other."

"Ah, Dillon, I've got a confession to make." She took a sip of her tea, grinned down at the few tea leaves on the bottom of the cup. "The pills you took, well, they're cold medicine. You see, I'd already stolen the pills and replaced them with Sudafed I found in the medicine cabinet."

Sometimes she just bowled him over. He toasted her with his tea. "I'm impressed, Sherlock. When did you switch them?"

"About five A.M. this morning, before anyone was stirring. Oh, yes, Mrs. Scruggins, the housekeeper, should be here soon. We can see what she's got to say about all this."

Mrs. Scruggins responded to Sherlock's questions by sighing a lot. She was a tall woman, nearly as tall as

Savich, and she looked strong, very strong, even those long fingers of hers including her thumbs, that each sported a ring. She had muscles. Sherlock didn't think she'd want to tangle with Mrs. Scruggins. She had to be at least sixty years old. It was amazing. There were pictures of her grandchildren lining the window ledge in the kitchen and she looked like she could take any number of muggers out at one time.

Savich sat back and watched Sherlock work her magic. "An awful thing," Sherlock said, shaking her head, obviously distressed. "We just can't understand it. But I'll bet you do, Mrs. Scruggins, here with poor Lily so much of the time. I'll bet you saw things real clearly."

And Mrs. Scruggins said then, her beringed fingers curving gracefully around her coffee cup, "I'd think she was getting better, you know?"

Both Savich and Sherlock nodded.

"Then she'd just fall into a funk again and curl up in the fetal position and spend the day in bed. She wouldn't eat, just lie there, barely even blinking. I guess she'd be thinking about little Beth, you know?"

"Yes, we know," Sherlock said, sighed, and moved closer to the edge of her chair, inviting more thoughts, more confidences.

"Every few weeks I'd swear she was getting better, but it wouldn't last long. Just last week I thought she was really improving, nearly back to normal. She was in her office and she was laughing. I actually heard her. It was a laugh. She was drawing that cartoon strip of hers, and she was laughing."

"Then what happened?"

"Well, Mrs. Savich, I can't rightly say. Before I left, Dr. Frasier had come home early and I heard them talking. Then she just fell back again, the very next day. It was really fast. Laughing one minute, then, not ten hours later, she was so depressed, so quiet. She just walked around the house that day, not really seeing anything, at least that's what I think. Then she'd disappear and I knew later that she'd been crying. It's enough to break your heart, you know?"

"Yes, we know," Sherlock said. "These pills, Mrs. Scruggins, the Elavil, do you refill the prescription for her?"

"Yes, usually. Sometimes Dr. Frasier just brings them home for her. They don't seem to do much good, do they?"

"No," said Savich. "Maybe it's best that she be off them for a while."

"Amen to that. Poor little mite, such a hard time she's had." Mrs. Scruggins gave another deep sigh, nearly pulling apart the buttons over her large bosom. "I myself missed little Beth so much I just wanted sometimes to lie down and cry and cry and never you mind anything else. And I wasn't her mama, not like Mrs. Frasier."

"What about Dr. Frasier?" Savich asked.

"What do you mean?"

"Was he devastated by Beth's death?"

"Ah, he's a man, Mr. Savich. Sure, he looked glum for a week or so. But you know, men just don't take things like that so much to heart, leastwise my own papa didn't when my little sister died. Maybe Dr. Frasier keeps it all inside, but I don't think so. Don't forget, he wasn't Beth's real father. He didn't know little Beth that long, maybe six months in all."

Sherlock said, "But he's been so very worried about Lily, hasn't he?"

Mrs. Scruggins nodded, and the small diamond studs in her ears glittered in the morning sunlight pouring through the window. Diamonds and muscles and rings, Sherlock thought, and wondered. Mrs. Scruggins said, "Poor man, always fretting about her, trying to make her smile, bringing her presents and flowers, but nothing really worked, leastwise in the long term. And now this." Mrs. Scruggins shook her head. She wore her gray hair in a thick chignon. She had lots of hair and there were a lot of bobby pins worked into the roll.

It occurred to Sherlock to wonder if Mrs. Scruggins really cared for Lily, or if it was all an act. Could it be that she was really Lily's companion, or maybe even her guard?

Now where had that thought come from? Hadn't Mrs. Scruggins saved Lily's life that first time Lily had taken the bottle of pills right after Beth's funeral? She was getting paranoid here; she had to watch it.

"I have a little boy, Mrs. Scruggins," Savich said. "I've only had him a bit more than seven months, and you can believe that I would be devastated if anything were to happen to him."

"Well, that's good. Some men are different, aren't they? But my daddy, hard-nosed old bastard he was. Didn't shed a tear when my little sister got hit by that tractor. Ah, well, I'm afraid I have things to do now. When is Mrs. Frasier coming home?"

"Perhaps as soon as tomorrow," Sherlock said. "She's had major surgery and won't be feeling very well for several days."

"I'll take care of her," Mrs. Scruggins said and popped her knuckles.

Sherlock shuddered, shot Savich a look, and thanked the older woman for all her help. She shook Mrs. Scruggins's hand, feeling all those rings grind into her fingers.

Just before they left the kitchen, Mrs. Scruggins said, "I'm real glad you're staying here. Being alone just isn't good for Mrs. Frasier."

Savich felt a deep shaft of guilt. He remembered he hadn't said very much when Lily had insisted on returning here after recuperating with their mother. She'd seemed just fine, wanted to be with her husband again, and he'd thought, *I would want to be with Sherlock, too,* and he'd seen her off at Reagan Airport with the rest of the family. Tennyson Frasier seemed to adore her, and Lily, it seemed then to Savich, had adored him as well.

During the months she was home, she hadn't ever called to complain, to ask for help. Her e-mails were invariably upbeat. And whenever he and Sherlock had called, she'd always sounded cheerful.

And now, all these months later, this happened. He should have done something then, shouldn't have just kissed her and waved her onto the flight to take her three thousand miles away from her family. To take her back to where Beth had been killed.

He looked down to see Sherlock squeezing his hand. There was immense love in her eyes and she said only, "We will fix things, Dillon. This time we'll fix things."

He nodded and said, "I really want to see Lily's in-laws again, don't you, Sherlock? I have this feeling that perhaps we really don't know them at all."

"Agreed. We can check them out after we've seen Lily."

At the Hemlock County Hospital, everything was quiet. When they reached Lily's room, they heard the sound of voices and paused at the door for a moment.

It was Tennyson.

And Elcott Frasier, his father.

Elcott Frasier was saying, his voice all mournful, "Lily, we're so relieved that you survived that crash. It was really dicey there for a while, but you managed to pull through. I can't tell you how worried Charlotte has been, crying, wringing her hands, talking about her little Lily dying and how dreadful it would be, particularly such a short time after little Beth died. The Explorer, though, it's totaled."

That, Savich thought, was the strangest declaration of caring he'd ever heard.

"It's very nice of all of you to be concerned," Lily said, and Savich heard the pain in her voice, and something else.

Was it fear? Dislike? He didn't know. She said, "I'm very sorry that I wrecked the Explorer."

"I don't want you to worry about it, Lily," Tennyson said and took her hand. It was limp, Savich saw, she wasn't returning any pressure.

"I'll buy you another one. A gift from me to you, my beautiful little daughter-in-law," Elcott said.

"I don't want another Explorer," she said.

"No, of course not," continued Elcott. "Another Explorer would remind you of the accident, wouldn't it? We don't want that. We want you to get well. Oh yes, we'll do anything to get you well again, Lily. Just this morning, Charlotte was telling me how everyone in Hemlock Bay was talking about it, calling her, commiserating. She's very upset by it all."

Savich, quite simply, wanted to throw Elcott Frasier out the window. He knew Frasier was tough as nails, that he was a powerful man, but Savich was surprised that he hadn't been a bit more subtle, not this in-your-face bludgeoning. Why? Why this gratuitous cruelty?

Savich walked into the room like a man bent on violence until he saw his sister's white face, the pain that glazed her eyes, and he calmed immediately. He ignored the men, walked right to the bed, and leaned down, pressed his forehead lightly against hers.

"You hurt, kiddo?"

"Just a bit," she whispered, as if she were afraid to speak up. "Well, actually a whole lot. It's not too awful if I don't breathe too deeply or laugh or cry."

"More than a bit, I'd say," Savich said. "I'm going to find Dr. Larch and get you some more medication." He nodded to Sherlock and was out the door.

Sherlock smiled brightly at both her brother-in-law and Elcott Frasier. He looked the same as he had the first time she'd met him, eleven months before—tall, a bit of a paunch, a full head of thick, white hair, wavy, quite attractive. His eyes were his son's—light blue, reflective, slightly slanted. She wondered what his vices were, wondered if he really loved Lily and wanted her well. But why wouldn't he? Lily had been his son's wife for eleven months now. She was sweet, loving, very talented, and she'd lost her only child and fallen into a deep well of grief and depression.

She knew Elcott was sixty, but he looked no older than mid-fifties. He'd been a handsome man when he was younger, perhaps as handsome as his only son.

There was a daughter as well. Tansy was her name and she was, what? Twenty-eight? Thirty? Older than Lily, Sherlock thought. Tansy—an odd name, nearly as whimsical as Tennyson. She lived in Seattle, owned one of the ubiquitous coffeehouses near Pioneer Square. Sherlock had gotten the impression from Lily that Tansy didn't come back to Hemlock Bay all that often.

Elcott Frasier walked to Sherlock and grabbed her hand, shook it hard. "Mrs. Savich, what a pleasure." He looked ever so pleased to see her. She wondered how pleased he was to see Dillon, since she knew, right to her toes, that Mr. Elcott Frasier had little respect for women. It was in his eyes, in his very stance—condescending, patronizing.

"Mr. Frasier," she said and gave him her patented, guileless sunny smile. "I wish we could meet again under less trying circumstances." Go ahead, she thought, believe I'm an idiot, worth less than nothing in brainpower.

"Your poor husband is very upset by all this," Mr. Frasier said. "Given all that's happened, I can't say I blame him."

Sherlock said, "Certainly he's upset. It's good to see you again, Tennyson." She went directly to sit on the side of Lily's bed. She lightly stroked her pale hair, which was getting oily now. Thick, lank strands framed her face. Sherlock saw the pain in her eyes, how stiffly she was holding her body. She wanted to cry. "Dillon will be back in just a moment, Lily. You shouldn't have to suffer like this."

"It is about time for a bit more pain medication," a nurse said as she came through the door, Savich at her heels. No one said a word as she injected the painkiller into Lily's IV. She leaned over, checked Lily's pulse, smoothed the thin blanket to her shoulders, then straightened. "The pain will lessen almost immediately. Call if you have too much more discomfort, Mrs. Frasier."

Lily closed her eyes. After a few minutes, she said quietly, "Thank you, Dillon. It was pretty bad, but not now. Thank you." Then, without another word, she was asleep.

"Good," said Savich and motioned for them all to leave. "Let's go to the waiting room. Last time I looked, it was empty."

"My wife and I are grateful to you for being here," Elcott Frasier said. "Tennyson needs all the support he can get. The past seven months have been very hard on him."

"That's just what I was thinking," Savich said. "Lily hitting that redwood gave us just the excuse we needed to come here and support Tennyson."

"My father didn't mean it the way it sounded, Dillon," Tennyson said. "It's just been difficult—for all of us." He looked down at his watch. "I'm afraid I have patients to see. I will be back to check on Lily in about four hours."

He left them with Elcott Frasier, who asked a passing nurse to fetch him a cup of coffee. She did without hesitation because, Sherlock knew, she wasn't stupid. She recognized the Big Man on the hospital board of directors when she saw him. Sherlock wanted to punch his lights out.

Savich leaned down, kissed Sherlock on the mouth, and said low, "No, don't belt him. Now, I've got all sorts of warning whistles going off in my head. I'm going to look at that car. Grill our brother-in-law's father, okay?"

"No problem," Sherlock said.

When Dillon found Sherlock two hours later, she was in the hospital cafeteria eating a Caesar salad and speaking to Dr. Theodore Larch.

"So do you think she was so depressed that she decided to end it? Again?"

"I'm a surgeon, Mrs. Savich, not a psychiatrist. I can't speculate."

"Yeah, but you see lots of people in distress, Dr. Larch. What do you think of Lily Frasier's state of mind?"

"I think the surgical pain is masking a lot of her symptoms right now—that is, if she has any symptoms. I haven't seen any myself. But what do I know?"

"What do you think of Dr. Rossetti?"

Dr. Larch wouldn't quite meet her eyes. "He's, ah, rather new here. I don't know him all that well. Dr. Frasier, however, knows him very well. They went to medical school together, I understand. Columbia Presbyterian Medical School, in New York City."

"I didn't know that," Sherlock said and tucked it away. She wanted to meet this Dr. Rossetti, the pompous man Lily didn't like and whom Tennyson appeared to be pushing very hard on his wife.

She smiled at Dr. Larch, took a bite of her salad, which was surprisingly good, and said, "Well, you know, Dr. Larch, if Lily didn't try to kill herself, then that means that just perhaps someone is up to no good. What do you think?"

Dr. Ted Larch nearly swallowed the ice cube he was rolling around in his mouth.

"I can't imagine, no, surely not—that's crazy. If she didn't do it on purpose, then it's more likely that something just went wrong with the car, an accident, nothing more than a tragic accident."

"Yes, you're probably right. Since I'm a cop, I always leap to the sinister first. Occupational hazard. Hey, I know. She just lost control of the car—maybe a raccoon ran in front of the Explorer and she tried not to hit it—and ended up smacking the redwood."

"That sounds more likely than someone trying to kill her, Mrs. Savich."

"Yes, the raccoon theory is always preferable, isn't it?"

Sherlock saw Dillon out of the corner of her eye. She rose, patted Dr. Larch on his shoulder, and said, "Take good care of Lily, Doctor." At least now, she thought, walking quickly toward Dillon, Dr. Larch would keep a very close eye on Lily because he wouldn't forget what she'd said. He would want to dismiss it as nonsense, but he wouldn't be able to, not entirely.

Savich nodded across the cafeteria to Dr. Larch, then smiled down at his wife. Her light blue eyes seemed brighter than when he'd left her, and he knew why. She was up to something. And she was very pleased with herself.

"What about the car?"

"Nothing at all. It's been compacted."

"That was awfully fast, wasn't it?"

"Yeah, sort of like cremating a body before the autopsy could be done."

"Exactly. Dr. Larch thinks Lily is just fine, mentally, thank you very much. Actually, I think he has a crush on her. It's Dr. Rossetti he doesn't like, but who knows why? Did you know that Dr. Rossetti and Tennyson went to medical school together? Columbia Presbyterian?"

"No. That's interesting. Okay, Sherlock. I know that look. You either want me to haul you to the nearest hot tub and have my way with you, or you've done something. No hot tub? Too bad. All right, then. What have you done?"

"I planted a small bug just inside the slat on Lily's hospital bed. I already heard some interesting stuff. Come along and I'll play it back for you. Hmmm. About that hot tub, Dillon . . ."

They went to Lily's room, saw that she was still asleep and no one else was there, and Sherlock shut the door. She walked to the window, fiddled with the tiny receiver and recorder, turned on rewind, then play.

"Dammit, she needs more pain medication."

Savich said, "Who's that?"

"Dr. Larch."

"I cut it back, just like you ordered, but it was too much. Listen, there's no need to make her suffer like this."

"She doesn't react well to pain meds, I've told you that several times. It makes her even crazier than she already is. Keep the pain meds way down. I don't want her hurt anymore."

Sherlock pressed the stop button and said, "That was Tennyson Frasier. What do you think it means?"

Sherlock slipped the tiny recorder back into her jacket pocket.

"It could be perfectly innocent," Savich said. "On the other hand, the Explorer has been compacted. The guy at the junked car yard told me that Dr. Frasier told him to haul the Explorer in and compact it immediately. Will this thing click on whenever someone's speaking?"

"Yes, it's voice-activated. It turns off when there's more than six seconds of silence. I got it from Dickie in Personnel. He's a gadget freak, owed me one after I busted his sister's boyfriend—you know, the macho drug dealer who was slapping her around."

"Sherlock, have I ever told you that you never cease to amaze and thrill me?"

"Not recently. Well, not since last night, and I don't think you had the same sort of intent then."

He laughed, pulled her against him and kissed her. Her curly hair tickled his cheek. "Let's call Mom and talk to Sean."

5

Clark Hoyt, SAC of the new Eureka FBI field office, which had opened less than a year before, handed Savich the bottle of pills. "Sorry, Agent Savich. What we've got here is a really common antidepressant, name of Elavil."

"Not good," Savich said and looked out the window toward the small park just to the left of downtown. The trees were bright with fall colors. If he turned his head a bit to the right, he'd see the Old Town section on the waterfront. A beautiful town, Humboldt's county seat, Eureka was filled with countless fine Victorian homes and buildings.

"Something I can help you with, Agent Savich? Sounds like something's happening you don't like."

Savich shook his head. "I wish there was something, but the pills are exactly what they should be. I guess it would have been really easy if they were something different. I told you that the Explorer my sister totaled has been compacted. I was really holding out big hopes for those pills. Oh yeah, call me Savich."

"Okay, Hoyt here. Now, the Explorer—that was done awfully fast."

"Yes, maybe too fast, but then again, my life's work is to be suspicious. Maybe it was just very straightforward. As of right now, it's all a dead end. However, I think it's time I did a bit of digging on my brother-in-law, Dr. Tennyson Frasier."

Clark Hoyt, who had heard of some of the exploits of Sherlock, Savich, and MAX, Savich's transgendered laptop, said, "Don't tell me that you didn't do a background search on this guy before he married your sister? Seems to me a brother would have checked out the fillings in his teeth."

"Well, yeah, sure I did. But not a really deep one. Just that he didn't have a record, hadn't ever been in rehab for drugs or alcohol, stuff like that."

"And that he wasn't a bigamist?"

"No, I didn't check on that. Lily told me he'd been right up front about the fact that he'd been married before and that his wife had died. You know something, Hoyt? I wonder now what the first wife died of. I wonder how long they were married before she died." His eyes brightened.

"Savich, you don't really think he's trying to kill his wife? The pills were just what they were supposed to be."

"They were indeed, and I'm not sure. But you know, information is just about the most important thing any cop can have." Savich rubbed his hands together. "MAX is going to love this."

"You know that the Frasiers are a really big deal down in Hemlock Bay and the environs. Daddy Frasier has dealings all over the state, I understand."

"Yeah. Before, I didn't see the need to check into Papa's finances and dealings, but now it's time to be thorough."

"Is your sister going to be all right?"

"Yes, she'll be just fine."

"I've got the names of some excellent psychiatrists in

the area—all women, just like you wanted. I hope one of them will be able to help your sister."

"Yeah, me too. But you know—no matter there's no proof of any funny stuff, that it really does look like she just drove the Explorer into that redwood on purpose—I simply can't believe that Lily tried to kill herself. No matter what anyone says, I find myself coming back again and again to the fact that it just doesn't fit."

"People change, Savich. Even people we love dearly. Sometimes we can't see the change because we're just too close."

Savich took another look at that lovely park and said, "When Lily was thirteen, she was running a gambling operation in the neighborhood. She would take bets on anything from the point spread in college football games to who could shoot the most three-point baskets in any pro game. Drove my parents nuts. Since my dad was an FBI agent, the local cops didn't do anything, just snickered a lot. I think they all admired her moxie, but they gave my dad lots of grief about it, called her a chip off the old block.

"When she hit eighteen, she suddenly realized that she liked to draw and she was very good at it. She's an artist, you know, very talented."

"No, I hadn't heard."

"Actually, her talent comes from our grandmother Sarah Elliott."

"Sarah Elliott? Good grief, *the* Sarah Elliott, the artist whose paintings are in all the museums?"

"Yep. Lily's talents lie in a different direction—she's an excellent cartoonist, lots of humor and irony. Have you ever heard of the cartoon strip *No Wrinkles Remus?*"

Agent Hoyt shook his head.

"That's all right. It's political satire and shenanigans, I guess you could say. She hasn't done much for the past seven months, since the death of her daughter. But she will, and once she gets herself back together again, I'm sure she's going to be syndicated in lots of papers across the country."

"She's that good?"

"I think so. Now, given her talent, her background, can you really believe that she would try to kill herself seven months after her daughter was killed?"

"A girl who was the neighborhood bookie, then a cartoon strip artist?" Hoyt sighed. "I'd like to say no, I can't imagine it, Savich, but who knows? Aren't artists supposed to be high-strung? Temperamental? You said she still can't remember a thing about the accident?"

"Not yet."

"What are you going to do?"

"After MAX checks everything out, we'll see. No matter what, I'm taking Lily back to Washington with my wife and me. I think it's been proved that Hemlock Bay isn't healthy for her."

"Everything could be perfectly innocent," Clark Hoyt said. "She could have simply lost control of the car."

"Yeah, but you know something? I saw my brother-in-law differently this time. I saw him through Lily's eyes, maybe. It's not a pretty sight. I want to strangle him. Actually, I wanted to throw his daddy through the hospital window."

Clark Hoyt laughed. "Let me know if there's anything I can do."

"I will, thank you, Hoyt. Count on it. Thanks for the names of the shrinks."

HEMLOCK BAY, CALIFORNIA

On the following Sunday afternoon, four days after her surgery, Lily was pronounced well enough to leave the hospital. She suffered only mild discomfort, because Dr. Larch had stopped by her room, looking determined, and given her some pills to keep the worst of the pain at bay. She still walked bent over like an old person, but her eyes were clear, her mood upbeat.

Sherlock had wanted to ask Dr. Larch about lowering Lily's meds temporarily on Dr. Frasier's orders, but Savich said, "Nope, let's just hold off on that for a while."

"Nothing else good on the tape," Sherlock said in some disgust as she removed the small bug from beneath Lily's hospital bed while Lily was in the small bathroom bathing. "Not even doctors or nurses gossiping."

Ten minutes later Savich said to his sister as he pushed her wheelchair toward the elevator, "I told Tennyson that Sherlock and I are taking you to see your new shrink. He wasn't happy about that, said he didn't know anything about this woman. She could be a rank charlatan and he'd lose all sorts of money, maybe even get you more depressed. I just let him talk on, then gave him my patented smile."

"That smile," Sherlock said, "translates into 'You mess with me, buddy, and even your toenails are gonna hurt.'"

"In any case, at the end of all his ranting, there was nothing he could do about it. He tried to get me to convince you to see Dr. Rossetti. I do wonder why he thinks the guy is so great."

"He's not," Lily said. "He's horrible." She actually shuddered. "He came back again this morning. The nurse had just washed my hair for me, so I looked human and felt well enough to take him on."

"What happened?" Sherlock asked. She was carrying Lily's small overnight bag. Savich pushed her wheelchair onto the elevator, punched the button. No one else was on board.

Lily shuddered yet again. "I think he'd talked to Tennyson some more. He tried to change his tactics. He actually attempted to be ingratiating, at least at first. When he slithered into my room—yes, that's it exactly, he slithered—Nurse Carla Brunswick had just finished blow-drying my hair."

Nurse Brunswick turned toward him and said, "Doctor."

"Leave us alone for a bit, Nurse. Thank you."

Lily said, "I don't want Nurse Brunswick to leave, Dr. Rossetti. I want you to leave."

"Please, Mrs. Frasier, just a moment of your time. I fear we got off on the wrong foot when I was here before. You were just out of surgery; it was simply too soon for you to want to hear about anything. Please, just a few minutes of your time."

Nurse Brunswick smiled at Lily, patted her hand, then left the hospital room.

"I see that I have little choice here, Russell. What do you want?"

If he was angered at her use of his first name, he didn't let on. He kept smiling, walked to her bed, and stood there, towering over her. She looked at his hands; his plump hands sported a ring this time—a huge diamond on his pinkie. She wished she could throw him out of her room.

"I just wanted to speak to you, Mrs. Frasier—Lily. See if perhaps we could deal better with each other, perhaps you could come to trust me, to let me help you."

"No."

"Are you in pain, Lily?"

"Yes, Russell, I am."

"Would you like me to give you a mild antidepressant?"

"My pain is from my ribs and my missing spleen."

"Yes, well, that pain will likely suppress the other, deeper pain for a while longer."

"I hope so."

"Mrs. Frasier—Lily—won't you come to my office, perhaps next Monday? That will give you another week to recuperate."

"No, Russell. Ah, here's Dr. Larch. Hello. Do come in. Dr. Rossetti was just leaving."

Savich looked ready to spit by the time Lily finished, but she just laughed. "No need to go pound him, Dillon. He left, didn't say another word, just walked out. Dr. Larch didn't move until he was gone."

"What I don't understand," Sherlock said thoughtfully, "is why both Tennyson and Dr. Rossetti want you as his patient so very much. Isn't that strange? You give Rossetti grief and he still wants you?"

"Yes," Savich said slowly, "it is strange. We'll have to see what MAX has to say about Russell Rossetti. He was ready to give you some antidepressants, right there, on the spot?"

"It seems so."

After Lily was in the car, a pillow over her stomach and ribs, the seat belt as loose as possible over the pillow, Savich said, "I have a psychiatrist for you, Lily. No, not someone to shrink you and give you more medication, but a woman who is very good at hypnosis. What do you think?"

"Hypnosis? Oh, goodness, she'll help me remember what happened?"

"I hope so. It's a start anyway. Maybe it will jump-start your memory. Since it's Sunday, she's coming into her office especially for you."

"Dillon, I think I just gained a whole ton of energy."

Sherlock heard her say under her breath, "I'll know, finally, if I'm really crazy."

"Yes, you'll know, and that's the best thing to happen," Sherlock said and patted her shoulder.

"Then we're off right now to Eureka."

Dr. Marlena Chu was a petite Chinese-American woman who looked barely old enough to buy liquor.

Lily was tall, nearly five feet eight in her ballet flats, which were what she was wearing today, and she wondered how she could trust someone so small she could easily tuck her beneath her armpit.

Dr. Chu met them in her outer office, since there was no one else there on Sunday. "Your brother has told me what has happened," she said. "This must be very difficult for you, Mrs. Frasier." She took Lily's hands in her own small ones and added, "You need to sit down. I can see that you're still very weak. Would you like a glass of water?"

Her hands felt warm, Lily thought; she didn't want to let them go. And her voice was incredibly soothing. She suddenly felt much calmer, and surely that was odd, but true nonetheless. Also, the nagging pain in her ribs seemed to fade. She smiled at Dr. Chu, hanging on to her hands like a lifeline.

"No, I'm just fine. Well, maybe a bit tired."

"All right, then. Come into my office and sit down. I have a very comfortable chair and a nice, high footstool so you won't feel like you're pulling anything. Yes, here we are."

Her inner office was perfectly square with soft blue furnishings and lots of clean, oak parquet floor. Again, Lily felt a wave of peace and calm wash through her.

"Do let me help you sit down, Mrs. Frasier."

"Please, call me Lily."

"Thank you. I'd like that." As soon as Lily was seated, Dr. Chu brought her chair alongside and took Lily's left hand in hers again. Dr. Chu watched Lily's eyelids flutter as warmth and calm flowed through her, and was pleased. She watched Mr. Savich ease the footstool beneath his sister's narrow feet and saw it immediately lessened the pull on her stitches. She studied her patient. Even though she was pale, her eyes were bright. Lovely eyes, a soft light blue that went very nicely with her blond hair. She was a lovely young woman, but that didn't really matter. What was important was that she was in trouble. What was more important was that she was soaking up the strength Dr. Chu was giving her. "Lily is such a romantic name. It sounds like soft music; it's the sort of name to make one dream of fanciful things."

Lily smiled. "It's my grandmother's name. Coincidence, maybe, but she grew the most beautiful lilies."

"It's interesting how some things work out, isn't it?"

"Yes, interesting, but sometimes it's also terrifying."

"True, but there is nothing here to harm you, Lily." She patted Lily's hand again. Dr. Chu knew that Lily Frasier was an artist, and that meant she was creative, probably very bright. Such folk usually went under very easily. She said in her soft voice, "You understand that I'm going to try to help you remember what happened last Wednesday evening. Do you want this?"

"Yes, I want to know very badly what really happened. Just tell me what to do. I've never been hypnotized before."

"It's nothing, really. I just want you to relax." She lightly squeezed Lily's hand.

Lily felt more warmth flow through her, all the way to her bones, felt herself becoming utterly calm. Those small hands of Dr. Chu's, how could they make her feel like this?

Savich pulled a chair next to Lily's and took her other hand. A strong hand, she thought, strong fingers. His hand didn't make hers feel warm, but it did make her feel safe. He said nothing at all, was just there beside her, there for her. Sherlock sat on a sofa behind Lily, quiet as could be.

Dr. Chu said, "You will perhaps believe this a bit odd, Lily, but I don't swing a watch in front of your eyes or let you lie on the sofa and chant this and that over and over. No, we'll just sit here and chat. I understand you draw a cartoon strip. *No Wrinkles Remus*? Such an interesting title. What does it mean?"

Lily actually smiled. She felt the familiar pain of Beth's death ease away. "Remus is a United States senator from the state of West Dementia, located in the Midwest. He's very bright, utterly ruthless, completely amoral, has overweening ambition, and loves to pull fast ones on his opponents. He's also known as 'Ept Remus,' as opposed to inept, because he's so fast to come up with a new angle to get what he wants. He's a spin master. He never gives up, just ignores what people say because he knows that soon enough they'll forget, ignores what the truth is, and continues until he gets what he wants. What he wants now is the presidency, and he's shafted a friend of his to get it."

Dr. Chu raised a thin, perfectly arched black brow and smiled. "An interesting character study, and not all that unfamiliar."

Lily actually chuckled. "I finished another strip just last week. His friend Governor Braveheart isn't taking being shafted well. He's fighting back. Although he's tough as hell, he's got one big problem—he's honest. It's good. At least I hope it is."

"Did you take it to your editor at the paper?"

Lily paused a moment and closed her eyes. "No, I didn't."

"Why not?"

"Because I started feeling bad again."

"What do you mean by 'feeling bad'?"

"Like nothing really mattered. Beth was dead and I was alive, and nothing was worth anything, including me and anything I did."

"You went from feeling great and creative, from smiles and laughter to utter depression?"

"Yes."

"In just a day?"

"Yes. Maybe less. I don't remember."

"On the day your husband left for Chicago, how did you feel, Lily?"

"I don't remember feeling much of anything. I was . . . just there."

"I see. Your husband called you the next day—Wednesday—and he wanted you to take some medical slides to a doctor in Ferndale?"

"That's right."

"And the only road is 211."

"Yes. I hate that road, always have. It's dangerous. And it was dusk. Driving at that time of day always makes me antsy. I'm always very careful."

"It makes me nervous as well. Now, you took two more antidepressant pills, right?"

"That's right. Then I slept. I had terrible nightmares."

"Tell me what you remember about the nightmares."

Dr. Chu wasn't holding her hand now, but still Lily felt a touch of warmth go through her, felt like it was deep inside her now, so deep it was warming her very soul. "I saw Beth struck by that car, over and over, struck and hurled screaming and screaming, at least twenty feet, crying out my name, over and over. When I awoke, I could still see Beth. I remember just lying there and crying and then I felt lethargic, my brain dull."

"You felt leached of hope?"

"Yes, that's it exactly. I felt like nothing was worth anything, particularly me. I wasn't worth anything. Everything was black, just black. Nothing mattered anymore."

"All right, Lily, now you're driving away from your house. You're in your red Explorer. What do you think of your car?"

"Tennyson yells every time I call it a car. I haven't done that for months now. It's an Explorer and nothing else is like it and it isn't a car, so you call it by its name and that's it."

"You don't like the Explorer much, do you?"

"My in-laws gave it to me for my birthday. That was in August. I turned twenty-seven."

Dr. Chu didn't appear to be probing or delving; she was merely speaking with a friend, nothing more, nothing less.

She was also lightly stroking Lily's left hand. Then she turned to Savich and nodded.

"Lily."

"Yes, Dillon."

"How do you feel, sweetheart?"

"So warm, Dillon, so very warm. And there's no nagging pain anywhere. It's wonderful. I want to marry Dr. Chu. She's got magic in her hands."

He smiled at that and said, "I'm glad you feel good. Are you driving on 211 yet?"

"Yes, I just made a right onto the road. I don't mind the beginning of it, but you get into the redwoods and it's so dark and the trees press in on you. I've always thought that some maniac carved that road."

"I agree with you. What are you thinking, Lily?"

"I'm thinking that when it's dark, it will be just like a shroud is thrown over all those thick redwoods. Just like Beth was in a shroud and I'm so depressed that I want to end it, Dillon, just end it and get it over with. It's relentless, this greedy pain. I'm thinking it's settled into my soul and it won't leave me, ever. I just can't stand it any longer."

"This pain," Dr. Chu said in her soft voice, holding Lily's hand now, squeezing occasionally, "tell me more about this pain."

"I know the pain wants to be one with me. I want to give over to it. I know that if I become the pain and the pain becomes me, then I'll be able to expiate my guilt."

"You came to the conclusion that you had to kill yourself because it was the only way you could make reparation? To redress the balance?"

"Yes. A life for a life. My life—worth nothing much—for her small, precious life."

Then Lily frowned.

Dr. Chu lightly ran her palm over Lily's forearm, then back to clasp her limp hand. "What are you thinking now, Lily?"

"I just realized that something isn't right. I didn't kill Beth. No, I'd been at the newspaper, giving my cartoon to Boots O'Malley, seeing what he thought, you know?"

"I know. And he laughed, right?"

"Yes. I heard the sheriff say later that Beth's body had been thrown at least twenty feet."

Lily stopped. She squeezed Dr. Chu's hand so tightly her knuckles whitened.

"Just stay calm, Lily. Everything is just fine. I'm here. Your brother and Mrs. Savich are here. Forget what the sheriff said. Now, you suddenly recognized that you didn't kill Beth."

"That's right," Lily whispered, her eyelids fluttering. "I realize that something is wrong. I suddenly remember taking those sleeping pills that Tennyson put on the bedside table. I took so many of them, felt them stick in my throat and I swallowed and swallowed to get them down, and I sat with that bottle and chanted, more, more, more, and then the bottle was nearly empty and I thought suddenly, *Wait, I don't want to die,* but then it was too late, and I felt so sorry for the loss of Beth and the loss of me."

"I don't understand, Lily," Savich said in that darkly smooth voice of his. "You told me about the pills you took just after Beth's funeral. Why are you thinking about that now, while you're driving?"

"Because I realize that I can't really remember actually taking those pills. Now isn't that odd?"

"It's very odd. Tell us more."

"Well, I realize I didn't want to die then, and I don't want to die now. But why is the guilt eating at me like this? What's inside my brain that's making me want to simply drive the Explorer right into the thick trees that line this horrible road?"

"And did you find an answer, Lily?"

"Yes, I did." She stopped, just stopped and sighed deeply. She was asleep. Her head fell lightly to the side.

"It's all right, Mr. Savich. Let's just let her rest awhile, then I'll wake her and we can carry on. She'll be back with us when she wakes up. We'll see if she needs to go under again.

"You know, Mr. Savich, I'm getting more and more curious about that first time when she took all those sleeping pills. Just maybe we should go into that as well."

"Oh, yes," Sherlock said from behind them.

However, they didn't have to wake Lily up. Not more than another minute passed when suddenly Lily opened her eyes, blinked, and said, "I remember everything." She smiled at Dr. Chu, then said to her brother, "I didn't try to kill myself, Dillon, I didn't."

Dr. Chu took both of her hands now and leaned very close. "Tell us exactly what happened, Lily."

"I came back to myself. I felt clear and alert and appalled at what I'd been considering. Then the road twisted, started one of those steep descents. I realized I was going too fast and I pressed down on the brake."

"What happened?" Savich said, leaning toward her.

"Nothing happened."

Sherlock whispered, "I knew it, I just knew it."

Savich said, "Did you pump the brakes the way Dad taught you way back when?"

"Yes, I pumped gently, again and again. Still there was nothing. I was terrified. I yanked up the emergency brake. I know it only works on the rear tires, but I figured it would have to slow me down."

"Don't tell me," Savich said. "The emergency brake didn't work either."

She just shook her head, swallowed convulsively. "No, it didn't. I was veering from the center toward the deep ravine on my left. I pulled back, but not too far because the redwoods were directly to my right, thick, impenetrable. I was going too fast, and the downhill grade was becoming even steeper. That stretch twists and wheels back on itself a whole lot before it flattens out at the outskirts of Ferndale."

Sherlock said from behind her, "Did you slam the shift into park?"

"Oh, yes. There was an awful grinding noise, like the transmission was tearing itself up. The Explorer shuddered, screamed, and all the wheels locked up. I went into a skid. I tried to let the side of the Explorer scrape against the redwoods, to slow me down, but then the road twisted again. I knew I was going to die."

Savich pulled her very gently into his arms, settling her on his lap. Dr. Chu never released her left hand. Lily lay against him, her head on his shoulder. She felt Sherlock's fingers lightly stroking her hair. She drew a deep breath and said, "I remember so clearly slamming head-on into that poor redwood, thinking in that split second that the redwood had survived at least a hundred years of violent Pacific storms but it wouldn't survive me.

"I remember hearing the blaring of the horn, so loud, like it was right inside my head. And then there just wasn't anything."

She pulled back and smiled, a beautiful smile, clean and filled with self-awareness and hope. "Now, this is a very strange thing, Dillon. The brakes didn't work. Did someone try to kill me?"

Since Dr. Chu was still holding her hand, Lily wasn't frightened. Actually, she felt good all the way to her toes. Her smile didn't fade a bit with those awful words.

"Yeah," Savich said, looking directly into her eyes. "Probably so. Isn't that a kick?"

"Now," Dr. Chu said, "let's just go back and see how it happened that you ended up in the hospital with all those sleeping pills in your stomach."

Lily felt peaceful and excited at the same time. "Yes, let's go back."

6

"All right, MAX, whatcha got?"

Sherlock walked over, looked down at the laptop screen. "Oh, dear, he's not doing anything. You don't think he's becoming MAXINE again so soon, do you, Dillon? He's in a mood?"

"Nah, MAX is still a he, and he's just concentrating. He's going to turn up something for us."

"You hope."

"MAX just shuddered a bit. That means he's digging deep. Is Lily asleep?"

"Yes, I just checked on her. She didn't want a pain pill. Said she didn't need it. Isn't that amazing?"

"Lily told me that a doctor who could make her feel good without hurting her was sure an improvement over a husband who can't. She said she still feels better for having met her."

"Since Dr. Chu didn't hold our hands, we'll have to work out our stress at the gym. Too bad." Then Sherlock laughed. "Remember when she asked Dr. Chu to marry her? That was good, Dillon. She wants out of this mess.

"Now, according to Mrs. Scruggins, Tennyson will be home in about two hours. She told me she's making a vegetarian dinner just for you—her special zucchini lasagna, and an apple-onion dish that she assured me would make you hum and help you keep your, er, physique perfect. I think she'd like to see you on a calendar, Dillon. What do you think?"

Savich just laughed, then smacked MAX very lightly on his hard drive with the palm of his hand.

"Not going to commit yourself, are you? Okay, she's got a big crush on you, Dillon. I think it struck when she saw you in your T-shirt this morning, your pants zipped up but not fastened. There was lust in her eyes when she said your name. She had her hands clasped on her bosom. That's a sure sign she wants you."

Savich cocked a dark eyebrow at his wife. "Don't go there, Sherlock, it scares me too much."

She thought about how she felt whenever she saw him in a T-shirt—or less—and didn't doubt Mrs. Scruggins's fast-beating heart one bit. She lightly touched her fingertips to the back of his neck and began to knead.

MAX beeped.

"He's jealous."

"No, that was a burp. Well, maybe he's telling me he's distracted, what with you draped all over me."

Sherlock leaned down to kiss the back of his neck, then just grinned at him as she did some stretching. "It really is time for the gym. Do you think there's one here in Hemlock Bay?"

"We'll find one. Tomorrow morning, if Lily's still feeling fine, we'll go get the kinks out and lower our stress levels."

She stretched a bit more, rubbing the back of her neck. "You think Tennyson was giving her pills to make her depressed, don't you? You think he changed the pills back, just to be on the safe side since her big brother Fed was here."

"Sounds good to me. After Dr. Chu couldn't get anything conclusive about Lily's so-called attempt to commit suicide right after Beth's funeral, I'm thinking that maybe she never tried to kill herself at all."

"It was strange how Lily sort of remembered, but she didn't really. If she didn't do it, then it had to be Tennyson, and that was the bastard's first try. They'd been married all of four months, Dillon. That's incredibly cold-blooded. It makes me really mad. Let's prove it so we can pound him."

"We'll try, Sherlock. Here we go. Good work, MAX."

Both of them read the small print on the screen, as Savich slowly scrolled. A couple of minutes later, Savich raised his head and looked up into Sherlock's blue eyes.

"Not really all that much of a surprise, is it? So, our Tennyson was married once before, just like he told Lily. Only thing is, he didn't bother to mention that his first wife committed suicide only thirteen months after they'd tied the knot."

Savich hit his palm against his forehead. "I'm an idiot, Sherlock. I shouldn't have given him the benefit of the doubt, shouldn't have respected his privacy. Some brother I am after that bastard first husband of hers. After Jack Crane, I should have opened every closet in his house, checked his bank statements for the past twenty years. You know something else? All I had to do was flat-out ask Tennyson just how his first wife died."

"He probably would have lied."

"It wouldn't have mattered. You know I can tell when someone's lying. Also, I could have done then what I'm doing now. My holding back, my respecting Lily's decision, could have cost Lily her life. I want you to flay me, Sherlock."

Sherlock was twining one curly strand of hair round and round her finger, a sure sign she was upset. He immediately took her hand between his two large ones. She said, "I'd just as soon flay myself, Dillon. Do you think Lily would still have married him if she'd known that the first wife killed herself?"

"We can ask her. You can bet she'll be asking herself the same question, over and over. But the thing is that this is now, and her eyes are wide open. Eleven months ago she believed she loved him, thought she'd found a really wonderful father for Beth. If Tennyson had told her, she'd probably have felt sorry for him—poor man—losing his wife like that. She probably would have married him anyway. If I'd told her, it probably would have pissed her off, she'd have resented me, and she would have married him."

"Okay, so no flaying. You know, Dillon, sometimes we women do think with our hearts, not like you men, who think with your . . . well, that's better left unsaid, isn't it?"

He grinned up at her. "Yep, probably so."

"All of it was an illusion. Look, the first wife—her name was Lynda—was rich, Dillon, had a nice, fat trust fund from her grandfather. Oh, my, she was only twenty-five."

"Ah, just read this, Sherlock." Savich stroked his fingers over his jaw and added, disgust thick in his voice, "That immoral bastard. It usually comes down to money, doesn't it? Daddy got himself into a mess and so his son tries to bail him out. Or maybe it was both of them in the mess up to their necks. That sounds more likely."

"Yes," Sherlock said. "It's so mundane, really, just a couple of greedy men trying to get what they want."

Savich nodded as he read to the end of MAX's information. He sat back a moment, then said, "It seems very likely to me that Tennyson killed his first wife as well as trying to kill Lily. Was Daddy in on it with him? Very likely. Doesn't matter. I don't want to take any more chances. I want Lily out of here. I want you to take her to that very nice bed-and-breakfast we stayed at once in Eureka. What was it?"

"The Mermaid's Tail, just off Calistoga Street. It's late

fall. Tourist season is over so they'll have room. What will you do?"

"I'm going to have a nice vegetarian dinner with Tennyson. I love lasagna. I'm going to see if I can get him to admit to anything useful. I really want to nail him. I'll join you and Lily later."

He rose and pulled her tightly against him. "Take MAX with you. Keep after him to find out all he can about Daddy Frasier's efforts to get that public road built to the lovely resort spot on the coast he's so hot to build. Without the state legislature passing it, the project would be doomed. He's having trouble. Maybe they ran out of bribery money."

"Don't forget the condos he's planning, too—Golden Sunset."

"Yes, lots of potential profit from those as well. Elcott Frasier has lots and lots of bucks already invested. I wonder if they ran into more roadblocks. Maybe that's why they wanted Lily out of the way. They were in deep financial trouble again. Now, let's get you guys packed up and out of this house."

But Lily didn't cooperate. She was awake, she still didn't hurt very much at all, and she was very clearheaded. She smacked her palm to the side of her head and announced, delight and wonder in her voice, "Would you look at me—I'm not depressed. In fact I can't imagine being depressed. Nope, everything inside there is rattling around clockwise, just as it should be."

They were in the hallway outside her bedroom. Lily was dressed in loose jeans and a baggy sweater, hair pulled back in a ponytail, no makeup, hands on hips, reminding Savich of his once sixteen-year-old sister who stood tall and defiant in front of their parents, who were dressing her down but good for her latest bookie scheme. "No, Dillon, I won't just turn tail and leave. I want to read everything MAX has come up with so far. I want to speak to Tennyson, confront him with all this. It's my right to find out if my husband of eleven months married me only to kill me off. Oh, dear. There's a big problem here. Why would he do it? I don't have any money."

"Unfortunately, sweetheart," Savich said, his voice very gentle, "you are very rich. All us kids tend to forget what Grandmother left us."

"Oh, my Sarah Elliott paintings. You're right, I forget about them, since they're always on loan to a museum."

"Yes, but they're legally yours, all eight paintings, willed to you. I just e-mailed Simon Russo in New York. You remember him, don't you? You met him way back when he and I were in college."

"I remember. That was way back in the dark ages before I started screwing up big time."

"No, you were screwing up then, too," Savich said, lightly punching her arm. "Remember that point spread you had on the Army-Navy game? And Dad found out that you'd gotten twenty dollars off Mr. Hodges next door?"

"I hid out in your room, under your bed, until he calmed down."

They laughed. It sounded especially good to Sherlock, who beamed at both of them. Lily depressed? It was hard, looking at her now, to believe that she'd ever been depressed.

Lily said, "Yes, I remember Simon Russo. He was a real pain in the butt and you said yeah, that was true enough, but it didn't matter because he was such a good wide receiver."

"That's Simon. He's neck-deep in the art world, you know. He got back to me right away, said eight Sarah Elliotts are worth in the neighborhood of eight to ten million dollars."

Lily stared at him blank-faced. She was shaking her head. "That's unbelievable. No, you're pulling my leg, aren't you? Please tell me you're kidding, Dillon."

"Nope. The paintings have done nothing but gain in value since Grandmother died seven years ago. Each of the four grandchildren got eight paintings. Each painting is worth about one million dollars right now, more or less, according to Simon."

"That's an enormous responsibility, Dillon."

He nodded. "Like you, I think the rest of us have felt like we're the guardians; it's our responsibility to see that the paintings are kept safe throughout our lifetimes and exhibited so that the public can enjoy them. I remember yours were on loan to the Art Institute of Chicago. Are they still there?"

Lily said slowly, rubbing her palms on the legs of her jeans, "No. When Tennyson and I married he thought they should be here, in a regional museum, close to where we lived. So I moved them to the Eureka Art Museum."

Savich said without missing a beat, "Does Tennyson know anyone who works in the museum?"

Lily said very quietly, "Elcott Frasier is on the board of the museum."

"Bingo," Sherlock said.

When Tennyson Frasier walked through the front door of his house that evening, he saw his wife standing at the foot of the stairs, looking toward him. She watched his eyes fill with love and concern. But it didn't take him long to realize that something was up. He sensed it, like an animal senses danger lying in wait ahead. His step slowed. But when he reached Lily, he said gently, as he took her hands, "Lily, my dear, you are very pale. You must still be in pain. After all, the surgery wasn't long ago at all. Please, sweetheart, let me take you up to bed. You need to rest."

"Actually, I feel fine, Tennyson. You needn't worry. Mrs. Scruggins has made us a superb dinner. Are you hungry?"

"If you're sure you want to eat downstairs, then yes, I'm hungry." He sent a wary look to his brother- and sister-in-law, who had just walked into the entrance hall from the living room. "Hello, Sherlock, Savich."

Savich just nodded.

"Hope you had a good day, Tennyson," Sherlock said and gave him a sunny smile. She hoped he couldn't tell just yet that she wanted to strangle him with his own tie.

"No, I didn't actually," Tennyson said. He took a step back from Lily and stuck his hands in his pockets. He didn't take his eyes off his wife. "Old Mr. Daily's medication isn't working anymore. He talked about sticking his rifle in his mouth. He reminded me of you, Lily, that awful hopelessness when the mind can't cope. It was a dreadful day. I didn't even have time to come visit you before you left the hospital. I'm sorry."

"Well, these unpleasant sorts of things occasionally happen, don't they?" Sherlock patted his arm and just smiled at the disgusted look he gave her.

Savich winked at her as they walked to the dining room.

Tennyson tenderly seated Lily in her chair in the long dining room. Lily loved this room. When she'd moved in, she had painted it a light yellow and dumped all the heavy furniture. It was very modern now, with a glossy Italian Art Deco table, chairs, and sideboard. On the walls were five Art Deco posters, filled with color and high-living stylized characters. Tennyson was no sooner seated than Mrs. Scruggins began to serve. Normally, she simply left the food in the oven and went home, but not this evening.

Tennyson said, "Good evening, Mrs. Scruggins. It's very nice of you to stay."

"My pleasure, Dr. Frasier," she said.

Sherlock, who was watching her pile food onto Lily's plate, knew that Mrs. Scruggins wasn't about to leave unless she was booted out. "I couldn't very well leave when Mrs. Frasier was coming home, now could I?"

Savich nearly smiled. Mrs. Scruggins wanted to hear everything. She knew the air was hot, even if she didn't know the reason, and would become hotter.

Lily took a small bite of a homemade dinner roll that tasted divine. She said to her husband, "Oh yes, Tennyson, you'll be pleased, I hope, to hear that I didn't try to kill myself by running the Explorer into the redwood. Actually, neither the brakes nor the emergency brake worked. Since I was on that very gnarly part of 211, I didn't stand a chance. Doesn't that relieve your mind?"

Tennyson was silent, frowning a bit over a forkful of lasagna, beautifully flavored, that was nearly to his mouth. He swallowed, then said slowly, his head cocked to the side, "You remembered, Lily?"

"Yes, I remembered."

"Ah, then you mean that you changed your mind? But it was too late because then the brakes failed?"

"That's it exactly. I realized that I didn't want to kill myself, but then it didn't matter, since someone had evidently disabled the brakes."

"Someone? Come on, Lily, that's absurd."

Savich said easily, "Unfortunately, the Explorer was compacted the very next day after the accident, so we can't check it out to see if it is or isn't absurd."

"Perhaps, Lily," Tennyson said very gently, "just perhaps you're wanting to remember something different, something that could alleviate the pain of the past seven months."

"I don't think so, Tennyson. You see, I remembered while I was under hypnosis. And then when I came out of it, I remembered the rest of it, all by myself. All of it."

A thick eyebrow went straight up. Savich had never before seen an eyebrow do a vertical lift like that. Tennyson turned to Savich and spoke, his voice low and controlled, but it was obvious to everyone that he was very angry. "You're telling me you took Lily to see a hypnotist? One of those charlatans who plant garbage in their patients' minds?"

"Oh, no," Sherlock said, taking Lily's clenched fist beneath the table. "This doctor didn't plant anything, Tennyson. She simply helped Lily to remember what happened that evening. Both Dillon and I were there the whole time, and he and I are very familiar with hypnotists as part of our work. It was all on the up-and-up. Now, don't you think it's strange that the brakes didn't work? Don't you think it's at least possible that someone disabled them from what Lily said?"

"No, what I think is that Lily disremembers. I'm not sure if she's doing it on purpose or if she's simply confused and wants desperately for it to be this way. Don't you see? She made up the brakes failing so she wouldn't have to face up to what she did. I don't think the brakes failed. I certainly don't think anyone cut the lines. That's beyond what is reasonable, and her saying that, claiming that that's what happened, well, it really worries me. I don't want Lily to even consider such a thing; it could make her lose ground again.

"Listen, I'm a psychiatrist—a real one—one who doesn't use hocus-pocus on people to achieve some sort of preordained result. I am not pleased about this, Savich. I am Lily's husband. I am responsible for her."

Sherlock pointed her fork at him and said, her voice colder than a psychopath's heart, "You haven't been doing such a good job of it, have you?"

7

Tennyson looked as if he wanted to throw his plate at Sherlock's head. His breathing was hard and fast.

Sherlock continued after a moment of chewing thoughtfully on a green bean, "I've also wondered at the timing. You remember, don't you, Tennyson? You called to ask Lily to deliver those medical slides to Ferndale, knowing it would be dusk to dark when she was on 211. Then the brakes failed. That sounds remarkably fortuitous, doesn't it?"

"Damn you, you both went behind my back, did something you knew I wouldn't approve of! Lily is fine now. She no longer needs you here. I repeat, I am her husband. I will take care of her. As for your ridiculous veiled accusations, I won't lower myself to answer them."

"I think you should consider lowering yourself," Sherlock said, and in that moment, Tennyson looked fit to kill.

Savich waited a moment for him to regain some calm, then said, "All right, let's just move along. Let's suppose, Tennyson, that Lily does remember everything exactly as it happened. That raises a couple of good questions. Why did the brakes fail? Perhaps it was simply a mechanical problem? But then the emergency brake failed, too. It's rather a difficult stretch to make if there's also a second mechanical problem, don't you think? And that means that someone had to have disabled the systems. Who, Tennyson? Who would want Lily dead? Realize, too, that if she had died, why then, everyone would have declared it a clear case of suicide. Who would want that, Tennyson?"

Tennyson rose slowly to his feet. Sherlock could see the pulse pounding in his neck. He was furious, and he was also something more. Frightened? Desperate? She just couldn't tell, which disappointed her. He was very good, very controlled.

Tennyson said, the words nearly catching in his throat, "You are a cop. You see bad things. You deal with bad people, evil people. What happened wasn't caused by someone out to kill Lily—other than Lily. She's been very ill. Everyone knows that. Lily knows that; she even accepts it. The most logical explanation is that she simply doesn't remember what happened because she can't bring herself to admit that she really tried to commit suicide again. That's all there is to it. I won't stand for your accusations any longer. This is my home. I want you both to leave. I want you both out of our lives."

Savich said, "All right, Tennyson, Sherlock and I will be delighted to leave. Actually, we'll leave right after dinner. Mrs. Scruggins made it just for me, and I don't want to miss any of it. Oh, yes, did I tell you that we know all about Lynda—you remember, don't you? She was your first wife who killed herself only thirteen months after marrying you?"

They hadn't told Lily about Lynda Middleton Frasier. She froze where she sat, her mouth open, utter disbelief scored on her face, any final hope leached out with those words. When her husband had spoken so calmly, so reasonably, she had wondered if it was possible that her mind had altered what really happened, that her mind was so squirrelly that she simply couldn't trust any thought, any reaction. But not any longer. Now she knew she hadn't dis-remembered anything. Oh, God, had he killed his first wife? It was horrible, unbelievable. Lily was shaking from the inside out—she couldn't help it.

She said slowly, holding her knife in a death grip, her knuckles white from the strain, "I remember that you told me you'd been married for a very short time, Tennyson, a long time ago."

"A long time ago?" Sherlock said, an eyebrow arched. "Sounds like maybe it was a decade or more, doesn't it? Like he ran away with a girl when he was eighteen? Actually, Lily, Tennyson's first wife, Lynda, killed herself two years ago—just eight months before you came to Hemlock Bay and met him." She looked over at Tennyson and said, her voice utterly emotionless, "However, you didn't say a word about your wife having killed herself. Why is that, Tennyson?"

"It was a tragic event in my life," Tennyson said calmly, in control again, as he picked up his wineglass and sipped at the Napa Valley Chardonnay. It was very dry, very woody, just as he preferred. "It is still painful. Why would I wish to speak of it? Not that it was a secret. Lily could have heard it from anyone in town, from my own family even."

Sherlock leaned forward, her food forgotten. The gaunt-let was thrown. This was fascinating. She smiled at Tennyson Frasier. "Still, doesn't it seem like it would be on the relevant side, Tennyson, for her to know, particularly after Lily tried to kill herself seven months ago? Wouldn't you begin to think, Oops, could there be something wrong, just maybe, with me? Two wives trying to do away with them-selves after they've been married to me only a short time? What are the odds on that, do you think, Tennyson? Two dead wives, one live husband?"

"No, that's all ridiculous. None of it was at all relevant. Lily isn't anything like Lynda. Lily was simply bowled over by her child's death, by her role in her child's death."

"I didn't have a role in Beth's death," Lily said. "I realize that now."

"Do you really believe that, Lily? Just think about it, all right? Now, as for Lynda, she had a brain tumor. She was dying."

This was a corker, Savich thought. "A brain tumor?"

"Yes, Savich, she was diagnosed with a brain tumor. It wasn't operable. She knew she was going to die. She didn't want the inevitable pain, the further loss of self, the deterioration of her physical abilities. Her confusion was growing by the day because of the tumor. She hated it. She wanted to be the one to decide her own end, and so she did. She gave herself an injection of potassium chloride. It works very quickly. As for the tumor, I saw to it that it was kept quiet. I saw no reason to tell anyone." He paused for a moment, looked at Savich, then at Sherlock. "There are, of course, records. Check if you want to, I don't care. I'm not lying."

"Hmmm," Sherlock said. "So you think it's better for a woman to be known as a suicide for no good reason at all?" Sherlock sat back in her chair now, arms crossed over her breasts.

"It was my call and that's what I decided to do at the time."

"Thirteen months," Savich said. "Married the first time only thirteen months. If Lily had managed to die in that accident, then she would have beaten Lynda to the grave by two months. Or, if she had died in her first attempt, right after Beth's death, then she would have really broken the record."

Tennyson Frasier said slowly, looking directly at his wife, "I don't find that amusing, Savich. You have judged me on supposition, on a simple coincidence, no evidence that would stand up anywhere, and surely a cop shouldn't do that. Lily didn't die, thank God, either time. If she had died in that accident, I doubt I would have survived. I love her very much. I want her well."

He was good, Savich thought, very good indeed. Very fluent, very reasoned and logical, and the appeal to gut emotion was surefire. Tennyson was certainly right about one thing—they didn't have any proof. He was right about another thing—Savich had already judged him guilty. Guilty as sin. They had to get proof. MAX had to dig deeper. There would be something; there always was.

Sherlock chewed on a homemade roll that was now cold, swallowed, then said in the mildest voice imaginable, "Where did Lynda get the potassium chloride?"

"From her doctor, the one who diagnosed her in the first place. He was infatuated with her, which is why, I believe, he assisted her. I knew nothing about any of it until she was dead and he told me what had happened, what he had helped her do. I didn't file charges because I'd known she'd wanted to end her life herself, on her own terms. Dr. Cord died only a short while later. It was horrible, all of it."

Lily said, "I heard about Dr. Cord's death from a woman in Casey's Food Market. She said he shot himself while cleaning his rifle, such a terrible accident. She didn't mention anything about your wife."

"The townspeople didn't want to see me hurt any more, I suppose, particularly since I had a new wife, so I guess they just kept quiet." He turned to his wife and said, his voice pleading, his hand stretched out toward her, "Lily, when you came to town, just over a year and a half ago, I couldn't believe that someone else could come into my life who would make me complete, who would love me and make me happy, but you did. And you brought precious little Beth with you. I loved her from the first moment I saw her, just as I did you. I miss her, Lily, every day I miss her.

"What you've been going through—maybe now it's

over. Maybe what happened with the Explorer, maybe that snapped you back. Believe me, dearest, I just want you to get well. I want that more than anything. I want to take you to Maui and lie with you on the beach and know that your biggest worry will be how to keep from getting sunburned. Don't listen to your brother. Please, Lily, don't believe there was anything sinister about Lynda's death. Your brother is a cop. Cops think everyone has ulterior motives, but I don't. I love you. I want you to be happy, with me."

Savich, who'd been finishing off his lasagna during this impassioned speech, looked only mildly interested, as if he were attending a play. He laid down his fork and said, "Tennyson, how long has your dad been on the board of the Eureka Art Museum?"

"What? Oh, I don't know, for years, I suppose. I've never really paid any attention. What the hell does that have to do with anything?"

"You see," Savich continued, "at first we couldn't figure out why you would want to marry Lily if your motive was to kill her. For what? Then we realized you knew about our grandmother's paintings. Lily owns eight Sarah Elliotts, worth a lot of money, as you very well know."

For the first time, Savich felt a mild surge of alarm. Tennyson was a man nearing the edge. He was furious, his face red, his jaw working. He readied himself for an attack, just in case.

But what Tennyson did was bang his knife handle on the table, once, twice, then a really hard third time. "You bastard! I did not marry Lily to get her grandmother's goddamned paintings! That's absurd. Get out of my house!"

Lily slowly rose to her feet.

"No, Lily, not you. Please, sit down. Listen to me, you must. My father and I are familiar with the excellent work of the folk at the Eureka Art Museum. They have a splendid reputation. When you told me your grandmother was Sarah Elliott—"

"But you already knew, Tennyson. You knew before you met me that first time. And then you acted so surprised when I told you. You acted so pleased that I had inherited some of her incredible talent. You wanted so much to have her paintings here, in Northern California. You wanted them here so you could be close to them, so you could control them. So that when I was dead, you wouldn't have any difficulty getting your hands on them. Or maybe your father wanted the paintings close? Which, Tennyson?"

"Lily, be quiet, that's not true, none of it. The paintings are great art. Why should the Art Institute of Chicago have them when you live here now? Also, administration of the paintings is much easier when they're exhibited locally."

"What administration?"

Tennyson shrugged. "There are phone calls coming in all the time, questions about loaning the paintings out, about selling them to collectors, the schedule for ongoing minor restoration, about our approval on the replacement of a frame. Endless questions about tax papers. Lots of things."

"There was very little of what you just described before I married you, Tennyson. There was only one contract with the museum to sign every year, nothing else. Why haven't you said anything about any administration to me? You make it sound like an immense amount of work."

Was that sarcasm? Savich wondered, rather hoping that it was.

"You weren't well, Lily. I wasn't about to burden you with any of that."

Suddenly, the strangest thing happened. Lily saw her husband as a grayish shadow, hovering without substance, his mouth moving but nothing really coming out. Not a man, just a shadow, and shadows couldn't hurt you. Lily smiled as she said, "As Dillon said, I'm very rich, Tennyson."

Savich saw that his brother-in-law was trying desperately to keep himself calm, to keep himself logical in his arguments, not to get defensive, not to let Lily see what he really was. It was fascinating. Could a man be that good a liar, that convincing an actor? Savich wished he knew.

Tennyson said, "It's always been my understanding that you simply hold the paintings in a sort of trust. That they aren't yours, that you're merely their guardian until you die and one of your children takes over."

"But you've been in charge of their administration all these months," Lily said. "How could you not know that they were mine, completely mine, no trust involved?"

"I did believe that, I tell you. No one ever said anything different, not even the curator, Mr. Monk. You've met him, Lily, up front, so pleased to have the paintings here."

Savich sipped at the hot tea Mrs. Scruggins had poured into his cup. "None of us hold the paintings in trust," he said. "They're ours, outright." He knew Mrs. Scruggins was listening to everything, forming opinions. He didn't mind it a bit. Just maybe she'd have something more to say to him or to Sherlock when this little dinner meeting was over. "If Lily wants to, she can sell one or two or all of the paintings. They're worth about one million dollars each. Maybe more."

Tennyson looked stunned. "I—I never realized," he said, and now he sounded a bit frantic.

"Difficult not to," Lily said. "You're not a stupid man, Tennyson. Surely Mr. Monk told you what they're worth. When you found out I was Sarah Elliott's granddaughter, it would have been nothing at all for you to find out that she willed them to me. You saw me as the way to get to those paintings. You must have rubbed your hands together. I left everything in my will to Beth, at your urging, Tennyson, if you'll remember, and I named you the executor."

"As it happened," Savich said, "Beth did predecease Lily. Who inherits?"

"Tennyson. My husband." She continued after a moment, so bitter she was nearly choking on it. "How easy I made everything for you. What happened? Big money troubles? You needed me out of the way, fast?"

Tennyson was nearly over the edge now. "No, no, listen to me. I suppose I just saw the paintings as your grandmother's, nothing more than that. Valuable things that needed some oversight, particularly after you became so ill. All right, I was willing to do that work. Please, Lily, believe me. When you told me that she was your grandmother, I was very surprised and pleased for you. Then I just dismissed it. Lily, I didn't marry you for your grandmother's paintings. I swear to you I didn't. I married you because I love you, I loved Beth. That's it. My father—no, I don't believe there could possibly be anything there. You've got to believe me."

"Tennyson," Lily said, her voice low, soothing, "do you know that I've never been depressed in my life until I married you?"

"Dammit, before Beth's death, you had no reason to be depressed."

"Well, maybe I did. Didn't I tell you a bit about my first husband?"

"Yes, he was horrible, but you survived him. But, Lily, it was completely different when your daughter was killed by a hit-and-run driver. It's only natural that you'd be overcome with grief, that you would experience profound depression."

"Even after seven months?"

"The mind is a strange instrument, unpredictable. It doesn't always behave the way we would like it to. I've prayed and prayed for your full recovery. I agree it's been taking you a long time to recover but, Lily, you'll get well now, I know it."

"Yes," she said very slowly and pushed back her chair. "Yes, I know I'll get well now." She felt her stitches pull, a tug that made her want to bend over, but she didn't. "Yes,

Tennyson," she said, "I fully intend to get well now. Completely well."

She pressed her palms flat on the table. "I will also love Beth for the rest of my life, and I will know sadness at her loss and grief until I die, but I will come to grips with it. I will bear it. I will pray that it will slowly ease into the past, that I won't fall into that black depression again. I will face life now and I will gain my bearings. Yes, Tennyson, I will get well now because, you see, I'm leaving you. Tonight."

He rose so quickly his chair slammed down to the floor. "No, dammit, you can't leave me... Lily, no! It's your brother. I wish my father hadn't called him; I wish Savich hadn't come here to ruin everything. He's filled your mind with lies. He's made you turn on me. There's no proof of anything at all, just ask him. No, none of it's true. Please, Lily, don't leave me."

"Tennyson," Lily said very quietly now, looking directly at him, "what sort of pills have you been feeding me these last seven months?"

He howled, literally howled, a desperate, frightened sound of rage and hopelessness. He was panting hard when he said, "I tried to make you well. I tried, God knows, and now you've decided to believe this jerk of a brother and his wife and you're leaving me. Dammit, I've been giving you Elavil!"

Lily nodded. "Actually, there doesn't seem to be any solid proof to haul you to the sheriff. The sheriff is something of a joke anyway, isn't he? When I remember how he tried so hard to apprehend Beth's killer."

"I know he did the best he could. If you'd been with Beth, maybe you would have made a better witness, but you—"

She ignored his words and said, "If we find proof, then even Sheriff Bozo will have to lock you away, Tennyson— no matter what you or Daddy say, no matter how much money you've put in his pocket, no matter how many votes you got for him—until we manage to get some competent law enforcement in Hemlock Bay. The truth of the matter is, I would leave you even if you didn't kill your first wife, if you hadn't, in truth, tried to kill me, because, Tennyson, you've lied to me; from the very beginning you lied to me. You used Beth's death to make me feel the most profound guilt. You milked it, manipulated me—you're still doing it—and you very likely drugged me to make me depressed, to make me feel even more at fault. I wasn't at fault, Tennyson. Someone killed Beth. I didn't. I realize that now. Were you planning on killing me even as you slid the ring on my finger?"

He was holding his head in his hands, shaking his head back and forth, not looking at anyone now.

"I found myself wondering today, Tennyson—did you kill Beth, too?"

His head came up, fast. "Kill Beth? Oh, my God! No!"

"She was my heir. If I died, then the paintings would be hers. No, surely even you couldn't be that evil. Your father could, maybe your mother could, but not you, I don't think. But then again, I've never been good at picking men. Look at my pathetic track record—two tries and just look what happened. Yes, I'm obviously rotten at it. Hey, maybe it's my bookie genes getting in the way of good sense. No, you couldn't have killed or had Beth killed. Maybe we'll find something on your daddy. We'll see.

"Good-bye, Tennyson. I can't begin to tell you what I think of you."

Both Savich and Sherlock remained silent, looking at the man and woman facing each other across the length of the dining table. Tennyson was as white as a bleached shroud, the pulse in his neck pounding wildly. His fingers clutched the edge of the table. He looked like a man beyond himself, beyond all that he knew or understood.

As for Lily, she looked calm, wonderfully calm. She didn't look to be in any particular discomfort. She said,

"Dillon and Sherlock will pack all my things while you're at your office tomorrow, Tennyson. Tonight, the three of us are going to stay in Eureka." She turned, felt the mild pulling in her side again, and added, "Please don't destroy my drawing and art supplies, Tennyson, or else I'll have to ask my brother or sister-in-law to break your face. They want to very badly as it is."

She nodded to him, then turned. "Dillon, I'll be ready to leave in ten minutes."

Head up, back straight, as if she didn't have stitches in her side, she left the dining room. Lily saw Mrs. Scruggins standing just inside the kitchen door. Mrs. Scruggins smiled at her as she walked briskly past, saying over her shoulder, "It was an excellent dinner, Mrs. Scruggins. My brother really liked it. Thank you for saving my life seven months ago. I will miss you and your kindness."

8

EUREKA, CALIFORNIA
THE MERMAID'S TAIL

Lily swallowed a pain pill and looked at herself in the mirror. She'd looked better, no doubt about that. She sighed as she thought back over the months and wondered yet again what had happened to her. Had she looked different when she'd first arrived in Hemlock Bay? She'd been so full of hope, both she and Beth finally free of Jack Crane, on their own, happy. She remembered how they'd walked hand in hand down Main Street, stopping at Scooters Bakery to buy a chocolate croissant for Beth and a raisin scone for herself. She hadn't realized then that she would soon marry another man she'd believe with all her heart loved both her and Beth, and this one would gouge eleven months out of her life.

Fool.

She'd married yet another man who would have rejoiced at her death, who was prepared to bury her with tears running down his face, a stirring eulogy coming out of his mouth, and joy in his heart.

Two husbands down—never, never again would she ever look at a man who appeared even mildly interested in her.

Fact was, she was really bad when it came to choosing men. And the question that had begun to gnaw at her surfaced again. Was Tennyson responsible for Beth's death?

Lily didn't think so—she'd been honest the night before about that—but it had happened so quickly and no one had seen anything at all useful. Could Tennyson have been driving that car? And then the awful depression had smashed her, had made her want to lie in a coffin and pull down the lid.

Beth was gone. Forever. Lily pictured her little girl's face—a replica of her father's, but finer, softer—so beautiful, that precious little face she saw now only in her mind. She'd just turned six the week before she died. Beth hadn't been evil to the bone like her father. She'd been all that was innocent and loving, always telling her mother any- and everything until . . . Lily raised her head and looked at herself again in the mirror. Until what? She thought back to the week before Beth was killed. She had been different, sort of furtive, wary—maybe even scared.

Scared? Beth? No, that didn't make any sense. But still, Beth had been different just before she died.

No, not died. Beth had been killed. By a hit-and-run driver. The pain settled heavily in Lily's heart as she wondered if she would ever know the truth.

She shook her head, drank more water from the tap. Her brother and Sherlock had just left, after she'd assured them at least a half dozen times that she still felt calm, didn't hurt at all. She was fine, go, go, pack up her things in Hemlock Bay. She hoped that Tennyson hadn't trashed her drawing supplies.

She drew a deep, clean breath. Yes, she wanted her drawing supplies today, as soon as possible. She wanted to hold her #2 red sable brush again, but it would be foolish to buy another one just to use today. No, she'd just buy a small sampler set of pens and pen points, inexpensive ones because it didn't really matter. Maybe she'd get a Speed-ball cartooning set, just like the one her folks had given her when she'd wanted to try cartooning so many years before. Those pens would still feel familiar in her hand. And a bottle of India ink, some standard-size, twenty-pound typing paper, durable paper that would last, no matter how many times it was shoved into envelopes or worked on by her and the editors. Yes, just some nice bond paper, not more than a hundred sheets. Usually, since she did political cartoons, she used strips of paper cut from larger sheets of special artist paper, thicker than a postcard—bristol board, it was called, well suited for brushwork. And one bottle of Liquid Paper. She could just see herself—not more than an hour from now—drawing those sharp, pale lines that would become the man of the hour, Senator No Wrinkles Remus, the soon-to-be president of the U.S., from that fine state of West Dementia, where the good senator has managed to divide his state into halves, to conduct the ultimate experiment with gun control. One half of the state has complete gun control, as strict as in England; the other half of West Dementia has no gun control at all. He gives an impassioned speech to the state legislature, with the blessing of the governor, whom he's blackmailed for taking money from a contractor who is also his nephew: "One year, that's all we ask," Remus says, waving his arms to embrace all of them. "Just one year and we'll know once and for all what the answer is."

And what happens in the west of West Dementia is that criminals auction off areas to one another since civilians aren't allowed to own any device that shoots a bullet out of a barrel. Criminals break-and-enter at their leisure, whenever the spirit moves them. Houses, banks, gas stations, 7-Elevens, nothing is safe.

In east West Dementia, every sort of gun abounds, from sleek pistols that fire one round a minute to behemoths that kick out eight hundred zillion rounds a second. There are simply no limits at all. Because of the endless supply, guns are really cheap. What happens surprises everyone: robbery stats go down nearly seventy percent after a good dozen would-be robbers are killed breaking in—to homes, banks, filling stations, 7-Elevens.

On the other side of it, killing abounds. Everything that moves, and doesn't move, gets shot—deer, rabbits, cars, people. Some people even take to target-shooting in the rivers. Many trout, it is said, die from gunshot wounds.

There are rumors of payoffs from both the National Rifle Association and the Mafia to No Wrinkles Remus, but like his name, no matter what he does—or people believe he does—that face of his remains smooth and absolutely trustworthy.

Lily was grinning like a madwoman. She rubbed her hands together. She wanted to draw *No Wrinkles Remus*—now, right this minute, as soon as she could get a pen between her fingers. She didn't need a drawing table, the small circular Victorian table in her room would be perfect. The sun was coming in at exactly the right angle.

She just didn't want to wait. Lily grabbed her purse, her leather jacket, and headed out of the bed-and-breakfast. Mrs. Blade, standing behind the small counter downstairs, waved her on. Lily didn't know Eureka well, but she knew to go to Wallace Street. A whole bunch of artists lived over in the waterfront section of town, and a couple of them ran art supply stores.

The day was cloudy, nearly cold enough to see your breath, a chilly breeze swirling about in the fallen autumn leaves that strengthened the salty ocean taste when you breathed in. She managed to snag a taxi across the street that was letting off an old man in front of an apartment building.

The driver was Ukrainian, had lived in Eureka for six years, and his high-schooler son liked to doodle, even on toilet paper, he said, which made you wonder what sort of poisoning you could get using that toilet paper. He knew just where to go.

It was Sol Arthur's art supply shop. She was in and out in thirty minutes, smiling from ear to ear as she shifted the wrapped packages in her arms. She had maybe eleven dollars left in her purse—goodness, eleven whole dollars left in the world. She wondered what had happened to her credit cards. She would ask Dillon to deal with it.

She stood on the curb looking up and down the street. No way would a taxi magically appear now even though she was ready to part with another four dollars from her stash. No, no taxi. Such good lightning luck didn't strike twice. A bus, she thought, watching one slowly huff toward her. The bed-and-breakfast wasn't all that far from here, and the bus was heading in the right direction. She jaywalked, but not before she was sure that no cars were coming from either direction. There weren't a whole lot of people on the street.

No Wrinkles Remus is looking particularly handsome and wicked, right there, full-blown in her mind again. He looks annoyed when a colleague hits on a staffer Remus himself fancies; he feels absolute joy when he discovers that the wife of a senator cheated on her husband with one of his former senior aides.

She was singing when the bus—twenty years old if not older, belching smoke—lumbered toward her. She saw the driver, an old coot, grinning at her. He had on headphones and was chair-dancing to the music. Maybe she was the only passenger he'd seen in a while.

She climbed on board, banging her packages about as she found change in her wallet. When she turned to find a seat, she saw that the bus was empty.

"Not many folk out today?"

He grinned at her and pulled off his headphones. She repeated her question. He said, "Nah, all of 'em down at the cemetery for the big burying."

"Whose big burying?"

"Ferdy Malloy, the minister at the Baptist Church. Kicked it, just last Friday."

She'd been lying in the hospital last Friday, not feeling so hot.

"Natural causes, I hope?"

"You can think that if you want, but everyone knows that his missus probably booted him to the other side. Tough old broad is Mabel, tougher than Ferdy, and mean. No one dared to ask for an autopsy, and so they're planting Ferdy in the ground right about now."

"Well," Lily said, then couldn't think of another thing. "Oh, yes, I'm at The Mermaid's Tail. Do you go near there?"

"Ain't nobody on board to tell me not to. I'll take you right to the front door. Watch that third step, though, board's rotted."

"Thank you, I'll be careful."

The driver put his headphones back on and began bouncing up and down in the seat. He stopped two blocks down, just in front of Rover's Drive-In with the best hamburgers west of the Sillow River, sandwiched next to a storefront that advertised three justices of the peace, who were also notaries, on duty 24/7.

Lily closed her eyes. The bus started up again. No Wrinkles Remus was in her mind again, playing another angle.

"Hey."

She looked up to see a young man swinging into the seat next to her. He simply lifted off the packages, set them on the seat opposite, and sat down.

For a moment, Lily was simply too surprised to think. She stared at the young man, no older than twenty, his black hair long, greasy, and tied back in a ratty ponytail. He had three silver hoops marching up his left ear.

He was wearing opaque sunglasses, an Orioles cap on his head, turned backward, and a roomy black leather jacket.

"My packages," she said, cocking her head to one side. "Why did you put them over there?"

He grinned at her, and she saw a gold tooth toward the back of his mouth.

"You're awful pretty. I wanted to sit next to you. I wanted to get real close to you."

"No, I'm not particularly pretty. I'd like you to move. Lots of seat choice, since the bus is empty."

"Nope, I'm staying right here. Maybe I'll even get a little closer. Like I said, you're real pretty."

Lily looked up at the bus driver, but he was really into his rock 'n' roll, bouncing so heavily on the seat that the bus was swerving a bit to the left, then back to the right.

Lily didn't want trouble, she really didn't. "All right," she said and smiled at him. "I'll move."

"I don't think so," he said, his voice barely a whisper now, and he grabbed her arm to hold her still.

"Let go of me, buster, now."

"I don't think so. You know, I really don't want to hurt you. It's too bad because, like I said, you're real pretty. A shame, but hey, I need money, you know?"

"You want to rob me?"

"Yeah, don't worry that I'll do anything else. I just want your wallet." But he pulled a switchblade out of his inside jacket pocket, pressed a small button, and a very sharp blade flew out, long and thin, glittering.

She was afraid now, her heart pumping, bile rising in her throat. "Put the knife away. I'll give you all my money. I don't have much, but I'll give you all I've got."

He didn't answer because he saw that the bus was slowing for the next stop. He said, low, "Sorry, no time for the money."

He was going to kill her. The knife was coming right at her chest. She tightened, felt the stitches straining, but it didn't matter.

"You fool," she said. She drove her elbow right into his Adam's apple, then right under his chin, knocking his head back, cutting off his breath. Still he held the knife, not four inches from her chest.

Twist left, make yourself a smaller target.

She turned, then did a right forearm hammer, thumb down smashing the inside of his right forearm.

Attack the person, not the weapon.

She grabbed his wrist with her left hand and did a right back forearm hammer to his throat. He grabbed his throat, gagging and wheezing for breath, and she slammed her fist into his chest, right over his heart. She grabbed his wrist and felt the knife slide out of his fingers, heard it thunk hard on the floor of the bus and slide beneath the seat in front of them.

The guy was in big trouble, couldn't breathe, and she said, "Don't you ever come near me again, you bastard." And she smashed the flat of her palm against his ear.

He yelled, but it only came out as a gurgle since he still couldn't draw a decent breath.

Only fifteen seconds had passed.

The bus stopped right in front of The Mermaid's Tail. The driver waved to her in the rearview mirror, still listening to his music, still chair-dancing. She didn't know what to do. Call the cops? Then it was taken out of her hands. The young man lurched up, knowing he was in deep trouble, scooped up his knife, waved it toward the bus driver, who was now staring back at the two of them wide-eyed, no longer dancing. He waved the knife at her once, then ran to the front of the bus, jumped to the ground, and was running fast down the street, turning quickly into an alley.

The bus driver yelled.

"It's okay," Lily said, gathering her bags together. "He was a mugger. I'm all right."

"We need to get the cops."

The last thing Lily wanted was to have to deal with the cops. The guy was gone. She felt suddenly very weak; her heart was pounding hard and loud. But her shoulders were straight. She was taller than she'd been just five minutes before. It hadn't been much more than five minutes when she'd first gotten onto that empty bus, and then the young guy had come on and sat down beside her.

It didn't matter that she felt like all her stitches were pulling, that her ribs ached and there were jabs of pain. She'd done it. She'd saved herself. She'd flattened the guy with the knife. She hadn't forgotten all the moves her brother had taught her after she'd finally told him about Jack and what he'd done.

Dillon had said, squeezing her so hard she thought her ribs would cave in, "Dammit, Lily, I'm not about to let you ever be helpless again. No more victim, ever." And he'd taught her how to fight, with two-year-old Beth shrieking and clapping as she looked on, swinging her teddy bear by its leg.

But he hadn't been able to teach her for real—how to handle the bubbling fear that pulsed through her body when that knife was just a finger-length away. But she'd dealt with the fear, the brain-numbing shutdown. She'd done it.

She walked, straight and tall, her stitches pulling just a bit now, into The Mermaid's Tail.

"Hello," she called out, smiling at Mrs. Blade, who was working a crossword puzzle behind the counter.

"You look like you won the lottery, Mrs. Frasier. Hey, do you know a five-letter word for a monster assassin?"

"Hmmm. It could be me, you know, but Lily is only four letters. Sorry, Mrs. Blade." Lily laughed and hauled her packages up the stairs.

"I've got it," Mrs. Blade called out. "The monster assassin is a 'slayer.' You know, 'Buffy the Vampire Slayer.' "

"That's six letters, Mrs. Blade."

"Well, drat."

Upstairs in her room, Lily arranged the small Victorian

table at just the right angle to the bright sun. She carefully unwrapped all her supplies and arranged them. She knew she was on an adrenaline high, but it didn't matter. She felt wonderful. Then she stopped cold.

Her Sarah Elliott paintings. She had to go right now to the Eureka Art Museum and make sure the paintings, all eight of them, were still there. How could she have thought only of drawing Remus?

No, she was being ridiculous. She could simply call Mr. Monk, ask him about her paintings. But what if he wasn't trustworthy—no one else had proved the least trustworthy to date—he could lie to her.

Tennyson or his father could have stolen them last night after they'd left the house. Mr. Monk could have helped them.

No, someone would have notified her if the paintings were gone. Or maybe they would just call Elcott Frasier or Tennyson. No, they were her paintings, but she was sick, wasn't she? Another suicide attempt. Incapable of dealing with something so stressful.

She was out the door again in three minutes.

9

The Eureka Art Museum took up an entire block on West Clayton Street. It was a splendid old Victorian mansion surrounded by scores of ancient, fat oak trees madly dropping their fall leaves in the chilly morning breeze. What with all the budget cuts, the leaves rested undisturbed, a thick red, yellow, and gold blanket spread all around the museum and sidewalks.

Lily paid the taxi driver five dollars including a good tip because the guy had frayed cuffs on his shirt, hoping she had enough cash left for admission. The old gentleman at the entrance told her they didn't charge anything, but any contributions would be gracefully accepted. "Not gratefully?"

"Maybe both," he said and gave her a big grin. All she had to give him in return was a grin to match and a request that he tell Mr. Monk that Mrs. Frasier was here.

She'd seen the paintings here only once, during a brief visit, before the special room was built, right after she'd married Tennyson. She'd met Mr. Monk, the curator, who had gorgeous, black eyes and looked intense and hungry, and two young staffers, both with Ph.D.s, who'd just shrugged and said there were no jobs in any of the prestigious museums, so what could you do but move to Eureka? At least, they said, big smiles on their faces, the Sarah Elliott paintings gave the place class and respectability.

It wasn't a large museum, but nonetheless, they had fashioned an entirely separate room for Sarah Elliott's eight paintings, and they'd done it well. White walls, perfect lighting, highly polished oak floor, cushion-covered benches in the center of the room to sit on and appreciate.

Lily just stood there for a very long time in the middle of the room, turning slowly to look at each painting. She'd been overwhelmed when her grandmother's executor had sent them to her where she was waiting for them in the office of the director of the Art Institute of Chicago. Finally, she'd actually touched each one, held each one in her hands. Every one of them was special to her, each a painting she'd mentioned to her grandmother that she loved especially, and her grandmother hadn't forgotten. Her favorite, she discovered, was still *The Swan Song*—a soft, pale wash of colors, just lightly veiling an old man lying in the middle of a very neat bed, his hands folded over his chest. He had little hair left on his head and little flesh as well, stretched so taut you could see the blood vessels beneath it. The look on his face was beatific. He was smiling and singing to a young girl, slight, ethereal, who stood beside the bed, her head cocked to one side. Lily felt gooseflesh rise on her arms. She felt tears start to her eyes.

Dear God, she loved this painting. She knew it belonged in a museum, but she also knew that it was hers—hers—and she decided in that moment that she wanted to see it every day of her life, to be reminded of the endless pulse of life with its sorrowful endings, its joyous beginnings, the joining of the two. This one would stay with her, if she could make that happen. The value of each of the paintings still overwhelmed her.

She wiped her eyes.

"Is it you, Mrs. Frasier? Oh my, we heard that you had been in an accident, that you were in serious condition in the hospital. You're all right? So soon? You look a bit pale. Would you like to sit down? May I get you a glass of water?"

She turned slowly to see Mr. Monk standing in the doorway of the small Sarah Elliott room, with its elegant painted sign over the oak door. He looked so intense, like a taut bowstring, he seemed ready to hum with it. He was dressed in a lovely charcoal gray wool suit, a white shirt, and a dark blue tie.

"Mr. Monk, it's good to see you again." She grinned at him, her tears dried now, and said, "Actually, the rumors of my condition were exaggerated. I'm just fine; you don't have to do a thing for me."

"Ah, I'm delighted to hear it. You're here. Is Dr. Frasier here as well? Is there some problem?"

Lily said, "No, Mr. Monk, there's no problem. The past months have been difficult, but everything is all right now. Oh, yes, which of these paintings is your favorite?"

"*The Decision,*" Mr. Monk said without hesitation.

"I like that one very much as well," Lily said. "But don't you find it just the least bit depressing?"

"Depressing? Certainly not. I don't get depressed, Mrs. Frasier."

Lily said, "I remember I told my grandmother I loved that one when I'd just lost a lot of money on a point spread between the Giants and Dallas. I was sixteen at the time, and I do remember that I was despondent. She laughed and loaned me ten dollars. I've never forgotten that. Oh, yes, I paid her back the next week when a whole bunch of fools bet New Orleans would beat San Francisco by twelve."

"Are you talking about some sort of sporting events, Mrs. Frasier?"

"Well, yes. Football, actually." She smiled at him. "I am

here to tell you that I will be leaving the area, Mr. Monk, moving back to Washington, D.C. I will be taking the Sarah Elliott paintings with me."

He looked at her like she was mad. He fanned his hands in front of him, as if to ward her off. "But surely, Mrs. Frasier, you're pleased with their display, how we're taking such good care of them; and the restoration work is minor and nothing to concern you—"

She lightly laid her fingers on his forearm. "No, Mr. Monk, it looks to me like you've done a splendid job. It's just that I'm moving, and the paintings go where I go."

"But Washington, D.C., doesn't need any more beautiful art! They have so many beautiful things that they're sinking in it, beautiful things that are stuck in basements, never seen. They don't need any more!"

"I'm very sorry, Mr. Monk."

Those gorgeous dark eyes of his glittered. "Very well, Mrs. Frasier, but it's obvious to me that you haven't discussed this with Dr. Frasier. I'm sorry but I cannot release any of the paintings to you. He is their administrator."

"What does that mean? You know very well the paintings are mine."

"Well, yes, but it's Dr. Frasier who's made all the decisions, who's directed every detail. Also, Mrs. Frasier, it's common knowledge here that you haven't been well—"

"Lily, what are you doing out of bed? Why are you here?"

Dillon and Sherlock stood just behind Mr. Monk, and neither of them looked very pleased.

She smiled, saying only, "I'm here to tell Mr. Monk that the paintings go where I go, and in this case, it's all the way to Washington, D.C. Unfortunately, he says that everyone knows I'm crazy and that Dr. Frasier is the one who controls everything to do with the paintings—and so Mr. Monk won't release them to me."

"Now, Mrs. Frasier, I didn't quite mean that."

Savich lightly tapped him on the shoulder, and when Mr. Monk turned, in utter confusion, he said, "The paintings can't be released to my sister? Would you care to explain that to us, Mr. Monk? I'm Dillon Savich, Mrs. Frasier's brother, and this is my wife. Now, what is all this about?"

Mr. Monk looked desperate. He took a step back. "You don't understand. Mrs. Frasier isn't mentally competent, that's what I was told, and thus the paintings are all controlled by Dr. Frasier. Appropriate, naturally, since he is her husband. When we heard that she'd been in an accident, an accident that she herself caused, there were some who thought she was dying and thus Dr. Frasier would inherit the paintings and then they would never leave the museum."

"I'm not dead, Mr. Monk."

"I can see that you're not, Mrs. Frasier, but the fact is that you aren't as well as you should be to have charge of such expensive and unique paintings."

Savich said, "I assure you that Mrs. Frasier is mentally competent and is legally entitled to do whatever she wishes to with the paintings. Unless you have some court order to the contrary?"

Mr. Monk looked momentarily flummoxed, then, "A court order! Yes, that's it, a court order is what's required."

"Why?" said Savich.

"Well, a court could decide whether she's capable of making decisions of this magnitude."

Sherlock patted his shoulder. "Hmm, nice suit. I'm sorry, Mr. Monk, as this seems to be quite upsetting to you, but she is under no such obligation to you. I suppose you could try to get her declared incompetent, but you would lose, and I'm sure it would create quite a stir in the local papers."

"Oh, no, I wouldn't do that. What I mean is that I suppose then that everything is all right, but you understand, I have to call Dr. Frasier. He has been dealing with everything. I haven't spoken to Mrs. Frasier even once over all the months the paintings have been here."

Savich pulled out his wallet, showed Mr. Monk his ID, and said, "Why don't we go to your office and make that phone call?"

Of course Savich had shown Mr. Monk his FBI shield. He swallowed, looked at Lily like he wanted to shoot her, and said, "Yes, of course."

"Good," Savich said. "We can also discuss all the details of how they'll be shipped, the insurance, the crating, all those pesky little details that Dr. Frasier doesn't have to deal with anymore. By the way, Mr. Monk, I do know what I'm doing since I also own eight Sarah Elliott paintings myself."

"Would you like to go now, Mr. Savich?"

Savich nodded, then said over his shoulder as he escorted Mr. Monk from that small, perfect room, "Sherlock, you stay here with Lily, make sure she sits down and rests. Mr. Monk and I will finalize matters. Come along, sir."

"I hope the poor man doesn't cry," Lily said. "They built this special room, did a fine job of exhibiting the paintings. I think that Elcott and Charlotte Frasier donated the money to build the room. Wasn't that kind of them?"

"Yes. You know, Lily, many people have enjoyed the paintings over the past year. Now people in Washington can enjoy them for a while. You need to think about where you want the paintings housed. But we can take our time there, no rush, let people convince you they're the best.

"Oh, Lily, don't feel guilty. There are a whole lot of people there who have never seen these particular Sarah Elliott paintings."

"Truth be told, I'm just mighty relieved that they're all present and accounted for and I'm not standing here looking at blank walls because someone stole the paintings. That's why I came, Sherlock. I just realized that since Tennyson married me for the paintings, maybe they were already gone."

Sherlock patted a cushion and waited until Lily eased carefully down beside her. "We didn't want to wait either." She paused to look around. "Such beauty. And it's in your genes, Lily, both yours and Dillon's. You're very lucky. You draw cartoons that give people great pleasure, and Dillon whittles the most exquisite pieces. He whittled Sean, newly born, in the softest rosewood. Whenever I look at that piece, touch it, I feel the most profound gratitude that Dillon is in my life.

"Now, I'm going to get all emotional and that won't help anything. Did I have a point to make? Oh yes, such different aspects of those splendid talent genes from your grandmother."

"What about your talent, Sherlock? You play the piano beautifully. You could have been a concert pianist, if it hadn't been for your sister's death. I want to listen to you play when we get back to Washington."

"Yes, I'll play for you." Sherlock added, without pause, "You know, Lily, I was very afraid that Tennyson and his father had stolen the paintings as well, and you hadn't been notified because you'd been too ill to deal with it."

"I suppose they had other plans. All of this happened very quickly."

"Yes, they did have time, but don't you see? If the paintings were suddenly gone, they would have looked so guilty San Quentin would have just opened its doors and ushered them right on in. I suppose they were waiting to sell them off when you were dead and they legally belonged to Tennyson."

"Dead." Lily said the word again, then once more, sounding it out. "It isn't easy to believe that someone wants you dead so they can have what you own. That's really low."

"Yes, it is."

"I feel shock that Tennyson betrayed me, probably his father as well, but I don't want to wring my hands and cry about it. Nope, what I really want to do is belt Tennyson in the nose, maybe kick him hard in his ribs, too."

Sherlock hugged her, very lightly. "Good for you. Now, how do you feel, really?"

"Calm, just a bit of pain, nothing debilitating. I believed I loved him, Sherlock, believed I wanted to spend the rest of my life with him. I trusted him, and I trusted him with Beth."

"I know, Lily. I know."

Lily got ahold of herself, tried to smile. "Oh yes, I've got something amazing to tell you. Remus was dancing in my head this morning, yelling at me so loud that I went out and bought art supplies. Then, strange thing, I get on this empty city bus to go back to The Mermaid's Tail and this young guy tries to mug me."

Sherlock blinked, her mouth open.

Lily laughed. "Finally I've managed to surprise you so much you can't think of anything to say."

"I don't like this, Lily. Tell me exactly what happened."

But Mr. Monk appeared in the doorway. "I will contact our lawyers and have them prepare papers for your signature. I've detailed to Mr. Savich how the paintings will be packed and crated in preparation to be shipped to Washington. You will need to inform us of their destination so that we can make arrangements with the people at the other end. There will be two guards as well for the trip. It's quite an elaborate process, necessary to keep them completely safe. I will phone you when the papers are ready. Did you plan to leave the area soon?"

"Fairly soon, Mr. Monk." Lily rose slowly, her stitches pulling, aching more now, and took his hand. "I'm sorry, but I really can't leave them here."

"It's a pity. Dr. Frasier said on the phone that you were divorcing him and that he had no more say in anything."

"I'm relieved that he didn't try anything underhanded," Lily said.

Mr. Monk looked profoundly uncomfortable at that. "He's a fine man, and so are his esteemed father and mother."

"I understand that many people think that. Yes, we're divorcing, Mr. Monk."

"Ah, such a pity. You've been married such a short time. And you lost your little girl just a few months ago. I do hope you're making this decision with a clear head."

"You still think my mental condition is in question, Mr. Monk?"

Mr. Monk seemed to pump himself up. He swallowed and said, "Well, I think that just maybe you're acting in haste, not really thinking things through. And here you are divorcing poor Dr. Frasier, who seems to love you and wants only the best for you. Of course, Mrs. Frasier, this is a very bad thing for me and for the museum."

"Well, these things happen, don't they? And I'd have to say that Dr. Frasier loves my paintings, sir, not me. I'm staying at The Mermaid's Tail here in Eureka. Please call when I can finalize all this."

Lily's last view of Mr. Monk was of him standing in the doorway to the Sarah Elliott room, hunched in on himself, looking like he'd just lost all his money in a poker game. The museum had run just fine before Sarah Elliott's paintings had arrived, and it would do so after they went away.

When they were walking down the stone steps of the museum, Savich on one side of Lily, her arm resting heavily on his, Sherlock on the other, Savich said, not looking at her, "I was wondering if Tennyson would be obstructive when we called him up. To be honest, if it had been you, Lily—by yourself on the phone—he would have been, no doubt in my mind about that. But he couldn't this time, not with two of us federal agents and one of them your brother."

He stopped abruptly, turned, and grasped Lily's shoulders in his big hands. "I'm not pleased with you, Lily. You should have let Sherlock and me take care of all this. I'll bet you pulled your stitches and now your belly aches like you've been punched."

"Yes," Sherlock said, "Dillon's right. You look like you're ready to fall over."

Lily smiled down at her sister-in-law—small, fine-boned, all that incredible curly red hair, and the sweetest smile—who could take down a guy three times her size. And she played the piano beautifully. She'd known from the moment they'd first met at her and Dillon's wedding that Sherlock's love for Dillon was steady and absolute. Beth had been three years old at the time, so excited to see her uncle Dillon, and so proud of her new patent-leather shoes. Lily swallowed, got herself together. She said, "Do you know that you and Dillon could finish each other's sentences? Now, don't fret, either of you. I am feeling a bit on the shaky side, but I can hold on until we get back to the inn." She hugged him tight, then stepped back. "You know what, Dillon? I've decided that I'm going to check into my own credit card situation."

"What does that mean?"

Lily just smiled. He helped her into the backseat, gently placed the pillow over her stomach, and fastened her seat belt. She lightly touched her fingertips to his cheek. "I'm glad you came to the museum. I don't think I had enough money to pay for a taxi back to the B-and-B."

Savich shook his head at her as he slipped his hand beneath the seat belt to make sure it wouldn't press too hard against her middle, got in the driver's seat, and drove off.

"Now then, Lily," Sherlock said, turning in her seat. "You can't put it off any longer. Dillon will want to hear all about this, too. I want you to tell us about the mugger who attacked you on that empty bus this morning. No more than two hours ago."

Savich nearly drove into a fire hydrant.

* * *

They were eating lunch in a small Mexican restaurant, The Toasted Taco, on Chambers Street, just down the block from The Mermaid's Tail, Lily having decided she was starving more than she was aching.

"Good salsa," Lily said and dipped in another tortilla chip and stuffed it in her mouth. "That's a sure sign that the food will be okay. Goodness, I don't think I've ever been so hungry in my life."

Savich said, "Talk."

She'd told them about the bus driver who had explained to her that the bus was empty because of the big burying and was having a fine time chair-dancing while he drove, headphones turned up high, and about the young man with three earrings in his left ear, the switchblade that was sharp and silver and nearly went into her heart.

Savich blew out a big breath, picked up a tortilla chip, and absently chewed on it. "I suppose it's occurred to you it may not have been a mugger."

"He talked like one, maybe, I'm not sure since I've never been mugged before. Then he ruined it by pulling this switchblade knife. One thing I'm absolutely sure of—there was death in his eyes. And you know what? I knew all the way to my stomach lining that it was the end of the line. But then I went after him, Dillon, wrecked him good—all the moves you taught me. I could hear your voice telling me things, 'Make yourself as small as possible,' stuff like that. I hammered him—my hand a tight fist and whap! Then I hammered him hard against his chest, then polished him off by slamming my palm against his ear. Unfortunately, he got himself together and jumped off the bus, got away. Hey, I smashed him, Dillon, really smashed him."

She looked so proud of herself that Dillon wanted to hug her until she squeaked, but he was still too scared. She could have been killed so very easily.

He cleared his throat. "Did you call the police?"

Lily shook her head. "To be honest, all I wanted to do was get back to the B-and-B. Then I thought of the paintings and got to the museum as fast as I could. Why don't you think it was a mugger?"

Savich was still shaking with reaction. "I'm upset about this, Lily, really upset. He most certainly wasn't a mugger. Listen, an empty bus, a guy starts with a throwaway line about taking your wallet to keep things real calm, then he brings out the knife? A mugger? No, Lily, I don't think so."

"The question is," Sherlock said, chewing on a chip that she'd liberally dipped in salsa, her right hand near her glass of iced tea, "who found him, got him up to speed and moving so fast? You told Tennyson just last night that you were leaving him. Talk about fast action—that really surprises me. Tennyson, his father, whoever else is involved in this—they're not pros, yet they got this guy after you very quickly. He must have been watching the B-and-B, then followed you to the art supply shop, got ahead of you and on the bus at the next stop. It was well planned, well executed, except, thank God, he failed."

"Yeah, they didn't know what Dillon had taught me." She actually rubbed her hands together, realized she'd gotten salsa all over herself, and laughed. "Can we have another basket of chips?" she called out to the young Mexican waitress, then, "I saved myself, Dillon, and it felt really good."

Savich understood then, of course. Her life had been out of control for so very long, but no longer. He patted her back. "I wonder if it would help to check hospitals. Did you hurt him that bad?"

"Maybe. Good idea, I didn't think of that."

"He's paid to think of things like that," Sherlock said and got out her cell phone. She looked up at them after a moment, "We've got a lot of possibilities here."

Savich said, "You know, I was going to call the cops.

But now that I think about it, I don't think the local constabulary is what we need just yet. What I want is Clark Hoyt from the FBI field office right here in Eureka. If he knows the local cops, thinks they could help with this, then we can bring them into it. But for the time being, let's use our own guys."

Sherlock said, as she dialed information, "Great idea, Dillon. I'm sure glad they opened up this field office last year. The one in Portland wouldn't be able to help us with much. Clark can get all the hospitals checked in no time. Now, Lily, tell me where you hit this guy. Be as specific as you can."

"Yeah, I can do that, and then hand me a napkin so I can draw the guy for you."

10

Savich flipped open his cell phone, which was softly beeping the theme song from *The Lion King,* listened, and said, "Simon Russo? Is this the knucklehead who shot himself in the foot with my SIG Sauer?" Then he laughed and listened some more. Then he talked. Savich realized quickly enough that Simon didn't like what he had been hearing, didn't like it at all. What the hell was going on here? He listened as Simon said slowly, "Listen, Savich, just get your grandmother's paintings safely back to Washington. Do it right away, don't dither or let the museum curator put you off. Don't take any shortcuts with their safety, but move quickly. I'll be down to Washington as soon as the paintings get there. I want to see them. It's very important that I see them. Don't take any chances."

Savich frowned into his cell phone. What was this all about? "I know you like my grandmother's paintings, Simon. She gave you your favorite when you graduated from MIT, but you don't have to come down to Washington to see them right away."

"Yes," Simon said, "trust me on this, I do." And he hung up.

Sherlock was standing on the far side of the bedroom, her own cell phone dangling from her hand. "Sweetheart," he called out to her, "strangest thing. Simon is all hot under the collar to see Lily's eight Sarah Elliott paintings. He's being mysterious, won't tell me a thing, just insists he has to see the paintings as soon as they arrive in Washington."

Sherlock didn't say anything. Savich felt a sharp point of fear. Jesus, she looked shell-shocked, no, beyond that. She looked drop-dead frightened, her pupils dilated, her skin as pale as ice. He was at her side in an instant. He gathered her against him, felt that she was as cold as ice as well, and held on to her tightly. "What's wrong? Tell me what's wrong. It's Sean, isn't it? Oh God, something's happened to our boy?"

She shook her head hard, but still no words.

He pulled back, saw the shock of fear still deep in her eyes, and shook her lightly. "Please tell me, Sherlock, talk to me. What's going on? What happened?"

She swallowed, and managed finally to get the words out. "Sean's all right. I checked in at the office. I heard Ollie yell in the background that he had to speak to us. Oh, God, Dillon, Ollie said that Tammy Tuttle just up and walked out of the jail wing of Patterson-Wright Hospital."

"No," Savich said, shaking his head in utter disbelief, "you've got to be kidding me." Things like that just didn't happen. She was very dangerous, and everyone at the hospital knew it. He continued to stare down at his wife, wanting to see some flicker of doubt that wasn't there. "That can't be possible," he went on slowly. The panic of it was nearly under control, but he just didn't want to believe it, to accept it. "She was in the jail ward. She was well guarded. The woman is nuts. Everyone knows what she's done. She couldn't just walk out."

"They were going to put her in restraints tomorrow or

the next day, when they thought she was well enough to be a danger to them. Then there was a screwup in the scheduling of the guards. Evidently, she was ready for something to give her a chance. When she got her break, she snagged a nurse, knocked her out cold, and took her white pantsuit. At least she didn't kill her. But she walked out."

"It hasn't been even a week since they amputated her arm. How could she have the strength to take down a nurse? They're used to violent patients; they're trained. She's got only one arm, for God's sake."

"Obviously no one thought she had the strength or the ability, and that's why when there was the scheduling foul-up, no one was really concerned. And that's why no one even discovered she was gone until a nurse went in to give her a shot and found another nurse tied up naked in the closet. They figure she got herself at least a two-hour window."

Savich shook himself. His brain was back in gear, finally. "All right. Where would she go? Do they have any leads?"

"Ollie says there are more cops looking for her than the hunt for Marlin and Erasmus Jones. Everyone knows she's really scary, that she's truly dangerous. No one wants her free again." Sherlock cleared her throat. "There's the question of those things you saw in the barn, Dillon—the Ghouls."

He squeezed her again and said against her temple, her curly hair tickling his nose, "I know what I want to do right this minute. I want to talk to Sean and listen to him gurgle. That little guy is so sane, and that's what we need right now, a big dose of normalcy." He didn't add that he just wanted to know for sure, all the way to his soul, that his little boy was all right. As for the Ghouls—if they were real, and Savich knew to his bones that they were—then it was possible there was more danger than anyone could begin to imagine. Would the FBI let all the people looking for

Tammy Tuttle know that she could have accomplices? Or were they just going to ignore everything he'd told them?

They took turns gurgling with their son, who was busy gnawing a banana, not a graham cracker. Then they called Ollie back to see if there was any news yet.

"Yes," Ollie Hamish said, "but not good." Sherlock could see him leaning back in his chair, spinning it just a bit, because he was nervous and scared. "Tammy Tuttle just murdered a teenage boy a block outside of Chevy Chase, Maryland. She left a note on the body. Well, actually, she didn't leave it *on* the body, she left it attached to the body. It's addressed to you, Savich."

"Read it, Ollie."

"Here goes: 'I'll get you and I'll rip your arm off and then I'll cut your fucking head off, you murdering bastard. Then I'll give you to the Ghouls.' "

"That's real cheery," Savich said. "Was it addressed specifically to me?"

"Yeah, which means she knows your name. How? Everyone thinks she probably heard people talking about you in the hospital. She left her fingerprints all over the paper and envelope, obviously didn't care. Oh yes, at the murder scene, there was also a black-painted circle, and the boy was inside it. She's loose, Savich. Everyone is shaken to their toes. It was a really gruesome crime scene. That poor kid, he was only thirteen years old."

"Black-painted circle," Savich said. "Tammy called to the Ghouls to come get the boys in the circle."

"I was hoping maybe you really hadn't seen anything, Savich, that maybe you'd just experienced a temporary vision distortion. Since the boy's body was a mess, maybe more of a mess than a single one-armed sick woman could have done, then maybe these things—these Ghoul characters—were somehow involved. Jimmy Maitland brought it up. And the bosses even had a big meeting about it.

They've all decided that what you saw in that barn were dust devils."

Savich said finally, "Mr. Maitland has my number here if he wants to talk about it. Now, here's something to do. Bring in Marilyn Warluski."

"We already went looking. She's long gone, no one knows where."

"MAX found out that she has an ex-boyfriend in Bar Harbor, Maine, name of Tony Fallon. Check there. Just maybe she'll be with him and know something. Tammy has to go somewhere, and Marilyn loaned her and her brother that barn for their use. Did Tammy steal any money?"

"Not at the hospital, but elsewhere? We haven't heard of anything yet. Also, there have been a dozen reports of stolen vehicles. We're checking all those out as well."

"Okay. Find Marilyn and wring her out, Ollie. I think you should be the one in direct contact with her. You know more than the others."

"Okay. Let me take a deep breath here. I'm very glad you aren't listed in the phone book and your phone number's private. It's unlikely she could find you where you are, but I want you to be careful, Savich, really careful."

"You can count on that, Ollie."

"Okay. How are things going out there with Lily?"

Savich said, "She managed to hurt a guy who tried to kill her on an empty bus a couple of hours ago. Clark Hoyt in the new Eureka field office is checking all the hospitals. No word yet. Lily drew a picture of him and we just heard from a Lieutenant Dobbs at the Eureka Police Department that the guy's a local hood-for-hire, a freelancer, who would kill his own mom for the right price. Name of Morrie Jones. Everyone's looking for him. He's a kid, just turned twenty."

Savich could see Ollie shaking his head back and forth

as he said, "Big troubles on both coasts. Ain't nothing easy anywhere in this world, is there?"

Lily slept for three hours—no nightmares, thank God—and awoke to see her brother seated on a big wing chair pulled near her lovely Victorian canopied bed, a gooseneck lamp beaming light over his right shoulder, reading through a sheaf of papers.

He looked up immediately.

"You're fast. I just opened one eye and you knew I was awake."

"Sean got both Sherlock and me trained in a matter of days. He yawns or grunts, and we're ready to move."

She managed a smile, but truth be told, the day's events had caught up with her. She'd gone from being euphoric about drawing Remus again, to nearly being murdered, to getting back her paintings. At least she'd had a great Mexican lunch and it hadn't made her sick to her stomach.

But now, even after a very long sleep, she still felt wrung out. Her side ached something fierce, and her head sat heavy and dull on her shoulders. "No, Dillon, don't get up. What are you reading?"

"Articles and reports MAX found for me on weird phenomena. I'm trying to find other reported crimes with similarities to the Tuttles' rampage and the Ghouls."

"You told me just a little bit about the Tuttles and these Ghoul things, Dillon. Tell me more."

"There were two of them, two distinct white cones that sometimes came together. You can imagine how the two boys—Tammy and Timmy Tuttle called them 'Little Bloods'—were reacting. I've never seen such terror. I nearly swallowed my own tongue I was so afraid. Then Tammy Tuttle called to the Ghouls, yelled for them to bring their axes and knives, their 'treats' were ready for them. The boys wanted out of that circle and Tammy pulled her knife. She was going to nail them to the barn floor, inside that damned circle. That's when I shot her, and the bullet nearly tore her arm off. Timmy pulled his gun then, but he wasn't going to shoot me, no, he was aiming at the boys, so I had to kill him clean and quick, no choice. Then one of those white cones was coming at us, and I shot it. Did the bullet hurt it? I have no idea. I pulled the boys out of that circle and then both of the white cones just whooshed out of there. No one outside the barn saw them. So it was just the two boys, me, and Tammy, who had called them."

"My God, that's scary."

"More than you can imagine."

Lily said, "I wonder, did their victims have to be inside that circle?"

"Good question. Since I was there and saw all of it, I think they did have to have their victims inside the circle. Or maybe it was just a ritual that they themselves had developed over time, a ceremony that gave the Tuttles more of a kick out of what they were doing. However, I didn't see that the Ghouls had any knives or axes, so why did they say that?" He paused a moment, thinking back. "You know, Tammy had a knife but I didn't see any axes anywhere."

"Maybe she was just speaking dramatically."

Savich thought about the teenage boy, his body mutilated. "Maybe. I don't think so."

"What sorts of things has MAX dug up?"

He paused for a moment, then gave a slight shake of his head as he said, "You'd be surprised what's turned up over the years."

"Yeah, I bet I would, only you're not going to tell me anything, are you?"

There was a knock on the door.

Sherlock's voice. "Quick, Dillon. Open up!"

She was carrying three covered trays, stacked on top of one another. "From Mrs. Blade, downstairs," she said and handed them to Savich. "Besides doing crossword puzzles, she likes to cook. She insisted that if we couldn't come down to the dining room, she was sending this up."

Two huge plates of spaghetti with meatballs, one huge plate without the meatballs for Savich, lots of Parmesan cheese in a big bowl on the side, eight slices of garlic bread, and three large bowls of Caesar salad.

No one said a word for at least seven minutes, just groaned with pleasure and chewed. Finally, Lily sat back, patted her stomach, and sighed. "That garlic bread makes your back teeth sing the Italian anthem. Goodness, that was nearly as good as our Mexican lunch."

Sherlock wanted to laugh, but her mouth was full of spaghetti. Savich said, "Nah, Lily, give me a salty tortilla and salsa hot enough to burn the rubber off my soles any day. I wonder which one of your in-laws is going to pay us a visit this evening?"

Lily turned a bit pale. "But why would any of them want to see me again?"

Sherlock took the tray off her lap and said matter-of-factly, "Because their pigeon is bent on flying out of the coop. You survived the attack on the city bus this morning. No more attacks since Dillon and I have been with you. Nope, now they've got to visit you and try to convince you that Tennyson can't live without you."

"A final shot," Lily said.

"Yes, that's right," Sherlock said.

Savich just smiled. "Only thing is, they also know that their little pigeon has two big crows guarding her. We'll see exactly what tack they take. Ah, look at that dessert Sherlock was hiding from us. Chocolate mousse, one of my favorites."

Tennyson and his mother showed up an hour later, at precisely eight o'clock.

Charlotte Frasier had come to the hospital only once, stood by Lily's bed, and told her at least three times that she desperately needed to see dear Dr. Rossetti, a fine doctor, an excellent man who would help her. She was so worried about her dear Lily, everyone was. No one wanted her to try to kill herself again. To which Lily had simply stared at her, not a single word coming to mind after that outrageous speech. This evening, she was beautifully dressed in a dark wine-colored wool suit, a pale pink silk blouse beneath. Her thick black hair, not a hint of white, was cut short and tousled in loose curls and waves around her face. It was a very young style, but it didn't look ridiculous at all. Her teeth were white and straight, her lipstick blood-red. Charlotte looked good; she always had.

As for Tennyson, he paid no attention to either Savich or Sherlock, just marched directly to Lily's bed, grabbed her hand, and held on tightly.

"Come home with me, Lily. I need you."

"Hello, Tennyson. Hello, Charlotte. What more could we possibly have to say to each other? Dillon thought you would come by this evening, but I have to admit I'm very surprised." Lily finally got her hand back and asked, "Oh yes, where is your father? Isn't he well?"

Savich said easily, "Maybe they don't think they need him. They're hopeful they can talk you around by themselves."

Lily said to her husband, "You can't."

Charlotte said in her rich-as-sin Savannah-smooth voice, "Elcott wanted to come tonight, but he had a slight indigestion. Now, listen to me for a moment, Lily. My son loves you very much. Since he's a man, it's difficult for him to speak from his heart—that's a woman sort of thing to do, so I am telling you for him that he really does need you."

"Actually, Charlotte, Tennyson can speak very eloquently. However, I don't think his heart has anything to do with it. No, Charlotte, what Tennyson really needs is my Sarah Elliott paintings."

"That's not true." Tennyson whirled about to face Savich. "You have filled her head with suspicions, doubts, with lies about me and my family and my motives. I don't have any ulterior motives! I love my wife, do you hear me? Yes, that is from my bruised and bleeding heart! I wouldn't do anything to harm her. She's precious to me. Why don't you and your wife just go back to Washington and fight criminals, you know, people who have really done bad things, not innocent people you've just taken a dislike to. That's what you're paid to do, not rip apart a loving family! Leave us the hell alone!"

"That was a very impassioned speech," Sherlock said, smiling and nodding in approval. She knew from the furious pulse pounding in Tennyson's neck that he would cheerfully murder her.

Charlotte's voice was still as silky and soft as gently flowing honey. "Now, now, my dears, all of you need to calm down. Lily dearest, you're a grown woman. My Tennyson is just as protective of his own younger sister as your brother is of you. But your brother and his wife have gone over the line. They dislike my son, for whatever reasons I'm sure I can't say. But there can simply be no proof to any of their accusations, not a shred. Mad accusations, all of them. Lily, how could you possibly believe such things of my son?"

Sherlock said, "I wouldn't call them particularly 'mad accusations,' but, yes, ma'am, you're right about proof. If we had proof, we'd haul his butt to jail."

Charlotte said, "So, then, why are you continuing to poison poor Lily's mind? You're doing her a disservice. She's really not well, you know, and you're pushing her farther down a road none of us want her to travel."

"Mother—"

"No, it's true, Tennyson. Lily is mentally ill. She needs to come home so we can take care of her."

Lily said in a loud, clear voice that brought everyone's

eyes back to her, "A young guy tried to murder me this morning."

"What? Oh, God, no!" Tennyson nearly jerked her up into his arms, but Lily managed to press herself against the headboard and hold firm. Even as she was struggling, she said, "No, Tennyson, I'm quite all right. He didn't succeed, as you can see. Actually, I beat the stuffing out of him. The cops know who he is. Do back away now before my sister-in-law bites you."

Sherlock laughed.

"That's right," Savich said. "His name is Morrie Jones. Ring a bell, Tennyson? Charlotte? No? Well, you certainly got to him quickly enough, set everything in motion with nary a wasted moment. The cops will catch him anytime now and he'll spill his guts to them, and then we'll have our proof."

Tennyson said, "It's another lie, Lily. The guy must have mistaken you for someone else; that, or more likely, the guy was just a mugger. Where did it happen?"

"That's right, you couldn't have known where he'd find me, could you? He got on a local city bus that was empty except for me and the bus driver, because of the funeral."

"Yes," Charlotte said. "Dear old Ferdy Malloy died, probably poisoned by his wife. Everybody knows it, but no one was about to insist on an autopsy, least of all the coroner."

"Yes, yes, but that's not important, Mother. Someone tried to hurt Lily."

"A sharp knife probably meant he was planning to do more than hurt me," Lily said. "Lucky for me that Dillon had taught me how to protect myself."

"Just maybe," Tennyson said now, his voice all soft and gentle, his patented shrink's voice, "just maybe there was this young guy who came on to you, maybe even asked you out. I know Dr. Rossetti believes that a young woman, vulnerable like you are, uncertain, her mind clouded, can imagine many different things to disguise her sickness—"

Lily, who'd been staring at him like he had sprouted a TV antenna from his head, said, "Why did I ever think I loved you? You're the biggest jerk."

"I'm not, I'm just trying to understand you, to make you face things. Besides, that's what Dr. Rossetti thinks."

Lily began laughing, rich, deep laughter that didn't stop for a good, long time. Finally, wiping her eyes, she said, "You're really good, Tennyson, both you and Dr. Rossetti. You combined all your shrink analysis with some pills to drive me over the edge, and no wonder I wanted to do away with myself. So I made the guy up to assuage my guilt. Do you know what, Tennyson? I think I'm just about over blaming myself."

Charlotte said, "Lily dearest, I'm glad to hear you say that, actually—"

Lily interrupted her mother-in-law. She was waving Tennyson away even as she said, her voice light, amused, "Please go now, both of you. I hope that I'm lucky enough never to see either of you again."

Sherlock said, "Oh, I hope we do see them again, Lily. In a courtroom."

Savich said suddenly, "Your first wife, Tennyson. I don't suppose Lynda's fondest wish was to be cremated?"

Tennyson was shaking so much from rage, Sherlock was sure he was going to go after her husband, a singularly stupid thing for him even to consider. She stepped quickly to him, laid her hand on his forearm and said, "Don't even think about it. You couldn't take me and I'm half your size. Even five days after surgery, I doubt you could take Lily either. So please just leave, Tennyson, and take your mother with you."

"I am appalled that you have relatives who are so very close-minded and obnoxious, Lily," Charlotte Frasier said, her words smooth out of her mouth. They left, not another word out of either mouth, but Tennyson did pause to give Lily a tormented look over his shoulder.

Sherlock said thoughtfully, "He was trying to reproduce a patented Heathcliff look there, all down-in-the-mouth and pathetic. He didn't do it well, but he tried."

Lily said, "Did you notice that lovely black turtleneck sweater Tennyson was wearing? I gave it to him for Christmas."

"You know what I think, Lily?" Savich asked, shaking his head at her. "I think the next time a guy appeals to you, red lights need to flash in your brain. Then we need to take him in for questioning."

"I was just thinking about that this morning. Maybe I'm too gullible. Okay, no more good-looking men; actually, no more men at all, Dillon, or I'll kick myself from here to Boston. Nothing but gnomes with pocket protectors for me in the future, and they'll just be friends."

That was going overboard, Sherlock was thinking, but for the time being, not a bad way for Lily to think about the opposite sex.

Lily said, "I wish I had a beer so I could drink to that."

Savich said, "No beer. Here's more iced tea."

"Thanks." Lily sipped the tea and laid her head back against the pillow. "I wonder where my father-in-law was. You think they really thought he'd be a liability?"

"Evidently so," Savich said. "What amazes me is they don't seem to realize what a liability the both of them are."

"I've never heard such a charming Southern accent," Sherlock said. She sat down on the bed beside Lily and lightly rubbed her arm. "Talk about candy coating."

"She frightened me more than Tennyson." She gave both of them a fat smile. "I held up," she said, gave a deep sigh, and said again, "I held up. He never guessed that I was so scared."

Savich felt her pain in his gut. He gathered her against him, very careful with her stitches. He kissed the top of her head. "Oh no, sweetheart, there isn't a reason for you to be afraid of him, ever again. I was proud of you. You held up great."

"Yes, you did, Lily, so no more talk about being scared. Remember, you've got your two bulldogs right here. You know something? I don't know what they thought they could gain by coming here. They didn't try to be very conciliatory. Are they stupid or was there some method to their approach?"

"I surely hope not," Lily said and closed her eyes.

Savich's cell phone rang.

11

◈ "You go to bed now, Lily. No arguments. You look like a ghost out of *A Christmas Carol*."

Lily managed a small smile and did as she was told. She was still weak, and the long plane trip back east had knocked her flat. She awoke an hour later to hear Dillon and Sherlock talking to Sean. They cuddled, hugged, and kissed him until finally he was so exhausted he hollered big time for about two minutes. Then he was out like the proverbial light. His nursery was right next to the guest room, where she lay quietly in the dim light. She didn't realize she was crying until a tear itched her cheek. She wiped it away.

She closed her eyes when she heard her door open slightly. No, she wasn't ready to see anyone just yet, although she loved them both dearly for caring about her so very much. She pretended to be asleep. When she heard them go downstairs, she got up and went into the baby's room. Sean was sleeping on his knees, his butt in the air, two fingers in his mouth, his precious face turned toward her. He looked just like his father, but he had his mother's dreamy blue eyes. She lightly rubbed her fingers over his back. So small, so very perfect.

She cried for the beauty of this little boy and for the loss of Beth.

Late that evening, over a good-sized helping of Dillon's lasagna, she said, "Have you checked back with your office? Did they find Marilyn Warluski?"

Savich said, "Not yet. They found the boyfriend, Tony Fallon, but he claims she hasn't contacted him. But there were a couple of folk in Bar Harbor who identified a photo of her, said they'd seen her recently. They're going back to put his feet to the coals. We'll know something soon."

"We hope," Sherlock said. Then she smiled. "You should have seen Dillon's mother when we picked up Sean—she didn't want us to take him. She said we'd promised her at least a week with him all to herself, but we'd lied; it was barely a week. She was shouting 'Foul' even as we were pulling out of her driveway."

Savich shook his head. "Now he'll be so spoiled that we'll actually have to say no to him a couple of times to get him grounded back into reality."

"I bet Mom would love to baby-sit him on a regular basis," Lily said.

"Well," Savich said, "she's got her own life. She's his treat; two or three times a week he gets big doses of Grandma. It works well that way. Our nanny, Gabriella Henderson, is the best. She's young, so she's got the energy and stamina to keep up with him. Believe me, he can wear you down very fast."

Lily was laughing, looking over at Sean, who was seated in his walker, a nifty contraption that let him scoot all over the downstairs. If he ran into something, he just changed directions.

Savich said, "Those wheels are bad for the floor, but Sherlock and I decided we'd just have them refinished when he moves on to crawling and walking."

Lily said slowly, "Isn't it strange? I never imagined you with a kid, Dillon."

Savich smiled and helped her down on his big stuffed chair. "I didn't either, but here came Sherlock, blasted right into my comfortable life, and it just seemed like the right thing. We're very lucky, Lily. Now, sweetheart, we've been traveling all day and you're jet-lagged, probably really bad what with the surgery a week ago. I want you to sleep at least ten hours before you face the world here in Washington tomorrow."

"You and Sherlock have to be jet-lagged too. Even though you travel a lot and you are FBI agents, you—"

The front doorbell rang.

Savich walked around Sean, who was speeding toward the front door. It was Simon Russo. Savich knew him as a man of immense energy and focus, a man who just didn't quit. And now Simon was looking beyond him to the living room.

"Simon, it's good to see you. What the devil are you doing here?"

Simon grinned at his friend, shook his hand, and said, "Yeah, good to see you, Savich. I came to see the paintings. Where are they? Not here, I hope. You don't have the kind of security to keep the paintings here, even overnight."

"No we don't. Come on in. No, the paintings are in the vault in the Beezler-Wexler Gallery, safe as can be."

"Good, good. I'd like you to arrange for me to see them, Savich."

"So you said. First, however, you need a cup of tea and a slice of apple pie. My mom made it."

"Oh, not your blasted tea. Coffee, please, Savich, I'm begging you. Coffee, black. Then we can see the paintings."

"Simon, come on in and say hello to Sherlock and meet my sister, Lily. You can see the paintings tomorrow."

Simon shook his head and asked, "Not until tomorrow? How early?"

"Get a grip, Simon. Come on in. Hey, guys, look who just flew through our front door? Simon Russo."

Lily's first impression of Simon Russo was that he was too good-looking, that he was a man who looked like a Raphaelesque angel, hair black and thick and a bit too long. Yeah, the angel Gabriel, probably, the head angel, the big kahuna. He was taller than her brother, long and lean, his eyes brighter and bluer than a winter sky over San Francisco Bay, and he looked distracted. He hadn't shaved. He was wearing blue jeans, sneakers, a white dress shirt, a yellow-and-red tie, and a tweed jacket. He looked like a gangster academic, an odd combination, but it was true. Or maybe a nerd gangster, what with a name like Simon. He also looked like he knew things, maybe dangerous things. Lily was sure all the way to her bones that she wouldn't trust him if he pledged his name in blood.

Red lights flashed in her brain. No, she wouldn't let herself even see him as a man. He was an expert who wanted to see her Sarah Elliott paintings for some reason. He was Dillon's friend. She wouldn't have to worry about him. Still, she found herself drawing back into the big chair, just in case.

"Simon!" Sherlock was across the living room in under three seconds, her arms thrown around him, laughing and squeezing him. She came barely to his chin. He was hugging her, kissing her bouncing hair. She pulled back finally, kissed his scratchy cheek, and said, "Goodness, you're here in a hurry. Yes, I know it isn't us you want to see, it's those paintings. Well, you'll just have to wait until morning."

Lily watched him hug her sister-in-law close once again, kiss her hair once again, and say, "I love you, Sherlock, I'd love to keep kissing you, but Dillon can kill me in a fair fight. The only time I ever beat him up, he was sick with the flu, and even then it was close. He also fights dirty. I don't want him to mess up my perfect teeth." He lifted her over his head, then slowly lowered her.

Savich said, crossing his arms over his chest, "You kiss her hair again and I'll have to see about those teeth."

Simon said, "Okay, I'll stay focused on the paintings, but, Sherlock, I want you to know that I wanted you first." He started to kiss her again, then sighed deeply. "Oh, what the hell."

Then he turned those dark blue eyes on Lily, and he smiled at her, far too nice a smile, and she wished she could just stand up and walk out of the room. He was dangerous.

"Why," she said, not moving out of her chair, actually pressing her back against the cushions, "are you so hot to see my paintings?"

Savich frowned at her, his head cocked to one side. She sounded mad, like she wanted to kick Simon through a window. He said easily, "Lily, sweetheart, this is Simon Russo. You've heard me talk about him over the years. Remember, we roomed together our senior year at MIT?"

"Maybe," Lily said. "But what does he want with my paintings?"

"I don't know yet. He's a big-time dealer in the art world. He's the one I called to ask how much Grandmother's paintings are worth in today's market."

"I remember you," she said to Simon. "I was sixteen when you came home with Dillon on Christmas your senior year. Why do you want to see my paintings so badly?"

Simon remembered her, only she was all grown up now, not the wily, fast-talking teenager who'd tried to con him out of a hundred bucks. He didn't remember the scheme—some bet, maybe, but he did remember that she would have gotten it out of him, too, if her father hadn't warned him away and told him to keep his money in his wallet.

Simon wasn't deaf. He heard wariness, maybe even distrust in her voice. Why would she dislike him? She didn't even know him, hadn't seen him in years. She didn't look much like that teenager, either. She still looked like a fairy princess, but this grown-up fairy princess looked ground under—alarmingly pale, shadows beneath her eyes. Her hair was pulled back in a ratty ponytail and badly needed to be washed. She also needed to gain some weight to fill out her clothes. Antipathy was pouring off her in waves, a tsunami of dislike to drown him. Why?

"Are you in pain?" he asked, taking a step toward her.

Lily blinked at him, drawing herself in even more. "What?"

"Are you in pain? I know you had surgery last week. That's got to be tough."

"No," she said, still looking as though she was ready to gut him. Then Lily realized that she had no reason at all to dislike this man. He was her brother's friend, nothing more, no reason to be wary of him. The only problem was that he was good-looking, and surely she could overlook that flaw. He was here to see her paintings.

The good Lord save her from good-looking men who wanted her paintings. Two had been more than enough.

She tried to smile at him to get that puzzled look off his face.

Now what was this? Simon wondered, but he didn't get an answer, of course. He didn't say anything more. He turned on his heel and walked to where Sean had come to a halt in his walker and was staring up at him, a sodden graham cracker clutched in his left hand. Crumbs covered his mouth and chin and shirt.

"Hi, champ," Simon said and came down on his haunches in front of Sean's walker.

Sean waved the remains of the graham cracker at him.

"Let me pass on that." He looked over his shoulder. "He's still teething?"

Sherlock said, "Yep, for a while yet. Don't let Sean touch you, Simon, or you'll regret it. That jacket you're wearing is much too nice to have wet graham cracker crumbs and spit all over it."

Simon merely smiled and stuck out two fingers. Sean looked at those two fingers, gummed his graham cracker faster, then shoved off with his feet. The walker flew into Simon. He was so startled, he fell back on his butt.

He laughed, got back onto his knees, and lightly ran his fingers over Sean's black hair. "You're going to be a real bruiser, aren't you, champ? You're already a tough guy, mowed me right down. Thank God you've got your mama's gorgeous blue eyes or you'd scare the bejesus out of everybody, just like your daddy does." He turned on his heel to say to Lily, "Are you the changeling or is Savich?"

Savich laughed and gave Simon a hand up. "She's the changeling in our immediate family. However, she looks just like Aunt Peggy, who married a wealthy businessman and lives like a princess in Brazil."

"Okay, then," Simon said, "let's see if she tries to bite my hand off." He stuck out his hand toward Lily Frasier. "A pleasure to meet another Savich."

Good manners won out, and she gave him her hand. A soft hand, smooth and white, but there were calluses on her fingertips. He frowned as he felt them. "I remember now, you're an artist, like Savich here."

"Yes, I told you about her, Simon. She draws *No Wrinkles Remus,* a political cartoon strip that—"

"Yes, of course I remember. I've read the strip, but it's been a while now. It was in the *Chicago Tribune,* if I remember correctly."

"That's right. It ran there for about a year. Then I left town. I'm surprised you remember it."

He said, "It's very biting and cynical, but hilarious. I don't think it matters if the reader is a Democrat or a Republican, all the political shenanigans ring so true it just doesn't matter. Will the world see more of Remus?"

"Yes," Lily said. "Just as soon as I'm settled in my own

place, I'm going to begin again. Now, why are you so anxious to see my paintings?"

Sean dropped the graham cracker, looked directly at his mother, and yelled.

Sherlock laughed as she lifted him out of the walker. "You ready for a bath, sweetie? Goodness, and a change, too. It's late, so let's go do it. Dillon, why don't you make Lily and Simon some coffee. I'll be back with the little prince in a while."

"Some apple pie would be nice," Simon said. "I haven't had dinner yet; it would fill in the cracks."

"You got it," Savich said, gave Lily the once-over to make sure she was okay, and went to the kitchen.

"Why do you want to see my paintings so badly?" Lily asked again.

"I'd just as soon not say until I actually see them, Mrs. Frasier."

"Very well. What do you do in the art world, Mr. Russo?"

"I'm an art broker."

"And how do you do that, exactly?"

"A client wants to buy, say, a particular painting. A Picasso. I locate it, if I don't know where it is already—which I do know most of the time—see if it's for sale. If it is, I procure it for the client."

"What if it's in a museum?"

"I speak to the folk at the museum, see if there's another painting, of similar value, that they'd barter for the one my client wants. It happens that way, successfully sometimes, if the museum wants what I have to barter more than the painting they have. Naturally, I try to keep up with the wants and needs of all the major museums, the major collectors as well." He smiled. "Usually, though, a museum isn't all that eager to part with a Picasso."

"You know all about the illegal market, then."

Her voice was flat, no real accusation in it, but he knew

to his toes that she was very wary of him. Why? Ah, yes, her paintings, that was it. She didn't trust him because she was afraid for her paintings. Okay, he could deal with that.

He sat down on the sofa across from her, picked up the afghan, and held it out to her.

Lily said, "Thanks, I am a bit cold. No, no, just toss it to me."

But he didn't. He spread it over her, aware that she didn't want him near her, frowned, then sat down again and said, "Of course I know about the illegal market. I know all of the main players involved, from the thieves to the most immoral dealers, to the best forgers and the collectors who, many of them, are totally obsessed if there is a piece of art they badly want. 'Obsession' is many times the operative word in the business. Is there anything you want to know about it, Mrs. Frasier?"

"You know the crooks who acquire the paintings for the collectors."

"Yes, some of them, but I'm not one of them. I'm strictly on the up-and-up. You can believe that because your brother trusts me. No one's tougher than Savich when it comes to trust."

"You've known each other for a very long time. Maybe trust just starts between kids and doesn't end, particularly if you rarely see each other."

"Whatever that means," Simon said. "Look, Mrs. Frasier, I've been in the business for nearly fifteen years. I'm sorry if you've had some bad experiences with people in the art world, but I'm honest, and I don't dance over the line. You can take that to the bank. Of course I know about the underside of the business or I wouldn't be very successful, now would I?"

"How many of my grandmother's paintings have you dealt with?"

"Over the years, probably a good dozen, maybe more. Some of my clients are museums themselves. If the painting is owned by a collector—legally, of course—and a museum wants to acquire it, then I try to buy it from the collector. Since I know what all the main collectors own and accumulate, I will try to barter with them. It cuts both ways, Mrs. Frasier."

"I'm divorcing him, Mr. Russo. Please don't call me that again."

"All right. 'Frasier' is a rather common sort of name anyway, doesn't have much interest. What would you like to be called, ma'am?"

"I think I'll go back to my maiden name. You can call me Ms. Savich. Yes, I'll be Lily Savich again."

Her brother said from the doorway, "I like it, sweetheart. Let's wipe out all reminders of Tennyson."

"Tennyson? What sort of name is that?"

Lily actually smiled. If it wasn't exactly at him, it was still in his vicinity. "His father told me that Lord or Alfred just wouldn't do, so he had to go with Tennyson. He was my father-in-law's favorite poet. Odd, but my mother-in-law hates the poet."

"Perhaps Tennyson, the poet—not your nearly ex-husband—is a bit on the 'pedantic' side."

"You've never read Tennyson in your life," Lily said.

He gave her the most charming smile and nodded. "You're right. I guess 'pedantic' isn't quite right?"

"I don't know. I haven't read him either."

"Here's coffee and apple pie," Savich said, then cocked his head, looking upward. He said, "I hear Sherlock singing to Sean. He loves a good, rousing Christmas carol in the bathtub. I think she's singing 'Hark! The Herald Angels Sing.' You guys try to get along while I join the sing-along. You can trust him, Lily."

When they were alone again, Lily heard the light slap of rain on the windows for the first time. Not a hard, drenching rain, just an introduction, maybe, to the winter rains that were coming. It had been overcast when they'd landed in Washington, and there was a stiff wind.

Simon sipped Savich's rich black coffee, sighed deeply, and sat back, closing his eyes. "Savich makes the best coffee in the known world. And he rarely drinks it."

"His body is a temple," she said. "I guess his brain is, too."

"Nah, no way. Your brother is a good man, sharp, steady, but he ain't no temple. I bet Savich would fall over in shock if he heard you say that about him."

"Probably so, but it's true nonetheless. Our dad taught all of us kids how to make the very best coffee. He said if he was ever in an old-age home, at least he'd know he could count on us for that. Our mom taught Dillon how to cook before he moved to Boston to go to MIT."

"Did she teach all of you?"

"No, just Dillon." She stopped, listening to the two voices singing upstairs. "They've moved on to 'Silent Night.' It's my favorite."

"They do the harmony well. However, what Savich does best is country and western. Have you ever heard him at the Bonhomie Club?"

She shook her head, drank a bit of coffee, and knew her stomach would rebel if she had any more.

"Maybe if you're feeling recovered enough, we could all go hear him sing at the club."

She didn't say anything.

"Why do you distrust me, Ms. Savich? Or dislike me? Whatever it is."

She looked at him for a good, long time, took a small bite of apple pie, and said finally, "You really don't want to know, Mr. Russo. And I've decided that if Dillon trusts you, why, then, I can, too."

12

Raleigh Beezler, co-owner of the Beezler-Wexler Gallery of Georgetown, New York City, and Rome, gave Lily the most sorrowful look she'd seen in a very long time, at least as hangdog as Mr. Monk's at the Eureka museum.

He kissed his fingers toward the paintings. "Ah, Mrs. Frasier, they are so incredible, so unique. No, no, don't say it. Your brother already told me that they cannot remain here. Yes, I know that and I weep. They must make their way to a museum so the great unwashed masses can stand in their wrinkled walking shorts and gawk at them. But it brings tears to my eyes, clogs my throat, you understand."

"I understand, Mr. Beezler," Lily said and patted his arm. "But I truly believe they belong in a museum."

Savich heard a familiar voice speaking to Dyrlana, the gorgeous twenty-two-year-old gallery facilitator, hired, Raleigh admitted readily, to make the gentlemen customers looser with their wallets. Savich turned and called out, "Hey, Simon, come on back here."

Lily looked through the open doorway of the vault and

watched Simon Russo run the distance to the large gallery vault in under two seconds. He skidded to a stop, sucked in his breath at the display of the eight Sarah Elliott paintings, each lovingly positioned against soft black velvet on eight easels, and said, "My God," and nothing else.

He walked slowly from painting to painting, pausing to look closely at many of them, and said finally, "You remember, Savich, that your grandmother gave me *The Last Rites* for my graduation present. It was my favorite then and I believe it still is. But this one—*The Maiden Voyage*—it's incredible. This is the first time I've seen it. Would you look at the play of light on the water, the lace of shadows, like veils. Only Sarah Elliott can achieve that effect."

"For me," Lily said, "it's the people's faces. I've always loved to stare at the expressions, all of them so different from each other, so telling. You know which man owns the ship just by the look on his face. And his mother—that look of superior complacency at what he's achieved, mixed with the love she holds so deeply for her son and the ship he's built."

"Yes, but it's how Sarah Elliott uses light and shadow that puts her head and shoulders above any other modern artist."

"No, I disagree with you. It's the people, their faces, you see simply everything in their expressions. You feel like you know them, know what makes them tick." She saw he would object again and rolled right over him. "But this one has always been my favorite." She lightly touched her fingertips to the frame on *The Swan Song*. "I really hate to see it go to a museum."

"Keep it with you then," Savich said. "I've kept *The Soldier's Watch*. The insurance costs a bundle as well as the alarm system, but very few people know about it, and that's what you'll have to do. Keep it close and keep it quiet."

Simon looked up from his study of another painting. "I

have *The Last Rites* hung in a friend's gallery near my house. I see it nearly every day."

"That's an excellent idea," Raleigh Beezler said and beamed at Lily, seeing hope. "Do you know, Mrs. Frasier, that there is an exquisite town house for sale not two blocks from my very safe, very beautiful, very hassle-free gallery that would accord you every amenity? What do you say I call the broker and you can have a look at it? I understand you're a cartoonist. There is this one room that is simply filled with light, just perfect for you."

That was well done, Lily thought. She had to admire Mr. Beezler. "And I could leave some of my paintings here, in your gallery, on permanent display?"

"An excellent idea, no?"

"I'd like to see the town house, sir, but the price is very important. I don't have much money. Perhaps you and I could come to a mutually satisfying financial arrangement. My painting displayed right here for a monthly stipend, a very healthy one, given that this house sits in the middle of Georgetown and I'd have to afford to live here. What do you think?"

Raleigh Beezler was practically rubbing his hands together. There was the light of the negotiator in his dark eyes.

Simon cleared his throat. He'd continued studying the rest of the paintings, and now he turned slowly to say, "I think that's a very good idea, Ms. Savich, Mr. Beezler. Unfortunately, there is a huge problem."

Lily turned to frown at him. "I can't see any problem if Mr. Beezler is willing to pay me a sufficient amount to keep up mortgage payments, at least until I can get an ongoing paycheck for *No Wrinkles Remus,* maybe even get it syndicated..."

Simon just shook his head. "I'm sorry, but it's just not possible."

"What's wrong, Simon?" Because he knew Simon,

knew that tone of voice, Savich automatically took Lily's hand. "All right, the floor's yours. You really wanted to see the paintings. You've seen them. I've watched you studying them. What's wrong?"

"No easy way to say this," Simon said. "Oh damn, four of them are fakes, including *The Swan Song*. Excellent fakes, but there it is."

"No," Lily said. "No. I would know if it weren't real. You're wrong, Mr. Russo, just wrong."

"I'm sorry, Ms. Savich, but I'm very sure. Like I said, the way Sarah Elliott uses light and shadows makes her unique. It's the special blend of shades that she mixed herself and the extraordinary brush strokes she used; no one's really managed to copy them exactly.

"Over the years I've become an expert on her paintings. Still, if I hadn't also heard some rumors floating around New York that one of the big collectors had gotten ahold of some Sarah Elliott paintings in the last six months, I wouldn't have come rushing down here."

Savich said, "I'm sorry, Lily, but Simon is an expert. If he says they're fake, then it's true."

"I'm sorry," Simon said. "Also, there were no Sarah Elliotts for sale that I knew of. When I heard *The Swan Song* as one of the paintings acquired, I knew something was wrong. I immediately put out feelers to get more substantial information. With any luck, I'll find out what's going on soon. Unfortunately, I haven't yet heard a thing about what happened to the fourth painting. Since I knew that you, Ms. Savich, owned them, and that they'd been moved from the Art Institute of Chicago to the Eureka Art Museum eleven months ago, I didn't want to believe it—there are always wild rumors floating through the art world. I couldn't be sure until I'd actually seen them. I'm sorry, they are fakes."

"Well," Sherlock said, her face nearly as red as her hair, "shit."

Savich stared at his wife and said slowly, "You really cursed, Sherlock? You didn't even curse when you were in labor, at least you didn't until the end."

"I apologize for that, but I am so mad I want to chew nails. This is very bad. I'm really ready to go over the edge here. Those bastards—those officious, murdering bastards. There, I don't have to curse anymore. I'm sorry, Dillon, but this really is too much. This is so awful, Lily, but at least we have a good idea who's responsible."

Lily said, "Tennyson and his father."

Sherlock said, "And Mr. Monk, the curator of the Eureka museum. He had to be in on it. No wonder he was near tears when you told him you were taking the paintings. He knew the jig would be up sooner or later. He had to know that in Washington, D.C., experts would be viewing the paintings and one of them would spot the fakes."

"So did Tennyson," Savich said.

Lily said, "Probably my father-in-law as well. Maybe the whole family was in on this. But they couldn't have known we would find out the very day after we got here." She turned to Simon Russo. "I'm madder than Sherlock. Thank you, Mr. Russo, for being on top of this and getting to us so quickly."

Simon turned to Savich. "There is one positive thing here. At least Tennyson Frasier didn't have time to have all eight of them forged. Now that I know for certain that we've got four forgeries, I can find out the name of the forger. It won't be difficult. You see, it's likely to be one of three or four people in the world—the only ones with enough technique to capture the essence of Sarah Elliott and fool everyone except an expert who's been prepared for the possibility."

Lily said, "Would you have known they were fakes if you hadn't heard about them being sold to a collector?"

"Maybe not, but after the second or third viewing, I probably would have realized something was off. They really are very well done. When I find out who forged them, I'll pay a visit to the artist."

"Don't forget, Simon, we need proof," Savich said, "to nail Tennyson. And his family, and Mr. Monk at the Eureka museum."

Sherlock said, "No wonder that guy tried to murder you on the bus, Lily. They knew they had to move quickly and they did. It's just that you're no wuss and you creamed the guy. I wanna lock them all up, Dillon. Maybe stomp on them first."

Simon, who had been studying *The Maiden Voyage,* looked up. "What do you mean she creamed the guy? Someone attacked you? But you were just out of surgery."

"Sorry, I forgot to mention that," Savich said.

Lily said, "There was no reason to tell him. But yes, I'd been five or six days out of surgery. I was okay, thanks to a psychiatrist who—well, never mind about that. But I was feeling just fine. A young guy got on an empty bus, sat beside me, and pulled out this really scary switch-blade. He was lucky to get away." And Lily gave him a big smile, the first one he'd gotten from her. He smiled back.

"Very good. Your brother taught you?"

"Yes, after Jack—No, never mind that."

"You have a lot of never minds, Ms. Savich."

"You may have to get used to it." But she saw him file Jack's name away in that brain of his.

Simon said, "As for the fourth painting, *Effigy,* I thought it was just fine at first, but then I realized that the same forger who did the other three did that one as well. No leads yet on *Effigy,* but we'll track it down. It probably went to the same collector."

Mr. Beezler, shaken, wiped a beautiful linen handker-chief over his brow and said, "This would be a catastrophe to a museum, Mr. Savich, like a stick of dynamite stuck in the tailpipe of my Mercedes. You, Mr. Russo, you are, I gather, in a position to perhaps get the original paintings back?"

"Yes," said Simon, "I am. Keep the black velvet warm, Mr. Beezler."

Savich said, "I'll speak to the guys in the art fraud section, see what recommendations they have. The FBI doesn't do full-blown stolen art investigations at this time, so our best bet is Simon finding out who acquired the paintings."

Simon said, "First thing, I'll do some digging around, hit up my informants to get verification on who our collector is, find the artist, and squeeze him. The instant our collector hears that I'm digging—and he'd hear about it real quick—he'll react, either go to ground, hide the paintings, or maybe something else, but it won't matter."

"What do you mean 'something else'?" Lily asked.

Savich gave him a frown, and Simon said quickly, shrugging, "Nothing, really. But since I plan to stir things up, I'll be really careful who's at my back. Oh yeah, Savich, I'm relieved you didn't use the shippers that Mr. Monk wanted you to use."

Savich said, "No, I used Bryerson. I know them and trust them. There's no way Mr. Monk or Tennyson or any of the rest of them could know, at least for a while, where the paintings ended up. However, I will call Teddy Bryerson and have him let me know if he gets any calls about the paintings. Simon, do you think anyone will realize that these four paintings are fakes if they're out in the open for all to see?"

"Sooner or later someone would notice and ask questions."

Lily said to Mr. Beezler, "I can't very well let a museum hang the four fakes. What do you think about hanging all of them here for a while, Mr. Beezler, and we can see what happens?"

"Yes, I will hang them," said Raleigh, "with great pleasure."

Lily said to Simon, "Do you really think you can get the paintings back?"

Simon Russo rubbed his hands together. His eyes were fierce, and he looked as eager as a boy with his first train set. "Oh, yes."

She imagined him dressed all in black, even black camouflage paint on his face, swinging down a rope to hover above an alarmed floor.

Savich said, "Just one thing, Simon. When you find out who bought the paintings, I go with you."

Sherlock blinked at her husband. "You mean that you, an FBI special agent, unit chief, want to go steal four paintings?"

"Steal back," Savich said, giving her a kiss on her open mouth. "Bring home. Return to their rightful owner."

Lily said, "I'll be working with Mr. Russo to find the person who forged them and the name of the collector who bought them. And then we'll have proof to nail Tennyson."

"Oh no," Savich said. "I'm not letting you out of my sight, Lily."

"No way," Sherlock said. "No way am I letting you out of my sight either. Sean wants his auntie to hang out with him for a while."

Simon Russo looked at Lily Savich and slowly nodded. He knew to his bones that when this woman made up her mind, it would take more than an offering of a dozen chocolate cakes to change it. "Okay, you can work with me. But first you need to get yourself back to one-hundred-percent healthy."

"I'll be ready by Monday," Lily said. She raised her hand, palm out, to her brother before he could get out his objection. "You guys have lots to worry about—this Tammy Tuttle person. She's scary, Dillon. You've got to focus on catching her. This is nothing, in comparison, just some work to track these paintings, maybe talking to these artists. I know artists. I know what to say to them. It won't be any big deal. I can tell Mr. Russo exactly how to do it."

"Right," said Simon.

Sherlock was pulling on a hank of curly hair, something, Savich knew, she did when she was stressed or worried. She said, "She's right, Dillon, but that doesn't mean I like it." She sighed. "And it's not just Tammy Tuttle. Oh well, I'll just spit it out. Ollie phoned just before we left the house this morning."

"He did?" Savich turned the full force of his personality on his wife, a dark brow raised. "And you didn't see fit to mention it to me?"

"It's Friday morning, Gabriella was at the dentist and running late; she's our nanny," Sherlock added to Simon. "Besides, you'd already told Ollie and Jimmy Maitland that you wouldn't be in until late morning. I was going to tell you on the way in."

"I know I don't want to hear this, but out with it, Sherlock. I can take it."

"Besides worrying about Tammy Tuttle, there's been a triple murder in a small town called Flowers, Texas. The governor called the FBI and demanded that we come in, and so we will. Both the ATF and the FBI are involved. There's this cult down there that they suspect is responsible for the murder of the local sheriff and his two deputies, who'd gone out to their compound to check things out. Their bodies were found in a ditch outside of town."

"That's nuts," Simon said.

"Yes," Sherlock said, "it is. Ah, Raleigh, would you mind visiting with Dyrlana for a moment? All this stuff is sort of under wraps."

Raleigh looked profoundly disappointed, but he left

them in the vault. At the doorway, he said, "What about your sister and Mr. Russo? They're civilians, too."

"I know, but I can control what they say," Savich said. "I really couldn't get away with busting your chops."

They heard him chuckling as he called out, "Dyrlana! Where is my gumpoc tea?"

"One problem is," Sherlock said, "that the cult has cleared out, split up into a dozen or more splinter groups and left town in every direction. Nobody knows where the leader is. They've pulled in a few of the cult members, but these folks just shake their heads and claim they don't know anything about it. The only good thing is that we have a witness, of sorts. It seems that one of the women is pregnant by the guru. Lureen was rather angry when she found him seducing another cult member, actually at least three or four other cult members. She slipped away and told the town mayor about it."

Savich said, "A witness, then. Did she identify the guru as the guy who ordered the murders?"

"Not yet. She's still thinking about it. She's afraid she'd screw up her child's karma if she identified the father as a murderer."

"Great," Savich said and sighed. "Like Ollie said, there doesn't seem to be anything in this life that's easy. Do we have some sort of name on this guy?"

"Oh, sure, that's no secret," Sherlock said. "Wilbur Wright. Lureen just wouldn't say his name out loud, but everybody knows it, since he was around town for a couple of months."

"Isn't that clever?" Savich rubbed the back of his neck, nodded to Simon, grabbed his wife's hand, and walked out of the vault. He said over his shoulder, "It's settled then. Lily, you rest and recuperate. Simon, you can stay at the house. I'd feel better if you did. Sherlock and I will call you guys later. Oh yes, don't spoil Sean. Gabriella is besotted with him already; she doesn't need any more help. Holler if you want MAX to check anything out for you, Simon."

"Will do."

"Oh, yes, there's one other thing," Sherlock said to Savich once they were out of the vault and in the gallery itself, alone and beyond the hearing of Lily or Simon. She glanced at Raleigh and Dyrlana, who were drinking gumpoc tea over by the front glass doors.

Savich knew he didn't want to hear this. He merely looked at her, nodding slowly.

"The guru. He had the hearts cut out of the sheriff and his two deputies."

"So this is why the Texas governor wants us involved. This guy has probably done something this sick before in other states. Ah, Sherlock, I just knew it couldn't be as straightforward as you presented it. So, is Behavioral Sciences also involved?"

"Yes. I didn't want Lily to have to hear that."

"You're right. All right, love, let's go track down Tammy Tuttle and Wilbur Wright."

Lily Savich and Simon Russo stood in the silent vault, neither of them saying a word. She walked to one of the paintings that was real, not forged—*Midnight Shadows*. She said, "I wonder why he tried to kill me when he did? What was the hurry? He had four more paintings to have forged. Why now?"

Savich had told Simon most of what had happened to his sister the previous evening, after she'd gone to bed, looking pale and, truth be told, wrung out. All except for the murder attempt on the city bus in Eureka. What had happened to her—what was still happening—was tragic and evil, and it all came on top of the death of her daughter.

But just perhaps they could recover the paintings. He sure wanted to. He said, "That's a good question. I don't know why they cut the brake lines. My guess is that something must have happened to worry them, something to make them move up the timetable."

"But why not just kill me off right away? Surely it would have been easier for Tennyson to simply inherit the paintings, to own them himself. Then he wouldn't have had to go to all the trouble and risk of finding a first-class forger and then collectors who would want to buy the paintings."

"Count on Mr. Monk to help with all that. I bet you Mr. Monk doesn't have all that sterling a reputation. I'll check into that right away."

"Yes," Lily continued, her head cocked to one side, still thinking. "He could have killed me immediately, and then he would have owned the paintings. He could then have sold them legally, right up front, with no risk that someone would turn on him, betray him. Probably he would have made more money that way, you know, in auctions."

"First of all, Lily, killing you off would have brought Savich down on their heads, with all the power of the FBI at his back. Never underestimate your brother's determination or the depths of his rage if something had happened to you. As for legal auctions for the paintings, you're wrong there. Collectors involved in illegal art deals pay top dollar, many times outrageous amounts because they want something utterly unique, something no one else on the face of the earth owns. The stronger the obsession, the more they'll pay. Going this route was certainly more risky, but the pay-off was probably greater, even figuring in the cost of the forgery. It was trying to kill you that was the real risk. As I said, something very threatening must have happened. I don't know what, but we'll probably find out. Now, you ready to go have some lunch before you go home to bed?"

Lily thought about how tired she was, how she could simply sit down and sleep, then she smiled. "Can I have Mexican?"

13

Savich was seated in his small office in the Jefferson dorm at the FBI academy when two agents ushered in Marilyn Warluski, who'd borne a child by her cousin Tommy Tuttle, now deceased, the child's whereabouts unknown. They'd nabbed her getting on a Greyhound bus in Bar Harbor, Maine, headed for Nova Scotia. Since she'd been designated a material witness, and Savich wanted to keep her stashed away, they'd brought her in a FBI Black Bell Jet to Quantico.

He'd never met her, but he'd seen her photo, knew she was poorly educated, and guessed that she was not very bright. He saw that she looked, oddly, even younger than in her photo, that she'd gained at least twenty pounds, and that her hair, cropped short in the photo, was longer and hung in oily hanks to her shoulders. She looked more tired than scared. No, he was wrong. What she looked was defeated, all hope quashed.

"Ms. Warluski," he said in his deep, easy voice, waving her to a chair as he said her name. The two agents left the office, closing the door behind them. Savich gently pressed a button on the inside of the middle desk drawer, and in the next room, two profilers sitting quietly could also hear them speak.

"My name is Dillon Savich. I'm with the FBI."

"I don't know nothin'," Marilyn Warluski said.

Savich smiled at her and seated himself again behind the desk.

He was silent for several moments, watched her fidget in that long silence. She said finally, her voice jumpy, high with nerves, "Just because you're good-lookin' doesn't mean I'm gonna tell you anythin', mister."

This was a kick. "Hey, my wife thinks I'm good-looking, but I'm wondering, since you said it, if you're just trying to butter me up."

"No," she said, shaking her head, "you're good-lookin' all right, and I heard one of the lady cops on the airplane say you're a hunk. They were thinkin' that a sexy guy will make me talk, so they got you."

"Well," Savich said, "just maybe that's so." He paused a fraction of a second, then said, his voice unexpectedly hard, "Have you ever seen the Ghouls, Marilyn?"

He thought she'd keel over in her chair. So she knew about the Ghouls. She paled to a sickly white, looked ready to bolt.

"They're not here, Marilyn."

She shook her head back and forth, back and forth, whispering, "There's no way you could know about the Ghouls. No way at all. Ghouls are bad, real bad."

"Didn't Tammy tell you that I was there in the barn, that I saw them, even shot at them?"

"No, she didn't tell me . . . ah, shit. I don't know nothin', you hear me?"

"Okay, she didn't tell you that I saw them and she didn't tell you my name, which is interesting since she knows it. But she did tell you that she wanted to have at me, didn't she?"

Marilyn's lips were seamed tight. She shook her head and said, "Oh, yeah, and she will. She called you that creepy FBI fucker. I don't know why she didn't tell me that you saw the Ghouls."

"Maybe she doesn't trust you."

"Oh, yeah, Tammy trusts me. She doesn't have anybody else now. She'll get you, mister, she will."

"Just so you know, Marilyn, I'm the one who shot her, the one who killed Tommy. I didn't want to, but they left me no choice. They had two kids there, and they were going to kill them. Young boys, Marilyn, and they were terrified. Tommy and Tammy had kidnapped them, beaten them, and they were going to murder them, like they've murdered many young boys all across the country. Did you know that? Did you know your cousins were murderers?"

Marilyn shrugged. Savich saw a rip beneath the right arm of her brown, cracked leather jacket. "They're my kin. I could miss Tommy—seein' as how he's dead now—but he killed our baby, cracked its poor little head right open, so I was really mad at him for a long time. Tommy was hard, real hard. He was always doin' things you didn't expect, mean things, things to make you scream. You killed him. He was one of a kind, Tommy was. Tammy's right, you're a creepy fucker."

Savich didn't respond, just nodded, waiting.

"You shouldn't have shot Tammy like you did, tearing her arm all up so they had to saw it off. You shouldn't have been there in my barn in the first place. It wasn't none of your damned business."

He smiled at her, sat forward, his palms flat on his desk. "Of course it's my business. I'm a cop, Marilyn. You know, I could have killed Tammy, not just shot her arm off. If I had killed her in the barn then she wouldn't have killed that little boy outside Chevy Chase. Either she did it or the Ghouls did it. Maybe the Ghouls did kill the boy, since there was a circle. Do the Ghouls have to have a circle,

Marilyn? You don't know? Were you with her when she took that boy? Did you help her murder him?"

Marilyn shrugged her shoulders again. "Nope, I didn't even know what she was going to do, not really. She left me at this grungy motel on the highway and told me to stay put or she'd bang me up real bad. She looked real happy when she got back. There was lots of blood on her nurse's uniform; she said she'd have to find somethin' else to wear. She thought it was neat that there was blood on the uniform, said it was a-pro-pos or somethin' like that. Now, I'm not goin' to say any more. I already said too much. I want to leave now."

"You know, Marilyn, your cousin's very dangerous. She could turn on you, like this." He snapped his fingers, saw her cower in the chair, saw her shudder. He said, "How would you like to be ripped apart?"

"She wouldn't turn on me. She's known me all my life. I'm her cousin, her ma and mine were sisters, at least half-sisters. They wasn't real sure since their pa was always cattin' around."

"Why did Tammy pretend to be Timmy?"

Marilyn focused her eyes on the pile of books along the side wall of the office and didn't answer. Savich started to leave it for the moment since it obviously upset her, when she burst out, "She wanted me, you know, but she weren't no dyke and so she played with me only when she was dressed like Timmy, but never when she was Tammy."

For an instant, Savich was too startled to say a word. What a wild twist. He said finally, "Okay then, tell me what kind of shape Tammy is in right now."

That brought Marilyn up straight in her chair. "No thanks to you she's going to be okay, at least she kept telling me that. But she hurts real bad and her shoulder looks all raw and swollen. She went to a pharmacy late one night, just when they was closing, and got the guy to give her some antibiotics and pain pills. He nearly puked when he saw her shoulder."

"I didn't hear about any robbery in a pharmacy," Savich said slowly. They'd been looking, but hadn't gotten any news as yet.

"That's because Tammy whacked the guy after she got the medicine from him, tore the place up. She said that'd make the cops go after the local druggies."

"Where was this, Marilyn?"

"In northern New Jersey somewhere. I don't remember the name of that crummy little town."

Local law enforcement hadn't connected the pharmacist's murder to the Tammy Tuttle bulletin the FBI had circulated all over the eastern seaboard. Well, at least now they'd find out everything the local cops had on the murder. He said, "Where did Tammy go after you went off to Bar Harbor?"

"She said she wanted some sun so's it would heal her shoulder. She was going down to the Caribbean to get herself well. No, I don't know where; she wouldn't tell me. She said there were lots of islands down there and she'd just find the one that was best for her. Of course she didn't have enough money, so she robbed this guy and his wife in a real fancy house in Connecticut. Got three thousand and change. That's when she told me she'd be all right and I could take off."

"Naturally she's going to call you, let you know how she's doing?"

Marilyn nodded.

"Where will she call you?"

"At my boyfriend's, in Bar Harbor. But I'm not there anymore, am I? My boyfriend will tell her that the cops came around and I left."

That was true enough, Savich thought, no hope for it. He just hoped that Tammy wouldn't call until they'd found out where she was in the Caribbean.

Marilyn said, "I'll bet she really wants to kill you bad because of what you done to her. She'll come back when she's really well, and she'll take you down. Tammy's the meanest female in the world. She beat the shit out of me every time I saw her when we was growin' up. She'll get you, Dillon Savich. You're nuthin' compared to Tammy."

"What are the Ghouls, Marilyn?"

Marilyn Warluski seemed to grow smaller right in front of him. She was pressed against the back of her chair, her shoulders hunched forward. "They're bad, Mr. Savich. They're really bad."

"But what are they?"

"Tammy said she found them when she and Tommy were hiding out in some caves in the Ozarks a couple years ago. That's in Arkansas, you know. It was real dark, she told me, real dark in that stinkin' cave, smelled like bat shit, and Tommy was out takin' a leak, and she was alone and then, all of a sudden, the cave filled with weird white light and then the Ghouls came."

"They didn't hurt her?"

Marilyn shook her head.

"What else did she say?"

"Said she knew they were the Ghouls, just knew, that somehow they'd got inside her head and told her their name, then told her that they needed blood, lots of young blood, and then they laughed and told her they were counting on her, and then they just winked out. That's what Tammy said: they laughed, spoke in her head, and just 'winked out.'"

"But what are they, Marilyn? Do you have any idea?"

She was silent for the longest time, then she whispered, "Tammy told me just a couple of days ago that the Ghouls were pissed off at her because she and Tommy hadn't given them their young blood in the barn, that if Tommy was still alive, they'd eat him right up."

"Do you think that's why Tammy got that kid? So the Ghouls could have their young blood?"

She didn't say anything, just looked at him and slowly nodded. Then she started crying, hunched over, her bowed head in her hands.

"Do you know anything else, Marilyn?"

She shook her head. Savich believed her. He also understood why she was shivering. He was close to shivering himself. He had goose bumps on his arms.

Two FBI agents escorted Marilyn Warluski out of Savich's office. She would remain here at Quantico, a material witness and the FBI's guest until Savich and Justice made a decision about what to do with her.

He was standing by his desk, deep in thought, looking out the window toward Hogan's Alley, the all-American town that the FBI Academy had created and used to train their agents in confronting and catching criminals, when Jeffers, a profiler in the Behavioral Sciences, housed three floors down here at Quantico, said in his slow, Alabama drawl even before he cleared the doorway, "This is about the strangest shared delusion I've ever heard, Savich. But what are the things to them? How do they interact with Tammy Tuttle? Marilyn said Tammy told her the Ghouls got in her head and told her to do things."

"What we've got to do is predict what Tammy Tuttle will do next given this belief of hers in the Ghouls," said Jane Bitt, a senior profiler who'd lasted nearly five years without burning out.

Jane Bitt came around Jeffers and leaned against the wall, her arms crossed over her chest. "Lots of other monsters but not anything like this. Tammy Tuttle is a monster. She's got monsters inside her—monsters within a monster. The problem is that we don't have any markers, any clues to give us even a glimmer of an idea of what we're working with here. We're faced with something we've never seen before."

"That's right," said Jeffers, the two words so drawn out in his accent that Savich wanted to say them for him, that or just pull them out of his mouth. "How do we get her, Agent Savich? I sure want to hear what she has to say about the Ghouls."

Savich said, "You heard Marilyn say that Tammy went to the Caribbean, to an island 'right' for her. She couldn't have walked there, and she sure can't be hard to spot. Just a moment, let me call Jimmy Maitland. They can get on that right away." He placed the phone call, listened, and when he finally hung up, he said, "Mr. Maitland was nearly whistling. He's sure they'll get her now. What else do you guys think from listening to her?"

"Well," Jane said as she sat down, crossing her legs and leaning forward, "it seems to be some sort of induced hallucination. Marilyn seems to think they're real, and both you and the boys saw *something* unusual in that barn, isn't that right, Agent Savich?"

"Yes," Savich said.

"Maybe Tommy and Tammy have some sort of ability to alter what you see and feel, some sort of hypnotic ability."

Savich said to Jeffers, "You did a profile on Timmy Tuttle before he turned out to be Tammy."

"Savich is right, Jane," Jeffers said. "We ain't got nothing useful that fits a psychotic cross-dresser who may have hypnotic skills."

Savich laughed, said, "You know what I want to try? I want to talk Marilyn into letting us hypnotize her. Maybe if you're right about this, she can tell us a lot more when she's under."

Jeffers laughed. "Hey, maybe the Ghouls are real, maybe they're entities, aliens from outer space. What do you think, Jane?"

"I like the sound of that, Jeffers. It'd perk up our boring lives a bit, add some color to our humdrum files. White cones whirling around black circles—maybe they're from Mars, you think?"

Savich said, "Actually, I've been reading articles, studies on various phenomena involved in past crimes."

"Found anything?" Jeffers asked.

"Nothing like this," Savich said. "Not a thing like this."

He added as he stood, "Joke all you want, but just don't do it in front of the media."

"Not a chance," Jane said. "I don't want to get committed." She rose, shook Savich's hand. "Marilyn told you that Tammy met up with the Ghouls in a cave. My husband is really into speleology and we usually go spelunking on our vacations. In fact, we were planning on visiting some of the caves in the Ozarks this summer. No matter how much I can laugh about this, I might want to rethink that plan."

WASHINGTON, D.C.

Lily was leaning over her drawing table, looking at her work. No Wrinkles Remus was emerging clear and strong and outrageous from the tip of her beloved sable brush. The brush was getting a bit gnarly, but it was good for another few weeks, maybe.

First panel: Remus is sitting at his desk, a huge, impressive affair, looking smug as he says to someone who looks like Sam Donaldson, "Here's a photo of you without your wig. You're really bald, Sam. I'm going to show this photo to the world if you don't give me what I want."

Second panel: Sam Donaldson clearly isn't happy. He grabs the photo, says, "I'm not bald, Remus, and I don't wear a wig. This photo is a fake. You can't blackmail me."

Third panel: Remus is gloating. "Why don't you call Jessie Ventura? Just ask him what I did to him."

Fourth panel: Sam Donaldson, angry, defeated, says, "What do you want?"

Fifth panel: Remus says, "I want Cokie Roberts. You're going to fix it so I can have dinner with her. I want her and I'm going to have her."

Lily was grinning when she turned to see Simon Russo standing in the doorway.

He looked fit, healthy, and tanned. She felt suddenly

puny and weak, still bowed over a bit. She wished he'd just go away, but she said, "Yes?"

"Sorry to bother you, but you should be in bed. I just spoke to Savich, and he said to check on you. He knew you wouldn't be following orders. You've got a strip nearly ready?"

"Yep. It's not the final version yet, but close. Remus is in fine form. He's blackmailing Sam Donaldson."

Simon wandered over to look down at the panels. He laughed. "I've missed Remus, the amoral bastard. Glad to see him back."

"Now I've got to see if the *Washington Post* would like to take me and *Remus* in. Keep your fingers crossed that they'll agree. I won't get rich anytime soon, but it's a start."

Simon said after a moment, looking down at the *Remus* strip, "I know a cartoonist doesn't make much money until he or she is syndicated. Hey, I just happen to know Rick Bowes. He runs the desk. How about I give him a call, go to lunch, show him the strips?"

Lily didn't like it, obvious enough, so he didn't say anything more until she shook her head. "All right, then, you bring some of these strips to show him and I'll take you both to a Mexican restaurant."

"Well," she said, "maybe that would be okay."

"Will you take a nap now, Lily? You should take some of your meds, too."

Sean hollered from the nursery down the hall. They heard Gabriella telling him that if he'd just stop chewing his knuckles as well as hers, she'd get him a graham cracker and they'd go for a walk in the park. Sean let out one more yell, then burbled. Gabriella laughed. "Let's go get that cracker, champ."

Lily heard Sean cooing as Gabriella carried him down the hall. She tried to swallow the tears, but it just wasn't possible. She stood there, not making a sound, tears rolling down her cheeks.

Simon knew about tragedy, knew about the soul-deep pain that dulled over time but never went away. He didn't say a word, just very slowly pulled her against him and pressed her face to his shoulder.

When the phone rang a minute later, Lily pulled away, wouldn't look him straight in the eye, and answered it.

She handed it to him. "It's for you."

14

It was nearly ten o'clock Sunday night. Simon was back in New York and had just finished a hard work-out at his gym. He felt both exhausted and energized, as always. He toweled off his face, wiped the sweat off the back machine, stretched, and headed for the showers. There were at least a dozen guys in the men's locker room, all in various stages of undress—cracking jokes, bragging about their dates, and complaining about injured body parts.

Simon stripped and nabbed the only free shower. It was late when he finally stepped out and grabbed up his towel. Only two guys were left, one of them blow-drying his hair, the other peeling a Band-Aid off his knee. Then, not three minutes later, they were gone. Simon had on his boxer shorts when the lights went out.

He grabbed for his pants. He remembered the circuit breaker was outside the men's locker room, right there on the left wall.

He heard something, a light whisper of sound. It was the last thing he remembered. The blow just over his right ear knocked him out cold. He fell flat to the locker room floor.

"Hey, man, wake up! Oh God, please, man, don't be dead. I'd lose my job for sure. Please, man, open your eyes!"

Simon cracked open an eye to see an acne-ridden face, a very young face that was scared to death, staring down at him. The young guy was shaking his shoulder.

"Yeah, yeah, I'm not dead. Stop shaking me." Simon raised his hand and felt the lump behind his right ear. The skin was broken, and he felt the smear of his own blood. He looked up at the kid and said, "Someone turned out the lights and hit me with something very hard."

"Oh, man," the kid said, "Mr. Duke is going to blame me for sure. I'm supposed to take care of this place, and I've only been here a week and he's going to fire me. I'm road-kill." He began wringing his hands, looking around wildly, as if expecting to see Mr. Duke, the manager, at any minute.

"The guy who hit me—I guess you didn't see him?"

"Nah, I didn't see any guy."

"All right. Don't worry, chances are he's long gone. Help me up, I've got to check my wallet." Once on his feet, Simon opened his locker door and reached for his ancient black bomber jacket that had seen its best days at MIT a dozen years before. His wallet was gone.

A robber trips the circuit breaker, then comes into the gym locker room to steal a wallet? He must have known only one guy was left, which meant that he'd had to look in, to check. A mugger in a men's locker room?

"Sorry, kid, but we should call the cops. Can't hurt. Just maybe they'll turn up something."

Simon canceled his credit cards while he waited for the cops to show up. The police, two young patrolmen, took a statement, looked around the gym and in the locker room, but—

Simon waited to call Savich until he was back at his brownstone on East Seventy-ninth Street.

Savich said, "What's happening?"

Simon said, "I had a bit of trouble just a while ago."

Savich said, "You leave my house this afternoon after you get a phone call, don't call me to tell me what's going on, and you're telling me you've already landed into trouble?"

"Yeah, that's about the size of it. Is Lily better?"

"Lily is indeed better, and she's pissed. She said tomorrow is Monday, her stitches are out in the morning, and she's coming up to New York, no matter what kind of excuses you try to pawn off on her."

"I'll have to think about that," Simon said.

"All right, tell me what happened."

After Simon had finished, Savich said, "Go to the hospital. Have a doctor check out your head."

"Nah, it's nothing, Savich, the skin's barely split. Don't worry about that. Thing is my wallet was taken, and I really don't know what to make of it all."

Savich said slowly, "You think some people know you're after my grandmother's paintings?"

"Could be. Thing is, when I got that phone call at your house, I wasn't exactly truthful with Lily. It wasn't an emergency with a client here in New York. It was from an art world weasel I do business with occasionally. I'd called him from your house earlier and he said he'd heard some things, too, and now he's put out some feelers for me on the Sarah Elliott paintings. He was expecting some solid results soon, would have something to show me, and he needed me up here in New York. I was supposed to meet him tonight, but he called earlier and said he didn't have everything together yet. So it's on for tomorrow night, at the Plaza Hotel, the Oak Room Bar, one of his favorite places. The guy's good, really knows what he's doing, so I'm hopeful."

"All right, sounds promising. Now, just in case you were wondering how good a liar you are, Lily didn't believe you for a minute. Your mugging, Simon, maybe it was just a mugging or maybe it was a warning. They didn't hurt you seriously, and they could have. I'll bet you a big one that your wallet is in a Dumpster somewhere near the gym. So take a look."

Simon could picture Savich pacing up and down that beautiful living room with its magnificent skylights.

"How's Sean?"

"Asleep."

"Is Lily asleep, too?"

"Nope. She's here, knows it's you on the phone, and wants to lay into you. I can't stop her from coming up, Simon."

Simon said, "Okay, give her my address, tell her to take a shuttle up here. I'll meet her unless there's a problem. I wish you could keep her with you longer, Savich."

"No can do."

Simon said, "I changed my mind, Savich. It may be turning dangerous, real fast. I really don't want Lily involved in this. She's a civilian. For God's sake, she's your sister. I take it all back. Tie her to a chair; don't let her come up here."

"Do you happen to have any suggestions about what I should do, other than tying her up?"

"Put her on the phone. I want to talk to her."

"Sure. She's about to rip the phone away from me in any case. Good luck, Simon."

A moment later, Lily said, "I'm here. I don't care what you have to say. Just be quiet, go to the hospital, get a good night's sleep, and meet my plane tomorrow. I'll take the two-o'clock United shuttle to JFK. Then we can handle things. Good night, Simon."

"But Lily—"

She was gone.

Then Savich's voice came on. "Simon?"

"Yeah, Savich. Well, I'd have to say it was a nonstarter."

Savich laughed. "Lily's my sister. She's smart, and they are her paintings. Let her help with it, Simon, but keep her safe."

Simon bowed to the inevitable. "I'll try."

He took two aspirins and went back to his gym. There was a Dumpster half a block away. Lying on the top was his wallet, with only the cash gone. He looked up to see two young guys staring at him.

When one of them yelled an obscenity at him, Simon started forward. They didn't waste time and swaggered away, then turned when they figured they were far enough away from him and gave him the finger.

Simon smiled and waved.

He was waiting for her, standing right in front of the gate, arms crossed, looking pissed.

Lily smiled, said even before she got to him, "I didn't want to carry much because of my missing spleen. I've got a bag down on carousel four."

"I've decided you're going back to Washington to draw your cartoons."

"While you find my paintings? Doesn't look like you started out very well, Mr. Russo. You don't look so hot. I think I did better on that bus than you did in your men's locker room last night. And I want to find my grand-mother's paintings worse than you do."

And she walked past him to follow the signs to Baggage Claim.

Simon didn't own a car, had never felt the need to, so they took a taxi to East Seventy-ninth, between First and Second. He assisted her out of the cab, took her purse and suitcase, grunted because it had to weigh seventy pounds, and said, "This is it. I've got a nice guest room with its own bath. You should be comfortable until you wise up and go back home. How are they doing on that cult case in Texas? They got him yet? Wilbur Wright?"

"Not yet. What Dillon does is feed all the pertinent information into protocols he developed for the CAU— Criminal Apprehension Unit. Put that eyebrow back down. So you already know what he does and how he does it."

"I should have asked, has MAX got Wilbur yet?"

"MAX found out that Wilbur Wright is Canadian, that he attended McGill University, that he's a real whiz at cellular biology, and that his real name is Anthony Carpelli— ancestry, Sicily. Oh my, Simon, this is very lovely."

Lily stepped into a beautifully marbled entryway, and felt like she'd stepped back into the 1930s. The feel was all Art Deco—rich dark wood paneling, lamps in geometric shapes, a rich Tabriz carpet on the floor, furniture right out of the Poirot series on PBS.

"I bought it four years ago, after I got a really healthy commission. I knew the old guy who'd owned it for well nigh on to fifty years, and he gave me a good deal. Most of the furnishings were his. I begged and he finally sold me most of them. Neat, huh?"

"Very," she said, a vast understatement. "I want to see everything."

There was even a small library, bookshelves to the ceiling with one of those special library ladders. Wainscoting, leather furniture, rich Persian carpets on the dark walnut floor. He didn't show her his bedroom, but guided her directly to a large bedroom at the end of the hall. All of the furniture was a rich Italian Art Deco, trimmed with glossy black lacquer. Posters from the 1930s covered the walls. He put her suitcase on the bed and turned. She said, shaking her head, "You are so modern, yet here you are in this museum of a place that actually looks lived in. This is a beautiful room."

"Wait till you see the bathroom."

He didn't tell her that he was leaving until he had the key in his hand that evening at 10:30.

"I'm meeting a guy with information. No, you're not coming with me."

"All right."

He distrusted her, she could see it, and she just smiled. "Look, Simon, I'm not lying. I'm not going to sneak out after you and follow you like some sort of idiot. I'm really tired. You can go hear what your informant has to say. Just be careful. When you get back, I'll still be awake. Tell me what you find out, okay?"

He nodded and was at the Plaza Hotel by ten minutes to eleven.

LouLou was there, pacing back and forth along the park side of the Plaza, beautifully dressed, looking like a Mafia don. The uniformed Plaza doormen paid him little attention.

He nodded to Simon, motioned to the entrance to the Plaza's Oak Room Bar. It was dark and rich, filled with people and conversation. They found a small table, ordered two beers. Simon leaned back, crossing his arms over his chest. "How's it going, LouLou?"

"Can't complain. Hey, this beer on you? Drinks aren't cheap here, you know?"

"Since we're in New York, I figured the Oak Room would be our venue. Yeah, I'm paying for the beer. Now, what have you got for me?"

"I found out that Abe Turkle did the Elliotts. Talk is he had a contract to do eight of them. Do you know anything about which eight?"

"Yeah, I do, but you don't need to know any more. I would have visited Abe Turkle second. You sure it's not Billy Gross?"

"He's sick—his lungs—probably cancer. He's always smoked way too much. Anyway, he took all his money and went off to Italy. He's down living on the Amalfi Coast, nearly dead. So it's Abe who's your guy."

"And where can I find him?"

"In California, of all places."

"Eureka, by any chance?"

"Don't know. He's in a little town called Hemlock Bay, on the ocean. Don't know where it is. Whoever's paying him wants nim close by where he is."

"You're good, LouLou. I don't suppose you'll tell me where you heard this?"

"You know better, Simon." He drank the rest of his beer in one long pull, wiped his mouth gently on a napkin, then said, "Abe's a mean sucker, Simon, unlike most artists. When you hook up with him, you take care, okay?"

"Yeah, I'll be real careful. Any word at all on who our likely collectors are?"

LouLou fiddled with a cigarette he couldn't light, even here in a bar, for God's sake. "Word is that it just might be Olaf Jorgenson."

This was a surprise, a big surprise, to Simon. He wouldn't have put Olaf in the mix. "The richest Swede alive, huge in shipping. But I heard that he's nearly blind, nearly dead, that his collecting days are over."

LouLou said, "Yeah, that's the word out. Why buy a painting if you're blind as a bat and can't even see it? But, hey, that's what I heard from my inside gal at the Met. She's one of the curators, has an ear that soaks up everything. She's been right before. I trust her information."

"Olaf Jorgenson," Simon said slowly, taking a pull on his Coors. "He's got to be well past eighty now. Been collecting mainly European art for the past fifty years, medieval up through the nineteenth century. After World War Two, I heard he got his hands on a couple of private collections of stolen art from France and Italy. Far as I know, he's never bought a piece of art legally in his life. The guy's certifiable about his art, has all his paintings in climate-controlled vaults, and he's the only one who's got the key. I didn't know he'd begun collecting modern painters, like Sarah Elliott. I never would have put him on my list."

LouLou shrugged. "Like you said, Simon, the guy's a nut. Maybe nuts crack different ways when they get up near the century mark. His son seems to be just as crazy, always out on his yacht, lives there most of the time. His name's Ian—the old guy married a Scotswoman and that's how he got his name. Anyway, the son now runs all the shipping business. From the damned yacht."

Simon gave a very slight shake of his head to a very pretty woman seated at the bar who'd been staring at him for the past couple of minutes. He moved closer to LouLou to show that he was in very heavy conversation and not interested. "LouLou, how sure are you that it's Olaf who bought the paintings?"

"Besides my gal at the Met, I went out of my way to get it verified. You know my little art world birdies that are always singing, Simon. I spread a little seed, and they sing louder and I heard three songs, all with the same words. One hundred percent? Nope, but it's a start. Cost me a cool thousand bucks to get them to sing to me."

"Okay, you done good, LouLou." Simon handed him an envelope that contained five thousand dollars. LouLou didn't count it, just slipped the fat envelope inside his cashmere jacket pocket. "Hey, you know what the name of Ian Jorgenson's yacht is?"

Simon shook his head.

"Night Watch."

Simon said slowly, "That's the name of a painting by Rembrandt. That particular painting is hanging in the Rijksmuseum in Amsterdam. I saw it there a couple of years ago."

LouLou cocked his head to one side, his hairpiece not moving a bit because it was expensive and well made, and gave Simon a cynical smile. "Who knows? Just maybe

Night Watch is hanging in Ian's stateroom, right over his bed. I've often wondered how many real paintings there are left in the museums and not beautifully executed fakes."

"Actually, LouLou, I don't want to know the answer to that question."

"Since Sarah Elliott just died some seven years ago, all her materials—the paints, the brushes—still exist. You take a superb talent with an inherent bent toward her sort of technique and visualization, and what you get is so close to the real thing, most people wouldn't even care if you told them."

"I hate that."

"I do, too," LouLou said. "I need another beer."

Simon ordered them another round, ate a couple of peanuts out of the bowl on their table, and said, "Remember that forger Eric Hebborn, who wrote that book telling would-be forgers exactly how to do it—what inks, papers, pens, colors, signatures, all of it? Then he up and dies in ninety-six. The cops said it was under mysterious circumstances. I heard it was a private collector who killed Hebborn because a dealer friend had sold him an original Rubens that turned out to be a fake that Hebborn himself had done. Supposedly the dealer died shortly thereafter in a car accident."

LouLou said, "Yeah, I met old Eric back in the early eighties. Smart as a whip, that guy, and so talented it made you cry. You wondering if it was Olaf Jorgenson who popped him? Hey, Simon, there's a whole bunch of collectors who'd cut off hands to have a certain medal or stamp or train or painting. They've got to have it or life loses its meaning for them. Look, Simon, when you get down to it, they're the people who keep us in business."

"I wonder if Olaf ordered all eight paintings. I wonder what he's paying for them."

"Huge bucks, my man, huge, count on it. All eight Sarah

Elliotts? Don't know. I haven't heard any other names floated around. Simon, I heard those eight paintings are owned privately by a member of the Elliott family?"

"Yes, Lily Savich owns them. And therein lies a very long, convoluted tale." Simon rose, putting a fifty-dollar bill on the table. "LouLou, thank you. You know where to find me. I think I'll be heading out to California soon to track down one of the major players—Abraham Turkle. He's English, right?"

"Half Greek. Weird guy. Very eccentric, said to eat only snails that he raises himself." LouLou shuddered. "You take care around him, Simon. Abe killed a guy who tried to rip him off with his bare hands, just a couple of years ago. So have a care. Hey, this Lily Savich hire you?"

Simon paused, cocked his head to the side. "Not exactly, but that's about it. I want to get those four paintings back."

"I hope the others are safe."

"Much safer than the snails in Abe's garden. Take care, LouLou."

"Why are you going after Abe?"

Simon said, "I want to see if I can shake something loose. It's not just the art scam. There are other folk involved in this deal who have done very bad things, and I want to nail them. Just maybe Abe can help me do that."

"He won't help you do squat."

"We'll see. His forging days in Hemlock Bay are over. I want to catch him before he takes off to parts unknown. Who knows what I can get out of him."

"Good luck shaking the wasp nest. You know, I've always liked the name Lily," LouLou said and gave Simon a small salute. Then, when Simon left, LouLou turned his attention to that very pretty lady at the bar who'd kept looking over at them.

15

Dr. Hicks said quietly, "Marilyn, tell me, how did Tammy look when she came back to the motel?"

"She had on a coat and she just ripped it apart and showed me her nurse's uniform. It was soaked with blood."

"Did she seem pleased?"

"Oh yes. She was crazy happy that she got away. She just kept laughing and rubbing her bloody hand against herself. She loves the feel of fresh blood."

"How did she get back to the motel? You said her hand was all bloody. Wouldn't somebody have noticed?"

"I don't know." Marilyn looked worried, shaking her head just a bit.

"No, no, that's okay. It's not important. Now, you said she was wearing a coat. Do you know where she got the coat?"

"I don't know. When she came to get me, she was wearing it. It was too big for her, but it covered her arm where she didn't have one, you know?"

"Yes, I know. Mr. Savich would like to ask you some questions now. Is that all right, Marilyn?"

"Yes. He was nice to me. He's sexy. I'm kinda sorry that Tammy's gonna kill him."

Dr. Hicks raised a thick brow at Savich, no look of shock on his face since he'd heard it all. He just shook his head as Savich eased his chair nearer to Marilyn's.

"She's well under, Savich. You know what to do."

Savich nodded, said, "Marilyn, how are you feeling about Tammy right now?"

She was silent, her forehead creased in a frown, then she shook her head and said slowly, "I think I love her; I'm supposed to since she's my cousin, but she scares me. I never know what she's going to do. I think she'd kill me, laugh while she rubbed my blood all over the only hand she's got left, if she was in the mood, you know?"

"Yes, I know."

"She's going to kill you."

"Yes, she might try, you told me. How do you think she contacts the Ghouls?" Savich ignored Dr. Hicks, who didn't have a clue who or what the Ghouls were. He just shook his head and repeated the question. "Marilyn?"

"I've thought about that, Mr. Savich. I know they were there when she killed that little boy. Maybe, from what she said, she just thinks about them and they come. Or maybe they follow her around and she just says that to prove how powerful she is. Do you know what the Ghouls are?"

"No, I don't have any idea, Marilyn. You don't either, do you?"

She shook her head. She was sitting in a comfortable chair, her head leaning back against the cushion, her eyes closed. She'd been staying in a room at the Jefferson dormitory at the FBI complex, watched over by female agents. She'd washed her hair, and they'd given her a clean skirt and sweater. Even hypnotized, she looked pale and frightened, her fingers continually twitching and jerking. He wondered what would happen to her. She had no other family, no education to speak of, and there was Tammy, in the Caribbean, who'd scared her all of her life. He hoped the FBI would find her soon and Marilyn wouldn't have to be scared of her anymore.

He said, "Has Tammy been to the Caribbean before?"

"Yeah. She and Tommy visited the Bahamas a couple years ago. In the spring, I think."

"Did they take the Ghouls with them?"

Marilyn frowned and shook her head.

"You don't know if they killed anyone while they were there?"

"I asked Tommy, and he just laughed and laughed. That was right before he got me pregnant."

Savich made a note to check to see if there'd been any particularly vicious, unsolved killings during their stay.

"Has Tammy ever talked about the Caribbean, other than the Bahamas? Any islands that she'd like to visit?"

She shook her head.

"Think, Marilyn. That's right, just relax, lean your head back, and think about that. Remember back over the times you've seen her."

There was a long silence, and then Marilyn said, "She said once—it was Halloween and she was dressed like a vampire—that she wanted to go to Barbados and scare the crap out of the kids there. Then she laughed. I never liked that laugh, Mr. Savich. It was the same kind of laugh that Tommy had after the Bahamas."

"Did she ever talk about what the Ghouls did to those kids?"

"Once, when she was being Timmy, she said they just gobbled them right up."

"But the Ghouls don't just gobble them up, do they? They maybe take an arm, a leg?"

"Oh, Mr. Savich, they just do that when they're full and aren't interested in anything but a taste. But I can't be sure because both Tommy and Tammy never really told me."

Savich felt sick. Jesus, did she really mean what he

thought she meant? That there were young boys who'd simply disappeared and would never be found because the Tuttles had eaten them? Were they cannibals? He unconsciously rubbed his arms at a sudden chill he felt.

He looked over at Dr. Hicks. His face was red, and he looked ready to be ill himself.

Savich lightly touched her forearm and said, "Thank you, Marilyn, you've been a big help. If you could choose, right now, what would you like to do with your life?"

She didn't hesitate for a second. "I want to be a carpenter. We lived for about five years in this one place and the neighbor was a carpenter. He built desks and tables and chairs, all sorts of stuff. He spent lots of time with me, taught me everything. 'Course I paid him just like he wanted, and he liked that a lot. In high school they told me I was a girl and girls couldn't do that, and then Tommy got me pregnant and killed the baby."

"Just one more question. Was Tammy planning to contact you from the Caribbean?" He'd asked her this before. He wanted to see if she added anything under hypnosis because now he had a plan.

"Yeah. She didn't say when, just that she would, sometime."

"How would she find you?"

"She would call my boyfriend, Tony, up in Bar Harbor. I don't think he likes me anymore. He said if the cops were after me, then he was out of there."

Savich hoped that Tony wouldn't take off too soon. He was still there, working as a mechanic at Ed's European Motors. He'd check in again with the agents in Bar Harbor, keep an eye on him, maybe some wiretaps. Now they had something solid. A call from Tammy.

"Thank you, Marilyn." Savich rose and went to stand by the door. He watched as Dr. Hicks brought her gently back. He listened as he spoke quietly to her, reassuring her, until he nodded to Savich and led her from the room, holding her shoulder.

Savich said, "It's time for lunch, Marilyn. We'll eat in the Boardroom, not the big cafeteria. It's just down the hall on this floor."

"I'd really like a pizza, Mr. Savich, with lots of pepperoni."

"You've got it. The Boardroom is known for its pizza."

EUREKA, CALIFORNIA

Simon was pissed. He'd sent Lily back to Washington. She'd been as pissed as he was now, but she'd finally given up, seen reason, and slid her butt into the taxi he'd called for her. Only she hadn't gone back to Washington. She'd simply taken the same plane he had to San Francisco, keeping out of sight in the back, then managed to make an earlier connection from San Francisco to Arcata-Eureka Airport. She'd waltzed right up to him at the damned baggage carousel and said in a chirpy voice, "I never thought I'd be traveling back to Hemlock Bay only two weeks after I finally managed to escape it."

And now they were sitting side by side in a rental car, and Simon was still pissed.

"You shouldn't have pulled that little sneaking act, Lily. Some bad stuff could happen. We're in their neck of the woods again, and I—"

"We're in this together, Russo, don't forget it," she said. She gave him a long look, then glanced out the back window of their rental car to study the three cars behind them. None appeared to be following them. She said, "You're acting like I've cut off your ego. This isn't your show, Russo. They're my paintings. Back off."

"I promised your brother I wouldn't let you get hurt."

"Fine. Okay, keep your promise. Where are we going? I was thinking it would be to Abe Turkle. You said maybe you could get something out of him, not about the collector he was working for, but maybe about the Frasiers. Since he's here, that pretty well proves he's involved with them, doesn't it?"

"That's right."

"You said Abraham Turkle is staying in a beach house just up the coast from Hemlock Bay. Do we know who owns it? Don't tell me it's my soon-to-be-ex-husband."

Simon gave it up. He turned to her as he said, "No, it's not Tennyson Frasier. It's close, but no, the cottage is in Daddy Frasier's name."

"Why didn't you tell me that sooner? That really nails it, doesn't it? Isn't that enough proof?"

"Not yet. Just be patient. Everything will come together. Highway 211 is a very gnarly road, just like you told me. Are we going to be passing the place where you lost your brakes and plowed into that redwood?"

"Yes, just ahead." But Lily didn't look at the tree as they passed it. The events of that night were growing more faint, the terror fading a bit, but it was still too close to her.

Simon said, "Turns out that Abraham Turkle has no bank account, no visible means of support. So the Frasiers must be paying him in cash."

"I still can't get over their going to all this trouble," Lily said.

"After we verify that Mr. Olaf Jorgenson of Sweden now has three in his possession—no, we want him to have all four of the paintings, it'd keep things simple—we may be able to find out how much he's paid for them. I'm thinking in the neighborhood of two to three million per painting. Maybe higher. Depends on how obsessed he is. From what I hear, he's single-minded when he wants a certain painting."

"Three million? That's a whole lot of money. But to go to all this trouble—"

"I can tell you stories you don't want to hear about how

far some collectors will go. There was one German guy who collected rare stamps. He found out that his mother had one that he'd wanted for years, only she wanted to keep it for herself. He hit her over the head with a large bag of coins, killed her. Does that give you an idea of how completely obsessed some of these folk are?"

Lily could only stare at him. "It's just hard to believe. This Olaf Jorgenson—you told me he's very old and nearly blind in the bargain."

"It is amazing that he can't control his obsession, not even for something as incidental as, say, going blind. I guess it won't stop until he's dead."

"Do you think his son Ian has the real *Night Watch* aboard his yacht?"

"I wouldn't be at all surprised."

"Are you going to tell the people at the Rijksmuseum?"

"Yeah, but trust me on this, they won't want to hear it. They'll have a couple of experts examine the painting on the sly. If the experts agree that it's a forgery, they'll try to get it back, but will they announce it? Doubtful.

"We've been checking out Mr. Monk, the curator of the Eureka Art Museum. He does have a Ph.D. from George Washington, and a pedigree as long as your arm. If something's off there, Savich hasn't found it yet. We're going deeper on that, got some feelers out to a couple of museums where he worked. You keep looking back there. Is anyone following us?"

Lily shifted in her seat to face his profile. "No, no one's back there. I can't help it. To me, this is enemy territory."

"You're entitled. You had a very bad experience here. You met Mr. Monk, didn't you?"

"Oh yes."

"Tell me about him."

Lily said slowly, "When I first met Mr. Monk, I thought he had the most intense black eyes, quite beautiful really, 'bedroom eyes' I guess you could call them. But he looked hungry. Isn't that odd?"

Simon said, "He has beautiful eyes? Bedroom eyes? You women think and say the strangest things."

"Like men don't? If it were Mrs. Monk, you'd probably go on about her cleavage."

"Well, yeah, maybe. And your point would be?"

"You'd probably never even get to her face. You men are all one-celled."

"You think? Really?"

She laughed, she just couldn't help it. He pushed his sunglasses up his nose, and she saw that he was grinning at her. He said with a good deal of satisfaction, "You're feeling better. You've got a nice laugh, Lily. I like hearing it. Mind you, I'm still mad because you followed me out here, but I will admit that this is the first time I've seen you that you don't look like you want to curl up and take a long nap."

"Get over it, Simon. We must be nearly to Abraham Turkle's cottage. Just up ahead, Highway 211 turns left to go to Hemlock Bay. To the right there's this asphalt one-lane track that goes the mile out to the ocean. That's where the cottage is?"

"Yes, those were my directions. You've never been out to the ocean on that road?"

"I don't think so," she said.

"Okay now, listen up. Abe has a bad reputation. He's got a real mean side, so we want to be careful with him."

They came to the fork. Simon turned right, onto the narrow asphalt road. "This is it," Simon said. "There's no sign and there's no other road. Let's try it."

The ocean came into view almost immediately, when they were just atop a slight rise. Blue and calm as far as you could see, white clouds dotting the sky, a perfect day.

"Look at this view," Lily said. "I always get a catch in my throat when I see the ocean."

They reached the end of the road very quickly. Abe Turkle's cottage was a small gray clapboard, weathered, perched right at the end of a promontory towering out over the ocean. There were two hemlock trees, one on either side of the cottage, just a bit protected from the fierce ocean storms. They were so gnarly and bent, though, that you wondered why they even bothered to continue standing.

There was no road, just a dirt driveway that forked off the narrow asphalt. In front of the cottage was a black Kawasaki 650 motorcycle.

Simon switched off the ignition and turned to Lily. She held up both hands. "No, don't say it. I'm coming with you. I can't wait to meet Abe Turkle."

Simon said as he came around to open her car door, "Abe only eats snails and he grows them himself."

"I'm still coming in with you."

She carefully removed the seat belt, laid the small pillow on the backseat, and took his hand. "Stop looking like I'm going to fall over. I'm better every day. It's just that getting out of a car is still a little rough." He watched her swing her legs over and straighten, slowly.

Simon said, "I want you to follow my lead. No reason to let him know who we are just yet."

When he reached the single door, so weathered it had nearly lost all its gray paint, he listened for a moment. "I don't hear any movement inside."

He knocked.

There was no answer at first, and then a furious yell. "Who the hell is that and what the hell do you want?"

"The artist is apparently home," Simon said, cocking a dark eyebrow at Lily, and opened the door. He kept her behind him and walked into the cottage to see Abraham Turkle, a brush between his teeth, another brush in his right hand, standing behind an easel, glaring over the top toward them.

There was no furniture in the small front room, just painting supplies everywhere, at least twenty canvases stacked against the walls. The place smelled of paint and turpentine and french fries and something else—maybe fried snails. There was a kitchen separated from the living room by a bar, and a small hallway that probably led to a bedroom and a bathroom.

The man, face bearded, was indeed Abe Turkle; Simon had seen many photos of him.

"Hi," Simon said and stuck out his hand.

Abe Turkle ignored the outstretched hand. "Who the hell are you? Who is she? Why the hell is she standing behind you? She afraid of me or something?"

Lily stepped around Simon and said, extending her hand, "I like snails. I hear you do, too."

Abraham Turkle smiled, a huge smile that showed off three gold back teeth. He had big shoulders and hands the size of boxing gloves. He didn't look at all like an artist, Simon thought. Wasn't an artist supposed to wear paint-encrusted black clothes and have long hair in a ponytail? Instead, Abraham Turkle looked like a lumberjack. He was wearing a flannel shirt and blue jeans and big boots that were laced halfway to his knees. There were, however, paint splotches all over him, including his tangled dark beard and grizzled hair.

"So," Abe said, and he put down the brushes, wiped the back of his hand over his mouth to get off the bit of turpentine, and shook Lily's hand. "The little gal here likes snails, which means she knows about me, but I don't know who the hell you are, fella."

"I'm Sully Jones, and this is my wife, Zelda. We're on our honeymoon, just meandering up the coast, and we heard in Hemlock Bay that you were an artist and that you liked snails. Zelda loves art and snails, and we thought we'd stop by and see if you had anything to sell."

Lily said, "We don't know yet if we like what you paint, Mr. Turkle, but could you show us something? I hope you're not too expensive."

Abraham Turkle said, "Yep, I'm real expensive. You guys aren't rich?"

Simon said, "I'm in used cars. I'm not really rich."

"Sorry, you won't want to buy any of my stuff."

Simon started to push it, then saw that Lily looked on the shaky side. Simon nodded to Abe Turkle and just looked at him.

"Wait here." Abe Turkle picked up a towel and wiped his hands. Then he walked past them to the far wall, where there were about ten canvases piled together. He went through them, making a rude noise here, sighing there, and then he thrust a painting into Lily's hand. "Here, it's a little thing I did just the other day. It's the Old Town in Eureka. For your honeymoon, little gal."

Lily held the small canvas up to the light and stared at it. She said finally, "Why, thank you, Mr. Turkle. It's beautiful. You're a very fine artist."

"One of the best in the world actually."

Simon frowned. "I'm sure sorry we haven't heard of you."

"You're a used-car salesman. Why would you have heard of me?"

"I was an art history major," Lily said. "I'm sorry, but I haven't heard of you either. But I can see how talented you are, sir."

"Well, just maybe I'm more famous with certain people than with the common public."

"What does that mean?" Simon asked.

Abe's big chest expanded even bigger. "It means, used-car salesman, that I reproduce great paintings for a living. Only the artists themselves would realize they hadn't painted them."

"I don't understand," Lily said.

"It ain't so hard if you think about it. I reproduce paintings for very rich people."

Simon looked astonished. "You mean you forge famous paintings?"

"Hey, I don't like that word. What do you know, fella, you're nothing but a punk who sells heaps of metal; the lady could do a lot better than you."

"No, you misunderstand me," Simon said. "To be able to paint like you do, for whatever purpose, I'm really impressed."

"Just hold it," Abe said suddenly. "Yeah, just wait a minute. You aren't a used-car salesman, are you? What's your deal, man? Come on, what's going on here?"

"I'm Simon Russo."

That brought Abe to a stop. "Yeah, I recognize you now. Dammit, you're that dealer guy...Russo, yeah, you're him. You're Simon Russo, you son of a bitch. You'd better not be here to cause me any trouble. What the hell are you doing here?"

"Mr. Turkle, we—"

"Dammit, give me back that painting! You aren't on any honeymoon now, are you? You lied to me. As for you, Russo, I'm going to have to wring your scrawny neck."

16

Lily didn't think, just assumed a martial arts position that Dillon had shown her, the painting still clutched in her right hand.

She looked both ridiculous and defiant, and it stopped Abe Turkle in his tracks. He stared at her. "You want to fight me? You going to try to karate chop me with my own painting?"

She moved back and forth, flexed her arms, her fists. "I won't hurt your bloody painting. Listen, pal, I don't want to fight you, but I can probably take you. You're big but I'll bet you're slow. So go ahead, if you want, let's just see how tough you are."

"Lily, please don't," Simon said as he prepared to simply lift her beneath her armpits and move her behind him. To Simon's surprise, Abe Turkle began shaking his head. He laughed, and then he laughed some more.

"Jesus, you're something, little lady."

Abe made to grab the painting from Lily's hand, and she said quickly, whipping it behind her back, "Please let me keep it, Mr. Turkle. It really is beautiful. I'll treasure it always."

"Oh, hell, keep the stupid thing. I don't want to fight you either. It's obvious to me that you're real tough. Hell, I might never get over being scared of you. All right, now. Let's just get it over with. What do you want, Simon Russo? And who is the little gal here?"

"I'm just here to see which Sarah Elliott you're working on now."

Abe Turkle glanced back at his easel, and his face blotched red as he said, "Listen to me, Russo, I barely heard of the broad. You want to look?"

"Okay." Simon smiled and walked toward Abe.

Abe held up a huge hand still stained with daubs of red, gold, and white paint. "You try it and I'll break your head off at your neck. Even the little lady here won't be able to hold me off."

Simon stopped. "Okay. Since there were no paintings missing from the Eureka Art Museum, you must be having trouble working from photographs they brought to you. Which one is it? Maybe *The Maiden Voyage* or *Wheat Field*? If I were selecting the next one, it would be either of those two."

"Go to hell, boyo."

"Or maybe you had to stop with the Sarah Elliotts altogether now that they're gone from the museum? So you're doing something else now?"

"I'd break your head for you right this minute, right here, but not with my new stuff around. You want to come outside?"

"You were right about the lady," Simon said. "She isn't my wife. She's Lily Savich, Sarah Elliott's granddaughter. The eight paintings that were in the museum, including the four you've already copied, belong to her."

"Are you finishing a fifth one, Mr. Turkle? If you are, it's too bad because you won't get paid for it. The real one is back in my possession so there won't be any chance to switch it."

Simon said, "Actually, I'm surprised you're still here in residence since the paintings have flown the coop. They're hoping they'll get them back? No chance.

"To be honest, Abe, the real reason we're here is that we want to know who commissioned you. Not the collector, but the local people who are paying you and keeping you here."

"Yes," Lily said. "Please, Mr. Turkle, tell us who set this up."

Abe Turkle gave a big sigh. He looked at Lily and his fierce expression softened, just a bit. "Little gal, why don't you marry me and then I could look at those paintings for the rest of my life. I swear I'd never forge anything again."

"I'm sorry, but I'm still married to Tennyson Frasier."

"Not for long. I heard all about how you just walked out on him."

"That's right. But even so, the paintings belong in a museum, Mr. Turkle, not in a private collection somewhere, locked away, to be enjoyed by only one person."

"They're the ones with all the money. They call the shots."

Simon said, "Abe, she's divorcing Tennyson. She wants to fry that bastard's butt, not yours. You'd do yourself a favor if you helped us."

Abe said slowly, one eyebrow arched up a good inch, "You've got to be joking, boyo."

Lily stepped forward and laid her hand on Abe Turkle's massive shoulder. "We're not joking. You could be in danger. Listen, Tennyson tried to kill me, and I wondered, Why now? Do you know? Did something happen to make him realize that I was a threat to him, before you'd finished copying all the paintings? Please, Mr. Turkle, tell us who hired you to copy my paintings. We'll help you stay safe."

"That really so? Your old man tried to kill you? I'm sorry about that, but I don't have a clue what you're talking about. Both of you need to just get out of here now."

He was standing with his legs spread, his big arms crossed over his chest. "I'm sorry you were almost killed, but it doesn't have anything to do with me."

"We know," Simon said, "that this cottage is owned by the Frasiers. You're staying here. It isn't a stretch to figure it out."

"I don't have anything to say about that. Maybe when this is over, the little gal will share some lunch with me, I'll marinate up some snails, then broil them. That's the best, you know."

Lily shook her head, then walked to the easel. Abe didn't get in her way, didn't try to block her. She stopped and sucked in her breath. On the easel was a magnificent painting nearly finished—it was Diego Velázquez's *Toilet of Venus,* oil on canvas.

"It's incredible. Please, Mr. Turkle, don't let some collector take the original. Please."

Abe shrugged. "I'm just painting that for the fun of it. I'm in between jobs right now. No, you don't want to say that it's because you took all the Sarah Elliott paintings away from the museum. Nah, don't say that. There's nothing going on here so I'm just having me some fun."

Simon came around and looked at the nearly completed painting. "The original is in the National Gallery in London. I hope your compatriots elect to leave it there, Abe."

"Like I said, this is just for fun. A guy's got to keep practicing, you know what I mean? Look, I painted this from a series of photos. If I were in it for bucks, I wouldn't have let her see it. I'd be in London, too."

Lily couldn't give up, not yet. "Won't you just tell us the truth, Mr. Turkle? Tennyson Frasier married me only to get his hands on the paintings. Then he tried to kill me. Did he tell you that, Mr. Turkle? It's possible that he murdered my child as well, I don't know for sure. Please, we won't involve you. Just tell us."

Abe Turkle looked back and forth between the two of them. He slowly shook his head.

"I wish you hadn't found me, Russo," Abe Turkle said, shaking his big head. "I really wish you hadn't." He turned then and walked out the cottage door.

"Wait!" Lily started after him.

Simon grabbed her sleeve and pulled her back. "Let him go, Lily."

They watched from the doorway as the big, black Kawasaki scattered rocks and dirt as it picked up speed. Then he was gone.

"We screwed up," Simon said.

"I wish he'd stayed and fought me," Lily said.

Simon looked down at her, remembering the image of her in a fighting position, with that painting in her right hand. He grinned. He lightly touched his hand to her hair. "You're all blond and blue-eyed, you're skinny as a post, your pants are hanging off your butt, and knowing you for just a short time, I know you've got more guts than brains. I swear to you, when I tell Savich how his little sister was ready to take on Abe Turkle, he'll— No, better not tell him how I nearly got you into a fight. Well, shit."

Lily punched him in the gut. "You jerk. I didn't see you trying to do anything."

Simon grunted, rubbed his palm over his belly, and grinned down at her. "I hope you didn't pull anything loose when you hit me. Not in me, in you."

"I might have, no thanks to you."

She didn't speak to him until they were back in the car and headed down to Hemlock Bay.

"We're going to see Tennyson?"

"Nope, we've got other fish to fry."

WASHINGTON, D.C.
THE HOOVER BUILDING
FIFTH FLOOR, THE CRIMINAL
APPREHENSION UNIT

It was one o'clock in the afternoon. Empty sandwich wrappers were strewn on the conference table, leaving the vague smell of tuna fish with an overlay of roast beef, and at least a dozen soda cans stood empty. They'd just finished their daily update meeting. Savich's second in charge, Ollie Hamish, said to the assembled agents around the CAU conference table, "I'm going to be going to Kitty Hawk, North Carolina, in the morning. Our research says that he not only took the real Wilbur's name, he's spent a lot of time in Wright's hometown. Chances are, though, that he's not going to Dayton, since everyone's looking for him there, but to Kitty Hawk. I've gotten all the data over to Behavioral Sciences, to Jane Bitt. We'll see what she's got to add, but that's it, so far.

"I'm going to our office down there, fill them all in, and get things set up for when he turns up."

Savich nodded. "Sounds good, Ollie. No more supposed sightings of the guru in Texas?"

"Oh, yeah," Ollie said, "but we're letting the agents there deal with them. Our people here believe guru Wilbur is already heading across country, due east to North Carolina. Our offices across the South are all alerted. Maybe we can get him before he hits Kitty Hawk. It might be that Kitty Hawk will be his last stand. We don't want him to bring real havoc when he gets there. We'll see if Jane Bitt agrees."

Sherlock said, "Have we got photos?"

"The only photo we've got is old and fuzzy, unfortunately. We're looking at getting more."

Special Agent Dane Carver, newly assigned to the unit, said, "Why don't you give me the photo, Ollie, and let me work on it. Maybe we can clean it up in the lab."

"You got it."

Savich looked around the conference table. "Everyone on track now?"

There were grunts, nods, and groans.

Millie, the CAU secretary, said, "What about Tammy, Dillon? Any sightings? Any word at all yet?"

"Not a thing as yet. It's only been a day since I spoke to Marilyn Warluski at Quantico. Our people are staying with Tony, Marilyn's boyfriend, in Bar Harbor. His phone's covered. If Tammy calls, we'll hear it all. He's cooperating." Savich paused a moment, then shrugged. "It's frustrating. She's not in good shape, yet no one's seen her. Chances are very good that she did indeed murder a pharmacist in Souterville, New Jersey. The other pharmacist checked and said someone had rifled through the supplies. Vicodin, a medication to control moderate pain, and Keflex, an oral antibiotic, a good three or four days' supply, were missing. Evidently she killed the guy because he refused to give her anything.

"As you know, we alerted police on all islands to Tammy's possible presence. Now they also know to keep a close eye on doctors and pharmacies, and why."

Ollie said, sitting forward, his hands clasped, "Look, Savich, she threatened you. I read you the note. She means it. We've all been talking about it, and we think you should have some protection. We think Jimmy Maitland should assign you some guards."

Savich thought about it a minute, then looked down the table to Sherlock. He realized that she was thinking about Tammy finding out where they lived and coming to the house. She was thinking about Sean. He said to Ollie, "I think that's a great idea. I'll speak to Mr. Maitland this afternoon. Thanks, Ollie, I really hadn't thought it through."

He called a halt, scheduled a meeting with his boss, Jimmy Maitland, within the hour, and kissed Sherlock behind a door. Then he went to his office and punched in Simon's cell phone.

Simon answered on the third ring. "Yo."

"Savich here. Is Lily all right? What's going on?"

"Yes, she's fine." Simon then told him about their meeting with Abe Turkle, omitting Lily's challenge to beat the crap out of Abe. Then he told him about their much shorter meeting in Hemlock Bay with Daddy Frasier. "That old guy's really something, Savich. The guy hates Lily, you can see it in his eyes, colder than a snake's, and in his body language. I think he would have threatened her if I hadn't been there."

Savich wanted details, and so Simon told him exactly what had happened.

They'd gone to Elcott Frasier's office because they wanted to get in the old man's face, scare the bejesus out of him, let him know that everyone was on to him. Since he was the president and big cheese of the Hemlock National Bank, he had the shiny corner office on the second floor, all windows, a panoramic view of both the ocean and the town. Simon had wondered if Frasier would see them. His administrative assistant, Ms. Loralee Carmichael, at least twenty-one years old, and so beautiful it made your teeth ache to look at her, left them to kick up their heels for only twelve minutes, acceptable, Simon decided, since they'd caught the old man off guard and he'd probably want to get himself and his stories together. But Simon was worried about Lily. He'd have given anything to put her on a plane back to Washington, D.C., where she'd be safe. She looked nearly flattened, her face pale and set. If there'd been a bed nearby, he'd have tied her down in it. She moved slowly, but she had that lockjaw determined look, and so he kept his mouth shut.

Elcott Frasier welcomed them into his office, patted

Lily's shoulder, his hand a bit on the heavy side, and said, "Lily, dear. May I say that you don't look well."

"Mr. Frasier." She immediately moved away from him. "Since you've already said it, I don't suppose there's anything I can do about it." She gave him a smile as cold as his own. "This is Mr. Russo. He's a dealer of art. He's the one who verified that four of my Sarah Elliott paintings are forgeries."

Elcott Frasier nodded to Simon and motioned to them to be seated. "Well, this comes as quite a surprise. You say you're an art dealer, Mr. Russo. I don't know many art dealers who can spot forgeries. Are you quite sure about this?"

"I'm not exactly an art dealer, Mr. Frasier, as in running a gallery. I'm more a dealer/broker. I bring buyers and sellers together. Occasionally I track down forgeries and return them to their rightful owners. Since I own a Sarah Elliott and know her work intimately, I was able to spot the fakes among the eight paintings that Lily owns, particularly since I knew which four had been forged."

Simon paused a moment, wondering how much to tell Frasier and if it would frighten the man. He'd known, of course, about the forgeries, didn't even try to act shocked. Why not push it all the way, since he had a pretty good idea of how it had gone down? It would have to make him act. He hadn't told Lily this and hoped she wouldn't act surprised. He smiled toward her, then added, "I originally thought that you initiated the whole deal. But then I got to thinking that you're really a very small man, with no contacts at all. There's a collector, a Swede named Olaf Jorgenson, who isn't a small man. He's very powerful, actually. When he wants something, he goes after it, no obstacle too great. I believe that it was Jorgenson who instigated the whole thing. It went this way: Olaf wanted the Sarah Elliott paintings when they were in the Art Institute of Chicago, but he couldn't pull it off and had to wait. He knew exactly when Lily Savich left Chicago to move to Hemlock Bay, California. He put out feelers and found you very quickly, and your son, Tennyson, who was the right age. Then you all cut a deal. Actually, I heard Olaf had only three of the paintings. I don't know where the fourth one is as of yet. Hopefully, he has it as well. It makes everything cleaner, easier." Simon snapped his fingers right in Frasier's face. "We'll get them back fast as that. So, Mr. Frasier, did I get it all right?"

Elcott Frasier didn't bat an eye. He looked faintly bored. Lily, though, who knew him well, saw the slight tic in his left eye, there only when he was stressed out or angry. He could be either or both at this moment in time. She was surprised initially at what Simon had said but realized that it had probably happened just as Simon had said. She said, "Jorgenson is indeed powerful, Elcott. He isn't a small man at all, not like you."

Simon thought her father-in-law would belt her. He was ready for it, but Frasier managed to hold himself in. He said, dismissively and as smoothly as a politician accepting a bribe for a pardon, "That's quite a scenario, Mr. Russo. I'm sorry to hear four of the paintings were forged. No matter what you say, it must have happened while they were at the Art Institute of Chicago. All this elaborate plot by this fellow Olaf Jorgenson sounds like a bad movie. However, none of this has anything to do with me or my family. I really don't know why you came here to accuse me of it."

He turned to Lily and there was a good deal of anger in those eyes of his. "As for you, Lily, you left my son. I fear for his health. He is not doing well. All he talks about is you. He says that your brother and sister-in-law slandered him, and none of it's true. He wants to see you, although if I were him, and I've told him this countless times, I'd just as soon see the back of you for good. You weren't a good wife to him. You gave him nothing, and then you just up and left him. His mother is also very concerned. The mere idea that he would marry you to get ahold of some paintings, it's beyond absurd."

"I don't think it's absurd at all, Elcott. It could have happened the way Mr. Russo said. Or maybe it was Mr. Monk who found Mr. Jorgenson. Either way, four of my paintings are fakes and you are the one responsible.

"Now, if Tennyson isn't doing well, I recommend that he pay a visit to Dr. Rossetti, the psychiatrist he very badly wanted me to see when I was still in the hospital. One wonders what he had to do with all this." Lily paused a moment, shrugged, then continued. "But of course you would know about that. How much did you pay Morrie Jones to kill me?"

"I didn't pay him a—" She'd snagged him, caught him completely off guard. He'd burst right out with it, then cut off like a spigot, but too late. Simon was impressed.

The tic was very pronounced now, and added to it was a face turning red with outrage.

"You're quite a bitch, you know that, Lily? I can see why you brought your bodyguard with you. This painting business, I don't know what you've done, but you can't lay it on me. I'm not to blame for anything."

Simon wanted, quite simply, to stand, reach over Mr. Frasier's desk, and yank the man up by his expensive shirt collar and smash him in the jaw. It surprised him, the intense wish to do this man physical damage. But when he spoke, he was calm, utterly measured. "Trust me, Mr. Frasier, Lily isn't a bitch. As for your precious son, what he is isn't in much doubt. Would you like to tell us why Abe Turkle is staying at your cottage?" Simon sat slightly forward in his chair, the soul of polite interest.

"I don't know who that is or why he's there. The real estate agent handles rentals."

"Naturally Abe knows you, Mr. Frasier, knows everything, since he's forged the paintings for you. I do know that he's expensive. Or perhaps Olaf is handling his payments as part of the deal?"

Mr. Frasier got to his feet. The pulse was pounding in his heavy neck. He was nearly beyond control, his hands shaking. Almost there, Simon thought. Elcott Frasier pointed to the door and yelled, "I don't know any damned Olaf! Now, get out, both of you. Lily, I don't wish to see you again. It's a pity that the mugger didn't teach you a lesson."

Simon said, "We'll return for a very nice visit, along with the FBI, when we have our proof. Not much longer. Consider this a reality check. You might want to consider cutting a deal right now, with us. If you don't, just think of all those big, mean prisoners in the federal lockups; they like vulnerable old guys like you."

"Get out or I'll call the sheriff!"

Lily laughed, couldn't help it. "Sheriff Bozo?"

Elcott Frasier yelled, "His name is Scanlan, not Bozo!" Then he nearly ran to the door, jerked it open, and left them staring after him. Simon said to Lily as he helped her to her feet, "It's been quite a morning, first Abe and now your soon-to-be-ex-father-in-law, both of them leaving us in their lairs and stalking off. But everyone is shook up now, Lily. We've stirred the pot as much as we can. Now we wait to see who does what. Just maybe old man Frasier will decide to cut a deal. Now, you ready for a light lunch, maybe Mexican?"

"There isn't a Mexican restaurant in Hemlock Bay. We'll have to go to Ferndale."

Loralee Carmichael looked them over very carefully as they left the reception area. Simon wiggled his fingers in good-bye to her. There was no sign of Elcott Frasier.

He said carefully, as he walked slowly beside her to the elevator, "I want you to consider leaving the rest of this to me. Can I talk you into going back to Washington?"

"No, don't even try, Simon."

"I had to try. When bad men are afraid, Lily, they do things that aren't necessarily smart, but are, many times, deadly."

"Yes. We will be very careful."

He sighed and gave it up. "Over tacos we can discuss our next foray."

"Do you really think that Olaf Jorgenson set this whole thing up?"

"When you think about it, he's the one with all the contacts and the expertise, unless our Mr. Monk knows more about the illegal side of the business than we're aware of yet. I'm sure that Frasier will be speaking to Mr. Monk if he hasn't already. I can't wait to hear what this guy with his bedroom eyes has to say."

Simon paused a moment, switched his cell phone to his other ear, then said, "That's all of it, Savich, every gnarly detail."

He waited for Savich to ask him questions, but Savich didn't say anything. Simon could practically hear him sorting through possible scenarios.

Simon said, "Lily did really good, Savich. She's tired, but she's hanging in. I've tried to talk her into going back to Washington, but she won't hear of it. I swear I'll keep her safe."

"I know you will," Savich said finally. "Just to let you know, Clark Hoyt, the SAC in the Eureka FBI office, is going to provide you backup. I figured you guys would stir everything up and that could be very dangerous. I don't want you to be on your own. If you happen to see a couple of guys following you, they're there to keep you safe. If you have any concerns, just give Clark Hoyt a call. Now, you make Lily rest. How many tacos did she get down?"

"Three ground beef tacos, a basketful of chips, and an entire bowl of hot salsa. We're going to hole up now, then see Mr. Monk in the morning. By then, they'll all have spoken together, examined their options, made plans. I can't wait to see what they'll do. Give my love to Sherlock, and let Sean teethe on your thumb. Any word on Tammy Tuttle?"

"No."

"I'll call you after we've seen Mr. Monk tomorrow."

"Clark told me they've got a line on Morrie Jones. It shouldn't be long before he's in the local jail."

"Thank God for that. I'll call the cops in Eureka and find out." He paused, then added, "I'm not planning on letting Lily out of my sight."

17

Lily was deeply asleep, dreaming, and in that dream, she was terrified. There was something wrong, but she didn't know what. Then she saw her daughter, and she knew Beth was crying, sobbing, but Lily didn't know why. Suddenly, Beth was far away, her sobs still loud, but Lily couldn't get to her. She called and called, and then Beth simply wasn't there and Lily was alone, only she wasn't really. She knew there was something wrong, but she didn't know what.

Lily jerked up in bed, drenched with sweat, and groaned with the sharp ache the abrupt movement brought to her belly. She grabbed her stomach and tried to breathe in deeply.

When she did, she smelled smoke. Yes, it was smoke and it was in her room. That was what was wrong, what had brought her out of the nightmare. The smell of smoke, acrid, stronger now than just a moment before. Then she saw it billowing up around the curtains in the window, black and thick, the curtains just catching fire.

Dear God, the bed-and-breakfast was on fire. She hauled herself out of the high tester bed with its drapey gauze hangings and hit the floor running.

Her door was locked. Where was the key? Not in the door, not on the dresser. She ran to the bathroom, wet a towel, and pressed it against her face.

She ran to the phone, dialed 911. The phone was dead. Someone had set the fire and cut the phone lines. Or had the fire knocked out the lines? Didn't matter, she had to get out. Flames now, in the bedroom, licking up around the edges of the rug beneath that window with its light and gauzy draperies. She raced, bowed over, to the wall and began banging on it. "Simon! Simon!"

She heard him then, shouting back to her. "Lily, get the hell out of there, now!"

"My door's locked. I can't get it open!"

"I'm coming! Stay low to the floor."

But Lily couldn't just lie down and wait to be rescued. She was too scared. She ran back to the door and pulled and tugged the door knob. She picked up a chair and smashed it hard into the door. The chair nearly bounced off it. It didn't matter, anything to loosen it from its frame. The door did shudder a bit. She realized that the damned door wasn't hollow. It was old-fashioned and solid wood. She heard Simon jerk his door open, heard him knocking on doors, yelling. Thank God he hadn't been locked in like she was.

Then he was at her door, and she quickly moved back. She heard him kick it, saw it shudder. Then he kicked it hard again, and the door slammed inward. "You okay?"

"Yes. We've got to warn everyone." She began coughing, doubled over, and he didn't hesitate. He picked her up in his arms and carried her down the wide mahogany staircase.

Mrs. Blade was in the lobby, and she was helping out a very old lady who was sobbing quietly.

"It's Mrs. Nast. She's a permanent resident. I tried to call nine-one-one but the line's dead, of all things. There are people on the third floor, Mr. Russo. Please get them."

"I've already called nine-one-one on my cell phone. They're on their way." Simon set Lily down and ran back up the stairs. He heard her hacking cough as he ran.

He didn't get to the top of the stairs alone. Beside him at the last minute were firemen, all garbed up and yelling for him to get back downstairs and out of the building.

He nodded, then saw a young woman struggling with two children, coughing, trying to pull them down the corridor. The two firemen had their hands full with other guests. Simon simply grabbed all three of them up in his arms and carried them downstairs. They were all coughing by the time they got out the front door, the kids crying and the mother holding herself together, comforting them, thanking him again and again until he just put his hand over her mouth. "It's okay. Take care of your kids."

They saved a lot of The Mermaid's Tail, thank God, and all of the ten people staying there. No serious injuries, just some smoke inhalation.

Colin Smith, the agent sent over by Clark Hoyt to maintain an overnight watch on the bed-and-breakfast, told them he'd seen two men sneaking around, followed and lost them, turned back to see the smoke billowing up, and immediately called the fire department. That was why most of The Mermaid's Tail was still standing.

Agent Smith left them, after making certain they were okay, to repeat his story to the fire chief and the arson investigator, who'd just arrived.

Simon was holding Lily close to him. She was barefoot, wearing a long white flannel nightgown that came to her ankles, and her hair was straggling around her shoulders. He'd managed to scramble into jeans and a sweater and sneakers before he'd left his bedroom. He blew out, but didn't see his breath. It was cold, probably just below fifty degrees, and the firemen were distributing coats and blankets to all the victims. Neighbors were coming out with more blankets and coffee, even some rolls to eat.

Simon said, "You okay, Lily?"

She only nodded. "We're alive. That's all that matters. The bastards. I can't believe they set the entire place on fire. So many people could have been hurt, even killed."

"Your brother realized before I did that they'd probably try something. You met Agent Colin Smith. Your brother got the SAC here in Eureka to send him to watch over us."

She sighed and just stayed where she was. She was exhausted, doubted that any part of her would move, even if she begged. "Yeah, I realized he was a guard for us. I sure wish he'd caught them before they set the fire."

"He does, too. He's really beating himself up. He was calling in his boss, Clark Hoyt, last time I saw him. Hoyt will probably be here soon. I'll bet you he's already called Savich."

"At four o'clock in the morning?"

"Good point."

"It's really cold, Simon."

He was sitting on a lawn chair that a neighbor had brought over. He pulled her onto his lap, wrapping the blankets around both of them. "Better?"

She just nodded against his shoulder and whispered, "This really sucks."

He laughed.

"You know, Simon, even Remus wouldn't go so far as to do this sort of thing. Someone so desperate, so malevolent, they don't care how many people they kill? That's really scary."

"Yes," he said slowly, "it is. I didn't expect anything like this."

"You got mugged in New York so soon after you left

Washington. These people work really fast. I'm beginning to think it's Olaf Jorgenson behind all this, not the Frasiers, just like you said. How would the Frasiers have even known about you or where you were?"

"I agree. But you know, the guy didn't try to kill me, at least I don't think he did."

"Probably a warning."

"I guess. This wasn't a warning. This was for real. We're in pretty deep now, Lily. I'll bet you that Clark Hoyt isn't going to let us out of his sight for as long as we're in his neck of the woods."

"At this point I'm glad. No, Simon, don't say it. I'm not about to leave you alone now." She fell silent, and for a little while he thought she'd finally just given out. Then she said, "Simon, did I ever tell you that Jeff MacNelly was my biggest influence for Remus?"

Who was Jeff MacNelly? He shook his head slowly, fascinated.

"Yes, he was. I admired him tremendously." When she realized he didn't have a clue, she added, "Jeff MacNelly was a very famous and talented cartoonist. He won three Pulitzer Prizes skewering politicos. But he never once said that they were evil. He died in June of 2000. I really miss him. It upsets me that I never told him how much he meant to me, and to Remus."

"I'm sorry to hear that, Lily." He realized then that she was teetering on the edge of shock, so he pulled another blanket around her. It was too much even for her. Her life had flown out of control when she'd married Tennyson Frasier. He couldn't imagine what she'd gone through when her daughter had been killed and she'd managed to survive months of depression. And then all this.

Lily said, "Jeff MacNelly said that 'when it comes to humor, there's no substitute for reality and politicians.' I don't like this reality part, Simon, I really don't."

"I don't either."

WASHINGTON, D.C.
HOOVER BUILDING

Savich slowly hung up the phone, stared out his window a moment, then lowered his face to his hands.

He heard Sherlock say, "What is it, Dillon? What's happened?" Her competent hands were massaging his shoulders, her breath was warm on his temple.

He slowly raised his head to look up at her. "I should have killed her, Sherlock, should have shot her cleanly in the head, just like I did Tommy Tuttle. This is all my fault—that boy's death in Chevy Chase, and now this."

"She's killed again?"

He nodded, and she hated the despair in his eyes, the pain that radiated from him. "In Road Town, Tortola, in the British Virgin Islands."

"Tell me."

"That was Jimmy Maitland. He said the police commissioner received all our reports, alerted his local officers, waited, and then a local pharmacist was murdered, his throat cut. The place was trashed, impossible to tell what drugs were taken, but we know what was stolen—pain meds and antibiotics. They don't have any leads, but they're combing the island for a one-armed woman who's not in good shape. No sign of her yet. Not even a whiff. Tortola isn't like Saint Thomas. It's far more primitive, less populated, more places to hide, and the bottom line is there's just no way to get to and from the island except by boat."

"I'm very sorry it happened. You know she's gotten ahold of a boat. By now she's probably long gone from Tortola, to another island."

"It's hard to believe that no one's reported a boat stolen."

"It's late," Sherlock said. "E-mail all the other islands, then let it go for a while. Let's go home, play with Sean, then head over to the gym. You need a really hard workout, Dillon."

He rose slowly. "Okay, first I've got to talk to all the local cops down there, make sure they know what's happened on Tortola, tell them again how dangerous she is." He kissed her, hugged her tightly, and said against her temple, "Go home and start playing with Sean. I'll be there in a while. Have him gum some graham crackers for me."

QUANTICO, VIRGINIA
FBI ACADEMY

Special Agent Virginia Cosgrove cocked her head to one side and said, "Marilyn, it's for you. A woman, says she's with Dillon Savich's unit at headquarters. I'll be listening on the other line, okay?"

Marilyn Warluski, who was folding the last of her new clothes into the suitcase provided by the FBI, nodded, a puzzled look on her face. She was staying in the Jefferson dorm with two women agents, just starting to get used to things. What did Mr. Savich want from her now? She took the phone from Agent Cosgrove and said, "Hello?"

"Hi, sweet chops. It's Timmy. You hot for me, baby?"

Marilyn closed her eyes tight against the shock, against the disbelief. "Tammy," she whispered. "Is it really you?"

"No, it's Timmy. Listen up, sweetie, I need to see you. I want you to fly down here, to Antigua, tomorrow; that's when I'll be there. I'll be at the Reed Airport, waiting for you. Don't disappoint me, baby, okay?"

Marilyn looked frantically over at Virginia.

Virginia quickly wrote on a pad of paper, then handed it to Marilyn. "Okay, I can do it, but it'll be late."

"They treating you all right at that cop academy? Do you want me to come up with the Ghouls and level the place?"

"No, no, Tammy, don't do that. I'll fly down late tomorrow. Are you all right?"

"Sure. Had to get me some more medicine on Tortola.

Lousy place, dry and boring, no action at all. Can't wait to get out of here. See you tomorrow evening, baby. Bye."

Marilyn slowly placed the phone in its cradle. She looked blankly at Virginia Cosgrove. "How did she know where I was? I need to call Dillon Savich. Damn, it's really late."

Assistant Director Jimmy Maitland called Dillon Savich to mobilize the necessary agents. He got it done in two hours and set himself up to coordinate the group leaving for Antigua.

Maitland called in the SWAT Team at the Washington, D.C., field office because they were bringing this all down very possibly in an airport, and there could always be trouble. He told Savich, "Yeah, I threw them some meat and they agreed to come out and play. We got one team, six really good guys."

Vincent Arbus, point man for the team, built like a bull, bald as a Q-tip, and many times too smart for his own good, looked at Savich, then at Sherlock, who was standing at his side, and said in his rough, low voice, "Call me Vinny, guys. I have a feeling that we're going to be getting tight before this is all over.

"Now, how the hell did this crazy one-armed woman know that Marilyn Warluski was holed up in Jefferson dorm at Quantico? How the hell did she get her number?"

"Well," Savich said slowly, not looking at Sherlock, "I sort of let it be known. Actually, I set the whole thing up."

18

Mr. Monk was gone, his office left looking as if he would be returning the next day. There were no notes, no messages, no telltale appointments listed in his date book, which sat in the middle of his desk. There was no clue at all as to where he'd gone.

Nor was he at his big bay-windowed apartment on Oak Street. He hadn't cleaned out his stuff, had just, apparently, taken off without a word to anyone.

Hoyt said to Simon when he opened his hotel room door, "He's gone. I just stood in the middle of that empty living room with its fine paintings by Jason Argot on the white walls, with its own specialized lighting, and I tell you, Russo, I wanted to kick myself. I knew we should have covered his place, but I didn't. I'm an idiot. Kick me. There's got to be a clue somewhere in there about where his bolt-hole is. Or maybe not, but I haven't found a bloody thing. Really, Russo, just kick my ribs in."

"Nah," Simon said as he zipped the fly on his new jeans and threaded his new belt. He waved Hoyt into his deluxe room with its king-size bed that took up nearly three-quarters of the space. Lily was right through the adjoining door. They were staying at the Warm Creek Lodge, both with an ocean view from one window and an Old Town view from the other. "I appreciate your checking him out for us first thing, since Lily and I didn't have any clothes at all. Though I wouldn't have minded paying the jerk a visit myself. Thank God I left my wallet in my jeans pocket last night or we'd be in really deep caca. Actually, if the credit card companies hadn't sent me replacement credit cards after my wallet was stolen in New York, we'd still be in deep caca. We're all outfitted now, real spiffy. Now, what about Monk's car? Any sign of it?"

"We've got an APB out on it—a Jeep Grand Cherokee, 'ninety-eight, dark green. And we're covering the Arcata airport. We've sent out alerts as far down as SFO, though I don't think he could have gotten that far."

"Problem is, we don't know when he bolted. Don't you think it would be better if you issued a tri-state airport alert?"

"Yeah, good idea. I'm thinking he probably got scared. I doubt he has a fake ID or a passport. If he tries to take a flight, we'll nail him."

Simon nodded. "Would you like a cup of coffee? Room service just sent some up with croissants."

Clark Hoyt looked like he would cry. He didn't say another word until he'd downed two cups of coffee and eaten a croissant, smeared with a real butter pat and sugarless apricot jam.

When Lily came in a few minutes later, Simon smiled at the sight. She looked even better than he'd imagined. She was wearing black stretch jeans, a black turtleneck sweater, and black boots. She looked like a fairy princess who was also a cat burglar on her nights off. Clark Hoyt, when he rose to greet her, said, "Quite a change from how you looked early this morning. I like all the black."

Lily thanked him, poured herself a cup of coffee, and

watched him eat a second croissant. He filled Lily in on what they hadn't found so far.

Hoyt said, "I called Savich back at Disneyland East and filled him in. He made me swear on the head of my schnauzer, Gilda, that you guys didn't have a single singed hair on your heads. It was arson, all right, but no idea yet who the perps were or who hired them."

"Disneyland East?" Lily asked, an eyebrow up.

"Yep, just another loving name for FBI Headquarters. Hey, thanks for breakfast. You guys still smell like smoke. It's really tough to get it all out. I should know, I was over-enthusiastic with my barbeque last summer and lost my eyebrows, although my face was so black you couldn't tell. Just lay low; keep out of sight until I get some news for you, okay?"

It was early afternoon when Hoyt came to get them from the lodge. Mr. Monk hadn't tried to fly out of harm's way. Actually, he hadn't flown anywhere. He was quite dead, head pressed against the steering wheel, three bullets through his back. The Jeep was in a sparse stand of redwood trees, and some hikers, poking around, had found him.

Lieutenant Larry Dobbs of the Eureka Police Department knew that the situation was dicey, that it involved a whole lot more than this one body, and even that the FBI was involved. He agreed to let Clark Hoyt bring out the two civilians, after the crime scene had been gone over.

Simon and Lily stood looking at the Jeep. "They didn't really try to hide him," she said. "On the other hand, it could have been a long time before someone accidentally came upon him. God bless hikers."

"The medical examiner estimates he's been dead about seven hours, give or take," said Clark Hoyt. "He'll know a lot more after the autopsy. Our lab guys will crawl all over that Jeep to see what's what. Ah, here comes Lieutenant Dobbs. You've met, haven't you?"

"We've spoken on the phone," Simon said and shook Dobbs's hand. Simon saw quickly enough that the lieutenant was impressed with how Clark Hoyt deferred to him.

"Do you think he was with someone?" Lily asked both men. "And that someone killed him and then moved his body to the driver's side?"

Lieutenant Dobbs said, "No. From the trajectory of the bullets, there was someone, the shooter, riding in the backseat, behind Monk. Maybe someone else riding in the passenger seat. I don't know. Maybe Monk knew they were taking him out to kill him. But if so, why did he calmly pull over? Again, I don't know. But the fact is he did pull off the road into the redwoods, and the guy in the backseat shot him."

Simon and Lily were given permission to walk over the area. They looked everywhere, but there wasn't anything to see. The hikers had made a mess of things in their initial panic. There were five cop cars and two FBI cars adding to the chaos. There weren't any tire tracks except the Jeep's, which meant that the other car must have stayed parked on the paved road.

Lieutenant Dobbs eyed Simon and Lily and said, "Agent Hoyt tells me you guys are involved in this up to your eyeballs. Let me tell you, you two have brought me more woes than I've had for the last ten years, beginning with that jerk who attacked you on the public bus, Mrs. Frasier. Oh, yeah, Officer Tucker just found Morrie Jones a couple of hours ago, holed up in a fleabag hotel down on Conduit Street."

"Keep him safe, Lieutenant," Lily said. "He was part of this, too, as was Mr. Monk. And look what happened to him."

"You got it." Lieutenant Dobbs said then, "You know, it hasn't been all bad. I've met Hoyt here, a real federal agent and all, and I haven't had to watch *Wheel of Fortune* with my wife. I haven't had a single bored minute since I got that first call from you guys. Only bad thing is this body over there. A body's never good." He sighed and waved to one of the other officers. He said over his shoulder, "Clark, try to keep these two out of more mischief, all right? Oh, yes, I'm going to be interviewing all the Frasiers, including your husband, Mr. Tennyson Frasier. Maybe it'll scare them, make them do something else stupid. I understand you've already tried, got them all riled up. Now let's see how they handle the law." He waved toward the body bag containing Mr. Monk. "This wasn't a bright thing to do."

"Don't forget Charlotte Frasier, Lieutenant," Lily said, "and don't be fooled by that syrupy accent. She's terrifying."

Hoyt said, "Then I'm going to wait until the lieutenant is through with them, wait until they're nice and comfortable at their homes in Hemlock Bay again, and then I'm going to pay them a little visit and grill them but good. Savich has sent me lots of stuff. I've been speaking to some of our representatives in Sacramento, checking real close into El-cott Frasier's financial situation. Lots of conflicting info so far, but there's been a lot of flow in and out of his accounts there. Something will shake loose; it usually does. Oh, yeah, I heard that Elcott Frasier has hired Mr. Bradley Ab-bott, one of the very best criminal lawyers on the West Coast, to represent him and his family." Hoyt rubbed his hands together. "This is going to be really interesting."

As they drove back to Eureka, Simon was brooding. Lily recognized the signs. He looked single-minded as he drove, looking neither right nor left, saying nothing to Lily, who was hungry and wanted to go to the bathroom.

"Stop it, Simon."

That jerked him around to stare at her. "Stop what?"

"You've got a look that says you're far away, like maybe the Delta Quadrant."

"Yeah, I was just thinking. About Abe Turkle. He's a

loose end, Lily, just like Mr. Monk. So is Morrie Jones, but he's in jail, and hopefully safe there. The lieutenant is going to put a guard on him."

Lily said, "I forgot to tell you, when you and Hoyt were talking back there, Lieutenant Dobbs told me that Morrie claims he doesn't know a thing, that a couple of thugs hurt him when he was minding his own business in a bar. He claimed no broad could ever hurt him. Oh yes, Morrie's got a big-time lawyer. I wonder how much money Morrie's being paid to keep his mouth shut."

Simon said, "Can Lieutenant Dobbs find out who hired the lawyer?"

"I asked him if he knew. He said he'd sniff around. Now, Simon, you're brooding because you think Abe Turkle might be in danger." In that instant, Lily forgot she was hungry, forgot she needed to go to the bathroom. "You've just made my stomach drop to my knees. Let's go see Abe, Simon."

He grinned over at her, braked, and did a wide U-turn.

"Hey," she said, "not bad driving. Won't this piece of garbage go any faster?"

Simon laughed. "You're the best, Lily, do you know that? Hey, I see someone doing another U-turn behind us. Must be our protection."

"Good. Hope he can keep up with us."

Simon laughed.

"My dad, Buck Savich, used to tell me that if I decided to become a professional bookie, I'd be the best in the business. Except for one thing."

"What's that?"

"He'd say my eyes changed color whenever I lied, and if anyone noticed that, my days as a bookie would be over."

"Your eyes are blue right now. What color do they go to when you lie?"

"I don't know. I've never looked at myself in the mirror and lied to it."

"I'll keep that in mind, though, and let you know."

Simon turned his attention back to the road. He saw big Abe Turkle in his mind, a paintbrush between his teeth, ready to beat the crap out of him. Then Abe's smile when he looked at Lily. The man was a crook, but he was an excellent artist. Simon didn't want him to get killed.

He sped up to sixty because his gut was crawling. Bad things, bad things. But he said in a smooth, amused voice, "You probably remember that I met your dad when Dillon and I were in our senior year at MIT. He was something else."

"Yes," she said. "He was the best. I miss him very much. All us kids do. As for Mom, she was a mess for a long time. She met this guy, a congressman from Missouri, just last year, still claims they're only friends, but she's a lot happier, smiles a lot more, just plain gets out and does more things. She adores Sean, too. He's the only grandkid close by."

"What did your mom think of all the legends about Buck Savich? There were so many colorful ones floating about long before he died."

"She'd just shake her head, grin like a bandit, and say she didn't think the tales were exaggerations at all. Then, I swear it to you, she'd blush. I think she was talking about intimate things, and it always freaked us kids out. You just can't think of your parents in that way, you know what I mean?"

"Yeah, I do. I guess, on the other side of the coin, our parents look at us and see little kids who will be virgins for the rest of their lives."

Lily laughed. "What about your parents? Where do they live?"

"My folks have been divorced for a very long time. My dad's a lawyer, remarried to a woman half his age. They live in Boston. No little half-brothers or half-sisters. My mom didn't remarry, lives in Los Angeles, runs her own makeover consulting firm. If they ever had any liking for each other, it was over before I could remember it. My sisters, both older than I am, told me they'd never seen anything resembling affection either." He paused just a moment, slowed a bit for a particularly gnarly turn, then sped up again. "You know, Lily, I have a hard time seeing you as a bookie. Did you make some money for college?"

She gave him a shark's grin, all white teeth, ready to bite. "You bet. Thing was, though, Mom decided it was better that Dad not know exactly what my earnings totaled from age sixteen to eighteen, especially since I hadn't paid any taxes."

"It boggles the mind." He looked at her then, saying nothing, just looking. "Do you know that you're looking more like a fairy princess again? I like you in all that black. How's your scar doing?"

"My innards are fine; the scar itches just a bit. It's no wonder you like all black since you bought all my clothes. You want me to look like Batgirl, Simon?"

"I always did like to watch her move." He grinned at her. "Truth is, I saw the black pants and knew it would have to be black all the way." He gave her a sideways look. "I don't mean to be indelicate, but did all the underwear fit?"

"Too well," she said, "and I don't like to think about it, so stop looking at me."

"Okay." For a couple of seconds, Simon kept his eyes on the road. Then he said, chuckling, "As I said, when I saw the black, I knew it was you. But you know, I think the biggest change was your getting all that ash and soot washed out of your hair and off your face."

Every stitch she was wearing was black, even the boot socks. She said, not intending to, "Why haven't you ever married?"

"I was married, a very long time ago."

"Tell me."

He gave her another sideways look, saw that she really wanted to know, and said, "Well, I was twenty-two years old, in overwhelming lust, as was Janice, and so we got married, divorced within six months, and both of us joined the army."

"That was a long time ago. Where is Janice now?"

"She stayed in the army. She's a two-star general, stationed in Washington, D.C. I heard she's gorgeous as a general. She's married to a four-star. Hey, maybe someday she'll be chief of staff."

"I wonder why Dillon didn't tell me."

"He would have been my best man in the normal course of things, but we eloped and he was off in Europe that summer, living on a shoestring, so I knew he didn't have the money to fly home, then back to Europe again." Simon shrugged. "It was just as well. Who was your first husband? Beth's father?"

"His name was Jack Crane. He was a stockbroker for Phlidick, Dammerleigh and Pierson. He was a big wheeler-dealer at the Chicago Stock Exchange."

"Why'd you split up?"

She tried to just shrug it off, give him a throwaway smile, but it wasn't possible. She drew a deep breath and said, "I don't want to talk about that."

"Okay, for now. Here we are. Keep your eyes open, Lily, I really have a bad feeling about this." He turned right onto the narrow asphalt road that led to the cottage, looked back, and saw their protection turning in behind them.

No motorcycle.

Simon did a quick scan, didn't see a thing. "I really don't like this."

"Maybe he just went into town to get some barbeque sauce to go with his snails."

Simon didn't think so, but he didn't argue as they walked up to the cottage. The door wasn't locked. He didn't say a word, just picked Lily up under her armpits and moved her behind him. He opened the door slowly. It was gloomy inside, all the blinds pulled down. The room was completely empty—no stacked paintings against the walls, no easel, no palette, not even a drop of paint anywhere or the smell of turpentine, just empty.

"Check the kitchen, Lily. I'm going to look in the bedroom." They met back in the empty living room five minutes later.

Agent Colin Smith stood in the open doorway. "No sign of Abe Turkle?"

Simon shook his head and said, "Nope. All that's left is a box of Puffed Wheat, a bit of milk, not soured, and a couple of apples, still edible, so he hasn't been gone long."

Lily said, "He's packed up and left. All his clothes, suitcase, everything gone, even his toothpaste."

"Do you think he went to London with that painting he was finishing?"

"I hope not. It was really very good, too good."

Colin Smith asked, "You were afraid he was dead, weren't you? Murdered. Like Mr. Monk."

Simon nodded. "I had a bad feeling there for a while. Let's tell Lieutenant Dobbs about this. Agent Smith, if you'll call Clark Hoyt, fill him in. You know, Abe had lots of stuff—at least thirty paintings leaning against the walls. All he had was a motorcycle. Maybe he rented a U-Haul to carry everything away."

"Or maybe one of the Frasiers loaned him a truck."

"Maybe. Now then, Agent Smith, Lily and I are off to pay a visit to Morrie Jones. I need to speak to Lieutenant Dobbs and the DA, get their okay. I've got an offer for Morrie he can't refuse."

Lily held up a hand. "No, I don't want to know. Maybe by now they know who's paying his lawyer." Simon closed the cottage door and waved to Agent Smith.

"Don't count on it," Simon said as he set the pillow gently over Lily's stomach and fastened the seat belt.

19

"It's so bright and hot and blue," Sherlock said,
scratching her arm. Then she sighed. "You know,
Sean would really like this place. We could strip him down
and play in that sand, build a castle with him, even a moat.
I can just see him rolling over on the castle, flattening it,
laughing all the while."

For the first time in as long as she could remember,
Sherlock realized Dillon wasn't listening. She could only
imagine what was going through his mind, all the ifs and
buts. It was his show, and naturally he was worried, impossible not to be. They were working through the American
Consular Agent with the Royal Police Force at Police
Headquarters located on, strangely enough, American
Road. But they were still in a foreign country, dealing with
locals who were both bewildered by the extreme reaction
of the United States federal cops—all fifty of them—to
one woman, who only had one arm and was supposedly
coming to their airport. But they were cooperating, really
serious now after Savich had shown the entire group pho-

tos of her victims, including the latest one on Tortola. That one really brought it home.

Tammy couldn't have gotten to Antigua before late morning, no way, even with a fast boat. Tortola was just too far away. The weather had been calm, no high winds or waves. She couldn't have gotten here ahead of them, except by plane, and they'd been checking air traffic from Tortola and nearby islands. And there was no indication at all that she knew how to fly. They'd had time to get everything set up, to get everyone in position.

Sherlock gave him a clear look. "We have time. Stop worrying. Marilyn will be here in about two hours. We'll go over everything with her, step by step."

"What if Tammy isn't alone? What if Tammy has been traveling around as Timmy this whole time? Remember, it was Timmy who called Marilyn at Quantico."

Sherlock had never before seen him so questioning of what he was doing.

When she spoke, Sherlock's voice was as calm as the incredible blue water not one hundred yards away, "One arm is one arm, despite anything else. No one on any of the islands has reported anyone jiggering about with just one arm. The odds are stacked way against her. You know all the local police in both the British Virgin Islands and the U.S. Virgin Islands are on full alert. The Antiguan authorities aren't used to mayhem like this, so you can bet they're very concerned, probably more hyper than we are, particularly after those crime-scene photos. Dillon, everyone is taking this very seriously."

"So you think I should just chill out?"

"No, that's impossible. But you're very smart, top drawer. Just stop trying to second-guess yourself. You've done everything to prepare. If we have to deal with something other than just Tammy, we will."

The local cops, of which there weren't many, had con-

verged on the airport. They were trying to look inconspicu-
ous and failing, but they were trying, a couple of them even
joking with tourists. All of them were used to dealing with
locals who occasionally smoked too much local product or
drank too much rum, or an occasional tourist who tried to
steal something from a duty-free store. Nothing like this.
This was beyond their experience.

Savich just couldn't help himself. He checked and
rechecked with Vinny Arbus on the status of the SWAT
team. If Tammy Tuttle managed to grab a civilian, they
were ready. Marksmen were set up, six of them, in strate-
gic spots around the airport as well as inside. Half the
marksmen were dressed like tourists, the other half, like
airport personnel. They blended right in.

Would Tammy come in by plane? Would she simply
walk in? No one knew. All hotels and rooming houses had
been checked, rechecked. Jimmy Maitland was seated in
the police commissioner's office with its overhead fan,
boiling alive in his nice fall suit.

There were nearly fifty FBI personnel involved in the
operation, now named Tripod. Special Agent Dane Carver
had picked the name because the perp had only one arm
and two legs, so Tuttle was the tripod.

A couple of hours later, Marilyn Warluski, scared to the
soles of her new Nike running shoes, pressed close to
Agent Virginia Cosgrove, her lifeline. Cosgrove was jit-
tery, too, but too new an agent to be as scared as she should
be. As she saw it, she was the most important agent present. It was to her that Tammy Tuttle would come. She was
an excellent shot. She would protect Marilyn Warluski.
She was ready.

"She's coming, Mr. Savich," Marilyn said, her voice dull
and flat when he checked in with her again at six o'clock
that evening. She was standing by the Information Desk in
the airport, the Caribbean Airlines counter just off to the
left.

"It will be all right, Marilyn," Virginia said, her voice more excited than soothing, and patted her hand for at least the thirtieth time. "Agent Savich won't let anything happen, you'll see. We'll nail Tammy."

"I told you it was Timmy who called me. When she's Timmy, she can do anything."

"I thought she could do anything when she was Tammy, too," Savich said.

"She can. He can. If they're both here, not just Timmy, then there'll be real trouble."

Savich felt a twist of fear in his guts. He said slowly, his voice deep and calm, "Marilyn, what do you mean if they're both here? You mean both Tammy and Timmy? I don't understand."

Marilyn shrugged. "I didn't think to tell you, but I saw it happen once, back a couple of years ago. We were in that dolled-up tourist town, Oak Bluffs. You know, on Martha's Vineyard. I saw Tammy comin' out of this really pretty pink Victorian house where we were all stayin' and she just suddenly turned several times, you know, real fast, like Lynda Carter did whenever she was goin' to change into Wonder Woman. Same thing. Tammy turned into Timmy, like they were blended together somehow, and it was the scariest thing I'd ever seen until Tammy walked into that motel room all covered in that little boy's blood."

Savich knew this was nuts. Tammy couldn't change from a woman into a man. That was impossible, but evidently Marilyn believed it. He said, carefully, "It seemed to you that Tammy and Timmy somehow coalesced into one person?"

"Yeah, that's it. She whirled around several times and then there was Timmy, all horny and smart-mouthed."

"When Tammy turned into Timmy, what did he look like?"

"Like Tammy but like a guy, you know?"

Virginia Cosgrove looked thoroughly confused. She

started to say something, but Savich shook his head at her. Savich wanted to ask Marilyn to describe Timmy. Marilyn was suddenly standing perfectly still. She seemed to sniff the air like an animal scenting danger. She whispered, "I can feel Timmy close, Mr. Savich. He's real close now. Oh, God, I'm scared. He's going to wring my neck like a chicken's for helping you."

"I don't understand any of this." Virginia Cosgrove whispered low, just like Marilyn had. "So Tammy is really a guy?"

"I guess we'll find out, Agent Cosgrove. Don't dwell on it. Your priority is Marilyn. Just protect Marilyn."

Marilyn leaned close and took Virginia's hand. "You won't let him take me, will you, Agent Cosgrove?"

"No, Marilyn, I won't even let him get close to you." She said to Savich, "You can count on me. I'll guard her with my life."

It was seven o'clock in the evening, just an hour later. Since it was fall, the sun had set much earlier, and it was dark now, the sky filling with stars and a half-moon. It was beautiful and warm. The cicadas and the coquis were playing a symphony if anyone was inclined to listen.

The airport looked fairly normal except it was probably a bit too crowded for this time of day, something Savich hoped Tammy Tuttle wouldn't realize. But he knew she would notice because the local cops looked jumpy, too ill at ease for her not to notice. Or for Timmy to notice. Or whichever one of them showed.

Savich drew a deep breath as he watched the crowd. He said, "Timmy is close, Sherlock, that's what Marilyn said. She said she could feel him. That was an hour ago. I think she's even more scared than I am. She also firmly believes—no doubt at all in her mind—that Tammy can change into a guy at will, into this Timmy."

Sherlock said, "If a Timmy shows up, then I'll check us both into Bellevue."

"You got that right."

There weren't that many tourists in the airport now, real tourists at least. The major flights from the States had arrived, passengers dispersed, and just a few island-to-island flights were going out in the evening. This was both good and bad. There was less cover, but also less chance that a civilian would be harmed.

When it happened, it was so quick that no one had a chance to stop it. A short, rangy man, pale as death itself, with close-cropped black hair, except for some curls on top of his head, seemed suddenly to simply appear behind Agent Virginia Cosgrove. He said against her ear, "Just move, sweetie, make any movement at all to alert all the Feds hanging around here and I'll slice your throat from ear to ear. What'll be fun is that you'll live long enough to see your blood gush out in a bright red fountain."

Virginia heard Marilyn whimper. How had he gotten behind her? Why hadn't someone alerted her? Why hadn't someone seen him? Yes, it sounded like a man, like this Timmy Tuttle Marilyn had talked about. What was going on here? She had to be calm, wait for her chance. She slowly nodded. "I won't make a move. I won't do anything."

"Good," the man said and sliced her throat. Blood gushed out. Virginia had only a brief moment to cry out, but even then it wasn't a cry, it was only a low, blurred gurgling sound.

He turned to Marilyn, smiled, and said, "Let's go, baby. I've missed my little darlin'. You ready, baby?"

Marilyn whispered, "Yes, Timmy, I'm ready."

He took her hand in his bloody one, and with his other hand, he raised the knife to her throat. At that moment, Savich, who'd been in low conversation with Vinny Arbus, saw the blood spurting out of Virginia Cosgrove's neck. He'd been looking at her just a moment before. How was it possible? Then he saw a guy dragging Marilyn with him, a

knife at her throat. A dozen other agents and at least a
dozen civilians saw Virginia fall, her blood splattering
everywhere, and saw a pale-as-death man dragging Marilyn Warluski.

All hell broke loose. It was pandemonium, people
screaming, running, frozen in terror, or dropping to the
floor and folding their arms over their heads. But what was
the most potent, what everyone would remember with
stark clarity, was the smell of blood. It filled the air, filled
their lungs.

It was a hostage situation, but it wasn't a bystander who
was the hostage. It was Marilyn Warluski.

Savich spotted the man, finally free of screaming civilians, and he'd recognize that face anywhere. It was
Tammy Tuttle's face—only it wasn't quite. No, not possible. But Savich would go to his grave swearing that it was
a man with the knife held to Marilyn's throat, and he had
two arms, that man, because Savich saw two hands with
his own eyes. It had to be someone else, not Tammy Tuttle dressed up like a man. Someone who looked enough
like Tammy to fool him. But how had that crazy-looking
man gotten so close to Virginia and Marilyn so quickly,
and no one had even noticed? Suddenly nothing made
sense.

Agents grabbed tourists who were still standing and
pushed them to the floor, clearing the way to get to the man
and his hostage.

A local police officer, a very young man with a mustache, closed with them first. He shouted at the man to stop
and fired a warning shot in the air.

The man calmly turned in the officer's direction, pulled a
SIG Sauer from his pocket so fast it was a blur, and shot him
in the forehead. Then he turned around and it seemed he
saw Savich, who was at least fifty feet from him. He yelled,
"Hey, it's me, Timmy Tuttle! Hell-ooooo, everyone!"

Savich tuned him out. He had to or he couldn't function.

He knew that the marksmen stationed inside the terminal had Tuttle in their sights. Soon now, very soon, it would be over.

He moved around the perimeter, slid behind the Caribbean Airlines counter with half a dozen agents behind him, and kept moving toward Timmy Tuttle.

Three shots rang out simultaneously. Loud, clear, sharp. It was the marksmen, and they wouldn't have fired without a clear shot at Timmy Tuttle.

Savich raised his head. He knew he couldn't be more than twenty feet from Timmy Tuttle. He couldn't see him. Could they have missed?

Then there were half a dozen more shots, screaming, and deep and ugly moans wrung out of people's throats from terror.

Savich felt something, something strong and sour, and he turned quickly. He saw Sherlock some ten feet away, just off to his left, with three other agents, rising from her kneeling position, her SIG Sauer aimed toward where Timmy Tuttle and Marilyn had been just moments before. She looked as confused as he felt. It took everything in him not to shout for her to stay back, please God, just stay back, he didn't want her hurt. And what would hurt her? A man who really wasn't a man, but an image in whole cloth spun from Tammy Tuttle's crazy brain?

Savich saw a flash of cloth, smelled the scent of blood, and he simply knew it was Timmy Tuttle. He ran as fast as he could toward a conference room, the only place Timmy could have taken Marilyn. He kicked open the door.

He stopped cold, his gun steady, ready to fire. There was a big rectangular table in the center and twelve chairs, an overhead projector, a fax, and two or three telephones.

There wasn't anyone in the room. It was empty. But even in here he smelled Virginia's blood; he could swear that he smelled her blood, rich, coppery, sickening. He swallowed convulsively as he took in every inch of the room.

So Timmy hadn't come in here. Another room then. Agents on his heels, he ran across the hall to see his wife, gun held in front her, pushing open a door with SECURITY stenciled on the glass.

He was across that hall and into the room in an instant. He saw Sherlock standing in the middle of the room, the three agents fanned out behind her, all of them searching the room. But Sherlock wasn't doing anything, just standing there staring silently at the single large window that gave onto the outside.

She turned slowly to see him in the open doorway, agents at his back, staring at her, shock and panic alive in his eyes. She cocked her head to one side in silent question, then simply closed her eyes and fell over onto the floor.

"Sherlock!"

"My God, is she shot?"

"What happened?"

The other three agents converged.

Savich knew he couldn't stop, but it was the hardest thing he'd ever done in his life. He yelled, "Make sure she's all right! Conners, check everyone out! Deevers, Conlin, Marks, Abrams, you're with me!"

He heard one of the agents shout after him, "She's breathing, can't see anything wrong with her. The guy wasn't in here, Savich. We don't know where he went."

The window, he thought, Sherlock had been staring at that window. He picked up a chair and smashed it into the huge glass window.

When they managed to climb out the window they'd cleared of glass, they knew, logically, that Timmy Tuttle and Marilyn Warluski couldn't have come this way since the glass hadn't been broken. But it didn't matter. Where else could Timmy Tuttle have gone? They covered every inch of ground, looked into all the buildings, even went onto the tarmac where one American 757 sat waiting, calling up to the pilot. But Tammy or Timmy Tuttle was gone, and Marilyn as well. As if they'd just vanished into thin air, with nothing left to prove they'd even been there except for Virginia Cosgrove's body, bloodless now, lying on her side, covered with several blankets, local technicians working over her. And the one local officer Timmy Tuttle had shot through the head.

He'd used his right hand when he'd shot that officer.

Savich had shot Tammy Tuttle through her right arm in that barn in Maryland, near the Plum River.

At the hospital, they'd amputated her right arm.

He wondered if they were all going mad.

No, no, there was an explanation.

Somehow a man had gotten into the airport, killed Virginia Cosgrove, and grabbed Marilyn. And no one had seen him until he had Marilyn by the neck and was dragging her away.

No one much wanted to talk. Everyone who had been in the airport appeared confused and looked, strangely, hungover.

Savich and his team went back to the security room. Sherlock was still unconscious, covered with blankets, a local physician sitting on the floor beside her.

No one had much to say. Jimmy Maitland was sitting in a chair near Sherlock.

Savich picked up his wife, carried her to a chair, and sat down with her in his arms. He rocked her, never looking away from her face.

"It's as if she's asleep," the physician said, standing now beside him. "Just asleep. She should wake up soon and tell us what happened."

Jimmy Maitland said, "We've put out an island-wide alert for Timmy Tuttle, with description, and Marilyn Warluski, with description. The three agents with Sherlock didn't see a single blessed thing. Nada."

Savich nodded, touched his wife's hair. He didn't think he'd be surprised by anything ever again.

A few minutes later, Sherlock opened her eyes. She looked up and, surprisingly, smiled. "You're holding me, Dillon. Why? What happened?"

"You don't remember?" He spoke very slowly, the words not really wanting to speak themselves, probably because he didn't want an answer.

She closed her eyes for a moment, frowned, then said, "I remember I ran into this room, three other agents behind me. No one was here." She frowned. "No, I'm not sure. There was something—a light maybe—something. I can't remember."

"When I came in, you were standing perfectly still, staring out that big window. The other agents were searching the room. But you didn't move, didn't twitch or anything, and then you just fell over."

Jimmy Maitland said, "Did you see anything of Timmy Tuttle or Marilyn?"

Sherlock said, "Timmy Tuttle—yes, that crazy-looking guy who was as pale as an apocalypse horseman—yes, I remember. He was holding Marilyn around her neck—a knife, yes, he had a knife. I was terrified when I saw Dillon go in after him into that conference room."

"You saw Timmy go into the conference room?"

"I think so. But that can't be right. Didn't he come in here?"

"We don't know. None of the agents saw him in here," Savich said. "No, Sherlock, that's okay. You just rest now. You'll probably remember more once you get yourself together. Does your head ache?"

"A bit, why?"

"You feel maybe a bit like you're hungover?"

"Well, yes, that's right."

Savich looked up at Jimmy Maitland and nodded. "Everyone I've spoken to, agents and civilians alike, everyone feels like that."

"Sherlock," Maitland said, crouching down beside her.

"Why was it just you who collapsed? You must have seen something."

"I'm thinking, sir, as hard as I can."

Dillon slowly eased her up until she was sitting on his lap. She started shaking. Savich nearly lost it. He pulled her hard against him, protecting her, from what, he didn't know. He just didn't want her hurt, no more hurt, no more monsters from the unknown.

Then she said, pulling away from him just a little bit, her voice firm and steady, "Dillon, I'm all right. I promise. I've got stuff to think about. Something really weird happened, didn't it?"

"Yes."

"It's there, in the back of my brain, and I'll get it out."

20

EUREKA, CALIFORNIA

Morrie Jones stared at the young woman who had taken him down, hurt him, dammit, before he could get away from her. He just couldn't believe it. She was skinny, looked like a damned little debutante with her blond hair and blue eyes and innocent face, like the prototypical little WASP. That damned lawyer of his had even told him that she'd been recovering from surgery and she'd still stomped his ass. He really wanted to hurt her. Hell, he'd even do it for free, this time.

He said to Simon, "You claimed I didn't need my lawyer, that you just wanted to talk to me, that you had something to offer that I couldn't refuse. You from the DA's office?"

Simon said, "No, but I have her approval. I see you remember Ms. Savich."

"Nah, I heard her name was Frasier. I know that's right because that's the name of the broad I'm going to sue for attacking me."

Lily gave him a big smile. "You go ahead and sue me, boyo, and I'll just smack your face off again. What do you think?" She cracked her knuckles, a sound Morrie Jones had hated since he was a kid and his old man did it whenever he was drunk.

"Stop that," Morrie said, staring at her hands. "Why'd the cops let you two in here?"

She cracked her knuckles again, something she'd rarely done since she was a bookie and some kid from another neighborhood had threatened to horn in on her territory. "What's the matter, Morrie? I still scare you?"

"Shut up, you bitch."

"Call me a bitch again and I'll make you eat your tongue." She gave him a sweet smile, with one dimple.

Simon said, "All right, that's enough. Listen up, Morrie. We want you to tell us who hired you. It could save your life."

Morrie started whistling "Old Man River."

Lily laughed. "Come on, Morrie, spare us. You got a brain? Use it. Herman Monk is dead, shot three times in the back."

"I don't know no Herman Monk. Sounds like a geek. Don't know him."

That could be true. Simon said, "Monk was a loose end. He's dead. You're a loose end, too, Morrie. Just think about your lawyer for a moment. Who is he? Who sent him? Who's paying his bill? Do you really think he's going to try to get *you* off?"

"I hired him. He's a real good friend, a drinking buddy. We watch the fights together down at Sam's Sports Bar, you know, over on Cliff Street."

Lily said, as she tapped her fingers on the Formica surface, split down the middle by bars, with Simon and Lily on one side, Morrie on the other, "He's setting you up, Morrie. You too stupid to use your brain? You know he told the sheriff that he took your case pro bono?"

"I want a cigarette."

"Don't be a moron. You want to die, hacking up your

lungs? He said he took you on for free, out of the goodness of his heart. I want you to just think about all this. What did your lawyer promise you?"

"He said I was getting out of here, today."

"Yeah, we heard," Simon said, and it was true, according to Lieutenant Dobbs. The judge had called and was prepared to set bail. "You know what's going to happen then?"

"Yeah, I'm going to go get me a beer."

"That's possible," Lily said. "I hope you really enjoy it, Morrie, because you're going to be dead by morning. These people really hate loose ends."

Morrie said, "Who did you say this Monk geek was?"

Lily said, "He was the curator of the museum where my grandmother's paintings were displayed. He was part of the group who had four of the paintings copied, the originals replaced with the fakes. When it all came out, when it was obvious that things were unraveling, he was shot in the back. That's why they wanted you to kill me. They want my paintings and here I am doing what they knew I'd do— stirring things up until I find out who stole my paintings. I wonder how long before they shoot you, Morrie."

"I'm leaving town, first thing."

"Good idea," Simon said. "But I see two big problems for you. The first is that you're still in jail. Your lawyer said he was going to get you out? Who's going to pay the bail, Morrie, and that's your second problem. Your pro bono lawyer? That's possible, what with all the money from the people who hired you in the first place. So, let's say you walk out of here, what are you going to do? Hide out in an alley and wait for them to kill you?"

Morrie believed him, Simon knew it in that moment. Simon waited a beat, then said, "Turns out I can solve both problems for you."

"How?"

"Ms. Savich here will drop charges against you, we'll get you out of here without your lawyer knowing about it.

To sweeten the deal, I'll give you five hundred bucks. That'll get you far away from these creeps, give you a new start. In return you give me the name of who hired you."

Morrie said, "Look, I'm going to sue her the minute I get out of here. Five hundred bucks? That's jack shit."

Simon's gut was good. He knew he was going to get Morrie. Just one more nudge. He turned on the recorder in his jacket pocket. "You know, Morrie, Lieutenant Dobbs and the DA don't really want me to cut any deal with you. I had to talk them into it. They want to take you to trial and throw your butt in jail for a long time. Since Lily hurt you pretty good, it's more than your word against hers. You'd be dead meat, Morrie."

It took only three more minutes of negotiation. Simon agreed to give Morrie Jones eight hundred dollars, Lily agreed to drop the charges, and Morrie agreed to give them a name.

"I want to see her sign papers and I want to see the money before I do anything."

Lieutenant Dobbs and the DA weren't pleased, but knew that Morrie was incidental compared to the person who'd hired him.

Lily, in the presence of Lieutenant Dobbs, an assistant DA, a detective, and two officers, signed that she was dropping the charges against one Morrie Jones, age twenty.

Once they were alone again, Morrie said, slouching back in his chair, "Now, big shot, give me the money before I say another word."

Simon rose, pulled his wallet out of his back pocket, and laid out the entire wad. There were eight one-hundred-dollar bills and a single twenty. "Glad you didn't wipe me out completely, Morrie. I appreciate it. That twenty will buy Lily and me a couple of tacos."

Morrie smirked as Simon started to slide the hundred-dollar bills through the space beneath the bars. "Tell me a story, Morrie."

"I don't exactly have a name. Hey, no, don't take the money back. I got just as good as a name. Look, she called me. It was this woman and she had this real thick accent, real Southern, you know? Smooth and real slow. She didn't give me her name, just Lily Frasier's name. She described her, told me where she was staying and to get it done fast.

"I went right over to the bank, picked up the money, then I went to work." He slid his eyes toward Lily. "It just didn't quite work out the way I wanted."

"That's because you're a wimp, Morrie."

Morrie half-rose out of his chair. The jail guard standing against the wall immediately straightened. Simon raised a hand. "How much did this woman pay you to kill Lily?"

"She gave me a thousand for a down payment. Then she was to have five thousand to me when it was done and on the news."

"This is not a good business, Simon." She stared at Morrie. "I was only worth six thousand dollars?"

Morrie actually smiled. "That's all. You know, I would have done it for less if I'd known you then."

Simon realized that Lily was enjoying herself. She was having a really fine pissing contest with this young thug. He pressed his knee against her leg.

But she had one more line. "What I did to you I did for nothing."

Simon just shook his head at her. "Morrie, which bank?"

"Give me the money first."

Simon slid the money all the way through. Morrie's hand slid over it, presto. He closed his young eyes for a moment, feeling the money like it was a lover's flesh. "Wells Fargo," he said, "the one just over on First Street and Pine. The money was there in my name."

"You didn't ask who had left the money waiting there for you?"

Morrie shook his head.

"Thanks, Morrie," Lily said as she rose. "Lieutenant

Dobbs thinks you'll be out sometime this afternoon. He's agreed not to tell your lawyer. My advice to you—get the hell out of Dodge. This time you don't have to be afraid of me. The woman who hired you—chances are good she wants you dead, and she's capable of doing it herself."

"You know who she is?"

Lily said, "Oh yeah, we know. She'd eat you with her poached eggs for breakfast. Hey, what happened to the thousand bucks she gave you?"

Morrie's eyes slid away. "None of your damned business."

Lily laughed, shook her finger at him. "You pissed it away in a poker game, didn't you?"

"No, dammit. It was pool."

Clark Hoyt was waiting for them in Lieutenant Dobbs's office. His arms were folded over his chest. He looked very odd. "I got a call from Savich. He was calling from Saint John's, in Antigua, of all places, said to tell you that all hell will break loose in the media really soon now, but that he and Sherlock are okay. It seems that Tammy Tuttle got ahold of Marilyn Warluski and they're gone. There was a big situation there at the airport. Savich called it a fiasco."

"Antigua?" Simon said. "I guess he couldn't tell us he was there."

Lily said, shaking her head, "Dillon will not be a happy camper about this."

Hoyt himself wondered what had happened, but he said only, "Savich didn't give me any details, said he'd call again this evening. I told him where you guys are staying now. Okay, tell me who hired Morrie."

"Yeah," Lieutenant Dobbs said as he came into his own office to see the two civilians and the Fed. "Who was it?"

"It was my mother-in-law," Lily said. "No doubt at all that it was Charlotte. She didn't give Morrie her name, but that accent of hers—it has so much syrup in it, you could sweeten a rock."

Lieutenant Dobbs shook his head. "So now you know, but there's still no case. Both Hoyt and I interviewed the Frasiers—all three of them—separately. In all three cases, their lawyer, Bradley Abbott, a real son of a bitch hard-nose, was present. The Frasiers refused to answer any questions. Abbott read a statement to us. In the statement, the Frasiers claim all of this is nonsense. They are sorry about Mr. Monk, but it has nothing to do with them, and this is a waste of everyone's time. Oh yeah, then their lawyer told us that you were nuts, Lily, that you'd do any-thing to get back at them, for what reason they don't know, but no one should believe a single word you say. We need more evidence before we can bring them to the station and put them in an interview room again."

Hoyt said to Simon and Lily, "We'll have two agents on Morrie Jones. Lieutenant Dobbs hasn't got a problem with that, especially since he's short officers right now. We won't let the little twerp out of our sight."

"Good," said Lieutenant Dobbs. "All right, listen up. I've got a murder to solve. As for you, Lily, you're just an attempted murder, so I guess I can let you slide just a bit. I understand this thing is more complicated than a Greek knot, and that all of it ties together."

Simon said, "If it's okay with you, Lieutenant, I'd like to go to Wells Fargo to see if there's a record of who gave Morrie a thousand dollars for the hit on Lily. That'd be too easy, but it's worth a shot."

Lieutenant Dobbs said, "She paid that little dip just a thousand bucks to off Lily?"

"Oh, no," Lily said. "I'm worth lots more than that. There was another five thousand bucks when the job was done."

Simon said, "Okay, then, let's get cracking."

On the way out the door, Lily looked at Simon for a mo-ment, at his too-long, very dark hair, and realized she hadn't really noticed before how it curled at his neck.

"Those little curls—they're cute," she said and patted his nape.

Simon rolled his eyes.

Hoyt, who was walking behind them, laughed.

Since Hoyt was along, they got instant cooperation at Wells Fargo. One of the vice presidents, who seemed more numerous than tellers at the windows, hustled onto the computer and punched up the money transfer transactions for the very morning Morrie had attacked Lily on the city bus.

Mr. Trempani raised his head, looked at each of them in turn. "This is very strange. The money was wired in care of Mr. Morrie Jones by a company called Tri-Light Investments. Any of you ever heard of them?"

"Tri-Light," Lily said. "I don't think Tennyson ever mentioned that company."

"Who are they?" Hoyt asked.

"All we have is an account number in Zurich, Switzerland. It simply lists Tri-Light Investments and the Habib Bank AG at 59 Weinbergstrasse."

"Curiouser and curiouser," Simon said.

Hoyt said, "I'll call Interpol and get someone to check this out. But don't count on finding anything out. The Swiss have duct tape over their mouths." He paused for a moment. "You suspect someone, don't you, Simon? And not just the Frasiers. Who?"

"If the owner of this Tri-Light Investments is a Swede by the name of Olaf Jorgenson, then we're confirming lots of things," Simon said.

"Makes sense," Hoyt said. "He's the collector, isn't he? That's how it all ties into Ms. Savich's paintings. You guys think he's the one who commissioned them."

"It's possible," Simon said.

Lily punched Simon in the ribs. "It's more than possible, Clark. Call us on the cell phone as soon as you know, okay?"

Hoyt said, "You promised no hotdogging. That means you don't go see Charlotte Frasier without having at least me along."

HEMLOCK BAY, CALIFORNIA

Lily pointed to the Bullock Pharmacy, and Simon pulled into an open parking spot in front of Spores Dry Cleaners next door. An old man was staring out at them from the large glass windows that held three hanging Persian carpets, presumably just cleaned.

Ten minutes later, Lily came out of the Bullock Pharmacy carrying a small paper bag. She eased into the passenger seat and drew a deep breath. "It's such a beautiful town," she said. "I always thought so. You can smell the ocean, feel that light sheen of salt on your skin. It's incredible."

"Okay, I agree, lovely town, lovely smell in the air. What happened?"

"I had a real epiphany going into that pharmacy." And then she told him what had happened. There'd been about ten people in the store, and all of them, after they saw her, were talking about her behind their hands. They stepped away if she came near them, didn't say anything if she said hello to them. Lily was frankly relieved when Mr. Bullock senior, at least eighty years old, nodded to her at the checkout line. Evidently he was the spokesperson. He looked at her straight in the eye before he rang up her aspirin and said, "Everyone is real sorry you tried to kill yourself again, Mrs. Frasier."

"I didn't, Mr. Bullock."

"We heard that you blamed it on Dr. Frasier and left him."

"Is that what everyone believes?"

"We've known the Frasiers a long time, ma'am. Lots longer than we've known you."

"Actually, Mr. Bullock, it's very far from the truth. Someone has tried to kill me three times now."

He just shook his head at her, waved the bottle of aspirin, and said, "You need something stronger than these, Mrs. Frasier. Something lots stronger. You'll never live to be as old as I am if you don't see to it now."

"Why don't you talk to Lieutenant Dobbs in Eureka?"

He just looked at her, saying nothing more. Lily didn't feel like standing there arguing with the old man to change his mind, with the dozen other people in the store likely listening, so she just paid and left, knowing those people were thinking she was one sick puppy, no doubt about it.

"That's it. Nothing much, really." She waved the bottle of aspirin. "Thanks, Simon." He handed her a bottle of diet Dr Pepper, and she took two of the tablets.

"Isn't it interesting that no one wanted to speak to me," she said, "except Mr. Bullock. They were all content just to hang back and listen."

"It's still a beautiful town. Tennyson, Mom, and Dad have been busy," Simon said. "How about some lunch?"

After a light lunch at a diner that sat right on the main pier, Lily said, "I want to visit my daughter, Simon."

For a moment, he didn't understand. She saw it and said, even as tears stung her eyes, "The cemetery. After I leave, I know I won't be back for a while. I want to say good-bye."

He wasn't about to let her go by herself. It was too dangerous. When he told her that, she simply nodded. They stopped at a small florist shop at the end of Whipple Avenue, Molly Ann's Blooms.

"Hilda Gaddis owns Molly Ann's. She sent a beautiful bouquet of yellow roses to Beth's funeral."

"The daffodils are lovely."

"Yes. Beth loved daffodils." She said nothing more as they drove the seven minutes to the cemetery set near the Presbyterian Church. It was lovely, in a pocket nestled by hemlock and spruce trees, protected from the winds off the ocean.

He walked with her up a narrow pathway that forked to

the right. There was a beautiful etched white marble stone, an angel carved on top, her arms spread wide. Beth's name was beneath, the date of her birth, the date of her death, and beneath, the words *She Gave Me Infinite Joy*.

Lily was crying, but made no sound. Simon watched her go down on her knees and arrange the daffodils against the headstone.

He wanted to comfort her but realized in those moments that she needed to be alone. He turned away and went back to the rental car. His cell phone rang.

It was Clark Hoyt, and he was excited.

21

There was nothing more for Savich to do in Antigua. Timmy Tuttle, with two healthy arms, had Marilyn, and Savich didn't want to even think of what he was doing to her.

Or maybe two different people had her, one wild-eyed man with black hair and two arms, and a woman with one arm and madness and rage in her eyes.

Savich couldn't stand himself. He'd set up Marilyn, gotten an FBI agent killed, along with a local police officer, and left chaos in his wake. He knew he'd see Virginia Cosgrove's sightless eyes for a very long time, and that long red gash that had slit her throat open.

Jimmy Maitland had taken his arm, trying to calm him down. "Batten down the guilt, Savich. I approved everything you did. We faced something or someone that shouldn't have been there. It happened. You've got to prepare to move on."

Maitland shook his head, ran fingers through his gray hair, making it stand on end. "Jesus, I'm losing it. There's nothing more we can do here. We're going home. I'm leaving Vinny Arbus and his SWAT team in charge. They'll keep looking for Marilyn and coordinate with local law enforcement. This confusion, Savich, it will unravel in time. There's an explanation, there has to be."

Savich didn't let Sherlock out of his sight. He realized soon enough that she was different—more quiet, her attention not on any of them, and he'd look at her and know she was thinking about what had happened, her eyes focused, yet somehow far away.

There was so much cleanup, so many explanations to give, most omitting the inexplicable things because they didn't help anyone to know the sorts of things that could drive you mad. And most important, there was no sign of the man who'd taken Marilyn Warluski from the Saint John's airport.

When they got back to Washington, Savich left immediately for the gym and worked out until he was panting for breath, his body so exhausted it was ready to rebel.

When he walked in the front door, feeling so exhausted each step was a chore, his son was there to greet him, crawling for all he was worth right up to Savich's feet, grabbing onto his pants leg. Savich started to reach down to pick him up when he heard Sherlock say, "No, wait a second."

Sean yanked hard on his father's pants, got a good hold, braced himself, and managed to pull himself up. Then he grinned up at his father and lifted one leg, then the other.

All the miserable unanswerable questions, all the deadening sense of failure, fell away. Savich whooped, picked up his son, and tossed him into the air, again and again, until Sean was both yelling and laughing, one and then the other.

It was Savich who wrote Sean's accomplishment in his baby book that evening. "An almost giant step for kidkind." Then "The leg lift, one at a time—he's getting ready to walk, amazing. His grandmother says I started walking early, too."

In bed that night, Sherlock nuzzled her head into Savich's neck, lightly laid her palm over his heart, and said, "Sean brings back focus, doesn't he?"

"Yes. I was ready to fall over from working out so hard when I walked in the house, and then he crawls over to me and pulls himself up. Then he lifts each leg, testing them out, nearly ready to take off. I didn't think I had any laughter left in me, but I guess I do."

"Don't feel guilty about it. You should have seen Gabriella. She was so tickled when I got home, so proud of both herself and Sean that she couldn't wait to show off what he could do. Those leg lifts, I haven't read about that in any baby books. Gabriella got some video of him doing that with me. I swear she didn't want to leave this afternoon. I expect her husband to call me and complain about what demanding employers we are."

Savich settled his hand on her hip, kneaded her for a moment, thinking she'd dropped weight, kissed her forehead, then turned on his back to stare up at the dark ceiling.

"Dillon?"

"Hmm?"

"I waited until Sean was in bed and we were lying here, all relaxed."

"Waited for what, sweetheart?"

She took a deep breath. "I've remembered some stuff that happened in that room at the airport."

HEMLOCK BAY

Hoyt said, "You'll never believe this, Simon!"

"Yeah, yeah, what, Clark?"

"Lieutenant Dobbs, he's got—"

Simon heard the slight shifting in sound, perhaps a small movement in the backseat of the car, but just as he knew something was different, he felt something very hard come down over his right temple. He slumped forward on the steering wheel, his forehead striking the horn.

It blared.

"Simon? Simon, where are you? What the hell happened?"

Lily heard the horn. Their rental car? But Simon was there, surely. Then she realized something was very wrong. She was on her feet in a second, racing down those beautifully manicured paths to the visitors' parking lot. She heard the man running behind her, just one man; she heard the deep crunching of gravel beneath his feet.

She ran faster, veering away from the parking lot, running back into the thick stand of hemlock and spruce trees. She was fast, always had been.

She heard the man shout, but not at her. He was shouting at his accomplice. What had happened to Simon? The horn was still blaring, but it was more distant now. And then she realized that he must have fallen on the horn. Was he dead? No, no, he couldn't be, he just couldn't.

She was through the trees, out the back, and there was the damned cliff, miles and miles of it, running north and south. She had been here before, and there wasn't any escape this way. What to do?

She ran along the edge of the cliff, searching for a way down, and found one, some yards ahead just before the cliff curved inward, probably from sliding and erosion over the years. There was a skinny, snaking trail, and she took it without hesitation. There was nothing ahead except empty land dotted with trees and gullies. They'd get her for sure, that or just shoot her down. Maybe there was something there on the beach. Anything was better than staying up here and being an easy target.

The path was steep, and she had to slow way down. Still she tripped a couple of times, and the last time, she had to grab a bush that grew beside the trail to halt her fall. It had thorns, and she felt them score her hands and fingers.

She vaguely heard birds calling overhead.

She knew the men had to be nearly at the top of the trail now. They'd come after her. What was down here except more beach? There had to be someplace to hide, some cover, a cave, anything.

Her breath was spurting out of her, broken, tight. A stitch ripped through her side. She ignored it. She had to be calm, keep herself in control.

She kept her eyes on the winding trail. Wouldn't it ever stop? She heard the men now, yelling from the top for her to come back up, they weren't going to hurt her.

She managed three more steps, then there was a shot, then an instant ricochet off a rock just one foot to her right, scattering chips in all directions. A chip hit her in the leg, but it didn't go through her jeans.

She hunkered down as much as she could, twisting to the left, then the right, going down until at last her feet hit the hard sand on the beach. She chanced a look back up to the top and saw one of the men start down after her. The other man was aiming his gun at her. It was a handgun, not accurate enough at this distance, she hoped.

It wasn't. He shot at her three more times, but none of the bullets seemed to strike close to her.

She stumbled over a gnarly piece of driftwood and went flying. She landed on her stomach, her hands in front of her face. She saw wet sand, driftwood, kelp, and even one frantic sand crab not six inches from her nose.

She lay there for just a moment, drawing in deep breaths, feeling the stitch in her side lessen. Then she was up again. She saw the man coming down the trail, but he wasn't being as careful as she'd been. He was a big guy, not in the best of shape. He was wearing those opaque wraparound sunglasses, so she couldn't really make out his features. He had thick, light brown hair and a gun in his right hand. She watched him stumble, wildly clutching at the air to regain his balance, but he didn't. He tumbled head over heels down the trail and landed hard at the bottom, not moving. His gun. His gun was her only chance. She'd seen it flying. She ran to his side in an instant. She picked up a big piece of driftwood, realized it was soggy and not heavy enough, and grabbed up a rock instead. She leaned over him and brought the rock down on his head as hard as she could. She slipped her hand inside his coat and pulled out his wallet. She shoved it into her pocket, then saw the gun some six feet back up the trail, just off to the side, lying on top of a pile of rocks.

The man on top was yelling, firing, but she ignored him. She got the gun, turned, and ran for all she was worth down the beach.

WASHINGTON, D.C.

Savich felt his heart pounding faster beneath his wife's palm. He shot up, turned on the bedside lamp, then faced her. "Tell me."

"I remember being scared for you when I saw you go into that conference room. Then I'm sure I saw Timmy Tuttle dragging Marilyn into that security room across the hall. I ran into the room, the three other agents behind me. The room was empty. At least that's what I thought at first.

"I saw this bright light, Dillon. It nearly blinded me, and I swear to you, for some reason I just couldn't move. The light was right in front of that big window, and I know I saw Timmy and Marilyn in the middle of that light.

"I could hear the other agents yelling at each other. I realized they weren't seeing what I was. Still I couldn't move. I was just nailed to the spot looking at that white light. Then Timmy Tuttle grabbed Marilyn tight around her neck, and..."

"And what?"

"Dillon, I'm not crazy, I swear."

He pulled her against him. "I know."

"They just disappeared. It was like they were right in front of me, then they were in front of the window, and the window was bathed in the white light. Then they receded through that white light until they were gone. Then everything just seemed to close down. That's all I remember."

Savich said, "That's just fine, Sherlock. Well done. It fits right into the rest of it. It seems logical to everyone that Tammy Tuttle used some sort of mass hypnosis. You know how David Copperfield walked through the Great Wall of China? How he got sawed in half with millions of people watching, most of them on TV?"

"Yes. You think Tammy has this skill?"

"It makes sense. There she or he was with Marilyn, and then she or he just wasn't there. I think the whole thing was this big performance that she worked out to show us we're dealing with a master. You know what else I think? I think Tammy knew I was trying to trap her and using Marilyn as bait. She knew we'd be at the airport waiting for her. She was ready for us. I also think she really wants us to believe that everything we saw was supernatural, beyond our meager brains. But it's not. She's just very, very good. She wanted to scare us all to death, paralyze us. I do wonder, though, why she didn't try to kill me."

Sherlock pulled away, stroked her fingers over his jaw, and said, "I think it's because she couldn't get close enough to you. I've given this a lot of thought, Dillon, and I think you're one of the few people Tammy's ever met whom she can't hypnotize or perform an illusion for when she's up close to you. And if she can't get close to you without your seeing exactly what she is, then she can't kill you."

"You mean if I had been close to her, I wouldn't have seen Timmy, I'd have really seen Tammy?"

"Yes, it sounds reasonable. If she can't get close enough to you without your seeing her exactly as she is, then she knows she's at a disadvantage. When you were in the barn in Maryland with her, how far away were you standing from her?"

"Maybe two dozen feet."

"And she was always just what she was? Tammy Tuttle?"

"Yes. She called the Ghouls, but she didn't change. When I shot her, I saw the bullet nearly rip her arm from her body. I saw her fall, heard her yells of pain. She remained exactly what she was and who she was."

Sherlock said, "Then at the airport, she just couldn't get close enough to you to kill you. And she realized, too, that she couldn't get too close or you'd see her as she really is and kill her. She's being really careful after what you did to her at the barn."

Savich said, "Jimmy Maitland called me at the gym, told me that Jane Bitt in Behavioral Sciences allowed that just maybe it is possible that Tammy is a strong telepath in addition to all her illusion skills. She won't swear to it, says she doesn't want to get mocked out, but we should consider it, given the incredible control Tammy was able to exert at the airport."

Sherlock said, "So maybe she's got both this talent and skill in creating illusions. I think you were right. Tammy knew that you were setting her up. She also knew that you would bring Marilyn. For whatever reason, she wanted Marilyn back. I'm just hoping that she didn't want her back to kill her. Maybe she really is fond of Marilyn. Maybe Marilyn feeds her ego, makes her feel powerful because she's so very malleable and suggestible. Tammy can make Marilyn see, make her believe anything she tells her to believe. Didn't you tell me that Marilyn firmly believes everything Tammy says?"

"Oh, yes, and it's genuine, Sherlock. Even under hypnosis, Marilyn was frightened of Tammy and she believed everything she said to Dr. Hicks and to me. She remembered it as fact, for heaven's sake, so she had to have believed it."

Savich threw back the covers and jumped to his feet. He grabbed a pair of jeans as an afterthought and pulled them on. "I'm going to do some research on this with MAX."

He walked back to the bed, grinned down at his wife, pulled her up tightly against him, and kissed her until she would have just as soon he waited until morning to visit MAX. But she knew that brain of his was working again, asking questions, wanting to know everything, and fast.

"I won't be gone too long."

She lay back down in bed, shut off the table lamp, pulled the covers to her chin, and smiled into the darkness when she heard Dillon speaking to MAX down the hall in his study. She heard him laugh.

22

There weren't any caves, not even one indentation in the rock where she could squeeze in and wait them out. Just a beach that went on and on, driftwood piled all over it, and slimy trails of kelp, dangerous when you were running.

But she had a gun. It was small and ugly, but she wasn't defenseless. From what she knew about guns, which wasn't much, it was a close-range gun, useless at a distance, but if you got near enough, it could kill a person quite easily.

The temperature dropped as the sun went behind gathering clouds, whirling rain clouds. Any minute now rain would pour down. Would that help her or not? She didn't know.

Had there been three men? One staying with Simon and the other two after her? Maybe there were just two men and Simon could get away and call for help. They'd been idiots—telling their FBI protectors that since they were just going to the cemetery and they wanted to be private, they'd meet them back in Hemlock Bay.

She stopped, bending over, her hands on her thighs, so tired her breath was catching and she was wheezing with the effort to breathe. She flattened herself in the shadow of the cliff and looked back.

Then, suddenly, she heard one of the men cup his hands around his mouth and shout, "Lily Frasier! We have Simon Russo. Come out now or we will kill him. That is a promise. Then we will call our friends to come at you from the other end of the beach. We will trap you, and you won't like what will happen to you then."

The man's words brought her breath back, straightened her right up. The man's voice was also thick with an accent—stilted, unnatural. Swedish. Well, damn, it seemed that Olaf Jorgenson himself had come, or sent his friends. She ran again, until she rounded a slight promontory and looked up. She had found her way out. Another narrow trail snaked up the cliff, much like the one she'd taken down. Two miles back up the beach? Three miles? She didn't make a sound, just shot up that trail, using her hands on rocks and scrubs, anything to keep her steady, knowing they couldn't see her until they came around the promontory themselves.

They couldn't kill Simon. They'd left him alone in the car. If there was a third man watching him, well then, they couldn't contact him. Unless they had a cell phone. Everybody had a cell phone. Oh, God, please, no. It had to be a bluff, it just had to be.

She slipped once, saw pebbles and small rocks gushing out from the cliff and pounding their way back down to the beach. She held still, then started up again. She was up to the top of the cliff in no time and running. The men would realize soon enough where she'd gone.

Hurry, she had to hurry. She hurt, really bad, but she thought of Simon, of his hair curling at his neck, and she knew nothing could happen to him. She wouldn't let it. Too much loss in her life, she couldn't bear any more. She came into the back of the cemetery, climbed the wrought-iron fence, and ran down the path toward the visitors' parking lot.

The horn wasn't blaring anymore.

Nearly there, she was nearly there. She saw their rental car, but didn't see Simon. She got to the car. He was stretched out on the front seat, unconscious. Or dead.

She pulled the driver's side door open. "Simon! Wake up, dammit! Wake up!"

He moaned, struggled to a sitting position. He blinked, finally focusing on her face.

"They're after us, two men, both with guns. I got away from them but we don't have much time. Scoot over, we're getting out of here. I'm going to drive us right to jail and have Lieutenant Dobbs lock us in. It's the only safe place in the world. No lawyers allowed. Just Lieutenant Dobbs. He can bring our food. We'll get Dillon and Sherlock out here. They'll figure this all out, and we can get the hell out of here."

As she spoke, she managed to shove his feet off the seat and push him toward the passenger door. "It will be all right. You don't have to do anything, see, I can drive now. Just rest, Simon."

"No, Lily, no more driving. You're not going anywhere, not anymore."

Lily turned slowly at that syrupy voice and stared up at Charlotte Frasier, who was pointing a long-barreled gun at her. "You've given us too much trouble. If I hadn't decided to oversee this myself, you would have escaped yet again. I always believed three times was a charm, and so it is. Get out of the car, Lily. Now."

Lily wasn't surprised, not really. Not Elcott, but Charlotte. Then she almost smiled. Charlotte didn't know she had a gun, too. Would Charlotte take the chance of killing them here, in the cemetery parking lot? She believed all the way to her gut that Charlotte was capable of anything. She was still free, and Mr. Monk had been dead for three days now.

Then she saw the men running toward them. She had to hurry, had to do something. She opened the door, lifting one arm, hiding the other hand slightly behind her.

"Where's Elcott?" she said, wanting to distract Charlotte, just for an instant. "And that marvelous son of yours? Who loves me so much he'd like nothing more than to bury me? Aren't they hanging back there, waiting for you to tell them what to do?"

"Don't you dare speak of my husband and my son like that—"

Lily was clear. She raised the gun and fired.

Washington, D.C.
FBI Headquarters

Ollie Hamish came running into Savich's office. "We got him! We got Anthony Carpelli, a.k.a. Wilbur Wright. He was right there in Kitty Hawk on the Outer Banks. He was kneeling in front of the monument at Kitty Hawk and we came up on him and he just folded down like a tent and gave it all up."

For an instant, Savich was so distracted he didn't know what Ollie was talking about. Then he remembered, the guru from Texas who'd had his followers murder the two deputies and the sheriff, the Sicilian Canadian who'd attended McGill University and had an advanced degree in cellular biology. Savich said slowly, "Sit down, Ollie. You said he was kneeling at the monument? As in worshiping?"

"Maybe so. All the agents were so relieved at how easily it went down, they were celebrating, drinking beers at eleven o'clock in the morning. We got him, Savich. He'll go back to Texas and fry, probably."

"Probably not," Savich said. "Remember that he isn't tied directly to those killings, just hearsay from a woman who was pissed off."

"Yes, Lureen. Evidently they're holding her as a material witness. They've also picked up two more of Wilbur's people who were in the cult. Everyone thinks his own people will finally nail his ass. At least we got him and he's not going to be killing anybody else.

"Hey, Savich, you should be really pleased. After all, it was you and MAX who predicted he'd probably go back to Kitty Hawk."

Savich realized he was so caught up with Tammy Tuttle that he didn't feel much of anything about Wilbur Wright. And it was a victory, a very clean win. Everyone would be very pleased. He smiled at Ollie. "I am pleased. MAX discovered sixteen more killings throughout the Southwestern U.S. that sound like the work of Wilbur. So there's lots of other crimes to tie in to this one; local law enforcement should be brought up to speed and get with the program. Dane Carver is heading that up. Now that you've got Wilbur Wright, you can get our doctors on him and see what makes him tick."

"I really don't want to know."

"Unfortunately a jury will demand to know. Meet with Dane and go over all the other cases, then head down to interview Wilbur."

"When we caught him, I looked at him, Savich. You know, I don't think I've ever seen such dead eyes, and I've seen lots of bad folk up close and personal; but Wilbur, he was just flat-out scary. You wonder what exactly he's seeing with those dead eyes. It won't be long before they extradite him back to Texas with more than enough evidence to fry his butt."

"You can bet the lawyers will fight extradition."

"Yeah, they'd prefer a state where there's no death penalty, but if we get enough evidence, it won't matter."

"We done good, Ollie. Now you and Dane sew it up, okay?"

"You got it." Agent Ollie Hamish leaned forward in his chair, clasping his hands between his legs. "I've heard all sorts of things, Savich, about what happened in Antigua. How's that going?"

Savich told him all of it. "We've got people working on where she learned her illusion skills so we can get a better handle on what she's capable of. There are more people scouring the airport in Antigua trying to find out how she managed to get away, questioning everyone in the area, searching all boats, all private charters."

Ollie said, "She's still got only one arm and, physically, she's in bad shape, right?"

"I don't know how bad it still is. Her surgeon said if she has an infection, she could be dead within a week without antibiotics. But if she doesn't have an infection, she could make it through just fine. He said she responded superbly to the surgery. I asked the doctor if anyone had ever reported seeing someone other than Tammy Tuttle or seeing her where she shouldn't be."

"Did he even understand what you meant?"

"Yes," Savich said slowly, "he did. He said that an orderly told him he'd just seen Tammy up and walking to the bathroom the day after surgery. When he went to check her, she was lying strapped down to the bed. Nobody believed the orderly. Then she escaped and no one could figure that out, either. Anyway, Ollie, how are Maria and Josh? He just turned two, right?"

"Yeah. He's running all over the house, opening every drawer, banging every pot. He yells 'no' at least fifty times a day, and he's cuter than the new puppy we just got, who peed on the shirt I was going to wear this morning."

Savich laughed. It felt good. He nodded Ollie out, then turned back to MAX.

A call came in an hour later. Tammy Tuttle had been

spotted in Bar Harbor, Maine, where agents had showed
her photo all over town, along with Marilyn's, and left
phone numbers. A local photo shop owner had called the
Bar Harbor police department to say she'd left film and
was going to come back.

"I've got to get close to her," Savich said to Sherlock. He
kissed her nose and left the unit, nearly on a run, shouting
over his shoulder, "I've got to see Tammy with one arm,
and not something she wants me to see."

"Please, not too close," Sherlock called out, but she
didn't think he heard her.

It took very little time for Savich and six other agents to
board a Sabreliner at Andrews Air Force Base for a flight to
Bar Harbor.

He spent the entire flight telling the agents everything he
could think of. It was time, Savich decided, feeling a
weight lift off his shoulders, to let everyone know exactly
what they were dealing with.

A psychopathic killer who is an illusionist, possibly a
telepath. He had never seen anything like it, and he hoped
he never would again.

He'd just finished telling all the agents about the Ghouls,
detailing what Marilyn had told him and what he himself
had seen. If they didn't believe him, they were cool enough
to keep it to themselves.

One agent, a friend of Virginia Cosgrove's, didn't doubt
a single word. As they were debarking from the jet in Bar
Harbor, she said, "Virginia told me some things Marilyn
Warluski had told her. It was terrifying, Mr. Savich."

"Just Savich, Ms. Rodriguez. I'm very sorry about
Agent Cosgrove."

"We all are, sir." Then she managed a grin. "Just Lois,
Savich."

"You got it.

"The thing is, guys," he said a few minutes later to all of
them, "if you see her or him again"—he waved the artist's

drawing under all their noses—"don't play any games. Don't even think about trying to take her alive. Don't trust anything you see happen, fire without hesitation, and shoot to kill. Now, I'm going to the photo shop, make sure there's no confusion. Then we'll get together at the local police department and get everything set up."

He wondered if the Ghouls would be with her, with Tammy as their head acolyte, their priestess of death.

He was becoming melodramatic. All he really knew as he walked into the photo shop, Hamlet's Pics, on Wescott Avenue, was that he was glad to his soul that Sherlock wasn't here, that she was at home, safe with Sean.

He spoke to the photo shop employee, Teddi Tyler— spelled with an "i" he was told—to verify what he'd said to the local police. Teddi repeated that the woman whose photo Savich was showing him had indeed been in the shop, just yesterday, late afternoon. He'd called the police right away.

"What did she want?"

"She had some film she wanted developed."

Savich felt his heart pound, deep and slow, and it was all he could do to remain calm and smooth. They were so close now. "Did you develop the film, Mr. Tyler?"

"Yes, sir, Agent Savich. The police told me to go ahead and develop it and hold the photos for the FBI."

"When did she say she wanted to pick the photos up?"

"This afternoon, at two o'clock. I told her that would be just fine."

"Did she look like she was in good health, Mr. Tyler?"

"She was sort of pale, but looked good other than that. It was pretty cold yesterday so she was all bundled up in a thick coat, a big scarf around her neck and a wool ski cap, but I still recognized her, no problem."

"Did you make any comment to her about how she looked familiar?"

"Oh, no, Agent Savich. I was really cool."

Yeah, I bet, Savich thought, praying that he'd been cool enough not to alert Tammy that he was on to her. One thing—Teddi Tyler was still alive, and that meant Tammy hadn't felt threatened, he hoped. Everything he'd told Savich so far was exactly what he'd told the local cops.

"I want you to think carefully now, Mr. Tyler. When she handed you the film, which hand did she use?"

Teddi frowned, furrowing his forehead into three deep lines. "Her left hand," he said at last. "Yes, it was her left hand. She had her purse on a long strap hanging over her left shoulder. It was kind of clumsy."

"Did you ever see her right hand?"

Again Teddi went into a big frown. "I'm sorry, Agent Savich," he said finally, shaking his head, "I just don't remember. All I'm sure about is that she stayed all bundled up—again no surprise, since it was so cold."

"Thank you, Mr. Tyler. Now, a special agent will take your place behind the counter. Agent Briggs will be in soon and you can go over procedures with him." Savich raised his hand, seeing that Teddi Tyler wanted to argue. "There's no way you are going to face this woman again, Mr. Tyler. She's very dangerous, even to us. Now, show me those photos."

Savich took the photo envelope from Teddi and moved away from the counter to the glass front windows. The sun was shining brightly for a November day. It didn't look like it was forty degrees outside. He slowly opened the envelope and pulled out the glossy 4x6 photos. There were only six of them.

He looked at one after the other, and then looked again. He didn't understand. All of them were beach shots, undoubtedly taken in the Caribbean. Two were taken in the early morning, two when the sun was high, and two at sunset. None of them was very well done—well, that made sense since she had only one arm—but what was the point?

All beach shots, no people in any of them. What was this about?

He held the photos up to Teddi. "Did she say anything about the photos? What they were? Anything at all?"

"Yeah, she said they were vacation photos she wanted to show her roommate. Said her roommate didn't believe her when she'd said how beautiful it was down in the Caribbean. She had to prove it."

If Tammy hadn't lied, then Marilyn was alive. She wanted Marilyn to admire the beaches in the Caribbean.

He told Teddi Tyler to take off as soon as Agent Briggs arrived. As for Briggs, he was a natural retailer, experienced in undercover jobs. He was fast, a good judge of people's behavior. Savich trusted him. Briggs knew how dangerous Tammy was, knew everything Savich knew.

They had three hours to get it all set up. There were three agents undercover near Marilyn's boyfriend's house just off Newport Drive. He doubted they would see either Marilyn or Tammy at the boyfriend's house. Of course not, Savich thought, that would be too easy.

Savich left, drew the salty air deep into his lungs, and called Simon Russo on his way to the meet with the other agents. He hadn't spoken to Russo or Lily in nearly thirty hours. He knew they were all right; otherwise Hoyt would have yelled out. Still, he wanted to know what was happening. He was worried about Lily, just couldn't help it. He knew Simon would protect her with his life, knew Hoyt and the Eureka police were with them all the way. But still, she was his sister, and he loved her deeply. He didn't want anything to happen to her. When he thought of what she'd already endured, he felt rage in his gut.

The more he thought about it, the more Savich worried.

He pulled his leather jacket collar up around his ears and dialed. Simon's cell phone didn't answer. Savich wasn't about to second-guess himself and try to believe that the battery was dead. He immediately put in a call to Clark Hoyt.

23

Clark Hoyt answered his cell phone on the third ring. "Savich? Good thing you called. We can't find Simon or Lily. Our guys have been sticking close to them, but when Lily wanted to go to the cemetery, everyone decided they'd be safe there, and so we agreed to give them some privacy. Jesus, Savich, they went after them in the cemetery!

"When they didn't show up in an hour at Bender's Café in Hemlock Bay, my agents called me, then drove to the cemetery. We found Simon's rental car and one of the Frasiers' cars in the parking lot. There weren't any other cars around. We know Lily visited her daughter's grave because the daffodils she'd bought were there."

Hoyt paused.

"What is it, Clark? What else did you find?"

"Some blood on the front seats, Savich, just a trace, but there was blood on the parking lot cement, a good bit more. We're testing it. We fucked up, Savich. Jesus, I'm sorry. We'll find them, I swear it to you."

Savich felt fear twisting in his belly, but when he spoke,

his voice was controlled. "The fact that you found the Frasiers' car there as well as Simon's—were the Frasiers taken, too? Or were the Frasiers a part of it and just left their car there? If they plan to come back, then why would they leave their car next to Simon's—that's a sure give-away that they were involved."

"That's what we think."

"At least you didn't find them dead. They've been taken. By whom?"

"We're trying to track down the Frasiers, but nothing yet. They must be with Simon and Lily. Lieutenant Dobbs and I went to the hospital to see Tennyson Frasier. He claimed he didn't know where his parents were. Seemed to me that he really didn't care one way or the other. When we told him that Lily was gone, I thought he'd go nuts. This Dr. Rossetti—you remember, the shrink who wanted to treat Lily when she was still in the hospital after the ac-cident? The guy Lily didn't like? Well, he was there with Tennyson. He got all huffy, said Tennyson was a fine man, a great doctor, and his wife was a bitch and didn't deserve him. He then gave Tennyson three happy pills while we were watching. I'll tell you, Savich, I think Tennyson re-ally doesn't know anything about the disappearance."

Savich was hearing everything, but he wasn't thinking a whole lot in that instant. He was flat-out scared. He wanted to leave Bar Harbor and fly immediately out to California, but he couldn't. He simply couldn't leave. It was that sim-ple and that final. He said, "I'm not sure what I think right at this moment, Clark. And I can't break free. I'm up to my eyeballs right now." He drew a deep breath. "Actually, we're about to confront a psychopathic killer right here in Bar Harbor, Maine, and I'm in charge."

"Look, Savich, there are a whole bunch of us on this. We'll find out who took them."

Yeah, yeah, Savich thought, then said, "If this Olaf Jor-genson is behind this, we're talking about a lot of resources, like a private Gulfstream jet here, with flight plans out of the country. It won't be hard to find them."

"We're already on that. I'll call you when we get something. Ah, good luck in Bar Harbor."

"Thank you. Keep me posted."

"Yes, I will. Look, Savich, I'm sorry. Dammit, I was supposed to keep them covered, keep them safe. I'll do everything I can with this. I'll call you every hour."

"No, Hoyt, call me only if it's an emergency for the next three hours. Otherwise, I'll get back to you when I can." Clark Hoyt didn't know what nuts was, Savich thought, as he punched off his cell phone. He had to call Sherlock, tell her what was going on. Thank God she was home and safe. He didn't want her to hear about Simon and Lily from Hoyt or Lieutenant Dobbs. He had two hours and forty minutes left to set up the operation. He walked over to Firefly Lane to the Bar Harbor Police Department. He knew he simply had to try to stop thinking about Lily and Simon now. He had to concentrate on killing Tammy Tuttle.

He wanted to press his fingers against the pulse point in her neck and not feel a thing.

Lily heard moaning, then a series of gasping curses that seemed to go on forever. Those curses sounded strange, long and drawn out. Then she heard crying. Crying?

No, she wasn't crying. Nor was she cursing. She felt movement, but it wasn't tossing her around; it was just there, all around her, subtle, faintly pulsing.

Simon. Where was Simon?

She opened her eyes slowly, not really wanting to because her head already hurt and she feared it would crack open when she opened her eyes.

There was a woman moaning again. Crying, then more of those soft, slurred curses.

It was Charlotte. Lily remembered now. She'd shot Charlotte, but she was still alive. And hurting. Lily at least felt some satisfaction. If her head hadn't hurt quite so badly, she would have smiled. She hadn't saved herself or Simon, but she had managed to inflict some damage.

She moved her head a little bit. There was a brief whack of pain, but she could handle it. She saw that she was sprawled in a wide leather seat, some sort of belt strapping her in. It cut into her belly and didn't hurt much, just a little tug, and that was a relief.

She saw Simon was seated next to her. He was strapped in, too. She realized then that he was holding her hand on top of his leg. He was looking toward Charlotte.

"Simon."

He made no sudden movement, just slowly turned his head to look down at her. He smiled, actually smiled, and said, "Shit, I knew I should have left you at home."

"And miss all this excitement? No way. I'm so glad you're alive. Where are we?"

"We're about thirty thousand miles up, a private jet, I'd say. How are you doing, sweetie?"

"I don't feel much like a sweetie right now. We're in an airplane? So that's that funny feeling, like we're in some sort of moving cocoon. Oh, dear, I guess maybe we're on our way to Sweden?"

"I guess it's possible, but why did you say it like you already knew."

"When those guys were chasing me down the beach, they shouted to me. They're foreign, very stilted English, Swedish, I think. I thought then that Mr. Olaf Jorgenson had gotten tired of waiting to have things done for him."

"You're right about their being Swedish." He was silent for a moment, then said, "You said you were running down the beach to get away from them?"

She told him what had happened, finding the trail back up, finding him unconscious, and then about Charlotte.

"If Charlotte hadn't been there, we would have gotten away and I would have moved us to the Eureka jail, no visitors allowed."

He picked up her hand and held it. "That crying and cursing—it's Charlotte Frasier. The pilot, who also seems to be a medic, has been working on her. You shot her through her right arm. Pity, but she'll be all right. Before you came awake, she was screaming that you were an ingrate, after all she'd done for you. She said she was going to kill you herself." He didn't add that she'd punctuated everything she said with the foulest language he'd heard in a long time.

She was thoughtful for a long moment, then said, "Are you all right?"

"Yes, just a slight headache now. How's your head?"

"Hurts."

"Ah, they see we're awake. Here comes Mr. Alpo Viljo. No, I'm not making it up, his name is Alpo. Sounds Swedish to me. He's an enforcer, a bodyguard maybe. I've never run into a real Swedish bad-ass before. From what I've heard, he's the one who smacked his pistol butt against your head."

Alpo Viljo was indeed one of the men who'd chased her on the beach near the cemetery. He was even bigger up close, but really out of shape, his belly hanging over his belt, unlike most of the Scandinavian people she'd met. At least he was blond and blue-eyed. Had to be some Viking blood in there somewhere.

He didn't say anything, just stood there, his arms crossed over his chest, staring down at her.

Lily said, "What's your partner's name?"

He started, as if he wasn't sure he understood her, then said in his stilted, perfectly understandable English, "His name is Nikki. He's a mean man. Do not do anything to piss him off."

"Where are we going, Mr. Viljo?"

"That is none of your business."

"Why is Mr. Olaf Jorgenson bringing us to Sweden?"

He just shook his head at her, grunted, turned, and walked back to the front of the cabin, where Charlotte Frasier was still muttering a curse every little while.

"You got that, Lily? No pissing off Nikki. As for Alpo, I think he likes you. You do look like a princess, and maybe Alpo's a romantic man. But don't count on it, okay?"

She had to grin, even though it hurt her head to move her mouth. She looked out the window at the mountains and canyons of white clouds. She said as she turned back to face him, "Simon, I really do like your hair. Even messed up, it's cool the way it curls at your neck. Long, but not too long. Sexy."

"Lily," he said, leaning closer, his voice very low, "you're not thinking straight at the moment. I want you to close your eyes and try to sleep."

"I think that's probably a very good idea. All right. Maybe I could have some aspirins first?"

Simon called out to Alpo Viljo, and soon Lily was downing a couple of aspirin and a very large glass of water. She gave him a silly grin as her eyes closed.

And in that exact moment, Simon knew it was all over for him. He'd met a woman to trust, a woman loyal to her bones. She sent his feelings right off the scale. His princess, all delicate and soft and pale as milk—well, not right now, since she was still damp from the rain, her clothes torn and splattered with mud, and that hair of hers, all limp and tangled around her head; it was his opinion that she looked superb.

What was a man to do?

He eased a small airplane pillow between her belly and the seat belt. He leaned back against the seat and closed his own eyes.

Lily awoke thinking of her brother, knowing he must be frantic. Surely Hoyt and Dillon knew they'd been taken.

But did they have any idea where? And, for that matter, why had they been kept alive at all?

She looked over at Simon's seat. It was empty. He was gone. But where?

She heard a man's deep voice say in halting English right next to her ear, "You eat now."

Nikki eased himself down into Simon's seat. He was holding a tray on his lap. It was the man who'd shouted to her on the beach, the man Alpo had said was mean.

"Where's Simon?"

The big man just shook his head. "Not your worry. Eat now."

She said very slowly, very deliberately, "No, I won't do anything until I see Simon Russo."

Nikki cupped his big hand around the back of her neck and dragged her head back. He picked up a glass of something that looked like iced coffee without the ice and forced her to drink it. She struggled, choked, the liquid spilling down her chin and onto her clothes, soaking in, smelling like coffee and something else. Something like pills went down her throat. She felt dizzy even before Nikki let go of her neck. "Why did you do that?"

"We land soon. Officials here. We want you quiet. Too bad you did not eat. Too thin."

"Where's Simon, you son of a bitch?" But she knew the words didn't sound right coming out of her mouth. She wished she'd eaten, too. She heard her stomach growl even as she fell away into a very empty blankness.

24

Special Agent Aaron Briggs, neck size roughly twenty-one inches, biceps to match, a gold tooth shining like a beacon in his habitual big smile, nodded from behind the counter at agents Lowell and Possner. Both agents were dressed casually in jeans, sweaters, and jackets, trying to appear like ordinary customers looking at frames and photo albums.

It was two o'clock, on the dot.

Savich was in the back. Aaron knew he had his SIG Sauer ready, knew he wanted Tammy Tuttle so bad he could taste it. Aaron wanted her, too. Dead was what Tammy Tuttle needed to be, for the sake of human beings everywhere, particularly young teenage boys. He'd listened to every word Dillon Savich had said on the flight up here. He knew agents who'd seen the wild-eyed guy in Antigua who'd slit Virginia Cosgrove's throat, agents who couldn't explain what they'd seen and heard. He felt a ripple of fear in his belly, but he told himself that soon she'd be dead, all that inexplicable stuff he'd heard she'd done down in the airport in Antigua would then be gone with her.

The bell over the shop door sounded as the door opened. In walked Tammy Tuttle, wrapped up in a thick, unbelted wool coat that hung loose on her. Aaron put out his big smile with its shining gold tooth and watched her walk toward him. He could feel the utter focus of agents Possner and Lowell from where he stood, his SIG Sauer not six inches from his right hand, just beneath the counter.

She was pale, too pale, no makeup on her face, and there was something about her that jarred, something that wasn't quite right.

Aaron was the best retail undercover agent in the Bureau, bar none, with the reputation that he could sell a terrorist a used olive-green Chevy Chevette, and he turned on all his charm. He said, "Hi, may I help you, miss?"

Tammy was nearly leaning against the counter now. She wasn't very tall. She bent toward him and his eyes never left her face as she said, "Where's the other guy? You know, that little twerp who spells Teddi with an 'i'?"

"Yea, ain't that a hoot? Teddi with an 'i.' Well, Teddi said he had a bellyache—he's said that before—and called me to cover for him. Me, I think he drank too much last night at the Night Cave Tavern. You ever been there? Over on Snow Street?"

"No. Get my photos, now."

"Your name, miss?"

"Teresa Tanner."

"No problem," Aaron said and slowly turned to look in the built-in panels, sectioned off by letter of the alphabet. Under *T,* he found Teresa Tanner's envelope third in the slot, which was exactly where he'd placed it himself an hour before. He picked up the envelope with her name on it, was slowly turning back to her, knowing Savich was ready for him to drop to the floor so he'd have a clear shot at her, when suddenly he heard a hissing sound, loud, right in his ear, and he froze. Yes, a hiss, like a snake, right next to him, too close, too close, right next to his neck, and its fangs would sink deep into his skin and...

No, his imagination was going nuts on him, but there it was again. Aaron forgot to fall to the floor so Savich could have his shot. He grabbed his SIG Sauer from beneath the counter, brought it up fast, just like he knew Possner and Lowell were doing, and whipped around. The photo envelope was suddenly in her hand; he didn't know how she'd gotten it, but there it was, and then both Tammy Tuttle and the envelope were gone. Just gone.

He heard Savich yell, "Get out of the way, Aaron! Move!"

But he couldn't. It was like he was nailed to the spot. Savich was trying to shove him aside, but he resisted, he simply had to resist, not let him by. He saw a harsh, bright glow of fire in the corner of the shop, smelled burning plastic, harsh and foul, and heard Agent Possner scream. Oh God, the place was on fire, no, just a part of it, but it was mainly Agent Possner. She was on fire—her hair, her eyebrows, her jacket, and she was screaming, slapping at herself. Flames filled her hair, bright and hot and orange as a summer sun.

Agent Aaron Briggs shoved Savich aside and started running, yelling as he ran toward Possner.

Agent Lowell was turning to Possner, not understanding, and when he saw the flames, he tackled her. They fell to the floor of the shop, knocking over a big frame display, and he was slapping at her burning hair with his hands. Aaron jerked off his sweater as he ran toward them, knocking frame and album displays out of the way.

Savich was around the counter, running toward the door, his gun drawn. Aaron saw him but didn't understand. Didn't he care that Possner was on fire? He heard a gunshot, a high, single pop, then nothing. Suddenly the flames were out. Possner was sobbing, in the fetal position on the floor, Lowell's shirt wrapped around her head, and Aaron saw that Lowell was all right, no burns that Aaron could see. He had his cell phone out, calling for backup, calling for an ambulance. And Aaron realized that his fingers looked normal. He thought he'd seen them burned, just like he'd seen Possner burned.

Savich was running, searching through the streets. There weren't that many folk around, no tourists at all, it being fall and much too chilly for beach walks in Bar Harbor. He held his SIG at his side and made a grid in his mind. He'd studied the street layout. Where would she go? Where had she come from?

Then he saw her long, dark blue wool coat, thick and heavy, flapping around a corner just half a block up Wescott. He nearly ran down an old man, apologized but didn't slow. He ran, holding his SIG Sauer against his side, hearing only his own breathing. He ran around the corner and stopped dead in his tracks. The alley was empty except for that thick wool coat. It lay in a collapsed pile against a brick wall at the back of the alley.

Where was she? He saw the narrow, wooden door, nearly invisible along the alley wall. When he got to it, he realized it was locked. He raised his SIG Sauer and fired into the lock. Two bullets dead on and the lock shattered. He was inside, crouched low, his gun steady, sweeping the space. It was very dim, one of the naked bulbs overhead, burned out. He blinked to adjust his vision and knew he was in grave danger. If Tammy was hidden in here, she could easily see his silhouette against the streetlight behind him and could nail him.

He realized he was in a storeroom. There were barrels lining the walls, shelves filled with boxes and cans, paper goods. The floor was wooden and it creaked. The place was really old. It was dead quiet, not even any rats around.

He swept over the room, hurrying because he didn't believe she'd stayed in here, no, she'd go through the door at the far end of the storeroom. It just wasn't in Tammy's nature to hide and wait.

He opened the door and stared into a bright, sunlit dining room filled with a late-lunch crowd. He saw a kitchen behind a tall counter on the far side of the dining room, smoke from the range rising into the vents, exits to the left leading to bathrooms, and a single front door that led out to the sidewalk. He stepped into the room. He smelled roast beef and garlic. And fresh bread.

Slowly the conversations thinned out, then stopped completely, everyone gaping at the man who was in a cop stance, swinging a gun slowly around the room, looking desperate, looking like he wanted to kill someone. A woman screamed. A man yelled, "Here, now!"

"What's going on here?"

This last was from a huge man with crew-cut white hair, a white apron stained with spaghetti sauce, coming around the kitchen counter to Savich's left, carrying a long, curved knife. The smell of onions wafted off the knife blade.

"Hey, fellow, is this a holdup?"

Savich slowly lowered his gun. He couldn't believe what he was seeing, just couldn't believe that he'd come through a dank storeroom into a café and scared a good twenty people nearly to death. Slowly, he reholstered his gun. He pulled out his FBI shield, walked to the man with the knife, stopped three feet away, and showed it to him. He said in a loud voice, "I'm sorry to frighten everyone. I'm looking for a woman." He raised his voice so every diner in the big room could hear. "She's mid-twenties, tall, light hair, very pale. She has only one arm. Did she come in here? Through the storeroom door, just like I did?"

There were no takers. Savich checked the bathrooms, then realized Tammy was long gone. She might have remained hidden in the storeroom, knowing he'd feel such urgency he'd burst into the café. He apologized to the owner and walked out the front door.

In that moment, standing on the Bar Harbor sidewalk, Savich could swear that he heard a laugh—a low, vicious laugh that made the hair on his arms stand up. There was no one there, naturally. He felt so impotent, so completely lost that he was hearing her in his mind.

Savich walked slowly back to Hamlet's Pics. When he got there, he stood a moment outside the shop, incredulous. There'd been mayhem when he'd burst out of there. But now there were no cop cars, no ambulance, no fire engines. Everything was quiet, nothing seemed to be out of the ordinary.

He walked into the photo shop. There were three agents standing on the far side of the shop just staring down, talking quietly among themselves.

Agent Possner wasn't burned. There was no sign that there had ever been a fire in Hamlet's Pics. Agents Briggs, Lowell, and Possner stared back at him.

Savich walked out. He sat down on a wooden bench on the sidewalk just outside the photo shop and put his head in his hands.

For the first time, he thought the FBI needed to assign someone else to catch this monster. He'd failed. Twice now, he'd failed.

He felt a hand on his shoulder and slowly raised his head to see Teddi Tyler standing over him. "I'm sorry, man. She must really be something to get past you guys."

"Yeah," Savich said, and he felt just a shade better. "She's something. We'll get her, Teddi. I just don't know how as of yet."

She was still somewhere in Bar Harbor with Marilyn, she had to be. He got slowly to his feet. He had to get a huge manhunt organized.

In that instant, he realized that even if they didn't find her, she had every intention of finding him. She would hunt him down, not the other way around. And the good Lord knew, he was much easier to find.

GOTHENBURG, SWEDEN

It was cold, so bloody cold Lily didn't think she could stand it. Strange thing was that she knew she wasn't really conscious, that she didn't really know what was happening or where she was, but her body just kept shuddering, convulsing with the cold. The cold was penetrating her bones, and she felt every shake, every shudder.

Then, suddenly, she felt Simon near her, no doubt it was him because she knew his scent. She already knew his damned scent, a good scent, as sexy as his hair curling at his neck. His arms were suddenly around her, and he hugged her hard against him, pulling her so close she was breathing against his neck, feeling his heart beat steady and strong against hers.

He was breathing deeply, and cursing. Really bad words that Savich had never said even when he was pissed off, which had been quite often when they were growing up. What a long time ago. Sometimes, like now, she thought as she shivered, being an adult really sucked. She pressed closer, feeling his warmth all the way to her belly. The convulsive jerks lessened, her brain began to function again.

She said against his collarbone, "Where are we, Simon? Why is it so cold? Did they leave us beside a fjord?"

His hands were going up and down her back, big hands that covered a lot of territory, and he rolled her under him so he could cover more of her.

"I guess we're in Sweden. It's sure too cold in this room for us to be in the Mediterranean near Ian's yacht. I just woke up a while ago. They drugged us. Do you remember?"

"Yes, Nikki forced something down my throat. I guess you were already under. How much time has passed?"

"A couple of hours. We're in a bedroom, and there isn't

even a heater working. The door is locked, and the bed is stripped, so we have no blankets or sheets. I didn't realize you were so cold until just a minute ago. Are you warming up now?"

"Oh yes," she said, against his neck, "definitely better."

He was silent for a long time, listening to her breathe, feeling her relax as she grew warmer. He cleared his throat and said, "Lily, I know this is an awfully unusual place and perhaps even a somewhat strange time to mention this, but I have to be honest here. You didn't do well picking your first two husbands. I'm thinking that you need a sort of consultant who could help you develop a whole new set of criteria before you try a third husband."

She raised her head, saw his bristly chin in the dim light, and said only, "Maybe, but I'm still married to the second one."

"Not for much longer. Tennyson is soon to be only another very bad chapter in your history. Then he'll be a memory, and you'll be ready to begin work with your consultant."

"He's scary, Simon. He married me to get to my paintings. He fed me depressants. He probably tried to kill me by cutting the brake lines in the Explorer. He's a very bad chapter, maybe the biggest, baddest yet, and my history isn't all that long. It's not particularly good for the soul to have both Jack Crane and Tennyson Frasier in your life."

"You'll divorce Tennyson just like you did Jack Crane. Then we'll figure out these new criteria together."

"You want to be my marriage consultant?"

"Well, why not?"

"I don't even know your educational background or your experience in this area."

"We can discuss that later. Tell me about your first husband."

"All right. His name is Jack Crane. He was even worse

than Tennyson. He knocked me around when I was pregnant with Beth. The first and last time. I called Dillon and he was there in a flash, and he beat Jack senseless. Loosened three of his perfect white teeth. Cracked two ribs. Two black eyes and a swollen jaw. Then Dillon taught me how to fight so if he ever came around again, I could take care of him myself."

"Did he ever come around after you divorced him so you could beat him up?"

"No, dammit, he didn't. I don't think he was scared of me. He was scared Dillon would get every FBI agent in Chicago on him and he'd be dead meat. You know, Simon, I don't think having a consultant to select new criteria would help. You can be sure that I thought long and hard about Tennyson, given that Jack was a wife beater."

"You didn't think long enough or hard enough. You have trouble with criteria, Lily, and that's why you need a consultant, to keep your head screwed on straight, to see things properly."

"Nope, it's more than that. I'm simply just rotten at picking men. Your counseling me wouldn't work, Simon. Besides that, I don't need you. I've decided that I'm never going to get married again. So I don't need to consult you or anyone else about it."

"A whole lot of men aren't anything like your first or second husbands. Just look at Savich. Do you think Sherlock ever has any doubts about him?"

He felt her shrug. "Dillon is rare. There are no criteria that fit him. He's just wonderful, and that's all there is to it. He was born that way. Sherlock is the luckiest woman in the world. She knows it; she told me so."

She was quiet for a moment, and he could feel her relaxing, warming up, and it was driving him nuts. He couldn't believe what he was saying to her.

She said into his neck, "You know, I'm beginning to

think that once I marry a man, he turns into Mr. Hyde. He sinks real low real fast. But I guess you'll tell me it's because of my lousy criteria, again."

"Are you saying that all guys would turn into a Mr. Hyde?"

"Could be, all except for Dillon. But you see my point here, Simon. Don't be obtuse. With both Jack and Tennyson, I didn't believe either of them was anything but what I believed them to be when I married them. I loved them, I believed they loved me, admired me, even admired my Remus cartoons. Both Jack and Tennyson would go on and on about how talented I was, how proud they were of me. And so I married them. I was happy, at least for maybe a month or two. About Jack—he did give me Beth, and because of that I will never regret marrying him." Her voice caught over her daughter's name. Just saying her name brought back horrible memories, painful memories she'd lived with for so very long. It had been so needless, so quick, and then her little girl was gone. She had to stop it, cut it off. It was in the past, it had to stay there. She pictured Beth in her mind, decked out in her Easter dress of the year before, and she'd been so cute. She'd just met Tennyson. She sighed. So much had happened and now poor Simon was caught up in all of it. And he suddenly wanted her?

She said, "You can't possibly want to consult with me on this, Simon. I think you could say we've got a situation here; we might die at any minute—no, don't try to reassure me, don't try it. You know it's very possible, and you're trying to take my mind off it, but talking about Jack and Tennyson isn't helping."

He just kept holding her and said finally, nodding against her hair, "I understand."

"Stop using that soothing voice on me. You know you're not thinking straight. You know what? I think God created

me, decided He'd let me screw up twice, and then He'd
keep me safe from further humiliations and mistakes."

"Lily, you may look like a princess—well, usually—but
what you just said, that was bullshit. I intend to make use
of some proper criteria. You'll choose really well next
time."

"Just forget it, Simon. I'm the worst matrimonial bet on
the planet. I'm warm now, so you can get off me."

He didn't really want to, but he rolled off and came up
on his elbow beside her. "This bare mattress smells new. I
can make out more of the room now. It's nice, Lily, very
nice."

"We're at Olaf's house, somewhere in Sweden."

"Probably."

"Why did..."

She let the words die in her mouth when the bedroom
door opened, sending in a thick slice of bright sunlight.
Alpo walked in, Nikki behind him. "You are awake
now?"

"Yes," Simon said, coming up to sit on the side of the
bed. "Don't you guys believe in heat? Is Olaf trying to
economize?"

"You are soft. Shut up."

Lily said, "Well, we don't have your body fat; maybe
that's the difference."

Nikki shouldered Alpo out of the way and strode to
where Simon was sitting. "You get up now. You, too," he
said to Lily. "A woman does not speak like that. I am not
fat; I am strong. Mr. Jorgenson is waiting for you."

"Ah," Lily said, "at last we get to meet the Grand
Pooh-Bah."

"What is that?" Nikki asked as he stepped back so they
could get up.

"The guy who controls everything, the one who believes
he's the big cheese," Simon said.

Alpo looked thoughtful for a moment, then nodded. "We will go see the Grand Pooh-Bah now." He said to Lily, "He will like you. He may want to paint you before he kills you."

Not a happy thought.

25

It had been nearly a whole day, and there was no sign of Tammy Tuttle or Marilyn Warluski. There'd been dozens of calls about possible sightings, all of which had to be investigated, but so far, nothing. It was the biggest manhunt in Maine's history, with more than two hundred law enforcement people involved. And always there in Savich's mind was Lily and where she was. Whether she was alive. He couldn't bear it and there was nothing he could do.

He was nearly ready to shoot himself when Jimmy Maitland called from Washington.

"Come home, Savich," he said. "You're needed here in Washington. We'll get word on Tammy sooner or later. There's nothing more you can do up there."

"She'll kill again, sir, you know it, I know it, and that's when we'll get word. She's probably already killed Marilyn."

Jimmy Maitland was silent, a thick, depressed silence. Then he said, "Yes, you're right. I also know that for the moment there's nothing more we can do about it. As for you, Savich, you're too close now. Come home."

"Is that an order, sir?"

"Yes." He didn't add that he was calling from Savich's house in Georgetown, sitting in Savich's favorite chair, bouncing Sean on his knee, Sherlock not two feet away, holding out a whiskey, neat, in one hand and a graham cracker in the other. Jimmy hoped the cracker wasn't intended for him. He needed the whiskey.

Savich sighed. "All right. I'll be back in a few hours."

If Sean had decided to talk while his father was on the phone, Jimmy would have been busted, but the kid had been quiet, just grinning at him and rubbing his knuckles over his gums. Jimmy hung up the phone, handed Sean to Sherlock, and said as she handed him the whiskey, "This is a royal mess, but at least Savich will be home sometime this evening. He's really upset, Sherlock."

"I know, I know. We'll think of something. We always do." She gave Sean the graham cracker.

Jimmy said, "Savich feels guilty, like he's the one who's failed, like the murders of all those people, including our own Virginia Cosgrove, are his fault."

"He always will. It's just the way he is."

Jimmy looked over at the baby, who was happily gumming the graham cracker. He said, "Sean reminds me of my second to oldest, Landry. He was a pistol, that one, gave me every gray hair I've got on my head. If you ever get tired of this little champ, just give me a call."

He downed his whiskey and stared for a moment at the marvelous Sarah Elliott painting hanging over the fireplace. "I've always wondered about the soldier in that painting, wondered what he was thinking at that moment when he was frozen for all time. I wonder if there was someone at home who would grieve if he died."

"Yes, it's excellent. Has Dillon kept you in the loop about Lily and Simon?"

"He told me earlier that Agent Hoyt found the flight plan for a private Gulfstream jet owned by the Waldemarsudde

Corporation that took off from Arcata airport bound for Gothenburg, Sweden. The CEO is Ian Jorgenson, son of Olaf Jorgenson, the collector we believe is involved in all this."

Sherlock nodded and said, "Did he also tell you that we think his son is a collector as well?"

"Yes," Jimmy said. "Interesting, isn't it, that Charlotte and Elcott Frasier were also taken? Or maybe they went willingly because the jig was almost up for them here. Tennyson is still in Hemlock Bay. There's not a shred of evidence yet to connect him to the attempts on Lily's life or Mr. Monk's murder, or any of the rest of it. Seems to me that Lily's husband is his parents' dupe."

"Maybe so," Sherlock said. "It doesn't matter. Lily's divorcing him. Oh yes, Dillon has already called two cop friends he has in Stockholm and Uppsala. We know that Jorgenson has a huge estate in Gothenburg called Slottsskogen, or Castle Wood. It's about halfway up the coast of Sweden on the western side. Dillon said that one of his friends, Petter Tuomo, has two brothers in the Gothenburg police. They're on it. We haven't heard anything back yet."

Jimmy said, "Good, things are moving. Does Savich have friends all over the world?"

"Just about, thank God." She sighed, kissed Sean, who was wriggling to get down, and shook her head. "Everywhere we look, there's something horrible ready to fall on our heads. We're terrified about Lily and Simon. We're praying that Olaf Jorgenson hasn't killed them."

"I can't see why he'd bother to kidnap them if he wanted them dead, Sherlock. There's got to be more going on here than we know."

GOTHENBURG, SWEDEN

An hour later, bathed, warm, and in fresh clothes, Lily and Simon preceded Alpo and Nikki down a massive oak staircase that could accommodate six well-fed people at a time.

They were led to the other side of an entrance hall that was a huge chessboard, black-and-white square slabs of marble, with three-foot-tall classic carved black-and-white marble chess pieces lined up along the walls.

They walked down a long hall, through big mahogany double doors into a room that was two stories high, every wall covered from floor to ceiling with books. There were a good half dozen library ladders. A fire burned in an exquisite white marble fireplace with an ornately carved mantel that was at least two feet wide and covered with exquisite Chinese figures. There was a large desk set at an angle in the corner. Behind the desk was a man not much older than fifty, tall, blond and blue-eyed, fit as his Viking ancestors. He was tanned, probably from days spent on the ski slopes. The man rose as Simon and Lily were brought in. He looked at them, his expression gentle and sympathetic. She drew herself up. That was nonsense, and she wouldn't underestimate him. The man nodded, and both Alpo and Nikki remained by the door.

"Welcome to Slottsskogen, Mr. Russo, Mrs. Frasier. Ah, that means Castle Wood. Our city's largest park was named after this estate many years ago. Won't you sit down?"

"What is the city?"

"Sit down. Good. I'm Ian Jorgenson. My father asked me to greet you. You both look better than you did when you arrived."

"I'm sure that's true," Lily said.

"Your English is fluent," Simon said.

"I attended Princeton University. My degree, as you might imagine, is in art history. And, of course, business."

Lily said, "Why are we here?"

"Ah, here is my father. Nikki, bring him very close so he can see Mrs. Frasier."

Lily tensed in her chair as Nikki pushed a wheelchair toward them. In the chair sat an impossibly old man, with just a few tufts of white hair sticking straight up. He looked frail, but when he raised his head, she saw brilliant blue eyes, and they were cold and sharp with intelligence. The brain in that head was not frail or fading.

"Closer," the old man said.

Nikki brought him to within inches of Lily. The old man reached out his hand and touched his fingertips to her face. Lily started to draw back, then stilled.

"I am Olaf Jorgenson, and you are Lily. I speak beautiful English because, like my son, I also attended Princeton University. Ah, you are wearing the white gown, just as I instructed. It is lovely, just as I hoped it would be. Perfect." He ran his fingers down her arm, over the soft white silk, to her wrist. "I want you to be painted in this white dress. I am pleased that those American buffoons failed to execute you and Mr. Russo."

"So are we," Lily said. "Why did they want to kill us so badly, Mr. Jorgenson?"

"Well, you see, it was my intention to let the Frasiers deal with you. I understand they bungled the job several times, for which I am now grateful. I hadn't realized what you looked like, Lily. When Ian showed me your picture, I ordered the Frasiers to stay away from you. I sent Alpo and Nikki to California to fetch you back to me. They were clumsy also, but it turned out not to matter because you, my dear, are here at last."

Lily said slowly, "I don't look like anyone special. I'm just myself." But she knew she must look like someone who mattered to him, and so she waited, holding her breath, keeping still as his fingers stroked her arm, up to her shoulder. She saw that his nails were dark and unhealthy-looking.

The old man said finally, "You look exactly like Sarah Jameson when I first met her in Paris a very long time ago, before the Great War, when the artistic community in Paris broke free and flourished. Ah yes, we enraged the staid French bourgeoisie with our endless and outrageous play, our limitless daring and debauchery. I remember the hours

we spent with Gertrude Stein. Ah, what an intelligence that
one had, her wit sharper than Nikki's favorite knife, and
such noble and impossible ideas. And there was the clever
and cruel Picasso—he painted her, worshiped her. And
Matisse, so quiet until he drank absinthe, and then he
would sing the most obscene songs imaginable as he
painted. I remember all the French neighbors cursing
through the walls when he sang.

"I saw Hemingway wagering against Braque and Sher-
wood—it was a spitting contest at a cuspidor some eight
feet away. Your grandmother kept moving the cuspidor.
Ah, such laughter and brilliance. It was the most flamboy-
ant, the most vivid time in all of history, all the major talent
of the world in that one place. It was like a zoo with only
the most beautiful, the wildest and most dangerous speci-
mens congregated together. They gave the world the greatest art ever known."

"I didn't know you were a writer or an artist," Simon
said.

"I'm neither, unfortunately, but I did try to paint, studied
countless hours with great masters and wasted many canvases. So many of my young friends wanted to paint or to
write. We were in Paris to worship the great ones, to see if
perhaps their vision, their immense talent, would rub off,
just a bit. Some of those old friends did become great; others returned to their homes to make furniture or sell stamps
in a post office. Ah, but Sarah Jameson, she was the greatest of them all. Stein corresponded with her until her death
right after World War Two."

"How well did you know my grandmother, Mr. Jorgenson?"

Olaf Jorgenson's soft voice was filled with shadows and
faded memories that still fisted around his heart, memories
he could still see clearly. "Sarah was a bit older than I, but
so beautiful, so exquisitely talented, so utterly without restraint, as hot and wild as a sirocco blowing up from the

Libyan desert. She loved vodka and opium, both as pure as she could get. The first time I saw her, another young artist, her lover, was painting her nude body, covering it with phalluses, all of them ejaculating.

"She was everything I wanted, and I grew to love her very much. But she met a man, a damned American who was simply visiting Paris, a businessman, ridiculous in his pale gray flannels, but she wanted him more than me. She left me, went back to America with him."

"That was my grandfather, Emerson Elliott. She married him in the mid-1930s, in New York."

"Yes, she left me. And I never saw her again. I began collecting her paintings during the fifties. It wasn't well known for some time that she'd willed paintings to her grandchildren, such a private family matter. Yes, she willed eight beautiful paintings to each child. I knew I wanted them all for my collection. You are the first; it is unfortunate, but we managed to gain only four of the originals before the Frasiers became convinced that you were going to leave their son, despite the drugs they were feeding you. They knew you'd take the paintings with you, so they decided to kill you, particularly since your husband was your beneficiary after your daughter's death."

"But I didn't die."

"No, you did not, but not for their lack of trying."

"You're telling me that my husband was not part of this plot?"

"No, Tennyson Frasier was their pawn. His parents' great hopes for him were dashed, but he did manage to make you his wife. It's possible he even fell in love with you, at least enough to marry you, as his parents wished."

She'd been so certain that Tennyson had been part of the plot. She asked, "Why didn't you just offer me money?"

"I knew you would turn me down, as would your siblings. You were the most vulnerable, particularly after your divorce from Jack Crane, and so I selected you."

"That's crazy. You invent this convoluted plan just to bilk me out of my grandmother's paintings?"

"Sarah's paintings belong with me, for I am the only one who can really appreciate them, know them beyond their visual message and impact, because I knew her, you see, knew her to her soul. She would talk to me about her work, what each one meant to her, what she was thinking when she was painting each one. I fed her opium, and we talked for hours. I never tired of watching her paint, of listening to her voice. She was the only woman I ever wanted in my life, the only one." He paused for a moment, frowning, and she saw pain etched into the deep wrinkles in his face. From the loss of her grandmother or from illness?

He said, his voice once again brisk, "Yes, Lily, I selected you because you were the most vulnerable, the most easily manipulated. Most important, you were alone. When you moved to Hemlock Bay, I had Ian approach the Frasiers. Tell them, Ian."

"I played matchmaker," Ian Jorgenson said and laughed. "It was infinitely satisfying when it all came together. I bought the Frasiers—simple as that. You married Tennyson, just as we planned, and his parents told him to convince you to have your Sarah Elliott paintings moved from Chicago to the Eureka Art Museum. And there our greedy Mr. Monk quickly fell in with our plans."

Simon said to the old man, "You managed to have four of them forged before I got wind of it."

Those brilliant blue eyes swung to Simon, but he sensed that the old man couldn't see him all that clearly. "You meddled, Mr. Russo. You were the one who brought us down. You found out through your sources, all that valuable information sold to them by an expatriate friend of mine who betrayed me, and then it was sold to you. But that is not your concern. If she had not betrayed me, then I would have all your paintings now, and you, Lily, would be dead. I am not certain that would have been best."

"But now you'll never get the other four," Lily said. "They're out of your reach. You won't be hanging onto those you do have very long. Surely you know that."

"You think not, my dear?" The old man laughed, then said, still wheezing, "Come, I have something to show you."

Three long corridors and five minutes later, Lily and Simon stood motionless in a climate-controlled room, staring at fourteen-foot-high walls that were covered with Sarah Elliott paintings. The collection held at least a hundred fifty paintings, maybe more.

Simon said as he stared at the paintings, slowly taking in their magnificence, "You couldn't have bought this many Sarah Elliott paintings legally. You must have looted the museums of the world."

"When necessary. Not all that difficult, most of them. Imagination and perseverance. It's taken me years, but I am a patient man. Just look at the results."

"And money," Simon said.

"Naturally," Ian Jorgenson said.

"But you can't see them," Lily said as she turned to look at Olaf Jorgenson. "You stole them because you have some sort of obsession with my grandmother, and you can't even see them!"

"I could see them all very well until about five years ago. Even now, though, I can see the graceful sweeps of her brush, shadows and sprays of color, the movement in the air itself. Her gift is unparalleled. I know each one as if I had painted it myself. I know how the subjects feel, the texture of the expressions on their faces. I can touch my fingers to a sky and feel the warmth of the sun and the wind caressing my hand. I know all of them. They are old friends. I live inside them; I am a part of them and they of me. I have been collecting them over forty years now. Since I want all of them before I die, it was time to turn to you, Lily. If I'd only known at the beginning that you were so like my Sarah, I wouldn't have allowed those fools to try to kill you. Because you are resourceful, you saved yourself. I am grateful for that."

Lily looked down at the old man sitting in his wheelchair, a beautiful hand-knitted blue blanket covering his legs. He looked like a harmless old gentleman, in his pale blue cashmere sweater over a white silk shirt with a darker blue tie. She didn't say anything. What was there to say, after all? It was crazy, all of it. And rather sad, she supposed, if one discounted the fact that he was perfectly willing to murder people who got in his way.

She looked at the walls filled with so many of her grandmother's paintings. All of them perfectly hung, grouped by the period in which they were painted. She had never seen such beauty in one room before in her life. It was her grandmother's work as she had never seen it.

She watched Simon walk slowly around the large room, studying each of the paintings, lightly touching his fingertips to some of them until he came to one that belonged to Lily. It was *The Swan Song,* Lily's own favorite. The old man lying in the bed, that beatific smile on his face, the young girl staring at him.

Olaf said, "That was the first one of yours I had copied, my dear. It was always my favorite. I knew it was at the Art Institute of Chicago, but I couldn't get to it. It was frustrating."

Simon said, "So it was the first one you stole from the Eureka Museum."

"Nothing so dramatic," Ian Jorgenson said, coming forward. He laid his hand lightly on his father's shoulder. "Mr. Monk, the curator, was quite willing to have the painting copied. He simply gave it to our artist, replacing it with a rather poor, quickly executed copy until the real copy was finished. Then they were simply switched. No one noticed, of course. You know, Mr. Russo, I had hopes for you, at least initially. You yourself own a Sarah Elliott painting. I had hoped to convince you to join me, perhaps even to sell me your painting in return for a generous price and my offer of a financially rewarding partnership in some of my business ventures."

Ian looked toward Simon and his eyes narrowed, but when he spoke, his voice was perfectly pleasant. "My father realized you wouldn't agree after Nikki and Alpo described your behavior on the long trip over here. You were in no way conciliatory, Mr. Russo. Actually, my father's desire to make use of you in his organization was the only reason we bothered to bring you to Sweden. My father wanted to test you."

"Give me a test," Simon said. "Let's just see what I would say."

"Actually, I was going to ask you to give me your Sarah Elliott painting, *The Last Rites;* it is one I greatly admire. In exchange, I would offer you your life and a chance to prove your value to me."

"I accept your offer, if, in return, you give Lily and me our freedom."

"It is just as I feared," Olaf said and sighed. He nodded to his son.

Ian looked at his hands, strong hands, and lightly buffed his fingernails on his cashmere sleeve. He said to Simon, "I look forward to killing you, Mr. Russo. I knew you could never be brought to our side, that you could never be trusted. You have interfered mightily."

Simon said, "You had your chance to get *The Last Rites,* Mr. Jorgenson. Freedom for Lily and me, but you turned it down. Let me promise you that you will never get that painting. When I die, it goes to the Metropolitan Museum of Art."

Olaf said, "I do detest making mistakes in a person's character. It is a pity, Mr. Russo."

Lily said to Ian, "Is it true that you have Rembrandt's *Night Watch* aboard your yacht?"

Ian Jorgenson raised a blond brow. "My, my, Mr. Russo

has many tentacles, doesn't he? Yes, my dear, I had it gently removed from the Rijksmuseum some ten years ago. It was rather difficult, actually. It was a gift to my wife, who died later that year. She was so pleased to look at it in her last days."

The old man laughed, then coughed. Nikki handed him a handkerchief, and he coughed into it. Lily thought she saw blood.

Ian said, "As my father said, the Art Institute of Chicago is a difficult place, more difficult than even I wished to deal with. In the past ten years they've added many security measures that make removal of art pieces very challenging. But most important, my only contact, a curator there, lost his job five years ago. It was a pity. I didn't know what to do until you moved to that ridiculous little town on the coast of California. This Hemlock Bay."

Olaf said, "My son and I spent many hours coming up with the right plan for you, Lily. Ian traveled to California, to Hemlock Bay. What a quaint and clever name. It was such a simple little town, generous and friendly to newcomers, such as you and your daughter, was it not? He liked the fresh salt air, the serenity of the endless stretches of beach and forest, the magnificent redwoods, and all those clever little roads and houses blended into the landscape. Who could imagine it would be so simple to find such perfect tools? The Frasiers—greedy, ambitious people—and here they had a son who would be perfect for you."

"Did they murder my daughter?"

26

"You think the Frasiers killed your daughter?" Ian Jorgenson repeated, his voice indifferent. He shrugged. "Not that I know of." Lily suddenly hated him.

Olaf said, "I know you felt sorrow over your daughter's death. But what does it matter to you now who is responsible?"

"Whoever struck her down deserves to die for it."

"Killing them won't bring back your little girl," Ian said, frowning at her. "We, in Sweden, actually in most of Europe, do not believe in putting people to death. It is barbaric."

What is wrong with this picture? Simon wondered, staring at Ian Jorgenson.

"No," Lily said, "it won't bring Beth back, but it would avenge her. No one who kills in cold blood should be allowed to continue breathing the same air I breathe."

"You are harsh," said Olaf Jorgenson.

"You are not harsh, sir? You, who order people murdered?"

Olaf Jorgenson laughed, a low, wheezy sound thick with phlegm, perhaps with blood.

"No, I always do only what is necessary, nothing more. Vengeance is for amateurs. Now, you do not have to wonder again if the Frasiers killed your daughter. They did not. They told me that they'd been concerned because your daughter, by ill chance, had seen some e-mails on Mr. Frasier's computer, communications that she shouldn't have seen. They, of course, assured the child that the messages were nonsense, nothing important, nothing to even think about."

So that was why Beth had been moody, withdrawn, that last week. Why hadn't her daughter come to her, told her, at least asked her about what she had seen? But she hadn't, and then she'd been killed.

Olaf Jorgenson continued, "I understand it was an accident, one of your American drunk drivers who was too afraid to stop and see what he'd done."

Lily felt tears clog her throat. She'd happily left Chicago and Jack Crane and moved to a charming coastal town. She couldn't believe what it had brought them.

Simon took her hand, squeezed her fingers. He knew she was feeling swamped with the memories of her loss and despair. She raised her head to look at Olaf Jorgenson and said, "What do you intend to do with us?"

"You, my dear, I will have painted by a very talented artist whom I've worked well with over the years. As for Mr. Russo here, as I said, I hold no hope now of bringing him into my fold. He is much too inflexible in his moral code. It is not worth the risk. Also, he seems taken with you, and I can't have that. Isn't that interesting? You've known each other for such a short time."

"He just wants to be my consultant," Lily said.

Simon smiled.

"He wants you in bed," Ian said. "Or maybe you're already lovers and that's why he's helping you."

"Don't be crude," Olaf said, frowning toward his son, then added, "Yes, I fear that Mr. Russo must take a nice, long boat ride with Alpo and Nikki here. We still have two lovely canals left from those built back in the early seventeenth century by our magnificent Gustav. Yes, Mr. Russo, you and my men here will visit one of the canals this very night. It's getting cold now, not many people will be about at midnight."

Simon said, "I can't say I find that an appealing way to spend the evening. What do you intend to do with the Frasiers?"

Olaf Jorgenson said to Lily, not to Simon, "At the moment they are my honored guests. They accompanied you here since they knew they could not remain in California. Your law enforcement, and so on. They expect to receive a lot of money from me. In addition, Mr. Frasier already has very nice bank accounts in Switzerland. They are prepared to spend the rest of their lives living very nicely in the south of France, I believe they said."

Lily said, "After you've painted me, then what will happen?"

He smiled then, showing her his very beautiful white teeth, likely false. "Yes, yes, I know I am an old man, but I do not have much longer to live. I want you with me until it is my time. I was hoping, perhaps, that you would see some advantage in marrying me."

"Oh, is that why I'm wearing white? To put me in the mood?"

"You want manners," Ian said. He was angry, she could see it as he stepped toward her only to stop when he felt his father's hand on his forearm. Ian shook off his father's hand and said, "She is disrespectful. She needs to see what an honor it would be to be your wife!"

Olaf only shook his head. He even smiled again as he said to Lily, "No, my dear, you are wearing white because that is a copy of the dress I last saw your grandmother wearing in Paris. It was the day she left with Emerson Elliott. The day I believed my world had collapsed."

"You are good at copies, aren't you?" Lily said. "I am not my grandmother, you foolish old man."

Ian struck her across the face. Simon didn't say a word, just hurled himself at Ian Jorgenson, slamming his fist into his jaw, then whirled back and kicked him in the kidney.

"Stop!" It was Nikki and he'd pulled a gun, which was aimed at Simon.

Simon gave him a brief bow, straightened his shirt, and walked away.

Ian slowly raised himself to his feet, grimacing in pain. "I will go with Nikki and Alpo this evening. I will be the one to kill you."

"All this," Simon said, marveling as he turned to Olaf Jorgenson, "and you raised a coward, too."

Lily lightly placed her hand on Simon's arm. She was terrified.

She said to Olaf, "Even if I found you remotely acceptable in matrimonial terms, sir, I couldn't marry you. I'm married to Tennyson Frasier."

The old man was silent.

"I don't ever wish to marry again, at least until I've seriously reconsidered my criteria. I don't think there's any way in the world that you would ever fit them. I'm married anyway, so it doesn't matter, does it?"

Still the old man was silent, thoughtfully looking at her. Then he slowly nodded. He said, "I will be back shortly."

"What are you going to do, Father?"

"I do not believe in bigamy. It is immoral. I'm going to make Lily a widow. Nikki, take me to my library." As Nikki wheeled him out of the huge room, Lily and Simon saw him pull a small, thick black book from his sweater pocket. They watched him thumb through it as he disappeared from their view.

"He's completely mad," Lily whispered.

WASHINGTON, D.C.

Savich walked through the front door of his home, hugged his wife, kissed her, and said, "Where's Sean?"

"At your mom's house—babbling, gumming everything in sight, and happy. I left your mom a two-box supply of graham crackers."

Savich was too tired, too depressed to smile. He raised an eyebrow in question.

She said, without preamble, "Both the Bureau and I agree with your plan. Tammy wants you, Dillon. She's focused on you. There's no doubt in anyone's mind that she will come here. I took Sean to your mother's because we don't want him in harm's way.

"Right before you got home, Jimmy Maitland issued a statement to the media that you were no longer the lead investigator in the manhunt for Tammy Tuttle. Aaron Briggs has replaced you as the lead. He said you were urgently needed to gather vital evidence in the Wilbur Wright case, the cult leader responsible for the heinous murders of a sheriff and two deputies in Flowers, Texas. You're traveling to Texas on Friday to begin working with local law enforcement."

He hugged her close and said against her hair, "You and Mr. Maitland got it done really fast. So I'm to leave on Friday? Today is Tuesday."

"Yes. It gives Tammy plenty of time to get here."

"Yes, it does." Savich streaked his fingers through his hair, making it stand straight up. "Have you got Gabriella safely stashed away?"

"Actually, she's at your mom's house during the day. Both of them are safe. She said she doesn't want to miss a single step that Sean takes."

But Sean's parents were missing his first steps, Savich thought. He felt brittle with rage, bowed with his failure.

He said finally, knowing that she wouldn't like or accept

it, "She's scary, Sherlock. I don't want her near you, either."

She nodded slowly as she stepped against him, pressing her face to his neck. "I know, Dillon, but I couldn't think of anything else. Jimmy Maitland told me you'd balk because of me and Sean, and I knew I couldn't allow that. Now we've gotten both Gabriella and Sean to safety. Don't even think you can send me away. We're in this together, we always have been, and we're going to get her. We have the advantage here because we control the scene. We can act and plan, we can be ready for her, not just wait to react to something she does."

He held her tightly. He wondered if she could smell his fear, there was such a huge well of it. Savich kissed her and hugged her until she squeaked. "We've got to be ready for her, Sherlock, and I've got some ideas about that. I've been thinking about this for a good while now."

"Like what?" she asked, pulling back, looking up at him.

"She has the power to create illusions, to make people see what she wants them to see. Whether it's some kind of magician's trick or a strange ability that's inside her sick brain, the end result is the same."

He let her go and began pacing. He looked at his grandmother's painting over the fireplace, then turned and said, "You believe that she can't fool me if I'm close enough to her. If we can get her here in the house, I'll be close enough."

He came back to her, smiled down at her while he ran his fingers through her curly hair.

"Kiss me, Dillon."

"Can I do more than just kiss you?"

"Oh yes."

"Good. Dinner can wait."

All the world can wait, Sherlock thought, as she held him to her. "After dinner, I want us to go to the gym. It'll relieve all the stress."

"You got it. But if you have much stress after I'm through with you, I'll have to reassess my program."

And he laughed, actually laughed.

GOTHENBURG, SWEDEN

Bloated clouds hung low, blotting out the moon and stars. They would bring rain, perhaps even snow, before the night was over.

Simon was sitting low in a small boat, his hands tied behind him. Alpo was rowing and Nikki was beside him, the gun pressed against his side. In a boat trailing them were Ian Jorgenson and a small man Simon hadn't seen before who was rowing.

The canal was wide, the town of Gothenburg on either side casting ghostly shadows in the dark light. There was just the rippling of the oars going through the water, smooth and nearly soundless.

The canal twisted to the right, and the buildings became fewer. There were no people that Simon could see.

He very nearly had the knot on his hands pulled loose. Just a few more minutes and his hands would be free, and a little more time after that to get circulation back into his hands and fingers.

If he had just a bit more time, he had a chance. But the buildings were thinning out too much. They could kill him at any time without worry.

He worked the knot, rubbing his wrists raw, but that didn't matter. His blood helped loosen the strands of hemp.

"Stop!"

It was Ian Jorgenson. His small boat pulled up beside theirs.

"Here. This is fine. Give me the gun, Nikki, I want to put a bullet through this bastard. Then you can put him in that bag and sink him to the bottom."

Simon could feel Nikki leaning toward Ian to give him the gun. It was his last chance. Simon jumped up, slammed against Alpo, and dove at the small man in the other boat. Both boats careened wildly, the men shouting and cursing. As Simon hit the water, he heard a splash behind him, then another.

God, there was nothing colder on earth than this damned water. What did he expect? He was in Sweden in November, for God's sake. He wondered how long he had before hypothermia set in and he died. He didn't fight it, just let himself sink, quickly, quietly, trying not to think of how cold he was, how numb his legs felt. He had to get free or he would die, from the frigid water or from a bullet, it didn't matter. He worked his hands until he hit the bottom of the canal, twisted away from where he thought the other men were. He swam as best he could with only his feet in the opposite direction, back down the canal, veering toward the side, back to where there was more shelter and a way to climb out of the water.

He was running out of breath and he was freezing. There wasn't much more time. There was no hope for it. He kicked upward until his head broke the surface. He saw Nikki and Ian both in the water, speaking, but softly, listening for him. Damn, his hands weren't free yet.

He heard a shout. They'd spotted him. He saw Alpo rowing frantically toward him. He didn't stop to get Ian or Nikki out of the water, just came straight toward Simon.

At last his hands slipped free from the frayed hemp. He felt his blood slimy on his wrists, mixing with the water. It should have stung like a bitch, but he didn't feel much of anything. His hands were numb.

He dove just as he saw Alpo raise a gun and fire. The frigid water splashed up in Simon's face, close. Too close. He dove at least ten feet down and swam with all his strength toward the side of the canal.

When he came up, his lungs on fire, the boat was nearly

on him. The second boat was behind him and now all the men were in it, searching the black water for a sign of him.

Ian shouted, "There he is! Get him!"

Gunshots split the water around him.

Then he heard the sirens, at least three of them.

He went under again, deeper this time, and changed direction to swim toward the sound of those sirens. It was so cold his teeth hurt.

When he couldn't hold his breath for another second, simply couldn't bear the water any longer, he came up as slowly as he could, his head quietly breaking the surface.

He just couldn't believe what he was seeing. A half dozen police cars screeched to a stop on the edge of the canal, not ten feet from him. Guns were drawn, men were shouting in Swedish, flashing lights on Ian and his crew.

A man reached out his hand and pulled Simon out of the canal. "Mr. Russo, I believe?"

27

Lily walked beside Olaf's wheelchair back to the main entrance hall with its huge black-and-white marble chessboard, its three-foot-tall pieces lining opposite sides of the board, in correct position, ready to be moved.

He motioned for a manservant to leave his chair right in the middle of the chessboard, squarely on the white king five square. He looked at Lily, who stood beside the white king, then glanced down at the watch on his veined wrist and said, "You didn't eat much dinner, Lily."

"No," she said.

"He's dead by now. Accept it."

Lily looked down at the white queen. She wondered how heavy the chess piece was. Could she heft it up and hurl it at that evil old man? She looked toward the silent manservant, dressed all in white like a hospital orderly, and said, "Why don't you get an electric wheelchair? It's ridiculous for him to push you everywhere."

Olaf said again, his voice sharper now, not quite so gentle, "He's dead, Lily."

She looked at him now and said, "No, I don't believe he is, but you soon will be, won't you?"

"When you speak like that, I know you aren't at all like your grandmother, despite your look of her. Don't be disrespectful and mean-spirited, Lily. I don't like it. I'm quite willing to present you the Frasiers' heads on platters. What more can I offer you?"

"You can let Simon and me leave with my grandmother's paintings."

"Don't be a child. Listen to me, for this is important. In a wife I require obedience. Ian, I'm sure, will help me teach you manners, teach you to curb your tongue."

"It's a new millennium, Olaf, and you're a very old man. Even if you died within the week, I would refuse to remain here."

He banged his fist on the wheelchair hard, making it lurch. "Dammit, you will do what you're told. Do you need to see your lover's body before you will let go of him? Before you accept that he really is dead?"

"He's not my lover. He just wants to be my consultant."

"Not your lover? I don't believe you. You spoke of him as if he were some sort of hero, able to overcome any obstacle. That is nonsense."

"Not in Simon's case." She wished that she really did believe him capable of just about anything, even if it was nonsense. But she was hoping frantically that Simon wasn't dead. He'd promised her, and he wouldn't break his word. When they'd taken him but two hours before, he'd lightly cupped her face in his hands and whispered, "I will be all right. Count on it, Lily."

And she'd licked her dry lips, felt fear for him moving deep and hard inside her, and whispered back, "I've been thinking about those new criteria, Simon. I admit I sure do need help when it comes to men."

He patted her cheek. "You got it."

She'd watched the three men take him out of that beautiful grand mansion, watched the door close behind them, heard the smooth wheels of Olaf Jorgenson's chair across the huge chessboard foyer.

Olaf brought her back, saying, "You will forget him. I will see to it."

She glanced at the two bodyguards, standing utterly silent. They'd both come with them from the dining room.

"Do you know I have an incredible brother? His name is Dillon Savich. He doesn't paint like our grandmother; he whittles. He creates beautiful pieces."

"A boy's hobby, not worth much of anything to anyone with sophistication and discrimination. And you spend your time drawing cartoons. What is the name? Remus?"

"Yes, I draw political cartoons. His name is No Wrinkles Remus. He's utterly immoral, like you, but I've never yet seen him want to murder someone." She paused for a moment, smiled at the motionless manservant. "I'm really quite good at cartooning. Isn't it interesting the way Grandmother's talent found new ways to come out in us, her grandchildren?"

"Sarah Elliott was unique. There will never be another like her."

"I agree. There will never be another cartoonist like me either. I'm unique, too. And what are you, Olaf? Other than an obsessed old man who has had too much money and power for far too long? Tell me, have you ever done anything worthwhile in your blighted life?"

His face turned red; his breathing became labored. The manservant looked frightened. The two bodyguards stood straighter and tensed, their eyes darting from Lily to their boss.

She just couldn't stop herself. Rage and impotence roiled inside her, and she hated this wretched monster. Yes, let him burst a vessel with his rage; let him stroke out. It was payback for all that he'd done to her, to Simon. "I know what you are—you're one of those artists manqué, one of those pathetically sad people who were just never good enough, who could only be hangers-on, always on the outside looking in. You weren't even good enough to be a pale imitation, were you? I'll bet my grandmother thought you were pitiful, yes, pathetic. I'll bet she told you what she thought of you, didn't she?"

"Shut up!" He began cursing her, but it was in Swedish and she couldn't understand. The bodyguards were even more on edge now, surprised at what the old man, their boss, was yelling, the spittle spewing out of his mouth.

Lily didn't shut up. She just talked over him, yelled louder than he was yelling, "What did she say to you that last day when she left with my grandfather? Because you went to her, didn't you? Begged her to marry you instead of Emerson, but she refused, didn't she? Did she laugh at you? Did she tell you that she would even take that woman-hating Picasso before you? That you had the talent of a slug and you disgusted her, all your pretenses, your affectations? What did she say to you, Olaf?"

"Damn you, she said I was a spoiled little boy who had too much money and would always be a shallow, selfish man!" He was wheezing, nearly incoherent, flinging himself from side to side.

Lily stared at him. "You even remember the exact words my grandmother said to you? That was more than sixty-five years ago! My God, you were pathetic then, and you're beyond that now. You're frightening."

"Shut up!" Olaf seemed feverish now, his frail, veined hands clutching the arms of the wheelchair, his bent and twisted fingers showing white from the strain.

The manservant was leaning over him now, speaking urgently in his ear. She could hear the words, but he spoke in Swedish.

Olaf ignored him, shook him off. Lily said, smiling, "Do

you know that Sarah loved Emerson so much she was always painting him? That there are six of his portraits in our mother's private collection?"

"I knew," he screamed at her, "of course I knew! You think I would ever want a portrait of that philistine? That damned fool knew nothing of what she was. He couldn't have understood or appreciated what she was! I could, but she left me. I begged her, on my knees in front of her, but it didn't matter—she left me!"

He was trembling so badly she thought he would fall from his wheelchair.

Suddenly, Olaf yelled something in Swedish to his manservant. The man grabbed the handles and began pushing the wheelchair across the huge chessboard.

"Hey, Olaf, why are you running away from me? Don't you like hearing what I have to say? I'll bet it's only the second time anyone's told you the truth. Don't you want to marry me anymore?"

She heard him yelling, but she couldn't make out the words; they were garbled, incoherent, some English, some Swedish. He sounded like a mad old man, beyond control. What was he going to do? Why had he left? She stood on the king one square, leaning against the beautifully carved heavy piece, shuddering with reaction, wondering what she'd driven him to with her contempt, her ridicule. She couldn't run because she didn't doubt the two bodyguards would stop her.

Where was the manservant taking him? What had he said to him? The two bodyguards were speaking low, so she couldn't really hear them. They stared at her again, and she saw bewilderment in their eyes. She wouldn't get three steps before they were on her.

Lily's rage wilted away and was replaced with a god-awful fear. But she'd held her own. She thought of her grandmother and wondered how like her she was. They'd both faced down this man, and she was proud of what they'd done.

She stood there, her brain squirreling madly about, wondering what to do now. She didn't have time to think about it. She heard the smooth wheelchair wheels rolling across the marble floor and saw Olaf coming toward her. This time he was pushing himself, his gnarled, trembling hands on the cushioned wheel pads. His two bodyguards took a step forward. He shook his head, not even looking at them. He was staring at Lily, and there was memory in his eyes, memory of that other woman, painfully clear and vivid. She knew that what had happened that day had struck him to his very soul, maimed him, destroyed what he'd seen himself as being and becoming. And now he saw what he had become after that day so very long ago.

Lily saw madness in his eyes; it was beyond hatred, and it was aimed at her. At her and her grandmother, who was dead and beyond his vengeance. Everything that had driven him, the decades of obsession with her grandmother as the single perfect woman, all of it had exploded when Lily had pushed him to remember the events as they'd really happened, forced him to see the truth of that day Sarah Elliott told him she was leaving with another man.

He came up to within six feet of her and stopped pushing the wheels. She wondered if he could make out her outline. Or was she a vague shadow?

He spoke, his voice low and steady as he said, "I've decided I won't marry you. I have seen clearly now that you don't deserve my devotion or my admiration. You are nothing like Sarah, nothing at all." He lifted a small derringer from his lap and pointed it at her.

"The Frasiers are dead. They weren't worth anything to me alive. And now, you aren't either."

The bodyguards took a step forward, in unison.

He'd had the Frasiers killed?

Lily ran at the wheelchair, smashed into it as hard as she could and sent it over onto its side, scraping against the marble floor. Olaf was flung from the chair.

Lily didn't hesitate. She ran as fast as she could, to fall flat behind the white king. She heard two rapid shots. The king's head shattered and fragments of marble flew everywhere.

She heard Olaf yell at the bodyguards, heard their loud running steps. She stayed flat on the floor. Several shards of marble had struck her, and she felt pricks of pain, felt the sticky flow of blood down her arm, rolling beneath her bra, staining the white dress.

She heard Olaf cursing, still helpless on the floor. He was screaming at his bodyguards to tell him if he'd killed her yet.

The bodyguards shouted something, but again it was in Swedish so she didn't understand. They didn't come after her, evidently because he wanted to have this pleasure all for himself, and they knew it.

She began moving on her elbows, behind the queen now, toward the great front door, behind the bishop. She looked out toward Olaf. One of his bodyguards was bending over him, handing him his own gun.

The bodyguard picked Olaf up and set him again in his wheelchair, then turned the chair toward her. And now Olaf aimed that gun right at her.

She rolled behind the knight. She wasn't any farther than ten feet from the front doors.

"I like this game," Olaf shouted and fired. The bishop toppled, shattering as it fell, falling over her ankles. She felt a stab of pain, but she could still move her feet, thank God. She moved solidly behind the knight and stilled.

Olaf shouted again. Then he laughed. Another shot, obscenely loud in the silence, and she saw a huge chunk of marble floor, not three feet from her, spew in all directions.

He fired again and again, sending the white king careening into the queen.

Lily was on her knees behind the rook now, close to the front door.

Another shot whistled past her ear, and she flattened herself. One of the bodyguards yelled and ran toward her. Why?

Then she heard more shots, at least six of them, but they weren't from Olaf or the bodyguard; they were coming through the front door. She heard yelling, men's voices, and pounding on the door until it crashed inward.

Olaf and the bodyguards were shooting toward the door.

Lily lurched to her feet, lifted a huge shard of the bishop's white miter, ran toward Olaf, and hurled it at his wheelchair.

It hit him. Olaf, his gun firing wildly, straight up now, went over backward. His bodyguards ran as policemen fired at them from the open front door.

More gunfire. So much shouting, so much damned noise, too much. Simon was there, just behind the third policeman. He was alive.

There was sudden silence. The gun storm was over. Lily ran to Simon, hurled herself against him. His arms tightened around her.

She raised her head and smiled up at him. "I'm glad you came when you did. It was pretty dicey there for a while."

She heard Olaf screaming, spewing profanity. Then he was quiet.

Simon said in her ear, "It's over, Lily, all over. Olaf isn't going anywhere. It's time to worry about yourself. You're bleeding a little. I want you to hold still; there's an ambulance coming."

"I'm all right. It's just cuts from the flying marble. You're wet, Simon," she said. "Why are you wet?"

"I was careless. Be still."

"No, tell me. How did you get away from them? What happened?"

He realized that she just couldn't let it go, and he slowed himself, keeping his voice calm and low. "I dove into the canal to get away, but I couldn't. Then there were all sorts of cops there to pull me out of the canal and take care of Alpo, Nikki, and Ian. Nobody was killed. They're all in the local lockup. It was your brother, Lily. He called a friend in Stockholm who happened to have two brothers living here in Gothenburg. The police were watching the mansion, saw Ian and the boys stuff me in the car, called backup, and followed."

"I want to meet those brothers," she said. For the first time, she felt like smiling, and so she did, a lovely smile that was filled with hope.

28

WASHINGTON, D.C.

Late Saturday night, it was colder in Washington than it had been in Stockholm. The temperature had plummeted early in the day and the skies had opened up and sprinkled a dusting of snow all over the East Coast. Lily was finally in bed, her shoulder and back no longer throbbing from the shards of marble that had struck her. "Nothing important here—all surface pain," the Swedish doctor had said, and she'd wanted to slug him. Now she would probably have more scars.

When she'd said this on a sigh to Simon, he'd said, as he'd eased some pillows around her on the roomy first-class seat, that he liked banged-up women. The scars showed character.

"No," Lily had said as she let him ease a thin airplane blanket to her chin, "what it shows is that the woman has bad judgment."

He'd laughed as he'd kissed her. Then he'd smoothed the hair off her forehead and kissed her again, not laughing this time.

Then Simon had cupped her face in his palm and said

very quietly, since the movie was over and everyone was trying to sleep in the dimly lit cabin, "I think we're going to make a fine team, Lily. You, me, and No Wrinkles Remus."

Lily snuggled down under the blankets. She hoped Simon was doing better than she was. Like her, he'd been ready to fall flat on his face from exhaustion. She hoped he was sleeping.

Actually, Simon was turning slowly over in the too-short cot, not wanting to roll himself accidentally off onto the floor. He had managed to get the blanket carefully wrapped around his feet, no easy thing, since his feet were off the cot and on the big side. He'd taken up temporary residence in Sean's room, just down the hall from Lily, since the baby was still with Mrs. Savich. A precaution, Dillon had said as he'd helped Dane Carver, a new special agent in his unit, carry in the narrow army cot that would be Simon's bed. He'd announced to both men that he didn't care if he had to fit himself into Sean's crib, if that's what it took to get to sleep.

He knew she was okay, just down the hall. Not near enough to him for the time being, but Simon had plans to change that. He could easily picture her in his brownstone, could picture how he'd redo one of those large upstairs bedrooms to make it her workroom. Great light in that room, just exactly right for her.

Simon was smiling as he breathed in the scent of Sean. Nice scent, but he would have preferred to be in the guest room with Lily, in her bed. He'd always been a patient man, which, he supposed, was a good thing, since he'd only known Lily for a little more than two weeks.

As for Lily, she didn't know why she couldn't sleep. It was after midnight in Washington, morning in Sweden. But she and Simon had been in Sweden such a short time, her body had no clue what time of day it was. She was beyond exhaustion, yet she couldn't sleep.

She was still very worried about her brother. Tammy

Tuttle hadn't shown up, hadn't come after Dillon, and both her brother and Sherlock were frustrated and on edge, at their wits' end.

On Friday afternoon, as announced, Dillon had taken a taxi to the airport and checked in for a flight to Texas. Then, at the last minute, he'd deplaned and slipped back into the house in Georgetown.

Now it was Saturday night, well beyond the deadline, and Lily knew there were still agents covering the house. Jimmy Maitland wasn't taking any chances, and the very sophisticated house alarm was set.

Lily hoped that Dillon and Sherlock were sleeping better than she was. She knew they missed Sean. When they'd all come up to bed, they'd automatically turned to go to Sean's room.

She rolled onto her side and sucked in her breath at a sudden jab of pain. She didn't want to take any more pain pills. She closed her eyes and saw that huge room again, its walls covered with her grandmother's paintings. So many to be returned to museums all over the world. Olaf Jorgenson and his son would not be able to stop it. Ian would be in jail for a very long time. Olaf was in the hospital, in very bad shape.

After a good deal of time, she was finally floating toward sleep, when her brain clicked on full alert and her eyes flew open. She'd heard something. Not Simon or Dillon or Sherlock moving around, something that wasn't right.

Maybe it was nothing at all, just a phantom whisper from her exhausted brain or only a puff of wind that had sent a branch sweeping against the bedroom window. Yes, the sound was outside, not in her bedroom. Maybe it was in Simon's bedroom, just down the hall. Had he awakened?

Lily continued to wait, gritty eyes staring around the dark room, listening.

She started to relax again when she heard a creak. Just a

slight pressure on the oak floor could cause a creak, but it
was there and it was close. In the air, no longer heard, but
she still felt it. Lily waited, straining to hear, her heart
pounding now.

The scattered carpets covering the oak floors would
mask any creaks, make someone walking hard to hear.

Lily lurched upright, straining to see. Too late, she saw a
shadow, moving fast, and something coming down at her.
She felt a deadening pain like a sharp knife driving into her
skull.

She fell back onto the pillow. Just before she passed out,
she saw a face over her, a woman's face, and she knew
whose face it was. The mouth whispered, "Hi, little sister."

Sherlock couldn't sleep. Dillon's arm was heavy over
her chest, and he was close and warm, his familiar
scent in the air she breathed, but it didn't help. Her brain
wouldn't turn off; it just kept moving, going over and over
what they knew about Tammy, what they imagined but
didn't know.

When she couldn't stand it anymore, Sherlock eased
away from Savich, got out of bed, and pulled on her old
blue wool robe. She wore socks to keep her feet warm
against the oak floor.

She had to check the house again, just had to, though
she'd already checked it three times, and Dillon had
checked probably another three. She had to be sure. It was
early Sunday morning, it was snowing, and Sean was at his
grandmother's, safe. When would she feel secure enough
to bring him home? Ever? It had to end. Tammy had to do
something; it had to end, sometime.

She hoped the four agents outside weren't freezing their
butts off. At least she knew they had hot coffee; she'd taken
them a huge thermos about ten o'clock.

She got to the end of the hall and paused for a moment,

feeling the house warm around her, breathing in its comforting smells. It took a moment, but Sherlock realized that something was different.

It was quiet in a way she wasn't used to. Too quiet. She realized that the alarm was off, the very low hum you could barely hear wasn't there. Panic lurched up into her throat.

She turned to look down the beautifully carved oak staircase. She saw dim light pooling at the bottom from the glass arch above the front door, snowflakes drifting lazily down. She took one step, then another, when a hand hit her square in the middle of the back. She screamed, or at least she thought she did, as she went head over heels down the stairs. Someone passed by her as she lay there facedown on a thick Persian carpet, the breath knocked out of her, barely hanging on to consciousness. She'd struck her head, struck everything on her body, and she could hardly move.

She thought she heard a moan, and then the figure was gone. The front door opened as she stared at it, yes, she was sure it was open, now fully open, because she felt a slice of cold air reach her face, and she shivered.

The front door stayed open. Only an instant passed before she realized what had happened. Someone had shoved her down the stairs. Someone had just gone out through the front door.

She managed to stagger to her feet, fear swamping her. Tammy Tuttle, it had to be her, but how? How had she gotten past the agents and into the house? Why hadn't Sherlock seen her?

She threw back her head and yelled, "Dillon! Oh God, Dillon, come quickly!"

Savich and Simon appeared at the top of the stairs at the same time, both wearing only boxer shorts. A light went on.

"Sherlock!"

Savich was beside her, holding her tightly against him, then gently pushing her down, afraid that he was hurting her.

Sherlock came back up, grabbed his arms. "No, no, Dillon, I'm okay. Tammy—she was here; she shoved me down the stairs. The alarm was off and I was just coming downstairs to check. I heard a woman's moan. It wasn't me. Where's Lily? Dear God, check Lily."

Simon was back up the stairs, taking them two, three at a time. They heard him yell, "She's gone!"

Dillon grabbed his cell phone to call the agents outside.

Simon turned on all the lights as Dillon was speaking to the agents. The front door was open and there was no sign of Lily. Somehow, Tammy had taken her out without Sherlock seeing anything.

Savich stood on his front porch in his boxer shorts, straining to see through the snow falling like a thin, white curtain in front of him, into the darkness beyond.

Jimmy Maitland said as he sipped his coffee, so blessedly hot that it nearly burned his tongue, "What do the folk in Behavioral Sciences have to say?"

Savich said, "Jane Bitt is guessing, she freely admits it, but as far as she knows, no one has ever before encountered anything like Tammy Tuttle. She may have some sort of genetic gift, be able to project what she wants you to see. What's amazing is the scope. She had everyone in that airport in Antigua believing she was a man, and this is what makes her so unique. Jane said that even given that, we shouldn't focus exclusively on it—there's just no percentage to it. She says there's no beating her that way. We should focus on a woman with one arm who's twenty-three years old. What would she do? If we can predict that, she's vulnerable."

"But we don't know what she'll do, where she'd take Lily," Sherlock said.

"She was supposed to come after *me* here, not Lily—to tear my fucking head off," Savich said slowly, staring at his hands, which were clasped tightly together around Sherlock's waist.

Jimmy Maitland blinked. He had never heard Savich utter a profanity before, and then he realized he was quoting Tammy.

Simon was on his feet, pacing in front of the two of them. He was wearing only wrinkled black wool slacks, no shirt, even his feet were bare.

"Listen, Savich, you know she took Lily because she figured it was better revenge than just killing you. Now, think, dammit. Where would Tammy Tuttle take Lily?"

It was nearly four o'clock in the morning and snow was still falling lightly. No one said a word. Savich sat in his favorite chair, leaned his head back, and closed his eyes. He felt Sherlock leaning against him.

Then Sherlock said very softly, "I think I know where she might have taken Lily."

29

Lily was colder than when she'd been lying on that naked mattress in Gothenburg. Her wrists and ankles were bound together loosely, with some sort of tape. She was lying on her side in a dark room, and it smelled funny. It wasn't unpleasant, but she didn't recognize it.

She was all right. She felt a dull throb on the side of her head, but it wasn't bad, and her side hurt, but that wouldn't kill her. No, it was the insane woman who had brought her here who could kill her.

Did she hear someone laugh? She couldn't be sure.

She gritted her teeth and tried working at her wrists. There was a little bit of movement; the tape wasn't all that tight. She kept pulling and twisting, working the duct tape.

Where was she? Where had Tammy Tuttle taken her? She knew Tammy was utterly mad and smart, since up to now she'd managed to evade Lily's brother. She'd taken Lily because she was Dillon's sister. She thought it was better revenge against Dillon than just killing him.

Lily knew she was right about that. Dillon was probably

driving himself mad with guilt. She kept working the duct tape.

What was that smell that permeated the air? Then she knew. She was in some sort of barn. She smelled old hay, linseed oil, yes, that was it, at least it was some kind of oil, and the very faint odor of ancient dried manure.

A barn somewhere. She remembered Simon asking Dillon where they'd first caught up with the Tuttle brother and sister, and he'd said it was at a barn on Marilyn Warluski's property near the Plum River in Maryland.

Maybe that was where she was. At least Dillon and Sherlock knew about this place. Was this Marilyn Warluski here with her as well? Was she still alive?

Dull, gray light was coming through the filthy glass behind her. It was dawn. Soon it would be morning.

Lily kept working the duct tape. She didn't want to think about how in all the years she'd used duct tape it had never broken or slipped off. But it was looser than before, she knew it.

Lily needed to go to the bathroom. She was hungry. Her side and shoulder were thudding with pain. Just surface pain, that damned doctor had assured her. She wished now she had slugged him. Let him feel some surface pain for a while, the jerk.

There was more light, dull, flat light, and she could see now that she was in a small tack room. There was an ancient desk shoved against the opposite wall, two old chairs near it. A torn bridle with only one rein was dangling from a nail on the wooden-slatted wall.

It was cold. She couldn't stop shivering. Now that she could see around her, see the cracks in the wooden walls that gave directly to the outside, she was even colder. She was wearing only her nightgown. At least it was a long-sleeve flannel number that came to her neck and down to her ankles.

But it wasn't enough.

She turned her head when she heard the door slowly open.

She saw a woman standing in the dim light. "Hello, little sister. How are you doing with the duct tape? Loosen it up a bit yet?"

And Lily said, "I'm not your little sister."

"No, you're Dillon Savich's little sister and that's more than close enough. That's just dandy." Tammy walked into the small room, sniffed the air, frowned for just a moment, then pulled one of the rickety chairs away from the desk and sat down. She crossed her legs. She was wearing huge-heeled black boots.

"I'm very cold," Lily said.

"Yeah, I figured."

"I also have to go to the bathroom."

"Okay, I don't care if you're cold, but I wouldn't make you lie there on your side and pee on yourself. That would be gross. I'm going to unfasten your feet so you can walk. You can go out in the barn and pick your corner. Here, I'll put the duct tape around your wrists in front of you. I wouldn't want you to pee on yourself." Lily didn't have a chance to fight her. Her ankles were bound. She could do nothing, just wait for the duct tape to go around her wrists again. At least they were in front of her now, even for just a short time.

"Here's a couple of Kleenex."

Lily walked ahead of Tammy into the large barn. It was a mess—overflowing rotting hay, random pieces of rusted equipment, boards hanging loose, letting in snow and frigid air. She quickly saw the big, black-painted circle. It was starkly clean. That was where Tammy and her brother had forced the two boys to stay while Tammy called her Ghouls.

"How about the corner over there? Hurry up now, you

and I have lots to do. I don't trust you not to be stupid but it won't matter if you are. Move, little sister."

Lily relieved herself, then turned to face Tammy, who'd been watching her.

"How did you get into the house? The alarm system is one of the best made."

Tammy just smiled at her. Lily saw her very clearly now in the shaft of strong morning light that speared through a wide slash in the wall. She was wearing black jeans over those black boots, and a long-sleeve black turtleneck sweater. One sleeve dangled where her arm should have been. She wasn't ugly or beautiful. She just looked normal, average even. She didn't look particularly scary, even with her moussed, spiked-up dark hair. Her eyes were very dark, darker than her hair, in sharp contrast to her face, which was very pale, probably made more pale with white powder, and her mouth was painted a deep plum color. She was thin, and her single hand was long and narrow, the fingernails capped with the same plum color that was on her mouth. Even thin, she gave the overwhelming impression that she was as strong as a bull.

"I'll just bet your brother and that little redheaded wife of his were chewing off their fingernails waiting for me. But I didn't come when they wanted me to. That announcement the FBI character made on TV, I didn't believe it, not for an instant. I knew it was a trap, and that was okay. I took my time, found out all about the alarm, how to disarm it. It wasn't hard. Sit down, little sister."

Lily sat on a bale of hay so old it cracked beneath her. "I don't think you could have done that alarm yourself, alone. It would require quite some expertise."

"You're right. People always underestimate me because they think I'm a hick." Tammy grinned down at her, then

began pacing in front of her, every once in a while looking
down at her empty sleeve, where her other hand should
have been. Lily watched her and saw the look of panic,
then bone-deep hatred, cross her face.

"What are you going to do with me?"

Tammy laughed. "Why, I'm going to put you in the circle and I'm going to call the Ghouls. They'll come and tear
you apart, and that's what I'll deliver back to your
brother—a body he'd rather not see." Tammy paused for a
moment, then cocked her head to one side. "They're close
now, I can hear them."

Lily listened. She could hear the faint rustling of tree
branches, probably from the constant fall of snow, the
movement of the wind. But nothing else, not even early-
morning birds, no animal sounds at all. "I don't hear anything."

"You will," said Tammy. "You will. We're going to walk
over to that black circle. You're going to sit down in the
middle of it. I won't even tie your hands behind you. Now,
move it, little sister." Tammy pulled out a gun and aimed it
at Lily.

"No, I'm not going anywhere," Lily said. "Will the
Ghouls still want me if I'm not in the circle? What if
you've already killed me with that gun of yours? Will they
still want me then?"

"We'll just have to see, won't we?" Tammy raised the
gun and aimed it at Lily's face.

Simon wished he were on his motorcycle, weaving in
and out of the heavy, early-morning traffic. Why
didn't Savich have a bloody siren? Why were there so
many people at this hour?

When there was finally a break in the traffic, Savich
pressed his foot hard on the accelerator. Simon looked
out the back window, saw six black FBI cars, one after

the other, coming fast, keeping pace with them.

"Tell me, Sherlock," he said, his heart thudding fast, hard beats. "We'll be there soon. Tell me about Tammy."

Slowly, Tammy lowered the gun. "You think you're pretty cute, don't you?"

Lily slowly shook her head, so relieved she was nearly sick. She'd been ready to feel a bullet go right through her heart, to just be gone, and that was it. Sudden and final and she was dead. But she was still here, still alive, with Tammy, who was still holding that ugly gun.

The circle—it appeared Tammy wanted her in that circle, still alive. "Where is Marilyn? She's your cousin, isn't she?"

"You want to know about my sweet little cousin? I'm not real happy with her right now. See, she told your brother everything about me. Then he used her for bait. That was ruthless of him. I like that in a guy. She was waiting for me right there in the open, in that airport, standing next to that stupid agent who was supposed to be guarding her. From me. What a joke that was. I cut the agent's throat, and everyone saw a crazy young man do it. Everyone believed it, but it was really me.

"You want to know why I hate your brother? It's not hard. He killed my brother, shot my arm off, just left it dangling by a few strips of muscle, and I saw it hanging there and I thought I was going to die. And they strapped me down to this bed because your brother told them I was bad trouble, and then they cut the rest of it right off in the hospital and I nearly died. All because of your damned brother."

Then Tammy let loose, screamed to the rafters, "One goddamned arm! Just look at me—my fucking sleeve is empty! I nearly died from the infection, damn him to hell. He shot my arm off! After I set the Ghouls on you, after they've gnawed you to a bloody mess, I'm going to get him, *get him,* GET HIM!"

Lily kept her mouth shut, tried to pull herself together enough to work on the duct tape. She wished she could raise her hands and use her teeth, but Tammy would notice that for sure. At least her hands were still bound in front of her; that might give her some chance.

Tammy drew a deep breath as she slowly lowered the gun. Her eyes focused again, on Lily. "You're like him— stubborn."

"How did you get past all the agents guarding the house?"

"Stupid buggers, all of them. It was easy. There's hardly any challenge anymore. I didn't let them see me."

Lily didn't want to believe anything that outrageous, but she said, "And they couldn't see me either?"

"Oh yes. Nothing to it. Just dragged you out, wearing that cute little nightgown—sorry I didn't get you a coat. But I figured after you realized what was going to happen to you, you'd want to feel the cold, better than being dead and not feeling anything at all. Now, little sister, move into the goddamned circle."

"No."

Tammy raised the gun and fired. Lily cried out, unable to help herself. She threw herself to the right, off the bale of hay, felt the hot whoosh of the bullet not an inch from her cheek, and rolled and kept rolling, pulling and twisting at the tape on her wrists. Another bullet hit a pile of moldering hay and spewed it upward.

Then Tammy stopped shooting. She walked over to Lily and stood still, staring down at her, the gun pointed at her chest. Lily looked up, frozen, afraid to move, afraid even to breathe.

Lily said, finally, "You have a problem, don't you, Tammy? The Ghouls won't come if I'm not staked like a tethered goat in that black circle, right? So get used to it. I'm not going anywhere."

Tammy didn't say a thing to that, just turned and walked away, her strides in those heavy, black boots long and solid. Lily watched her disappear into the tack room and close the door behind her, hard.

It was so silent that Lily could hear the barn groan as the rising wind hit it. Then Lily heard a scream, a woman's scream, Tammy's scream and two gunshots, loud, sharp.

Dillon ran out of the tack room toward her, his SIG Sauer in his hand, yelling, "Lily! Oh my God, are you all right, sweetheart? Everything's okay. I got into the tack room, shot her before she saw me. Oh God, are you hit?"

She felt such relief she thought she'd choke on it. She yelled, "Dillon, you came! I kept her talking, knew I had to keep her talking. Oh God, she's so scary. Then she started shooting at me and I thought it was all over—"

Lily stopped cold. Dillon was nearly to her, not more than six feet away, when suddenly Lily didn't see her brother anymore. She saw Tammy. She wasn't holding Dillon's SIG Sauer; she was holding that same little ugly gun that was hers. Her brain froze. Just simply froze. She couldn't accept what she was seeing, what was right in front of her, she just couldn't. Oh, God.

"Honey, are you okay?"

It was Tammy's voice, no longer Dillon's.

Then Lily realized it really was Tammy. She thought she'd seen Dillon because she wanted to so much, and Tammy wanted her to. And Tammy thought it was working.

Oh God, oh God.

Lily said, "I'm okay. I'm so glad you're here, Dillon, so glad."

Tammy dropped to her knees beside Lily and turned her onto her side. "Let me get that tape off you, sweetheart. There, let me just slip the knife under the tape. Good,

you've already loosened it. You could have gotten yourself
free and away, couldn't you?" Then Tammy Tuttle pulled
Lily against her and hugged her, kissed her hair. Stroked
her single hand down her back. Lily felt Tammy's slight
breasts against hers.

Tammy had laid the gun on the ground, just a hand's
length away from her, not more than six inches. "Just hold
me, Dillon. Oh, God, I was so scared. I'm so glad you
came so quickly."

She cried, sobbed her heart out, felt Tammy squeeze her
and kiss her hair again. Lily's hand moved slowly toward
the gun, slowly, until her fingers touched the butt.

Tammy swept up the gun, tucked it into her waistband,
and said, "Let me help you up, honey. That's right. You're
okay now. Sherlock is just outside with the other agents.
Let's go see them."

Tammy was holding her tightly against her side, walking toward the barn doors. No, not really toward the doors.
She was swerving to the left now, toward that big black
circle.

Just as Tammy flung her onto her back and into the circle, Lily grabbed the gun from Tammy's waistband, raising
it at her.

Tammy didn't seem to notice that Lily had her gun, that
she was pointing it at her. She'd turned toward the barn
doors, raised her head, and yelled, "Ghouls! No young
bloods for you this time, but a soft, sweet morsel, a female.
Bring your axes, bring your knives, and hack her apart!
Come here, Ghouls!"

The barn doors blew inward. Lily saw whirling snow
blowing in, and something else in that snow. A dust devil,
that was it. That was what Dillon had seen as well, wasn't it?

The snow seemed to coalesce into two distinct forma-
tions, like tornadoes, whirling and dipping, coming toward
her. But they were white, twisting this way and that, in

constant motion, coming closer and closer. Lily felt frozen in place, just stared at those white cones coming closer, not more than a dozen feet away now, nearly to the black circle now. She had to move, had to.

Tammy saw that something was wrong. She pulled a knife out of her boot leg, a long, vicious knife. She raised that knife and ran toward Lily.

Lily didn't think, just raised the gun and yelled, "No, Tammy, it's over. Yes, I see you. The minute you got close, I saw you, not my brother. The Ghouls won't help you."

Just as Tammy leaped at her, the knife raised, the blade gleaming cold, Lily pulled the trigger.

Tammy yelled and kept coming. Lily pulled the trigger again and again, and Tammy Tuttle was kicked off her feet and hurled a good six feet by the force of the bullets. She sprawled on her back, gaping holes in her chest. Her one arm was flung out, the empty sleeve flat on the ground.

But Lily didn't trust her. She ran to her, breathing hard and fast, nearly beyond herself, and she aimed and fired the last bullet not a foot from Tammy's body. Her body lurched up with the bullet's impact. She fired again, but there was only a click. The gun was empty, but Tammy was still alive, her eyes on Lily's face, and Lily couldn't stop. She pulled the trigger, like an automaton, again and again, until, finally, only hollow clicks filled the silence.

Tammy lay on her back, covered with blood, her one hand still clenched at her side. Even her throat was ripped through by a bullet. Lily had fired six shots into her. Lily dropped to her knees, put her fingertips to Tammy's bloody neck.

No pulse.

But her eyes were looking up at Lily, looking into her. Tammy was still there, still clinging to what she was. Her lips moved, but there was no sound. Slowly, ever so slowly, her eyes went blank. She was dead now, her eyes no longer wild and mad, no longer seeing anything at all.

There was utter silence.

Lily looked up, but the Ghouls were gone. They were gone with Tammy.

30

FBI specialists from the evidence labs went over every inch of the barn at the Plum River in Maryland.

They found candy wrappers—more than three dozen—but no clothing, no bedding, no sign that Tammy Tuttle had been there for any time at all.

There was no sign of Marilyn Warluski.

"She's dead," Savich said, and Sherlock hated the deadening guilt in his voice.

"We can't be sure of anything when it comes to that family," Sherlock said matter-of-factly, but she'd moved closer and put her hand on his shoulder, lightly touching him.

TWO DAYS LATER

It was late afternoon, and the snow had stopped falling. Washington was covered with a blanket of pristine white, and a brilliant sun was overhead. People were out and about on this cold, crystalline Sunday even as the national media announced the shooting death of the fugitive killer Tammy Tuttle in a barn in Maryland.

Lily came into the living room, a cup of hot tea in her hand. "I called Agent Clark Hoyt in Eureka. He said that Hemlock Bay was rife with gossip over the deaths of Elcott and Charlotte. The mayor, the city council, and the local Methodist church are holding meetings to plan a big memorial service. No one, he said, really wants to delve too deeply into why they were killed, but it's possible that the floating rumors could even exceed the truth."

Lily paused for a moment, then added, "I also called Tennyson. He's very saddened by his parents' death. It's difficult for him to accept what they did, that they used him—used both of us—to gain their ends. He said he knows now that his parents were feeding me depressants all those months and that they had been the ones to arrange for my brakes to fail when I was driving to Ferndale."

"But how did they know what you would be doing?" Sherlock asked.

"Tennyson said he called them from Chicago, just happened to mention that he'd asked me to drive to Ferndale, and when. I feel very bad for him, but I wonder how he could have been so blind to what his own parents were."

"They fooled you as well," Savich said. "At least enough. No one wants to see evil; no one wants to admit it exists."

Lily said, "I've decided to fly to California for the memorial service. I'm going for Tennyson. He's been hurt terribly. I feel that I must show him my support now, show everyone that I believe he was innocent of everything that happened. He knows I'm not coming back to him, as his wife, and he accepts it." She sighed. "He said he was leaving Hemlock Bay, that he never wants to see the place again."

"I can't say I blame him," Simon said.

Savich said, "Please tell Tennyson for us that we are very sorry about what happened."

"I will." Lily raised her head, listened, and smiled. "Sean's awake from his nap."

Both Savich and Sherlock were up the stairs, side by side, their hands clasped.

Simon smiled at Lily, sipped his coffee. Savich had made it, so it was excellent. He sighed with pleasure.

"So, Lily, as your new consultant, I think it's very good for you to go back for his parents' memorial service. It will put closure on things. It will be over. Then you will begin to move forward. Now, I've been thinking hard about this."

"And what did you decide, Mr. Russo?"

"I think the first step is for you to move to New York. It's never wise for a client to be any distance at all from her consultant."

Lily walked across the living room, gently placed her teacup on an end table, and sat down on Simon's lap. She took his face between her hands and kissed him.

Simon sighed, set down his own cup, and pulled her close. "That's very nice, Lily."

"Yes, it is. Actually it's better than just nice." She kissed his neck, then settled herself against him. "I just wanted to tell you that you're the best, Simon. I can't believe it's all really over—that I'm even going to get all my paintings back. But you know what? I want to stay in Washington for a while. I want to settle down, let the past sort itself out, and when I'm ready for the future, I want it to be with a clean slate, no excess baggage dragging along with me. I want to launch No Wrinkles Remus again. I want to be my own boss for a while, Simon."

She thought for a moment that he'd argue with her, but he didn't. He rubbed his hands up and down her back and said, "Our time together hasn't had many normal moments, like this. I think the consultant will need frequent visits, lots of contact, and both of us can think about things looking forward, not back."

She kissed him again and pressed her forehead to his. "Deal," she said.

Simon settled back and wrapped his arms around her, her cheek pressed against his neck. He said, "I forgot to tell you. An art dealer friend e-mailed me, said Abe Turkle is in Las Vegas gambling, and winning. He said Abe looked and acted like some big lumberjack; no one would believe for an instant he's one of the top forgers in the world."

"I wish I could remember what happened to that painting he gave me at his cottage."

The doorbell rang.

Dillon and Sherlock were still upstairs playing with Sean. Lily pulled herself off Simon's lap and went to answer the door. When she opened it, a FedEx man stood there, holding out an envelope. "For Dillon Savich," he said. Lily signed the overnight receipt and brought the envelope back into the living room.

She called out to Dillon. Shortly, Savich, carrying Sean over his shoulder, Sherlock at his side, came downstairs.

Dillon patted his sister's cheek. "What you got, babe?"

"An overnight envelope for you, Dillon."

Savich handed Sean to Sherlock and took the envelope. He looked down at it, bemused, and said, "It's from the Beach Hotel in Aruba." He opened the envelope, pulled out a sheaf of color photos. Slowly, he looked at each of them.

"Come on, Dillon, what is it?"

He raised his head and said to Sherlock, "These are the photos that Tammy took in the Caribbean to show to Marilyn." There was a white sheet of paper behind the last photo, just a few lines written on it. He read aloud.

"Mr. Savich, Tammy was right, the beaches here are very beautiful. I'm glad she didn't kill you."

MARILYN WARLUSKI

Turn the page for a preview of
Catherine Coulter's new FBI thriller,

ELEVENTH HOUR

Coming soon from G. P. Putnam's Sons

SAN FRANCISCO

Nick sat quietly in the midnight gloom of the nave, upper body hunched forward, her head in her arms resting on the pew in front of her. She was here because Father Michael Joseph had begged her to come, had begged her to let him help her. The least she could do was talk to him, couldn't she? She'd wanted to come late, when everyone else was already home asleep, when the streets were empty, and he'd agreed, even smiled at her. He was a fine man, kind and loving toward his fellow man and toward God.

Would she wait? She sighed at the thought. She'd given her word, he'd *made* her give her word, known somehow that it would keep her here. She watched him walk over to the confessional, watched with surprise as his step suddenly lagged, and he paused a moment, his hand reaching for the small handle on the confessional door. He didn't want to open that door, she thought, staring at him. He didn't want to go in. Then, at last, he seemed to straighten, opened the door and stepped in.

Again, there was utter silence in the big church. The

deep black shadows weren't content to fill the corners of the church; they crept down even the center aisle, and she was swallowed up in them. There was a patch of moonlight coming through the tall stained-glass windows. And the air had seemed to settle after Father Michael Joseph stepped into that small, confined space.

It should have been peaceful, but it didn't feel that way. There was something else in the church, something that wasn't restful, that wasn't remotely spiritual. She fidgeted in the silence.

She heard one of the outer church doors open. She turned to see the man who was going to make his confession at midnight walk briskly into the church. He looked quite ordinary, slender, with a long Burberry raincoat and thick dark hair. She watched him pause, look right and left, but he didn't see her; she was in the shadows. She watched him walk to the confessional where Father Michael Joseph waited, watched him open the confessional door and slip inside.

Again, silence and shadows hovered around her. She was part of the shadows now, looking out toward the confessional from the dim vague light. She heard nothing.

How long did a confession take? Being a Protestant, she had no idea. There must be, she thought, some correlation between the number and severity of the sins and the length of the confession. She started to smile at that, but it quickly fell away.

She felt a rush of cold air over her, covering her for a long moment before it moved on. How very odd, she thought, and pulled her sweater tighter around her.

She looked again at the altar, perhaps seeking inspiration, some sort of sign, and felt ridiculous.

After Father Michael Joseph had finished, what was she supposed to do? Let him take her hand in his big warm ones, and tell him everything? Sure, like she'd ever let that happen. She continued to look up at the altar, its flowing

shape blurred in the dim light, the shadows creeping about
its edges, soft and otherworldly.

Maybe Father Michael Joseph wanted her to sit here
quietly with nothing and no one around her. She thought in
that moment that even though he wanted her to talk to him,
he wanted her to speak to God more. But there were no
prayers inside her. Perhaps deep in her heart there were,
but she really didn't want to look there.

So much had happened, and yet so little. Women she
didn't know were dead. She wasn't. At least not yet. He
had so many resources, so many eyes and ears, but for now
she was safe. She realized sitting there in the quiet church
that she was no longer simply terrified as she'd been two
and a half weeks before. Instead she'd become watchful.
She was always studying the faces that passed her on the
street. Some made her draw back, others just flowed over
her, making no impact at all, just as she made no impact on
them.

She waited. She looked up at the crucified Christ, felt a
strange mingling of pain and hope fill her, and waited. The
air seemed to shift, to flatten, but the silence remained absolute, without even a whisper coming from the confessional.

Inside the confessional, Father Michael Joseph drew
a slow deep breath to steady himself. He didn't want
to see this man again, not ever again, for as long as he
lived. When the man had called Father Binney and told
him he could only come this late—he was terribly sorry,
but it wasn't safe for him, and he had to confess, he just
had to, of course—Father Binney had said yes. The man
told Father Binney he had to see Father Michael Joseph, no
one else, and of course, Father Binney had again said yes.

Father Michael Joseph was very afraid he knew why the
man had come again. He'd confessed before, acted con-

trite—a man in pain, a man trying to stop killing, a man seeking spiritual help. The second time he'd come, he'd confessed yet again to another murder, gone through the ritual as if he'd rehearsed it, saying all the right words, but Father Michael Joseph knew he wasn't contrite, that—that what? That for some reason Father Michael Joseph couldn't fathom, the man wanted to gloat, because the man believed there was nothing the priest could do to stop him. Of course Father Michael Joseph couldn't tell Father Binney why he didn't want to see this evil man. He'd never really believed in human evil, not until the unimagined horror of September 11th, and now, when this man had come to him for the first time a week and a half ago, then again last Thursday, and now tonight, at nearly midnight. Father Michael Joseph knew in his soul that the man was evil, without remorse, with no ability to feel his own, or another's, humanity. He wondered if the man had ever felt truly sorry. He doubted it. Father Michael Joseph heard the man breathing in the confessional across from him, and the man said, his voice a soft low monotone, "Forgive me, Father, for I have sinned."

He'd recognize that voice anywhere, had heard it in his dreams. He didn't know if he could bear it. He said finally, his voice thin as the thread hanging off his shirt cuff, "What have you done?" He prayed to God that he wouldn't hear words that meant another human being was dead.

The man actually laughed, and Father Michael Joseph heard madness in that laugh. "Hello to you too, Father. Yes, I know what you're thinking. You're right, I killed the pathetic little prick. This time I used a garrote. Do you know what a garrote is, Father?"

"Yes, I know."

"He tried to get his hands beneath it, you know, to try to loosen it, to relieve the pressure, but it was nice strong wire. You can't do anything against wire. But I eased up just a bit, to give him some hope."

"I hear no contrition in your voice, no remorse, only satisfaction that you committed this evil. You have done this because it pleased you to do it—"

The man said in a rich, deep, sober voice, "But you haven't heard the rest of my tale, Father."

"I don't want to hear anything more out of your mouth."

The man laughed, a deep belly-rolling laugh. Father Michael Joseph didn't say a word. It was cold and stuffy in the confessional, hard to breathe, but his frock stuck to his skin. He smelled himself in that sweat, smelled his dread, his fear, his distaste for this monster. *Dear Lord, let this foul creature leave now, leave and never come back.*

"Just when he thought he had pulled it loose enough so he could breathe, I jerked it tight, really fast, you know, and it sliced right through his fingers all the way to the bone. He died with his damned fingers against his own neck. Grant me absolution, Father. Did you read the papers, Father? Do you know the man's name?"

Father Michael Joseph knew, of course he knew. He'd watched the coverage on television, read it in the *Chronicle*. "You murdered Thomas Gavin, an AIDS activist who's done nothing but good in this city."

"Did you ever sleep with him, Father?"

He wasn't shocked, hadn't been shocked by anything for the past twelve years, but he was surprised. The man had never taken this tack before. He said nothing, just waited.

"No denial? Stay silent, if you wish. I know you didn't sleep with him. You're not gay. But the fact is, he had to die. It was his time."

"There is no absolution for you, not without true repentance."

"Why am I not surprised you feel that way? Thomas Gavin was just another pathetic man who needed to leave this world. Do you want to know something, Father? He wasn't really real."

"What do you mean 'he wasn't really real'?"

"Just what I said. He didn't really ever exist, you know? He wasn't ever really here—he just existed in his own little world. I helped him out of his lousy world. Do you know he contracted AIDS just last year? He just found out about it. He was going nuts. But I saved him, I helped him out of everything, that's all. It was a rather noble thing for me to do. It was a sort of an assisted suicide."

"It was vicious cold-blooded murder. It was real, and now a man of flesh and blood is dead. Because of you. Don't try to excuse what you did."

"Ah, but I was giving you a metaphor, Father, not an excuse. Your tone is harsh. Aren't you going to give me my penance? Maybe have me say a million Hail Marys? Perhaps have me score my own back with a whip? Don't you want me to plead with you to intercede with God on my behalf, beg for my forgiveness?"

"A million Hail Marys wouldn't get you anywhere." Father Michael leaned closer, nearly touched that evil, smelled the hot breath of that man. "Listen to me now. This is not a sacramental confession. You believe that I am bound by silence, that anything anyone tells me can go no further than the confessional. That is not true. You have not made a sacramental confession; you are not contrite, you seek no spiritual absolution, and I am not bound to silence. I will discuss this with my bishop. However, even if he disagrees with me, I am prepared to leave the priesthood if I have to. Then I will tell the world what you have done. I won't allow this to continue."

"You would really turn me over to the cops? That is very impassioned of you, Father. I see that you are seriously pissed. I didn't know there was a loophole in your vow of silence. I had wanted you to be forced to beg and plead and threaten, but realize you're helpless and let it eat you alive. But how can anyone predict someone's behavior, after all?"

"They'll throw you in an institution for the rest of your miserable life."

The man smothered a laugh, managed a credible sigh and said, laughing, "You mean to imply that I'm insane, Father?"

"No, not just insane. I think you're a psychopath—ah, I believe the correct term is *sociopath*, isn't it? Doesn't make it sound so evil, so without conscience. It doesn't matter, whatever you are, it's worse than anything doctors could put a tag to. You don't give a damn about anybody. You need help, although I doubt anyone could help the sickness in you. Will you stop this insanity?"

"Would you like to shoot me, Father?"

"I am not like you. But I will see that you're stopped. There will be an end to this."

"I fear I can't let you go to the cops, Father. I'm trying not to be angry with you for not behaving as you should. All right. Now I'm just mildly upset that you aren't behaving as you're supposed to."

"What are you talking about—I'm not acting like I'm supposed to?"

"It's not important, at least it isn't for you. Do you know you've given me something I've never had before in my life?"

"What?"

"Fun, Father. I've never had so much fun in my life. Except, maybe, for this."

He waited until Father Michael Joseph looked toward him through the wire mesh. He fired point-blank, right through the priest's forehead. There was a loud popping sound, nothing more because he'd screwed on a silencer. He lowered the gun, thoughtful now because Father Michael Joseph had slumped back against the wooden confessional wall, his head up, and he could see his face clearly. There was not even a look of surprise on the priest's face, just a flash of something he couldn't really understand. Was it compassion? No, certainly not that. The priest despised him, but now he was shackled for all eternity, without a chance for him to go to the police, no opportunity for him even to take the drastic step of leaving the priesthood. He was silent forever.

Now Father Michael Joseph didn't have to worry about a thing. His tender conscience couldn't bother him. Was there a Heaven? If so, maybe Father Michael Joseph was looking down on him, knowing there was still nothing he could do. Or maybe the priest was hovering just overhead, over his own body, watching, wondering.

"Good-bye, Father, wherever you are," he said, and rose.

As he eased out of the confessional and carefully closed the narrow wooden door, he realized what the look on the Father's face was—the look of someone who'd won. But that made no sense. Won what? The good Father had just bought the big one. He hadn't won a damned thing.

There was no one in the church, not that he expected there to be. It was dead silent. He would have liked it if there had been a Gregorian chant playing softly. But no, there was nothing, just the echo of his own footsteps on the cold stones.

What did that damned priest have to look happy about? He was dead, for God's sake.

He walked quickly out of St. Bartholomew's Church, paused a moment to breathe in the clean midnight air, and craned his neck to look up at the brilliant star-studded sky. A very nice night, just like it was supposed to be. Not much of a moon, but that was all right. He would sleep very well tonight. He saw a drunk leaning against a skinny oak tree set in a small dirt plot in the middle of the sidewalk just across the street, his chin resting on his chest—not the way it was supposed to be—but who cared? The guy hadn't heard a thing.

There would be nothing but questions with no answers for now, since the cops wouldn't have a clue. The priest had made him do things differently, and that was too bad. But it was all close enough.

But the look on the priest's face, he didn't like to think about that, at least not now.

He whistled as he walked beneath the street light on Filmore, then another block to where he'd parked his car, squeezed it between two small spaces, really. This was a residential area and there was little parking space. But that too was just the way it was supposed to be. It was San Francisco, after all.

One more stop to make. He hoped she'd be home, and not working.

The blade, *Illusion*, flashed in the dim light. . . .

Naked, sword in hand, Tristen faced the window into the shadowed night and saw all the town of Henas'amef flared up in Lines. There were all the wards, all the magic of craftsmen and householders warding their own doors and walls; the common magic of parents and homekeepers and the pure trust of children . . . all these things Unfolded to him in that unworldly glow, block by block, house by house, outward toward the great defensive wall of Henas'amef itself, a bright blue Line often retraced and constantly tended. Something had challenged them.

But they held. For now, they held. . . .

FORTRESS OF OWLS
C. J. CHERRYH

By C. J. Cherryh

Fortress in the Eye of Time
Fortress of Eagles
Fortress of Owls
Fortress of Dragons *

Published by HarperPrism

*coming soon

C. J. CHERRYH

FORTRESS OF OWLS

HarperPrism
A Division of HarperCollins Publishers

🏭 **HarperPrism**
A Division of HarperCollins*Publishers*
10 East 53rd Street, New York, NY 10022-5299

This is a work of fiction. The characters, incidents, and
dialogues are products of the author's imagination and are not to
be construed as real. Any resemblance to actual events or
persons, living or dead, is entirely coincidental.

ISBN 0-06-102008-7

HarperCollins®, 🏭 ®, and HarperPrism®
are trademarks of HarperCollins Publishers Inc.

Cover type design © 1999 by Michael Sabanosh
Cover illustration © 1999 by Matthew Stawicki

A hardcover edition of this book was
published in 1999 by HarperPrism.

First HarperPrism paperback printing: March 2000

Printed in the United States of America

Visit HarperPrism on the World Wide Web at
http://www.harperprism.com

❖ 10 9 8 7 6 5 4 3 2 1

To my editor, Caitlin,
whose belief in this story carried it to print—

To Jane,
who patiently read and remarked,
version after version—

And to Beverly,
who compiled the constantly growing lexicon
out of all these pages—

Thank you

THE ZEIDE

West Gate

Armory

Blacksmith

Barracks

Shrines & Tombs

South Gate

W E N S

PROLOGUE

There is magic.
There is wizardry.
There is sorcery.
They are not now, nor were then, the same.

Nine hundred years in the past, in a tower, in a place called Galasien, a prince named Hasufin Heltain had an inordinate fear of death. That fear led him from honest study of wizardry to the darker practice of sorcery.

His teacher in the craft, Mauryl Gestaurien, seeing his student about to outstrip his knowledge in a forbidden direction, brought allies from the fabled northland, allies whose magic was not taught, but innate. These were the five Sihhë-lords.

In the storm of conflict that followed, not only Hasufin perished, but also ancient Galasien and all its works. Of all that city, only the tower in which Mauryl stood survived.

Ynefel, for so later generations named the tower, became a haunted place, isolated within Marna Wood, its walls holding intact the horrified faces of lost Galasien's people. The old tower was Mauryl's point of power, and so he remained bound to it through passing centuries, though he sometimes intervened in the struggles that followed.

The Sihhë took on themselves the task of ruling the southern lands—not the Galasieni, whose fate was bound up with Ynefel, but other newcomers, notably the race of Men, who themselves had crept down from the north. The Sihhë swept across the land, subduing and building, conquering and changing all that the Galasieni had made, creating new authorities and powers to reward their subordinates.

The five true Sihhë lived long, after the nature of their kind, and they left a thin presence of halfling descendants among Men before their passing. The kingdom of Men rapidly spread and populated the lands nearest Ynefel, with that halfling dynasty ruling from the Sihhë hall at unwalled Althalen.

Unchallenged lord of Ynefel's haunted tower, Mauryl continued in a life by now drawn thin and long, whether by wizardry or by nature: he had now outlasted even the long-lived Sihhë, and watched changes and ominous shifts of power as the blood and the innate Sihhë magic alike ran thinner and thinner in the line of halfling High Kings.

For of all the old powers, Shadows lingered, and haunted certain places in the land. And one of them was Hasufin Heltain.

One day, in the Sihhë capital, within the tributary kingdom of Amefel, in the rule of the halfling Elfwyn Sihhë, a queen gave birth to a stillborn babe. The queen was in mourning—but that mourning gave way to joy when the babe miraculously drew breath and lived, warmed, as she thought, by magic and a mother's love.

To the queen it was a wonderful gift. But that second life was not the first life. It was not the mother's innate Sihhë magic, but darkest sorcery that had brought breath into the child—for what lived in the babe was a soul neither Sihhë nor Man: it was Hasufin Heltain, in his second bid for life and power.

Now Hasufin nestled in the heart of the Sihhë aristocracy, still a child, at a time when Mauryl, who might have known him, was shut away in his tower in seclusion, rarely venturing as far as Althalen, for he was finally showing the weakness of the ages Hasufin had not lived.

Other children of the royal house died mysteriously as that fey, ingratiating child grew stronger. Now alarmed, warned by his arts, full of fury and advice, Mauryl came to court to confront the danger. But the queen would not hear a wizard's warning, far less dispose of a son of the house, her favorite, her dearest and most magical darling, who now and by the deaths of all elder princes was near the throne.

The day that child should attain his majority, and the hour he should rule, Mauryl warned them, the house and the dynasty would perish. But even that plain warning failed to persuade the queen, and the king took his grieving queen's side, refusing Mauryl's unthinkable demands to delve into the boy's nature and destroy their own son.

In desperation and foreseeing ruin, Mauryl turned not to the halfling Sihhë of the court, but to the Men who served them. He conspired with Selwyn Marhanen, the warlord, the Sihhë's trusted general, and encouraged Selwyn and other Men to bring down the halfling dynasty and take the throne for themselves.

In that fashion Mauryl betrayed the descendants of the very lords he had raised up to prevent Hasufin's sorcery.

Hence they called Mauryl both Kingmaker, and Kingsbane.

And with the help of Men and with wizards drawn from all across the kingdom, Mauryl seized the chance, insinuating both the Marhanen and his men and a band of wizards into the royal palace. Then Mauryl and his circle held magic at bay while a younger wizard, Emuin, killed the sleeping prince in his chambers—a terrible and bloody deed, and only the first of bloodshed that night.

Destroying Hasufin, however, was the limit of Mauryl's interest in the matter. The fate of the Sihhë in the hands of Selwyn and his men, even the fate of the wizards who had aided him, was beyond his reach, and Mauryl again retreated to his tower, weary and sick with age. Young Emuin took holy orders, seeking to forget his deed and find some salvation for himself as a Man and a cleric.

Given this opportunity, Selwyn's own ambition and Men's fear of magic they did not wield led them to rise in earnest against Sihhë rule: province after province fell to the Marhanen.

The district of Elwynor across the river from Althalen, however, though populated with Men, attempted to remain loyal to the Sihhë-lords, and raised an army to bring against the Marhanen, but dissent and claims and counterclaims of kingship within Elwynor precluded that army from ever taking the field. The Marhanen thus were able to take the entire tributary kingdom of Amefel, in which the capital of Althalen had stood, and treat it as a tributary province.

But rather than rule from Althalen, remote from the heart of his power, and equally claimed by all the lords of Men, Selwyn Marhanen established a capital in the center of his home territory, declared himself king, and by cleverness and ruthlessness set his own allies under his heel, creating them as barons of a new court.

From the new capital at Guelemara, Selwyn dominated all the provinces southward. He and his subjects, mostly Guelenfolk and Ryssandish, were true Men, with no gift for wizardry and no love of it either, lean-

ing rather to priests of the Quinalt and Teranthine sects. Selwyn raised a great shrine next his palace, the Quinaltine, and favored the Quinalt Patriarch, who set a religious seal on all his acts of domination.

Of all Men loyal to the Sihhë, only the Elwynim held their border against the Guelenmen . . . for that border was on the one hand a broad river, the Lenúalim, and on the other, the haunted precincts of Marna Wood, near the old tower.

So the matter settled . . . save only the question of Amefel, the province on the Guelen-held side of the Lenúalim River: Selwyn's hope of holding his lands firm against the Elwynim rested on not allowing an Elwynim presence on that side of the river. So holding Amefel was essential.

Now the history of Amefel was this: Amefel had been an independent kingdom of Men when the first Sihhë-lords walked up to its walls and demanded entry. The kings of Amefel, the Aswyddim, had flung open their gates and helped the Sihhë in their mission to conquer Guelessar, a fact no Guelen and no Guelen king could quite forget. In return for this treachery, the local Aswydd house had enjoyed a unique status under the Sihhë authority, and always styled themselves as kings, as opposed to High Kings, the title the Sihhë reserved for themselves alone.

Having conquered the province, but fearing utter collapse of his uneasily joined kingdom if he became embroiled in a dispute with the Aswydds over their prerogatives, Selwyn Marhanen accorded the Aswydds guarantees of many of their ancient rights, including their religion, and including their titles. So while the Aswydds became vassals of the king of Ylesuin, and were called dukes, they were styled aethelings, that is to say, royal, within their own province of Amefel. This purposely left aside the question of whether the other earls of Amefel bore rank equivalent to the dukes of Guelen and Ryssandish lands. Since Amefin and Guelenfolk generally avoided appearing in one another's courts, the question remained tacit and unresolved.

Selwyn thus had Amefel; but the opposing district of Elwynor formed a region almost as large as Ylesuin was with Amefel attached; and its independency from Ylesuin over that first winter had given Elwynor's lords time to gather forces. By the next spring, with Selwyn in Amefel, the river Lenúalim had become the tacitly unquestioned border. To secure Elwynor as part of Ylesuin remained Selwyn's unfulfilled dream to his dying day.

The Elwynim meanwhile, having declared a Regency in place of the lost High King at Althalen, were ruled not by a king, but by one of their earls, himself with a glimmering of Sihhë blood, who styled himself Lord Regent. The people of Elwynor took it on stubborn faith that not all the royal house of the Sihhë-lords had perished, that within their lifetimes a new Sihhë-lord, the one they called the King To Come, some surviving prince, would emerge from hiding to overthrow the Marhanen and reestablish the Sihhë kingdom. This time the kingdom would have faithful Elwynor at its heart, and all the loyal subjects would live in peace and Sihhë-blessed prosperity in a new golden age.

The Elwynim, therefore, cherished magic and prized the wizard-gift. But outside the Lord Regent's line there were far too few who could practice wizardry in any degree. Certainly no one possessed such magic as the Sihhë had used, and there were few enough wizards who would even speak of the King To Come . . . for the wizards of this age had had firsthand experience of Hasufin Heltain, and they remained aloof from the various lords of the Elwynim who *wished to employ them. Those few who had any Sihhë blood whatsoever were likewise reticent, for fear of becoming the center of some rising that could only end in disaster.*

So the Elwynim, deserted by their wizards and by those who did carry the blood, became too little wary of magic and those who promised it . . . and still the years passed into decades without a credible claimant in Elwynor.

Selwyn died. Ylesuin's rule passed to Selwyn's son Ináreddrin . . . and this, after Ináreddrin was a middle-aged man with two previous marriages and two grown sons.

Now Ináreddrin was Guelen to the core, which meant devoutly, blindly Quinalt—his mother's influence. As prince, he had no love of his uncivil warlord father, but a great deal of fear of him. He grew up with no tolerance for other faiths, despite the exigencies of the Amefin treaty. He lost patience with his wild eldest son, Cefwyn, for Cefwyn took his grandfather's example and clung to the Teranthine tutor, Emuin (that same Emuin who had aided Mauryl at Althalen), whom Selwyn had appointed royal tutor for his grandsons.

This was no accident: Selwyn as a reigning king had found priests and the Quinalt a convenient resource, and to that end he had supported them—they kept the Guelenfolk obedient. But to safeguard his kingdom for the years to come, and with at least some fear of what he had faced at Althalen, Selwyn had wanted his grandsons never to dread priests or wizards—rather to understand them, and to have one of the best on their side.

This was a source of bitter argument within the royal house: the queen died, Ináreddrin grew more alienated from his father, and the very year Selwyn

died and Ináreddrin became king, Ináreddrin per-
suaded his younger son Efanor into the strictest
Quinalt faith—lavishing on him all the affection he
denied the elder son.

So did the highest barons, notably of the provinces of
Ryssand and Murandys, favor Efanor, and there was talk
of overturning the succession—for the more Efanor
became religious, the more Cefwyn, the crown prince and
heir, consoled himself with wild escapades, sorties on the
border, and women . . . very many women.

Still, by Guelen law and custom, even by the tenets
of the Quinalt itself, Cefwyn was, incontrovertibly, the
heir.

So Ináreddrin, either in hopes that administrative
responsibility would temper Cefwyn—or, it was whispered, in hopes some assassin or border skirmish
would make Efanor his heir—sent Cefwyn to administer the Amefin garrison with the courtesy title of
viceroy, thus keeping a firmer Marhanen hand on that
curiously independent province.

Now, ordinarily and by the treaty, there was no
such thing as a viceroy in Amefel, and the duke of
Amefel, Heryn Aswydd, was not at all pleased by this
gesture . . . but Heryn kept his discontent to himself,
even agreeing to report to Ináreddrin regarding the
prince's behavior, and on the worsening situation
across the river—for there was a reason Ináreddrin
had felt a need for a firmer Guelen presence in Amefel.
The Regent in Elwynor had no children but a daughter
of his old age. The lords of Elwynor, weary of waiting
for the appearance of a High King, were now saying
the Regent should choose one of them to be king, as he
was advanced in years . . . and the only way for one
earl to gain any legitimate connection with royalty was
by marrying the Lord Regent's daughter.

The Regent, Uleman Syrillas, refused all offers,

swearing that his only child, his daughter Ninévrisë, would wield the power of Regent herself... unprecedented, among the Elwynim and the Sihhë kings, that a woman should rule in her own right. But Uleman had prepared his daughter to rule... and when the day came that a suitor tried to enforce his demands with arms and carry Ninévrisë away, the Regent refused to bow.

Elwynor sank into civil war... and that war insinuated itself across the river into Amefel: there were families with kin on both sides of the river.

So it was into this situation that Ináreddrin sent Prince Cefwyn to strengthen the garrison.

And it was entirely characteristic of Ináreddrin that he told Heryn he was to watch Cefwyn and told Cefwyn to watch Heryn, who was, after all, a heretic Bryaltine.

Unbeknownst to the king, in fact, Duke Heryn was in league with one of the rebel earls in Elwynor.

Others of the Elwynim rebels, those who lacked force of arms, were keen to have wizardly sanction.

And Hasufin Heltain, once again dead, as Men knew death, was waiting only for such a moment of crisis and a condition in the stars. Through the situation in Elwynor, that ancient spirit found his way closer and closer to life.

Mauryl, however, had foreseen the hour, and had saved his strength for one grand, unprecedented spell, a Summoning and a Shaping, a revenant brought forth from the fire of Mauryl's hearth—not a perfect effort, however, nor mature nor threatening. To Mauryl's distress the young man thus Summoned lacked all memory of what or who he had been.

Mauryl called his Summoning... Tristen. And the day Mauryl lost his struggle with Hasufin, Tristen, a young man with the innocence of the newly born, set forth into *the world, hoping to do the things Mauryl intended.*

The Road which began from Ynefel led Tristen not to a wizard, who would teach him, as Tristen had hoped, but straight to Prince Cefwyn, on a night when, despising his host, Heryn Aswydd, Cefwyn was sleeping with Heryn's twin sisters, Orien and Tarien.

Tristen was as innocent a soul as ever Cefwyn had met . . . incapable of anger, feckless, and utterly outspoken, but wizardous at the very least. When Tristen confessed he was Mauryl's, Cefwyn's curiosity was immediately engaged; and when Cefwyn began to deal with Tristen, he found himself snared indeed—for after his grandfather's anger and his father's cold dislike of him, after the northern lords' wish for Efanor and his own brother's desertion, this was the only wholehearted offer of a stranger's friendship he had ever met.

Meanwhile Tristen continued to learn . . . for he was a blank slate on which Mauryl's spell was still writing, Unfolding new things in wizardous fashion, at need, and providing him knowledge unpredictable in its scope and its deficiency. Tristen wondered at butterflies . . . and asked questions that shot straight to the prince's heart.

Cefwyn's affection toward this wizardous stranger made Duke Heryn Aswydd hasten his plans . . . for Cefwyn was growing fey and difficult. Heryn used King Ináreddrin's suspicion of his son to lure the king and Prince Efanor to Amefel . . . hoping then to do away with Cefwyn and the younger prince in the same stroke as the king, and thus overthrow the Marhanen dynasty.

Prince Efanor, however, had not ridden with the king; he had ridden straight to Cefwyn to accuse and berate his brother, determined to find out the truth ahead of their father's arrival, to spring any trap upon himself if one existed. It was a brave act. And when

Cefwyn knew his father had listened to Lord Heryn, he was horrified, and rode at once to prevent the ambush, no matter the danger.

He arrived too late, and was almost overwhelmed by the force that had killed the king; but the knowledge of warfare Unfolded to Tristen that day, on that battlefield, and the gentle stranger turned warrior. He rescued the princes, defeated Heryn's allies—and when Cefwyn reached Henas'amef not only unexpectedly alive, but king of Ylesuin, Heryn paid with his life for his treason.

Tristen, however, strayed into the hills, where he fell in with the Lord Regent of Elwynor, who was dying, in hiding from the same enemies as had killed his old enemy Ináreddrin. The old Regent's last wish was to bring his daughter Ninévrisë to Cefwyn Marhanen—as his bride . . . for the only hope for the Regency now was peace with Ylesuin.

So Tristen brought Lady Ninévrisë to Cefwyn, and Cefwyn Marhanen, new king of Ylesuin, fell headlong in love with the new Regent of Elwynor.

Tristen, for his services, became a lord of Ylesuin, no longer mocked for his simplicity, but now feared, for no one who had seen him fight could discount him. And Heryn's sister Orien became duchess of Amefel, since Cefwyn was not ready to set aside the entire dynasty, and had seen none but ordinary flaws in Orien. Orien, however, was bent on revenge and lied in her oaths. Lacking armies, lacking skill in war, she sought another means to power . . . and became prey to sorcerous whispers from the enemy, Hasufin Heltain.

Hasufin's immediate goal was an entry into the fortress of Henas'amef, but because of Tristen and Emuin, he could not breach the wards: so he moved his pawn Orien to make an attempt on Cefwyn's life, moved another pawn to attempt Emuin's life, and at the same time drew the rebel army across the river in all-out war.

The first two failed. The third was aimed at Tristen, whom Hasufin recognized as Mauryl's last and most effective weapon. Sorcery would be at its strongest in a moment of chance and upheaval, and there was no moment of upheaval greater than the shifting tides of a battlefield: thus Hasufin made his strongest bid to break into the world and destroy Tristen, who stood between him and life and substance.

In the world of Men, at a place called Lewenbrook, near Ynefel, the Elwynim rebels, under Lord Aséyneddin, met Cefwyn Marhanen's opposing army. That was the conflict Men fought.

But when Aséyneddin faltered, Hasufin sent out tides of sorcery in reckless disregard. A wall of Shadow rolled down on the field, and those it touched it took and did not give up. It was Hasufin's manifestation, and all aimed at Tristen's destruction.

Tristen, however, took up magic as he took up his weapons, when the challenge came. When Hasufin Heltain loosed his sorcery, Tristen rode into the Shadow, penetrated into Ynefel itself, and drove Hasufin from his unsteady Place in the world.

Cefwyn meanwhile had prevailed in the unnatural darkness, and when the sun broke free of the Shadow, he had held his army together. Aséyneddin's forces, such as survived, shattered and ran in panic.

It was a long way back to the world, however, from where Tristen had gone. Exhausted, hurt, at the end of his purpose, Tristen resigned his wizard-made life, finished with Mauryl's purpose, too weary to wake to the world of Men.

But he had once given his shieldman Uwen, an ordinary Man with not a shred of magic in him, the power to call his name. This Uwen did, the devotion of a simple man seeking his lost lord on the battlefield, and Tristen came.

There was a moment, then, when Cefwyn stood victorious over the rebels, that he might have launched forward into Elwynor: the southern lords had rallied to the new king, and would have followed him. But Cefwyn saw his army badly battered and in need of regrouping, he knew the enemy was on the run, meaning they would sink invisibly into Elwynor, and he knew, as a new king, he had left matters uncertain behind him. The majority of his kingdom did not even know they had changed one king for another, and the treaty he had made with Ninévrisë had never reached his people.

It was the end of summer. Good campaigning weather still remained, but harsh northern winters could make fighting impossible. So for good or for ill, Cefwyn opted not to plunge his exhausted army, lacking maps or any sort of preparation, into the unknown situation inside Elwynor, which had been several years in anarchy and still had rival claimants to the Regency. Instead he chose to regroup, settle his domestic affairs, marry the lady Regent, ratify the marriage treaty, and rally the rest of his kingdom behind him in a campaign to begin in the spring.

He went home, trusting his father's trusted men, gathering up his brother Efanor, and attempting simply to take up the power of the monarchy as it had been. But when he reached his capital, he discovered his father's closest friends among the barons meant to wrest the power into their own hands . . . as his father had let them do much as they pleased for years. It was no longer a matter of the northernmost barons preferring Efanor. They had had a king they could rule, they meant to have another one, and in their minds Cefwyn was a wastrel prince who would be a weak king: he could be managed, they had said among themselves, if they kept him diverted.

That was not, however, the king who came home to

them: Cefwyn arrived surrounded by their southern rivals, who were clearly in favor, and allied to Mauryl's heir, betrothed to the Elwynim Regent, and proposing war on the Elwynim rebels. This was not Ináreddrin's dissolute son: it was Selwyn's hard-handed grandson, and the barons were appalled.

So they took a new tactic . . . they were older, cannier, more experienced in court politics. They would use the priests, prevent the marriage, treat the lady Regent as a captive—and seize land in Elwynor.

Cefwyn was as determined to bring them into line and shake the kingdom into order. He sent the southern barons home to attend their harvests and prepare for war, all but Cevulirn, whose horsemen had less reliance on such seasons and who stayed as a shadowy observer for southern interests.

In Elwynor, meanwhile, another of the rebel lords, the survivor of all the others, took advantage of the confusion to bring his army out of the hills, besiege his own capital of Ilefínian, and declare the lady Regent captive in the hands of the Marhanen king.

Cefwyn took measures to ensure that the Quinalt would approve the marriage and the treaty by which he would agree to put Elwynor in the hands of Ninévrisë as lady Regent, independent of the Crown of Ylesuin.

The barons retaliated with an attempt to limit the monarchy over them.

And if Tristen had been feared in the south, he found he was abhorred in the north. He kept to the shadows . . . for Cefwyn, fighting for his right to wed the woman he loved and trying to wrest back sovereignty in his own capital, feared Tristen's being caught up in the fight.

Obscurity, however, only increased the mystery. The barons saw Tristen as an influence on Cefwyn that must be eliminated. On a night when lightning, whether by chance or wizardry, struck the Quinalt roof, a penny in the offering in the Quinaltine was found to be Sihhë coinage, with forbidden symbols on it; and the charge was forbidden wizardry, attacking the Quinalt and the gods.

Cefwyn suspected that His Holiness the Patriarch was devious enough to substitute the damning coin, and Cefwyn moved quickly to force the Patriarch into his camp. But the coin together with the lightning threw the wider court into such alarm that Cefwyn felt compelled to remove Tristen from controversy. In what he thought a clever and protective stroke, he sent Tristen back to Amefel not as a refugee in disgrace, but as duke of Amefel . . . a replacement for the viceroy he had left in charge.

Now this viceroy was Parsynan, appointed on the advice of some of these same troublesome barons, notably Murandys and Ryssand . . . for Cefwyn had exiled Orien Aswydd and her sister to a Teranthine nunnery for their betrayal, and had never appointed another duke, until now.

Hearing that Tristen was going to Amefel, and that Parsynan was recalled, Corswyndam Lord Ryssand panicked, fearing that certain records might fall into the king's hands. So he sent a rider to advise Parsynan of his imminent replacement.

Corswyndam's courier rode hard enough to reach the town of Henas'amef, the Amefin capital, ahead of the royal messenger bearing the official notice. Parsynan quite naively brought his local ally Lord Cuthan, an Aswydd by remote kinship, into his confidence, since this man had supported him against his brother earls before.

Cuthan, however, was in on a plot by the Elwynim to create war in Amefel, a distraction for Cefwyn, and the plan was to seize the citadel, on the promise Elwynim troops would then invade and engage with the king's *forces. Cuthan not only failed to warn Parsynan it was coming . . . but he also said nothing to warn his brother lords that a detachment of the king's forces was about to arrive. One or the other would happen first, and Cuthan meant to stay safe.*

So, ignorant of important pieces of information, certain Amefin lords, led by Earl Edwyll of Meiden, seized the South Court of the fortress of Amefel to wait for Elwynim support.

In the same hour, losing courage, Cuthan told the other earls the king's forces were coming, and there were as yet no Elwynim.

The other earls failed to join Edwyll . . . which suited Cuthan: he and Edwyll were old rivals, and now Edwyll was guilty of treason, sitting in the fortress with the king's forces approaching. And none of the rest of them were guilty of anything.

In a thunderstroke, before anyone had thought, Tristen arrived and, to the cheers of the populace, moved swiftly uphill to the fortress to take possession. The earls of Amefel rapidly set themselves on the winning side.

Edwyll, meanwhile, died, having enjoyed a cup of wine out of Orien Aswydd's cups, untouched since the place was sealed at her exile . . . and whether Edwyll's death was latent wizardry attached to Orien's property, or simple bad luck, the command of the rebels now devolved to Edwyll's son, thane Crissand, who was forced to surrender. Tristen now had the fortress in his hands.

Not satisfied with the death of Earl Edwyll, however, Parsynan, in command of the garrison troops, seized the prisoners from Tristen's officers and began executing them.

Tristen found out in time to save Crissand . . . and dismissed Lord Parsynan from the town in the middle of the night and without his possessions, scandalous treatment of a noble king's officer, but if there was anything wanting to make Tristen the hero of Henas'amef, this settled matters: the people were delighted, wildly cheering their new lord. Crissand, Edwyll's son, himself of remote Aswydd lineage, swore fealty to Tristen in such absolute terms it offended the Guelen clerks who had come with Tristen, for Crissand owned Tristen as his overlord after the Aswydd kind, aetheling, a royal lord, reopening all the old controversy about the status of Amefel as a sovereign kingdom. Crissand had become Tristen's friend and most fervent ally among the earls of Amefel . . . who, given a lord they respected, came rapidly into line, united for the first time in decades.

In the succeeding hours Tristen gained both the burned remnant of Mauryl's letters, and Lord Ryssand's letter to Parsynan. The first told him that correspondence Mauryl had had with the lords of Amefel might have some modern relevancy . . . one archivist had murdered the other and run with the letters. The second letter revealed Corswyndam's connivance with Parsynan.

Tristen sent Ryssand's letter posthaste to Guelessar, while Cuthan, revealed for a traitor to both sides, took advantage of Tristen's leniency to flee to Elwynor.

In the capital, Ryssand knew he had to move quickly to lessen the king's power against any baron, and one of his clerks had reported that the office of Regent of Elwynor, which Ninévrisë claimed, included priestly functions. So at Ryssand's instigation, the Holy Quinalt rose up in protest of a woman in priestly rites, which would break the marriage treaty.

Cefwyn countered with another compromise and a trade of favors with the Holy Father: Ninévrisë agreed to state that she was and had always been of the Bryaltine sect, that recognized though scantly respectable Amefin religion, and if she agreed to accept a priest of that faith as her priest, leaving aside other difficult questions, the Quinalt would perform the wedding.

The barons now came with the last and worst: charges of infidelity, Ninévrisë's with Tristen, laughable if one knew them . . . but Ryssand's daughter Artisane was prepared to perjure herself to bring Ninévrisë down, and Ryssand's son Brugan brought the charges to Cefwyn, along with a document giving much of his power to the barons, which was clearly the alternative.

Therein Ryssand overstepped himself: it gave an excuse for a loyal baron, Cevulirn of Ivanor, to challenge Brugan and, by killing him, change the character of the effort. The gods had let a man of the king's kill the man who made the charge, and if Ryssand should make public the attack on Ninévrisë, that fact would come out.

But if it should, someone would challenge Cevulirn, and another and another . . . or if it did not, Ryssand could not be expected to deal civilly with the man who had killed his son. Cefwyn still hoped to deal with the other barons, and would cast the killing as a private quarrel to prevent the issue becoming public.

But that meant Cevulirn had to leave court, and Cefwyn girded himself for a confrontation in court with a powerful baron who had just lost his son . . . a confrontation that might yet tear the kingdom apart if the other barons stood with Ryssand.

Into this situation Ryssand's incriminating letter arrived secretly into Cefwyn's hands . . . and Cefwyn thus had the means to suggest Ryssand retire to his estates immediately, or have all his actions made public to the other barons.

So the treaty stood firm, Cefwyn and Ninévrisë married, and Tristen settled in to rule in the south as lord of Amefel, lord of the province containing old Althalen and bordering Ynefel and Elwynor across the river.

And rule he does, in the first glorious winter of his wizard-summoned life.

BOOK
ONE

CHAPTER 1

Master Emuin had packed in a night, when His Majesty in Guelemara had decreed a new duke for Amefel. Baskets, barrels, and bundles had gone out of master Emuin's tower room in the Guelesfort in the heart of Guelemara and into wagons that night of storm and departure, and after a slow transit between provinces, up they had come, a week and more later, into the appointed tower in the fortress of Henas'amef.

But when master Emuin's new tower room had reached its apparent limits, as it had on the day following his arrival, why, baskets and bundles coming up for the week afterward had necessarily accumulated on the stairs and on the very small landing, hardly more than a step, that gave a servant, a petitioner, or the new duke of Amefel himself scant place to stand and knock for admittance.

"Master Emuin?"

"Leave it on the stairs! Gods bless, fool, there's no more room!"

"Master Emuin, it's Tristen, if you please."

Footsteps crossed the floor. The door opened. The old man peered out, hair disarrayed and gusting past his face in a cold wind and a white daylight that said the shutters were open despite the snow sifting down outside.

"Master Emuin, you'll freeze." Tristen pushed through the door into the round tower room, where, indeed, shut-

ters were wide to the winds and windows were blazing
white with winter sky. Emuin was wrapped in a heavy
traveling cloak, and so was Tristen, but for different reasons, Tristen was sure. Master Emuin had kept his room
in the Guelesfort in similar state, but in the milder days of
autumn, and, however new to his authority over the old
man, Tristen was certainly not disposed to tolerate that
state of affairs here.

Consequently, he began closing shutters.

To Emuin's clear indignation: "And how am I to
see, pray?"

"Candles. Lanterns. As other people do, sir! People
account *me* the simpleton, and you the wizard and
wise man, and you have the hall full of baskets and
this tower so cold it gusts cold wind into the lower
hall. Whence this notion not to have candles?"

There followed a small, uncomfortable pause in
which Emuin looked elsewhere.

"It *is* that?" Tristen asked, surprised to have happened on the truth. Then he added that favorite, persistent question that always found so little patience
among ordinary folk: "*Why*, sir?"

"Plague and bother of lighting fires! Leave my shutters alone! The place is dark as a cave."

"If you'll not have Tassand arrange this, then *I*
shall, sir. I *will*, with or without your leave." It was a
great impertinence to defy the old man, but he had
learned of Cefwyn how to argue, and argue he was
prepared to do.

"The duke of Amefel will not carry baskets and
build shelves! There are simply too many baskets to
fit! They used to fit! I don't know how it came to be so
much. Leave one shutter, I say! How can a man see?"

"Then you'll accept Tassand's help." He faced an
obdurate, weary old man, one who had not planned to
reestablish his workshop twice, a man at his wits' end after

a hard journey . . . an old man who still, a week after coming all this journey specifically to advise him in his new office, at least as Emuin had said to him, continually found reasons not to speak to him frankly on far more important matters than baggage obstructing the stairs. "And you *shall* have it, sir, his help or mine. You may choose which, but the lower hall is full of drafts, and the candles blow out when someone opens the east doors."

A tremor of weariness had come into Emuin's mouth, and more wrinkles than usual mapped the territory around his eyes. He trembled on the verge of yielding. Then: "No! No, *you* will not be arranging baskets or carrying them."

"Then Tassand, sir. His Majesty set me in charge. I must have the baskets up the stairs and the shutters shut."

A second surly glance.

"I'll have them set in whatever order you wish," Tristen said, "a fire laid, candles lit. Please have all the windows shut by this evening, sir, at least by the time the sun goes down."

"Beeswax. None of your tallow candles, young lord, nothing stinking of slaughter. I will have beeswax."

Then there was more in it than candles, as there was more in Emuin's insistence on open windows than a desire for daylight by day and a view of the stars at night. Master Emuin was not a man who chose luxury or spent money profligately, beeswax being the luxury, above tallow. But he *was* a wizard, and the question of beeswax or tallow passed not without note and not without significance in Tristen's thoughts.

"Beeswax," Tristen said, "you shall have, sir." He was pressed for time in this small foray up the stairs, and let the precise reason of the candles escape comment, but he marked it for inquiry at some quieter moment. "You'll have Tassand's earnest attention to whatever things you need, clothing for attendance in hall . . . and all set in order in a proper clothespress." He saw that the one that did exist was crammed so full of bottles and papers the doors stood open.

"Nonsense."

"Tassand need not retrieve your robes out of baskets."

"I have no room, I say! Hang them on a peg. For a peg, I have room!"

"Join me at supper this evening, where it's warm. Cook will have meat pies."

"When I have found my charts, young lord! *If* I have found my charts, which at the moment seems unlikely!"

Emuin shouted in frustration, and Tristen found his own amiability tested. "They might be in those baskets on the stairs, sir. Dogs might come at them. There *was* a dog about. I saw him below." That this had been far out in the yard, from the window, he failed to say. Whatever moved master Emuin to accept help and hasten his baskets up the steps was a benefit.

"Perish the creature! Very well, very well, *send* Tassand! Gods *bless*!" Master Emuin cracked his shin against a bench in the dimmed light. "Leave me one window, if you please! I have old eyes. Gods, what a contentious lad you've become!"

"For your health's sake, sir, and the servants', and the downstairs candles, and to have your advice for a long time to come, without your taking ill up here, yes, I have become extremely contentious." Tristen relented, leaving one leeward shutter ajar on stiff metal hinges so that the room was not altogether in twilight. He had had a fire laid in the hearth and wood provided in advance of his teacher's arrival, and it had burned far too fast, thanks to the gusts, he was sure.

The tower room had a fireplace which shared a duct with the guardroom below and the hall below that, three flues and one common stonework that led to the wayward and now wintry winds above the fortress roof. It was thanks to the warm stonework, with other rooms' smoke passing through, that there was any comfort at all in the room. "You need more firewood. Have you asked?"

"No, no. And I don't need a fire. The damned wind kicks up a gale in here when the flue's open. Damn." Master Emuin had found a pot of powders spilled in the bottom of a basket, and was not in a good humor. "Damn, damn."

It seemed time for even the lord of Amefel to make a quiet retreat, out the door and down past the numerous baskets of herbs and birds' nests and down again the rambling East Stairs, with its little nooks and shelves and half levels, themselves piled high with stray baskets. His guard, four men, his constant and trusted companions, had waited below, and followed him from there.

It had not been an entirely satisfactory meeting. He had come upstairs intending to set the fortress generally under master Emuin's surveillance, had found himself distracted into argument about the shutters.

Distraction in master Emuin's vicinity was not an uncommon occurrence. He would have liked to have asked master Emuin about the archives and the problems there. He would have liked to consult master Emuin about the vacant earldom of Bryn, but they had ended arguing about other things. He saw no likelihood that all the baskets and bundles were ever going to fit into the tower. Now he walked the hall uneasy in this requirement regarding the candles, which echoed off his own dislike of Emuin's open and unwarded windows . . . and there was another piece of unfinished business he had not yet had a chance to discuss with Emuin: the wizard-work that had left the fortress more open than some to wizardous attack.

He most of all wished that master Emuin would leave his charts in whatever disorder they fell, look at events around him, and provide a steady and sober counsel to him in his new rule over the province of Amefel.

Yes, Emuin had advised him in some limited particulars, but there remained the flood of mundane matters which he had not yet been able to persuade the old man to hear, such as the pile of petitions regarding land settlements, and several very much greater ones, involving the king and the situation in Elwynor.

But no, Emuin would not be at peace to hear anything so important until his workshop was in order, which it was not, and showed no prospect of being. Tristen began asking himself where he could find storage outside the tower, which master Emuin thus far refused to consider; he had come upstairs to gain advice about the affairs of the fortress, and instead found himself wondering where he could set a clothespress.

Now he found himself wondering why he had ever thought he could spare an afternoon to leave the fortress and ride outside the walls.

But Earl Crissand had pleaded with him and cajoled him to take some relief from the demands on his attention. He had a need and a duty, Crissand said, to see the people and be seen by them, a duty he could not accomplish inside the fortress. The ducal seat at Henas'amef had become remote and estranged from the commons even under its recent duke and duchess, and the last authority, Lord Parsynan, had brought the land nothing but grief and bloodshed. It was time the people saw hope for better days.

So here they were, he and his guard all cloaked and gloved and equipped for winter riding—an unexpectedly appropriate weight of clothing for venturing the tower room—bound for the west doors and the stable-court. The escape seemed both more attractive and less responsible since the conversation above; and he only hoped to reach the stables.

All through the lower hall the household staff with mops and buckets fought back the thin gloss of mud soldiers and workmen brought from the snowy yard. And around the central doors, that mud mixed with the shavings and dust of workmen repairing the damages of their new lord's accession. It was a second source of draft in the fortress, where wind leaked through the nailed patches, and it was a hazard to his escape, a source of overseers with questions.

He foresaw it: now a well-dressed master craftsmen intersected his path and showed him a paper, the requests of craftsmen for an order of oak planks.

Consult Tassand, was his answer to no few. He was sure his chief of household knew no more about oak planks than he did about wizardry and herb lore—less, in fact—but Tassand at least knew how to send petitioners to appropriate places. From being merely a body servant, Tassand had become a duke's master of household, did the office of chamberlain and half the office of seneschal.

Tassand seemed to know, moreover, when an order was excessive or excessively expensive, which his lord did not. He did know that money represented hours and quality of a man's work, and that dukes did not have an endless supply of it.

But today, faced with an order for wood which seemed reasonable for carpenters, and anxious to reach the doors: "Yes," he said, and moved on. "Yes," he said, to a further request, and he had no more than sent that man off, than a third man in court clothes appeared in his path, unrolling drawings of the carvings of the new main doors, and asking whether the design pleased him.

"The Eagle of Amefel in the center panel, do you see, Your Grace, and the border of oak leaves, for endurance . . ."

He had no idea why he should be asked about the carving for the main doors, which he had simply ordered repaired to stop the draft. The only usefulness of the carving might be a kind of magical seal, and everyone from earls to servants to his close friends had assumed that common doors would not do . . . nothing common ever suited. Endurance seemed a reasonable, a happy wish, to which he certainly consented, and with a wish of his own he reinforced it . . . he helped the craftsmen as he could, not knowing what he was supposed to do.

But by now he was sure he was overdue in the stable-court, and he was more and more sure Crissand was right in urging him to ride out for a day: he grew weary and short of patience. His court did everything in a great deal of fuss and uncertainty, and questions seemed to come to him faster than he could learn. Wishes for solutions aside, he had not enough officers, not enough servants, no clear lines of appeal—and, as Tassand had informed him, unhappily there was no other person established as the authority. What had existed, Parsynan and Edwyll between them had destroyed; and now both were gone, and he was there.

Consequently everyone wanted his attention, everyone wished to establish their connections and their favor with the new duke, and in the process their demands pressed on him until his head fairly swam with questions. He did not know *who* should do these things. He had no idea. And under the incessant demands for his attention, he could not find answers.

Indeed he was so overwhelmed he feared even Crissand had motives in stealing him away for several hours in private . . . points to press, favors to gain at the worst; and in agreeing to go, he knew it would wound him to the heart if that was all Crissand's reason in seeking his company. He hoped for less selfish notions in this young man who seemed so inclined toward him. He hoped for some beacon in this sea of demands, but he had been disappointed before, discovering even master Emuin set his own will ahead of friendship and promises, and that Cefwyn, whom he loved, had as many demands on his time as he had.

He understood Cefwyn's situation, now, in a way he never could have before.

But knowing that turned him desperately to seek warmth and company where it seemed to offer. And, oh, that might be foolish of him, and expose him to hazards such as he had seen in Cefwyn's court.

But he went. He trusted. He stormed through the last stretch of hallway toward the stable-court before more questioners could close about him—for he had been indoors for an entire fortnight now, imprisoned in his duty, in men's squabbles and difficulties, while all the wonder of snow spread across the land outside his misted, frosty windows.

And now the chance was on him. He rushed toward freedom in simple, undilute curiosity, eager to meet the sights that had tantalized him and eager to have a horse under him for a few hours . . . eager most of all to have Crissand beside him and the sound of a friendly voice without a single demand for favor or approval of some document.

Cefwyn had made him duke of Amefel . . . and of all pleasures the high office might have afforded (the prior lord, Heryn, had ordered gold dinnerplates, and the viceroy, Lord Parsynan, had coveted a lady's jewels), he discovered that the greatest and least attainable of all his treasures was time, time to ride out in the sparkling white and time to be with friends.

And when he and his accustomed bodyguards, Lusin and the rest, escaped out the west doors into the snowy damp air and thumped down the steepest steps in the fortress—he found himself both free and faced with a yard he had forgotten would be teeming with soldiery and oxen and carts.

"The lord's come down!" A trio of stablehands scampered at the sight of them, dodging through the confusion of ox teams and heaps of equipment bound for the bottom of the hill, all shouting for the duke's horses as they went. Tristen regarded the commotion with some dismay: nothing he did these days was circumspect or secret, and no one went sluggishly to accommodate him; the carts were going to the border, the army was going, this was the day he had appointed, and such had been his haste this morning he had not even realized his ride and the carts' being loaded overlapped each other.

Almost as they cleared the bottom step, one of the stablemaster's lads came laboring through the press with the tall ducal standards bundled together, brought from their storage near the armory, a heavy burden for a slight lad. It was a heavy burden, too, for the grown men appointed to carry them when they were unfurled. They were inevitably cumbersome, and in the wish of his heart, Tristen would have bidden the boy put the banners back in their safekeeping so he and Crissand could simply ride free and enjoy the day in anonymity . . . but those banners were part and parcel of their honest excuse for riding forth today. They would show them abroad, ride through the town of Henas'amef in brave display, and visit the nearest villages, likewise: and all that was to confirm that, indeed and at last, Amefel had a lord watching over them and doing the sort of things a lord did. In a winter ominous with war and its preparations, Crissand had reasoned with him, the people needed to see him. Banners were for courage, and they had to see them fly.

War . . . he did understand. Doors and orders for oak were another question altogether.

Perhaps Crissand might show him that, too.

Carts maneuvered with ponderous difficulty, one loading, one waiting. Uwen Lewen's-son arrived through the gap between with bay Gia at lead—Uwen bundled up in a heavy cloak and with a coif pulled up over his silver-streaked hair. Tristen recognized the horse but not immediately his own right-hand man.

Uwen was more sensible than he was, Tristen thought, feeling the nip of the wind, in which his hair blew free. It was not a dank cold, but a crisp, invigorating one, with the sky trying its best to be blue. It was better weather than they had enjoyed for a week; but it might turn, and while he came from his hasty passage through the lower hall all overheated, he had his coif and cowl, his heavy gloves and lined boots, foreseeing wind among the hills.

"A fine day," Uwen said. "Weather-luck is with us."

"A bright day," he said, his heart all but soaring. He had dreaded winter as a time of death, then seen it advance during their passage from Guelessar in an unexpected glory of frost . . . from his high windows he daily saw snow lying white and pure across the land and had wondered would it look as white close at hand.

And was snow like water, into which it turned, and did it change colors according to the sky like a pond? He saw it take on the glories of sunrise and sunset, such as there were under a leaden sky. He waited to see what the sun would bring.

And with the arrival of the sun for the first time in days he saw the promise of wonders. Even in the brawling confusion of the carts and the limited vantage of the stable yard, he saw Icicles, which he had only just learned as a Word, and never seen so glorious as just now, on this morning of sun breaking through the clouds. They decorated every ledge and eave, and sparkled. The most casual glance around at the yard showed how a frosting of snow glossed all the common things of the stable into importance. He had never noticed the curious carving about the stable door, for instance, an unexpectedly fine decoration for a humble building: the lintel was beautiful edged in the sifting of snow, a carving of flowers and grain, appropriate enough for horses.

All around him such details leapt up, from the pure snow lying on the stonework edges, white instead of mortar, to the way it made a thick blanket on the stable roof.

With Uwen accounted for and his guard waiting for their horses, he stared about him in a moment of delighted curiosity, seeking other wonders, finding beauty even in the lion-faced drain spouts above them, that he had never seen.

He wished, of course, not to be seen gawping about, as Uwen called it: the duke of Amefel had to rule with dignity and become like other lords, immune to wonder, attentive to serious matters, never easily distracted from the solemn business of his rank.

Oh, but so many things were new in this, his first winter in the world. The eaves of the gatehouse and its roof slates shone so bright in a moment of clear sunlight that they hurt the eyes. Never in the world was light so powerful, and yet the air itself was cold.

Meanwhile the lad with the standards had delivered them to Sergeant Gedd, foremost of the standard-bearers riding with him today, and was about to pursue his own business. But Tristen, seeing those two young, strong legs, pounced on the messenger he needed and nipped the lad's sleeve before he could quite escape.

"My lord!" Eyes were round and cheeks were cold-stung to a wondrously fiery blush. "May I serve m'lord?"

"Go inside, go upstairs to my apartments, and tell whoever comes to the door that I've spoken to master Emuin, do you have that? Say that Tassand is to go up to the tower as soon as possible and set it in order. Do you have all that?"

"Yes, m'lord! Tassand's to go to the tower!" The lad was solemn now, and puffed up with importance, and, dismissed, bowed and raced up the outside steps in frantic haste, slipping on the ice there.

There went more mud into the halls, but certainly the boy was no worse than the soldiers. Advising Tassand might have waited until he returned from the ride: he had all but forgotten his agreement in the distraction of the hallway. But now Tassand would attend master Emuin before master Emuin could forget he had ever agreed, so they would not have that argument again. He might have the stairs clear and master Emuin's noxious pots and powders out of the stairwell before evening, which might let Cook's servants reach the old man with food without breaking their necks.

On such chance encounters and with such chance-met messengers he did business, and that, he was sure, was part of the trouble. When they had set out from the capital he had felt overwhelmed with the size of the staff he had brought along, and now he found it a very scant number to accomplish the running of a province. Cook, an Amefin woman, had found him several reliable new servants for the halls; Ness at the gate, who was Amefin, had found two more for the storerooms; and the clerk they had brought from Guelemara, a Guelenman who nevertheless looked to make a home here in Amefel, was looking for likely lads with suitable training.

The house staff he had inherited from Parsynan came from service in or to noble Amefin houses, each one of which had its ambitions and each one of which would hear reports from those they lent. Such servants as had served Lord Heryn and Orien had mostly fled across the river, some in fear of the king, some in fear of their neighbors and rivals . . . and those servants that did remain of the original staff had to be watched by the servants he trusted.

But still he gathered them—all the servants, all the folk who in some way had dealt with him in his first days. He counted them part of Amefel, and his, even searching after the lad who had first met him as a stranger in Amefel and guided his steps to the gate-guards. He sought them out, guided them into his safe-keeping . . . and thus out of the hands of malign working from across the river, not enough of a staff yet, and those missing pieces were well scattered and hard to find again, which the more persuaded him it was necessary. He was *here*. He had a Place in the world. Certain things and persons had led him to that Place, and having done so, they were snared in magic: therefore, they had to be found.

Meanwhile, waiting for the lost to return and for the staff to reknit itself, they were short-handed.

"So master Emuin is havin' Tassand's help after all," Uwen said, standing beside him at the bottommost step, looking over the yard from that slight advantage, taller than he by that means, when ordinarily that was not the case.

"If he admits he ever agreed," Tristen said. "But I've learned. I press my advantage while I have it."

"Gods know what's in them baskets o' his," Uwen said. "I ain't pokin' into 'em, an' I hope Tassand's careful. Gods know what'll crawl out."

The boys were bringing the horses up by now, and the guardsmen that were serving as his escort arrived, already ahorse, passing in front of one of the wagons. Its ox team backed away from the crowding of half a dozen horses, not something an ox hitch or its wagon did well, and its left wheel aimed for a stack of barrels.

"Hold there!" Uwen shouted at the standing driver, seeing it in the same instant, and ran to slap the nearer ox on its rump and start it forward. The driver with his goad saw his dilemma and diverted his team on around the small circle of free space to face the gate, cart wheels not making the turn well, where Uwen again got to the fore, holding up both hands. "'At's good. Now ye hold that cart right here, man, no matter who says otherwise, until His Grace is down the hill. Don't ye be blockin' the road."

That effectively blocked all the other carts behind, who could not come through to load, but it saved them having that lumbering vehicle before them all the way down the hill . . . an incongruous precedence for a show of the ducal banners that would have been. The carts were gathering up the tents and heavy stores to take them down the hill, a slow process, that evidently had not started at dawn, when the ice was hard: they must have waited for the sun.

And that raised a question where Captain Anwyll was, who was supposed to be dealing with the drivers and the setting forth of the supplies to the river. Tristen observed Uwen's crisp passing of instructions, faulted Anwyll for his absence from the scene, then realized that he himself as the lord of Amefel had been more properly looking out for such considerations as the order of precedence, rather than gazing at the icicles.

Mooncalf, His Majesty's commander had been wont to call him.

"Where is Anwyll?" he asked Uwen.

"Dunno, m'lord. I'll find out."

The safety of others depended on him. He saw numerous failings in himself which he was resolved to mend, and knew that, no, it was not usually the grand things in which he failed: he had very reasonably, if high-handedly, contradicted the king's orders, taken the wide risk with the weather in sending Cefwyn's carts to the border with necessary supplies instead of back to Cefwyn, where they would wait idle all winter. The carters were irate: they had expected to be done and back on the road in the opposite direction, headed for Guelemara and their homes before the snows blocked the roads for good and all, and instead they were out on Amefin roads, which were little more than cattle-traces.

More, while the carts would not move in the deep winter, they were still Cefwyn's, and the king needed those wagons in Guelemara for very much the same reason as he himself was fortifying the border in the south. He hoped that he was right in his estimations—that no sudden Elwynim incursion on Cefwyn's west would make them necessary in the north, for he was not only keeping Cefwyn's carts for one more duty, he had also appropriated to border defense the detachment of Dragon Guard that had escorted him to Amefel.

But he had had no choice. When Cefwyn had sent him to take command of the garrison of Guelen Guard, neither of them had foreseen the situation, that the Guelen Guard of the garrison would have so bloodily offended against the Amefin that the Amefin would no longer deal with them. The Guelens had to be set down, the Dragons sent to do their work.

Nor had he been able to ask Cefwyn what to do. Messages went slowly and unpredictably between Amefel and Guelessar, and with the weather, more so. He had not had a reply to his last message from the capital, it was six days to send and obtain an answer, at least, and meanwhile he could only solve the problems he had at hand: keep the disgraced Guelens under tight rein, in garrison at the capital, and send the reliable Dragons to hold the river to be sure the Elwynim did not keep their promise to the earls of Amefel and invade.

More, if the weather turned a little worse for a little longer, the river could freeze, and if it froze, there would *be* no division between Amefel and Elwynor. For that reason he wanted reliable men there to watch . . . especially over the main road at Anas Mallorn, north of Modeyneth, which was the only road that would carry a large force rapidly to the heart of Amefel.

And that meant the men he was sending to the river had to have supply enough to last the winter in case the weather turned worse.

So he had no choice but to borrow the king's carts, weighing one disaster against another, and knowing Cefwyn was better served by a southern border in good order than by strict, uninformed obedience to his orders.

Such decisions, strategy, and maneuvering of armies, he could make with a clear head and strong confidence. He had done all that, and it weighed very little on his mind. It was the daily and moment-by-moment details of the operation that eluded him, and the details from which the sights and the sparkle of the sun claimed his attention. He knew the captains should have argued more strenuously about this day's outing, about the carts, about the decisions he made, but no one had, and that was his abiding concern. They took his orders so well that no one told him his mistakes these days, and Uwen came back to him with no more than a shrug and a glance back at the drivers.

"Fools," Uwen said, tugging his hand into a gauntlet.

Uwen should be here, administering the town. But Uwen would not let him ride out alone, and on the other hand, Amefel was too volatile a command, the feeling against Guelenfolk far too bitter to leave Captain Anwyll in charge of the capital. He left command to Lord Drumman, whom he trusted, an Amefin, and he hoped the Guelen Guard would create no new difficulty about it . . . not mentioning the other earls. He was only now learning which earl resented which other one in what particular respect.

But Drumman was generally liked. Therefore, he sent Anwyll to do the one thing a determined Guelenman might do with the goodwill of the earls: guard the river; Uwen he set in as much authority as Uwen was willing to take, but today Uwen went with him . . . his guard did, too, Guelen and conspicuously fair amid the generally darker Amefin.

"There's Lord Meiden, m'lord," Lusin said, and indeed, a little late himself, Earl Crissand had just ridden under the gate and past the rear of the inbound carts.

But not just the earl. The earl brought with him his own escort, the men of Meiden all cloaked and armed, and now completely obstructing the small courtyard around the oxcarts . . . indeed, Crissand's guard turned out to exceed his own, a show of force from a decimated house . . . he did not fail to notice it himself, as all around him the men of his own, Guelen-born, escort stiffened their backs and stared with misgivings.

Crissand, too, seemed to realize he had made a misstep, and rode up much more meekly than he had ridden in. "My lord," Crissand said, above the discontent lowing of oxen, and dismounted to pay his respects. "I had expected far more men. Forgive me. Shall I send back my guard?"

Did Crissand think so many guards prudent, and was Crissand right in estimating safety and risk out in his own rural land?

Crissand was young as he, at least in apparent years, and did many things to excess, but he had never seemed to be a fool regarding Amefel, and knew his land. They were Crissand's villages they proposed to visit. Tristen's eyes passed worriedly over the situation, as confusion reigned for a moment in the small yard and the Guelenmen of the Dragon Guard eyed the Amefin of Crissand's household in suspicious assessment amid the oxcarts.

In the same moment a stableboy oblivious to all the rivalry of Guelen and Amefin escorts brought red Gery up, holding out the reins. Tristen found it easier to set his foot in the stirrup and be under way than to sort out the excess of guards and weapons and precedences and this lord's sensibilities and that lord's distrust. He was not unarmed, standing naked in his bath. He did not fear Crissand.

"Bring them," he said to Crissand's anxious looking up at him.

In truth he would be solely an Amefin lord, relying only on these men, once he dismissed his Guelen forces back to Guelessar, as he must when he had raised sufficient Amefin units. Was that why Crissand had brought so many—that Crissand had proposed to supply the escort for him?

How he would have a ducal regiment in any good order by spring without setting one earl against another was another question—which earldom would contribute men and how many? But it was not today's question . . . for once he was up and had Gery's lively force under him, the motion and the prospect of freedom chased all more complex thoughts from his head. He was in the right place; he had done the right things. He ached from too much sitting in chairs and far too many difficult and contentious decisions in recent days. He knew he had sat blind to the land he was supposed to be governing, and hearing his choices only from the lips of advisers. Now he had that saddle under him and Gery willing and eager to move, he was eager to go, and circled Gery about with an eye to the gate as Uwen and his guard mounted up. The two troops muddled ranks for a moment, then began to sort out in fair good spirits.

The Dragon Guard themselves had been glad to have an outing away from the barracks, and good humor prevailed, though Tristen suspected a sharp rivalry still manifested in the haste and smartness with which the banner of Amefel unfurled in Sergeant Gedd's hands. The Eagle on its red field made a brave splash of color against the whites and browns and grays of the yard; and after it the two black banners of his other honors unrolled from their staffs, the Tower of the Lord Warden of Ynefel and the Tower and Star of the Lord Marshal of Althalen . . . both honors without inhabitants, but Amefin ones, so the Amefin made much of them. It was a brave show; and protocol held the banner of the Earl of Meiden to unfurl second: a blue banner with the Sun in gold, as brave and bright as Earl Crissand himself, dark as his fellow Amefin but with a glance like the summer sky. He might have been embarrassed for a moment in the relative size of their guards; but the day was so brisk and keen there was no resisting the natural joy in him. There was love in

Crissand Adiran, of all the earls, a disposition to be near him, to seek his friendship—and how could he have thought ill of Crissand's reasons?

There was love, a reliable and a real love grown in a handful of days, and Tristen did not know why it was: friendship had happened to both of them, on the sudden, completely aside from Tristen's both endangering and saving Crissand's life. It was no reason related to that, it was no reason that either of them quite knew. Crissand had simply risen on his horizon like the sun of his banner . . . and that was that. Prudence aside, putting by all worry for master Emuin and his advice, and for the workmen and for all the household, all in the friendship that had begun to exist, they were together, and there was a great deal right with the day simply in that.

With banners in the lead they rode out the iron-barred gates of the Zeide, gate-guards standing to sharp attention to salute them. The racket of their hooves echoed off the high frontages of the great houses around about as, wasting no time in the square, they began the downward course . . . numerous enough for an armed venture rather than a ride for pleasure, and they drew curious stares from those with business about the fortress gates, but as they entered the street the sun broke from a moment of cloud, shining all the way down the high street to midtown, lighting a blinding white blanket on gables of the high frontages, and that glorious sight gave no room for worry.

Traffic had worn off the snow in the streets to a little edge of soiled ice, and the brown cobbles ran with disappointingly ugly melt down that trace of sunlight, but above, about the eaves, all was glorious. The houses grown familiar to Tristen's eye from the summer were all frosted with snow and hung with icicles, and the sunlight danced and shone on them as they rode, shutters dislodging small falls of snow and breakage of ice as they opened for townsmen to see. The cheer in the company spread to the onlookers, who waved happily at this first sight of their new lord outside the fortress walls, and in company with Amefin. Already they had encouraged high spirits.

And, oh, the icicles . . . small ones, large ones, and a prodigious great one at the gable of the baker's shop, on a street as familiar to Tristen's sight as his own hallway atop the hill . . . familiar, yet he had never noticed that gable, never noticed half the nooks and crannies and overhangs of the high buildings that carried such sun-touched jewelry today.

It seemed wondrous to him, even here in the close streets. He turned to look behind them, gazing past the ranks of ill-assorted guardsmen and cheering townsfolk as dogs yapped and gave chase. It gave him the unexpected view of the high walls and iron gates of the Zeide, all jeweled and shining as if enchantment had touched them.

Lord Sihhë! someone shouted out then, at which he glanced forward in dismay. Others called it out from the windows, *Lord Sihhë and Meiden!* in high good cheer. The sound racketed through the town, and people shouted it from the street.

Lord Sihhë indeed. That, he had not wished. The Holy Father in Guelessar would never approve that title the people gave him; and the local Quinalt patriarch, before whom he had to maintain a good appearance, was sure to get the rumor of what the people shouted. Feckless as he had been, he had learned the price words cost, and he wished he could hush those particular cries . . . but they did it of love, nothing ill meant, and it was all up and down the street. The old blood might be anathema to the Guelen Quinalt; but among Amefin folk, who were Bryaltines, it was honor they paid him. They shouted it in delight: *Lord Sihhë and Meiden!* as Crissand waved happily at the onlookers, the partnership of the oldest of Amefin houses with the banner of Althalen, as it had been a hundred years ago, when Meiden was the friend of the Sihhë . . . was it that they thought of?

Past the crossing at midtown, they gathered speed on the relatively clear cobbles and jogged briskly downhill past a last few side streets and the last few shops and trades, down to the rougher, more temporary buildings near the walls. The town's lower gates stood open: they ordinarily did so by broad daylight; and consequently there was no delay at all to their riding out, no more concern for townsfolk and titles or the determined town dogs. The wide snowy expanse beyond the dark stone arch was freedom for a day.

He found himself lord of a changed land as he rode out . . . white, white, where the brown of autumn had been, and before that, the green and gold of enchanted summer . . . all gone, all buried and blanketed and tucked away for the winter.

All the knotty questions of armies and rivalries and titles and entitlements of lords fell away in broad, bright wonder, for if breath-blurred windows had shown him the surrounding fields and orchards as hazy white, the utter expanse of it had until now escaped him. There just was no cease of it. Boundaries that all summer and fall had said here is one field and here another, here a meadow, there a field . . . all were overlain until stone fences and sheep-hedges made no more than ridges.

But while those grand lines had blurred, he had never, at the distance of his windows, imagined the wealth of details written in the new snow, the record of farmers' traffic that told where men and beasts had walked hours, even days ago. The landing of a bird left traces, like marks on parchment.

Shadows of birds, too, passed on the snow, prompting him to look up, and then to smile, for his birds flew above them, outward bound, his silly, beloved pigeons, faring out on their business, as by evening they would fly home to the towers and ledges of the fortress, looking for bread and their perches. They circled over once, and flew out ahead, seeming to have urgent business in mind . . . a barn, perhaps the spill of a granary door: the woods never suited them. The woods were Owl's domain.

"Are they the ones from the tower?" Crissand asked, himself looking up.

"I think they are."

"Do they follow you?" Crissand asked.

"They go where they like. I don't govern them."

Did his birds fly sometimes far afield, and did they sometimes meet the pigeons that nested at Ynefel?

He was not sure, indeed, that anything lived at Ynefel. He saw them sweep a turn toward the west, indeed, away, away toward the river . . . and equally toward the stony hills around ruined Althalen. Ruins suited them well: they liked ledges and stonework. Certainly birds that dared nest at Ynefel, if they were the same birds, would never fear Althalen.

"Nothing of omen," Crissand wondered in some anxiousness.

"No," he said as they rode, "only birds."

A cloud came, passed. Many clouds came and went, and fields blazed white after shadow. Snow on bare gray apple branches made lacework of the eastern view. Moving shadows grayed the hills, and the sky was an amazing clear blue with fat wandering clouds, while the morning's fall cast a winter glamour on common stones and roadside broom. The horses' nostrils flared wide, their ears pricked forward in the bracing air. Their steps were willingly quick and light.

"Is it the South Road we use all the way?" he asked Crissand at a certain point. He had looked at maps; but the hills were a maze of small trails, some missing from the charts, he much suspected, and he was very willing to use a shortcut and go up into the wonderful hills if Crissand knew one.

"Yes, my lord, south an hour," Crissand said, "to Padys Spring. There's an old shrine, and the village track to Levey comes in there, only over the ridge. We'll leave the main road there."

Padys rang not at all off memory, neither the village of Levey, nor Padys Spring . . . though he was sure there should be water where Crissand described a spring being.

But, also, to his vague thought, the name of the place was not quite Padys.

"Bathurys," he said suddenly, pleased to have caught it.

"M'lord?"

"Bathurys," he said. It seemed increasingly sure to him that that was the proper name of the spring, as sometimes the very old names came to him. There was a shrine, Crissand had already said; but he was less sure of that fact.

But there at least should be a spring at a place called Bathurys, and when he set a right name to it, he far better recalled the lay of the land . . . thought of a village of gray stone, and flocks of sheep.

It was not so far a ride, then. He felt happy both in Gery's free and cheerful movement and in the increasing good temper of the company around him. He even heard laughter among the soldiers behind, and beside him, Uwen, who habitually was shy of lords' company, was not shy in Crissand's presence, and bantered somewhat with Crissand's captain, riding near them.

The two guard companies, the Dragons and the men of Meiden, had fought each other with bloody determination the night of his arrival; but the Dragons had also rescued Crissand and his men from execution, so with this particular Guelen regiment, the tally sheet of good and bad was mixed. Besides, the Dragons were a Guelen company the Amefin held in higher regard than they had ever held for the Guelen Guard, even before Parsynan's rule here: the Dragons, better disciplined, had never been hard-handed with the townsfolk, never stolen, never done any of the things the Guelens had done, so he had it reported. So, warily, cautiously, goodwill grew, in the amity of the officers and the lords, so in the ranks.

And, truth, by the time they had passed the first rest and ridden over the icy bridge, Uwen and the captain of Meiden's house guard were cheerfully comparing winters they had known, and arguing about the merits of sheep, while the men in the ranks had proceeded to local autumn, local ale, the taverns in Guelemara and those in Amefel, and the women they knew.

The men found their ways of talking. But Tristen labored in his converse with Crissand as if they were strangers, for all their prior dealings had been policy and statecraft. Now they talked idly, as common men did, about the autumn, the land, the flocks, and the apples. Uwen, who had been a farmer before he was a soldier, knew far more about any of these things, Tristen was sure, but Crissand knew everything there was to know about apples, their type, and their value. All Tristen found to do was ask question and question and question. Crissand did know his people's trade, down to the tending of apple orchards and sheep, which he had done with his own hands, and had no hesitation in the answers.

"The flocks are most of my people's living," Crissand said, "more so than the orchards in the last five years, since the blight. Lord Drumman's district is all orchards of one kind and another. So is Azant's. But we fared well enough in Meiden, since we have both sheep and apples: the barley never does well, to speak of: that comes from the east and from Imor and Llymaryn."

And again, after a time, Crissand said, "Lewenbrook was hardest on Levey of all Meiden's villages. Fourteen dead is a heavy toll for a village of two hundred, six more wounded, seven lost with my guard, a fortnight gone. That's a quarter of all the village, and every man they had between sixteen and thirty."

Tristen had not reckoned the dead in those terms, but it came clear to him, such a hardship.

"A great many widows for a small village," Crissand said, "and them to do the spring plowing, except I gift younger sons from some of my other villages to go and plant for the widows when they've seen to their own fields."

"We will not have Amefel for a battlefield again," Tristen vowed, with all knowledge Cefwyn was going to war and that he must. He would not have the war cross the river. He was resolved on that.

"Gods grant," Crissand said fervently.

Sun flashed about them when Crissand said it. It had been a moment of cloud, which passed . . . and indeed now there was certainly no tardiness in the heavens, though the wind was still. Spots of sunlight came and went with increasing rapidity across the land, glorious patches of light and gray shadow on the snow.

The talk was, albeit puzzling to him, also enlightening, even in this first part of their ride, of the things Crissand

and the other lords had suffered, and what the villages needed. They had a certain shyness of each other at the first, and Crissand seemed to worry about offending him, telling the truth as Crissand would, but everything Crissand said, he heard. From orchards and sheep they talked on about this and that, gossiped about various of the lords, but none unkindly: Drumman's ambition for a new breed of sheep, Azant's daughter's two marriages, her widowed at Lewenbrook, only seven days a bride—but not the only tragedy. Parsynan, so he had no difficulty understanding at all, had done nothing to mend the situation in the villages, nothing to recover Emwy from its destruction, nothing to help Edwyll's heavy losses, only to collect taxes for the coronation levy and further punish the villages that had helped win the day.

"Then the king's men came counting granaries and sheep again," Crissand said, "and that was the thing that pushed my father toward rebellion, my lord. We've no villages starving yet, but by next year they'd be eating the seed corn, and that, that, my lord, there's no recovering. So the Elwynim offer tempted my father, and the king's men made him angry. That's the truth of it. I don't excuse our actions, but I report the reason of them."

"I've yet to understand all Parsynan's reasons," Tristen said, "but at least by what I've seen, he built nothing. And I want the repairs made and no great amount spent, and no gold ornaments, and none of this. Yet they want to carve the doors, which is a great deal of expense, and more time, yet everyone, even the servants, say I should do it . . . while the villages want food. Is that good sense?"

"Our duke shouldn't have plain doors," Crissand said, "and if he understands the plight of the villages and sees to it they have grain, there's no man will complain about the duke's doors."

"I need troops to the riverside more," Tristen said in a low voice, still discontent with the delays for wood-carving, more and more convinced he should never have been persuaded to agree to it at all. "Any door would do to shut out the cold. I need canvas, I need bows, and I need horses and food."

"To attack Elwynor, my lord?"

"To keep the war out of Amefel. And the armory. There's another difficulty. Parsynan did nothing to maintain it; Lord Heryn kept it badly; Cefwyn set it to rights, and when the master armorer left to go with the king, Parsynan set no one in charge of it, and there's no agreement between the tally and what's there. I brought a good man back with me, Cossun, master Peygan's assistant, and he can't find records there or in the archive."

"I fear there was theft," Crissand said. "I even fear my men did some of it. But those weapons we have . . ." Crissand did not look at him when he added, ". . . even today. But Meiden wasn't the only one to take weapons. The garrison made free of it, if my lord wants the truth. The Guelen Guard."

"Yet where are the weapons?"

"Sold in the town, and pledged for drink, and such, in the taverns. The weapons are there, my lord, just not in the armory. Except if there was gold or silver, and that might have gone gods know where. To the purveyors of wine and ale and food, not to mention other things."

It was a revelation. So were many things, in this fortnight of his rule here. Everywhere he looked there was another manifestation of Parsynan's flagrant misrule, another particular in which a self-serving man had stripped the town and the garrison of whatever value might have served the people of Amefel. The Guelens, lax in discipline under Parsynan's rule, had seemed to view the Amefin armory as a place from which to take what they would—and knowing what he knew, yes, he could believe no officer had prevented it.

"Did you hear that, Uwen?"

"Aye," Uwen said, soberly. "An' I ain't surprised if those weapons is scattered through town, an' I ain't surprised if a lot of legs has helped 'em walk there, not just the Guelens. Metal's metal, m'lord, an' a good blade for a tanner or a wheelwright, that ain't unlikely at all. Is it?" Uwen asked of the Meiden captain.

The man agreed. "I wouldn't be surprised."

"And the archive?" Tristen asked Crissand.

"A man who wanted to remove a deed or change one," Crissand said, "could do that, for gold. That was always true. Which is as good as stealing, but in one case it was done twice, once by Lord Cuthan, and then by a lord I'll not willingly name, my lord, changing it back, so it never went to trial, because the archivist was taking money from both, and the last won. So I'd not believe any record that came to the assizes, my lord, because any could be forged. Some lands have two deeds, both sworn and sealed, and only the neighbors know the truth. So it comes to the court, and so my lord will decide on justice."

He had not yet dealt with the question of contested lands, of which he knew there were several cases pending, and he found it even more daunting by what Crissand said.

And now he knew at least two things he was sure Crissand had drawn him out here to say, and none of it favoring the Guelen Guard or the viceroy's rule here. The lord viceroy was gone; but the Guelen captain was not, and since the war needed the Guelen troops, their usefulness presented him a dilemma, two necessities, one for troops, the other simply not to have theft proceeding, especially of equipment.

The province had mustered for the war, he began to understand, and the weapons had just not gone back to the armory: the town was armed, and had been so, and yet the young men had no great skill in using the weapons. Hence so many of them had died at Lewenbrook. He did not like what he heard, not of the treatment of the contents of the armory, not of the forgery of records.

"They should not go on doing this," Tristen said with firm intent. "They will not go on doing it."

"Your Guelen clerk has taken no bribes," Crissand said. "An honest man in office has thrown certain lords into an embarrassing position: the last man to change a document may not be the right man, as everyone knows him to be, and there's a fear the whole thing will come out. Trust none of Cuthan's documents, and be careful of Azant's, on my honor . . . he's a good man, my lord, but he's done what he had to do, to counter Cuthan's meddling. He regrets it, and now he's afraid. If Your Grace asked all of them to return the deeds to what they were under Lord Heryn, it might be a fair solution. I say so, knowing I'll lose and Azant will gain by that, but I think it's fair, and it would make Azant very happy with Your Grace."

He heard that. He heard a great many things of like import.

"This is all Levey's care," Crissand said finally, as they came over a hill. Gray haze of apple trees showed against the snow, acres of them. "These are their orchards. But the hills about here are sheep pasture . . . good pasture, in summer. A prosperous village, if it hadn't lost so many men. The spring's not far now, my lord."

The snow had confounded all landmarks. He knew

he had ridden past this place before, but it was all strange to his eye, and no villager had stirred, here . . . the snow ahead of them was pure, trackless, drifted up near the rough stone walls of the orchard.

"Do you hunt, my lord?" The wind picked up, and Crissand pulled up the hood of his cloak. "There's fine hunting in the woods eastward, past the orchards. Hare and fox."

"No," Tristen said, flinching from the thought, the stain on the pure snow. "I prefer not."

None of your tallow candles, master Emuin had said. Nothing reeking of blood and slaughter. Nothing ever, if he had his way. He had seen blood enough for a lifetime.

There was a small silence. Perhaps he had given too abrupt a refusal. Perhaps he had made Crissand ill at ease, wondering how his lord had taken offense.

"Yet Cook must have something for the kitchens, mustn't she?" Tristen said, attempting to mend it. "So some will hunt. I don't prefer it for myself."

"What do you favor for sport, my lord?"

He blinked at the shifting land above Gery's ears and tried to imagine all the fair things that filled his idle hours, a question he had asked himself when he saw laughing young men throwing dice or otherwise amusing themselves, cherishing their hounds or hawks.

Or courting young women. He was isolate and unused to fellowship. Haplessly, foolishly, he thought of his pigeons, and the fish sleeping in the pond in the garden, and of his horses, which he valued.

Riding was something another young man might understand, of things that pleased him.

"His Grace is apt to thinking," Uwen said in his long silence. Uwen was wont to cover his lapses, especially when his lord had been foolish, or frightened people.

"Forgive me," Tristen said on his own behalf. "I

was wondering what I do favor. Riding, I think." That was closest. So was reading, but it was rarely for pleasure, more often a quest after some troubling concept. "So long as the snow is no thicker than this, we might ride all about the hills and visit all the villages, might we not?"

"Snow never comes deep before Wintertide, not in all my memory."

"And I had far rather wade through this than answer questions about the doors."

"As you are lord of Amefel you may have carved what you like, and do what you like. The people do love you. So do we all, my lord, all your loyal men."

That rang strangely, ominously out of the air, and lightly as he knew it was meant, he felt dread grow out of it, dread of encounters, dread learned where strangers feared other strangers, and encounters were mostly unpleasant. He felt shy, and afraid of a sudden, afraid of his own power over men's lives. He felt afraid because Crissand felt afraid of him, and it should not be so. The other lords feared him. So did the common folk. He recalled the breaking forth of Sihhë stars on doorways, the cheers in the streets. "Love?" He thought on that a moment.

There was a small silence this time on Crissand's side. "That you are Sihhë is no fault in their eyes."

"I am a Summoning and a Shaping," he said with more directness of his heart than he had ever used on that matter, even with Uwen, who rode close on his other side, Crissand's captain somewhat back in the column for a word with another man. "That I may be Sihhë seems mere afterthought to being a dead Sihhë."

"M'lord," Uwen protested, and Crissand:

"You are our fair lord. None better. None better!"

"A Shaping, and a fool. Uwen knows. Cefwyn's captain tells me so."

"Spite."

"No, I value that in him. And Uwen bears very patiently with my mistakes, knowing all my flaws, and keeps me from the greatest disasters . . ."

"M'lord!" Even Uwen was scandalized and did not return his fond smile.

"But you do so, and it is true, Uwen. I value your counsel as I value the Lord Commander's, and your protection above his."

"M'lord," Uwen muttered, embarrassed. But it was still true. What Uwen gave him was beyond price or valuation; and he wished ever so much that he might have that kind of honesty from Crissand. He thought he had had it for a moment, and then it had turned to the flattering and the worship Crissand gave him, and he felt that change like a wound.

"Uwen is my friend," Tristen said to Crissand, riding knee to knee with him, "and Lusin and my guards are my friends, and Tassand and my servants are my friends. And so is king Cefwyn and master Emuin and Her Grace of Elwynor; they know I'm a fool. His Highness Prince Efanor was kind to me, too, and gave me a book of devotions he greatly values. He thinks I'm a heretic. Commander Idrys of the Dragons, too; he calls me a fool and a danger, and I regard his advice. Annas, and Cook, here in Amefel, master Haman, all were kind to me, and I think they regard me as somewhat simple. But Guelessar was a lonely place. Lords, ladies, the servants in the halls and the cook and his men and all, all used to gods-bless themselves and didn't deal with me."

"They're Quinalt," Crissand said, as if that explained all the world.

"So is Uwen."

"Not that good a Quinaltine," Uwen said under his breath.

"And Cefwyn is my friend," Tristen continued doggedly to his point. "If you wish to be my friend, Crissand Adiran, if you become my friend, you should know that I hold Cefwyn in friendship."

"For your sake I give up all complaint against him."

"And will bear him goodwill?"

He had the gift, Emuin had advised him, of both asking and telling too much truth, challenging the polite lies that kept men from inconveniencing each other and the great lies that kept men from each other's throats. He had learned to moderate that, and wield silence somewhat more often.

But with this young earl who had first met him at sword's edge and then sworn to him more extravagantly than all the other earls, with this young man who had brought him here to pour half-truths into his ear, he cast down the question like a gage, to see whether Crissand would pick it up or find a polite and empty phrase to avoid allegiance to the Marhanen . . . and truth to him. Either way, he would thus declare the measure of their friendship.

"What will you, my lord?" Again Crissand attempted to dance sideways, disappointingly so. "I bear all goodwill to the king."

Uwen cleared his throat and said in a diffident tone, and without looking quite at Crissand: "His Grace is inclined to want the plain truth from a man on any number of points, your lordship, more 'n some is used to, but he ain't ever apt to hold the truth again' a man. Bein' as he's no older 'n last spring, when he come into this world, he'll ask ye things ye might wonder at, meanin' no disrespect by it. But ye'll have the truth from 'im, if ye will to have it."

It took courage for Uwen to speak up as he had, a common man, to what Uwen called his betters. But Uwen had shepherded him through courts and village streets and knew him as no other man did, and sometimes spoke for him when the going had gotten too tangled. Not even Cefwyn, nor even Emuin, knew him as Uwen did.

"Then I must tell the truth," Crissand said in that silence that followed, "and this is the foremost truth: His Majesty's law may call my father a traitor, and it's true, traitor to the Marhanen; and so am I. Nor do I repent anything I did. You would have saved my father, I well know. I would that my father had lived and that the lord viceroy had died. From the time I was accountable of anything, my father told me no good could come to Amefel while a Marhanen sat the throne in Guelessar and Heryn Aswydd in Henas'amef. And, yes, Heryn was kin of ours. But no one of my house mourned him—nor were we surprised when the king in Guelemara sent Heryn's sisters to a nunnery and set the viceroy over us. Nor were we at all surprised when the viceroy was a thief. Need he be better than Heryn Aswydd?"

All of that Tristen well understood. But the conclusion of it he did not. "Did you hope for better from Tasmôrden?"

"No. We hoped Tasmôrden would set my father in power. And after that, my father would see to Amefel. None other would. I'm not surprised to know there were no troops, nor would there be, coming to our relief. And when Cuthan betrayed us and you came and when the Guelen viceroy ordered us killed, I had no more hope. But I was not surprised." A small silence followed. It was no good memory, and Crissand gathered a deep breath and a brisker voice. "But when you came into that courtyard and rescued us, and you did *justice,* my lord, for the first time in a hundred years, someone did *justice* for men of Amefel, I knew my father didn't die in vain, that after all we

have a lord I will follow. And if you bid me be loyal to
the king, for your sake, my lord, then gods save the
king in Guelemara, I say it with all my heart."

That was a very great thing for an Amefin to say.

And when Crissand said gods save the king, Tristen
unthinkingly resorted to the gray space in simple
startlement, a recourse for a wizard's Shaping as easy
as a next breath or a wondering beyond the words and
into the real motion of a man's heart. He sped into
that space with an awareness of the men closest on
either hand, a feather-touch of awareness, of the familiar.

Uwen, for instance: Uwen was rather like a rock,
steady, ordinary, incontrovertible, neither there nor
quite aware of the things in that space, but coming
quite close to reaching it, at times, through familiarity
with him. The Meiden captain was dimmer in his
awareness. So with the rest of the guards.

But Crissand *glowed*, faintly but incontrovertibly
there. Crissand Earl Meiden himself was distant cousin
to the aethelings of Henas'amef, and, with the
aetheling blood came wizard-gift. Crissand to all seeming had not a glimmering awareness of the gift that
was in him . . . a gift perhaps enough to bend luck in
Crissand's favor. Luck had failed Crissand's father,
whose heredity was at least half the same; yet Crissand
said it: the cause had prospered. Luck had allowed
Crissand's men to save him from the viceroy's order,
so that Crissand and his mother both had lived.

And on that thought Tristen took a small pause, a
cold small thought, that Crissand's slight gift, his luck,
was a pivot on which greater things turned, and when
things were free to move, then wizardry had its best
chance. On a small pin, a great gate swung.

Whose wizardry had it been? Or might it be magic
at work, that sense that, somewhere, long ago, he had

known Crissand Adiran, or someone very like him?

But Crissand in the gray space now had not a glimmer of ill will. Rather Crissand shone with a pure, plain, and dangerous folly of adoration, a heady wine for anyone who drank.

Like Emuin's insistence on beeswax, it came with wizard-force, and sober as he had grown this autumn, such blithe excess of adoration frightened him. But in the reckless outpouring of Crissand's heart, he found Crissand's happiness and hope spread about him. Even the house guard and the Dragons had made a sort of conversational peace, and the world was incredibly fair and bright despite the grim talk of recent moments. Sunlight through the scudding, gray-bottomed clouds cast sparkling detail where it touched, random grains of snow shining like dust of pale jewels to left and to right of an untrodden road, and every hill and every copse of trees offered new beauty. Creature of a single year, he had imagined winter when it came would be deathly still, and instead he discovered it full of sparkle and motion and wonder around him, and he was warmed by unquestioning love.

Could there be a snare in too much beauty? Could there be too much expectation of good, and too much faith?

Could ever there be too much love?

And could love require lies?

He asked himself that. He had drawn Crissand once into the gray space himself, though he doubted Crissand had since ventured it on his own. He doubted, too, that Crissand had any least notion what had happened to him in that moment, or how he had found himself confronted while absent and, coatless and desperate, sent out into the snow.

He could teach Crissand, he thought, how to reach that place where concealment was very difficult. He was sure Crissand's gift was strong enough. But to set Crissand at liberty in that place . . . there were dangers in it, dangers in the gift, dangers in the wandering. Dared he believe Crissand would never venture it on his own?

But Crissand's attention was suddenly for a snowy ridge. He pointed to it and said, with a whitened barleyfield on the one hand and a bare-limbed apple orchard on the other, that they were coming to the crossroads.

"There is Padys Ridge, and the shrine and the spring just below it."

A very old oak, winter-bare, fronted that ancient outcrop, sole wild representative of his kind in an otherwise tame land of orchards and small, pruned trees. Just beyond it, still within the reach of its limbs, snow-covered, was the slight evidence of a road.

"There's our turn to Levey, my lord."

"Banners!" Uwen ordered, as they turned onto that track beside the oak, and the banners, dark and bright, unfurled.

Crissand had said there was a shrine of sorts. Indeed, with the scouring of the morning's wind, a small pile of man-set stones was peeping out from its snow blanket. It recalled one near Emwy village far to the west. That had been summer. The spring here was frozen where it flowed out of the natural rock, and had made a glorious mass of icicles.

"Padys Spring and the shrine, my lord. One of the last of the old places. The king's men overthrew most, wherever they found them. I ask you'll keep it. The village sets great store by it."

"A shrine of the Bryalt?" he asked, largely ignorant of gods, study as he would in Efanor's little book.

"Perhaps older, my lord. Though Bryalt offerings may turn up here, the king's law and the Quinalt notwithstanding." Crissand spoke in the hearing of Guelenmen, in Uwen's hearing most of all, and was surely aware it. "We go uphill from here, a clear, smooth road, as I recall it, no ditches or pits to fear on either side."

No track disturbing the snow since the last snowfall, either, but the blanket sank down considerably in a long line through the ridge, showing where the road was, and the stone sheep walls on either side, visible ahead of them, confirmed it. They rode past old stones, and many of the Guelenmen made a small sign against harm.

"The farmer folk are staunch Bryaltine," Crissand began to say as they rode past.

But just as they passed under the spreading branches of the oak a fierce gust of wind blew past them, driving the banners sideways and startling the horses with a pelting of snow from laden branches.

"ods!" Crissand said in dismay, and reined up sharply . . . for an old woman stood by the shrine, so gray and brown in her shawl and skirts she might have been part of the oak in the last blink of their eyes. She had drawn her shawl over her gray head, but hanks of her hair flew in the gale and the driven snow. She had a necklace hung with smooth river stones and knots of straw. Her skirts were weighted with braided cords and coins, and the fringes of her shawl flew wild as the icy wind skirled up.

"Gods!" Crissand said a second time, with an anxious laugh, soothing his horse with his off hand. "You gave me a fright, mother. I don't know you. Are you from Levey?"

She was no stranger and no common woman, Tristen knew it, and held Gery still: Uwen had halted beside him. So had all the column behind halted, and the banner-bearers ahead had turned back to face the woman in dismay.

"Auld Syes," Tristen said, for to name a thing was to have some power to bid it. "What brings you so far from Emwy?"

"Why, I come to bring the lord of Amefel to his senses," the old woman said, and pointed a bony bare arm from out of the clutch of flying fringes, stark and commanding as the wind continued to blow. "Lord of Amefel and the aetheling! Why do I find the twain of you riding west like common fools, when your road lies south? South for friends, lord of Amefel, north and east for foes, and blest the lord who knows one from the other! Mistake them not again, lord of Amefel!"

North for enemies and south for friends was no news; but east was Guelessar, and the king . . . and many another enemy, the barons not least. Tristen doubted nothing, and listened with ears and heart. Auld Syes had told him truth before.

And *aetheling* she said, the lord of Amefel and the aetheling, as if they were not the same thing . . . *the twain of you,* she said, *lord and aetheling*—which met his heart with a loud echo of all the wonderings he had had to himself. The guards who heard might not have heard that salutation in the same way: the common folk attributed both titles to him. Perhaps even Crissand failed to gather that implied duality.

But he did, and sat staunchly holding the red mare still between his knees, resolved not to flinch no matter the news out of the east.

"Lord of Amefel I am now. What shall I do for you, lady of Emwy?"

"Can truly you do aught, new lord? Have you true power, or is it only illusion you wield?"

A second shot winged home with an accuracy that might miss all attention but Uwen's: *Illusion* was one of the two words hammered in silver on the blade of the sword he bore at his side; *Truth* was written on the other, in bright letters of long ago, and of all men present, only Uwen knew what the writing on the blade signified: Uwen, and this old woman.

Of a sudden he found himself afraid, trembling with the old woman's challenge not in the gray space but on the earth and in it, and under his horse's feet. The blade he had rarely drawn, that dark metal presence that generally lurked quiescent at his hearthside.

Truth . . . and illusion. He was both, and would she show him the division in himself?

"If I have power to grant anything for you, lady, that will I."

"The living king at last sits in judgment. South, south, lord of Amefel, fare south today. And when you find my sparrows, my little birds, lord of Amefel, warm them, feed them. The wind is too cold."

His bones shook. He could not obtain his next breath.

"Find my sparrows!" Auld Syes cried, or the wind cried to him. "Find my sparrows when you have found your friends!" A brutal gust slammed into the banners, tilting them despite the struggles of the bearers, who swung them into the teeth of the gale. Horses shied up, some fighting to bolt, but battle-trained Gery danced in place, head up, ears flat. Auld Syes still stood at the center of the gale, her fringes and her necklaces flying about her as the winds circled round and round her, winding her strings of amulets and charms, tangling their yarns. Streaks appeared in the snow around her, short, broad gouges that kicked up new-fallen snow, passing around and around her like the skips of dancers. Whatever veil Auld Syes had parted to reach into the world was closing with a vengeance, and other spirits flowed along the edges of her power, spirits more dangerous and less wise.

"Lad!" Uwen cried in alarm, and the wind dislodged snow from the oak above them, a thicker and thicker curtain of white that hid the old woman in its heart, a gray shadow.

"Auld Syes!" Tristen shouted, disturbed by this talk of sparrows, friends, and kings. "Auld Syes, I am not done with questions for you! May I hold you?"

"Bid me under your roof, lord of Amefel!" The voice was fading now, obscured in the wind. "Dare you do so?"

"Come at your will, Auld Syes!"

"Gods," someone breathed. It might have been Crissand. It might have been Uwen. He himself invoked no more power than already roared about them as the veil of snow collapsed.

Then the wind slacked enough to clear the air, and to their eyes there was no woman, only tear-shaped streaks in a great broad ring, around and around where she had stood. Of Syes' feet there was no track at all: pure and undisturbed, the snow lay in the center of that ring, and the snow that fell now in fat clumps plopped down onto the stacked stones. A plain clay bowl, filled with snow, sat atop that pile, as the bowls had stood on the altar table in the Quinaltine, this open to the sky and filled with a winter offering, to what gods was uncertain.

"Gods save us." That was Lusin, chief of his guards, and Uwen with a rapid gesture signed safety to them all, a Guelenman, a Quinalt man by upbringing, asking, "Lad, are we safe here?"

"We ride south," Tristen said, turning Gery's head. "I think that was what she wanted." He beheld guardsmen's faces as shocked as Crissand's. Snow had stuck to the sides of helmets and stuck in the eyelets of mail coats and the coats of the horses, while more was falling from the sky, thicker and thicker, not the knife edge of sleet, now, but soft, wet clumps that stuck where they landed. Banners hung limp, all in the shelter of the oak.

"This *is* the road to Levey," Crissand said faintly and foolishly, as if his guidance were called in question along with their safety. "I am not mistaken in this."

"Then our journey is not to Levey," Tristen said, and by the folly of that protest guessed that Crissand was far yet from understanding Auld Syes or any other spirit that might go about her, some of them dangerous to more than life. "Ride back to the town, you and your men, before the weather becomes worse. Uwen and I will go on, with my guard. I can't say what we may meet."

"No, my lord! And the woman said, did she not, *friends* to the south? What should we fear?"

What indeed? Much, he answered the question in his own heart. "So she did," he said aloud, "but I can't speak to what sort of friends."

The Guelenmen in the company, his own standard-bearers, and his four guards, looked more dismayed than Crissand and his men, and Uwen, who had met Auld Syes before this, bore a willing but worried frown.

"Last time she came, m'lord," Uwen said, "there were no good event, and men died for 't."

"Yet *she* never did us harm," Tristen said. Truth: a king and a Regent had fallen, and men had died at her first appearance; at her second appearance, which Uwen had not seen, he had been in peril of his own life, but he had found Ninévrisë as a result of it.

Now he saw no choice: Auld Syes warned them, yes, but to his understanding of her nature she was not responsible for what then followed. And with a touch of his heels on Gery's sides, he threaded the column back through itself to reach the main road.

There he turned south, and Sergeant Gedd and the two other men carrying the banners urged their horses through low drifts and up the side of a ditch to get to the fore of him. The Guelenmen were bound by their honor and the king's order to go on if he would; but true to his word and also for honor's sake, Crissand and his men did not part their company, either. No more did he forbid them as Crissand came riding up the slant of the ditch to catch up with him and Uwen, the Amefin captain trailing him and slipping on the steep.

Snow began to fall more finely and more quickly from the sky, graying all the world as the wind swept down with a renewed vengeance, scouring blasts that carried so much snow that in a moment the trees of the apple orchard stood like gray ghosts, and the low wall was a faint shadow. The standard-bearers had never yet furled the banners. Now they rode with them tilted doggedly forward as if they defied the wind itself, a knife-edged and formless enemy that whisked their cloaks away from their bodies while they struggled two-handed and half-blind to keep the banners from being torn away.

"Furl the standards!" Tristen called out to them, dismayed at such gallant folly. What did they think they fought? he asked himself; and the next gust shook even the horses, and in better sense than their masters they tried to turn their backs; but riders forced them around into it by rein and heel. Meanwhile the imperiled banners came safely in, and the banner-bearers snatched their cloaks about their bodies. The cold had grown bitter. Crissand struggled with his coif and the reins and an escaping cloak edge, and Tristen was glad of both coif and heavy cloak.

"We'll be off the road in another such," Uwen said through chattering teeth. "An' fallin' in the ditch an' not found till spring. I hope to the gods ye can see our way, m'lord; I can't."

Tristen knew his way, sure at least that he knew where south was, but he pitied the men and the horses. He had never truly dared the gray space with Auld Syes, and only for his men's sake and justice did he try it now. "*Auld Syes!*" he said aloud, here and there alike, to whatever might be listening. "*We're doing as you wish! What more will you? Is this your doing, Auld Syes?*"

The wind had a voice, and it spoke, but not so any

man could understand it. What Auld Syes would and would not was without care for mortal discomfort or men's lives . . . so he feared: Auld Syes had made her effort and had left them to their fate.

But one there was not immune to pity.

"Seddiwy!" he called out. *"Speak kindly to your mother!"* For as he thought of it, Auld Syes' daughter might well be in this capricious upheaval of the elements, a shadow, certainly, if she still played skip and raced about the old woman's skirts. The wind itself might be a child's game, a game of shadows, sometimes prankish, sometimes deadly to her mother's foes . . . small willful child in dangerous company.

But potent child, for all that.

"Seddiwy! Cease this!"

It seemed someone heard, for the gale fell away so suddenly that the wall of wind against which they leaned was suddenly absent. Gery threw her head up, whinnied at the empty air, and gave a little skip in startlement.

Crissand set a hand behind him and looked all about, as if looking for apparitions or worse.

"She's a shadow," Tristen said, "a little girl. She means no harm to us. The elements are overturned with her mother's goings and comings, at least that may be the cause."

"A little girl!"

"A mischievous one. But good-hearted."

"I take you at your word, my lord." Crissand's voice was hushed and thin, and no less than the guards and the other captain, Uwen looked warily about him . . . justly so: more than a child might manifest about Auld Syes.

But now that the gusts had ceased, the snow began to congeal in great soft lumps as it fell, so that now they could see the road and the roll of the ditches alongside it quite clearly through a veil of fat, white puffs.

"There's a moment," Crissand said at last, breathlessly, in their apparent rescue. "There's a moment I shan't forget so long as I live. Good gods, you keep uncommon allies, my lord."

"She's Amefel's ally," Tristen said, for so it had always seemed to him. The air was less cold where they rode, now, yet a glance confirmed a shadow, an impression of dark in the all-enveloping gray, boding storm in the west. "Uwen's right that she's warned of ambushes before now. She spoke to me in the woods at Emwy near such a spring, and it may be, such a shrine."

He suspected he had never told that to Uwen, and did not explain now, but brought all his faculties to bear on the road southward, searching through the white distance and testing within the gray space unseen to the rest of them whether there was any presence on the road behind or ahead.

He felt all the cold-stung men beside him quite clearly, the faint and distant presence of what must be Levey village away and to the west.

He felt Gery under him and the horses around him, and he felt the dim presence of living things out across the orchards, small creatures, perhaps a rabbit in its burrow, or in a brush heap. Auld Syes spoke of sheltering birds; but he knew it to mean something else, and urgent, as he distractedly hoped for the safety of his birds and all creatures who had set out so blithely unforeseeing a storm such as this.

He had not foreseen it. Emuin had not. And all the wizard-sense he owned felt something ominous in the west this hour, something that otherwise should make them turn now and fare home quickly, to put themselves behind walls and wards.

And now he recalled how he had felt foreboding even before he had set out from Guelessar: a sense of threat, from a hill above the king's forest.

Do you find anything amiss? he had asked Emuin today, and had no answer, only talk of beeswax candles.

And why? Why indeed? And why no warning of storm or magic today, when the like of Auld Syes arrived out of the winter with warnings and directions to venture out?

He was not comforted, even while he pressed red Gery forward in the snow.

—*Do you hear me, sir?* he asked Emuin. *Do you yet hear me? Do you know what's happened?*

Was it anger that moved him? He was close to it, beset like this and taken without warning. He had found baffling Emuin's deserting the king to come with him in the first place, and yet never having advice for him, nor even traveling with him on the road.

He found Emuin's dereliction more and more portentous and troubling in light of Auld Syes' appearance just now, and still he rode through this storm telling himself that, of course, wizards had their ways and their necessary silences.

Oh, yes, Emuin had warned him . . . warned him Emuin feared his wishes and his will, and wished him to use either as sparingly as possible. So it was perfectly understandable that Emuin kept silent on all manner of things.

But something, perhaps even the extremity of the effort, had sent Auld Syes away with an appeal to him to invite her past the wards that surrounded him, and now violence boded in the west, and still Emuin said *nothing*, though others had acted. This was beyond prudence regarding what *he* would do. This silence encompassed what others intended, and he grew vastly out of sorts with it.

Conversation had meanwhile ceased among the guardsmen behind him, except the Guelenmen asked in the quiet of the fall was there ever the like, and the Amefin swore they had never seen anything to equal this weather.

"Are we still in Meiden lands?" Uwen wanted to know, and, yes, the Amefin captain said, they were still in his lord's lands, but only scarcely. Past the next brook Meiden's lands ceased, and the aged earl of Athel held sway.

It was a distant sound to him, their talk, in the strange quiet of the snowfall, like the floating silence of a dream, as if some magic had made an isle of calm around them and kept the dark of the storm elsewhere at bay. Seddiwy's lingering mischief or merely the troubling of nature Auld Syes had wrought, flurries of white appeared, but confined themselves to the hills and the horizon, small opaque patches beyond which they could not see.

They rode thus for an hour, at least, in such gentle snowfall, meeting no great accumulation on the road, which seemed unnaturally spared of the drifts that deepened on the hills, and the men's wonder informed him that, no, this was not the ordinary conduct of snowstorms.

They began to ride out of their area of peace as they rode into the sheep-meadows of the southern hills. A wind almost as fierce as the first stung their faces with sleet like icy sand and made the horses go with halfshut eyes and flattened ears.

"How far shall we ride?" some guardsman complained, and Uwen said, "Far as His Grace wishes it, man. Bear wi' it."

Soon now, was Tristen's increasing conviction. And now it seemed to him that the opposing storm was not all troubled nature, but that someone, somewhere, troubled nature deliberately, opposing Auld Syes, never wishing her to speak to him: she had asked his summons, his leave, which opened his wards to her, as a fugitive might ask a door be left unlocked.

It was dangerous, what she had asked; so was what he had granted; and yet thus far the only penalty of his venture was a dusting of snow and the chill that numbed and made decision difficult. Someone else, someone opposed to Auld Syes, instead of Seddiwy, might have roused this weather to make things difficult, but had no power or no desire to make it worse, and that someone else might even be master Emuin, angry at the venture, but he did not think so.

With sudden sureness, however, he knew the friends Auld Syes had warned him of were just the other side of the hill. Awareness of a presence reached through the gray of his Sight and into his heart . . . a faint glow about Crissand and another such glow of presence in the storm-blown haze ahead of them, blue and soft, advisory of wizard-gift.

There, his heart said. It was someone uncommon.

And a friend? Almost he dared guess, and his heart lifted. *Welcome,* he said to the white before them, and just then, on a hill made invisible by the blowing white, shadows of riders appeared as if in midair, three riders who approached them, each with a second, shadowy horse at lead.

Then came four, five, and two more out of the white, men whose colors were the snow and the storm themselves.

Gray cloaks and mingled gray horses, the foremost horse near to white. And, yes, here indeed were friends, Ivanim, from the province neighboring to the south.

Perhaps they had set out north as a courtesy to him, once the news of his accession in Amefel had reached Ivanor: that was the natural thought.

Yet did something so simple come heralded by Auld Syes, at such effort?

Clearer and clearer they came, both sides continuing to move, and the foremost rider proved no less than the lord of Ivanor himself, Cevulirn . . . who should not have been in the south at all, but eastward, in Guelessar, with Cefwyn.

That portended something in itself ominous.

"Ivanor!" Tristen called out, though the men with him made pious gestures against ghosts and shadows.

"Is it Tristen?" came the answering shout.

There was no need to break out the banners for reassurance in this murk, but Gedd had done so; and now the banners of Ivanor came forth, the White Horse; and Crissand's own, Sun on a blue whitened like ice.

"Welcome," Tristen called out to the lord of Ivanor, as their two parties met. He offered Cevulirn his hand as they met, the clasp of gauntlets well dusted with snow and frozen stiff with ice. "Welcome, sir. But how does Cefwyn fare?"

"Safely wedded, so I had word. I lingered at Clusyn monastery to know, on my way home. And how are matters in Henas'amef?"

"Very well. Very well, sir." It struck him only then that other courtesies were due, and he made them, self-conscious in his new lordship. "Your Grace, Crissand, Earl of Meiden; our friend, the duke of Ivanor."

"I've seen you in hall," Crissand said, "but as my father's son. Lord Cevulirn, count me your friend as devotedly as you are my lord's friend."

"Your Grace," Cevulirn said. That Crissand was earl had told a tale in itself, one Cevulirn would have no trouble reading: a father's death, the son's accession to the earldom, but there was no leisure here for asking and answering further than that. The wind tugged at cloaks and pried with icy fingers into every gap, and they were standing hard-worked horses in a chilling storm. "I take it your journey is to me," Tristen said above the buffeting of the gale, for there was nowhere else of note this road led, before it came to Henas'amef. "You're very welcome, you and your men. Shall we have the horses moving?"

"Indeed," Cevulirn said, and they reined about and Cevulirn with them. The wind came more comfortably at their backs as Tristen began to thread his own column again back through itself, and Ivanim sorted themselves out among Guelenmen and Amefin.

"Does His Majesty need me in Guelemara?" Tristen asked, first and clearest of his worries once they were faced about and headed home. "Are you here because things are going well, or because they aren't?"

"Well and ill. His Majesty sent me south for my health. It's high time His Majesty's friends put their heads together."

Cevulirn did not readily give up words, not before strangers, most of all. He only knew that Cevulirn had purposed to stay by the king this winter, to report to the southern lords any untoward demand of their rivals of the north, and to make it clear to the ambitious north that the south would not see its interests trampled. Yet Cevulirn had heard of the wedding only from the vantage of the monastery at Clusyn, and had come home contrary to his firm intentions.

So whatever had happened in the capital, it was not according to plan.

"Earl Crissand is trustworthy," Tristen said. "What do you mean we should put our heads together?"

"The northerners are rid of me," came the answer. "As they are of you, and yet they could not prevent the wedding. So at least half their plans came to naught, but gods know what Ryssand's done."

"Surely lightning hasn't struck the Quinalt." He was half in jest, but that was how the barons had been rid of him: he could not imagine how they had proceeded against Cevulirn, who was one of the greatest men in the land.

"Would lightning had struck Ryssand. No. But *I* struck him a grievous hurt, hence my ride south, hence a winter for us to arrange things more to His Majesty's liking. Hence my visit to you. How have you fared here?"

There was far too much to tell, and much of it bitter to Crissand, of whose witness he was entirely conscious. "Well enough," Tristen said, "considering all that's happened. Meiden lost a good many men. There were Guard killed. I sent Lord Parsynan out afoot, since he stole Uwen's horse; and I sent His Majesty's wagons to the border to fortify the bridges—or I had sent them this morning. The weather may have prevented them going."

"Have you, indeed?" Cevulirn's tone was flat, implying neither approval nor disapproval, only, for him, query. "Has there been difficulty there?"

It was another matter that touched heavily on Crissand's pride.

"My father, sir," Crissand said before he could speak, "had correspondence with Tasmôrden. The rebels offered to come in to support rebellion, and rebellion there was, to my father's grief and misfortune, sir."

"But no sight of Elwynim," Tristen said. "Yet I fortify the bridges, and kept the Guard, having no Amefin troops. The wagons . . . Cefwyn can spare them a fortnight more, so I hope, if nothing happens northerly."

"A fair risk," Cevulirn said after a moment of silence, leaving Tristen less than certain Cevulirn approved all he had done.

"Cefwyn told me," he said, "that he wishes to attack

Tasmôrden from the eastern bridges and not the south, for glory to the northern barons. And I've no wish to take any glory at all, or to have another battle at planting time, when the last was at harvest."

So Crissand had just told him, but Crissand was by no means the first to explain that with men drawn away from their farmsteads season after season, no crops grew and the lambing this spring would already go hard . . . he had not drawn men off the land, not yet. Amefel's losses had been heaviest, at Lewenbrook, a muster of peasant farmers and herders, where other provinces had sent well-trained troops.

"So I don't intend to cross the river," he said, "but I intend they shan't cross here, either."

"His Majesty's plan is to set Murandys and Ryssand and Guelessar in the field, all the heavy horse and all the gear," Cevulirn said. "It's the warfare Guelenfolk know. And I've urged His Majesty have a thought to the light horse, and getting a force over those roads, which by all Her Grace has said are none so fine and broad as those in Guelessar. Mud. And difficulty for those wagons His Majesty sets such store by, with all that heavy gear. March to Ilefínian and bring them to bloody battle . . . with all respect to your good captain, Amefel: the heavy horse will suffer in that plan, every league they travel. It's too far a march, too many hills that give vantage to archers."

"A bloody passage it'll be," Uwen said in a low voice, for Cevulirn he knew well. "An' I agree wi' Your Grace, and wi' my lord, I'd send the light horse."

"I've said the same," Tristen said.

"But that's not the king's wish in the matter," Cevulirn said, "for his Guelenfolk. So bloodily they'll win through, granted Ryssand doesn't stab our king in the back. The king sets all hope on Ryssand and Murandys, where least it should rest, and here am I in the south, where least I should rest, and His Majesty never so in danger from a knife in the dark when he was sleeping in Henas'amef, his guards notwithstanding."

A great deal was amiss. Tristen heard that very clearly as they rode. Cefwyn had wished to set Ninévrisë on her throne with no war at all, deeming the rebels broken at Lewenbrook. But a lesser lord, Tasmôrden, had leapt to the fore of the rebellion, and the rebels that had not yet crossed into Cefwyn's battlefield had simply swept aside and fortified a camp inside Elwynor, raising an army out of the stones there, as best they could surmise: certainly it had taxed the villages hard to raise the force it was now.

Set Ninévrisë on her throne Cefwyn would.

But Cefwyn averred he had no choice but exclude the south from the war and call this time on the north. Ryssandish folk and Guelenmen were the heart of his Guelen kingdom: the south was of *tainted* blood . . . had he not heard it from Cefwyn's lips?

And did that not still shiver through his memory? So thoroughly had Cefwyn remembered he was Guelen, and wanted their favor, when he could have called on the likes of Cevulirn and Sovrag. Having Cevulirn and Sovrag with him, he had sent home the Olmernmen; and him; and now Cevulirn?

The gray space remained untroubled; Tristen's heart did not.

Was it a visit without meaning, that Auld Syes guided? He thought not. They two were the king's friends, and Crissand had pledged himself through him, and so all the earls of Amefel, and Auld Syes herself had heralded Cevulirn's coming to him. Was it without meaning?

He was Lord Marshal of Althalen, Lord Warden of Ynefel, titles all but lost in his assumption of the dukedom of Amefel . . . meaningless and vacant of inhabitants, men said.

Men said. But might those be the honors Auld Syes called him to attend . . . when she as good as hailed Crissand aetheling?

The King he come again, she had said to Prince Cefwyn in his hearing, and that lanced through his memory like a lightning stroke.

Had not Uleman, who stood for a King, Lord Regent of Elwynor, also come to Amefel, and died? Young king, Uleman had called *him*, when he was dying, but in the gray space all things had questionable meaning. Uleman had charged him with defense of the innocent, Uleman, who lay now in ward of Althalen, a power not quite departed from the earth. Cefwyn made him lord here, in Amefel . . . the keystone in the arch that held Elwynor off Ylesuin's soil.

"Look, will ye?" he heard Uwen say as they passed the hill and rode down past the road to Levey, and all through the ranks men blessed themselves or spoke softly to their gods, for the old oak had fallen, its roots uptorn from the muddy ground, great clods fallen all about, and the branches cracked and ruined.

"Ain't no wind might topple an oak wi' that girth," a Guelenman said. "Gods bless, here were sorcery."

"Quiet wi' your 'sorcery'!" Uwen said sharply. "Wet ground an' a gale an' an old tree, aye, and a wizard-woman, but sorcery's another thing altogether. My lord don't dabble in that, so careful how ye use words."

"Gods bless us all the same," said Crissand, and Tristen regarded the uprooted oak, the very symbol of Amefel, asking himself whether wind could in fact have done it.

"An uncommon sight, to be sure," was Cevulirn's judgment.

"So the witch that foretold your journey stood there, Your Grace," said Crissand, "and warned us to look for you, and now see the ruin of the tree."

"There's nothing here now," Tristen said, "nothing harmful, nothing of threat. It's a very great tree to be rooted up. But the lady of Emwy is no slight matter either. Ride by."

That they did, and curious as he was and questioning in his own mind what might have befallen the oak, he did not unsettle his men further by turning in the saddle to gawk like an innocent. He was the stay of the guardsmen's confidence and their courage to confront strange things, and there were strange things enough for a week of gossip once they all reached town.

There was one more strange sight on the other side of the next hill, for their tracks, hitherto utterly blotted out by the snowfall, reappeared, never covered by any fall there, nor all along that earlier part of their road. The storm had never reached there, and they could see all the land before them from that height, with a thick snowfall behind them and none before.

"Not a natural storm," the soldiers said with anxious looks at the west, which still showed dark. "There weren't nothin' natural about it."

"As we met fair weather," Cevulirn remarked, "until an hour before our meeting."

"I think the carts must have gone out, after all," Tristen said, for he had been convinced until now that Anwyll's party could not possibly have set out into the teeth of that storm.

But nothing here would have prevented it.

—*Master Emuin?* he asked the nearest wizard he knew. *It's snowed, have you noticed? Or did snow fall at all in town? I think it did not.*

—*Have you ever seen an oak overthrown, master Emuin? Some might take it for ominous, and surely the soldiers do. What shall I tell them?*

No answer came to him, but that was, lately, no great surprise, though disheartening. At the same time he heard Lusin and Gedd saying to each other, with better cheer, well, that was a relief, no drifts between them and a warm fire.

It was a leaden sunset in the west and a blue evening in the northwest shot through with fire as they came up to the walls, over the tracks of farmers and the heavy tracks of the departed wagons.

They rode through the gates in close order, Lord Crissand making quiet, last-moment converse with Lord Cevulirn, explaining the streets were quiet and peaceful, and their visitor should fear no rebellion. They were well within the town, before the gatekeepers, caught by surprise, began to ring the bell that advised the hill fortress of visitors.

Then the curious began to peer out of shops and windows. The return of their party from a venture all the town had seen go out might not have drawn any but the hardiest out of doors on a frosty evening. But the bell drew attention, and the banners had unfurled, the White Horse of Ivanor among the banners belonging to the town and its own lords, and townsfolk threw on cloaks and mittens and came out into doorways, or peered out from well-situated windows, for not since summer had the White Horse banner been seen in the streets, when Cevulirn among other lords of the south had camped in that broad expanse outside.

Loaded carts had gone out for the border, where war was bruited about, a great lord had come guesting with their new lord and the new lord of Meiden . . . it surely made for talk, on an evening remarkable only for a light snowfall.

CHAPTER 3

The herald trumpets faded tremulously from the air, the harpers harped, the pipers piped, and the king and Royal Consort, settling on their dais in the great hall, looked out over the assembled nobles of Ylesuin, as happy as a bride and groom might be, who knew what all their guests were thinking. The king sat above the stone Ryssand had installed under the Dragon Throne, a lasting and symbolic legacy of Ryssand's attempts to prevent the wedding. That stone remained, though Ryssand was gone at least for a season; that stone would acquire the voice of baronial anguish if removed, for removing that handbreadth height would lower the king of Ylesuin to the height of his bride's chair of state, and that would unravel all the convolute and, in the end, bloody agreements that had let the court accept the marriage.

In Cefwyn's glum reckoning, the presence of that stone would only grow more, not less, a necessity, wearing itself into habit and memory until the damned thing was all but sacred. The majesty of Ylesuin must sit higher than his wife Her Grace of Elwynor, or northern baronial noses would be sorely out of joint, and when the barons' noses were out of joint then the barons would gather in corners and whisper, which at the moment and only of very late date, they dared not do without careful smiles on their faces and occasional sweet-faced bows toward enthroned majesty.

So all in all, the cursed stone was likely to remain, preserving Guelen pride and making it clear that the woman beside the king, his wife, his consort, his bride, and the love of his heart, was *not* the queen of Ylesuin.

In fact ever since he had come back from Amefel and the fighting at Lewenbrook to inform the barons that his father was dead and he was king, and that he had, moreover, betrothed himself to the daughter and heir of their old enemy, the Regent of Elwynor, he had met a resistance not only greater than he had anticipated, but more clever and dangerous than he had imagined. He had thought these men simply agreeable to his late father's unpleasant opinions, had realized too little and too late how very extensively these men were accustomed to having their will of his father and directing those opinions . . . and nowadays he wondered how many of the worst decisions of his father's reign had been his father's and how many were in fact Ryssand's instigation.

Certainly he had come to court in blither certainty and confidence of the world than he held now. Yet it was Ryssand, ultimately, who had rued the clash of wills . . . and Cefwyn could congratulate himself on having had his way in all meaningful things. Save this one.

Save this one, for at last, on the eve of the wedding and with the Quinalt granting all else and reconciled to performing the ceremony, he had slipped in the word *queen*, and a small delegation of lords and priests had presented him in turn the last, the most stringent and inflexible objection of the clergy: royal expectation aside, there had never quite *been* a queen of Ylesuin, even counting his father's mother and his, and Efanor's, and the Quinalt had come armed with chapter and verse to prove its case, a veritable parade of clerks and clerics.

It was true. It might be Cefwyn's argument that the omission was never intended for precedent, only that his grandmother had died before his grandfather's rule began and his mother and Efanor's mother had both been of Guelen burgesses and not royal, only wellborn. It was circumstance, not intent, in his argument, that had kept Ylesuin from having a queen, but that mattered little, when down to the day and in the toppling of all other obstacles, they had come to dicing words and titles and listening to long recitations of clerkly records. Facing the possibility of another disaffection of the Quinalt Patriarch, whom he had bought in costly coin of favors given, Cefwyn had had to admit that perhaps the reluctance to crown the king's wife was not an insurmountable slight to his bride, who would reign in Elwynor with or without the acknowledgment of Ylesuin, and who was, moreover, pleading with him to accept that slight and get on to the wedding. What she wanted for herself and her people was the alliance, and an army potent enough to drive Tasmôrden from his siege of her capital. She wanted no delays and she wanted that army to set its first contingents in order at the bridges immediately after the wedding. To that he agreed, for the situation in Elwynor had been growing grim then and was growing grimmer to this hour.

She would reign, indeed, as he willed: as they did not make her queen, so they could not trammel up her claim to the Regency of Elwynor, and he would provide—was providing—the army even tonight with his first forces camped on riverside.

And it would be her kingdom, separate from his. *That* was the unfortunate seed in what his barons had done: they had made it impossible for him to persuade her, win her, contrary to the provisions of the marriage treaty, to an early union of their kingdoms. She had insisted on her independency and her own lordship over neighboring Elwynor in the nuptial agreement . . . and that, most precisely, she had, thanks to the barons, without any possibility of argument on his part. Reign she would, in her land, during the summers, so they planned, leaving winters to a vice regent in her land, and gods hope they could ply rowboats between often enough or they would both go mad.

The raising of armies and the defense of their separate kingdoms aside, they loved one another madly, passionately, and to the edge, but not quite over the brink, of complete folly, and their passion had not abated since the wedding night. There was no having enough of one another. They were entirely happy in their nest upstairs. They would neither one act to the detriment of their separate kingdoms . . . but their fingers met whenever they found the chance, and had he ever seen eyes light as hers did whenever he came within her presence?

Gods, how had he lived his life this far without her?

They still walked through their dream of candlelight and flowers, at least in private. They still existed in the singing and the bells, and saw the garlands and the bright banners that were all he in good truth remembered of the wedding . . . well, there had been the satisfying and uncommon sight of certain of his unhappy barons trying valiantly to smile through the ceremony, and the equally uncommon sight of the Quinalt Patriarch's cousin Sulriggan, Duke of Llymaryn, positively aglow with happiness: Sulriggan's return from near exile having been the coin for the Patriarch's acceptance of Her Grace, the two were not unrelated circumstances.

That glow on Sulriggan's countenance continued to this very hour.

Looking out over the barons who were in attendance this evening, he saw the same sources of discontent, and expressions of gloom on those he had destined for retribution when he found the means . . . policy, not utter self-indulgence: the barons would learn him, or by the gods make way for those who would.

One of those acts of retribution, in fact, he would deal out this very evening, and contemplating that prospect, he could sit on the cursed stone and smile down on his court in honest contentment. Conspiracies to overthrow him would come to nothing, while he held a certain damning letter and while he had the loyalty of such as Tristen of Amefel and Cevulirn and the rest of the lords of the south. Even the middle lands had gained courage from the resolute muster of the south this summer's end, and might see their own affairs as safer in the hands of a strong monarch than in the hands of the northern tier of self-serving barons.

Unlikeliest allies of all, he now had the Patriarch and Lord Sulriggan to draw upon . . . securely bought, and safe so long as they stayed by the agreement: perhaps intruding just a little far upon his patience, but they were learning one another's limits.

Sulriggan was clinging close to Efanor, whose friendship he again courted . . . and would not win. Efanor was once betrayed, and would not listen. Dubious prize as Sulriggan was in most points of courage on a battlefield, however, in the conflicts within the court the man was as agile and as clever as one might ask. That generous nose of Sulriggan's could gather impending shifts in the wind with great sensitivity, and his cowardice in the field manifested as a sensible discretion of utterance once he knew his own interests were at stake.

Most central to all considerations of behavior, the lord of Llymaryn had learned once and for all that his wastrel prince would not sit the throne as a lax and tolerant sovereign . . . having not his father's inclination to agree to every document that reached his desk, some unread.

Nor, Sulriggan had discovered, did his prince, now king, like the sight of unwarranted expense, even extravagance of dress, when he had a war to fund and lords obliged to arm and equip their share of it.

Accordingly Sulriggan, the bane of his stay in Amefel, the lord who had mortally offended him, was modestly dressed tonight, a Quinalt sigil piously and ostentatiously displayed about his neck . . . clearly to remind everyone who his cousin was.

A marriage banquet was a time for forgiving and forgetting. And Sulriggan was not the only member of the court to return to grace. Tonight marked another act of royal clemency and courtly redemption.

Oh, indeed Prichwarrin, Lord Murandys, was here . . . Prichwarrin, whose niece, Luriel, was that second matter of royal compassion tonight. Luriel had indeed arrived in Guelemara, in court, and on this evening, all exactly as her sovereign had requested. Luriel would have walked here barefoot through snowdrifts at that invitation, Cefwyn was quite sure, quite as surely as Prichwarrin, Lord Murandys would have walked barefoot through hell to prevent it.

The pipers played a lively tune, and Cefwyn, reaching aside for his bride's hand, met eyes (gray with a deception of violet) that danced with candlelight. What more than such a look could a man want, and what need a king fear from any former love, when love so sure and serene looked back at him? If there was anything more than love a man dared wish in a bride, he had it all in Ninévrisë, and the thought of offense to her was the only consideration that remotely gave him pause tonight.

Not queen, indeed, but *Royal* Consort . . . the Quinalt and the barons had denied her the queenship, but in a last round of argument had agreed to *royal*, acknowledging the difference between burghers' daughters and a sovereign with her own lands to rule. It was not queen, and the lords were satisfied; it was a distinct precedent, and he was satisfied, for Ninévrisë had, in the absence of good *Quinalt* records, no proof of any royal descent . . . a ridiculous objection. The house of Syrillas, her house, might be a lineage older than his own . . . a lineage older, and magic-gifted and gods-knew-what-else that the orthodoxy of the Quinalt had rather not know or acknowledge it knew. But the house of Syrillas had not been listed in the Quinalt's documents, so it had not been *royal* until the Quinalt wrote it down, sealed, and incontrovertible in Quinalt records for all cases yet to come.

So her dignity was assured in whatever challenges his quarrels with the barons might bring . . . safe as the sanctity of the Quinaltine Patriarch, such as it was, purchasable as it was: lo, Sulriggan, now beaming with his restoration, and perhaps about to advance to the throne at this very moment to express his gratitude.

Appalling sight, and one he had as lief not face. He stood, to forestall that predatory advance, drew his Royal Consort to her feet, and called to the musicians for a romantic paselle. With Ninévrisë he descended the dais to the floor, and the heraldic and festive array of the court spun slowly, gracefully, beautifully into a pause before him.

The music sparkled into the courtly and intricate dance, as couples bowed aside from them and gave them the floor to themselves.

Ninévrisë danced with grace and delighted assurance. Cefwyn counted himself at least no discommoding partner; and the sparkle and flash of dower jewels by candle-gleam scarcely equaled the amused flash of her eyes as the dance wove them past one another and arm in arm and hand in hand and out and back again in this public display, this *challenge* to the interests that had tried to prevent this night. The single petticoat which had so scandalized the court did so again, with the king as willing accomplice, and Ninévrisë was the center of all attention, all gossip, all estimation . . . what *would* she do? What *would* she say? ran the hall like a current under the music.

And when the dance was done he lingered to bestow on his bride a very public and passionate kiss that wrung first a murmur of dismay and then laughter and applause from no few young folk of the court. Laughter of that sort was their friend if they could countenance it without blushing; and along with the wilder, less pious young folk, it was the burgess wives that most accepted Ninévrisë's royalty, they, and the rural lords and their common-born ladies, most older women, wed above their station in a day when customs were more forgiving than in this modern narrowness of doctrine. Many of the old midlands couples understood a lovers' kiss within marriage, and approved and applauded with the young folk; and many knew, too, what the great lords of the north had done to prevent the marriage. Certainly the northern lords' applause was late and limp and brief.

"This is my bride," he said defiantly to the assembled court, holding forth their joined hands. "This is my very dear bride," he said as they ascended the dais a second time, and he turned to face the court. "My bride whose forces fought beside us at Lewenbrook . . ." It was not quite so, since her few men had perished before the main battle, but it was a good turn of speech and true as far as noble sacrifice. "This is our neighbor, this true and pious and puissant lady, sole heir of the house of Syrillas, joined in love and amity to the Marhanen line. Peace, peace and an end to the wars that have been the rule of all our years;

peace on our borders, good hope to our descendants, justice to the righteous, and reward to the pious . . ." This last was for the priests. *"Gods bless Ylesuin!"*

"Gods bless the king," was the appropriate response, which came from one throat first, then in a general murmur that might cloak any less enthusiastic recital on the part of, say, Murandys.

Ninévrisë's black-robed priest yonder, so conspicuous in his darkness by the pillar, saluted them, too, wine cup in hand, gods help them . . . not that he had lacked a full cup at the common supper. Father Benwyn was a Bryaltine, that one priest given sober charge of Her Grace's soul in spiritual counsel; a male priest, most specifically, from a creed at least recognized by the Quinalt records. It satisfied the Patriarch, gave him a way to avoid admitting the priesthood of women, and necessitated no further bending of the already ravaged rules. Get me a Bryaltine, Cefwyn had said, in haste and urgency on almost the last night before the wedding, so we can sign this damned agreement.

But, good gods, Cefwyn thought, could they not have found me a sober one?

Gods bless the king, indeed. There might not be another Bryaltine within the court, except this one . . . maybe not another this side of Assurnbrook: Bryaltines did not prosper among Guelenfolk, and did not expect converts. That one existed at all had been a relief.

He signed quietly to a page, leaned forward. "Bid the guard assist Father Benwyn to his quarters. Give him a pitcher there."

That would keep him safely in the room and snoring until dawn, gods willing.

And that cleared the way for the other loneliest man at court: Prichwarrin, who occupied a place by a column, and not a soul willing to come close to him and converse, either.

The king and Royal Consort had had their dance, and satisfied custom by public celebration, proclaiming the royal marriage a sennight old and, by implication, consummated. This exhibition of the blissful couple was the Guelen custom, from throne to village commons, in varying degrees of drunken revelry . . . hence, too, the ready applause of the country gentry, whose tradition was all but bawdy. The rustic romantics of the court, none of them, alas, in ducal office, had come in their simplicity to sigh over their happiness, the sots like Father Benwyn had come to sup wine and eat . . . the young folk had come to dance and show their finery; and the great dukes who had survived the royal betrothal with their influence intact had gathered to plot next steps around Prichwarrin's fate.

For something had to happen. The king had paid many of his debts, but not the one that was on carefully shielded lips and in the whispers that ran beneath the music. A lady had come to this festivity, ostensibly to celebrate with the rest, but was not in the hall . . . and now, now or surely soon came that matter of retribution and satisfaction. The whole court knew that the king had summoned his former, unwed, and disgraced lover to court to meet his bride on this festive occasion, a matter for the delectation of every scandalmonger and gossip in court.

And it lent some hope of seeing Ninévrisë of Elwynor offended: that, too, in the harder, colder eyes of the great ladies of the realm.

But Ninévrisë smiled and talked to a page who offered her water in a crystal vessel. The pipers and harpers, following custom, had immediately begun a dance in which all could join. Movement swirled through the hall, the glitter of jewels and the rich color of festive finery as couples made their lines, still casting looks toward the dais to be sure they missed nothing.

And sure enough, amid the flash and gleam of brocades and velvets Cefwyn coldly caught Prichwarrin's eye, and this time beckoned, the slight crook of a finger, the true potency of a crowned, wedded, and lingeringly angry monarch. The second most powerful lord in the north cast his king an anxious look, as if there could be any doubt of the summons, then slunk forward from the side of the room, past the dancers, doubtless hoping for anonymity beneath the music.

But lords and ladies about the fringes of the hall spied that movement and their hawk-sharp stares attracted others, so that heads turned in a moving silence that spread across the hall. Even the dancers craned and maneuvered for view amid their turns, then slowed, and the fine order of the complex dance was broken. The pipers, just having begun, squalled off to silence.

Silence and attention was not what Lord Prichwarrin had wanted. The lord of Murandys had rather be snowbound in a drift twixt here and Sassury as standing before his monarch, the cynosure of every conversation and movement in the hall.

Cefwyn reached to the side and across the arm of his chair to rest his hand, publicly and pointedly, on his Elwynim bride's hand, while Prichwarrin, at the foot of the dais and standing even farther below his king by reason of the stone block his ally, Ryssand, had insisted on, looked as if he had something caught in his throat, something he foreknew would be indigestible . . . perhaps even fatal.

"Lord Murandys."

"Your Majesty," Prichwarrin said, and such was Lord Murandys' disarray and so deep was his isolation and his fear at the moment that he even added, "Your

Grace," for Ninévrisë, and nearly choked on it.

"Lord Prichwarrin," Cefwyn said, his hand thus set on Ninévrisë's. "We were anticipating your lovely niece. We were given to understand she had come from your capital. Is she here?"

"Yes, Your Majesty."

"Then in what doubt does she delay?"

It was all a show of relative powers, his, and Prichwarrin's. He, Ninévrisë, and everyone in the hall knew very well that Luriel had come to court, and why she had come to court, and under what cloud she had come to court. As his Lord Commander of the Guard, that black crow, Idrys, had informed him from the very beginning of the evening, the lady was awaiting a summons in the outer hall, but the great lords of the north and their ladies behaved as if they truly believed their king and his bride were ignorant of her presence and her waiting.

He might at any moment choose to become so, of course, thus wrecking the lady and setting Prichwarrin in a yet more uncomfortable position, one from which he must defy the king or deal with the scandal in his house.

Perhaps, the listening courtiers must think, that was the intent here, and they were about to witness a destruction . . . perhaps Her Grace's revenge on a rival.

Yet Lady Luriel had traveled to Guelemara on her hope and on her high pride, bravely so, for there was no private royal assurance what her welcome would be, whether cruel, public disgrace, or (some even whispered) to take up her former position within the court and within reach of the king's bedroom, to the bride's sure discomfort. Certain women and certain men would not believe otherwise, by their own natures; and the supposition was even reasonable: the king might have his foreign bride and yet maintain a northern

Guelen mistress to keep Murandys close to his side . . .
if he were so inclined, or less in love with his bride.

Even to this hour Murandys was not utterly sure of
his intentions, Cefwyn was sure, and he enjoyed every
instant of it, modest recompense for the damage
Murandys had done in his obdurate opposition to the
marriage. That opposition had not stopped short of
slander, which was why Lord Ryssand was home
mourning a son this winter season; but since
Murandys had gotten off alive and unscathed, and
vengeance was yet unvisited, Murandys was learning
that the king, like his grandfather, observed, remembered, and had very sudden limits to his tolerance.

"Shall I bring her?" Prichwarrin asked faintly, not
loudly enough for the satisfaction of every listener
leaning forward to hear, and Cefwyn cocked his head
on a side, affecting not to hear, himself, so Prichwarrin
said it again, clearing his throat. "She accepts Your
Majesty's gracious invitation."

Oh, there still *was* a defiance. Indeed, and depend on it,
the bitter bile could still from time to time seep out of
Murandys . . . not a grand, battlefield sort of spirit, rather
a mean dagger on the stairs sort of courage.

Luriel, his niece, had both kinds.

"Invitation?" Cefwyn echoed him, casting mild
aspersion, loudly enough to be gossiped about, and
gave Prichwarrin no chance to amend himself . . . fool,
to challenge him here, and under the circumstances; but
Prichwarrin had not proved himself the keenest wit in
court, and the lack of Ryssand's guidance tonight was
evident. "Bring your niece in," Cefwyn said, "yes, pray
do. Let us see her."

"Your Majesty," Prichwarrin said, his face quite
rigid, and turned and walked through a widening
gauntlet of spectators toward the doors. A small whisper of anticipated misfortune followed him.

The doors opened, and the hall stayed fixed on the sight of Prichwarrin going out, and immediately on Prichwarrin coming back, not escorting his niece, rather stepping aside as if he had just admitted the plague.

Luriel had evidently waited cloaked, for a moderate gasp went up as she appeared: the lady came not in modest repentance, but in jewels and a russet gown that blazed in the soft candle glow of the hall. Her fair hair was swept up in braids and pinned with gold; her cloak was trimmed with fox and embroidered in gold thread.

Fox-colors to cover a vixen heart, Cefwyn thought, well remembering that wonderful hair tumbled on a pillow, and that silken body luxuriant by faintest candlelight . . . how could a man not recall those nights, even a man faithful and sworn? Luriel wore the russet gown like a bright blazon in a hall listening and watching for her destruction. She wore it before all the good Quinalt women who would die rather than yield the virtue she had freely abandoned in a Marhanen's bed; and she wore it before all the good pious Quinalt men who now longed to breach that defense for themselves. She was a battle cry in motion as she walked to the steps of the dais, and there with a pale, set countenance, she bowed her head and sank in a deep reverence from which majesty alone could bid her rise forgiven or damned.

"Lady Luriel," Cefwyn said, "rise. We delight to see you. Welcome, most happily."

"My lord king," she said, looking up and rising indeed with a high flush on her cheeks. He had not been king when last they had seen one another, when she had left Henas'amef in grand dudgeon and ridden home . . . all because he would not pass last winter in revels and spend the Amefin treasury on her gowns.

She had hated the provincials of Amefel, calling them heretics, hated their rusticity, and despised the generally dark-haired Amefin lords and their ladies, calling them peasant farmers no matter their ancient blood.

Luriel now looked up at an Elwynim woman, the Elwynim being closer kin to the Amefin than not, a dark-haired, gray-eyed woman who was her rival in beauty, who had every motive to detest her, and who sat where she had hoped to sit as a crowned queen.

And what bitter and foreboding thoughts might not pass through Luriel's heart? Or seeking what redress had she written those letters asking him to bring her to court, when her uncle's order held her immured in his hall, in disgrace for her adventure?

Of all the ploys her uncle had used to prevent the wedding of him with Ninévrisë, however, her uncle had *not* brought Luriel's lost virtue into it, and with reason: Luriel hated her uncle Prichwarrin from childhood and would take any opportunity to set him at disadvantage.

The question in everyone's mind, however, was not Lord Murandys' view of his niece: power lay in other hands at this moment. Cefwyn maintained a studiedly calm benevolence as his bride and his former lover first crossed glances.

"Lady," Ninévrisë said, and gallant and wise as she was, even held out her hand, bidding Luriel come toward her. She rose from her lesser throne as Luriel mounted the steps like a prisoner to the scaffold. The whole great hall held its collective breath as Ninévrisë took Luriel's hands to prevent her second, confused curtsy.

To a stunned murmur from the hall, Ninévrisë leaned down and kissed Luriel of Murandys on either pallid cheek.

No one might ever have gotten the better of Luriel, her weak father's and feckless mother's despair in all her life, certainly the thorn in her uncle's flesh; but Luriel stood eye-to-eye with Ninévrisë, and found not a word to say, beyond a faint, "Your Grace," as the court maintained its deathly hush.

"How lovely you are," Ninévrisë said. "I shall look forward to seeing you among the ladies in my court. No, better still, I *command* it."

"Your Grace," Luriel said again, blushing, actually blushing in confusion and perhaps in dread of women's vengeance. Thus released, russet skirts gathered, she ebbed down the steps, having been publicly welcomed at highest authority into the society of the consort's court, women who must under other circumstances ostracize her for her breach of rules; a society which, perversely, would have welcomed her with discreet silence on her sins were she to become the king's mistress, and under the king's protection. But *absent* the king's furtive approval, she could not enter that society without the consort's express invitation or some man's patronage. Her kinship to Murandys was not sufficient for a woman under such a cloud. She would have had to find a connection or a liaison, probably furtive, likely less than her station, so that she could breach that female society on someone else's privilege.

And lo! instead, acceptance and respectability was handed her in her own right, without struggle, from her enemy's very hand, and Luriel was confounded *and* indebted to the Royal Consort at one stroke. As she backed from the foot of the dais perhaps her hard little heart even beat in gratitude; Cefwyn dared entertain that hope . . . at least of a calculated, weighed, and measured gratitude mingled with fear, for Luriel was, in terms of her own safety, no fool.

Her advantage most certainly now lay down a different path than she must have envisioned when she had written him letters pleading for royal rescue, and she must see that, either in gratitude or in fear . . . unless her scheming had turned one more corner than *he* had yet discovered.

His invitation to court was not a summons back to his bed, above all else. From the time they were lovers he had known that her true and deepest passion was for the throne, and that only Luriel's mirror ever saw love in those blue eyes. No, no one touched Luriel's well-armored little heart, no suitor ever so much as dented it, and no one could be more aware of that quality than her former lover. It was perhaps tragic that she was incapable of wanting power in a useful and sensible way, for what power itself could do— move armies, build cities, leave a legacy to the ages . . . but alas! all that wit and cleverness bent toward the trappings of power, the jewels, the music, and the festivities. She was no wiser than her mother in that respect.

But as of this moment and by reason of Ninévrisë's action possibilities of such luxury lay before Lady Luriel, an entire array of possibilities which had not existed before she was bidden join the consort's ladies: respectability, acceptance, clothes and music, festivities, the attention of handsome men, all the things that were Luriel's life . . . all the ambitions that made her so cursed boring once the sun rose.

The eyes of various gentlemen about the room, too, had kindled with interest, unmarried men and married alike, poor bedazzled fools. And Luriel when she retreated from the royal presence did so with all her powers of charm and wealth newly restored about her, a serpent having shed its old skin, leaving it now in the dust of her former disgrace. She glowed. Her uncle Prichwarrin now came seeking her hand, oh, yes, eager to assert *he* governed Lady Luriel, and ruled her fortunes. She had been damaged by her willful daring, and now was repaired and shining new. Lord Murandys had a marketable commodity again, granted he could bid his niece with any better success than before.

But almost before Lord Murandys could claim her hand, there was, yes, Rusyn, second son of Panys, offering *his*.

It was no accident. Panys had agreed, when offered royal blessing for a swift and successful courtship, and the lad was more forward than even Cefwyn had anticipated, eager, his royally commanded act of chivalry now become the public and swift appropriation of a prize many men envied.

And though Panys had never been overly friendly with the lands above Guelessar, young Rusyn immediately entered into polite converse with Prichwarrin and the lady, pressing his respects on the king's former mistress with vigor and bright determination.

Marry her, was Cefwyn's private word on the matter. Marry her, bed her, and keep her from further scandal and rest assured that great estates go with her. A married and well-disposed Luriel, he had assured Rusyn's father, would enjoy high royal favor . . . and a son of Panys would be in the approved line of inheritance in Murandys' much larger lands and honors.

"Well-done," Cefwyn said to Ninévrisë under the general buzz of conversation, and the uncertain start of musicians who first thought and then doubted they had received a royal cue. He gave a second, indubitable, and added, "I love you."

"And is this Panys' younger son?" Ninévrisë asked.

"Yes. That he is. Rusyn is the name. A scholar and a fine horseman."

Whatever could he have seen in Luriel? He swore he had been ten years younger last year, a fool defiantly posed in his own perverse folly: rebellion from his father.

Yet he had escaped marriage with Murandys' niece. That was some credit to his wit.

He had unraveled Heryn Aswydd's treachery.

He had lived to be king, against all odds, and to the barons' great disappointment, who had hoped for gentle, biddable, devoutly Quinalt Efanor.

But one remarkable year had seen him bed Luriel of Murandys and Heryn Aswydd's twin sisters . . . and fill his nights now with the woman he truly loved, whose name and image he could not put in the same thought with that unholy threesome.

The music brightened into a country dance, the son of the lord of Panys dancing a wild turn with Luriel amid the whirling ranks of the young and breathless.

Solitary and out of sorts, Murandys went off to scowl by his column.

CHAPTER 4

Servants set out supper, prepared plain glass goblets . . . not Lady Orien's cups, to be sure, although her dragons supported the table and loomed insistently from the ceiling of the ducal apartment, brazen, silent listeners recalling to any who knew her the presence of a woman and a household less than friendly to Cefwyn Marhanen, or to Mauryl. Tristen had ordered new cups, new service, and replacement from unquestioned sources for any foodstuff that might be about the place, all this before he would consent to live in this apartment; and plain pottery would have served him very well. But Tassand had come up with sturdy pewter plates and the green glass and argued it was more fitting a duke's private table.

The furnishings, however, had remained what they were, massive and costly and part of the ducal trappings that were, unfortunately so in Tristen's opinion, the pride of Amefel. The furnishings, the drapes, green velvet, he longed to replace, to exchange Aswydd green and gold for the proper deep red of Amefel.

But as he had said to Crissand and Uwen, the essential matters of his rule here did not involve the color of the drapery. An army of workmen was already underfoot repairing the expensive scars of his accession, and the presence of a few dragons and green drapes seemed tolerable and harmless, oppressive as they might be to his spirit. Accordingly he resolutely pretended the dragons were his, determinedly found a certain beauty of line in the snarling strike of scaled bodies, and told himself that green, besides being the Aswydd color, was the color of forest and hills.

Now he prepared to receive a guest, dragons and all . . . had asked Cevulirn to come here, rather than to the great hall, on the excuse of Cevulirn's exhaustion. But it was the privacy he courted, a chance to talk outside all hearing . . . while gossip flew through the town and in and out among the great houses. Everyone wanted to know what dire circumstance had stirred Ivanor out of Guelessar. The earls of Amefel (and by now everyone in Henas'amef) knew the same thing: that, alone of the southern barons, Cevulirn had stayed in Guelemara to promote southern interests; and now he was here, conferring with their new lord.

An urgent message from the king?

A breach between the king and the south?

Were the Elwynim about to pour across the river, taking advantage of what they might deem was still a valid agreement for influence in Amefel? For the town by now knew that the rebels in Elwynor had agreed to come across the river in Edwyll's scheme. Were they across and was the duke of Ivanor come as a prelude to a winter war?

All these tales Uwen reported from his tour of the stable yard and kitchens on their return. Uwen was deft at sifting rumors out of the very air: more, he was a common man good at talking to common folk who heard them, and gaining the truth from them.

"Bid the soldiers not gossip," Tristen had said to Uwen from the moment they had come home, but as well bid the pigeons not to fly and not to profane the Quinalt steps. The soldiers simply did not understand and simply could not refrain.

So he took for granted the soldiers would in an hour or so have spilled all they saw and half what they imagined (they would have some discretion) in the barracks and the kitchens to persons of great trustworthiness. From there it was an easy step to the taverns. And back again, by servants, to the noble ears . . . which would engender more questions.

But the earls would have to content themselves with what Crissand could tell them, at least until the morrow. He had Cevulirn to himself. Only Emuin had he asked to be there . . . itself a remarkable event. And a private word with Emuin Tristen earnestly wished for, too, on different but related business.

But as yet there was not a whisper of wizardly attention, not in the gray space nor at his apartment door. *Auld Syes* was the name he had sent hurtling into the gray space when he had reached the inside of the wards and nearness to Emuin; and after it he had sent all that Auld Syes had said to him, with hopes that that name in itself would rouse Emuin out.

To his profound disappointment, no. But for Cevulirn . . . yes. Emuin would come.

Now with a quiet stir at the door, Cevulirn arrived and disposed his small escort with the guards outside, the four who watched over his door by night. He came in, modestly dressed, escorted by the youngest servant.

"Ah," Cevulirn said when he looked toward a set and ready table, and his weathered face relaxed in pleasure as, his cloak scarcely bestowed on one servant's arm, Tassand set a cup of wine in his hand.

"Please sit, sir," Tristen said, with a gesture toward the table and its four places, one reserved for Uwen and one for Emuin. "I thought supper might come welcome."

"Very welcome, after days of hard biscuit and bad ale. And this," said Cevulirn, lifting his wine cup, "is *not* bad ale."

"I'm pleased," Tristen said, as they took their places. He relied on Tassand for such choices, limiting his own instructions to the request for something simple and hot, after the freezing ride. "We needn't wait. Uwen and Emuin may come, but then, they may not." He settled at table, let the servants serve the meal, and his guest have at least a taste of supper before he began with what his friends called *his questions.* "Did His Majesty send any message, sir?"

"I've heard nothing worse than the situation I left," Cevulirn said, and this, in privacy, Tristen took for the whole, if not reassuring truth. "Say that His Majesty sent me home to Toj Embrel, and Ryssand mourns a son, *hence* my wintering at home."

"Brugan?"

"Fair fight. Ryssand, however, will not see it that way." Cevulirn, a man of few words, found a few more of them. "Brugan and Lord Murandys came with a document for the king's seal . . . Do you wish to hear this during supper, or after?"

"During, if you will. I shouldn't enjoy a bite, wondering."

"So, then," Cevulirn said. "Brugan and the document. Brugan came into the Guelesfort with Murandys, bringing this document which would strip the monarchy of power."

"Cefwyn wouldn't sign such a thing."

"Ah, but they had a charge to make, if he would refuse. This was before the wedding, and they said if he wouldn't sign, they'd bring proof of Ninévrisë's unfaithfulness."

"Unfaithfulness? There's no one more faithful to him."

Cevulirn, soup spoon in hand, gave him a lengthy and sober look. "I think Your Grace means in the ordinary way of honorable behavior, in which the lady is unassailable. Their meaning was the traditional one, men with women, that manner of betrayal."

"Ninévrisë?"

"Your Grace, neither you nor I would think so. But there are those ready to believe ill of her, as of you. It was never their intent to besmirch Her Grace's reputation . . . no. It was the king's signature they wanted, and he'd granted all else they came demanding. They were emboldened to have it written out, with all manner of seals, a guarantee of the Quinalt's power . . . but instead of doing it himself, Ryssand, who has a wit, sent Murandys and his own son, Brugan, who, denied private audience with His Majesty, were fools enough to say it all before me, before Prince Efanor, and Idrys."

Tristen was appalled, not least at the folly of it. But Murandys had surely counted on Cefwyn and Efanor restraining Idrys, who would assuredly do whatever served Cefwyn.

Cevulirn had not, evidently, been restrained.

"And Brugan is dead? Directly as a result?"

Cevulirn laid down the spoon and regarded him in great seriousness. "Let me spread it all out for you, Your Grace. The precise charge was that Ninévrisë had a lover. Brugan's sister Artisane was ready to swear to it . . . that Her Grace had *you* for a lover, plainly put."

"Lover, sir?" The word fell at first confused on his hearing and then Unfolded in its carnal nature. He was disturbed enough by the word. Then he understood the rest of it, and his heart might have stopped. At very least it skipped a beat. "No, sir."

"I said that it was false," Cevulirn continued, "and Brugan having said it was true, he died. Hence His Majesty suggested I ride out of Guelemara that night. I would not have assented, but I feared if Ryssand had my presence to inflame him, he might press His

Majesty with the same charges in public, and then the good gods know I would have had to remove the most pernicious influence in the court. To His Majesty's detriment, he would insist, though I have a different opinion. So I honored my oath and left, against my will, and I have no knowledge how that fell out or whether the charge ever came public . . . but I know the wedding took place, which argues that it didn't. And of you and Her Grace, I assure you, no one who knows either of you could credit such a thing. Unfortunately, many do not know you or Her Grace."

"Ninévrisë is my friend," he said lamely and at disadvantage, he, who had never had more than a fleeting glimpse of the flesh of women . . . and that, in Lady Orien Aswydd, whose allure was a dark and dangerous one. He failed entirely to compass the thought, he was so astonished and appalled. "How can they have said so?"

"Artisane lied," Cevulirn said simply, "to please her father." Cevulirn tore off a piece of bread. "Now are you sorry not to have had supper first?"

"I think I should be ill. I should go to Guelemara!"

"By no means! The lie, such as it is, is at least silent enough that I believe the wedding took place. No more can we do. Your presence there would break it all open again, to what result none of us can predict. And listen: you will be amazed. *Efanor* was willing to draw, he was so outraged."

Efanor. Prince Efanor, who had given him the little book of Quinalt devotions, which he had by his bed. Efanor the pious, who thought so much of the gods he would never act inconsiderately: *Efanor* would draw his sword and fight for Her Grace's innocence. To such desperate violence the court had come, and so far had Efanor gone to side with his brother against Ryssand's lie.

"I am astonished," he said, finding the presence of mind to pick up his spoon.

"So His Majesty has married the Lady Regent, and I delayed at Clusyn until I had firmly and clearly received that report."

"Then you went home to Ivanor . . . and came here."

"Here I wished to come. But I'd been long absent from my own hall, and things there wanted at least a glance and a question. In these times, to ride the true road, straight west to you, was to invite comment . . . and a certain hazard, for a man feuding with Ryssand. I regard my men too highly to do that. Yes, I went home, advised my folk to prepare even against a raid from the north, or assassins. Then came I here, with no delay, hearing rumors of unrest in Amefel. I'm glad to find it settled."

Cevulirn's spies were nothing less than skilled, and in every court in the land, Tristen suspected, for little as the man said on most occasions, he always was well informed.

"The rebellion was against Lord Parsynan's vice regency," Tristen said directly. "Earl Edwyll had a promise from Tasmôrden to bring Elwynim forces across the river to support a rebellion; but Tasmôrden is still besieging Ilefínian. He only looked for Edwyll to make war here and keep Cefwyn's attention away from him."

"I'm hardly surprised in Tasmôrden's actions. Only in Edwyll's simplicity. I had thought him wiser."

"He was desperate."

"He died."

"Of accident. In this very apartment, while his men awaited an answer on their surrender. He'd drunk Lady Orien's wine . . . have no fear," he said, at Cevulirn's lifted brow. "We've changed the cups and drink from no other vessel she ever used. You heard this evening how Edwyll's son Crissand surrendered the citadel to me on a promise of safety. But the lord viceroy killed the men who surrendered; and almost Crissand himself. So I sent Parsynan out of Amefel, and retained the Guelen and the Dragon Guard until I can find Amefin enough to make a guard."

"Prichwarrin counseled Cefwyn to put him in office. He's of *that* faction; I would wager any sum you like that he's Corswyndam's man."

"I have proof of it," Tristen said. "Ryssand had sent Parsynan a message warning him I was to have Amefel, and the messenger rode to reach here and deliver it before the king's herald. Uwen and Anwyll and Emuin all say it's against the law to do that."

"Treason to do so, unquestioned."

"More, the lord viceroy called in only one of the earls to warn him, Lord Cuthan, Earl of Bryn, and Cuthan also knew Edwyll was about to seize the citadel; but Cuthan was Edwyll's rival. So when Parsynan warned Cuthan a change was coming Cuthan kept both sides' secrets until *after* Edwyll had attacked the viceroy's forces. Then he told the rest of the earls. That way all Edwyll's support failed, and no matter whether the Elwynim crossed the river to support the rebels or whether Cefwyn's troops took the town back, Cuthan would be safe. Some of the others held back to see whether the Elwynim would in fact come in, but I don't mention that to them, and they know now it was a bad notion. The other earls never hesitated to join me. They pretend they didn't know they were supposed to be rebels, and I pretend I don't know either, and so they feel safer about it. Crissand, too: he stood by his father, waiting for a message to let him do differently, but it never came. At the last he surrendered to save his men. Now he's sworn to me, and I've had no cause to doubt him."

That lengthy report drew a long, a solemn look. "You've grown very wise, Amefel. I am impressed."

"I hope so, sir."

Cevulirn knew him to a degree Amefel did not, and knew his failures and his follies. And Tristen felt his heart beat hard at Cevulirn's gray, assessing stare.

"Protect yourself. You must protect yourself," Cevulirn said. "And recall that Aswydd blood runs in both young Crissand and in Cuthan, just outside the degree that would have seen them banished in Cefwyn's order."

He knew. He certainly knew; and Auld Syes' salutation rang in his memory. Lord of Amefel and the aetheling . . .

"Too," Cevulirn said, "the ladies Aswydd are still alive, just across the border in Guelessar, learning sanctity in a nunnery . . . messengers might go between here and there with no trouble at all."

The Aswydd dragons looming over them and about them seemed ominous, and the very air grew close, full of foreboding. "I never forget it." He gave a glance, a lift of his hand at the dragons. "They remind me."

"That they do," Cevulirn said. "In this very room Orien practiced her sorcery, wizardry, gods-know-what."

"There's a difference, sir."

"I am aware there is. She began in one and set one foot in the other, gods send she tries no worse where she is. But that's why we have you and master Emuin. —I trust Emuin is in good health. I trust that's not behind his absence tonight."

"In good health, but locked in his tower. He will not see us after all, it seems." Tristen forbade himself the peevishness he felt about it. Anger was not safe for him: Emuin had warned him so, then provoked him, more than anyone else close to him. "I posed him questions, several questions. I don't doubt he's deep in his books. Or he's forgotten what hour it is. Whether he will answer my questions, I've no idea."

"A difficult post you've been given."

"Difficult in every point. One I haven't told you, sir. I've banished Lord Cuthan."

"Banished him! Where? To Guelessar? To Cefwyn?"

"To Elwynor, which he accepted; but we found the archivist was dead during the commotion, and someone had both dug out and stolen Mauryl's records . . . we suspect the second archivist. But Cuthan may have been to blame for it . . . at least some of the documents turned up in Cuthan's house. We searched his goods that he removed to take with him, but the guards might well have missed a scroll or two."

"Mauryl's records?"

"Letters to Amefel. I have the pieces of what they burned, but they say very little. Others may have said more."

Cevulirn drew a long, deep breath. "Wizard-work. Cuthan banished. Edwyll dead. Wagons bound for the border. And now records of Mauryl's time. Unnatural storms. And you just a fortnight in office, lord of Amefel. An active neighbor you will be to my lands, I do foresee it. Well that I lost no more time in coming here."

"M'lord," Tassand said, arriving in the room, and Tristen became aware there had been doings at the outer door. He had supposed it was another course of their supper being brought; but behind Tassand, Emuin came trailing in, late, with one of the servants still fussing his robe onto his shoulders, and with Uwen briskly behind him.

"Well, well," Emuin said, "all manner of birds before the storm, and a gray gull from the south, this time. News from the capital? They are wed?"

"So far as I do know," Cevulirn said. "I rode up from the south, having visited my hall briefly, and turned north to present a neighbor's greetings before the snow fell. —And to see whether Lord Tristen had levered His Majesty's viceroy out the gates, or whether he might need help." Cevulirn could be urbane and quick when he wished. Cevulirn also liked and trusted Emuin, Tristen had no doubt of it, but this was a very brief account, passing over more than it said. "I'd not bargained for deep winter in the hills."

Emuin's face changed, very subtly.

"So Uwen said," Emuin replied, and settled at table. So did Uwen, diffidently, though less abashed in small company, and the servants served the next course, while the talk drifted momentarily to the fare before them.

"Auld Syes met me on my way," Tristen said, "and advised me a friend was southward. Then the storm began, which I'm sure Uwen told you. It stopped when I called Seddiwy's name."

—I told you what Auld Syes said, he challenged the old man in the gray space, quietly and close at hand, disturbing as little as possible. This business about kings and aethelings. And friends to the south.

—With this great storm about. When wizardry stirs up forces, some other wizard may nip in and use them. I mislike it. I tell you I do.

—The storm came out of the west, sir.

—So does the evening sun, young lord. Does the heavenly orb belong to Mauryl or any other?

—But who sent the storm, then, sir?

—I'm sure I don't know. Was I there? Did you consult me? You did not.

The servants had brought in their meat and served it, and Tristen, frowning, cut a bit of cheese, out of appetite for dead creatures.

"There is opposition to us," Emuin said in a muted voice, aloud. "I have difficulty determining whence it comes, whether collective, of many interests, or whether single, directing all. I cannot say, nor see a way to determine what we face."

"In the storm?" Cevulirn asked, who had heard nothing of the lightning flash of exchange they had just had.

"It may be," Emuin said.

—Shelter my birds, Auld Syes told me, master Emuin. Yet I saw no birds. My pigeons flew out and back in safety. They were about the ledge this evening.

Emuin's face was very solemn. *One trusts those birds, if any, would return.*

"Cevulirn was caught in the storm," Tristen said. "He's killed Lord Ryssand's son, and left Guelemara, and come here to see whether I needed his help."

"Storms aplenty in this season, between wars," Emuin said. "But they are wed and done with protests, is it so?"

"Charges of unfaithfulness, sir," Cevulirn said, "naming Tristen, which no sane man credits."

"Sanity is not requisite in Guelemara," Emuin said. "Only orthodoxy. So Brugan is dead. Small loss."

"I was about to say," Tristen said, "which Lord Cevulirn doesn't know, about the letter."

"Mauryl's letters?" Cevulirn asked.

"Ryssand's to Lord Parsynan," Tristen said. "Ryssand sent warning Parsynan I was coming. What I did not say . . . I sent the letter to Idrys, in hope it would reach Cefwyn more quickly that way."

Cevulirn arched a brow, and a slow pleasure spread across his face. "Oh, His Majesty will be very pleased to have that in his hands. He *has* them. He *has* Ryssand in a noose, by the gods; and Ryssand will not find this easy."

"I hoped it might be of some use to Cefwyn."

"Of use to him! You've secured us all a quiet winter, and possibly saved Ylesuin. Oh, you'll be far better a neighbor than Heryn Aswydd, sir."

Considering Heryn Aswydd, and Duchess Orien, it was certainly no extravagant compliment, but Tristen felt warmed by that approval all the same. "I'm very glad to have you for a neighbor, sir. I counted on your help in the spring, but I'd no expectation you'd come here this winter."

"His Majesty was very wise to send you south. As he sent me, I think, knowing I might find you, and lo, here we are with our heads together and apprising each other of the actions of our enemies. If there was inspiration aloft in the lightning that night that cast you from the capital, it had to be in that stroke. His Majesty knows how weak his support is in the north, that at any moment these Guelen reeds he leans on may break and pierce his hand if not his heart. He won't grudge you the use of the carts, not in the least, though for the northern barons' eyes he may look askance at it. His Majesty can't say so, but I think he is amply warned and wary of just such treachery as you sent him proof of."

"Yet he'll not have me go cross the river," Tristen said unhappily. "Tasmôrden is assailing Ilefínian at this very hour, or worse, and you and I and a troop of your light horse could prevent it; I said so before I left Guelemara. But Cefwyn expressly forbade it."

Cevulirn's eyes kindled and shadowed. The lord of the Ivanim was a man of grays, grays in his dress, grays of hair that reached to his shoulders, and frosty eyes that had perhaps the faint heritage of the old Sihhë lineage in them. Perhaps, in the terms Men reckoned such things, they were at least remote kin, he and Cevulirn. It was certain they were of like mind.

And in all this exchange, Emuin quietly ate and listened.

"His Majesty may be less inclined to walk softly past Ryssand now that he has that letter in his hand," Cevulirn said. "Gods, that was a fine stroke. And were you not so explicitly enjoined against it, Amefel, I swear I would have my men here in short order, snow, storms, and all."

"No," Emuin said suddenly, and they all stopped and stared.

"*No, sir?*" Tristen asked.

Emuin seemed to have spoken on impulse, and now seemed to be as taken by surprise as they were.

"No," Emuin said again more thoughtfully and more slowly. "It will not be. It must not happen. I cannot see it, and I distrust any such notion for the two of you alone."

Tristen knew himself for the creature of less than a year, less adroit than Men, and ignorant. But Emuin had not only bewildered Cevulirn, he had even astonished himself, to judge by the puzzled crease of Emuin's brow.

"Is Cefwyn in danger from such an action?" To that sort of subtlety he had ascended, out of his former ignorance. "Would it set wizardous matters amiss?"

"Matters amiss with the northern barons, without a doubt," Emuin said in a distant tone. "But no, their discomfort is nowhere a concern in what I feel. Something will come, perhaps out of the north, I have no knowledge, nor can say what, but come it will, and we cannot be caught napping, or venture too recklessly across the river."

"Assassins?" Such had been known, or claimed, in Amefel, in Cefwyn's tenure. So Heryn Aswydd had claimed . . . falsely.

Emuin shook his head. "I don't know. Nor even

from which side of the river it might come."

"I put nothing past these northern barons," Cevulirn said, himself a southerner. "They'd slip a dagger in our good king's back and have a new dynasty . . . if Ryssand dared, if Ryssand didn't know there'd be war, war within, and war pouring over Ylesuin's border. This letter you gave into Idrys' hands will set the fear in Ryssand, and it may have quieted him for a space. Treachery from the Elwynim? Easily aimed at Cefwyn. Or at Her Grace. No need even to warn His Majesty of *that* danger. He knows with whom he has to deal. And as for the rest of the barons . . . those who once thought Efanor would be a more tractable king . . . I think Prince Efanor would be far other than they once thought him, if ever he came to the throne. There's an anger in Efanor that never yet has come out, and I think if no other has, Ryssand may have begun to perceive it, that day Brugan died. If anything should befall Cefwyn, Ryssand would not benefit by it."

Hard words, very hard words, even to contemplate Cefwyn fallen. Tristen's heart beat faster, and he saw extremities of anger in himself he had never contemplated, a door he very quickly shut fast and barred, holding to the calm Cevulirn spread abroad.

"Cefwyn is my law, sir. If they harmed him, or Her Grace, they would find *me* at their door. I'm not Guelen. Nor Ryssandish. And I don't care for the things they care for."

A small silence followed, Cevulirn's stark stare, and Emuin's, alike directed at him, as if they knew that door existed.

"I believe that," Cevulirn said. "Nor am I Guelen, or Ryssandish, for that matter. But make no such threats openly."

"Shall I allow them to plot against him and do him harm?" He found it all but impossible to sit calmly in his chair, a province removed from Cefwyn. "I won't."

"You would rouse Guelessar in arms against Amefel and Amefel against Ryssand and have all the realm in civil war," Emuin said, "if you bruited such a threat about. No, indeed you are not Guelen, young lord, nor Ryssandish, and by the evidence of witnesses, including Uwen Lewen's-son, I've no doubt you'd strew dead in windrows if they provoked your anger, but that's not what His Majesty needs of you at this pass. No. Contain your temper and your imagination. I *pray* you, contain it. There's no need for it yet. Only for cleverness and clear thought, which are in lamentable short supply in the north."

"Do you know what we ought to do? Tell me what Cefwyn does need, master Emuin, and I'll gladly do it."

"So will we both," said Cevulirn.

The servants were near, but they were his own, Tassand foremost of them, all brought with him from Amefel to Guelessar and back again. They were men loyal to him. Uwen, who had come late, had his meal in silence, and stayed silent throughout, but now Uwen's keen glance went to one of them and the other, a wise, common man who doubtless was thinking his own thoughts, and who looked grim and afraid, beyond easy reassurance.

"Yet you left Guelemara not of your own will," Emuin said, "lord of Ivanor. As did Lord Tristen. I'd say you had well-thought reason to obey His Majesty in that regard."

"If I could have steadied His Majesty's power by staying," Cevulirn said, "I would have done it; but nothing's served if we weaken the kingdom in fighting among ourselves. If Ylesuin stays strong and if Her Grace comes to Elwynor soon, the common folk across the river will rally to her banner despite her marrying a

Marhanen king. If she fails to come to their relief at first opportunity, the hope becomes less and less she will ever come. In that case, support for her cause will fall away to Tasmôrden quick as the wind can turn. So if we here begin any dissent that delays Her Grace returning to Elwynor and keeping her pledge to her people, then anything we do does the king harm, not good."

It was very clear what Emuin had wished Cevulirn to argue to him: his reasons, clearly given, to retreat and not contest his dismissal. And he heard them as good reasons.

"Yet," Tristen said with a sidelong, defiant glance at Emuin, "if we could prevent Tasmôrden altogether . . . and bring him down . . ."

"Even so," Emuin said, "gods know where that would lead. To a rising in the north, very possibly. Very likely the barons' failure to answer the king's call to arms. He might call and they might bid the king enforce his orders how he might. No, young lord, listen to Cevulirn in this. We dare not defy the king, we the loyal subjects. If we don't obey him, who will? And if you ride across the river and take Ilefínian, what in the gods' good name will you do with it?"

"Yet," Cevulirn said before Tristen could answer, "I *have* sent riders to Lanfarnesse and Olmern, and even to my neighbor Umanon in Imor."

Emuin was less pleased with that news.

"Also," Cevulirn went on, "I've left my second-in-command clear instruction to take the dukedom and swear to Cefwyn in the field should aught befall me untimely on the road: I'll not risk my successor by sending him to Guelemara as things sit now. In good truth, I expect Ryssand to attempt my life before the year's out, and I advise my allies as well as my appointed successor to look to their own backs. To you I came personally, as you see. To Idrys I have already spoken, and you know his opinion of Ryssand. To the risk of his own life, Idrys would proceed against Ryssand and Murandys; but not if Ryssand moderates his threats, and I understand that reasoning. It's Ryssand's compliance the king needs. Ryssand's gone as far as the king will permit, and Ryssand knows his head doesn't sit securely. Let him worry of nights whether Idrys will act in absence of orders. It will keep him out of mischief."

"To the kingdom's peril if Idrys should take it on himself to act," Emuin said darkly. "There's no succession in Ryssand now, once Corswyndam's gone."

"Tasmôrden has already attempted to divide Amefel from the rest of the kingdom," Tristen said. "And he may well seek some means to unsettle us. Wouldn't he rather see Ylesuin fighting inside its own borders instead of crossing the river in the spring?" All the uncertainty of the day brimmed up in him like flood. "And wizardry, if it does work on Tasmôrden's side, would press for that. Wouldn't it strike at the stone that will move, if it wants to bring the wall down?"

Cevulirn cast him a stark, a calculating look.

"Oh," said Emuin, "you would be astonished what understandings come to our young lord in dreams these days."

"I've understood nothing in dreams," Tristen said, disturbed even to think of them. "I dream of dragons, sir. And Owl."

"You don't dream as men dream, no," Emuin said, "yet all the same you do find curious notions, young lord, and keep me in continual suspense what understandings you may come by. You ask advice. In this I'll give it. Don't encourage Ryssand to greater adventures. That's considerable advice, young lord. Kings could profit by it. I pray ours does."

"That's what I must *not* do," he said. "But what shall we *do*, sir?"

"Why, you both shall do wisely, I hope, as each event demands."

"Wisely."

"But tell you what to do or what to purpose, that I will not, young lord, storm as you will. You say I don't listen to you; I assure you to the contrary. I have *been* listening."

"I do not storm, sir!"

Emuin held up a palm to heaven. "I think I felt a raindrop."

"I assure you, sir, I am not demanding."

"Ah," said Emuin, and reached for his cup, from which he took a slow sip of wine in a deep silence at the table. "Then let me be less humorous, at your pleasure. Cefwyn will ride among the first troops across the river. Not prophecy: he's Marhanen, and that sort of folly is his notion of kingship. If all else went well and if Cefwyn fell, it would very likely prevent any crossing at all, and it would make Ninévrisë a widow without a king to enforce her rights. *There* is your danger. Against all prudence, Cefwyn will afford Tasmôrden that chance at his life . . . if he ever comes to the river. Yes, Tasmôrden's made one try here in the south, not a great one, with no expenditure of men. But I do agree: it shows the inclination of the man to proceed by indirection and tricks. He's more subtle than his predecessor, Aséyneddin. He doesn't go straight to his objective, but in a slow and curving path. In many regards, he's more dangerous than Aséyneddin."

"The south will not rebel, thanks to His Grace," Cevulirn said. "That's failed, let us hope, and now our enemy has to take Ilefínian and subdue it before he can turn his attention to other objectives. But he has shown the ability to pursue two courses at once."

Cevulirn said that, and said something more, but the candlelight had gone to brass and the sound had dimmed. Tristen sat still, saw Emuin looking at him, and yet was not in that gray space. It was as if the ordinary world had slid from under him. He felt his senses slipping from him, and fought to have them back again . . . he was not the youth who had slipped away in sleep when too great things had Unfolded and startled his senses, but it was like that. He clenched his hand on the arm of the chair and drew a deep breath as darkness closed in.

He saw a dim cell that he had known himself, first of all places in the fortress of Henas'amef, save the gatehouse. He did not know what the gatehouse of the stable-court and the west stairs should have to do with Tasmôrden and sieges and intentions, but it did.

And he saw the lower hallway, that in front of the great hall, with light of day broken in where no light should be in the middle of the night, a dusty great light coming from a boarded end.

He heard a sound like the sound of his own heart beating in his ears, as if he had been climbing a high, high stairs, into dark, and into the gray space, where someone waited for him.

He would not go.

There was that Place.

And there was the cell beneath the west stairs. It was a different thing. It was related, but only discernible because the lower hall had disturbed him. Things tottered, chances poised that might go amiss tonight, and he felt flaws in his own safety. He had a lump on his head and had just waked, in fear, and in pain.

"M'lord?"

Uwen's voice, Uwen, whom he had given the gift to

Call him, Uwen, whose hand seized with gentle strength on his shoulder, so that he became aware first of Emuin's presence, bright and glowing, and Cevulirn's, dimmer, and Uwen's, common as stone, and as inert, and as solid. Of them all, Uwen was plain, unequivocal earth, strong and constant.

"It's one of his takin's," Uwen said. "He ain't had one o' these in a while. M'lord, do ye hear me?"

He did, perfectly well, but he could only press Uwen's hand for the moment. Then he found a breath. "I'm going to the west stairs cell."

"The west stairs cell?" Emuin asked sharply.

Uwen's face, close to his, showed deep concern, but no refusal. "Aye, m'lord, if ye will, and shall we do something in particular while we're there?"

"I think so," he said, and knew that Uwen would keep the rest of them from thinking him mad, but he had acquired something he had been looking for, and he refused to let go. He was acutely aware of Emuin weaving a tight net about them all, a safety within this dreadful room; and aware of Cevulirn, whose attention was wary and sure as a sword blade . . . no wizard, but no easy venture for a wizard, either, edged with a gift he had never himself brought forth into use.

"I've seen a shadow of sorts before this," he said to Cevulirn and to the two he trusted readily with such information. He tried to look at them as he spoke, and yet could not look away from the brazen dragon that loomed across the entry to the next room; it drew his attention, and his heart beat in his fingertips. He could scarcely muster his voice, and had half lost command of his limbs. The dragon meant something. It had something of its own to tell him, one more clamor for his attention.

"M'lord," said Uwen, and almost pried him from that wide awareness, but not quite. It was not that he was bound: it was that it was important, that matter in the cell, inside the wards that defended them.

"We should, perhaps, go," said Cevulirn, "and let His Grace rest. We were the second encounter of the day, so I understand."

"No!" Tristen said, then realized that utterance had been too fierce. He moderated it, with the vision of the dragon in his eyes: "No. Hear this. Hear it and remember it for me, for I shall forget once this is past. It's not the same as the Shadow at Lewenbrook, but all the same it troubles me. I see it to the east, at times . . . mostly east, sometimes to the west, like the storm today. Emuin says if it's a storm, it must come from the west, because storms do, and that's only sensible: I believe him. But I'm not sure that's the only reason or that it's always the same shadow. Shadows exist within the wards, in the hall below, too . . . I saw them in the first days I came to Henas'amef. Emuin knows what I mean. Emuin has seen them. There's something there. And there's another thing in the cell beneath the stairs, by the stable-court."

"The guardroom."

"The cell. We should go there."

"Of course," Emuin said with a fey desperation. "Of course we must, and gods save us all, young lord, what are we looking for?"

"A thief," he said, not knowing why he thought so, for it did not regard Mauryl's letters, and that search. He was sure of that. He rose from an unfinished supper, still gazing at the dragon, but able to look away now, from moment to moment, aware that he had in Lord Cevulirn a man who had been many days on the road and who could well do with that supper that to him had turned cold and unimportant. "I beg you stay, sir, enjoy your meal. This regards a very small thing I must attend, no present danger, nothing that will keep me long, I think. I'll come back when I'm done, and we'll share a cup before bed."

Social graces, social words, such as he had heard others make. But he had told the truth. He knew, at least, that the summons was brief, and that someone essential, someone looked-for, waited for him in that cell.

CHAPTER 5

᭱

Yes, m'lord," was the word from the Amefin guard . . . Ness, the man's name was. Ness had followed them unbidden from his post, his comrade left to stand guard above. "M'lord, Selmwy and I found 'im, only on account o' the Guelenmen we lost 'im . . . so's by Your Grace's order I got the keys back."

What Ness said made no particular sense to Tristen, and echoed off the walls of the small area outside the few cells the same way Ness's voice had echoed to him a certain night this early summer, that night when he himself, a prisoner, had sat in the endmost cell battered and bruised and sadly bewildered.

Then he had been afraid of Ness, and of this place. Now the tables were altogether turned, and Ness, fearing him, protested something done or not done by the Guelen Guard, and hoped his lord would forgive the confusion.

Forgiveness was easy. Forgiveness meant simply putting from his thoughts all anger toward Ness, who had never been a bad man, only a hasty one, and who had thought on that day last summer he was protecting the prince from thieves and assassins. Now Ness had brought down the keys, which he had fought over with the Guelens in the hall above, and in trembling haste opened the door to show him the object of contention between the two guard companies.

Uwen, practical man, had brought the lantern down from upstairs, a shielded light reliable in the gusts that swept these stairs. Meanwhile, still indignant, robbed of keys and charge, a Guelen guard had followed Uwen down the steps to watch the proceedings.

It was a jealous battle of authorities, and within it all, Lusin and Syllan had posted themselves upstairs, household officers, deliberately standing between the Guelen Guard, king's men, and the Amefin gate-guard, duke's men, who had claimed the royal prisoner and written him down as theirs. Emuin had stayed above with the opposed guardsmen, too, declaring it too much of a crowd on the narrow stairs.

In fact the squabble of guards and authorities like pigeons over a morsel of bread, and all of them so earnest, began to be a comedy . . . or would have been so, except for the wizard-feeling trembling in the air, and the fact that, jests and foolishness aside, the young man in this cell was in peril of his life.

The door opened into dark and showed them the morsel in question . . . a small lump of knees and elbows in the light of the lantern Uwen held high. The lump moved . . . a boy who hid his face and squinted at the light, then, vision obtained between knee and elbows, let out a startlingly pitiful sound and attempted to be completely invisible. Terror lanced through the gray space, and Tristen drew in a sharp breath and forbade the boy that invisibility, on all levels.

"Be still!" he said, and now he knew why he had bidden his guard gather this boy along with all the missing staff. Wizard-gift was in him.

"M'lord!" the waif cried and flung himself on his face in the dirty straw, and there all things stopped, in the gray space and in this place that stank with a remembered stench, and that held all the terror he himself had felt here.

"Paisi," Tristen said more gently. "Paisi is your name."

"No, no, m'lord, 'at's somebody else."

"Look up. Look at me."

Emuin should have come down, Tristen thought now, because the wizard-feeling rattled off the walls. But then, Emuin hardly needed to, for he *was* there, having an ear to the gray place, reserving himself from the gusts of fear and alarm that blew wildly about the cell.

In Amefin blood, the Guelenfolk said, was no little amount of the Sihhë. And he would not be surprised, in better light, and if the lad would look up at all at the lantern, if Paisi's eyes were gray as old glass.

"Paisi," he said again. "Never hide from me." Had not Mauryl said something of the sort to him, once?

And indeed the boy did venture half a look, furtive and fearful.

"See, you're not harmed. You're not to *be* harmed."

Terror still flooded forth, and defense, angry defense, but not denial.

"Boy," Uwen said, at his shoulder, a slow and tolerant voice, "your new lord's been huntin' ye high and low for a fortnight, an' set some great store by findin' ye, so's ye might as well bring your head up an' face 'im as near like a good, respectable lad as ye can manage. Get up, an' make a proper respect to His Grace. Ye're half a man . . . be all o' one."

The youth, stung, did get to his feet, but kept his back against his corner, as if the wall was safety, or needful support.

"What's the charge again' 'im, exactly?" Uwen asked with a glance over his shoulder at Ness. They had heard a confused account of theft, above, but Uwen asked particulars.

"Pilferage from m'lord's wagons," Ness said.

"A thief," Tristen said, recalling his impression above.

"A hungry boy, m'lord," Ness said, bravely. "Bein' afraid to come to the gate where he usually got a bit o' bread an' a meal or two off the kitchen leavin's, an' carry messages for the guard. We ain't seen 'im since the order went out to find 'im."

"And he guides strangers, do you, Paisi?"

"M'lord," was all the boy was willing to say, and the fear in the gray space was overwhelming.

"They been chasin' 'im all the day. An' was in the way o' hangin' 'im," Ness said. "For theft o' personal goods."

"They will not hang him," Tristen said. He had seen men hang, and had no desire to see this boy meet such a fate. "Not this boy, and no one else, will they hang. If there are thieves or hungry folk, send them to me."

"M'lord," Ness said faintly and fearfully, acknowledging the order.

Paisi, too, stared at him with the same wide-eyed look the young villagers in Guelessar had had, burning curiosity and stark fear commingled. It was a summer and a fall since they had looked at one another, and Tristen was not sure he would have recognized Paisi by the look alone . . . a boy, of what years Tristen had no idea how to reckon by looking at him. But this was indeed the boy who had found him wandering in the streets of the town and guided him to Cefwyn, and now he knew it was no happenstance that had drawn Paisi to him, though neither of them had known it then. Ness had been there. And surely Ness remembered.

"How old might you be?" he asked Paisi: nearly, but not quite a man, was the reckoning his eye made, and Paisi himself only shrugged as if that, like other things, escaped him.

"Little as fourteen, much as sixteen winters," Uwen said in the subject's silence. "An' he don't have proper manners for ye to bring 'im into a fine house, m'lord. 'E might do well in the guard if he learnt to stand an' look at a man."

What *should* he do with the boy now he had found him? He had never yet reckoned that part of his search. It had only mattered to him to know where Paisi was, and to know that he was close to him and could not fall into the hands of anyone else. He had added Paisi to his list of those souls he wanted found, and found for the same reasons as he would secure wards and latch windows, gathering the power of the household close in one place, not scattering it abroad, available to any ill intention that wandered in from Elwynor.

But he had never, when he had first met Paisi, been aware of the gift in him. He had been very marginally aware of the gift in himself, on that confused evening. But he had no doubt at all now why Paisi of all boys in Henas'amef had happened across him, and guided him to Cefwyn's gate. No chance, but wizardry had brought him to Cefwyn. He had wondered was there somewhere else he was supposed to have gone, perhaps to Elwynor or to the Lord Regent . . . but meeting Paisi now, he knew it *was* no chance, and that Cefwyn's court was where Mauryl had intended him to go.

That was a profound realization, one that led him astray to Ynefel and back, so that he needed Uwen's touch on the arm to remember what was essential, to find the boy someplace other than a straw-lined cell.

He did not want the boy loose and unwatched, no more than Mauryl's letters or Mauryl's books or a staff that Mauryl had leaned on. The wizardry that had sent *him* into the world had brushed past this boy and made of the boy a pivot-point on which so much else turned.

"He might help Tassand with Emuin's tower, if he were of a mind. I think I would prefer him in the house and not out of it."

"He'll steal the silver, m'lord. He wouldn't want to, but I fear temptation'd be too much for the lad. He can't rightly reckon his prospects. What ye hold up to 'im is so far beyond his ken as the sun and the stars is, and he just don't know how to think of silver an' hungry folk an' what he wants all at the same time."

"Nor do I," Tristen said, bringing silence all around him. "Yet I try." It was firmer and firmer in his mind that with all else unhinged in the world, any piece of his own left unclaimed could become an adit for sorcery, a danger as great as a broken ward. He had not been prepared to find Paisi so urgently claiming his attention. He had certainly not been prepared to find him in trouble with the king's guard and arrested for theft. But he was not utterly surprised, either. Uwen was right. Paisi was not a boy easy to love.

In fact he wondered if anyone but Ness had ever cared for him. And he wondered for what reason outside the common goodness of Ness's heart anyone had seen him fed and clothed. He had had Mauryl when he was foolish and helpless. But who had cared for Paisi's needs? And why?

"Is he yours?" he asked Ness. "Is he kin of yours?"

"M'lord," Ness said faintly, unsure, it was likely, what claiming Paisi might entail, or wherein he might be deemed at fault. "No, he ain't kin. He ain't no one's kin, that I know. But we an' the lads at the gate, we took care of 'im, an' he kind of slipped about the streets an' told us if there was somethin' amiss."

"Then he has had a use."

"Aye, m'lord, sort of a use. An' 'e ain't stole except once. Or twice."

"Has he lied to you?"

"Not so's ever mattered. 'E tells tales. 'E's a boy. Boys do."

"Then take him at least for the night. —Go to Ness," Tristen said to the young prisoner, "and do as he bids you. Have a bath at the scullery, have something to eat, and I'll send someone for you in the morning who'll tell you what you have to do. You've protected the town before. You'll go on protecting it. And you'll be an honest boy and not steal anything again, or Emuin will turn you into a toad."

Paisi cast frantic glances at Ness and at him, and at Uwen. Whether or not he believed the threat of being a toad he surely knew by now he was deep in wizards' business, and in danger.

"I have enemies," Tristen said softly, "and only honesty and my service may protect you. Dishonesty will deliver you to my enemies as surely as if you walked to Tasmôrden's gates."

"I don't know about lords an' wizards!" Paisi protested, for the first time finding a string of words. "I don't know about bein' in the Zeide!"

"Learn," Tristen said, "and make as few mistakes as you can. Steal *nothing*." He gave a nod to Ness. "Find him a bed. And supper. I left mine, for this, and left my guest, too. I must go back upstairs." He had only just realized the extent of his dereliction: strongly as he had felt the need here, he knew now he must go back and beg Cevulirn's pardon. "I'll send Tassand in the morning."

"Scrub under them fingernails," Uwen said, "as don't seem likely 'e ever has. Show 'im how to stand like a soldier and speak up like one, too. It ain't so different for His Grace's servants."

"Aye, Captain," Ness said in a hushed tone.

And that was the end of the matter, with Ness and Paisi at last. Increasingly it seemed he had done the right, the necessary thing.

"M'lor'," the young voice pursued him, a-tremble.

He stopped and looked back. Paisi had reached the bottom step, and came another step up.

"M'lor', if it's anything ye wish to hear . . . there's talk, there's talk I heard."

"And what talk?"

The silence after said perhaps the boy was too eager, foolishly eager, to prove himself useful; and all he had was dubious. Ness seemed to think so, too, for he overtook the boy and set a cautioning hand on his shoulder.

"In the market they said . . . They said you was goin' to raise up the old tower."

"Ynefel?"

"That 'un, yes, m'lor'. —An' ye'd bring back the magic."

"Who says so?"

"The gran'mothers say 't."

"He means the hedge-wizards," Uwen said. "Mostly they're midwives. Herb-witches."

He hardly knew what to say to that charge. Likely it was already true, in the sense that he came from Ynefel. But it was nothing he wanted bruited about the streets: the Quinalt was not that well-disposed to him, and Idrys had warned him of it.

"I don't know," he said, "and I know nothing about these grandmothers. What else do you know?"

"There's them carts gone out," Paisi said, "an' folk is talkin' about war and maybe ye'll call the muster."

"I don't intend to have war here. It's far from my intention."

"That's what I know, m'lor'."

The words were more than the words. The very stones rang with them . . . a sense of things to which ordinary men were deaf.

Of a sudden he reached across the gray space and seized on Paisi's notice, startling his soul half out of him, and facing him there, in the gray . . .

—*I think you hear me, Paisi.*

"Gods bless!" Paisi cried, and in the one world fell to his knees and in this one whirled away on the winds of panic . . . flat into Ness's arms.

Tristen pursued, a mere step down the stairs, and had him at close attention.

—*M'lor'* . . .

"Don't lie," he said, in this world and the gray one. "If you'll do a service for me, ask the grandmothers what they would say to me."

He had Emuin's attention, and knew it; and Emuin was utterly aware of the waif, and of him. In that moment Paisi seemed to see Emuin, for he turned his head all in a jerk and fled.

In the world of Men Paisi missed the step and tumbled to his knees on it.

"M' lord," Paisi said, trembling.

"Go with Ness," Tristen said aloud, and added, "Boy?" It echoed to him with Mauryl's voice, kind and commanding at once. When had the tables turned? "I'll never hurt you."

"My lord," Paisi whispered, on his knees.

"Send to Tassand in the morning," Tristen said to Ness, "and let him have the run of the town as he has had. I've given him something to do for me."

With that he had done all that was profitable to do, and he turned and went up the stairs with Uwen.

*   *   *

Emuin was there, with a handful of the Guelens, Emuin with hands in the sleeves of his gray robes, beneath the fitful light of a lantern, shielded light there in the drafty stairs. And even so the wind gusted the little flame and cast Emuin's face in ominous shadow.

"A thief, you say," Emuin prompted him aloud.

—*And what more? Emuin confronted him in the gray space as well, and the gray clouds were roiled with the storm of Emuin's distress.*

—*A boy, Tristen answered. He guided me to Cefwyn: should I leave him loose and unwarded? He's an open threshold. Now he's ours.*

—*Yours. Yours, young lord. I have nothing to do with him!*

Paisi had led Tristen straight as an arrow from the town gates to Cefwyn's doorstep, the night he had arrived. Wizardry went for weak points, and Paisi's hunger was that; it went for movable points, and there was none more unstable than a boy with no bed at night; it went for persons with a glimmer of the gift and no knowledge how to use it. And if there was malice afoot in the gray space at large, seeking any approach, any weakness in his Place in the world, he had just mortared in that stone with strong wards. He had meant what he said to Paisi: if hostile force attempted this boy who had so basic and early a connection to his presence here, he would know that threshold had been crossed. But the boy was himself harmless as the old women Uwen named.

—*Harmless! Emuin echoed his thought. Harmless now. Bring back the magic indeed.*

—*Is there truth in it, sir? Can you see? I can't. Who are these grandmothers?*

—*The truth, gods, the truth! The cursed truth is the magic's worn thin and raising it is* work, *young lord, wearying work, until a draught of your presence*

*pours down, and a wizard who ought to know better
finds it headier and headier wine, gods save me. Gods
save us all.*

The Guelen Guard, who had lost their prisoner to
higher orders, stood frowning, meanwhile, and all the
distressing exchange was in an eyeblink, leaving him
staring at Emuin and Emuin conspicuously evading his
eyes.

"The boy is a thief," the Guelen officer said, "and
will steal from Your Grace, if he goes free."

"He will go free . . . in my service." Tristen had no
idea what the boy had stolen or whether they had gotten it back. The wagons bound for the border had
been laden with all manner of things, supplies, soldiers' belongings, tents and fittings as well as grain for
horses. Paisi, however, would not have made off with
a grain sack. Likely it was something smaller.
"Whatever he stole," Tristen said, "have the owner
come to Uwen, and I will pay it."

"Your Grace," the sergeant said, "it was a man's
kit, an' we ain't ever found it."

"Then Paisi will tell where he hid it." He saw no
profit in long debate with the officer, and pursued his
way doggedly toward the lower west hall, having
learned to disentangle himself from the importunate:
solve a matter and move on, disentangling his guard
and those with him at the same time, and leaving firm
orders behind him.

But even so he felt himself constrained and hemmed
about.

"What in the gods' good name possessed you to
ride out today?" Emuin asked. Not: why have we left a
supper upstairs? That he took in stride. But riding out
with Crissand . . . that was in question.

"Crissand asked," he said simply. "Have you
marked it, sir, he has the gift?"

"As does that boy. This is Amefel. Half the province has the gift in some measure!"

"Not to that measure."

"No. That's true."

"I've done what I see to do. I ask, sir, this time I ask very strongly, that you advise me."

"And still, I say I will not—"

"I *know* what you will not, sir! But consider . . . the harm is out across the river. It *is* across the river, is it not?"

"It seems to be."

"Yet it was a great storm out there!" He needed exercise no discretion in front of Lusin and Uwen, who had been there, but he kept his voice low with great effort, lest it echo to the guards elsewhere, who surely could hear that they argued, if not *what* they argued. "Crissand urged me go, Auld Syes met me, Cevulirn had been on his way long before I took the notion to ride out. I say I felt disturbance in the west and you say not in the west. So where shall I look for it, sir? And what shall I do about it when I do find it?"

"I'm sure I don't know. Nor do I care to, young lord. I've told you that."

"And yet came with me back to Amefel."

"Someone needed to."

"And having arrived here, you do nothing, all for fear of involving yourself in Mauryl's spells. And what if Mauryl *wished* you to advise me?"

"I know he *did,* young lord! That's the bloody point! He had the cursed gall to leave you and me equally ignorant of his purposes and you ignorant of *your* purposes, and wherein am I to substitute mine? If mine were adequate, why am I not ruling Ynefel at this hour? No, no, and no! I am not Mauryl's successor, and I am most certainly not your master! Rail on *him,* that he failed to advise you! But on *me*? Why, I do as he did! I leave you ignorant as a new-whelped pup and trust the unwinding of his spell to inform you of your reasons or his intent . . . so where am I at fault more than he, pray?"

Now they were well beyond what the guards should witness, even Lusin and Syllan, and some consciousness of witnesses and the echoing halls seemed to return to Emuin, and he moderated his voice. "Forgive me. But think on statecraft and moderate behavior, young lord. I've every suspicion the knowledge of that art is in you, and does Unfold at need. You *are* the lord of Amefel. Conduct yourself so! Hold audience for your people and don't complain of me that I fail to advise you, when you will not act on the simple advice I have given you! And what do I tell you? Establish a court! Settle in one place and let entreaty come to you, not the other way about, none of this haring about the countryside looking for trouble! We are not yet at that need, that we must find troubles out by some country shrine."

"I mentioned no shrine."

There was a moment of silence then, and Emuin did not meet his eyes.

"You knew. You expected her," Tristen said accusingly, "and never told me."

"Say I'm not surprised at her," Emuin confessed, "since she precedes trouble, and trouble we shall have by spring, young lord, so she might as well have the winter's start on it. I say act on the advice I do give and then we will proceed to the advice you complain I do *not* give."

"And establish this *court*, sir?"

"That, for a beginning."

"And spend my days settling the design for carved doors, and debating with craftsmen? Hard enough to see to the things I need to."

"Better that than raising storms in the countryside.

Stay out of mischief! Provoke nothing before its time."

"Provoke *what*, sir? And in what *time*?" It was the very question he pursued, whether Emuin knew there was something on the horizon, or whether he was equally baffled and casting about for hints of what opposed them. "Storms may always come from the west, but Ynefel lies that way, too, and whether the tower is vacant or not concerns me. I have felt it vacant. I've thought that it was. Do you know?"

"Yes, it is vacant! I am certain of its vacancy, as I am certain there is no active shrine at Levey, and no hallow nor shadow beneath the oak that fell, not tonight, whatever may have been true at dawn this morning. But I'll be most grateful, young lord, if you and yours could refrain from poking and prying under every stone in the province. Follow the advice I do give, and don't rush into other things and then run to me for advice, as if I should have foreseen everything! I don't. I can't. I won't. So there! I'm out of need for supper this evening, and far from polite converse. Entertain your guest. I'll go back to my tower, by your leave, my good and gracious lord, and let you younger hearts plan the downfall of Tasmôrden. I'm weary."

"You've not had all your supper. And your advice would be welcome. Come upstairs with me and have the rest of your supper. Please, sir."

Another lengthy silence, Emuin seeming distracted and weary. "You don't hear me, do you? Nothing's come to you? *Crissand* lured you out there. *Crissand* brought you to this shrine. And who is Crissand? *What* is Crissand?"

"My friend, sir. My loyal friend." Dread afflicted him at the hearing. "Do you say otherwise?"

"Not so far as he wills." Emuin's lips trembled in the dim light, as if he would say more, and refrained. "He is Aswydd. And Amefin. And you are Mauryl's.

And have ever been.—Go to your guest. His arrival, too, is momentous, like this ragabones from the streets that you send to trouble the wisewomen. I'll go to my room."

"You're angry, sir. I only wish the truth."

"I'm in perfectly good sorts. I want my own tower. That number of stairs I can climb, none of this traipsing up to yours and down and up again. I grow weary of this up and down of this stairs, that stairs, come down to dinner, down to the guardroom, up again, pray. Your bones don't know the pains of age, young sir. The steps yonder are a mountain, my tower equally so, but at least it leads to bed."

"Sir." Contrition moved him. He had raised his voice to Emuin, and wished nothing more than to have Emuin's trust, and did not know how to win it. "I'll have your supper sent."

Emuin looked at him, old eyes, much the image of Mauryl's, worried, and shaded by wrinkled lids. Flesh had fallen away, the lines had gone deeper since the summer. Emuin looked at him, however, and there seemed fire in the shadow of his eyes, the lively dance the candles made.

"Master Emuin, Auld Syes told me things. I've tried to tell them to you. Have you heard me?"

"Oh, indeed I've heard. Have you?"

"As much as I can understand."

"Then more than I," Emuin said. "I'll go to my tower, in all goodwill, young lord."

"Have I done well?"

Again that long stare. "You've done very well," Emuin said unexpectedly, and walked away, leaving him to his puzzlement, but hugging that last as dearly as a cloak against a bitter wind. The old man looked frail as he walked away, frail and fragile, in that hallway that had never felt safe.

It did not feel safe tonight, less so than ordinarily. Many of the candles were out. It was the east wing draft, again, and the servants battled it, lighting and relighting the candles, and never yet had they found the reason of it: for years and years, the servants said, candles there had gone out.

And the stairs to Emuin's tower equally well suffered from it, especially when Emuin opened his door.

"Syllan," Tristen said.

"M'lord."

"Go with him. See he's provided for. Make tea for him."

Tristen was never to be without at least two guards, but Uwen counted among them. Syllan bowed his head and went after master Emuin, while he and his armed companions continued up the stairs.

"Master Emuin's sayin' there's troubles," Uwen muttered on the way up to his apartment. "An' dangers, an' what good are we simple lads when it's wizards?"

"I don't think that's to fear now," he said. "The things we have to fear I hope are all across the river at the moment."

"If that was so, ye wouldn't need us."

Uwen had right on his side.

"I wish I had been more moderate with him," Tristen said. "I made him angry." He had been angry himself, and that had never been his habit. He regarded the past moments with some dismay, and recalled he had been angry with Parsynan, for good reason, and angry at the archivist's murder, and angry at the workmen underfoot. He had been angry, in fact, for days, and felt as if never yet had he been able to lay aside the sword . . . that was the feeling he had. He was different from Men. He was different still when he took up the sword, and until he laid it down, and he felt as if he had taken it up at the gates of Amefel and never since been able to let it go.

And now he had fairly shouted at Emuin, or would have, if there were not the witnesses, and he had cast Cuthan out, and sent Parsynan on his way afoot, and done very many things that he would never have done until he had unsheathed the sword at the gates of Henas'amef.

He did not know what to do about it, save to continue to carry it, and to defend the town as he had begun to do. But, he said to himself as he came to the level of the hall, he could not go about full of temper. He had yet to learn how to carry the sword and not use it, that was the thing. He supposed that Cefwyn managed, and that Uwen did, and other men who had soldiering for a profession . . . for that he was very good with the sword did not mean it entirely protected those who were on his side.

Had he not gone alone across the field at Emwy? Had he not endangered all those trying to protect him?

There seemed a sober lesson in that, and he thought that Emuin might have delivered that lesson to him without a word, only by his absence. It was with a far quieter tread that he came up on the doors where his other guards waited, Aren and Tawwys, with the Ivanim escort . . . and the presence of the latter advised him that Cevulirn had not left, for which he was humbly grateful.

"I need guards against assassins," he said to Uwen as they walked into the foyer. "I think the Elwynim will try, at least. I fear more for my friends. For you. Be on your guard."

"Wi' Tasmôrden in charge over there," Uwen said, "I expect 'em, aye, before all's done; and now ye take in that light-fingered boy, which worries me for other reasons. He'll gossip all to Ness, an', m'lord, ye ha' rumors enow."

It was true. And it was worth considering.

Cevulirn sat, done with his supper, a cup of wine in hand, his feet before the fire . . . Tassand's arranging, certainly: Cevulirn's head was bowed, and he looked tired; but Cevulirn looked up with a level and completely wary stare as Tristen arrived at the fireside.

"It's settled," he said to Cevulirn, and sat down in the matching chair, waving Uwen and also Lusin on to the remnant of their supper. "Thank you for waiting."

"Will my lord eat?" Tassand asked, quietly at his elbow.

"I've had enough," he said, in every effort to answer his staff kindly; and deftly as a whisper of soles on the floor Tassand set a cup of wine in his hand and a plate of sweet cakes on the small table within carry of his hand. "Thank you, Tassand."

"My lord." Tassand absented himself then. They held the fireside to themselves, and still Cevulirn asked no questions, but curiosity . . . that was in the air.

"It was a boy I'd been looking for," Tristen said.

"Ah."

"A boy with the gift. As you have," he said to Cevulirn, chasing a small gray thought into the tangle of intentions. *Cevulirn* was one like Paisi, one he was reluctant to give up, a man essential also to Cefwyn's safety.

And Cevulirn glanced down, a momentary veiling of that gray stare, and that was as much truth as needed be between them. There was no need to press him. Cevulirn knew why he was here, knew his own value, at least that he had been moved enough to act. Crissand, also gifted, had felt ill at ease in the ride, and taken a small army for an escort. The boy Paisi might deny he had anything but luck after being taken up by the guard, but all these things had come on one day: the winds were blowing as they would and the coincidences of their meeting diminished to none.

And tonight, when his heart searched the gray space and the land around him, he knew unfinished tasks, unanswered questions . . . all these things, and knew the evening had provided him more essential pieces than he had had in the morning, even in his visit to stir Emuin forth from his tower. He knew all the gaps in the wards, both of the Zeide and of Henas'amef; and such faults in his defense as he could shore up, he had repaired.

But he felt uneasy in Auld Syes' appearance; uneasy in the overthrow of the oak; uneasy in the fact that he lacked officers and lords fit to maintain order while he fared out; uneasy that he lacked an army at his disposal when the border was a long, wooded, unobserved river between his fields and Elwynor, and he had never so much as seen those lands.

"Will you stay with me?" he asked Cevulirn. "Or must you ride south again?"

"I have affairs to set in order in my own land," Cevulirn said, "and a muster to raise, considering the spring: this in the chance His Majesty will call me."

The tainted south, Cefwyn had said. That phrase would not leave Tristen's thinking: wrong, wrong, wrong, it was, and yet there was Cefwyn's reasoning.

"And if he will not, and will not call me," Tristen said, "yet the border is my border; and I will not permit Elwynim to fight on Amefin soil. Cefwyn says the north must win the war; but I say the south mustn't lose it."

"Well said; very well said; and if Your Grace wished me to winter here, and my men and horses under canvas, here or at the border, that we might do, if you deem it needful . . . or even convenient . . . so the south should not lose the war."

Perhaps it was that hint of wizard-gift he had felt in

Cevulirn, that among the lords of the south and north, he had always felt greatest affinity for this lean gray man.

"Tasmôrden in besieging Ilefínian," Tristen said, "promised the Amefin aid if they would rebel. But that's failed. Now I have the province, and I only wish Cefwyn would let us cross to Ilefínian."

"So I urged on His Majesty and His Majesty's Commander," Cevulirn said.

"I begged Cefwyn send the both of us, but he still said the attack must come from the north."

"For *fear* of Ryssand and Murandys." Tristen shook his head. "And yet he relies on them."

"He is Guelen," Cevulirn said. "He has that firm idea that heavy horse and pikemen are the secure heart of his army. He and I have argued that point long and hard. But that's what he says to hide the truth of his reasons . . . the real reason he went home this summer. He had dissent within the Guelens. He saw danger in Murandys, danger in Ryssand's ambition, and most of all in Ryssand's influence with the Quinalt. If we had driven north to Ilefínian this summer, if we had set Her Grace on the throne and all had gone as smoothly as we could wish—*he* would have had to come home to Guelemara and present them an alliance with Elwynor which Ryssand would have opposed. And *that* would have stirred the north to join Ryssand, and Nelefreissan, Isin, Murandys for a certainty . . . the kingdom would have split. He faced them to fight for the Elwynim treaty and his marriage on level ground, and by all evidences, he's won over most of the lords. Only when Ryssand assailed Her Grace's honor, *then* he would have drawn and broken with Ryssand and Murandys, to the ruin of all the kingdom if they took up arms. Gods help the realm—and thank the gods for the letter you sent him. *There* we have our hope of being called and Ryssand being sent home. But *we* must be ready . . . ready to move so quickly the north can muster no objection."

"To stand under arms this winter? Cefwyn forbade us because he had to forbid us. But might not lords come here to hold a council—with very large escorts? We border Elwynor. Crissand thought it necessary to have a large escort. Might not others?"

"Lord of Amefel, you've grown very devious."

The stillness had become so great that the crackle of the fire was a third voice. From Uwen and Lusin, somewhat removed, came not a sound.

"What we did this summer, we could do again," Tristen said. "Could we not? Keep the signal fires ready, as we did at Lewenbrook, have all preparation made, so if Tasmôrden thinks of coming this way he daren't. Do we feast at Midwinter? Have I heard that right? Might I invite my friends to supper? Is that the way lords conceal their intentions?

"With polite pretenses, none of which anyone of sense believes, and which no one dares question to one's face?"

It was what he had seen at Guelemara, and it was heart and soul of the pretenses he had seen Cefwyn and Ryssand make over and over again. The practical use of it had Unfolded like a new word, sure as a well-balanced blade.

"But if we have all those escorts sitting here," Tristen said, "and if we have an army, won't the northern lords know then we're loyal to Cefwyn? And might not Lord Umanon come to us, rather than to the rest of the Guelens? And if *he* comes, wouldn't Llymaryn and Marisel listen to Cefwyn rather than Ryssand? And if Tasmôrden had to worry what we intended, might he divide his attention between us and Cefwyn? And might not the Elwynim who support Her Grace take heart?"

Again that small silence. "Your Grace," Cevulirn said, "you are no fool."

"Emuin says I am. So does Idrys. I was a fool only an hour ago, and made Emuin angry with me. But I know that Corswyndam and Prichwarrin will lie and do everything to their own benefit and none of Cefwyn's, and if Cefwyn has only them to rely on, they'll make demands at every moment Cefwyn needs something from them."

"That's true."

"So let him have us. Cefwyn says he can't muster the south for fear of offending the north. But the north doesn't approve of us whether we muster or not. *We've* marched together. We know our order in camp. We know all those things. We don't have to argue the way the northerners argue. We can just set up a camp, and this spring, when Cefwyn moves, we move across the river, set *our* camp on the far shore, and let Tasmôrden make what he will of it. Cefwyn forbade us to win the war. But he set me here to guard the border. I'll guard it—from Tasmôrden's side of the river."

"You have Ivanor with you," Cevulirn said with the fire shining in his eyes. "Olmern, Lanfarnesse . . . all will come."

"*Will* Imor, do you think?" Lord Umanon had always stood off from the others, in his brief experience, and detested the newly made lord of Olmern. "I'm least sure of him; but it seems he's more one of us than he is fond of Murandys. And if we had him with us, we'd have the entire middle of Ylesuin listening to him."

"He detests Murandys. That's certain. Let *me* send letters. If I summon them in my name, it won't forewarn the north. Nothing unusual at all in my messengers going back and forth . . . gods know the northern lords would like to know what we say to one another, but they'll imagine far too much if you sent the messages. —Your health, Amefel." Cevulirn lifted his cup and drank deep, here among the brazen dragons and green draperies that had been the scene of fatality with such cups. "Your long rule . . . Lord Sihhë, lord of Amefel and Althalen."

"Never say so." He felt heat touch his face, ill at ease with Cevulirn's fey and talkative mood. "The people do. I discourage it."

"You are what you are. And fortunate for His Majesty that you've been a faithful friend. *I* don't stand in your path, nor wish to."

"Emuin says the like, and I wish he would. I need his advice."

"I bestow mine. His Majesty is in dire danger, and the danger isn't at all that you're Sihhë, lord of Amefel. The danger isn't even that our king is Guelen and wed to an Elwynim. The danger is that Selwyn Marhanen established his throne on his blackguardly betrayal of a trusting lord, and Ináreddrin Marhanen established *his* throne on the unsatisfied ambitions of his father's rivals, both of them playing one lord against the other and one son against the other all for fear of assassination . . . exactly what happened to Ináreddrin, as it turned out; but a man makes his fate, and so do kings."

"What do you say?"

"That Cefwyn's throne, mark you, is set on a stone Ryssand demanded of him . . . and *never* was there a greater mistake than granting that and granting Ryssand *any* power. Expediency, expediency, expediency, grant this, grant that, all in the name of this marriage, this war, and all on the excuse of dire threat from Tasmôrden, who has only *become* a threat worth the name at all because Cefwyn would not cross the river immediately after Lewenbrook and take the

Elwynim capital for Her Grace. Now, yes, Tasmôrden has slaughtered his rivals, increased his army, and will slaughter Her Grace's partisans such as exist this winter when the capital falls. Next spring, we will slaughter his, as last summer, Aséyneddin and before him, Caswyddian, slaughtered all who opposed him. Another year of this and there'll be no man alive in Elwynor but starving peasantry and liars and weathercocks who swing to every wind that blows . . . no fit population for greatness, that. *There*, Amefel. I'm not reputed a man of many words, and I've just spent my entire store, the distilled opinion of six months in His Majesty's close company."

"He does regard your opinion."

"Regard it he may. But His Majesty has had my good advice, Idrys' good advice, Her Grace's good advice, and your good advice, and ignored it for bad, all to please Corswyndam of Ryssand, who had a kinglike power in the last reign and to no one's wonder is our monarch's rival for authority in this one. *There* is the man who will yet do us greater harm than Tasmôrden, mark me. His Majesty believes he may subdue that man by wit, not force, and I say a stout fence is the only solution to an ass that will not keep its pasture."

He had heard the truth. Everything he had himself observed said that Cevulirn told the matter fairly, and reached some conclusion of his own.

"What does a good lord do with the like of Ryssand, sir?"

"To whom is it necessary that a lord be *good*, Amefel?"

"To his people, sir."

"So say I. And Cefwyn knows the answer. He only hopes the answer to Ryssand's defiance will be something different if he can be more clever tomorrow. But the plain truth is, his good and loyal subjects should not be subject to Corswyndam's spite today. The king has his bride and his treaty now. He has no more leisure to temporize with a self-seeking baron, and his people have none for him to do so." Cevulirn set down an empty cup. "I'm well content to have Ryssand for an enemy. I prefer that man facing me, not at my back, for my people's sake as well as my own. Would Cefwyn would come to his senses."

"I understand everything you say, sir," Tristen said. "And I agree."

"So share a second cup, and I'll go tamely to my bed, having committed treason enough for an evening. I'll stay with you the few more days, go home to set things in order, and by Midwinter . . . ride back here again, with all necessary force if you aren't in jest."

"I am not in jest. Henas'amef will supply you with every need, firewood, canvas, grain, whatever you will have. I have a hundred of the Guelen Guard and two hundred of the Dragons, who must go back when spring comes. In the meantime they're at my orders. Lord Parsynan did nothing to raise a muster, and he did nothing to replace the weapons and equipage after Lewenbrook." He had not intended to enumerate Parsynan's failings, and went instead to his point. "My promise to Cefwyn didn't mean letting Tasmôrden cross before we stopped him. We'll have the bridges in our hands."

Something in the exchange pricked Cevulirn's odd humor. "Indeed," Cevulirn said. "And before I go . . . perhaps I should have a view of those bridges myself."

Tristen had no idea whether Emuin had listened to what he and Cevulirn said, but it was his impression the old man had withdrawn from all of it in truth, shut the door to his tower and held aloof from lords making plans he would not advise.

Uwen, however, had heard everything.

"Is it folly?" he asked Uwen, in consequence, after Cevulirn had left and when Tassand and the servants were disrobing him for bed. "I think he means nothing but good to Cefwyn, and I don't think he's a fool. I trust him."

Uwen had long since inured himself to questions of that nature, and passing judgment on what Uwen called his betters. Uwen would do it, in private, and quietly. "He ain't a fool, that 'un, never was." But the look Uwen gave him after was still troubled, something unsaid, and Uwen waited, gazing into the small fire in the bedchamber, until Tassand and the servants, trusted as they were, had left the room.

So Uwen would do, if he had something to say in absolute privacy, and Tristen gathered a robe about himself for warmth and went to the fireside. The light cast a fire glow over Uwen's face, brightest on the silver of his hair, which nowadays he wore clubbed, growing longer after the fashion of a man of rank.

"'At boy, an' his lordship the earl, an' Cevulirn," Uwen said, "is all of a piece, m'lord, that woman an' all . . . the witch."

"Wise or not wise?"

Uwen's face turned profile to him, eyes set on the fire. "Wisht I knew, lad. I ain't th' man to advise a duke."

"You called me lad."

"That I did, an' beg pardon. I shouldn't have done 't."

"Call me that, and tell me the truth. Am I a fool?"

Uwen's gaze swung back to him, earnest, surreal in the firelight and shadow. "I ain't th' one to say that, m'lord."

"Uleman called me *king*. Auld Syes said the lord of Amefel *and* the aetheling; and the second she meant was *Crissand*. I know it was. *Crissand* is the aethelings' heir. She meant he should be lord here. And what should I be? What should *I* be, Uwen?"

"What she said was a lot muddled," Uwen said soberly, "but there ain't but one king in Ylesuin, and anything else is treason, lad, just so's ye know 't. I'd follow ye at any odds, but so's ye know, I don't think His Majesty wants to hear any *king* in Amefel. I don't think His Grace of Ivanor wants to hear it either, and His Grace of Ivanor won't follow you over that brink. *I* would, but he won't."

It was dire to think of any king but Cefwyn; and he would not think it. "I *know* that. And I would never do anything against Cefwyn."

"Yet I think His Majesty has his own idea what ye are, lad, an' His Majesty's Commander ain't in doubt."

"Has Idrys talked to you? Can you say?"

"Oh, I'll say, m'lord. Ye're my lord, an' the Lord Commander don't expect otherwise when he talks to me, as I confess he did, before we left Guelemara."

"What did he say?"

"Oh, reasonable things. Sayin' I should have a care, an' not let ye do anything rash, an' to watch your back, m'lord. The Lord Commander wishes ye better 'n ye might think. Ye may be what ye are, but ye ain't Lord Ryssand, an' ye ain't ever *asked* for Amefel: it was His Majesty give it to ye, wi' His blessing an' His Holiness's blessing to boot, so, aye, His Majesty was the one who made the Holy Father willin'. It weren't the other way around. And ye can rest a' nights knowin' His Majesty knows what ye are, an' still stands by ye, 'gainst Ryssand an' the Quinalt and all of 'em."

The low music of Uwen's voice was sweet to him, stilling fears, allaying anxieties and doubts, and telling him things he longed with all his heart to believe.

"You don't fear me, Uwen."

"Ye keep askin', an' it's the same answer, m'lord. Ye should have answered master Emuin a wee bit softer, but 'e understands, same as me, it's a man's weight ye carry now, an' a burdensome weight it is: small wonder if ye feel it. Yet ye should answer him softer."

"I know. I repent of it. I repented the moment I'd done it."

"M'lord, I ain't findin' fault."

"No. *Fool*. *Fool* is what Idrys would say. *And* Mauryl. Auld Syes frightened Emuin. And yet, yet she only warns, by all I know. What wizards *do* . . . that's another question."

"It's above me, m'lord. Far above me . . . what wizards do."

"What *I* do, what Mauryl's done, what Emuin's done . . . all these things . . . tie one to the other. Cevulirn didn't come because Auld Syes wished it. *And who raised the storm*, Uwen? Who raised the storm?"

"It damn sure weren't natural, m'lord. An' whatever happened at that place, it ain't what it was when we rode in. That great tree uprooted . . . like whatever were there, was all done, old as it was: 'at was what I thought of. It was old, an' it was all done and broke."

"That it was." He saw in memory the ancient tree, its roots ripped from shadow to light, out of whatever secret places they had grown, deep in the earth, under it, among the old stones. Shadows might well have broken out. They might have followed Auld Syes, or her daughter. That, too, Emuin must have seen, as he had seen it.

He shivered, barefoot on the warm stones, beset by the draft in the room. The dragons loomed above them, and cast fire-shadow of dragons on the ceiling, all points and coils, enveloping all they did.

"I should write soon," he said. It was scarcely a fortnight since the last letter, which must move by courier over snowy roads, and at hardship to man and horse.

"To His Majesty?"

"To Cefwyn, yes. Idrys said as often as I wished, I should write. The last I wrote was about Cuthan."

"Letters has a way of strayin', m'lord. And for the sweet gods' sake don't write about meetin' wi' Ivanor."

"I know." He was not so new to the world he did not imagine what Ryssand would do with such a letter in his hands. "I expected Cefwyn would write to me."

"A man new-married don't think o' writin' letters, m'lord. On the other hand . . . maybe he has. The last king's messenger didn't have all that luck, did he?"

It was true. Edwyll's men had killed him. Edwyll, Crissand's father.

But with Cevulirn here, and the other lords to come . . . he found himself wondering what he could say, or should say, and knew no one he could send who would get a spoken confidence assuredly to Cefwyn. Even among the king's heralds . . . some had been the old king's men; and those could as well be Ryssand's, even if they came to him. Fool he might be, but he had understood that.

"I'll write," he said, "such as I can, and wish him to understand what I can't set down by pen. I'll write, when I know how things stand at the river."

CHAPTER 6

Cefwyn's head hurt, where the crown had pressed on it. On this bleak, cold morning he sat at solitary breakfast at a small table near windows which gave far too much light, and craned his neck painfully askew to look at his black-humored Lord Commander of the Guard.

"Tea," he muttered to the nearest page. "Now. For the Lord Commander as well. Sit down, master crow, you're a spot against the sun."

Idrys drew back one of the three chairs and settled his armored body carefully on brocade and painted wood. Idrys had appeared like toadstools in the morning, showing no evidence of headache or other inconvenience . . . a countenance that rarely changed, be it calamity or triumph Idrys had to relay.

"So what's amiss?" he asked Idrys.

"Did I say aught was amiss?" Idrys countered. "There might be good news."

"And horses will learn carpentry," Cefwyn said, "before master crow bears *all* good news. Spill it. Out with it. Where's Tasmôrden this morning?"

"Freezing outside Ilefínian, to this hour, if luck holds. No, my news is not Tasmôrden. Nor even Lord Tristen."

"Thank the gods."

"Luriel."

"I make my thanksgiving provisional."

"No, no, quite appropriate, my lord king. The lady established herself very well with Panys last night."

"Established."

"Spent the night in his chambers."

Cefwyn arched a brow, in spite of the sun, and meanwhile the page arrived with the new pot and a second cup. He let the lad pour, waggled fingers, sent him out of the range of gossip.

"She certainly wasted no time in that siege. *Tasmôrden* should employ her."

"Half the men in the hall last night entertained similar ambitions."

"Only half?"

"The rest know Prichwarrin."

"And doubtless some have known Luriel.—In his chambers, you say. Playing at draughts, you say? Discussing sanctity?"

"She does have a certain forwardness," Idrys remarked drily.

"Gods. How could I have been so blind?"

"As what? To have entertained a notion of marriage?"

"As to have had the vixen in my bed, gods save me, and gods save Ylesuin."

"Panys doesn't mind. The lady's dowry will be Murandys, her uncle's detestation notwithstanding, so long as she keeps her head."

"That lovely head is very well protected," Cefwyn muttered, and grimaced at the bitterness of the tea. Or was it the headache? "A wedding is almost certainly in the future, then, and agreeable to the lady as well."

"It would seem so."

"So master crow becomes the messenger of weddings." He furrowed his brow against the glare of sun. "I thought it was a dove."

"A crow is quite enough for Murandys," Idrys said,

buttering a bit of bread. "The lady's dear uncle is not utterly pleased. His niece won't easily forgive him her sojourn in disgrace . . . little likelihood of any reconciliation there until it's to the lady's clear advantage, as we both know of this lady. There's every likelihood that the lady will divulge all manner of his secrets to her new love, who, though young, is no fool. He'll bring them all to his father, and his father will most likely approach Your Majesty or Your Majesty's duly appointed representative, with all manner of these tidbits, in due course. This, granted Murandys finds no way to buy his niece's silence. Yet what can Murandys do but put a good face on it? His one offspring gets only daughters. And he'll no more beget another heir himself than horses will fly. Once Luriel produces a son, he'll put as good a face on it as the lady will allow."

"She'll spend Panys dry and move on to her uncle's treasury."

"Your Majesty's support would, of course, sustain Panys against the lady's depredations . . . and make sure whose ear those early reports find."

She would not spend rustic Panys completely dry, to be sure: their wealth was in apples, not gold, and her tastes were extravagant, requiring other than cider barrels: the orchards were Crown grant and could not be sold. But she would drive Panys' offspring to an importance within the royal councils and a passion for trade and gold that Panys could never otherwise hope to attain . . . and that was good for the monarchy, for Murandys linked with rustic Panys instead of Ryssand would guarantee him a far more tranquil reign.

Could he justify the expense of a gift to Panys, say, an establishment of some additional income, and cloak it from Murandys' objections?

"The lady herself is no fool," Cefwyn said. His own

liaison with the lady had been, at that time, a practical necessity, the heir of Ylesuin with the niece of a powerful baron of that unholy Ryssandish alliance, until the marriage had shipwrecked on a riskier, more advantageous match with a better-dowered woman he also loved, deeply and passionately. "What more can we ask?"

Idrys took a sip of tea, put the cup down, set his forearms before him on the table, and looked very sober. "Shall I answer that, my lord king?"

This was not good news. He foreknew it, and waved a hand in signal that Idrys should speak.

Idrys did. "We might ask discretion of Lord Tristen. He's done very well in sending the letter that silenced Ryssand, in subduing the rebellion that prevented a southern war. But my very reliable informant says charms are sold in the market again, and that the people hail him *Lord Sihhë* whenever he rides in the streets."

"So they did when I rode with him. This is nothing new."

"That the son of Meiden *knelt* to swear him allegiance and hailed him aetheling."

That was worth a moment of silence, at least. "To spite Guelen authority. I did read your report."

"The Quinalt there is distressed, and sent a letter to the Holy Father, who has *not* brought it to my lord king."

"I trust the Holy Father in Guelessar knows where his safety is and will reassure this priest. Good gods, the Quinalt in Amefel is used to witchery. Whence this complaint?"

"Whence, indeed?"

"Ryssand?"

"Oh, his letters also go to the Quinaltine." Idrys took a sip of tea. "But far more feet than two leave the

Quinalt every day, and I can't follow all of them at once."

"Those that go to Ryssand would be a benefit."

"That I have done. Unfortunately, I cannot follow through the doors."

"Well find the way! Where is your invention?"

"Time. Time, my lord king. One of Ryssand's servants met with mischance, a kettle of oil in the kitchens. Another dead, a fall on the stairs. I've other ears there, but none so well placed, and I reserve them against greater need than my suspicion that priests from the Quinalt go to Ryssand's priest. I know that conduit, and I assume that sewage flows. Beware Ryssand, I say. Beware his priests, and watch their actions."

"The damned northern orthodoxy."

"The northern orthodoxy, indeed. I've warned Lord Tristen. I warned him before he left, to make public gestures of favor to the Amefin Quinalt. More, I advised his advisers."

"Well done in that." The whole question of Tristen's innocence wandering through the maze of Quinalt, Teranthine, and Bryalt ambitions in Amefel was enough to curdle milk. "I'd suspect Ryssand's fingers are inside Amefel in more than Parsynan's case. The Quinalt there I never did trust."

"And Tristen is not utterly circumspect. I have also to report, unless something intervened, Parsynan's baggage is still in Henas'amef, and the carts have gone to the river."

"*My carts?*"

"He sent all your carts to the river, whence reports may be more scant: he also sent my informant there, who could not, of course, protest the mission, except to dispatch a man to advise me about the orders. I assume they've gone."

"And what does he think he's doing?"

"Dispatching supply to the borders. He's also declined to send home the Guelen Guard or Anwyll's detachment of the Dragons. They are not delayed. He's *kept* them all, and it seems he's reinforcing the river border. In all honesty, in my opinion, a service."

Cefwyn heaved a heavy, a considerate sigh. "He'll have my carts stranded in drifts, and then what will we do? But he doesn't think of that."

"Or he hopes to banish the snow. Conjure it from his path."

He was unsure whether that was humor. "Reinforcing that border is no sin, I agree. Good for him, I say, carts and all. And he has no house guard but the Guelens in the garrison, and my troops. He's not the mooncalf now. And regarding this mission to the river, pray, you never told me. I trust you told no one else."

"At this moment, in Guelessar, Anwyll's courier knows. But, of course, the Quinalt father in Amefel knows . . . which does add possibilities to the list of the knowledgeable."

"Priests! Priests at every turn. I grow very weary of priests."

"At least the Holy Father has remained constant to his best interests. But priests disaffected from Your Majesty will not go to the Holy Father, and I doubt ones alarmed by Tristen's doings will go to him."

"Where will they go?"

"Where indeed?"

"No wide guess, is it? I'll tell you, master crow, the Holy Father *fears* Ryssand; so does Sulriggan." He considered the alliances involved and heaved a sigh. "Damn him! —Why am I here, with all my friends exiled to the south, in favor of fools and grasping old men in the north whiom I little love? Tell me that, crow."

"Your grandfather weeded his garden severely from time to time. Your father was too complacent. I've no idea what you will be, my lord king, but if you prove complacent, I fear for us."

He knew precisely what Idrys counseled. "There's Murandys, keystone of the entire effort in the spring, the staging point of our advance. Shall I remove him, pray, and have *Luriel* lead my forces? Or young Panys, straight from his mother's arms? I need these conniving old men, damn them. At least they've fought in the border war."

"So has all the south."

"Yet I rule *here*."

"Move the capital."

He gave a rueful, startled laugh. "You jest."

"You say your power is in the south. Rule there."

The Marhanen had no welcome in Henas'amef–to parade through its streets, perhaps. But to rule? "Not for living there," he admitted. "Not possible."

"Then rule *here*," was Idrys' succinct counsel, "and don't look to do otherwise, my lord king."

Idrys had a way of slipping past his guard with a telling argument. And therein he did. Rule here. *Rule Ryssand*. That was the point wherein Idrys thought he failed as a king. It stung.

Idrys meanwhile finished his cup and rose, unbidden. "I've business downstairs, my lord king. I beg your leave."

"Go," he said, but his stare was meanwhile at the white, wintry light, the frosted panes.

Rule, *indeed*. As if he did not. Rule here. As if he did not.

Was not Murandys in check, and Ryssand home, disabled? And had he not set the south firmly in order, with Cevulirn attending business and Tristen there, in charge.

Gods knew what Tristen would *do* in ruling

Amefel, but he knew what things Tristen would *not* countenance, one such being dishonesty in the taxes and the other being any hostile incursion into the territory he was set to guard. Any adventure of Elwynim across the river would turn out to Tasmôrden's extreme regret, Cefwyn had every confidence. He had less in Tristen's forbearance from magic, but at least it would be magic outside the witness of Guelenfolk; and by the time the rumors did get to common lips they would have the flavor of ordinary gossip, a little less credible by their remove from Guelen lands and ordinary sights and doings.

Idrys chided him, and advised him to harsh measures, but he had secured the southern frontier with two broad strokes, not an arrow expended. That was the very point of what he considered wise rule, that things happened quietly and without fuss. Was Idrys not the master of such strokes, and did Idrys decry his quiet management of the south, which had defied his father and ultimately killed him?

No. It was not the south where Idrys faulted him. It was the north where he had not covered himself with glory, and Idrys was right, at least in his observation. That Ryssand was home and out of mischief was thanks to Cevulirn's sacrifice more than by his own cleverness; and by that stroke he might have been rid of Ryssand's poisonous influence in court for the winter, but he had lost Cevulirn's valuable presence, the last southern presence in his court, at least for the winter, and had a blood feud between two of his barons as a consequence. Luriel was holding Murandys in check and keeping him from uniting with Ryssand, but, gods, that was no stable situation, all teetering on the edge of Luriel's whims, her uncle's spite, and the cleverness of Panys' young son.

Marry the baggage off in haste, he thought. An

estate to Panys, a royal wedding present to dazzle
Luriel and keep her happy. He had the house of
Aysonel in Panys, royal lands his remote kin had held,
fine land, a good, anciently maintained chase among
the oldest oaks in the north. The Crown could ill
afford to diminish its holdings, but the Crown had
them precisely for gifts of state importance: Panys was
sensible and loyal, at least in this generation . . . gods
knew what Luriel's example could make of their
mutual offspring in the next.

But by the time Luriel's descendants were old
enough to commit their indiscretions, the Elwynim
question would be settled, granted the gods' goodwill.

And there was Panys' older brother, who would
inherit Panys itself, another sober, reasonable lad, gods
save him and his sire from accidents and Ryssand's
ambition.

He supped down a cold remnant of tea, setting his
thoughts on a second court wedding, as soon as practi-
cable . . . and the couple not yet having presented
themselves and their request.

"Call Annas," he said to a passing page, and when his
chamberlain appeared, even in advance of Ninévrisë's
venture forth on the day: "Strongly suggest to the son of
Panys that I suggest discretion and haste. Midwinter.
Midwinter would not be too soon."

There was no way to have held the men silent on the
sights they had seen, not with the presence of the lord
of Ivanor to inspire close questions: so Uwen said, and
so Tristen gathered of the things that echoed back to
him; by noon of the bright, blue day after their ride it
was certain in every tavern in Amefel that the men had
seen a witch at Levey crossing in flashes of lightning
and claps of winter thunder, that immediately after,

ghostly trumpets had heralded Lord Ivanor and his party, who had left Toj Embrel only that hour . . . folly, but the heart of the matter was the same: the lord of Amefel had ridden out with the earl of Meiden and come back attended as well by Ivanor and his men; and on the way a witch had appeared to them, with portents as yet disputable.

Meanwhile the earls were all astir to know the meaning of it, and anxious to see the lord of Ivanor and hear from his own lips the doings in the Guelen court, as they called it. So it was Cevulirn's door they beset, one visitor and another, all of which Tristen knew, and none of which he prevented.

It left him oddly free of petitioners and questions, so that he quietly fed the pigeons that came to his window, and even had leisure to watch their antics for a time, their pressing and shoving one another, the silly waddle about the ledge when they were sated. Their wings had quite cleared the snow from the ledge in that area, and the place below was only the courtyard, which was free of hazard and remarkably clear.

Boys ran and flung snowballs where lately men had battled and murder had been done, against that very wall.

How careless they were, he thought; with what lightness of heart they stalked one another and arranged their ambushes, and how sorrowful that later age filled their hands with iron. They were innocent, and thought it all a matter for laughter.

Through their midst, however, came a dark and purposeful figure, in a course from the South Gate toward the main doors. An angry man, Tristen thought, and recognized the cloaked and bundled portliness of His Reverence of the Quinalt as snowballs flew perilously close and spattered across the track just behind the man, prankish disregard of priestly authority.

It could not have sweetened the man's mood.

He had the least but growing premonition the matter would reach him. He could think of no excuse to avoid it, and no one to whom the patriarch of the Quinalt might apply in such anger but to him.

And within a very little time, indeed, he received word from Tassand that His Reverence had lodged a protest with the provost and with the guard, and called for the arrest not of the boys with the snowballs, but of certain women in the market.

He knew what it was, then, and surmised even that the small, furtive shaft he had launched in that direction had not gone unremarked by the priests. At very least he had released a prisoner of the Guelen Guard, he had known he left men discontent at his back; and Guelenmen discontent and now a Guelen priest manifestly angry and lodging charges against old women in the market did assume a certain strange relationship in his thoughts.

And dared he forget the rumors Uwen said were running the town? The priest seemed to have said nothing about witches and storms or the lord of Ivanor, only old women and trinkets.

"Tell Emuin," he said, for Idrys in his leaving Guelemara had warned him about priests, and advised him to cultivate their favor with gifts. He had made the gifts. He still had an angry priest on his doorstep . . . and Emuin was, if somehow not a priest, at least a sort of one, among the Teranthine. By his own preference he would wish to draw in the Bryalt clergy as well, for the sake of having yet one more priestly opinion to spread thin the Quinalt sense of absolute power and right to command everyone. He was not sure Emuin would come, in point of fact, but no Bryaltine had been near the guard last night; Emuin had, and he wished he had made the summons more absolute and more urgent. Uwen was out and about the duties of the garrison, something to do with the armory, and he was otherwise alone, but for Lusin and his guard.

So Tassand sped, and dispatched word downstairs to His Reverence of the Quinalt that there would be an audience as he petitioned, and went himself to advise Emuin he was urgently requested.

Meanwhile Tristen called one of the younger servants and decided on ducal finery . . . not so much that he cared to appear in splendor, as that he wished to allow Tassand the time it took to rouse Emuin out . . . likely from sleep, for the old man waked more of nights than by day, and kept his hours topsy-turvy of habit. In consideration of the priest, he chose not the black of Ynefel, but his new coat, Amefin red—his only such coat, as happened, but he counted it wise not to receive the Quinalt bearing the colors and symbols of a Sihhë lordship he well knew were anathema to the Quinalt.

And at his own pace and hoping for Emuin's swift arrival, he came downstairs with Uwen, to the little audience hall, the old one, where servants had lit candles. It had been cold when Cefwyn had it and it was cold now, where the patriarch waited in his outdoor cloak, tucked up like an angry winter sparrow. To Tristen's great relief Emuin had arrived in greater haste than he had shown for any business since his arrival in Amefel, appearing in spotless gray robes and orderly, except the wind had caught his white-streaked hair and had it standing wispily on end.

"Your Grace," said the patriarch in no good cheer.

Tristen walked to the ducal throne and sat down. "Sir."

"I have come from the market."

"I am aware, sir. And from the provost and with a complaint of some nature regarding women in the market."

That might have cut short half an hour's oration. At least having his business set in sum caused the patriarch's mouth to open and shut and reset itself, while Emuin tucked his hands in his wide sleeves and looked for all the world like an owl roused by daylight.

"Your Grace, Your Grace, not *merely* old women, but a danger to the town, and I pray Your Grace's sober attention to this matter. These otherwise laughable trinket-sellers are out openly in the square in daylight, with forbidden goods, flouting His Majesty's law and canon law alike, and selling poisons and other noxious powders in the open. I ask Your Grace order the provost to act on it forthwith."

"Poisons," he said. He had expected nothing of poisons.

—So do I sell them, said Emuin quietly, for rats and mice, given the snows do drive the creatures out of the fields and into granaries. They're generally better than charms, even mine.

"I have come here in all seriousness, Your Grace, expecting a hearing from a man reputed the friend of His Majesty!"

"I am listening, sir." It was, in fact, a small lapse he had committed, in wondering, and master Emuin in answering. He saw a peril in seeming distracted; but he had no intention of arresting the grandmothers with their small traffic: if there were magic, it was nothing that afflicted anyone that he could tell.

"These women, Your Grace, generally they are women of dubious station and practice . . ."

"Widows," said Emuin. "Earning a small living from herbs and cures, and the poisoning of rats."

"If it please you," the patriarch said sharply, "allow

me to speak in my turn and you in yours, brother
cleric."

"I take your reproof," Emuin said, hand on the
Teranthine sigil which hung in view on his breast. He
made a respectful little bow, or half of one. "Pray
inform His Grace about the poisons. He has no knowledge of rat-killing."

"For rats or whatever they be!" the patriarch said in
great vexation. "The good gods know how they're
commonly used, to rid wives of unwanted husbands,
or granaries of mice. Mice are not in question here.
Witchcraft is."

It had been fair weather in Henas'amef, given the
cold. The trinket-sellers he had seen in his limited faring out in the town braved the cold in far thinner
cloaks than His Reverence wore for this room. And
His Reverence had walked down the hill the morning
after he had set Paisi at liberty. That coincidence
seemed less strange beneath, than on the surface of
matters.

"Wizardry is not forbidden, either by king's law or
by the gods' law," Emuin said. "Your Reverence mistakes the law."

"We speak here of witchcraft, of sorcery . . ."

"Witchcraft and wizardry are one; it's Guelenfolk,
not wizards, who've made that division, and the king
will support me in it, I well know the law and the rule
of my order, Your Reverence: trust that I and my order
know whereof we speak. And sorcery? These pitiful
women couldn't raise a sot from his slumbers, let alone
master a shadow of any potency."

"They trade in forbidden coinage, in which His
Majesty surely has an interest."

"Only in seeing good silver come out of hoards and
into his revenues, *if* it were traded, which it is not. The
amulets are half at least fraudulent, copper, brother,

mere copper, which raises the worth of the copper, but the silver when they do find it is commonly melted and worn for bangles and rings here, as by your long tenure you might know."

"The king's law forbids that traffic! As you should know in your tenure in the capital, sir!"

"The late Lord Heryn enforced the king's law only when the king's son was in the town to see it, and the king has no interest whatsoever in confiscating trumpery trinkets and piddling *rat-charms*. Ask where half the Amefin treasury found its metal. *There's* your question."

"This is pointless talk! The issue is the law, brother, however blithely your all too tolerant order may wink at sorcery, both as a concept and a practice!"

"Sir," Tristen said. "Master Emuin will not countenance sorcery. Nor will these women."

"Selling charms!"

"Wizardry," Emuin retorted. "Honest wizardry, which is within the tenets of their faith, recognized by the king and council and perfectly legitimate, however you disapprove it."

"It's a thin line," the patriarch said stiffly, "crossing right over to blackest practice."

"No, sir," said Emuin, "it is not. It is not a thin line, it's a gaping chasm! That's the very point here, and those women with their little charms work *against* sorcery, not for it . . . as good maintain a rushlight against the darkest night of winter, but there they are, these poor folk, to tend a baby with the colic or drive the rats from a poor man's store of seed grain. Sorcery destroys. Sorcery corrupts. Sorcery empowers the shadows and a man whether gifted or not is a fool, sir, who seeks to reach into the shadows and gain knowledge. A greater sorcerer is still a fool, who seeks to reach there and bring something across for his own benefit. Greatest of *all* fools, Hasufin Heltain, who sought to steal *himself* from the shadows and have them all, the living and the dead, in the clutch of his greedy fingers!"

The walls rang with Emuin's anger, and silence followed it, a deep, troubling silence. Emuin had never been so forward with the truth, and Tristen heard it in a profound distress.

No less so the patriarch, whose face had gone red with anger, then pale with what he had heard.

"And what brings such dangers, but wizardry!"

"The greed of men, of which we have plenty in the world! And, aye, I practiced wizardry in those days, and do now, brother, and shall continue to do, whereby we shall not see another shadow roll down on Amefel, to gobble up the defense of good men and pious. Your Duchess Orien was the one to look to, subtle *and* dangerous, but ultimately evident to us by her workings, as I assure Your Reverence any sorcery in the lower town would make itself felt in short order."

"You say so. I don't have your source of confidence, I thank the gods for it."

"Thank your young Lord Tristen, who stood between you and the fall of this province. Thank those of us who detected sorcery in practice and stopped it! And thank your Lord Tristen and His Majesty, bearing arms against an invasion that would have swept through this province like flood. And yes, *that* was sorcery, on its way to Guelessar and all provinces else. It was that near a thing, this summer, brother, and whether or not you compass it with your philosophy, those selfsame women with their little charms likewise prayed with you, along with the incense that went up from Amefin shrines of every sect, while the Quinaltine sat ignorant on its hill in Guelessar and knew nothing of the threat until it was banished. *You* were a hero among the rest, brother, along with those who took up arms; you kept the candles lit and raised up prayers in *this* province against the danger we all faced. Stand with us. Let us have no quibbles of old women and charms in the marketplace, when your temporal lord could well use your prayers."

"His Grace is Sihhë," the patriarch said in a faint voice, as if that argued all; and perhaps it did: Tristen heard, and knew that, Prince Efanor's little book availing what it could, this man had set him on the side which that little book called *evil*.

"I shall never," Tristen said, "work any sorcery, sir. And these women are not our enemy," he added, to have that clear. "I read your book of devotions. His Highness gave it to me. Doesn't it say that the gods made all the world and the rain and the mountains? So surely they made Sihhë, too."

He had hoped to turn the patriarch's sure conviction at least to some doubt; and saw that he had had effect, at least that the patriarch seemed taken aback. So did Emuin, which warned him that it might not be the effect he had hoped.

"His Grace will attend the matter," Emuin said. "I assure you no sorcery will have effect in this town, nor anywhere His Grace can find it. He may be Sihhë: that remains unproven; he is certainly Mauryl Gestaurien's successor, legitimate and a friend to the realm, and will not permit harm to the souls or substance of honest folk."

"These things bring no good fortune," the Quinalt father said. "His Grace can have little sympathy in such practice, himself, but for the sake of the common folk of this town who have no commerce with wizards and who petition me with prayers for the safety of their souls, I beg you ask His Grace, since you have influence with him, to honor His Majesty's well-thought and reasonable laws and forbid the display of such symbols."

"Difficult, since the ducal arms contain them, at His Majesty's gift."

The patriarch drew in a breath. "Within the religious context, sir!"

"No common coin will damn any of your flock, father, nor lead any astray to Bryalt beliefs except they be Bryaltine from the cradle, which Your Reverence must admit is tolerably common in Amefel."

"I beg you take this seriously," the Quinalt father said. "And lead His Grace at least as strait and seemly a path as may be."

"His Grace has all manner of favor in His Majesty's eyes, *and* the approval of the Holy Father in Guelemara, who blessed him at his oath-giving, and commended him to Your Reverence's hands in all good faith. I will tell you, brother, for fair judgment and care of your flock's rights and dues, and for keeping the less savory influences . . . wizardous and sorcerous alike . . . from out of the dangerous marches westward, you should be grateful to him. There's none of the haunts and unhallowed goings-on as *might* find opportunity here, considering the very injudicious activities of Her now deposed Grace Orien Aswydd."

"We have never countenanced Her Grace's doings."

"Well enough, since she let the very fiend into the apartment His Grace has now warded beyond any opportunity for such maleficent spirits. I've tested his wards, and they are subtle and wonderfully made . . . should you wish to know?"

"I do not!" It was strange to stand to the side and hear himself discussed and argued about. But now the Quinalt father looked at him with a wide and distraught stare, and matters had gone askew from what was prudent, and at Emuin's hands, none other.

"Sir," Tristen said with a nod and a will to placate this distressed man, "if I have done anything amiss, I will always hear you, and tell me, tell me if I do wrong. I don't think Cefwyn ever feared the women in the marketplace, and I know there's no sorcery that I can feel. But if you have misgivings, I'll certainly walk there myself and see if there's any cause for alarm."

"Your Grace. In your gifts, in your observance of protocols, I find no fault. But I doubt Your Grace will take alarm in such small matters as frighten my flock."

That last was pointed and sharp-edged: he was not so naive as to miss it. "His Highness instructed me and gave me a book of devotions. He said it was good I read it, and find the gods, and avoid evil. I agree. I by all means wish to avoid evil." He had asked himself why the priest came to him now about the market just when the market and the grandmothers had entered his concern, and if it was not magic that made the connection, it was Men. "There was a boy, wasn't there, Your Reverence?"

"A boy."

"It was mischief for Paisi to steal a soldier's kit, but it was greater mischief for that man to come to you and suggest there was something amiss in the market, when the truth was that he wished someone to die for the theft, when it wasn't even his kit, as I understand: it belonged to a man of the Dragon Guard."

"I know nothing of any of this, Your Grace!"

"Didn't a soldier come to you?"

"He by no means told me about any boy."

"I doubt he did. But you should ask him what the truth is."

"Your Grace," the patriarch said, as if he had taken a dismissal in that, his case in disarray and his words turned back on him. But the patriarch blessed himself with a gesture, as Uwen would when he saw wizardry or magic. Clearly the patriarch wished to leave, and Tristen wished just as strongly that this priest would go away. "I shall ask, Your Grace."

And with a bow and a murmured courtesy, the man edged toward the door until, with a second bow, he was out it.

"Uwen," Tristen said.

"M'lord."

"I'll speak to that soldier. The sergeant."

"Aye, m'lord."

"I could almost tell you the man's name," Emuin said. "And you're quite right, young lord: it wasn't piety that moved His Reverence. Well guessed, and I guess exactly as you do, with small wizardry about it—but I fear His Reverence believes you just worked sorcery and stole it out of his thoughts. You've frightened that man. And you'll frighten the man you bring in to question, never doubt it."

"I guessed, sir. It was not by magic."

"Damned for the one time it wasn't," Emuin said. "But in the Guelen garrison, there's a captain who doesn't want to be in this town or in this province. He followed Parsynan's orders and had them overthrown, and hasn't been happy since, if you want my further guess. And that sergeant and no few of his men think like him. I may live in my tower, but I'm not deaf to what goes on in the yard."

"I wish the patriarch were in Guelessar," Tristen said, "if I could choose. But the soldiers in the garrison wouldn't be happy without him. I wish I might send the sergeant and all those men back to Guelessar, but he'd be at Ryssand's ear, do I understand how he would act? I think I do."

"I fear ye understand very well," Uwen said, "an' master Emuin's right, too. I'd have set that sergeant to the watch on the bridges, an' let the troublemaker tell 'is notions to them as has no way to send back to Ryssand, but soldiers is in a surly enough state in winter, wi' nothin' to do but pass rumor, as is. There'd be toads rainin' from heaven in the rumors they'd have about ye, m'lord, an' wi' the captain of the Guelens, too, who, by me, ain't any better. I've tried to reason wi' this man, and I know this sergeant. I wisht I'd found a place to set this fellow where he couldn't find mischief. I'm sorry it got to His Reverence."

"I wish I might send all the men home."

"An' defend the land wi' Ivanim?" Uwen asked.

"That is the choice," he said. They equally well knew the choices he did have. The Amefin villages would have a hard winter, a harder spring and famine in the fall if he mustered the men to winter camp. For half a century the king's law had allowed no establishment of men-at-arms in Amefel, entrusting the defense of the province to the Aswyddim's personal guard, and to a garrison of Guelen Guard, of the four Guelen companies the roughest and commonest. Now at urgent need and with the Aswydd guard fled across the river or back to their local lords for fear of Cefwyn's justice, Amefel had no men of its own but an irregularly armed peasant muster that belonged to the earls, and them needing to do their planting and lambing at the time the army would be engaged across the river.

Therefore, among other reasons, he had retained the Guelen Guard. But now he had evidence of Guelen disaffection, not an unreasonable discontent: the weather had turned, they were held here against expectation and in disgrace from their service with Parsynan, and now faced with the rise of Amefin to positions of authority, when it was Amefin they had once held in check as Parsynan's iron fist. They were not the guard he would have chosen. Was he at fault? Might another lord have managed better than he had done?

Certainly Parsynan had not improved these men; and Uwen had pleaded for them, saying only a better lord could redeem them. They were Uwen's old company; and they, Uwen argued, had been misused and misled.

"I will speak to their captain," he concluded. "Privately."

"You should do so," Emuin said, "privately. But you see the seed of discontent in these men, young lord, and it comes of slighting them."

"My slighting them?"

"And no few of the lords and burgesses. Where might they learn anything of your intent except from rumor? Become approachable. Hold audience. Do more in public."

"I speak with a half a score of them every time I venture the hall." He had rarely failed to answer chance questions, and on this he was very sure he was on firm ground. "I speak to soldiers and to workmen and servants in the kitchen. All these folk, as well as to the lords. I answer their questions."

"Yet make all decisions in chambers. Therein *you* are at fault. You asked advice: *now* I advise you."

"I've called the earls for supper."

"Hold audience beforehand and hold it today. This is where you fail. The people believe in you while the sun shines and they have enough to eat; but when things go harder, they have to *know* their lord to follow him. Worship is not enough, young lord. Care for their concerns. Care for their fears. Hear the quieter voices. We have His Reverence on our doorstep with rumors and accusations; but what more should you hear? You must sit a certain time every day in the great hall, no more of this dealing in the hallways of the Zeide and granting this and granting that to the loudest and most importunate. You'll miss the quiet and the desperate. Yes, ride out to the villages, and hear them as well. And don't neglect Henas'amef and your own court."

"His Grace already don't sleep enough," Uwen said. "Where's he to rest?"

"And you, Uwen Lewen's-son, you have your own fault in this! You are not Lord Tristen's body servant or his guard . . . you are his *captain*. Give me no excuses: take command of the Guard, march them up and down until they have no breath for gossip."

"Uwen does very well," Tristen said.

"Well is not good enough. And *you*, young lord, must be approachable for your people other than in the hallways, or prepare to do the business of the province there, on every chance approach and by all comers. You should *never* have been summoned by His Reverence to come down to hall, as if you were some truant lad with a lesson to read. I find it outrageous in him, and I find you far too accommodating of approach on the one hand and far too secret and unapproachable on the other. What you will tell to the earls separately, tell to them all in common council. Hear debates, once and together, not once for each man. Sit in state, and let petitioners see how their business weighs against other appeals to Your Grace's resources. If the matters they bring are trivial, they may take shame of it and ask less. Two problems may be each other's answer. And I will tell you *Cefwyn* could benefit by that advice. He cannot rule from his chambers. Indeed he cannot. He avoids the likes of Ryssand by shutting himself in chambers, but he fails to hear the town reeve, and this with a war in the offing. He is the *worst* example."

"Have you told him so?"

"I told his father, who had the same fault: oh, deal with every man in private, tell one man one thing, another the other, and thus Lord Mistrust rules all! Idrys, the most furtive man alive, *Idrys* concurs with me in this.

Ylesuin cannot have the ghost of the last king presiding over it, no more than Amefel can have Suspicion for a duke and Rumor for leader of its armies. You have His Reverence listening to sergeants of the Guard and soldiers whispering with the gate-guard, and gods alone know what tales they obtain from the kitchens. But fault none of them until you demand and they refuse. Captain Anwyll and his command left yesterday to sit and endure the snow on the river . . . good riddance, say I. Anwyll will never say good morning but he asks permission for it of someone. Of him I expect nothing but good compliance; but *you,* Uwen Lewen's-son, you've waited last night and all morning long and not seized the Guelens and shaken them into order. *Seize command!*"

"Aye, sir."

"And, young lord, duke of Amefel, until you assemble your court and rule it with a firm hand, I look for you to be a profound concern to your captain, who knows your kind civility with fools. Lordship does not bind you to give away the treasury or to consent to every request. I saw hope in Lewen's-son last night; I see it today. What of you?"

"Is that why now you advise me, when since summer Cefwyn and I alike have asked and asked and gotten nothing? Can you fault *me,* sir, when of *your* advice I've had precious little come down from the tower? You say I should leave my chambers and sit in hall. Cannot you come down and stand by me?"

That drew a tilt of Emuin's head and a wary look. "I advise as I see to advise. Now I see a stirring of will, young lord, in you and in your honest captain. Employ it."

"I have the earls' goodwill. The Guelen Guard is a harder matter."

"Parsynan appointed their officers, m'lord," Uwen said, "an' master Emuin's right, best we can do to keep

'em out of mischief is march 'em up an' down. Ye
daren't send a man of 'em home: they'd be straight to
Parsynan wi' gods know what tale. If ye wisht my soldierly opinion, it's the captain an' the seniormost
sergeant is the poison in the cup, him in the hall last
night. Gellyn's the sergeant's name. I suspect he was
the one went to the patriarch: and maybe ye can put
the fear in the sergeant, but small hope for the captain,
say I, who's a Quinalt man, an' a hard-nosed Quinalt
at that. 'E won't change, an' it ain't right you talk to
'im before me. You want the men that leapt right
quick to Parsynan's order to slaughter the prisoners,
m'lord, it was this captain an' this sergeant, an' the
rest was swept along wi' what they had no heart for,
otherwise."

Emuin had come forward with advice, and now
Uwen was stirred to report to him, when before he had
been swathed in silence.

And it was no shocking news, what Uwen said
about difficulties with the Guelen officers: he had
heard it before in bits and pieces. But now Anwyll was
out of the town, and his learned and lettered Guelen
efficiency was neither a restraint on the Guard officers
of the garrison nor on Uwen's command of them. He
had worked for a fortnight to have Anwyll out the
gates; and lo! now all the stones that had refused to
move tumbled at once.

"I do hear," he said, "and I'll take your advice,
yours and master Emuin's. I'll have Tassand teach
Paisi how to beg the soldier's pardon, for the soldiers'
sake, so they understand and he understands. He
mustn't do it again."

"That comforts me," Emuin said. "By this afternoon, do you say, Tassand is to have wrought this miracle?"

"I take your advice, sir," he said, for it seemed to

him a little salve for the soldiers' pride and for grudges might mend something of what was amiss with the Guelen Guard: a better lord, Uwen had said the night of the slaughter, might let these men regain their honor.

But gaining what he had of advice, and being told to establish a court, he pressed further on forbidden ground, this time with Emuin. "What of Auld Syes, then, sir, if advice is possible today?" He abandoned fear of asking or saying anything at all before Uwen, or even Lusin. "Have you advice on that, sir, and what when one of the earls asks me who she was or signifying what? I know the men have spread it about. And what do *you* think I should do about the sergeant?"

"Advice? Advice now, when you've gone out and stirred up the spirits of this land? Gods save us, say I, gods save us all. Discipline your sergeant or march him and his captain out to join Anwyll; set up a second camp with the discontents and leave *Uwen* sole captain here."

"Can they?"

"Can they what?"

"Can the gods save us? I've found nothing in Efanor's book to say so."

"Oh, young lord," Emuin said with a sober look and a shake of his head, "that is *not* the question. Certainly not in this matter. Set things in order. That's what you're here to do. Set all things in order that Parsynan and Cuthan disordered. All you know should tell you the danger in disorder. And with that, I'm back to my tower *and* my shuttered and warded windows, young lord. I've said enough. *Order* is what's needed. *Order* is the only saving of us. I pray you, establish one soon, any sort of order you like, so long as it's no one else's order."

Something in that, touching on what they both understood, breathed a cold breath out of the gray space.

"Do *you* see sorcery, sir? Or have you seen it?"

Emuin turned again and looked at him, but it was in the gray space that answer came to him, not aloud.

—Does it not always seek the crack in the wall, young lord?

So ruin had begun at Ynefel, subtly, an old, familiar crack beneath his own small window; and from that small fracture of the stone, grown greater, all calamity came. He could not but remember it, for the thunderclap that had riven the Quinalt roof could have shaken him no worse than did Emuin with that one word.

Yes, the Zeide's heart had many cracks, of every sort, not least the bloody rift between Meiden and the Guelen Guard.

Now the Quinalt, at a Guard sergeant's instigation, came lodging complaints aimed at Amefin.

"No more dare I say," Emuin proclaimed, and began to go his way.

Emuin denied him again, again stopped short of the whole truth; or perhaps it was all the truth Emuin had now to give him.

Uwen gave a twitch of his shoulders and a shake of his head, and began to say something. But all the light had gone to brass, and the gray space was all but with them.

He could reach out and have Emuin's attention from here. He asked himself what he would say when he did, what authority he would seize unto himself, and do *what* with it?

Invade Elwynor? He had Cefwyn's authority to raise an army unprecedented in the dealings of Ylesuin with Amefel; but Crissand pleaded the summer war had left the province bereft as was. Yet Cevulirn *happened* to come to him.

Who has done this? he asked the unresponsive void,

and the old man who was by now walking back to his tower, with feeble and arthritic steps.

—*Who has done this, Emuin? Have* you *called Ivanor to me?*

"Wizards is pricklish folk at best," Uwen was saying, in the world of substance and color and the smell of candles, cold stone, and the incense that lingered where the Quinalt had been. "I'll find the boy an' I'll find the one who talked to the priests, as ye say, m'lord. Master Emuin's entirely right to chide me: busy soldiers is better soldiers, an' the sergeant and the captain's better shoveling snow in the river camp. Ye've given 'em fair trial since they went again' your given word; an' if they've been behind your back a second time, don't gi' 'em a third chance. The river's the place for 'em, an' a warnin' to Captain Anwyll to go with 'em."

"What orders you see fit. At any time you see fit." Yet it seemed unfair to him, to damn a man unheard. "But before that, I'll hear the sergeant's reasons, and if I have no good answer from him, then send them all to Anwyll's camp."

"'At's just," Uwen agreed. "I'll bring 'im, sayin' ye want to have a word wi' 'im. And I'd ask did his captain approve what he did, m'lord, that I would, but I suspect I'd already know the answer. The poison there ain't all the sergeant. The sergeant wouldn't be what he is, 'cept for the captain."

"I trust your advice," he said. "Bid the sergeant come to my chambers, and after him, the captain, in private. And send to the earls. Say I'll hold court today."

Such was the plan; and so the sergeant was due to come at midafternoon, and the captain of the garrison directly after him, but by somewhat past the expected time, Uwen came to his apartment to say personally that there was no sight nor report of either man.

"It ain't ordinary the captain should be unfindable," Uwen said, "and right now I'm inquirin' in the lower stables."

"As if they should have fled?"

"Or should be attendin' of their horses or pretendin' so," Uwen said. "It's the only thing a soldier's got need of, wi'out orders to be out an' away from the garrison. If they ain't drinkin' or about the town . . . an' if they ain't at the stables, there's the whole damn town to search."

"Inquire," he said. The gray space might have told him something, if he had well known the men they were searching for. Ranging through the whole population of the town and finding soldiers was like searching for certain kinds of pebbles in a pile of them . . . it would mean sorting a good many other pebbles in the process, disturbing them and discovering more of their privacy and peace than seemed just, and taking time, that, too.

"Do you have the Guard searching for them?" he asked.

"I ain't ask't it, let alone ordered. It's their officers, m'lord. I'm inquirin' by way o' the Amefin guard an' the staff. An' talkin' to the undersergeants, the while, just getting the look o' men I used to know, m'lord, an' I do know some of 'em."

"But not all?"

"The Guelen Guard comes from more 'n Guelessar, m'lord. Panys, Murandys. *Murandys*' province. Any second and third son, as ain't apt to inherit, that man's apt to come to the standing companies. The lords' kin'll go to the Dragons or the Prince's Guard, but the common lads . . . an' them as ain't quite lads, like me . . . they're for the Guelen Guard. An', aye, some of these I marched to Amefel with; an' some I knew when His Majesty was here; an' some I knew for scoundrels, too, the senior sergeant bein' no better."

"But some you don't know?"

"A good many's come in since summer's end, when His Majesty marched home to Guelessar an' Parsynan came in. Some are good men an' one an' the other I've me doubts of. All's Quinalt, but some's too Quinalt, if ye take my meanin', m'lord, an' don't like Amefin."

"Set the garrison in order," he said. "Marching them to the river's not all the answer. Have the captain and the highest sergeant gone off and left *no one* word where they are? Or are men not telling?"

"Seems, m'lord, they left no instructions of who *is* in command, 'cept as there's seniority. The man who's second senior, *he* ain't informed where they are, an' I think I believe 'im. An' Your Grace is right: it ain't the way it ought to be."

"Did Anwyll allow such things?"

"Captain Anwyll didn't interfere much."

"You command the garrison," Tristen said. "And all the Zeide. Set them in order."

"Them's His Majesty's troops," Uwen said distressedly. "I can't just dismiss His Majesty's officers, m'lord. I ha'nt the authority, wi' all goodwill. I begun in the Guelens and came to the Dragons, unlikely as ever was; and then I could ha' ordered 'em: a Dragon sergeant can order a captain of the common companies. But I left the Dragons an' come wi' you, m'lord, which means I'm provincial an' not a king's man anymore. An' if them troops hadn't got a captain, I could, if you ordered, in your province. But not so long's there's a king's captain in charge. *Anwyll* could have ordered 'em. But ye sent him to the border."

That His Majesty's troops did as they pleased and did wrong to Amefin folk within a stone's cast of the Zeide was not tolerable to him; in his mind the captain had forfeited his command the night he had obeyed Parsynan's word against his. When he and the senior sergeant disappeared at the same time, leaving no orders behind them he knew what to call it: irresponsibility was a Word he had learned in one place and another. Treason, he had learned very well, here in Amefel.

And with the town's well-being and Amefin justice resting on the garrison's proper conduct, Anger rushed up, twice in two days, now.

Uncommon, he thought. And *that*, the anger, he carefully lifted out of its place to examine later, in some quietness of heart. To have anger give the next orders was unwise, even if it was just.

—*Do you hear?* he asked Emuin, across the insulating weight of stone. *Do you know that the captain and the sergeant have disappeared, and do you count it coincidence, good sir? Shall I be angry about it?*

There was no answer, as he had in his heart expected none. Oh, Emuin heard. Unquestionably he heard. Emuin was settling into his chamber, poking up the fire, which had gone to embers, and gave him attention, but no answer.

He had, he recalled, said to the patriarch himself that he guessed the source of the advisement about the trinket-sellers.

And was it unreasonable that the patriarch should have sent word to the sergeant, who might have told his captain? He himself had had little dealing with either man, and it was still the matter of a search after pebbles among pebbles; but he began to suspect that the pebbles in question were no longer in this heap.

"Perhaps they've taken horses," he said to Uwen, who waited quietly for his answer, "and then you would have authority."

"I am askin' that," Uwen said, "an' word ain't come yet."

"Only from the bottom of the hill?"

"There's a lot of shiftin' about, especially wi' the Ivanim in wi' sixty-odd horses an' them needin' room; master Haman's got lads movin' horses out to the far meadows and makin' winter shelter. It's over an hour's ride out an' back to some of them places, an' till we've counted, an' horses tendin' to wander off in copses an' stream cuts for windbreaks, even when ye built 'em a fair shelter . . ."

"We won't know by evening," he said, "unless the captain turns up before that."

"I asked the gate-guards, too. An' they just ain't sure whether the men is in or out. They don't much notice the soldiers comin' and goin'. I put it to 'em they should notice such things an' look sharper. They *are* under my command, and I apologize for that, m'lord."

If the captain had taken horse and gone, there was no question *where* he had gone: to Guelessar, to Parsynan, to unfriendly ears.

"We won't know, then, until we hear from Haman," Tristen said. "And the lords are coming, within the hour?"

"Aye, m'lord. Word's passed."

He had been remiss in letter-writing. Idrys had bidden him write often, very often; and now in Uwen's report he thought he should write that days-delayed letter.

"Go do what you can do," he said, "but be back when I go down to the hall."

"Aye, m'lord."

So Uwen went off to find those he was now sure were unavailable and well away, and Tristen sat down at the desk with dragon legs and under the brazen loom of dragon jaws, and took up pen to warn Idrys directly of all that had happened. He was all too aware now that along with the Dragons he had dismissed all his most reliable Guelen messengers, except his private guard. The Amefin guard would not be able to traverse Guelessar unquestioned or unremarked, and might not so easily reach Idrys. He had retained not a one of the Dragons at hand; and under the circumstances, trusting the Guelens to report ill of their own officers seemed folly. There was Gedd. He might well send Gedd.

Uwen, however, might well find an honest man or two in the unit of which he had been a part as late as midsummer. Not all of them had marched home, of those who had fought at Lewenbrook; and, Cevulirn's help notwithstanding, he could not afford to dismiss the Guelen Guard. Honest men must be the heart of what he should have done by now and must now urgently do with the Guelens: depose or assign elsewhere officers who had carried out the massacre. Now that the sergeant and the captain had fled, if that was indeed their course, then all the harm their reports could do would have been done ... and he was increasingly convinced that they had fled, and that the Quinalt had warned them.

Overtake the fugitive officers on the road, frighten the horses from under them ... *that* he might do, as he had done to Parsynan.

But it had not prevented Parsynan getting to Guelessar, as he was well sure Parsynan had done; and he found himself more than reluctant to invade the gray space with such a reckless assault.

And when he realized that in himself, he let the pen pause, asking himself why he did hesitate.

Fear of killing: there was that. There was no guarantee how they would fall, and a fall was chance and chance was the realm of wizards.

There was no guarantee such an act would in any

wise prevent the gossip arriving at a bad time; when it arrived was now a matter of a horse's strength, reasonably certain. But to bring it into the realm of chance also laid things as open as a window flung wide to whatever influences might be seething just out of reach of his inquiries.

There was Ivanor . . . arrived the very day he sent the Dragons to the border.

And arrived on the heels of portents and omens, word of lords and aethelings, himself and Crissand and prophecy.

Now Paisi, a waif detestable to the Guelens and sheltered by the Amefin gate-guard, had become the cause of upheaval in the Guelen Guard, the garrison that was Amefel's surest and readiest defense.

His hand trembled somewhat as he dipped the quill in ink. The thoughts that came to him were not quiet ones, nor assured in their direction. Emuin's sudden spate of advice to him and to Uwen assumed the character of a milestone reached, a point at which Emuin would speak; and now, now he was aware of Emuin's eavesdropping.

—*You know,* he said to Emuin, and had nothing but Emuin's retreating presence, refusing to utter a thing.

Anger came back, a blinding anger, and he smothered it, quickly, as some foreign and hostile thing.

To find Emuin standing at distance, watching him.

Watching, saying nothing, power intact.

Emuin *could* still keep secrets from him.

Had not Emuin always said he would not stand in the path of his intentions? Yet Emuin did exactly that, refusing his demands, keeping him from leaping from one stepping-stone of advice to the next, distracting him . . . *leading* him, by his frustrated questions, to examine things for himself, letting things Unfold to him. And leading him yet again, by his affection, by his anger, by his very conviction that Emuin held secrets from him . . .

While he had no answers from Emuin . . . he delayed acting. While he delayed acting . . .

He found other courses to take.

The anger subsided, grew cool. Master Emuin still said not a word to him, but he stood in the winds of the gray space and detected a certain small satisfaction wafting on the winds.

—Is that your tactic, sir?

Emuin did not ignore him, rather watched him warily, and he ignored Emuin, mostly, at least, aware that time was short and the earls would be gathering.

He wrote, in the time he had. And paused, the feather brushing his lips, and gazed at the candleflame, recalling how, in the mysterious ways of wizards, once at Mauryl's hearth he had been allured by fire. His hand still bore that small scar. He never forgot that he could not grasp the flame, only feed it or extinguish it.

Such was wizardry. Such had been Mauryl.

Such was Emuin, uncatchable, even by such a power as he had in himself. If his power was the wind and the whirlwind, Emuin's, like Mauryl's, was the fire, small as a spark, leaping up to consume whole houses, and moving aside from a curious finger.

And had not Mauryl been very like that? Mauryl, whose half-burned letters still contained only requests for supply and observations on the weather? A murderer had thought to find far more in Mauryl's writings, and yet . . . what could they learn of Mauryl or any wizard in the small exchanges? It was the long work that said more, the persistence of the little spark smoldering outside its hearth, the one, slight, unnoticed act of chance.

—I respect you, he said to one he was sure had his

ears well stopped and his heart warded. *I respect your working, sir, nor am such a fool as to ignore it. When I transgress, you will not tell me; but should I transgress against you, sir, I beg you continue to call me a fool. I fear the silence more than the shadows.*

I will to do good, sir. But we are, are we not, something different one from the other? If I am the wind, you are the fire, and may burn, but mine is the stronger force.

I am Sihhë. Is that the lesson I am finally to learn, that I am not a Man and that I should not *practice wizardry?*

If that's so, sir, it would seem I need you. I need you very much.

The captain of the Guelens has very likely fled, and mischief will come of it, and wizardry might prevent him.

But do you say I should not wield it? That magic *is my skill, and I should avoid wizardry?*

He listened until the ink dried on the quill tip, and he heard no answer, none, at least, in words.

But there was a sense of presence grown more peaceful, a touch softer than the feather and more subtle than a word. The dragons that loomed over this place threatened that peace: creatures of fire, reared in angry postures.

Yet was the carving oak, or horse?

Was the image bronze, or all that a dragon might be?

The nearest of them loomed, a spell in its own right, and warred against the peace. It leered across his shoulder, flanked him, stared outward with him, with its bronze and dreadful countenance, an Aswydd beast, witness of all that had happened here . . . and trying, so it seemed, to be his ally.

Do I command the dragons? he asked that silent, wizardly witness, with none but an afterthought to the king's men who bore that name, or to the arms of the Marhanen, the golden dragon on the red field, which was the emblem of the kingdom as well. His immediate question was to what extent he could reach back into Aswydd power, and rely on it; but in the way of such questions, it answered itself differently.

The echo of understanding the question raised in him was that the Aswydd dragons extended their reach into Guelessar, and that they backed the Marhanen throne, not Sihhë emblems . . . never the Sihhë emblems. The dragons were solely the emblems of Men and kings and lords of Men. This room he had never felt he owned. This room he had warded by his presence, as much as lived in it. It was useful to everyone's safety that he lived here and kept the wards.

Yet it came to him, yes, he did command the dragons, now, and only so long as these creatures of fire and passion failed to rouse his anger, or his passion, or his fear. That long, and only so long, did he command them, and only that long did he command those who were their masters.

The dragons and those who commanded them must not break that condition. They must never break it. With wind and fire alike they could deal, but never break that condition. He was writing a message to the Lord Commander, with the local garrison in disarray; he was facing a meeting of the lords of Amefel, to sit and do justice, and the dragons loomed above, reminding him their anger was fire, and his will was wind.

He felt that silent and wizardly witness to his musings, sealed as he was, and deliberately withdrawn from the soundless sound in the silence that lapped about this room of his refuge. This, too, Emuin witnessed.

The quill when he dipped it and wrote scratched like claws on stone, as if the dragons stirred on their perches. Shadows, the tame ones that had a right here, lurked and crept under tables and in the folds of green drapery, within cabinets and in corners as he shaped his report.

He owned magic as his birthright. Having it, he knew he must be careful of it. He never loosed the shadows that belonged here, never, in fact, allowed the lights to be extinguished: candles always burned here, and he never shut the drapes by day. The ones who had died in this room were not wholly his men; but they were faithful to Amefel, and he willingly lived under their witness, conscious of their leanings, and sure now, as in Auld Syes' salutation to him and Crissand, that he held what would not forever be his.

Emuin heard that, too, and tried very quietly to slip away. But Emuin could not elude him now: often as Emuin might have watched, unseen, mistrustful of him before this, he was not unseen now, and might never be again.

—*Know that*, Tristen said, *wounded, and know I have heard at least one and two of your lessons, master Emuin. And because I have heard, I'm about to hear the demands of stonemasons and of the earls. I wish the Guelens and the house of Meiden will not go at each other's throats.*

Why, why, *master Emuin, do wicked purposes seem to slide by so easily, and these men escape me to do mischief and Mauryl's letters burn, and reasons for all this wickedness slip through my fingers? Is this the way of things in the world? Or is there cause aside from me and you?*

Is that the reason of your mistrust?

And is that mistrust of me the reason you came here, after all?

CHAPTER 7

There was no miraculous word of the fugitives by the hour the court convened . . . and that was not to Tristen's surprise or Uwen's. The readiness with which the court assembled did somewhat surprise Tristen: the summons had gone out to the earls to come early and present their petitions, such as they had, before the banquet . . . a feast which had already been planned for their guest for the evening, and on which Cook had labored since yesterday evening, to a mighty shouting and commotion around the kitchens. That event Tristen expected would see no tardiness.

But the earls all came, every one, even earlier than the requested hour; and so Cevulirn attended the audience of his neighbor province, dressed in his plain, serviceable gray and white, yet no lord in the hall was more dignified by his finery than Cevulirn by his demeanor. He drew every eye by his mere presence in hall, and stood at the side of the steps of the dais to give his account of doings at the court, the marriage of His Majesty and Her Grace, and the death of Brugan, son of Corswyndam, Lord Ryssand. There was no restlessness at all in his hearers, and all hung on the account of a man who doled words out like coin, well weighed and sparingly.

"What shall we do?" Drumman was quick to ask, when he had heard Cevulirn's account of his dismissal from the king's court. "This is an attack on the south and on all of us, our privileges, our rights, soon enough our land. We have in king Cefwyn a monarch who at least respects our soil and look how these damned northerners deal with him!"

"Aye," said no few, from among the ealdormen of the town, too, for Cefwyn had ruled Ylesuin from Henas'amef for some few weeks.

"Let 'im favor us in the least and here's the barons with their noses out of joint!" someone shouted out of turn. "Earl Drumman has the right of it. We fought wizards and the Elwynim at Lewenbrook, and buried our sons, where we could find 'em, an' where's bloody Ryssand?"

"Safe," said Cevulirn, in a fleeting still moment of the shock of that forwardness. "Safe, sir, and hopeful of comfort and power for himself, which does *not* come with a marriage to Ninévrisë of Elwynor, who will strengthen Cefwyn Marhanen. You see very clearly. Ryssand is my enemy. I assure you he is the enemy of your lord as well."

"Lord Sihhë!" someone was bold enough to call out. "Lord Sihhë can teach Ryssand a lesson or two!"

It was not what Tristen wished, this stir about the northern lords, and he saw matters sliding away from his hand in the very first moments of the audience Emuin had advised him to hold. He knew that was not by intent, nor by Cevulirn's intent, and he lifted his hand from the arm of the chair to seize a breathwide silence.

"I am the king's friend. All I've done is to establish Amefel's borders, and prevent war from coming here again . . . which I don't permit and which I don't think Cevulirn will permit."

"We will not permit it," Cevulirn said staunchly. "But that's my tale, such as it is, sirs."

"Long live the lord of Ivanor," Crissand said, and everyone said the same.

It was a high beginning, the matters of kings and the doings of barons. But it was not all that waited attention: "My lord," said Tassand, who had a list of things they should see to in the gathering, and brought it to the steps of the dais, "the matter of the Guard, the search after the officers. The dereliction of the command of the garrison: Your Grace's captain's come with his report."

"Are they found?"

Tassand ascended a step to lean close. "The lord captain's taken the sergeants," Tassand whispered, while every ear in the hall attempted to overhear. "And has them all an' some of the soldiers with him, an' Paisi . . . all to come in the hall, my lord duke, at your order."

"Bring them," he said, reluctant to have all this spread before the earls and the chance carpenter with a request for supply: but so Emuin had advised him he should rule. He settled himself for a lengthy proposal of the case, and the debate of the earls on every point of it, including Paisi's requisite apology.

But he had not reckoned with Uwen Lewen's-son, who marched in the soldiers in proper military order, saw them stand smartly to attention, and had Paisi trailing all with a hangdog look and a bundle in his arms. And then he said to himself that by Emuin's advice he should let his men speak, in public, and do business under everyone's witness.

"Uwen," Tristen said. "*Captain* Uwen. What do you have to report?"

"First is the justice wi' this lad," Uwen said, not at all abashed, "m'lord. An' he's to give the property back to the man in good order. Jump, boy. Do it!"

"M'lord," Paisi said in a faint voice, "I can't. He ain't here."

"And where is he?" Uwen asked the foremost of the men.

"At the border," said that man.

"Then give the kit to *him* in trust," Uwen said, "and apologize like a man, on your lord's order."

Paisi all but ran to bestow the kit on the Guard officer, and blurt out: "On account of I was wrong, sir, an' will never be a thief, an' I beg your pardon, sir, for the captain's sake and m'lor's."

"Given," came the short response, not entirely in good grace.

"He'll do duty for a fortnight," Uwen said, "an' stand wi' the guard at night, besides 'is duties in the house. An' when the Dragons march home again he'll come an' get that kit and beg pardon again, an' lucky I don't send 'im to the border to carry it."

"Sir," the soldier said, in far better humor. There was, as it were, a breath and a shifting in the ranks, even at attention, as if every man had found satisfaction in that.

"Yes, sir," Paisi said.

"'At's one thing," Uwen said, and strode along the polished pavings in boots a little short of absolute polish, unlike the lords', and with his silver hair windblown out of its tie. But in his broad, work-hardened body and use-scarred armor and the brisk sureness in the orders he gave, there was no doubt at all this was a man sure of his authority. "There's honest men in this company. But, m'lord, the captain an' the senior sergeant is very likely bound for Guelessar wi'out leave, which is a disgrace an' a shame to these honest men, especially as they did it only hearin' ye wisht t' speak to 'em. An' while it's true there's some good men find this a hard duty an' ain't happy in Amefel, and some has been forward in sayin' so, I told 'em on my honor an' your authority, m'lord, they was free to follow the captain an' the master sergeant and take their horses an' all an' leave wi' no let nor hindrance nor slight to their honor, on one condition: that they have the face to come here an' stand on two feet an' ask leave of the lord of this province like soldiers, not desertin' like some damn band of brigands. So's here's a fair number o' decent soldiers what ain't content to be here, an' if ye'll grant 'em leave, they'll go. An' here's others as is content and proud o' this company, an' will stay. Also, m'lord, here's a sergeant I served with, Wynned, who's come to ask leave on a different account, on account of his mother is ailin', an' he wants leave to see 'er, an' he'll come back soon's he's paid his respects an' seen to her wants."

"What Uwen says," Tristen answered quietly, and not without careful looks at the men, "I do agree to, and if you will go, go with whatever supply you need." The gossip was already sped and the harm was done; and he was glad to know Uwen had sifted the garrison for chaff.

"Your lordship," one said, "horses and lodging on our way."

"Horses and lodgin's is fair," Uwen said. "Seein' the weather. Tents an' the packhorses is needed here."

"What Uwen says, I support," Tristen said.

"They stood their part an' discharged their oath," Uwen said, "an' by me they're free to go."

"Go, then," Tristen said, "and bear my goodwill to the Lord Commander. I wish you good weather.— And, Wynedd, I wish your mother well."

"Your Grace," the man named Wynedd said, blushing bright red, and Tristen thought to himself that in Wynedd Uwen might have found his messenger.

"They'll be on their way in the hour," Uwen said. "Face! An' *turn*! An' bear yoursel's like soldiers, no farewells in the taverns!—Lewes!"

"Sir." One man stood fast as the others left, and Uwen waved him forward.

"This here's Corporal Lewes, who's a likely man, and who I'd set in a sergeant's place, among this list here. Lewes is Wynedd's corporal; an' I'll name others, by your leave, m'lord."

"As you see fit," Tristen said. He was amazed. Uwen, so shy and soft-spoken with him and within lords' gatherings was something else entirely in the field; and, it turned out, in a gathering of soldiers. He did recall that when Idrys had dealt with the Guard in Cefwyn's court he had not quite summoned such a large troop of them, but he had seen very little of court: he found the entire matter of the Guard dealt with and disposed of in far shorter a time than seemed the rule of things in council. His newly assembled earls looked with wonder at this public exchange and the trading of appointments in the garrison.

But had not Emuin said to proceed in public? There was good reason the province should know the quality of the men who kept order in the town, and no one looked displeased to witness the departure of the disaffected men; and not displeased at Wynedd's reasons or Lewes' recommendation, either, or with Uwen's handling of matters. There had been talk behind hands, but more for politeness and quiet, it seemed, than hostility.

"'At's my report, m'lord," Uwen said in conclusion, as the noise of soldiers faded in the hall.

"Well-done," Tristen said, and looked to the rest of Tassand's list, which proved thereafter the small business of petitions, the sort that had overtaken him in the hall, and requests, one for a marriage of a ducal ward.

"Am I in charge of this person?" he asked, and truth, as Lord Azant explained, the ducal ward was a relative of Lord Cuthan, a young girl, as Tassand knew and interjected, left behind in Cuthan's flight. Merilys was her name, and she was twelve years old.

"Twelve," he said. Ages of Men eluded him, but this seemed young. "A child."

"Indeed, my lord," said another, elder man. "In need of guidance and direction, and protection of the estate she can in no wise manage."

"And you, sir?"

"Thane of Ausey, Your Grace. Dueradd, thane of Ausey, betrothed to the lady in question."

"My lord," Earl Azant said, edging forward. "I stand remote kin to the child. In the absence of the earl, and his dispossession, all obligations of kinship are fallen on Your Grace. The marriage—"

"The marriage is contracted by the lady of Idas'aren," said the groom, "and agreed and sealed by the earl of Bryn, as m'lord can see if he will be so kind . . ."

"All agreements by the earl are abrogated," Azant said, "and this marriage is not in the girl's interest."

"Not all the earl's agreements are abrogated. His market agreements are being honored . . ."

"The lady of Idas'aren is not a heifer at market, and her mother, my cousin, is against this union!"

"What does the lady of Idas'aren say?" Tristen asked, lost in the back-and-forth of rights and arguments.

"My lord, she's too young to know her advantage."

"Then until she's old enough to know her advantage . . ." Tristen said. He found all sympathy for a young soul tossed and bartered about without her understanding or her consent. He had no idea of marriages. But he did, of being set about and ordered here and there. ". . . may I have the marriage wait?"

There was a murmur, and Tassand, a mere servant

in Guelessar, and now in charge of the household, said quietly: "I'm sure Your Grace can do whatever Your Grace pleases."

"Then I say let the marriage wait until she's older and can say what she wishes."

Azant made a small ha! of triumph, and the thane of Ausey retreated with a mutter of angry protest, drowned in the murmur of the hall. No one else looked unhappy, and no few looked well satisfied.

Meanwhile Tassand read out the next matter, stone for repair near the gate, ". . . requiring," Tassand said, "only Your Grace's word to pay the workmen, which seems justified here."

"I give it," he said, as he had agreed to a hundred such requests.

Had he done justice to the young girl? He felt a motion of his heart and he did as seemed right to him. He assented to what for some reason needed his assent. The other matters were as mundane as the request for payment . . . a request of the town clerks for Zeide records, and that, he knew was impossible.

"They're likely lost," he said, and saw the Guelen-born clerk who had come with him from the capital come forward, just to the edge of the gathering. "Are they not?"

The clerk gave a little bow. "M'lord, there's progress, but I beg to say, no, my lord, we still can't provide all the records. It's property and inheritance the magistrates want, and it's all a muddle, for reasons Your Grace knows."

The archives had been kept in disorder, or at least the semblance of it, even during Lord Heryn's life, so no king's clerk could find proof of Heryn's doings, that was what Cefwyn had said. Now the disorder was real, for Parsynan had done nothing to set the place in order that he could detect; and the senior archivist who might have kept the whereabouts of important papers and books set in memory was dead, murdered by the younger, who had fled.

"We make lists as quickly as we can," the clerk said, "but to tell the very truth, Your Grace, two more clerks or even a boy to carry and climb would speed the work; and Your Grace to rule on disputes, supplanting records."

"Tassand," Tristen said, out of his own competence.

"I'll inquire, m'lord," Tassand said, and he trusted it would come to some good issue, or Tassand would report to him. He had no idea what it cost to pay clerks, but he knew the books, which now were jumbled in towering stacks on tables, exceeding the shelves that existed, needed better care than Heryn had given them: not only inheritance and tax records, but works of philosophy, of history, of poetry, all gathered into one confused pile. There were treasures still in that place, he was convinced of it, and no knowing what Lord Cuthan might have destroyed or taken. As he understood, they had hardly a list of what the king of Ylesuin might have taken . . . nothing would Cefwyn destroy, no question there. But Cefwyn had certainly taken the tax records, and a history or two.

Cuthan had done the worst.

And wondering about Cuthan's dealings with the library led to other questions, and the welfare of Cuthan's people, which, if he had arranged the matters under discussion, would have been the foremost thing to do. But it seemed a discussion more appropriate to the lords alone, not to this hour when burghers from the town and clerks and common soldiers rubbed shoulders.

So when Tassand reported the list of petitioners exhausted and asked whether he would say anything he found nothing in particular to say. Now that he had taken up the broom to sweep difficulties and cobwebs off his doorstep, there was one paving stone missing from a complete and unscarred structure in Amefel: there was one outstanding fault, and he had thought of the man in two problems which had come before him, even in one audience.

Cuthan. Cuthan, Lord of Bryn.

Cuthan, Edwyll's betrayer.

Cuthan, Crissand's enemy, who had fled to Tasmôrden.

INTERLUDE

In the old scriptorium that served as solar in these cold winter days the consort's court stitched and gossiped. Lady Luriel was a primary subject of interest; but Ninévrisë said nothing, only attended her small, precise stitches, gathering news of Luriel's previous and current indiscretions, sure that in her own absence the subject of gossip was herself, and Father Benwyn, and Cefwyn.

Luriel found no mercy with these women. There was some whisper about "His Majesty," which a matron swiftly hushed; but mostly the ladies buzzed like bees about Panys' sister Brusanne, a plain, awkward, and myopic girl whose stitching always suffered from untimely knots. Brusanne was not accustomed to being the focus of attention, and said, clearly without thinking, regarding her brother, "His Majesty said he might have Eveny Forest and Aysonel if he married her."

Every eye turned to Ninévrisë, quick as a lightning stroke, and they were all trapped, looking at one another, exposed and naked, on a point of common dismay.

Then Ninévrisë calmly snipped a thread. "What a nice notion," she said blithely, feigning ignorance. "She's been so unhappy. Murandys is a rocky place, is it not? And Panys is full of forests."

"Yes, Your Grace," Brusanne said, blushing deep red.

"I look forward to her joining us here," Ninévrisë said. "She's very well read, so I hear."

"*I think she's sleeping late,*" said the shameless widow of Bonden-on-Wyk, and there was a general stir.

"*Madiden!*" said the Lady Curalle, thoroughly Guelen, and staunchly virtuous.

"*Well, so she may be,*" said the widow. "*She'll be wed, never a doubt. That one's set at marriage and escaping her uncle's hand, and would not I? Would not you? Small wonder.*"

"*Well, I'd dance with Murandys himself!*" said Byssalys with a wicked look. "*Jewels can excuse every fault else, oh, and that man has treasury.*"

"*His last wife had a lovely funeral,*" said the irrepressible widow Madiden.

Perhaps another lady of highest rank might have stilled the unseemly gossip, but Ninévrisë listened, and gathered knowledge, of Murandys, of Panys. It was a court far more tolerable, and more informative, with Lady Artisane in retreat. It informed her, as she listened, that Murandys was indispensable to Cefwyn's plans, and yet was not a man worth leaning on or relying on. Here was a man whose treatment of three wives was in question, whose management of his tenants was notorious, and she was distressed that Cefwyn tolerated this man . . . habit, and his father's policies, all that aside: if she were king of Ylesuin, she would not tolerate him.

But events had not made her a reigning monarch, nor even a reigning queen, and she could not claim that Elwynim nobility was in any regard better. A third of the lords of Elwynor had rejected her claim as a daughter to succeed her sonless father, Caswyddian and Aséyneddin had tried to marry her by force of arms, and if not all of the lords of Elwynor had rebelled, and if a brave handful had died in her defense and a brave handful more still held Ilefínian against

Tasmôrden, still she could not say that Murandys or even Ryssand was a worse lord. She would have to take the Regent's throne by blood and iron, with Guelen troops. It would not come to her on a waft of love and tossed roses.

Her needle pricked her finger and a spot of blood welled up. She evaded the bleached linen, but it stained the thread, and she sucked the finger clean and snipped the spoiled thread, tasting copper of blood in her mouth as she looked up to an arrival in the doorway.

Luriel had indeed come to her small court, and made a deep and formal curtsy.

"Your Grace," said Luriel.

"Lady." She impulsively extended the wounded hand with the damp finger, and Luriel came to take it and to bow again in a rustle of fashionable petticoats, a cushioning flower of velvet and wool blossoming about her. Ninévrisë smiled on purpose when Luriel lifted her gaze to meet hers; and, reminiscent of the night of the fox-hued gown, she saw a strong-chinned countenance with brows like soaring wings, eyes full of cautious wit and defense and hope.

"Welcome," she said, not altogether a matter of duty to Cefwyn: in some part, in a dearth of sharp wits in her small gathering, she indeed held hope of this woman Cefwyn had once thought of marrying. "Have you brought your stitching? Make room, make room for the lady, all of you."

It was in immaculate consideration of precedence, who moved aside and who did not, and Luriel found a stool between Bonden-on-Wyk and Brusanne of Panys, who cast her curious, shortsighted looks, and above Dame Margolis, a knight's lady, common as the earth and as generous.

"And how was the journey?" Bonden-on-Wyk wanted to know, and Luriel, delving into a fashionable *little sewing basket, gave the widow a bland, curious look.*

"Very well, Your Grace," Luriel said. "As any return must be. I have no dissatisfactions ... not a one."

Did she not? Brusanne was not quick as some, but counting the rumors of last night, she blushed rosy pink.

Oh, indeed, Luriel was no dullard, no starched Quinalt virgin. This was the girl who would very gladly have been queen, and who was far from blind to the substance and the claim in her remarks.

"How fine that a thaw preceded your arrival," *Ninévrisë returned the shot.* "And how fortunate."

Their glances crossed like rapiers, and her husband's former mistress engaged with a look sober as a salute.

"I found it so."

"Confusion and bad weather to my enemies one and all, and kind winds to my friends that come to this court: is that linen you have? What a lovely shade! Let me see it."

Luriel brought the frame close to her, and for a moment they were very close. "Your Grace is very kind."

"To my friends. I value loyalty very greatly."

The others had fallen silent, listening to the passage between them, and Bonden-on-Wyk said, "A winter wedding, will it be?"

"Madiden!" *said Olwydesse.*

"Well, will it?" *Bonden-on-Wyk asked, and Luriel gave a small, fierce smile.*

"Ah, gossip never waits an hour in this room, does it?"

"Well?"

"He's handsome," *Luriel said, gathering her frame*

and setting it toward the light, "and has very fine prospects."

She did not say, in this room, what those prospects were. Ninévrisë saw the glances and the lips nipped shut just in time, the widow Madiden's head tilted like a wise carrion crow's above a likely morsel.

Oh, Cefwyn, Ninévrisë thought, feeling still the prick of the fine steel. Lucky escaped, lucky this one's not with child.

Jealous? No, not of such a narrow escape: he knows, he well knows this lady. Cold steel for a bedmate, this one: not one ever to trust.

Nor to envy . . . why should I ever envy Luriel? She had her moment and lost it, and is wise enough to take charity from me, while it profits. I would I could like her, but she is only wiser than Artisane.

Give me my kingdom, give me land across the river from Murandys, and we'll see whose fisheries supply the court; give me an army at my beck and call and see if Ryssand's daughter brings another lying accusation of me.

Needles in and needles out, gold flowers and green leaves on the linen while winter frosts the glass and the heavens glow white with fire. Winter weddings and springtime war.

Give me the soil of my land underfoot, and let my husband see he's married no fool. Meanwhile I smile on his mistress and let the vixens in my hall wonder for a season: they see my husband's foreign wife, but not yet my father's daughter.

My father, sealed in stone in Althalen's ruined walls, my father, who wards the seat of kings from strayed Amefin sheep and attends shepherds in their wanderings . . . father who saved me from marriages to cowards and to his dying hour helped me to the husband I have. Wise father, brave father, see me sit *and stitch so patiently, making wishes with every thread. Luriel has until spring to win my friendship: I will allow her that fair trial.*

Father, who had the Sihhë blood and passed it down to me, bind wishes in the threads that make meadow flowers in this cold white day. Bespell me the bright blue of the Lines you keep, the palace you ward, all Lines and light. I do not forget. How could I forget?

Father, Uleman, Regent for all these years, I love him. I do love. I forgive him all the past, all his grandfather's works and all his father's: I love, and forgiving is natural for one who loves. I make him these silly flowers, I stitch the meadows of the spring when we will go to war, he and I, and when I pray the people believe in me. I stitch the blue Lines for a border, your palace of light, dear Father.

They give me this silly, sotted priest, Father, because the Quinalt fears my skirts, have you heard this foolishness, where you lie? Or has a rumor of it gotten to you? You said I had the Gift, in small part. If I have it, in small part, however, small, I sew my wishes into this linen cloth, smiling at my husband's mistress, and thinking we must be allies, we two, against the folly abundant in this room.

I sew wishes for an early spring. And for your easy rest, and for the rest of the dead at Ilefínian, for there will be many, many dead. Give Tasmôrden no peace and the faithful dead at least the hope of rescue.

I sew wishes that Tristen be well, my husband's best ally, and the one he dares not regard. He would cross the river and my husband forbids it, all for Murandys, and Ryssand, who threaten him: when I am Regent in Elwynor, I will remember all of this against them.

The sun passed the edge of the glass, just, and light grew less intense.

"*I don't like this green,*" *said Bonden-on-Wyk.* "*I think a brighter shade.*"

"*Too bright,*" *said Panys' daughter, who was a creature of pale shades about her dress, always faded.*

"*Not too bright,*" *said Luriel.* "*Add a darker for contrast. That other green. There's a match. —What do you think, Your Grace?*"

The girl who had worn vixen colors to reconcile with the king asked her opinion.

"*Oh, I think you're quite right,*" *Ninévrisë said, willing to be an ally. Give her a run at the leash, and see where she went, Ninévrisë thought, and consciously smiled.* "*I approve.*"

"*Well, well,*" *said Bonden-on-Wyk, peering at the combination of greens.* "*Who'd have thought those two would go together?*"

BOOK TWO

CHAPTER 1

∾

Two lords of Ylesuin rode out under a sky filled with scattered clouds, a heaven pasturing fat, misdirected sheep. It portended fair if fickle weather as they went out the gates of Henas'amef, two lords with a mingled guard of Ivanim and Guelenfolk . . . a mixed guard, and a startled flock of pigeons, winging out and out toward the still-sleepy west.

Hold court, Emuin had said, and that Tristen had done, if hastily. Take account, Emuin had said, and that accounting, given Cevulirn's brief but essential personal presence, had seemed the most pressing thing.

Other matters were already attended: the garrison flag flew atop the hill they had left, no longer under the same captain, but firmly in the hand of Uwen Lewen's-son, who had some distress at being left behind this morning, but there he was.

"I ain't troubled for you, m'lord," Uwen had said last night, "as ye manages things right well when they come to ye, but ye do have this way o' findin' the trouble in a place. An' pokin' about the north, lad—are ye sure we're ready for 't?"

Tristen had laughed, as Uwen could make him laugh even considering such a dire possibility. But he thought they were indeed ready. It was the river he proposed to visit, and Captain Anwyll, and his intention was not to provoke Tasmôrden.

"I fear worse if we leave Bryn to its own devices

even another day," he had said to Uwen this morning, just at the top of the hill, when they were setting out, "and you've Drumman, and Azant to advise you, so you should do very well even if the king's officers come visiting. Never fear."

"It's the Elwynim come visitin' concerns me," Uwen said. And standing very near him, face-to-face before he set his foot in the stirrup: "Ye take care, lad. Ye take great care."

"We will," Tristen had assured him, and they had parted with an embrace . . . no man else would he have trusted so much, not with the chance that the flight of the officers to Guelessar might rouse some inquiry. The better men of the Guelen Guard had come into line once Uwen had walked in with fire in his eye and set the garrison barracks in order, and indeed, some rode with him now. Uwen would shake the Guelen Guard until order fell out: he might have evaded command all this time, but he had waded into the matter with a clear notion of what he expected, as he said, from otherwise good soldiers, and he had the loyalty of the remaining sergeants: that was of great importance.

Accordingly Tristen had far less worry leaving the town than when the former captain had commanded all the armed might in his capital, and them a foreign, hated presence. He had no doubt his letter would reach Idrys, either, in the good sergeant's hands . . . and the Lord Commander, once warned, was completely capable of dealing with the Guelen captain.

So he and Cevulirn, Amefel, and Ivanor, rode out together to see the riverside, taking their course around to the north of the town and its hill.

There they turned off on the snowy, lesser-used road that wended through low hills toward the north and its villages. The road they took now was the same that led to Elwynor, the same that, once across the river by the bridge Anwyll guarded, led on to Ilefínian.

Theirs was not the only party going out from Henas'amef today. He had sent Crissand to Levey and to his other villages, and southward, as his right hand . . . for the pieces and parts of a policy had begun to fall into place, and messengers of various sort were carrying word of decisions taken. Before Cevulirn had come in, he had feared he might have no choice but to call up men a second time in a year and fling them against a better-armed, trained enemy to support the Marhanen king. The Amefin had faced yet one more unwanted war, if not on their own soil, then just across the river, with their backs to the water, in no enviable position and without the strength to carry an attack on foot to any great distance at all. They would become the anvil to Cefwyn's hammer from the northeast.

But with Cevulirn's promise of defense, came the hope that southern villages like Levey might keep their sons and plant their fields and expect to enjoy the harvest of them. Now they had a chance to bring troops to bear on the riverside, make firm that defense, and set a camp this spring on Tasmôrden's side of the river. For with the fast-moving light horse Cevulirn could supply, and with other lords coming in from the south, they would become a force that could strike hard and deep from such a camp and, with support from behind and bridges in their control, never be pinned with their backs against the river.

So, a situation with which he was far better pleased, they were riding north to inform the riverside villages that Ivanor was with Amefel, and to let them see with their own eyes that they had a strong force protecting them.

And, second and not the least reason for his going

this direction himself, *Bryn's* lands lay between here and the river. From the small region nearest the town and for a good distance more had been Lord Cuthan's land, a district foremost in Amefel's councils, their lord able to secure whatever he wished, even from the viceroy.

Now suddenly these villagers of Bryn were left as worse than lordless men, unrepresented in council; they were left with their oaths of fealty connecting them to an angry and embittered exile across the river. . . and they were left, as Lord Drumman had said, without any confidence in their new duke's disposition toward them, whether under a new duke of Amefel they would become the spoils of some angry rival of Cuthan's who might be granted the earldom, or whether they might simply be neglected and set at disadvantage among the earldoms. At very least, they might doubt the enthusiasm of their new duke for drawing his firmest defense to include them.

That situation of doubt, he and all the council were resolved, could not continue. Lord Cuthan was now formally dispossessed, by vote of the council of peers, nothing coerced, and that settled any claims of succession. So the other earls had taken other resolutions to sever the ties and the claim Cuthan had on them, and had those resolutions witnessed and sealed by the Bryaltine abbot. Those documents also Tristen had in hand, on a very important purpose of their riding out, if not the only one.

Far faster for a troop of riders to traverse this road to the river than it was for laden oxcarts. The deep frozen traces they followed were those of heavy wheels, inconvenient for the horses, who paced beside the ruts. Their course took them among low hills and within view of small woods, cut back from the road. Lord Heryn had removed all potential cover for banditry from roads and from rides: so Crissand had said. Lord Heryn had done most of the clearing, having no forester such as Cefwyn had over the extensive Crown lands, preserving and maintaining the woods, but simply directing where trees might be cut and where wood rights might be let to various earls for money. Removing the woods might have been a mistake, and Tristen wondered what the land might have been before Heryn; but still, the forces Amefel might raise were infantry that were accustomed to stand in lines, not slip through forest. Fighting among trees disordered their ranks and confused their signals: he had no difficulty understanding Heryn's reasons. The forces Cevulirn lent, too, light horse, were such as might use the Aswydds' roads to good advantage, riding with lightning speed as the Ivanim did, each with a horse in reserve . . . overland at need, but at no point through woods.

Still, if he could bring in Lanfarnesse, who used the woods and hills very willingly, he might yet bring force through the wooded lands to the west, assuring Amefel that no Elwynim army could slip in unseen.

And if he could bring in the help of Sovrag of Olmern, who could bring supply right to the bridgeheads by river barge, he could bring daunting force to bear on Tasmôrden's underbelly, while Tasmôrden's face was toward Cefwyn. Tasmôrden would not like it, not in the least, to be forced to face Cefwyn and the Guelen heavy horse on Cefwyn's terms, on the flat ground the maps showed in Elwynor's middle.

So Tristen said to Cevulirn, divulging his thoughts in this privacy of two riders with their guard some little distance behind.

"Tasmôrden thought he could create distraction here in Amefel," Tristen said, "and if I have your help, we'll make it so this border is no choice for him."

"A very good prospect," Cevulirn agreed, while the ground passed beneath them at a good, brisk clip.

Tristen rode Petelly, with Gery in reserve; and Cevulirn on the elder of the pair of dapple grays, the best of Ivanim breeding, a horse near white, gloriously beautiful even in winter coat . . . which no one could say of bay Petelly. All the horsemen behind were Ivanim, wearing colors of gray and green, on horses mostly that Crysin breed that was the pride of the Ivanim, light and quick and docile in handling, intelligent on the trail and willing and brave in the heat of battle. Even Petelly's willful stubbornness abated in the Ivanim's influence, and Gery went as calmly as the others at lead. If the Ivanim's skill with horses was magic, it was a magic Tristen set himself to learn, but he despaired ever of teaching it to his Amefin folk, who were devoted to the earth, kept their feet generally on it, and were only stable in battle as long as they were going forward. Count the Guelens much the same, but heavy-armed and deliberate, a great force once they arrived, but slow. It was the Ivanim which Tristen envied their lord, the Ivanim whose fast-moving help had revised all possibilities.

Crissand, he feared, was jealous, left behind, jealous and concerned, yet proclaiming for himself the visit to Levey. Crissand went alone and was possibly out of sorts, being no help such as Cevulirn could be, having no horse, only a depleted infantry and a store of weapons.

"I'll assure Your Grace of their loyalty," Crissand had said, in the dawn, "and take them your goodwill."

Clearly Crissand had wished to go where Tristen went, and was downcast in his hopes.

"I rely on you," Tristen had said to him, and, a word he still found troubling to have uttered, "as aetheling when the time comes."

Then Crissand had looked taken vastly aback, and

all vestige of resentment fled his face and his demeanor.

"My lord," Crissand had said then, and taken himself off to Levey, as stunned to have heard it as Tristen found himself, having said it, riding out with the cavalry he far more coveted, and with Cevulirn, whose alliance gave him a weapon he could wield with far greater subtlety than the blunt, brute force of the Amefin and Guelen foot.

What had possessed him, to have said it?

Yet he had seen the resentment, and felt there was justice in that resentment, and he knew that Crissand had heard the word aetheling the same as he, when Auld Syes had said it. So he brought it into the light, and let Crissand know he had a place with him, and that he was not dispossessed, either of friendship or of inheritance. Crissand had ridden off on his mission with a great possibility in his hands, and he had caught the fear of it as well as the honor.

But now, this morning, having cast *that* knowledge into the light, and riding free and with the Ivanim around him, he felt a lightness of spirit he had not felt since summer. He had done the thing he needed do. He had found a missing boy and confirmed a friend's place in his heart. The snows of winter lay all about, the cold made everything difficult, and yet he soared on a sense of hope, as if this morning important things were at last going as they ought.

They made good time in such good weather, such uncommon cooperation of the heavens. They made change and change about with the horses, after the Ivanim custom . . . and they went so much faster than the oxcarts he had sent out on the day of meeting Cevulirn that they passed two camps the ox train had used before the sun stood high over the western hills.

"We may yet overtake the captain," Cevulirn said. "He may not have his camp built yet."

But toward evening, and without overtaking Anwyll, they reached the place they had aimed for as their way stop . . . and their first destination, a small huddle of huts in a snowy surrounds of sheep-meadow and forest-crowned hills. The huts centered around a rustic, modest hall with a stubby stone tower at its north end for defense and lookout—its sole truly warlike feature a wooden archer's gallery around the tower summit. That wooden scaffold might be the only recollection of the summer's threats, a demonstration that these sheds and huts, yes, and the sheep and the small produce of its summer gardens, would be defended. Bandits or Elwynim intruders might find Modeyneth village too difficult a resource.

The snow in the vicinity was trampled, quite thoroughly, by men and sheep. Of the ox train there was no sign but the continuing ruts in the road, so they were sure that Anwyll had pressed on, nothing delaying . . . commendable in him, Tristen thought, as many things in Anwyll were indeed commendable. He had ordered haste, and haste Anwyll had managed.

But dare he think, far less worthily, that Anwyll had rather camp on the road than come under a rustic Amefin roof and ask hospitality of a rural lordling? Guelenmen were not loved here; and perhaps the place with its archer-platforms had felt too cold to a company of king's men.

At their riding in, however, with banners displayed, with the jingling of harness and the blowing of horses anxious for rest, first one door and then another cracked and faces appeared, cautiously.

Then the thane of Modeyneth himself, a young

man, ran out into the yard of the manor, not pausing for a cloak, pale of face and completely astonished at the visitation . . . though he could not be astonished, after Anwyll had passed this way, that the lord of Ynefel and Althalen now held all Amefel.

And the White Horse of Ivanor informed any eye the other lord in question was Cevulirn of Toj Embrel, who had never been anything but a friend . . . amazing indeed that he was here, but friendship of the armed men who had ridden into his village was not in question.

"Your Grace," was the thane's salutation: not *my lord,* that might acknowledge fealty, but the *Your Grace* that any man might pay to him and to Cevulirn. The Amefin were independent souls, and the thane clearly reserved his devotion. "How may we serve?"

He was Cuthan's man; but he was the best of the thanes of the honor of Bryn: so the earls all agreed. A young man with a common wife, he had marched his contingent to join the muster of Amefel, when by simple expedient of geography he might have evaded the call. He had fought at Lewenbrook, when Bryn had otherwise been reluctant and scant of appearance. In the recent troubles he had stayed to his land and made no requests of the duchy, nor appeared in court at all during the viceroy's rule . . . or yet come to town during his rule.

"Lodging," Tristen requested of the thane, aware as he did so that Uwen was accustomed to speak for him and he had become so accustomed to having Uwen do so that he felt uncertain of proprieties, making himself coequal with Cevulirn, speaking for himself and the small guard that rode with him. "Food."

"Safety on this house," Cevulirn added, at which the young thane drew a breath, much as if he had doubted their reasons . . . perhaps with thoughts of that great convoy of carts that had gone down the road to the river, the same direction his vanished earl had gone, right through this village.

"Your lordship," the thane replied to Cevulirn. "Your Grace. Welcome to Modeyneth." Inevitably, the young and curious had gathered; but so had their elders, mothers bundled in skirts and heavy shawls and scarves, some carrying babes in arms almost indistinguishable from their own bulk; old men, alike wrapped in heavy cloaks; and craftsmen and herdsmen with the signs of their trade about them and in their hands. "There's stabling for a few, shelter for more. Come in, let the boys tend the horses, and come in out of the wind."

The Ivanim assuredly would not abandon care of their horses or their gear to anyone, and in their example, the Guelens of Tristen's guard thought the same, so they all went to the stables, Tristen as well, settling Gery and Petelly together into the endmost large stall, with his own hands and the village boys' help seeing to their food and water.

After that, the manor opened its doors to him and all the company, and provided warm water for washing by a rustic, rough-masoned fireplace large enough for a sheep. To the stew cooking on the other hook, the women of the house added more water and more turnips and potatoes, while the young men of the house arranged benches and brought more in from storage, served up ale and bread to stave off hunger, all in a hall so small and quaint the rafters were hung with farming implements and the hounds had worn a small track in the earthen floor, with their restless circling the table and the surrounding benches against the walls. The dogs were shameless beggars, and in the way of men and dogs men fed them morsels and became less the strangers.

In that warmth and ease armor buckles were loosened, men lounged about the walls on the low fixed benches that embraced the room, and young folk brought in a snowy table-plank from outside, with its supports, to add more seats with the lords. There followed another bustle of preparation, village women in their aprons and winter wraps turning up at the door of the great house to offer additional spoons and bowls from their own hearths, as Tristen was curious to see . . . one or two apiece, for this was by no means the Zeide, and very far even from one of the great town houses in luxury.

When they sat down it was at a plain, scarred table among several tables, at the head of the room, and with the dogs hanging close by their master's elbow, waiting in tongue-lolling hope as the young folk brought the pottery bowls and the bread. More of that was baking, and the ale had already found approval. The stew went down with comforting warmth, all with small talk of the day, the weather, and, of greater import to the village, the news out of Henas'amef: the arrival of the Ivanim, the disaster to Meiden, and the aid to the southern villages.

That, and the great wagon train that had passed, only using the well, taking offered ale, but bound resolutely for the river. "Guelens," the thane's older cousin said, as if that summed up everything, "fitted out for war."

"And bearing Your Grace's orders," said the thane himself. "And leaving a great curiosity behind them. Is it war before spring, and on this road?"

"Not so soon, sir," Tristen said, "and if I have my will, not on this land. I wish to prevent the war from crossing into this district. Did your former lord advise you, passing through, what had happened?"

"Our lord," the thane said, a man anxious and troubled from before their arrival: he gave that impression; and having seen Guelen forces going through his land, followed by wagons and supply as of some great force, he had sure reason to regard it all with doubt. "Our lord, Your Grace, passed in the dawn a fortnight back, with Guelen soldiers about him, and no happy look."

"Did he speak?"

"Not that the soldiers would allow. I took it for some mission to the Elwynim." Perhaps the thane did not now so take it: he had a worried look, and his eyes shifted from one to the other of them . . . for as it turned out, he knew nothing of what had transpired to cause his lord's exile.

"You fought at Lewen field," Cevulirn said.

"Yes. I did." This with a small lift of the head, a motion of pride.

"Those of us who did saw things, did we not?" Cevulirn said. "Such things as give a man an understanding of our enemy that the court in Guelemara does not have. The southern lords were there, to a man; all the south takes it of great importance to end this matter with the Elwynim, before some wizard or other finds Tasmôrden's side and gives us a far worse enemy at our threshold. Your new lord attracts that sort of opposition, sir, being what he is. I think you may understand that, too."

The thane cast a wary look Tristen's way.

"But it was not a mission to the Elwynim your former lord had," Tristen said.

"Our *former* lord, Your Grace?"

The guard they had with them along with the thane's men had found place on the benches around the sides of the rustic hall, with ale and wooden platters. Conversation there had fallen away in a great listening hush so deep even the hounds stood still from their restless pacing.

"Your lord is banished. There is no lord of Bryn."

All breath in the hall seemed stifled.

"And what then brings Your Grace?" the thane asked.

"Lord Cevulirn is right: the longer Elwynor fights, the more likely some force will take advantage of Tasmôrden's danger . . . when the king comes. You've not asked me why I dismissed your lord."

Modeyneth's face became guarded and still. "It's in your right and your gift to do so, Your Grace, and so with us all."

"You have yet to call me your lord. *Am* I that?"

The hush deepened, if it were possible, and lasted a moment longer. "For my people's sake you are my lord, and within your right."

"Will you swear to me, sir?" This across the bread and cups of ale, the remnant of an excellent stew which the thane's young wife had provided. "Lord Cuthan hasn't released you, but I release you from your oath, and as of a fortnight ago you've had no lord. Will you swear to me, sir, or cross the river to join Lord Cuthan? I'll give you safe passage if that suits you."

"These people can't cross, with their land and their livestock. This *land* can't cross."

"Lord Cuthan might cross here to take it back."

There was another space of silence.

"Your Grace is asking me for my oath against my lord."

"Yes, sir, for your oath, and your loyalty to me and to whomever I grant the lordship of Bryn. Lord Cuthan betrayed Meiden and held knowledge from him which cost his life and a good many other lives, besides other crimes. Therefore I exiled your lord, and therefore I took back the title and honor. If you still are Cuthan's man, I give you leave to take whatever goods and men you wish and join Cuthan across the river, to share his fortunes, whatever they may be. He is my enemy, and he became the council's enemy, and Meiden bled for it."

That the thane hesitated long spoke well for his honesty. He rested his elbows on the scarred wood of the table and clasped his hands before his mouth, his eyes bright and steady, if troubled. "I marched behind you at Lewenbrook."

"I know."

"That the king in Guelessar sent you is on the one hand not astonishing. But it is unexpected, if Your Grace will forgive my saying so. It bodes better than Parsynan."

"Him I sent away. He was a thief, not alone of the jewelry we found. That Cuthan worked against him I find no fault at all. But that Cuthan conspired with Tasmôrden and betrayed Meiden to the king's soldiers, I do not forgive, and will not forgive. Nor will the other earls he failed to advise that the king's men were coming forgive him, either."

"Did he do such a thing?"

"That, yes. And more."

"So I've heard, too," Cevulirn said, "from young Meiden, and others of the earls."

All this the young thane heard with a sorrowful face, and a thoughtful one, and at that last, he nodded. "Then you'll have my oath to whatever lord you appoint. I do swear it and will swear, and will obey the lord you set over us. How may I serve my lord duke?"

"Build a wall, between the two hills beyond this village, and be ready to hold it if trouble comes. Let those hills be your walls."

Modeyneth leaned back from the table with a wary look. "The king's law forbids Amefin to fortify, except at Henas'amef."

"The king hasn't told me so," Tristen said, "and I

say you should build a wall, and this is the lord of Bryn's charge."

"But the lord of Bryn is across the river, Your Grace."

"Is he? I think not. *You* are the lord of Bryn, sir. You are my choice."

"I?" The thane now earl bumped an ale cup and all but overset it. "Gods save."

"The earls in Henas'amef recommend you. So I make you earl of Bryn, and I wish to have all the arms you can find in good order, fit, if war comes to Amefel. As I hope won't happen, if you build the wall I ask for and build it quickly. I am in great earnest, sir."

"My lord." The thane's own name was Drusenan; and now Earl Drusenan, and this rustic place had become an earl's estate. A woman who might be Drusenan's wife had heard and come to his side, drying her hands on her apron; and the new-made earl was still pale and trembling. "What shall I say to this?"

"Say that Tasmôrden will not pass," Tristen said. "That this road will be protected. That all the lands of Bryn will have justice and good advice."

"My lord, they will."

"Then you'll have done all I ask," Tristen said, and the new earl set his wife beside him, the woman's face with a hectic flush and her hands making knots of her apron. She was a lady with work-reddened hands and sweat on her brow, and by the laces of her midriff, swelling with child. Tristen had learned such signs. So the new earl would have an heir to defend. Drusenan, being young, would be earl for years if he lived so long as summer, and that was the question for all this district . . . for the bridge down the road was a likely place where Tasmôrden's forces might try to drive straight for Henas'amef by the shortest route.

"Gods save you and your house," Cevulirn said, the sort of thing Men said to one another, but Tristen had learned he could not utter it . . . being, Cefwyn had always said, a bad liar . . . so he simply ducked his head and let Cevulirn pay courtesies in a land that was not his.

Meanwhile the lord's men had caught up the enthusiasm and brimmed over with it; and in very short time the word slipped out of the small hall on serving boys' feet . . . hasting, doubtless, to pass through the village.

No doubt at all, when men turned up at the door, with ale broken out and every house in the village having turned out in the snowy yard. Out of nowhere in particular a piper came to the hall, and the new earl turned out the dogs and cleared back the tables, making a small space in which the determined might dance.

It was a commotion about the event which Tristen had not foreseen, though he said to himself it was foolish not to have realized how quickly word would spread and how excitedly Men would receive it. The dancing imperiled the best pots and a persistent dog, both of which the new earl's lady hastened out of the way . . . and the ale flowed free with noise and commotion until the mid of the night, or so it seemed to saddle-weary men with a long ride tomorrow.

But none of the Ivanim was drunk, nor were the Guelens, not nearly so much as the villagers . . . for, as Cevulirn had said under the cover of the noise, "I trust our host, but I don't *know* our host. That says all."

The drunkenness, however, grew noisy and inept among the villagers, and continued in the yard, after the new lady of Bryn chased out the celebrants in favor of pallets for the soldiers and a bed for their noble visitors.

"We've ample place for ourselves," young Bryn said. "Take our hospitality and our bed in the upstairs, and welcome, very welcome."

For his part, Tristen, and, he was sure, Cevulirn, would have far rather spread a pallet near the men he knew and trusted. But how was it possible to refuse when the couple, having received such an honor from him, was so set upon offering their best? And when this was the man to whom he had entrusted the sleep of an entire district of Amefel, should he not cast himself on his decision and trust the man?

"Thank you," Tristen said, and the lady without a word rose and began to lead the way.

A word, a single word, passed between Cevulirn and his lieutenant: wariness still, on Cevulirn's part, and Tristen bent his attention to the gray space on the instant.

Nothing. Nothing but the sense of Men in the vicinity, some dulled and sleep-beguiled, others not, and anxious . . . but how should Men not be, when their peace was so disturbed? He trod the worn wooden stairs up to the loft, with the new lady of Bryn in the lead, and Cevulirn went behind him.

The hall offered a floor for men to sleep on, and so the men would, but a sort of bedchamber was snugged in as a half loft above, wooden-floored, and lit and warmed by the light of the fire in the hall downstairs. It was a sensible and comfortable arrangement, assuring warmth and even a certain dim light, which was not the case in most rooms in the Zeide.

There the lady left them. Cevulirn never needed say aloud that he was ill at ease in this separation from his men . . . Cevulirn, who had a little of the wizard-gift, and perhaps a sense of things in the gray space, still was a troubled presence.

"I find no threat to us," Tristen said aloud, and Cevulirn said nothing, but cast him a resolutely comforted glance and sat down and took off his boots.

Tristen did the same, all the while listening, listening, surmising the anxiousness he still felt was the villagers' anxiety, and most of all the new-made lord's and his lady's, all disturbed at the storm that had swept down on their peace. Drusenan might be troubled at his lord's banishment and fall; at his own accession to unexpected heights in the same brief space. He might be mulling over the instruction to muster and build. All these things were possibly in Drusenan's agitated mind, and two wizard-gifts in their midst could only gather it up with unusual force. And their concern might cause others' concern by their frowns.

Yet the house did settle, and the presences in the house went out one by one as the fire downstairs was banked. Tristen settled beside Cevulirn in the soft feather bed. For a short time they talked of the river and the bridges, and then fell away to a mutual silence, both of them courting sleep in a house which had grown quiet and dim around them.

Cevulirn at last dropped off to a faint, drowsing presence, a light sleep, it was: Tristen was aware of presence, and that meant some awareness lingered. He himself failed to rest quite as easily, still uneasy in the unfamiliarity around him and in his responsibility . . . and in his daylong separation from Uwen, who had been beside him or accessible to him almost since he had come among Men. He found himself wondering what Uwen Lewen's-son might be up to in Henas'amef, how his first day of solitary command of the town might have gone; whether he was asleep, by now, in his bed, and whether Uwen also missed him.

Such questions he might satisfy. He might reach out to Emuin, from here, and through Emuin learn at least some things; but a thought prevented him: that they were a day closer to the river now, and that more powerful effort meant more exposure to wizardry than he liked.

He felt strangely unprotected, despite his access to wizardry, despite the sword on the floor next his bedside, despite the very formidable companion asleep at his side, one of the bravest and most skillful fighters in all Ylesuin, and despite all the guards below. He had not even brought Lusin and Syllan and his ordinary guard on this venture, but rather his night guard, good men, all, and brave and loyal to him, taking turn about bearing the ducal banner. Lusin and the rest of his day guard had come to have other duties more essential than standing at his door, and were more and more absent, one or the other managing the domestic things about the Zeide that they had come to manage very well, becoming the extra hands and eyes he had come to need so much in dealing with the ordinary business of the place.

Least of all could he withdraw those men at the very time Uwen might need them. And there was no reason to fear for himself, not with Cevulirn beside him, though the unaccustomed presence kept him from sleep.

So he rested, gazing at the eye-teasing glow of a distant banked fire on unfamiliar rafters, beams so low he could all but touch them. The same beams extended out over the hall where his men were sleeping, and he watched shadows move among the beams, tame and well-behaved shadows, as it happened, nothing ill feeling at all about the house itself.

He looked further into the shadows and saw the Lines that established the house, all well made, some brighter and older than others. That meant the house had known several changes, but each had observed the Lines of the one before, so far as his sleepy inquiry could ascertain.

He shut his eyes, courting sleep now with a determined wish, considering how long a ride they had on the morrow, on snowy roads.

But something else touched him, light as a summer breeze, awareness of lives, the way he was aware of a hawk aloft or a badger under a ledge, a horse in the stable, or men slipping about something very, very quietly out in the yard.

He listened to it, and asked himself was it innocent? And should he wake Cevulirn?

At the very thought, Cevulirn was awake, and a presence strong as a lit candle in the dark.

"Something's outside," Tristen whispered, and they both, having slept mostly dressed, put on their boots and took up their cloaks and their swords in the dimness of the loft.

There was not as yet any reason to call out an alarm to all the men below. They two came down the worn wooden stairs, the fire in the downstairs fireplace lighting the stairs just enough for night-accustomed eyes.

And just so the light showed a shadowy, cloaked figure, the new-made earl closing his front door, after a look or a venture into the yard outside.

Young Drusenan looked around, and up, saw them both, and stood stricken and still, on all sides of him a carpet of Ivanim guard sleeping, but not ale-dulled enough a spoken word would not rouse them.

Tristen came the rest of the way down the steps, sword bare in his hand, and Cevulirn joined him. No one had made a sound. The wife was awake, and had come out of her curtained nook, her braids all undone.

The earl might have been seeing to a horse, or himself investigating the unease outside, but the stricken look on his face said otherwise, and he had not the face to lie.

And now, roused by the faint sounds of their movements, one man of the guard stirred, and after that two, and half a dozen, and all the rest, reaching after arms and rising to cast long shadows around the walls.

Drusenan's face showed a pale sweat in the firelight. His wife wove her way through the guards, her hair unbound, a shawl about her, and reached her husband's side.

"I hear something," Tristen said, for there was a stirring, remote from him. Others looked puzzled, and Cevulirn looked doubtful. But Drusenan drew a breath like a man meeting cold water.

"My lord, the truth: I have other visitors . . . fugitives, helpless fugitives out of Elwynor. I should have confessed it, but I'd sworn to keep them secret, on my honor, my lord, and how could I break my oath? They're by no means enemies of yours. Women and children, old men. We've fed them, given them warmth in the cold."

"Hardly a surprise," muttered Cevulirn. "So I'm sure the borderers do and have always done."

So Ninévrisë's father's company had found Amefel their natural recourse, and gained help from the village of Emwy. Likewise the rebel Caswyddian had crossed, pursuing, and foraged off Amefin land, bringing death with him. There was no way to tell Elwynim friend from Elwynim foe when they all came for shelter and killed one another on Amefin soil.

"I beg my lord's mercy," the wife said, and added, faintly, "Lord, I am Elwynim, and have a cousin with them. How could I turn her away?"

"Blood is mixed here," Drusenan said. "And kinship binds us, even with other loyalties we keep. Your Grace, in your own good heart, help them. Shelter them. Feed them."

Feed my sparrows, Auld Syes had said.

These were Auld Syes' birds. The gray space echoed with the memory, the witch of Emwy, the uprooted oak.

"Show me these fugitives," he said.

There were indeed mostly women with small children, bundled against the cold, and very frightened to be hunted out of their refuge in the stable. They had been warm and snug among the many horses that had filled the stalls and the aisle. Now they stood exposed to view of armed men, roused out into the wind and shivering with fright.

"Small wonder the village wanted to stable the horses," Cevulirn said dryly. Since it was never the Ivanim habit to surrender that task to anyone, Tristen had no trouble guessing, the fugitives had had to hide elsewhere until the visitors were all abed. Then they had come creeping back to the lifesaving warmth, where hay and horses far in excess of the stable's capacity had made a very warm haven until the dawn.

And that was the mysterious coming and going in the night he had heard, the sense of presence more than he had accounted for, that had kept him awake.

But they were not a warlike group . . . less than a score in number, one a babe in arms, the rest anonymous bundles of heavy cloaks and wraps of every sort, at least three others of them children.

"They are no threat," Tristen said.

"Until asked questions by those who are," Cevulirn said. "Best not to have them on this route to the river, where they see all the coming and going of your supply. Bryn's villagers know where to go if trouble comes. These have fewer resources."

To have a contingent of Elwynim next Henas'amef or within it was no comfort, either. A gathering of Elwynim fugitives, however pitiful, afforded a resting place where Elwynim spies might come and go. There was nowhere completely safe to settle them, none of the river villages within reach wherein an Elwynim band that might include those sympathetic to Tasmôrden could not work some sort of harm: lights and signals, even daggers in the night, or at very least, one taking to his heels to go back across the river with news.

Yet the wind blew with a whisper to his thoughts . . .

What had Auld Syes said? Magic had a way of diverting one's attention, the things most needful to know slipping through one's fingers like water.

The living king at last sits in judgment.

And again, which he had already remembered: *When you find my sparrows, my little birds, lord of Amefel, warm them, feed them. The wind is too cold.*

Birds before the storm, not his birds, not the fat, silly pigeons that he daily fed at his windowsill, the foolish pigeons which had won him the Holy Father's ire in Guelemara, on account of the Quinaltine steps. No, these were certainly those other birds, Auld Syes' sparrows, come to him in want of shelter.

And wherefore should prudent birds lack shelter? When their nests were windblown down, when their homes were destroyed, when armies marched and villages burned and greedy men seized power. Those were the birds that flew on Auld Syes' storm . . . the winds blew, edged with winter and killing, and there was magic and wizardry behind his coming here and these fugitives seeking help of him.

And what direction would Elwynim loyal to Ninévrisë run?

They would never go to Guelessar for refuge, that was certain. Their lady Ninévrisë might have wed Cefwyn and might have Cefwyn's promise of aid, but for Elwynim noble or common to cross the river and deliver themselves into the hands of Guelenmen, their old enemies, that, they feared more than they feared Tasmôrden's army.

No, if Elwynim sought shelter, of course they would seek it among a folk allied by blood and history. Of course they would go south; and that was the duty Auld Syes had laid on him, to receive these folk and safeguard them, no matter what happened within Elwynor.

He looked at the pitiful band by torchlight, helpless and shivering, a close-wrapped band that looked for all the world like drab winter birds, and all looked fearfully at him, who held their lives and safety in his hands.

"Let's go back to the stables," he said, "out of the wind. That first. And you'll tell me what brought you here. I'll protect you, but if you wish me to, tell me the truth." He had not forgotten how Crissand's father Edwyll had contrived with Tasmôrden, who had promised to send Elwynim forces across the river . . . and indeed, in these, Tasmôrden had, but a force of the starving and desperate, whom Tasmôrden would be well content to see plundering Amefin resources: such cruelty he added to the tally of Tasmôrden's doings.

"Light a lantern," he said at the stable door . . . they should not bring the fire-dripping torches inside with the hay. And a man found a lantern and lit it, so they could go in among sleepy horses, gray and brown backs pressed side by side, and wary dark eyes shining back the lamplight in wonder what Men were doing.

Within the stable, barriered against the wind and in the warmth of so many horses and the bedding straw, Tristen appropriated a stack of grain sacks for a ducal seat; Cevulirn chose a barrel.

Drusenan stood and held the lantern himself, a circle of light which fell on faces that, indeed, freed of their muffling wraps, were all women, old men, and children.

"This is Tristen of Ynefel, our new lord duke of Amefel," Drusenan said, "and this is Duke Cevulirn of Ivanor, who's the best of the lords of the south, and they ask me why I've sheltered you."

"Our homes are burned, lords!" came the anguished reply. And from another: "We had no choice but cross to Amefel!"

"Where is your home?" Tristen asked quietly.

"Nithen, lord." A young woman spoke, a thin woman bearing a recent and ugly scar of burns on a hand clenched on her cloak of straw-flecked wool. "We come from Nithen district, mostly. One from Criess." Another head nodded, a young woman with a closely bundled child at her skirts. "Tasmôrden's men took our stock and our seed grain. We couldn't live there."

"My cousin," Drusenan's young wife spoke up. "Where else should she go, but to me?"

"Wife," Drusenan interposed; and then with a glance at his judges: "So they came for food, harmless and unarmed. How could we refuse them?"

Tristen was ignorant of farmers and shepherds, but he knew the map of Elwynor, such as they had. Nithen was not on the map he had, but Criess was, near the border. Cevulirn, however, asked shrewd and knowledgeable questions of the fugitives, how large a village was Nithen, what was its sustenance, where were the men . . . and how many men they had seen making the assault, riding what sort of horses, whether they had killed the men of the villages or forced them into service. All these things Cevulirn asked, and yes, there had been perhaps a hundred, and they had taken some men of various villages to serve Tasmôrden, but some who resisted, they had killed. An old man from Nithen had lost a son, and others shouted out their own losses with tears and anger.

Cevulirn's questions quickly assumed a shape in Tristen's understanding, an image of the number and condition of the enemy and the very weather of the day they had moved through the district. All the significance of Cevulirn's questions Unfolded to him in troublingly vivid order, and told him when, and how, and with what result. And he wished calm and comfort on the innocent.

"When Tasmôrden marched on the capital," Tristen said, "he went through Nithen; and that was above a fortnight past, is that so?" He was convinced both that they told the truth and that pity was justified for these desperate people. Nithen was a hamlet attached to Ilefínian, an estate of the Lord Regent himself.

And as for the day on which these folk had crossed over, no, they replied to his question, they were aware of no muster of Tasmôrden's forces to the border to aid any Amefin rebellion: it had all poured in on Ilefínian.

So Tasmôrden's promises of support to Edwyll were indeed a lie: only this hungry and desperate band had crossed the river, allowed to escape not out of mercy, but because their presence and that of other disordered bands of refugees might just as well aid Tasmôrden with no expenditure of troops. They might be a burden on Amefel's supplies, perhaps would steal from Amefin villages—at best, given Tasmôrden's promises to Edwyll and the rest, might confuse the king's troops. They were cast away to die.

But pitiful as they were, he would not be surprised if armed men began to flee the war and cross, too, and some of them might be Tasmôrden's men.

Most certainly, on Cevulirn's advice and his own clear sense, he should not leave these folk here to multiply on his supply route to the border.

And if Modeyneth was the village with connection to them, Modeyneth would still willingly feed them, Auld Syes' sparrows . . .

And what better refuge than in Emwy district, which was in Auld Syes' hands and under her potent wards, hers, and the late Lord Regent's? Ninévrisë's father, though a Shadow now, would know the true from the false.

"West of Modeyneth, in the hills," he said, "the war will not so likely come. There are walls and vaults at Althalen that would keep the wind out, and if we sent canvas and timbers, the old walls could well shelter them. I know the place is well warded against harm from the outside." He did not add that he himself would know sure as a shout and as instantly if any untoward thing happened there . . . he did not think there could be any intrusion at Althalen without his knowing it.

"Your Grace," Drusenan protested. "It's forbidden even to set foot in that place."

"So much the safer. I don't forbid it, and I'm lord of the place."

"The king forbade it, as he forbade—" It was to Drusenan's credit that he forbore to say, *the wall.*

"The king is my friend, and I know he'd bring these folk to Althalen himself if trouble threatened. There's nothing harmful there, not to the harmless. A little girl rules it, and the Lord Regent. If you can manage only canvas and straw, they'll be safe and warm within the walls. The stone there is thick, and reflects warmth if they have a fire."

"If they had leave to cut wood . . ." Drusenan said. "Plenty grows there."

"If we had your leave to cut it, my lord."

Why should you need it? he all but asked, but from Guelessar's example, he understood the jealousy with which lords guarded their wooded lands . . . and he knew the reason of it, that indiscriminate cutting would ruin the land and kill the game. "You have my leave," he said, looking at the women, "and if there should be haunts, don't fear them. Uleman's grave is there. The wards of that place are stronger than any common place."

The Regent's name greatly affected the women. One seized his hand, pressing her brow to it, hugging it to her.

"Gods bless Your Grace." The woman's wounded hands clasped on his so he could not force them off without touching seared flesh. She bore amulets, he saw as her shawl fell open, much like Auld Syes. She was a witch, but had no power, or none that he could feel. Cevulirn had far more, and glowed softly in the gray space. He touched her hands, wished her flesh to heal as soon as possible, and with no more hardship. She pressed her tearful face against his hand, and fell to her knees . . . he hoped because he had done some good.

"The king's law forbids settlement at Althalen," Cevulirn said in a hushed voice, at his other hand, "so you should know, Amefel, though I agree His Majesty would ride right over that law at his need. The king's law also forbids the raising of walls and defenses in Amefel."

"Is it all *Cefwyn's* law?"

"His grandfather's."

That was very different. "His giving me the banner of Althalen was against his grandfather's law, too, but he did, all the same. And he told me do justice, and I swore to him to do it. So I have to find these people a place." Tristen cast a look at Drusenan. "Settle them there tomorrow. Quickly as you may." It struck him between the lordship, the wall, and the fugitives that he had settled a double and a triple burden on Modeyneth. "Don't bear it alone. Call on the help of all Bryn's resources, up to the walls of Henas'amef and inside, and tomorrow send to all of Bryn and say this is my instruction, and the council decree says the same."

"My lord." There was fervent intent in Drusenan's voice. "I swear it. And your wall you shall have, my lord."

"With a gate in it, and two towers for archers." He had in mind exactly how he wished it would look, smooth white stone, with great towers; but he knew sensibly that in haste and with unskilled labor, it would be rough stone and wood.

"There is the ruin there," said Drusenan. "There, shall we build? Of the old stone?"

He was confounded for a moment, and then Cevulirn said, "Whatever serves to raise that wall faster, I think His Grace will approve."

They went inside, and back up to their chilled blankets, he and Cevulirn, while the men settled in the lower hall, with understanding, now, of the village secrets and the loyalty of Bryn, alike.

"A wall has stood there," Cevulirn said, "where you direct the wall to be. It's on the oldest maps. Did you know?"

"A Sihhë one?" He had not known. He was troubled to think so, but not altogether so.

"Barrakkêth raised it, and at other . . ."

. . . *points in the hills*, Cevulirn said, but he already

knew what Cevulirn would say. He could see his wall as he had seen it in planning, a string of small outposts which in some degree corresponded with the villages that stood there now, linking a series of steep-faced hills.

These villages had once been a source of supply to powerful garrisons. *That* had been the importance of Bryn, their ancient duty to the Sihhë kings. That was the source of their prominence in Amefel. The system of defenses Unfolded to him, with unwalled Althalen in the heart of such a bristle of defenses no enemy could prevail . . .

Instead Althalen had rotted at the heart, and the interest of the halfling kings in the people that toiled in uninteresting peace in the countryside had failed: long peace, and stability, and long, long dearth of ambition or purpose in existence.

Had it been good . . . or otherwise . . . for the villages under their rule?

Crissand spoke for the villages, and understood the farmers, and pleaded for attention to them. Crissand . . . aetheling, by the same blood Cuthan shared, that might even run in Drusenan of Bryn.

He said nothing after that, only felt a chill through the blankets and his clothing and despite the body lying next to him.

What had he done, in ordering these things? One moment he had been sure; and now he lay close to shivering at the thought of what he had commanded to exist, and at a title he had all but promised to bestow.

He, who had read the Book that Mauryl had given him . . . or that Mauryl had *returned* to him, whichever was the case: Barrakkêth's book, outlining the principles of magic, the fluid character of time and place, on which wizards so profoundly depended and which they attempted to nail in place.

False, Barrakkêth would say: nothing is so certain. The patterns were what mattered. The patterns and not the substance. A village *is* the realm, the realm a village, and the kingdom fares as well as any of its parts.

Might he then heal Althalen?

In a morning aglow with clouds, they brought out their horses, disturbing the sleep of the exiles from Elwynor. The village wives had made a great pot of porridge in the open air, and every man and every villager and the fugitives as well had hot porridge steaming in the wintry breeze. Faces stung red with cold all bore smiles this morning.

"Fare well," everyone called after them when they set out, and "Gods keep Your Lordship and Your Grace!" wafted after them as they rode out. "Gods save Amefel and gods save Ivanor! And gods save the lord of Bryn!"

The new lord of Bryn rode with them a short way to the two hills in the distance. It was a stream-riven cut through a wall of similar hills, and a shallow ford near two graceful, winter-bare beeches.

And there, too, icicled and snow-bedight, stood the ruin of two towers, one on either side, rock cut from the two hills. The quarry, too, was picked out in snow on the nearer hill.

"My wall," Tristen said, amazed at how exactly it answered to his vision. He could imagine the fallen blocks in place, and the gates of bronze, figured with forbidding faces.

"Gates to let honest comers through," he said to Drusenan. "And men to stand guard."

"With the old stone already cut," the new earl said, "by spring your towers will stand." Then Drusenan added, "As a boy I played among these hills, in and out these towers. So with every boy in Modeyneth. We made troops and fought battles."

"Against whom?" Having never been a boy, he could scarcely imagine what boys knew or did.

"Oh, the sheep. Scores of enemies."

"Guelens," Cevulirn supplied wryly, not a Guelen himself, and drew a chagrined look from the young lord of Bryn.

"I think so we imagined," Drusenan said.

"This time, against Tasmôrden," Tristen said quietly, uncertain of the currents that flowed here. "But not against the like of those folk you shelter. I'll give orders to Captain Anwyll at the river to watch out for others. He's a good man, and if he comes here, as he and his messengers must, trust him. His reports will do you no harm."

"I take your word, my lord, with all goodwill. As I give you mine. What more can words do?"

In such small exchanges of politeness Tristen found himself lost more than not, but in this saying, in this moment between himself and the new lord of Bryn, he felt the currents in the gray space moving and roiled, and the very stones so tinged with power he could draw it into his nostrils along with the scent of snow and cold rock.

He looked up the snowy rock face, and at the towers, and at the skeletal beeches, which were not part of his vision.

Green things had come here and grown in peace; and a barren place looming with threat had existed only for the games of children and the pasturage of sheep for decades.

His orders changed it back. It would stand and threaten again, and children would not play here: soldiers would stand guard; and a forbidden wall would stand here as it had stood before. He rode along it, eyes at times shut to the wall as it was, but old Lines answered him, old Lines leapt up at his touch, and would grow stronger with the work of Men's hands.

Cefwyn would forgive him. Cefwyn forgave him and would forgive, no matter the mind of his northern barons.

"I had not thought," Tristen said to Cevulirn as they rode away to the north, leaving the lord of Bryn to his task, "I had not even known stones had stood there when I ordered it. What brought it down? Do you know?"

"Oh, easily. Selwyn Marhanen ordered the Amefin fortresses cast down . . . and the northern defenses went with them. Folly," Cevulirn said to the brisk rhythm of the horses at a walk, "folly to have dismantled the defenses with Elwynor continually at war, but the prospect of having the wall held from the other side doubtless entered into the king's decision."

If that were so, the Elwynim would have seized territory far into Amefel . . . and by the Red Chronicle, there had been Amefin who hoped for that, many of them.

"You've given leave for the raising of walls," Cevulirn said. "But Cefwyn will agree, I think, and best the word of it reach him quietly. The northern barons certainly won't like it. And His Majesty should know beforehand and not be surprised by your breaches of law."

"Yes," he said, determined to send a messenger on the heels of the last, as soon as he reached home and the most direct route.

But his wall, he was resolved, should stand, and even in its early stages, would check any advance by way of the main road toward Henas'amef.

And with small intrusions stopped, and only the sheepwalks and the meadows and stony hillsides for a route into the land, no large force could move with any speed, certainly none with the great engines Cefwyn feared. Henas'amef's old walls were not fit for modern war, so Cefwyn had said; and unhappily, neither was Ilefínian across the river, so Ninévrisë had said.

Walls built for magic, Cefwyn had also said. In those days, in their pride, the halfling Sihhë had had even Althalen as an unwalled city, and trusted to their magic.

So he had done, and whether Cevulirn had guessed what he did, he had no knowledge. All wishes aided the wards, and he thought he had had wishes from that quarter, such as they were.

Oh, he longed for leave to be riding this road with a troop of light cavalry, more than followed them now . . . as he would, if Cefwyn had simply failed to forbid him.

And all along the way his eyes swept the snow-bleached hills for likely routes and lookouts.

Cevulirn, too, saw more than spoke.

They paused to change about horses in due course, and by noon, at a place where signs said Anwyll had camped even last night, they shared the bread and cheese the village had sent with them, Cevulirn's men grown easier, and more inclined to laughter in the evident success of their venture in this snowy land.

By afternoon the road had passed through that ridge of hills that contained the Lenúalim's broad stream; their riding began to be generally downhill, easier on the horses. From one last rise they could see far and wide across the land, to the sunset and white hills and the small woods, and the smoke of village fires somewhat to the darkening east.

Here, too, was a sight that Unfolded names and places: Asfiad, and Edlinnadd, but when he asked Cevulirn whether the names were thus, Cevulirn said Aswyth and Ellinan were the names.

So it was like reading the Book, written in a hand he had not recognized until the words themselves came back, and then it seemed he had known not alone the hand, but every flaw in the pages, every place where the hand had compromised a letter to avoid a roughness.

So when he thought of Asfiad, he thought of a well and a dark-eyed woman, as if it were yesterday, and he shivered in the cold wind the evening sent, under a gray and fading sky. All the colors of the sunset had faded.

Yet he knew this land, and so the river shore Unfolded to him, never seen, but there in his heart of hearts . . . indeed he had pored over maps before this, and had sure knowledge of some of the places; but now it spread out, winterbound, and white, dulled with evening, and full of names not in the maps, memories of springtime and summer and autumn so vivid they took his breath.

"We may not reach the camp," Cevulirn said, "but Anwyll must have gotten there. He's had good luck with the carts."

The oxcarts carried a great deal, but moved excruciatingly slowly: would move slowly on their way to Guelessar, too, and the weather was a question. Tristen considered the matter of Cefwyn's carts, gazing out above red Gery's ears. Sometimes he thought he rode black Dys, which was foolish: Dys was at home. Sometimes, too, he heard the rumble of armor, which was surely the recollection of Lewenbrook: the noise of the muster of the south and the heavy horse at full charge, armor a-rattle and hooves beating on late-summer sod. Had this place ever seen a battle?

But underfoot this evening was the soft, crisp fracture of unblemished snow under Gery's feet, a walking pace beside Cevulirn's gray, the banners all furled now that they were in desolate territory, with no eye to see.

He shivered despite the thick cloak. Perhaps it was like the wall, like the Book, and Mauryl's spell that had Called him into the world was written everywhere across the land, ready to Unfold to him with frightening immediacy.

There was little time, something kept saying to him: there was so little time to seize this Pattern and make it move as he wished.

CHAPTER 3

To the royal desk came all the accustomed trivia and the daily urgencies that faced the Crown: the proposed fishing weirs across Lissenbrook, among the accounting of fletchers requesting goose quills, which Cefwyn saw no reason should rise above the level of concern of the Commander of the Guard, except he had asked to be informed of any deficiency in the preparations or the movement of carts.

Besides that small crisis of goose feathers, he had a report from the royal forester regarding the condition and take of deer from the royal preserve, in a winter not as bitter as feared, the condition of the forest and the abundance of hare.

And from a tenant the usual complaint of foxes making depredations into domestic stores, and a request to hunt them. Besides there was a wall wanting mending in Imor, on royal lands he had not seen since taking the throne and which he despaired of seeing in the future: he loved that hunting lodge and its command of the southern hills.

He thought of the woods near Wys, saw in his mind's eye the afternoon light coming through winter branches. He smelled the moist, sweet air after a snowfall . . . and envied the life of the foresters who had the care of it for their sole duty, hunting deer, when his own task was, endlessly, fruitlessly, hunting Elwynim rebels.

What would it be, to know on rising for the day, that one's duty was to walk in the woods, take account of deer and hare and badger, watch the flight of the birds and understand the weather? He was sure the office was somewhat more troublesome than that: no life was as simple as it seemed. But what did the forester think? Did he think how splendid it would be to be the king, and rise leisured to the worship of countless courtiers, dine from a golden service, and be fawned upon continually?

The golden service was true, but golden cups made hot tea go cold. He preferred humble pottery, thought it luxurious for a king otherwise damned to cold tea, and maintained a set of the cheapest by the fireside. As for the fawning . . . ask Ryssand. A morning where the letters abounded with nothing more grievous than fishing rights or requests for petty permissions was itself luxury, compared to the convolute dealings of his lords, and gods save him, his almoner, who he knew was only waiting his chance for complaint.

He did not hold audiences often enough. Men had no choice but to approach him with letters, and Emuin reproached him for it. But it was far quicker to read about the foxes than to hear about them from some dyspeptic squire who'd had to wait his turn in a cold audience hall. The Sihhë-lords themselves had insisted on written petition, and had had an immense archive of records . . . which had flamed up mightily in the fall of Althalen, so he supposed: all that efficiency and good order sent up in smoke in an hour by his grandfather, who came of a sturdy people whose farmers felt entitled to complain to the king and send him gifts. Denied, they sent him letters, and more letters, paying a clerk, or worse, a priest, to write them up fair if they had no skill to do so.

And if the High King of Althalen had heard his

common farmers and paid attention, Emuin had said peevishly, he might have heard what would have saved him and his realm from your grandfather, who at least listened to *his* farmers, for all his other faults. Paper and parchment are no substitute for faces and the sight of fields.

They were not a substitute. And when he thought of it, he had rather look at turnip fields than the face of Lord Murandys. But common farmers did not easily get past the guards of the Guelesfort these days. The great barons had ceased to rub sleeves with such common fellows, during his father's reign, except on feast days.

"Your Majesty." A page flitted near. "The Lord Commander is here."

A page had kept the Lord Commander standing in the foyer. His staff had taken his admonition to preserve the king's privacy for his slugabed bride a shade too literally.

The page proffered a sealed letter, with Ryssand's colors.

All the ease went out of him. "I'll see the Lord Commander," he said, and in the same moment his bride came through the door from the inner chambers, a second dawn in his day. He had read, waiting for her; and now . . .

"Idrys is on his way in," he said. "Forgive me."

"Ilefínian," she surmised in immediate concern.

"No. I don't think so. But Ryssand is no good news. Sit by me."

Idrys arrived in the room before she had quite seated herself, Idrys, Lord Commander of the household, the black harbinger of disaster.

"Ryssand dares send to me," Cefwyn said, taking up his knife to loose the seal. "Do you know what the matter is?"

The seal proved breached. Idrys regularly did so. It was his duty to know.

"I confess so," Idrys said. "But Your Majesty should read it."

A moderately bland missive, until his eye struck the line:

seeking Your Majesty's understanding regarding the actions of Your Majesty's obedient subject in Amefel, in the protection of Your Majesty's interests . . .

and then:

I seek an early audience for a man Your Majesty once favored with his trust on matters of utmost urgency . . .

He looked up at Idrys, already angry . . . not at the news, which was not news to him, but at the brazenness of it. "He's speaking for *Parsynan* . . . I sent him from court on that account. How dare he?"

"Oh, read to the end."

He read further, finding a formal complaint of Tristen's theft of Parsynan's property and charges of threats against a Crown officer's life.

"Am I surprised? Recount to me the causes whereby I am surprised at this sweet union of purpose, master crow. Parsynan and Ryssand! I'm only astonished at my credulity, taking this man's recommendations to put that damned thief in office in the first place! Good loving *gods*!"

"The gods are allied with His Holiness, one would suppose . . . and that devotion is still firmly bought. I do keep an ear to it."

"Gods hope." He scanned the letter. "Abuse of his person. *Sorcery* aiming at Parsynan's life?"

"His horse threw him."

That was there to read. Indeed, oh, and the innocent horse had been ensorcelled to do murder on Lord Parsynan, as the rioting Amefin, encouraged by Bryalt priests, had assaulted a king's officer in the streets of Henas'amef.

That could be believed. So, for that matter, could the actions of the horse, but it was not sorcery, if Tristen had done it: Emuin, his old tutor, had taught him that fine distinction.

"And Ryssand commits his honor to this complaint," he asked Idrys.

"Oh, more, more than that, my lord king. Read on."

. . . the urgent representation of Your Majesty's loyal officers who will swear to these facts, as we who have honorably and loyally supported the Crown and the gods are greatly alarmed. We seek redress of grievances and, putting aside our own bitter mourning, wish to consult with Your Majesty regarding measures that may lead to greater, not less, unity of purpose.

"Bother and damnation. Unity of purpose. Bitter mourning. Hell!"

Your Majesty witnessed the circumstances that have left Ryssand bereft, and casting now all our care upon our remaining treasure, our daughter, whose alliance with a powerful house will shield Your Majesty's Ryssandish province, accordingly we have thought of various alliances. But we deem no union more glorious and none more beneficial to the tranquillity of Ylesuin than to join the Marhanen line to that of Ryssand, forging an alliance that will bring us to the spring in one mind and with one purpose. Accordingly I have written to His Highness . . .

"Good loving gods! He's lost all his wits!"

"Which part in particular has caught my lord king's eye?"

"Is he proposing *marriage*? Marriage?"

Ninévrisë leaned to see.

"Artisane," Cefwyn said, "loving gods! To my brother Efanor . . ."

"I suspect His Highness will be here shortly," Idrys said in his low voice. "The courier carried two letters to court. And how will my lord king respond to this sage and selfless proposal of peace?"

He lacked words. Launching the army not at Tasmôrden's forces, but at Ryssand, was ever so fleetingly the wish of his heart. "I detest this man. I truly detest him."

"Efanor surely doesn't favor him," Ninévrisë said. "And Artisane is clever, but not wise."

"Much like all that house." The blood ran calmer in Cefwyn's veins by now, on two further breaths and the consideration that, on the one hand, it was a calculated piece of effrontery, set to make him angry, and on the other hand . . . that Efanor, while gullible where it came to priests, was nonetheless Marhanen in blood and bone. Efanor was not clever, but he was wise: gentler, but not dull-witted, nor, once the Marhanen temper had slipped the bounds of religious restraint . . . was gentle Efanor necessarily slow to offense.

And if Ryssand took this insolent letter as a sort of threat, a not so subtle reminder of the scope of his power in Ylesuin, Ryssand sadly mistook both the sons of Ináreddrin.

In fact the commotion at the hall door, which opened to some visitor without overmuch ado of pages, led him to suggest, visitor as yet unseen, that they repair to the adjacent room and the table there. "Your counsel will be welcome," he said to Idrys, and signaled a page. "Wine and a number of cups. Gods know how far this conference will extend. We may have half the kingdom here before all's done." The commotion was imminent in the hallway. Cefwyn rose at some leisure, taking Ninévrisë's hand, and had not quite settled at the table when Efanor arrived in the room, color high in his face.

Cefwyn sat, Ninévrisë sat, and Idrys, who rarely sat with his king, bowed.

"Brother," said Efanor. "Your Grace, Lord Commander." Efanor had a rolled parchment in his fist.

"Brother, good morning," Cefwyn said. "I take it you've received the match of this correspondence."

"I have," Efanor said, and took the gestured invitation to join their small council. "I doubt it was in any hope of favorable consideration."

"And?" Cefwyn asked.

"And I take it as a gibe at you. He clearly expects no good of it," Efanor said.

"I take it for an outrage," Ninévrisë said. "The man is your bitter enemy."

"He is my royal brother's bitter enemy," said Efanor airily, which was to say he was angry and pretending calm. "*I* have fallen from his consideration, and therefore he writes such a large stroke, caring nothing for my opinion. There is Ryssand's gage, if you will, cast in our faces."

"Unfortunately," said Idrys, "we have no adequate reply."

"I know I have a certain reputation among the northern barons, which I never sought."

Their father had wished Efanor to rule, but never found the means to secure the throne to his younger, more placid, son. So had Ryssand wished it, once, estimating Efanor would be biddable, lost in his contemplations and his studies. All the world estimated Efanor as a monkish sort, inclined to celibacy and scholarship, and the religiosity that had dominated their grandfather's later years, in his excessive fear of hell. In Selwyn the court had seen the utmost of religious terror, in his last year.

The truth was that Efanor did not so much fear hell

as love his expectations and imaginations of the gods, and yet . . . and yet at this moment, the clear, steady look Efanor had, the color high in his face, recalled the impish brother who had helped filch sweets from the banquet trays, the brother who had hidden with him in a haystack, frustrating the captain of the Dragon Guard.

"So what if I were to be so gullible as to write to him," Efanor asked, "as if I believed every word, and considered his offer?"

There *was* the Efanor who had conspired with him, the Efanor his bride had never met, in the few months of a new kingship. *There* was his brother. Cefwyn found himself on the one hand all but breaking into a grin.

"That would set the fox in the henhouse," Idrys had said, who *had* seen that other Efanor, often . . . while Ninévrisë sat amazed.

"Ryssand might think twice about what he has and what he might lose," Efanor said.

"He might think twice and three times," Ninévrisë said, "but Artisane is a wicked girl. Truly, truly I counsel against this."

Cefwyn moved his hand to hers. "I would not countenance it," he said to Efanor, "for one reason: the affront she paid Nevris, whether young Artisane contrived it or whether she only said what her father dictated. I can't forgive that, or bring her into Nevris' presence, not for any advantage. Nor will I sacrifice my brother's happiness."

"Oh, never a qualm for me, brother. That Her Grace can't forgive the lady . . . that's a difficulty."

"If I could assure the troops to save my land and my lord's good heart," Ninévrisë said, "I'd kiss her and forgive in full view of the court. I account her that little. But for you, dear Efanor, my dear friend, you have a good heart; too good. For your own sake, don't make light of it. The woman is a serpent, and she has a sting. Gods forbid, that you might ever carry through such a marriage."

"As for me," Efanor said, with a ruddy color to the roots of his hair, "my reputation is largely deserved: women have never moved me to the extent..." Efanor's voice trailed off, but Cefwyn had no reticence.

"You are not tempted to follow me," Cefwyn said, "in my previous folly."

"I could remain lastingly indifferent to the lady, and, being good Quinalt, she is chaste."

Ninévrisë laid her hand on Efanor's sleeve. "No. Never throw away love."

"I'm half a monk," Efanor said, "don't they say so? What should I lose? And she's young. She may learn to be pleasant."

"Pleasant!" Cefwyn said, for he could bear no more.

Efanor gave him one of those glass-clear looks in his turn, innocent as Tristen's eyes at this challenge to his priests and his holy aspirations. "Kings and princes marry for policy, not love. Would you not have married Luriel, if there were no other prospect? The girl is young, and Quinalt at least in observance, and by the gods' grace the true faith might give us something in common. Ryssand's offered. He cannot object to being taken up on it."

"Gods, what a recommendation of a bride. I'll not have the brother I love fling himself between me and Ryssand's ambition."

"I'd give her no heir," Efanor said with quiet assurance. "And I assure you 't would be as good as a nunnery and no inconvenience to me. My life is simple . . . monastic, in most points. It can remain so. And we only speak of responding favorably to Ryssand's offer . . . not of the actual marriage. Take Luriel as an example. No marriage resulted."

He had never imagined such cold depth under Efanor's calm good humor: somehow, in some way, Ryssand had stirred Efanor's absolute detestation. Efanor had all but drawn in his defense and Ninévrisë's, and while Efanor would not take up the sword with any good cheer, this was indeed the brother he knew, who had planned at least half the forays of their childhood . . . and who had become his enemy when Efanor had believed him guilty of sedition.

Now it was Ryssand who had made Efanor angry. And monkish Efanor might style himself, but he was Marhanen.

"I will countenance a courtship," Cefwyn said, "but never a marriage. I will find fault with it. I'll find some flaw in any arrangement."

"As they did," Ninévrisë said. "And yet we married."

"Because we *willed* to marry, as gods know Efanor has no such desire. Gods. Gods. Idrys, you've been silent. What say you?"

"That nothing Ryssand plans favors anyone but Ryssand. But I'm not sure he's planned His Highness's acceptance. That will worry him."

"Write," Cefwyn said to Efanor, "and I shall. His own damnable arrogance may lead him to believe *we* think it a good idea. But gods save us, Nevris, if that baggage *ever* affronts you in the remotest . . . I'll have her head *and* her father's."

"That baggage is *feared*, mark me. Cleisynde fears her, as much as follows her. But Luriel—"

"Luriel hates her cousin, and always has."

"Luriel is new-crowned queen of all eyes,"

Ninévrisë said, "and is also clever, but not wise; and there have been great changes since Artisane left. If Artisane returns, when Luriel's all a-flurry over Panys and a prospect of *her* grand wedding, and all of us stitching on Luriel's wedding gown, oh, now there's the fox and the weasel in the same sack, with the neck tied."

He had had small understanding of the women's court, which he had thought of as sheep without a shepherd since Efanor's mother's death. Weasels in a sack seemed more apt since Ninévrisë's ascendancy.

And he gave what Ninévrisë said his careful consideration, for while Artisane and Luriel led no troops, wielded no swords, nor had good Quinalt ladies a voice in the councils of state, a quarrel between the niece of Murandys and the daughter of Ryssand would unsettle the relationship between those two houses. And that relationship, however unholy their recent acts, was the rock on which the north was built.

It was also the reef on which the kingdom might shipwreck itself for good and all. Quarrels in the women's court where the king could not directly intervene had their own potency.

"If Luriel gained a firm rule over Artisane," Cefwyn said, "the whole kingdom would be the safer. But neither the fox nor the weasel will threaten *you*, Nevris, and that I swear. There is one intervention I *can* make in your secret realm upstairs, and that is to see Luriel in one convent and Artisane in another at the other end of Ylesuin if ever you find their quarrels tiresome. You may not be queen of Ylesuin, but by the blessed gods the ladies of this court will know they have you to please, and none other.—So likewise for your peace, brother. I swear it, quite, quite solemnly."

"So shall we disturb Ryssand's?" Efanor asked with—Cefwyn could all but see it—the old sparkle in the eye and the old flare of the nostril that meant Efanor had decided and was bent on the deed.

"Be careful," Ninévrisë wished them both, and from Idrys, that dark eminence: "Hear her. Very carefully hear her, my lord king."

By evening of an easy ride, Tristen at Cevulirn's side came in sight of the river and of the camp, orderly rows of tents beneath their high vantage on the hill: there was one of the several bridges that led into Amefel . . . or its pylons and framing, for the deck was stripped of planking and that planking stored on this side of the river in sections, under guard. There was the camp, long-established with several sheds and a small company of guards, that had maintained their guard over the bridge before Anwyll had come here. Now the sheds that must have been all the camp were swallowed up in the brown and gray tenting that spread along the shore, and the fires which before now must have been modest and few sent up a blue haze of smoke which hung low above the water.

There, too, across the river, was their first view of Elwynor, a shore that, far from being ominous, looked very like their own, with snowy low hills and wooded crests. There, Tristen said to himself, there was Ninévrisë's kingdom. Ilefínian, under siege, lay far away over the hills. The dark Lenúalim, which had lapped like an old serpent about the stones of Ynefel in the spring and summer, ran here as a broad, cold river, sided by ice.

They rode down toward the camp in a light sifting of snow from the heavens. Banners unfurled, and showed to the camp who had come, which sent the soldiers scrambling to their feet. Men ran, and the camp answered with a brisk and anxious welcome.

Captain Anwyll, only just arrived himself, came half-dressed from the largest tent to meet them in the main aisle of the camp.

"Your lordships," Anwyll said, looking up at them on their horses. Anwyll's breath steamed in small, hurried puffs. "Is there trouble?"

"No. Only a visitor to see the camp," Tristen said, for he had no complaint of what he saw. "His Grace of Ivanor has come to see our situation."

"Honored," Anwyll said, though most likely, Tristen thought, their visit was not entirely welcome tonight, while order was not complete; Anwyll still looked distressed and caught at a loss. But he sent for a cloak and his coat and showed them about his small command.

"I'd see the bridge," Cevulirn said, "the captain's good grace extending that far."

Anwyll cast Tristen a glance as if to see was there contradiction, and receiving nothing contrary, led them to the bridgehead, where great timbers stood skeletal against the wintry sunset and the empty pylons stood tied by timbers, which alone lent the structure strength.

"There's some concern about the spring flood," Anwyll said, "We've the planking under guard; I'm told we should cross-brace when the floods come if the decking's not in place by then."

If they lost pylons or decking, they could not cross without considerable delay and difficulty; and Tasmôrden would very much aim at that destruction if he could spare the men from his siege: the bridges might well be his next attack.

"By no means must we let the bridges go," he said. Anwyll was shivering, and sneezed in reply. "Be well," he said, and Anwyll blessed himself with a worried look. "We should go where it's warm," Tristen said, and on their walk back to the center of camp observed Anwyll pressing a hand to his heart, where no few soldiers wore their Quinalt amulets, or Teranthine ones, beneath their coats, and so Anwyll had had, on a gold chain.

But worried or not, Anwyll ceased the small cough that had troubled him on their walk to the bridge, and there were no more sneezes.

Anwyll's tent was a spare, snug, and modest affair, with a forechamber large enough for a small chart table and field chairs, such as assembled out of pegs and parts. Twilight was deep, and the lighting of lanterns made a fair contribution to the pungent air, the smoke, and the warmth in the place . . . a smell that conjured other tents, and the battle at the end of summer . . . not, curiously, an unpleasant stench, that of oil and leather and horses, and the nearby river, only one that carried the implication of weapons advanced, battles possible, the enemy opposed.

Ale added its own aroma, ale provided from Anwyll's own store; and at that table and in Cevulirn's company, Tristen provided the news he had, the confirmation of Drusenan as Lord Bryn.

To the appointment of a lord of Bryn, Anwyll said nothing, nor likely knew whether Drusenan was good or otherwise; but to the mention of fugitives at Modeyneth, he frowned, doubtless not pleased to have Elwynim between him and his capital; and chagrined, it was likely, to have marched his force of elite Guard past a band of Elwynim without knowing they were there.

It was a fault. Tristen neglected, however, to mention it.

"I've moved these folk over to Althalen, across the hills," Tristen said, "to have them safe within walls and not let them gather in numbers on this road."

"To Althalen," Anwyll echoed, in mild dismay.

"Women and young children. But with the siege of Ilefínian there may be more seeking to cross."

"And what shall we do with them?"

"Let any cross who will cross," Tristen said, "if they swear to Her Grace."

"Armed troops as well?"

"If they've Tasmôrden at their backs," Cevulirn said dryly, "they'll be in a considerable hurry, and reluctant to discuss. And very difficult it will be to sort out Tasmôrden's men from the rest."

"If that should happen," Tristen said, "by no means receive armed men into your camp. Have them draw off to the east on the shore, and not up the hill, under any circumstance: occupy that, and be sure. If they obey orders, they may camp and not stir out of that camp. And should it happen, advise me of it as quickly as you can. You can change horses at Modeyneth: Drusenan would provide you what you need."

Anwyll looked much more content with that instruction, yet a little anxious all the same. "I understand so, Your Grace. And welcome news." Over all, Anwyll looked more content than he had been in coming here, and seemed particularly friendly toward Cevulirn's presence, as if, Tristen thought, Anwyll had not quite trusted his orders; but now seeing the duke of Ivanor, had more confidence in what he was bidden do.

That was very well: whatever comforted Anwyll could only make him a surer captain in this post; and until late hours and by lanternlight, with the snow sifting down from the heavens, they sat in Anwyll's tent and talked of Bryn's wall and of extending the river-watch all along the border.

"In both cases," Cevulirn said, "no prevention to any small force bent on mischief, and going through the hills, but no great force can cross."

Such forces needed heavy transport, and therefore needed roads, and well-maintained ones, with gravel and rock to fill the soft places. And that, too, Tristen knew as he knew that it was not the kind of warfare he and Cevulirn would use, if there were not Cefwyn's express order in the way.

"The men of Nithen district in Elwynor were forced to join Tasmôrden's army," Tristen said, "and so may others be with him by no choice of their own. Such men may well find occasion to slip across by ones and twos. Question carefully any Elwynim you find, man or woman, and treat them kindly. But be wary. Limit what they can see here. If you get the chance, learn where Cuthan has gone, whether he joined Tasmôrden, and doing what; and what the situation is in Ilefínian, and what kind of force Tasmôrden has. All that manner of thing."

And after their small gathering dispersed to their beds, "Captain," Tristen lingered to say.

"Your Grace." Anwyll's shoulders were at once drawn up, wariness as quick as an indrawn breath.

"The highroad passes by Henas'amef on its way to Guelessar," Tristen said. "Don't send Idrys dispatches by the riverside. There's no gain in speed and a great risk to the couriers."

"I assure Your Grace . . . there is no disloyalty . . ."

"I know there is not, sir, and I regard Idrys as a friend. He's an honest man, as I know you are, and I know you are his man. Send to him what you will, with my goodwill. I ask only your courier gather messages from me as well, so we need not have two men risking life and limb on the roads in bad weather."

Anwyll showed himself overwhelmed, and if manners had allowed it would surely have sat down. "Your Grace, I have never reported anything against you."

"Yet have reported to Idrys."

"Yes, Your Grace."

"I know you have your own orders. The Dragon Guard is mine only for the season. You should know Uwen has sent home certain of the Guelen Guard, men who wished to be released. I've had him take command himself, for the while, until I can muster a force to defend the province."

"Which officers were dismissed, if Your Grace please to say?"

"The captain and the senior sergeant, both, and certain of the other officers whose names I did not inquire." He found himself on the edge of his knowledge of what, as duke of Amefel, he could order; and had ordered, by those senses of danger which sometimes ruled his actions. Nothing had Unfolded to him in so doing except the small, steady unfurling of logical steps: take command, hold command, shape it until it fit the hand and the man that must lead it. "I said to the Lord Commander that Uwen Lewen's-son would be my captain. So he is. And the garrison is what is his to command, since king Cefwyn set me over it."

"The Lord Commander so advised me," Anwyll said, with a resolute look. "And I am to command the Dragons, over which I am instructed Your Grace has *no* authority."

That was Idrys' caution, which far from offending, had a warm and familiar feeling. He smiled, hearing it.

"Fair," he said. "Yet you came here."

"I'm instructed to obey reasonable orders, in the king's interest."

"And will you name officers for the Guelens? Uwen gave me a list. He says he can't appoint new officers, but you can. Who do you think is the best man?"

"Wynned."

"Will return when his mother mends, which I wish she does soon. He seems a good man."

"A wall in Bryn's lands and a guard captain dismissed. Your Grace, I had as lief not become adviser to this. And I will send to the Lord Commander, I advise you so."

"Idrys wishes me to do what keeps the king safe . . . have this province strong and ready, and not to admit a flood of Tasmôrden's men or to have Her Grace's men slaughtered against the river." It was very clear to him, clearer than all the debates they had had in councils before this, now that he had seen this place by the river, and that identical, snowy shore. "Did you approve the Guelens' officers, the things they did?"

"No, Your Grace, I didn't, nor do. If they were my command, they'd be set down."

He became aware, though how he was not himself sure, that the captain thought himself superior to the Guelen officers, and well he might: it was the truth. But Anwyll was wellborn, and Uwen was always daunted and quiet when Anwyll was about, falling back on his claim he was a common man.

And that was also behind his decision to send Anwyll to the river, that there was a certain reluctance in the man to deal with Amefin, Teranthines, Bryaltines, common sergeants, or peasants. It seemed a fault in him, one hard to lay hands on or to catch with the eye.

As now, Anwyll was sure he would have dealt differently with the Guelens, yet would likely defend them against any charge laid against them in the town.

He gazed at Anwyll, and Anwyll seemed entirely disquieted.

"What they've done was wicked," Tristen said. "I don't quite know all that the Quinalt means by wicked, but to kill prisoners was wicked. The men they led aren't bad soldiers, Uwen says so, and he should know, having been one."

Again that small hesitation, as if what Uwen said and Uwen thought was not, perhaps, what Anwyll thought.

"Wynedd is a good man," Anwyll said. "I have no trouble naming him. And Ennyn to hold as his second. I'll write out orders and place them in your hands."

Anwyll continued to be troubled, and wished he were not in Amefel. Tristen took that thought to his tent afterward.

"I've no doubt Anwyll will write to Idrys tonight," Tristen said when he joined Cevulirn in the soldiers' tent they had claimed for the night, all their guard sleeping the night in the mess tent which, against a shed now devoted to equipment, had a solid wall for a windbreak.

Cevulirn occupied his half of the tent, sitting on his pallet, their only light from the general fire outside.

"Should he not?" Cevulirn said.

"He should. But I mean so urgently he'll likely slip a rider out before morning, and I only hope he sends him by the Modeyneth road. He doesn't trust me, and I wish I could mend that. He doesn't quite trust Uwen, either, or doesn't think he should command the garrison, and to that I don't agree."

"You should have no illusions, Amefel: he is Guelen, wellborn, and Quinalt, and sees much that troubles him."

"He's Idrys' man, and I do trust Idrys."

That drew a silent, rare laughter from the gray lord of the Ivanim. "As I think Idrys trusts you, but beware of that trust of his."

"Why do you say so?"

Cevulirn, looking at him in the almost-dark and leaping light of the fire outside, was all shadows and surmise. "Because, lord of Amefel, Idrys *trusts* you on grounds of your honesty and your friendship for His Majesty, and if he ever doubts the friendship, or the honesty, or the gift Mauryl Kingsbane gave you, that trust will go with it. And you will never know at what moment. That's the difficulty of trusting loyal men."

"Why do you call him that?"

"Mauryl? Or Idrys?"

"Kingsbane. King*maker*, in the Red Chronicle."

"Bane to Elfwyn, at very least. Kingmaker, Kingbreaker. Words."

"Wizards' words mean things."

"That they do," said Cevulirn. "And so I say again, *Idrys* is aware what they called Mauryl Gestaurien, and he thinks on it daily, I do assure you, Amefel."

"I shall *never* betray Cefwyn."

"You," Cevulirn said, "are Mauryl Kingmaker's Shaping. And you are Lord Sihhë of the grateful Amefin. With the best will in the world toward Cefwyn, and all love, do you deny either?"

Perhaps it was a chill draft that wafted through the tent, but it was like Mauryl's questions. They sat in shadows, and shadows flowed all about them. He trembled when Cevulirn said that; and the trembling would not let him, for a long, long moment, utter any objection.

"I know your heart and your intent," Cevulirn said relentlessly, "and with the best will to His Majesty in the world, I *will* answer your summons this Wintertide, and bring the lords of the south with me. That, too, will trouble the good captain, beyond any news the two of us have brought him. But I don't trouble my sleep over the fact. Anwyll for all his good traits is a Guelenman to the least hair on his head. So I am Ivanim, and southron, and have blood of the Sihhë in my veins. And good Guelen will I never be, lord of Amefel, but a strong friend of His Majesty and friend to you, yes, I shall be.

For that matter, Idrys himself is southron, Anwyll's Guelen loyalty notwithstanding; a man, a Man, and not of the old blood, nor will he trust me or thee entirely, but trust *him*, I say, and write him often and keep him apprised of what you do. Above all His Majesty must not lose faith in the south, and just the same as that, neither must Idrys. There. Do I go too far?"

"No. No, sir, you do not."

He understood, both that he was right about Cevulirn, and that he was mapping a dangerous path through Guelen resentments. The northern barons wanted nothing more than to find a cause against him. They would not like the river camps, would far less like his breaching of the king's law to build the wall near Modeyneth.

Bring your men, he wished to say to Cevulirn, tonight, the two of them alone to hear, and plan. *Bring me the army, and we'll cross the river and bring aid to Ilefínian.*

But the words would not come. When it came to defying Cefwyn's direct order, he had a sudden vision of blood, of fire, and if he were not anchored by Cevulirn's still-waking presence and Cevulirn's next, unanswered question, he might have gone wandering to learn what he was almost certain of just now, a desperate, a sinking feeling.

"What's wrong?" Cevulirn.

"The gates," Tristen said, for he saw tall gates and fire and figures moving in the light.

"What gates?" Cevulirn asked, for there were none here.

Tristen drew a sharp breath, seeking the place where he was instead of the riot of fire and the clash of arms. "The gates have come open. At this very moment."

"Where?" Cevulirn asked. "Whose gates?"

"Ilefínian has fallen."

Cevulirn heard him in utter silence.

"We are too late to prevent it," Tristen said. "I don't know how I should know, or how I do know, but I think someone has opened the gates." He thought, more, that a breath of wizardry had pressed the situation, working quietly and for the merest instant flaring forth. He thought it the more strongly when he had formed the thought, and then flung a defense up in the gray space, strongly, strongly, nothing subtle.

Then the smothering feeling lifted.

"Now the birds will come," he said, thinking on Auld Syes. "That was what she foretold. We should send to Cefwyn ourselves. Tonight."

No question it must be one of Anwyll's men, to hope to get to Idrys.

"Your lordships?" Anwyll asked when they called on him, and he came, roused from bed and with a cloak clutched about him in the dim forechamber of his tent.

"Ilefínian has fallen," Tristen said, with Cevulirn at his back, and both of them determined.

"Did Your Grace receive a courier?" was Anwyll's reasonable question.

"No," Tristen said, "but I'm sure it's so. Deck the bridge."

"Your Grace—" Clearly Anwyll had had his wits shaken, and smoothed hair out of his eyes, trying to compose arguments. "You mean to let them across?"

"The ones to come first will be Her Grace's forces."

"His Grace thinks Tasmôrden's men are in the town," Cevulirn said, "and if that's so, devil a time holding them from the ale stores."

"Aye, my lord, I understand, but no messenger, as you say . . ."

"Disarm any soldiery," Tristen said, "and send them under escort to Modeyneth. He'll escort them to refuge. I need a rider to go to Guelemara, to His Majesty, to tell him."

"Word from the watchers on the river northward may get there first, Your Grace."

"And if something befalls the messengers, no word at all. There must be a messenger."

"Yes, Your Grace."

"For seven days leave the decking in place on the bridge. Then take it down again."

"Yes, Your Grace." Anwyll had the look of a man utterly confounded. "And what if the Elwynim come, the wrong Elwynim, and the bridge is decked?"

"You can hold them, Captain," was Cevulirn's short answer. "There's more than enough force here."

"Your Grace," Anwyll answered, passion rising. "We did not plan to stand with the bridge open! We need archers!"

"We'll have them here," Tristen said, "from Bryn."

"Amefin, Your Grace."

"This *is* Amefel," Cevulirn said. "Amefin are in good supply here."

"Your Grace." Whatever Anwyll had been about to say he thought better of, and collected himself. "I'll have you a rider immediately, Your Grace."

Tristen penned a letter in haste and gave it to Anwyll's messenger. Anwyll added another dispatch, and the rider left. There was little to do then but return to beds and rest what of the night remained, he and Cevulirn, in quiet converse for the better part of two hours into the dark, coming to no conclusion but that they must set a force here sufficient to hold, and that archers and a muster of Bryn to the wall-building and the defense of the bridge was inevitable.

And if Elwynim arrived who had a disposition to fight their war on Amefin soil, there was a hard choice, separating the two sides and being sure, as Cevulirn said, that the ones they might let abide in Amefel accepted the authority in Henas'amef.

"I'd hoped still a small force might have reached through and broken the siege," Tristen said in the shadowed dark, all the troubling visions roiling and leaping in the firelight that came through the flap. "But that won't happen now. Now it's Cefwyn's war, the sort he wanted."

"I'll post my guard here," Cevulirn said. "It's the only reasonable choice. A handful, but the best. They can use the bows."

"I thank you," Tristen said into the dark, having no idea else where he could lay hands on more troops this side of Assurnbrook, besides the troubled Guelens. And for a moment the small glow that was Cevulirn in the gray space was a greater one, and the bond of wizard-craft touched one and two out in the camp, smaller lights, but true.

Then, quietly, secret in the deep of night, Tristen set himself to wish such fugitives well and guide them to the river.

And he began to wish snow about Ilefínian, thick, blanketing snow, not so far as the river, where fugitives might strive to cross, but all about the sack of the town, a white blanket to cover the ugliness of death and fire and wounds.

A pure and pristine white, to cool angers, drive men indoors, and give Tasmôrden an enemy that would not yield to the sword.

He did so, and it seemed he was not quite alone in his effort, that in utter silence something in Cevulirn answered, and something in Henas'amef reached out to him, and something in the tower there waked and listened.

Ilefínian is fallen, was the burden of the night. And on the road, two riders, Anwyll's, and the one Anwyll had sent for them, on to Modeyneth, to Henas'amef, and to Guelessar.

CHAPTER 4

&\infty&

In the morning was time enough to discuss explicit orders with Captain Anwyll, who had heard the news in the middle of the night with doubt and anger.

But Anwyll had not failed his instructions, and had ordered the bridge decking restored at first light. His men, the elite Dragon Guard, accustomed to clean quarters and the finest fare, swore and struggled and pressed into service the oxen that should this very day have been moving the long-purloined carts back to Guelessar. The drivers were angry, and protested, and were pressed into service, handling the oxen, so Anwyll reported. Where there was not snow and ice, there was mud.

The drivers would be angrier yet to hear they needed remain to take the decking off in another sevenday, Tristen was well sure. They would need the oxen for that, and the carts would not move.

That the Ivanim guard, who were fair shots with a bow, would also remain until the bridge was closed and undecked again, however, improved Anwyll's mood marvelously.

And that Cevulirn's lieutenant would remain to lead those men heartened Anwyll even more so, for by that establishment of another senior officer, not all the burden of decision and judgment was on him. Cevulirn's lieutenant was veteran of numerous independent actions, as Anwyll was not; he was brisk, decisive, and confident, as Anwyll was not; and he was capable of distinguishing one band of Elwynim from another, as Anwyll was not, which made Tristen easier in his mind.

Since the Ivanim lieutenant had set to work, in fact, there was already a different sense of order, men and horses rapidly establishing a more permanent camp with no resources to begin with and abundant resource within an hour, and the Ivanim seemingly everywhere at once, considering winter stabling and timbers they might use for the purpose, if the weather worsened over their week. They accomplished wonders of organization before the morning fires had produced water hot enough for porridge, and by then Anwyll was in far better humor.

So with farewells to Cevulirn's men, and setting out by a good hour with only Tristen's small Guelenish guard force and bodyguard around them, they put the river at their backs in short order.

They kept the horses not to a courier's pace, for their armor and arms and heavy saddles were too much weight on the horses for that kind of riding. But all the same they pressed hard, and reached the ruined wall near Modeyneth at midafternoon, where the area around the old wall and towers already showed signs of clearing, timbers cut, fallen stone swept clean of snow.

The new earl himself was overseeing bands of workers in the brushy woods that had grown up about the old stones.

"My lords!" it was, when Drusenan saw them; and then a more sober reckoning when he saw how they came, without their guards.

"Grave news," Cevulirn said, and reported what they knew, regarding Elwynor and Ilefínian.

"Captain Anwyll of the Dragon Guard will deliver any fugitives to you, and he may ask you to raise a local muster," Tristen said. He was keenly aware how great a burden he had put on a new man, one time experienced in battle, yes, and a dreadful battle, but not having directed anything more than a village levy on the march. "I'll ask Lord Drumman to move to your assistance, with carts and oxen, as soon as I reach Henas'amef. I need all the oxen I have at the river. Above all, be very certain whoever you set at Althalen bears no weapons. Collect them if you find them. I'll have none of the war there brought here."

"My lord," Drusenan said in great earnest. "All that you wish, I'll do. Let me get my horse, and I'll ride with you to the village."

"No stopping tonight," Tristen said, but the reason of their overwhelming haste, that would send Cevulirn riding hard for the south, he did not confess even to this well-disposed and honest man. Rumors enough were likely to fly and would fly, no few of them to the Elwynim, and whence next, there was no limit of possibilities.

All the same Lord Drusenan rode with them as far as Modeyneth and some beyond, after a welcome cup of mulled wine and a breath for the horses.

"I've already sent out word to the villages," Lord Drusenan reported to them, "and told them the state of affairs in Bryn, and our charge from Your Grace, as I'm sure they'll come to help."

"You have Bryn's town resources to draw from," Tristen said, "and no few men there, with its treasury: I didn't let it go. I'll send what I can with Lord Drumman. And horses, which Anwyll may need, if you'll send them on in good order."

Another man, Tristen thought, might have sped straight for the town and the court and bought himself fine clothes, but Lord Drusenan had not even delayed for a ceremony, owning his modest swearing as binding on him as any in the great hall. He had gone to the wall to clear brush and snow from about the fallen stones and plied an axe until his hands were blistered. His lady, Ynesynë, had set up great kettles in the center of the village, expecting, she said, a hundred men from surrounding villages to come to the work. She had made provision for them to lodge in the stable and in the hall and wherever the village houses could find a little room.

Besides that, the village wives were packing the village's sole horse cart with supply for the fugitives in the ruins, while two of the local men had gone ahead with axes, so Drusenan had reported, to prepare shelters and firewood, and added, as everyone did, if only the weather held good.

It should, it must, it would, unless some wizard opposed him; and he might meet that challenge and hold it, too.

"I wish the snow will fall north of us," Tristen said, with great insistence in his heart, for all the while he and Cevulirn had ridden since dawn, he had held that determination, for whatever force it had, and now he was sure it would.

He wished health and good fortune on the village; and also on Syes' sparrows, traveling by now afoot to the ruins at Althalen, where other men of the village would guide them.

"And excuse Anwyll," he said. "He's a good man. He has a better heart than one might think. No one of Meiden would have survived at Henas'amef, if not for him coming to advise me what Parsynan was up to. Meiden owes him their lives."

"I take your advisement, my lord, and will remember."

But the new lord of Bryn, understanding their haste to reach Henas'amef by dark, few as they were, had no inclination to delay in debate, only offered himself and two of his young men to add to the guard they had.

"You've enough to do," Tristen said, as they were getting to horse, "and I fear nothing from bandits. See to the wall, that's what I most wish."

"See the young men exercised in arms as well as building," Cevulirn advised Drusenan, too. "If there's any place Elwynor might attack early and hard, it's this road, and that bridge, with the wall building. Tasmôrden won't like the look of that at all, and won't like the rumors out of the south of a strong rule here."

Amefel, which had used to be the softest approach to Ylesuin, was shored up with stone and soon to be edged with steel and muscled with horses and Ivanim cavalry. And that, Tristen thought, served Cefwyn better than carts and a company of the Dragons.

They made speed homeward bound after Modeyneth, camped but briefly and late, and that more for the sake of the horses that carried them, were on their way again at the first light of a clear, bright dawn, and laid their specific plans on the way, for the guard they had closest to them were trusted men. Cevulirn would write to the other lords, and surmised what force and support they might look for from each . . . Midwinter Day was the day they set for the lords and their escorts to gather at Henas'amef, a festive day, a time when friends gathered and saw in the new year—could the Quinalt fault a gathering of friends, be they lords with numerous men in their escort? The lords who had fought in Amefel this summer past would gather to give thanks, to share the feast, no less than peasants did around their year-fires, and noble families across the land.

That they might lay their plans then, that, their enemies would know.

But their coming depended on the will of the lords . . . and on what the weather might hold.

And the latter, Tristen thought, might lie within his hands. But while he might wish the snow away from them, or a moderation in the weather, he was far from certain he could manage something on the scale of hastening a season.

Yet wish he did. They had a great deal to accomplish, and instead of a long time to Midwinter, they found the days until Midwinter a very short time for them to bring together all they wished . . . for what they wished and planned was to have a force capable of striking through to Ilefínian and threatening the rebels' gains.

If they could do no more than embarrass Tasmôrden and make him look the fool, that would raise hopes of defying him, and raise men in support of Ninévrisë's claim . . . and that would also support Cefwyn's heavy cavalry and strong force coming from the east . . . for Cefwyn's reliance on heavy horse with the roads uncertain as they were alarmed him. Every sense he had of warfare, every sense he gained from the maps said that there was a reason Selwyn Marhanen had not pressed into Elwynor from the east, where roads were not up to Guelen standards, where brush was thick along the roads . . . he had never been there, but he was sure that was the nature of the land, as sure as if he had seen it, and anything he could do to the south to distract Tasmôrden onto two fronts eased his fears for Cefwyn.

"So the king and the north will have the victory and Murandys may look a valiant soldier," Cevulirn said in a tone of derision. "Let him, only so we have free rein here, and can raise an army out of the stones of Elwynor."

"If only Umanon will join us," Tristen said, for Umanon was the chanciest of their former allies, a heavy horse contingent, in itself, but a valuable one, with their light horse to probe the way. More, Pelumer of Lanfarnesse was not certain, especially if Umanon should hold back. Pelumer, Cefwyn had said, managed to be late to every fight, and they feared he would manage to be late to this one.

"But Sovrag will come," Tristen said. "I do rely on him."

"The man was a river pirate," Cevulirn said, "and the Marhanens ennobled him and granted him the district he holds because that rock of a fortress of his was too much trouble to take. *And* they needed his boats. As we do."

"Yet he's an honest man."

"An honest thief, nowadays. A reformed thief. Which turned the Olmernmen," Cevulirn added, "from brigandage against my lands and Umanon's toward occasional brigandage in the southern kingdoms, a great improvement for us, if it brings us no angry retribution. That in itself was a wonder. More than that, they've even planted small fields. That we never thought to see. I confess I like the man better now than two years ago. And he's learned things from being in Amefel. He's seen how farmerfolk live fairly well on the land. And he's learned how to sit a horse, if it's old and docile."

"What do you say of Pelumer?" Tristen asked, intrigued by Cevulirn's reckoning of the brigand lord, whom he did understand. Pelumer, however, blew both hot and cold, to his observation.

"Hard to catch," Cevulirn said of Pelumer. "Both

the rangers of Lanfarnesse *and* their lord. Apt to take the cautious view, apt not to risk his men. Late to every battle. Yet no coward."

Pelumer's light-armed forces were better suited to moving in small bands among the trees, skills of little use in a pitched battle, as Cefwyn had tried to use them. In some measure he did not blame Pelumer for his reluctance to throw them onto the field: for all Cefwyn's virtues of courage, he had a hardheadedness about the way to win a battle, which was a great deal of force moving irresistibly forward. Pelumer did not like the notion . . . nor, he found, did he, and he feared for Cefwyn, locking in that reliance on the Guelen forces.

Of Umanon of Imor Lenúalim, canny and Guelen and Quinalt, unlike all the rest of the southrons, he had the most doubt. He was the most like Cefwyn in some regards, but independent and interested primarily in his own province. "And Umanon?" he asked. "Will he agree with us, or with Ryssand?"

"He detests Corswyndam. And since Lewenbrook, he despises Sulriggan." This was the lord of Ryssand, and the lord of Llymaryn, two of the principal forces in the north. "He's capable of surprises. And he's more a southerner where his alliances and his purse are concerned. Nor is he that much enamored of the northern orthodoxy."

"The Quinaltines?"

"The doctrinists among the Quinaltines. A handful of troublesome priests, clustered around the northlands, some in Murandys, strict readers of the book and strict in interpretation . . . neither here nor there for you or me, here in the south. But it's a reason Umanon doesn't stand with Ryssand and Murandys. He detests the priests that espouse it, since the orthodoxy, mark you, faults Umanon's birth."

"How might they do that?"

"Oh, that Umanon's mother and her folk are Teranthines, and stiff in their faith as Umanon is in his. He won't condemn his mother and his aunt and her house, nor his cousins, who are wealthy men and the owners of a great deal of the grainfields that are Imor's wealth: he trades grain for northern cattle and the cattle for southern gold, to the seafarers, down the Lenúalim. His dukedom may be Guelen and Quinalt as you please, but the Teranthines are best at dealing with foreign folk and best at trade. They fear nothing, accept the most outrageous of foreign ways."

"And wizards? They accept them."

"Look at Emuin."

"Are there wizards in the wild lands south?" He had never read so.

"Assuredly. Perhaps even fugitive remnants of the Sihhë. We Ivanim trade along the border in silk and horses, with the Chomaggari, and farther still. And a modicum of wizardry has never troubled us."

"You yourself have some gift," Tristen observed with deliberate bluntness, and Cevulirn regarded him with a sidelong glance. "You use it. You used it during the business at Modeyneth. I think you know you have it."

"Our house is admittedly fey," said Cevulirn, "and I confess it, to one I think will never betray that confidence. We aren't wizards. But the gift for it is there."

"Between the two of us," Tristen said, "we might have no need of signal fires. I think you would hear me even in Toj Embrel."

Cevulirn regarded him a long few moments in silence, and the gray space seethed with Cevulirn's strong forbidding.

"I will not," Cevulirn said, "not unless at great need. I have trusted you, Amefel, as never I have trusted, outside Ivanor. And so if you need me, call by any means you can."

"I think that I did call you," Tristen said after a moment of thought on that point, "though not by intent and not by name. I needed an adviser, and here you are. And you'll come back, that I believe, too." It was in his mind that even his own wish might not be all the reason for Cevulirn's coming to him, for there were many wizards, Emuin had said, wizards living and dead, their threads crossed and woven, and hard to say which juncture mattered most to the fabric.

Wizardous elements came together in his vicinity, gathered by common purpose, common loyalties, common necessity . . . Emuin in his tower, he and Cevulirn; Crissand and Paisi; Ninévrisë in Guelemara and Uleman in his grave at Althalen.

Not discounting Mauryl . . . or Hasufin, though both were dispelled.

We are all here, Tristen thought to himself.

And all through the journey the sky stayed brilliant blue and the land gleaming white, except to the north, where clouds gathered dark and troubled, and pregnant with winter.

The sun was low when their reduced band drew in sight of Henas'amef, and it was a welcome sight, with lights beginning to show, peaceful and familiar with its skirt of snowy fields. A curiously warm feeling, Tristen thought, and how many faces it had, in summer, in winter, by day and by twilight.

Most of all he felt a warm expectation when he saw the Zeide's tower and knew that a friend lived there, and other friends waited for him and that his own bed was in that upper floor, and that Uwen would welcome him, and Tassand, and all the ones who cared for him. They would do thus, and thus, he imagined, weary of body but happy in the anticipation. All the comforts of his household would fold him in and care for him, knowing him as he knew them. Crissand might be back, might well be back, from his riding out. They would talk, sitting comfortably by the fire.

This was homecoming, he said to himself, a homecoming such as ordinary Men felt, a touch of things remembered and familiar after days of difficulty and strange faces and cold fingers and toes, of chancy food and watching sharply the movements of men he did not know.

They rode through the streets to the easy greetings of craftsmen, with the tolling of the bell at the gate to advise all the town and the height of the hill that the lord of Amefel had come back.

They had come back with far fewer Ivanim than before, it might be, but home safe and sound, all the same, and likely to the gossip and interest of every townsmen that beheld them and the banners.

Where are the Ivanim? they might ask among themselves, and, Was there fighting? But they would see no signs of battle about them, and they would ask until the answer flowed downhill from those in a position to know.

Best of all was Uwen waiting in the stable-court when they had come in under the portcullis of the West Gate . . . to do no more than change horses in Cevulirn's case, as Cevulirn had purposed to ride on even tonight. Master Haman would provide the lord of the Ivanim with horses, and Cevulirn would take a small, reliable escort of the best of the Guelen Guard as far as his hall in the south, at Toj Embrel.

So Tristen ordered.

"He's left his own men at the river with Anwyll," he added, speaking to Uwen on the matter. "He'll camp on the road, and we can surely provide him all he needs going home."

"Aye, m'lord," was Uwen's response to the request, and he rattled off names and sent a boy smartly after horses. Just as quickly he sent a soldier after the men he wanted for the escort, naming them by name almost in one breath.

So the yard broke into great and cheerful confusion, Haman's lads bringing out horses and gear, and assisting Lord Cevulirn, who saw to his own pair of grays, and who had precise requests for their feeding and watering, for he would take them on home with him, never parted from those horses.

But Uwen said, to Tristen alone and with a grim face, "M'lord, I ain't done well, I suspect. His Reverence took off, an' I couldn't stop 'im."

"Left?" Tristen asked in dismay. "His Reverence left Henas'amef? For Guelessar?"

"The hour you had the town at your back," was Uwen's answer. "He ain't no great rider, but I give him one of the men to see to 'im. I didn't know what else to do."

CHAPTER 5

Efanor's letter had gone out. No answer as yet had had time to come back. There was only, for Cefwyn, the mingled dread of Efanor's game and the delicious thought of Ryssand's consternation—since Efanor had written in the same letter that he meant to announce the engagement at some unspecified time, unprecedented breach of mourning for the Lady Artisane, and worse, far worse for the lady's reputation, if a royal match once announced were for any reason mysteriously broken off. Dared one suspect the lady's virtue? Artisane had escaped Ninévrisë's banishment by her immediate flight into mourning, and now dared she cast herself back into the affairs of the court, and expect immunity? Ryssand had a great deal to worry about.

He knew, and Efanor knew, that the betrothal Efanor pretended to accept would be lengthy in arrangement, fragile in character, and consummated in marriage only, *only* in the successful conclusion of the Elwynim war and in a moment of advantage: Cefwyn was still unconvinced that the house of the Marhanens could or should weave itself into Ryssand's serpentine coils.

And if the news of a royal betrothal should get abroad, it might somewhat steal the fire from Luriel's highly visible betrothal and hasty Midwinter marriage . . . that also would be regrettable if it happened. But if it set the formidable Luriel at Artisane's throat, so much the better.

That Lord Murandys wished audience with His Majesty in light of all this was no surprise at all, since the spies that lurked thick as icicles on the eaves had surely noticed this uncommon exchange of messages from both sides and might even have gotten wind of the content. Luriel's uncle Murandys danced uncertainly these days between the hope of his own advantage in Luriel's sudden amity with the Royal Consort and the king, on the one hand . . . and the more workaday hope of maintaining an alliance much as it had been with his old ally Ryssand. Ryssand was generally the planner and the schemer, having the keener wit by far . . . and Prichwarrin, who was not quite that clever, must feel very much on his own these days, very much prey to others' gossip and vulnerable to the schemes of all those he had offended, a list so long he might not even remember all the possible offenses.

Now to have any exchange in progress between the royal house and Ryssand in which he was not a participant must necessarily make him very, very anxious.

To be refused audience with the king must make him even more so. In fact, Prichwarrin must be fairly frothing in his uninformed isolation.

But Cefwyn was not at all sorry. He stood at the frosty, half-fogged window nearest his desk in a rare moment of tranquillity, a silence in his day, in fact, which his rejection of Prichwarrin's approach had gained him. He contemplated with somewhat more equanimity the general audience in the offing . . . there were judicial cases, among others waiting his attention, one appeal for royal clemency, which he was in a mood to extend: he'd spared greater thieves and worse blackguards than some serving-maid who'd stolen a few measures of flour.

Mostly, in this stolen moment of privacy, he watched the pigeons on the adjacent ledge.

Dared he think they were Tristen's few spies, remaining in Guelessar? Most of the offending birds had gone, miraculously, the very day Tristen left, and the Quinalt steps were sadly pure. He wished the birds back again, with their master, and wished with all the force of a man whose wishes only came true when Tristen willed it . . . useful talent, that.

No Emuin, no Tristen. His life was far easier without them drawing the lightning down, literally, on the rooftops. But it was far lonelier. He deluded himself that he had time on his hands, even that he could find the time to take to riding again, with Tristen, with Idrys . . . oh, not to hunt the deer: Tristen would be appalled. No, they would ride out simply to see the winter and to hear what Tristen would say of it, how he would wonder at things Men simply failed to look at, past their childhoods.

But, oh, how precious those things were! To look at the sky, breathe the cold wind, have fingers nipped by chill and skin stung red and heart stirred to life, gods, he had been dead until Tristen arrived and asked him the first vexing question, and posed him the first insoluble puzzle, and marveled at hailstones and mourned over falling leaves. What miracles there were all around, when Tristen was beside him . . . and damn Ryssand! that he had had no choice.

He had Tristen's letter. Gods damn Ryssand, gods bless Tristen, he had good news out of Amefel . . . and Ryssand dared make only small and cautious moves, a man on precarious ground.

Likewise precarious, atop the snowy roofing slates on a pitch the height of four ordinary houses, small, dogged figures had heaved up ladders across from the royal windows and tied scaffoldings aslant the steep, icy slope of the Quinalt roof, attempting to mend the lightning stroke that had assaulted the gods' home on earth.

Carts moved below, bringing timbers . . . carts which might well serve getting supply to the troops, except His Holiness owned these few, and guarded them jealously.

Odd, how avariciously he had begun to look at such mundane things. The carts Tristen had still not returned to him might not come back at all if the weather set in hard, and gods knew what Tristen thought he was doing with them.

Not moving Parsynan's belongings back to Guelessar, that was clear.

But being a resourceful king and understanding that trying to keep Tristen to a predictable, even a sensible course was like chasing water uphill, he had found ways, and with carts such as he could lay hands on, even those of the minor houses of Guelemara and the trades, he had moved men in greater numbers to the river bridges, using his personal guard and the Guelen Guard, men of Guelessar, not yet calling on the provinces for their levies.

He was merely setting the stage, putting necessary elements in place . . . keeping a watch on the river the while.

The weather had been surprisingly good, clouds dark to the west during the last two days, darkness over Elwynor, and fat gray-bottomed clouds speeding for the second frantic day across the skies of Guelessar, failing to drop snow or even to shade the sun. The whole season had been warmer than usual . . . and late as it was, and despite a few evening and morning snowfalls, winter had not set in hard this side of the river. He, who had learned to count wizards among the possible causes, looked at the situation in the west and wondered how much of the good weather was natural.

It was natural, however, that unseasonable warmth,

otherwise pleasant, produced its own miseries . . . for blight had entered a set of granaries in Nelefreissan, royal stores he had planned for support of the army. Mice were fat and prosperous, mites afflicted the mews and the poultry yard alike, fleas had become the kennelmaster's bane and, worst of all, had spread to the barracks, where they were execrated but not exorcised . . . remedies of burning sulfur and priests' blessings had done far less for the men's relief than a wizard might have done, Cefwyn was sure of it, and he perversely hoped that fleas afflicted all the pious, good Quinaltines who had contributed to Tristen's and Emuin's exile this winter.

If Emuin were here, there would not be fleas, and he had remarked that to the clerks and officers, failing to add, if Tristen were here, since wizardry in Emuin was faintly respectable, but wizardry in Tristen reminded everyone why Tristen and Emuin were *not* here this winter.

Meanwhile Annas, scandalized and fearing the spread of the vermin, drove the household harder than their habit, and wanted afflicted premises scrubbed to the walls.

Mixed blessings indeed. No one had seen such a mild winter, wherein stores of wood were far in excess of current need and ice stayed off the small ponds, to farmers' relief: no need to go out with axes to enable livestock to drink and no need yet to keep cattle close in byres. Autumn had stayed late, and later. There remained the chance, still, of the howling gray blast that would freeze all in a night and obscure the sun for days, but it had not happened yet . . . leaving them just snow enough to drive the vermin indoors, and the damned fleas with them, such was his own theory . . . not mentioning the notion of hostile wizardry and ill wishes from across the river, without a wizard left this side of the river.

Damned defenseless, Ryssand's quarrel had left them, and not alone to the fleas. If there was worse than vermin, if those scudding clouds heralded some wizardous storm in the making, they might well regret the actions that had sent all the wizards south.

All but one. *Ninévrisë* had the wizard-gift. He had neglected her in his reckoning. Perhaps, he thought with a wry laugh, perhaps he should appeal to his bride to attempt the banishment of mice. Perhaps the court might forgive her her small flaw, for that benefit.

But it was not a matter for jest, the small gift she had, and that he knew she had. More, and far more serious a matter, all the officers who had come back from Lewenbrook knew there was wizardry in the house of Syrillas and that it had not failed in the daughter. But Quinalt roof slates, mice, and fleas and all be damned, he was not about to prompt them to gossip it to the Quinaltine, who doubtless had heard already.

All the veterans, therefore, kept their counsel, even in the taverns seldom admitting there had been mani-festations at Lewenbrook and since, oh, nothing of the sort. One would have thought they had fought on some other field, to hear how it was this company or that which had driven back the enemy and cast their ranks in confusion.

Pigeons now battled for narrow space on the ledge, buffeted one another with gray wings. The losers wheeled away and lit in another patch of snow, unruly, disrespectful of each other, now their master was in exile.

So much odd had happened in those days the living witnesses knew not who had been responsible, or even what they had seen. The apparitions of dead men, the strange lights, the darkness by day . . . memories of that day shifted and changed like oil on water, so that none of them who had been there quite remembered all of it . . . nor truly wished to. Men pushed and shoved one another for position, but none of them acknowledged the battles of wizards.

He gave a small shiver, finding his hand chilled to ice by the glass. He drew back his fingers, folded them into a fist to warm them, finding his memories not so pleasant after all. For the pigeons, the silly, gray-coated pigeons, he was tempted to send for bread and take them under royal patronage for Tristen's sake, never mind what the court would say. It would be simple kindness to poor, dumb things.

But gossip . . . gossip would pick it up, saying the damned birds *were* messengers, wizardous in behavior, suspecting them of eavesdropping, gods knew. He could not harbor pigeons without the town imagining darkest sorcery.

In fact, as of yesterday and Efanor's message, he had emerged from the haze of recent matrimony and the confusion of Ryssand's attempt to prevent it, suddenly to realize he and Ninévrisë were whole, but that very dangerous things had happened around them . . . to realize, too, that those they relied on, like Idrys, had only been marking time, waiting for them to face the world at large and realize how few their numbers had grown to be.

So they did, now missing the absent faces, the voices, the counsel of those who should have shared their new life. Gaining each other, gaining a union that should make all the world the richer, they had lost what they most treasured, and might never see the court come back to what it had been. The reports he had out of Amefel spoke alarmingly of rebellion crushed and decisive actions taken . . . all well within Tristen's ability, if they challenged him.

But that side of him was dire and frightening: it had

shown itself at Emwy, and at Lewenbrook, not the gentle mooncalf, his defender of pigeons and his friend who marveled at a sunbeam . . . but the soldier, the revenant, whose martial skill spoke of another life, one long, long past.

Parsynan was at someone's ear, up in Ryssand, but he had passed through the midlands to get there. The Quinalt consequently was busy as the kennel fleas, at this lord's ear and at that one's, complaining of wizardry and heresy on the borders, of a populace that hailed Tristen their Lord Sihhë and raised forbidden emblems.

Silence it, he had said to the Patriarch yesterday, with no patience whatever. I need Amefel steady and peaceful, and however Tristen obtains it, well and good.

That last he had found himself adding as if he had to justify his order, as if some *value* for Tristen should make a difference to the Holy Father.

He wished peevishly he had not been so weak as to add that argument, wished that he had his grandfather's gift for stopping argument short of justifying himself.

If he were his grandfather he would have said, "The king's friend is the king's friend and whoever slights him will have me for an enemy. Damn the lot of you anyway."

Tristen's message, precious as it was, had stated in amazingly few words the overturn of all he had arranged in Amefel. He had feared Tristen might prove such a sparse letter writer. Master Emuin had his tower back. A lord of ancient lineage had suffered exile.

Tristen had exiled an Amefin earl. The lamb had assaulted the lion.

And let the rest of them, from Henas'amef to

Lanfarnesse, beware their sedition and their scheming, these rebel southrons who had never yet been willing to recognize a Marhanen king. With that gray-glass stare and a question or two, Tristen could assail their very souls, snare them, entrap them in a spell of liking that had no cure . . . he could attest to that, for he missed sorely the man who had done all this to him.

He had sent his own messenger to Tristen, and another to Cevulirn, asking after their health, professing his gratitude . . . asking after his carts, in Tristen's case, and hinting at a readiness to march in Cevulirn's. He had a province of Amefel rescued from rebellion due to Tristen's quick action; he had the Amefin people cheering his choice and not throwing rocks at his troops, which was also worth gratitude . . . if it were only a little less fraught with rebel Bryaltine sentiment for vanished kings.

All these things he had said, in letters to his two dearest friends, and realized thus far, muddleheaded with courtship and marriage, he had been very fortunate until this day simply to have had no disasters.

And as for Tristen, Tristen, whom wizard-work had raised or Shaped or whatever wizards minced up for words . . . there was no safer place to put him. Mauryl Kingmaker had sent them a gift thus double-edged, a soul who might be Barrakkêth incarnate.

And the Elwynim had long prophesied their King To Come, thinking some surviving one of halfling Elfwyn's sons might creep out of the bushes and byways to proclaim his thread of Sihhë blood and claim the crown of the old High Kings.

It was, after all, safest that he had himself fulfilled all the prophecies he could lay hands on, naming Tristen lord not only of Ynefel, to which he most probably had right, but to Althalen, and to heretic Amefel, where they might proclaim him lord of most anything in relative quiet. The Teranthines could embrace such heresy. He . . . even . . . could bear with a neighboring king, even a High King, did Tristen somehow stray into power.

Dared he, however, could he, should he . . . ever mention such thoughts to a bride he hoped would remain on this side of the river, in his realm, a peaceful, not a reigning, wife? Among all the preparations he had laid, the moving of troops, the marshaling of aid in council, the hammering-out of titles to bestow on Ninévrisë Syrillas, and this cursed business of priests, sodden or sober . . . dared he even think the thoughts when he had a bride so gifted as Tristen hinted she was, who might pluck his guilty imaginings out of the very air? He was a king. It was his fate, his duty, to make as much as he could favorable to himself, and therefore to his people.

Pigeons flew up of a sudden, battering each other with their wings at a movement, a sound. The door had opened, and a messenger had come in, and two of his ordinary guards, and Ninévrisë, she . . . white and frightened, carrying her skirts as if she had been running, all this in a trailing attendance of two anxious maids, Cleisynde and Odrinian, both Murandys' kin. The man in a Guelen Guard's colors was still mud-flecked from a hard ride, had wiped smears of it across his freckled young face, and looked exhausted and dazed.

"Your Majesty," the young man had gotten out, before Idrys, too, arrived with his own aide in close attendance, and the young man looked around to see.

Disaster, and he and Ninévrisë alike could guess from what source. This young officer had come from downstairs, from the stable-court, from the road, from hard riding, and he was Lord Maudyn's man, a messenger from his commander at the river.

"Your Majesty," the courier said in a breath, "Ilefínian has fallen."

Cleisynde was first at Ninévrisë's elbow, of all the women, the cousins from Murandys, who poised their cupped hands under Ninévrisë's arms, awaiting a fall, an outburst.

There was none. There were not even tears, only the evident pain.

Not an unexpected blow, Cefwyn thought, nor was it; but, black weather over there notwithstanding, Tasmôrden had carried the siege to the end, meaning the death of Ninévrisë's loyal folk in the capital, her childhood friends, her supporters, her kin, cousins, remote to the least degree, all, all doomed and done in a stroke.

And yet she stood pale and composed, a queen in dignity and in sharp sense of the immediate needs. "When and how?" she asked the messenger.

"My lord had no word yet," the man said anxiously, certainly knowing who Ninévrisë might be, but still caught, damn him, in a gap of stiff Guelen protocol that turned the messenger to him. "Your Majesty, I took horse as soon as the fires were lit. My Lord Maudyn will send to you with each new report he receives, but at the time I left, we knew nothing but the signal fires."

It was tormenting news, disaster, and yet nothing of substance to grasp, no word whether the town was afire or whether there was an arranged surrender, or what the fate of the defenders and the nobles there might be.

"Rest for the messenger," Cefwyn said. He had his standard of what ought to be provided for men and horses that bore the king's messages, and his pages knew what to do for any such man. "Fetch Annas."

"Your Majesty," it was, and: "Yes, Your Majesty,"

and all the world near him moved to comply; but nothing in his power could provide his lady better news, and what use then was it, but the ordering of armies that could bring her no better result?

"We knew it would come," was all he found to say to her, with a stone weighing in the pit of his own stomach.

"We knew it would come," she agreed, and turned and quietly dismissed her maids on her own authority. "See to the messenger yourselves," she bade them, "in my name. And tell Dame Margolis."

In *tell Dame Margolis* was every order that needed be made in Ninévrisë's court . . . as *fetch Annas* summed up all his staff could do. The news would make the transit to the court at large, the comfort of courtiers and true servants would wrap them about with such sympathy as courtiers and lifelong servants could offer. At least the gossip that spread would have the solid heart of truth with those two in charge of dispersing it.

But the Regent of Elwynor would stand as straight and strong as the king of Ylesuin stood, and not be coddled or kissed on the brow by her husband, even before the Lord Commander.

"*Is* that all we know?" Cefwyn asked of Idrys as the door shut and by the maids' departure left them a more warlike, more forceful assembly.

"Unhappily, no more than the man told," Idrys said, "but more information is already on the road here, I'm well certain we can rely on Lord Maudyn for that. There's some comfort in what the message didn't say: no force near the river, no signal of wider war coming on us. The weather's been hard, by reports. Nothing will move down those roads to the bridges."

"Thank the gods Amefel *isn't* in revolt at the moment," Cefwyn said. "Well-done of Tristen. Well-done, at least on that frontier."

There was now urgent need, however, to move troops west, to the river, in greater numbers, and the transport was stalled in Amefel.

And to Amefel, the thought came to him, the fugitives of Ilefínian were very likely to come, unsettling that province and appealing to the softest heart and most generous hand in his kingdom for shelter and help. That, too, was Tristen's nature, and it was damned dangerous . . . almost as sure as a rebellion for drawing trouble into the province that was Ylesuin's most vulnerable and volatile border with Elwynor.

"We'll have no choice but wait for more news," Cefwyn said. "But we will move the three reserve units into position at the river." With a scarcity of carts and drivers, the vast weight of canvas necessary for a winter camp was going to move very much slower than he wished, and therefore men who relied on those tents would not move up to their posts except at the pace of their few carts.

Damn, he thought, and then, on his recent thoughts and his praise of Tristen for steadying the province, gave a little, a very little momentary consideration that where Tristen was, wizardry was, too . . . far more than in the person of Emuin. Nothing untoward would happen there, that Tristen could prevent.

There followed a very small and more fearful thought that the hole in the Quinalt roof was not coincidence and the withholding of those carts was not coincidence, either. He knew it was never Tristen's intent to hamper the defense in the north. Tristen might well have gotten wind of the impending events in Elwynor, too; but the timing of it all had the queasy feeling of wizard-work, all of it moving the same direction, a tightening noose of contrary events.

He knew, for all the affairs of Ylesuin, a moment of panic fear, a realization that all the impersonal lines on maps and charts were places, and the people in them were engaged in murdering one another at this very moment in a mad, guideless slide toward events he did not wholly govern and which those maps on his desk yonder no longer adequately predicted.

They were on the slope and sliding toward war, but even who was on the slope with them was difficult to say.

Difficult to say, too, who had pushed, or whether anyone remained safe and secure and master of all that had happened above them. Tristen's dark master of Marna Wood, this Hasufin Heltain, this ill-omened ghost, as Tristen described him—devil, as the Quinalt insisted—was defeated and dispelled at Lewenbrook, his designs all broken, and *he* or *it* was no longer in question. The banner of Ylesuin had carried that field.

But Tristen had fought among them up to a point, and then something had happened which he did not well understand, or even clearly remember to this day. Darkness had shadowed the field, an eclipse of the light, night amid day; and so the sun sometimes was shadowed, and so wizards could predict it to the hour and day.

But had something been *in* that darkness? It seemed that the heart of the threat had been not the rebel Aséyneddin, but Hasufin Heltain, and when Hasufin retreated and Tristen cast some sort of wizardry against him, then Aséyneddin had fallen and that war had ended, the darkness had lifted, and all the forces of the Elwynim rebel Aséyneddin had proved broken and scattered in the darkness. Light had come back on a ground covered with dead, many of them with no mark at all.

A man who had fought at Lewenbrook had a good many strange things to account for, and memories even of men in charge of the field did not entirely agree, not even for such simple things as how they had turned Aséyneddin's force or ended up in the part of the field where they had seen the light break through. They could only say that in the dark and the confusion they had driven farther than they thought and won more than they expected.

Yet . . .

Yet none of it seemed quite stable, as if they had not quite deserved their good fortune and did not understand how they had gotten there.

They had won, had they not? Yet here he stood with a bereaved wife and no less than Idrys saying there was little they could do.

And if someone pushed them over the precipice toward another conflict, with lightning striking the roof and Tristen driven in apparent retreat . . . still, they had won the last encounter.

Had they not?

And would they not win against whatever lesser wizard Tasmôrden dragged out of the bushes?

Would they not?

Damn the Quinalt, whose fear of wizardry gave him no better advice than to avoid magic . . . when the whole of the Quinaltine combined could do nothing of the sort Tristen had done on that field, and nothing of the sort Tristen could do again.

And damn the Quinalt twice: *they* had sent Tristen to Amefel, even if it was his good design, and done only in time to avert the whole province rising up in arms.

Was *that* not good fortune . . . save his carts, which the weather would not let them take across the bridges anyway?

So here they were . . . committed, and before the winter forced the siege to a fruitless end; and before any white miracle of the gods could intervene to save

Ninévrisë's capital. It was not contrary to their unhappy predictions, at least . . . none of them had held out infallible hope.

He sent Idrys and Annas away with orders. And only when they stood alone did Ninévrisë allow tears to fall, and only a few of them.

"He will not hold it," was all he could say to her. At least without witnesses he could gather the Regent of Elwynor in his arms and hold her close against his heart.

"I have never wished I had wizardry," Ninévrisë said, hands clenched on his sleeves. "Until now. *Now* I wish it, oh, gods, I wish it!"

"Don't," he said, frightened, for she knew what she wished for, and the cost of what she wished, and reached after it as a man might grasp after a sword within his reach . . . very much within his reach; and no swordmaster, no Emuin, no Tristen to restrain her. He touched her face, fingers trembling with what he knew, he, a Man and only a man, and having no such gift himself. He took her fine-boned fist and tried to gain her attention. "Don't. I know you can. I believe you can. You can go where I can't follow, and do what I can't undo, being your father's daughter. I *know*. I *know* what you do have, I've never been deceived, and if Emuin were here . . . gods, if Tristen were here, *he'd* tell you to be careful what you wish."

She gazed at him, truly at him, as if she had heard Tristen say it himself, in just those words. Then she grew calmer in his arms. She reached up and laid fingers on his lips, as if asking silence, peace, patience. The tears had spilled and left their traces on her cheeks in the white, snowy light from the window, and all the world seemed to hold a painful breath.

"I love you," she said. "I'll love you, forever and always. That says all."

"It will always say all. And they won't win, Nevris. They won't win."

"But oh, my friends, all my friends . . . my family . . . my home and my people . . ."

"I know." He set his arms about her, let her rest her head against his shoulder, and she heaved a great, heartbroken sigh with a little shudder after. "Gods save them. We'll go. We'll take the town. We'll have justice."

If he had gone to Elwynor in pursuit of Tasmôrden at summer's end, if he had not insisted on dealing with his own court, his father's court, and all the old men, *believing* he would have loyalty from men who had hoped he would never be king.

Folly, he could say now: the might of Ylesuin had been readier then than it was now, if he had only taken the south on to a new phase of the war, and damned the opinions of the old men who supported the throne in the north. If even two or three of the midlands barons had come behind him and gathered themselves for war along with the southern lords, they might have crossed the river, carried through to the capital . . . he had had *Tristen* with him, for the gods' sakes.

But what had he done with Tristen's help? Set it aside. Tried to silence him for fear of his setting northern noses out of joint. Kept him out of view instead of using his help. And not demanded Emuin come down out of his tower and forewarn him. He had delayed for deliberations with men he had thought reliable and necessary and respected their arguments and their long service to his father, telling himself that their opposition to him had ended when he took the crown. Well now he had the consequence of it.

Yet crossing the river thus and relying on Tristen's help with Althalen's black banners flying would have offended the north, scandalized the Quinalt, alienated the commons, and *that* might have led to disaster and weakened Ylesuin, on whose stability all hope of peace rested . . . there was that truth. There was that.

Yet what might he have made of Ylesuin if he had not stopped at Lewenbrook and not forbidden magic and never come home to Guelemara until he had come as High King and husband of Elwynor?

What might he and Ninévrisë have become with the strength he had had in his hands in those few days? Everything he had done, he had done to get a legal, sanctified, recognized wedding that would secure an unquestioned succession, sworn to by the Quinalt and legally incontestable.

And, doing that, he had given Ninévrisë no way to win him and his aid except to cross every hurdle he set her. What else was she to do, having no army, having nothing but a promised alliance with him on condition of their marriage?

He owed her better, he thought, holding her close and cherished within his arms. Damn Tasmôrden and damn Ryssand and his allies, and damn his own mistaken trust in his own barons, but he owed her far, far better than this.

The baskets had disappeared from master Emuin's stairs long since—Tassand's managing—and Tristen left his guard below as he climbed up and up the spiral stairway on this day after his arrival home.

A door opened above before he could reach it, letting out not daylight this time, but warmth and candle glow, and a rapidly moving boy . . . who had not expected to see him there, face on a level with his feet. Paisi came to an abrupt halt and tried to make himself very small against the wall of the landing.

"M'lor'," Paisi whispered, as Tristen climbed up to stand there, far taller than Paisi.

"Paisi," Tristen said. "I trust master Emuin is in."

"Oh, that 'e is, m'lor', an' 'is servant sent me after wood an' salt, which I'm doin', m'lor', fast as I can."

"Other servants from the yard will carry the wood up for you, understand. You have only to ask them. The salt you must manage. Cook's staff will not come up these steps. They complain of ghosts."

"Yes, m'lor'." A deep, deep bow, and a wide-eyed, fearful stare. "Yes, m'lor', an' I will, m'lor'."

"Emuin won't harm you."

Paisi seemed to have lost all powers of speech. He had only added a good coat to his ragged shirt and worn boots to his bare feet; but he had had a bath, despite his uncombed and unclipped look.

"Didn't I send you to the guard and to Tassand," Tristen asked on that sharper look in the imperfect light, "and is this the dress they gave you?"

"I been i' the market, m'lor', an' beggin' Your Grace's pardon, listenin' as ye said, so I kep' the clothes, as they'd point at me if I was in a fine new coat."

There was a small disturbance of the gray space, a gifted boy trying to become invisible, as, in those clothes, he looked very much the boy he had always been . . . except a fine new coat.

"Go, do what he asks," Tristen said, not willing to deny master Emuin's instructions, whatever they might be, and not willing to plumb the convolutions of Paisi's reasons this morning. He had far more serious matters to deal with.

Paisi ran past him, and Tristen stepped up into the doorway of a tower room in far better order than last he had seen it.

"Good morning," Emuin said from the hearthside. Emuin sat on a low stool, stirring a pot and not looking at him, but the faint touch of wit was there, in the gray space, and it was the same as a glance. Tristen took it so.

"So Cevulirn is riding south," Emuin said, "leaving his guard at the river, and you have made your agreements for Bryn, for the raising of a wall, and for the settling of a band of fugitives at the old ruins."

"To Cefwyn's good. Do you say otherwise?"

"Not I," Emuin said. "No."

It was always the same reply, whether a refusal or a denial of objection always unclear. Emuin never rose quite as far as agreeing with his choices, and this refusal to contradict him was as halfhearted.

"I have ordered the watch fires ready," Tristen said,

coming to stand over the old wizard. "Which is a great hardship on the men that keep them. Consequently I wish all bad weather north of the river. I could reach Cevulirn otherwise, but it seemed better to use the fires, and to extend them to the view of Lanfarnesse, Olmern, and Imor."

Emuin nodded.

"Was that wrong?" Tristen asked. "*Is* it wrong?"

Emuin gave a shrug and never abated his stirring. Whether it was a spell or breakfast was unclear by the pot's sluggish white bubbling. It smelled like porridge.

"I'm sure I don't weep for Tasmôrden's discomfort," Emuin said. "It's no concern of mine, and none of my doing."

He could lose his temper entirely at this resumed silence. Almost. But Mauryl had taught him patience above all things, and he gathered it up in both hands.

"Porridge?" he asked, a tactical change of subject.

"Barley soup."

"How does the boy do?"

"He's a scoundrel," Emuin said, "but deft. He won't steal from me. As for why you've come—you wished His Reverence in Guelessar, as I recall. So to Guelessar he's gone."

A shot from the flank. It was not entirely why he had come, but he knew he was in the wrong, and badly mistaken in the way he had dealt with the man. "Uwen couldn't stop him."

"Short of your man arresting him or sitting on him, I doubt Uwen could have done anything to prevent him. What a cleric will, that he will, and a duke's authority through his man or otherwise can't stop him . . . short of lopping his head, that is, and that creates such ill will among the clergy."

"I've written to Cefwyn," he said meekly.

"Good. You should."

"And to Idrys, more plainly."

"Regarding?"

"Ilefínian."

"*That* . . ."

"Ninévrisë's people are dying, sir! Don't you know that? *That's* why I came."

Emuin looked at him from under his brows. "I say *that* because it was foredoomed to happen.—So, perhaps, was your settlement at Althalen. Oh, yes . . . *that* matter, while we're at it."

"You might have advised me."

"Advised you, advised you . . . were you ignorant what Althalen means, and what it signifies to have that site of all sites tenanted again?"

He drew a deep breath. No, he could not say he was ignorant of that.

"Were you unaware?"

"No, sir. But there was nowhere else I knew to put them. *Here* wasn't safe."

"In that, you may be right."

"Am I wrong, sir?"

"Wrong? I think it must have been fated, from the hour Cefwyn, the silly lad, handed you *its* banner and *his* friendship. What more could he think?"

"Have I done wrong, sir?"

"I don't think right and wrong figure here. If Althalen was foredoomed to fall and foredoomed to rise, damned little he or I could do about it."

"And I, sir?"

"At least this manner of rebirth does no harm to him."

From the edge of the water to very, very deep waters indeed, and shattering accusations.

"I *am* his friend, sir!" Tristen dropped to a bench near the fire, rested his elbows on his knees, and met the old man face-to-face, seeking one level, honest look from him. "Look at me, master Emuin! Have I given anyone any reason to think otherwise? Have I ever given you or Cefwyn any reason to think otherwise of me?"

"This boy you found," said Emuin, shifting the tide of question again onto a former shore, "this boy who's provoked His Reverence to disastrous measures and brought us all manner of trouble also happens to inform me of various things. A wisewoman, one of the grandmothers, has mothered young Paisi since he was left as a babe at her door. I'm fairly sure there's the old blood in him, which doubtless frightened his unfortunate mother into abandonment. That, or she had the Sight herself and saw him tangled with your fate."

"I wasn't here yet! Mauryl hadn't Summoned me."

"All the same."

"*Why? Why* should anyone fear me?"

"Why *should* anyone fear you? What do you think? And considering the small matter of His Reverence, tell me what you think he's apt to do."

"Spread trouble in Guelessar."

"Is it absolution you want or a better answer?"

"What shall I do about it?"

"Why did you bring Paisi out of gaol? Why was it important to find him?"

Wizards. Like Mauryl, Emuin shifted the ground under his feet and answered questions with questions on an utterly different matter: aim at him, and the shot came back double . . . and with terrible, dreadful surmises.

He mustered his wits to answer that question, as levelly and patiently and completely as he could: no lies, no evasions with master Emuin . . . to lead his guide to wrong conclusions served no good at all.

"He was my first guide when I came from Mauryl to Henas'amef. Paisi was. Should I leave him free, sir, counting all you've taught me of wizardry, to fall to other influences? Something moved him to bring me to the right place on the right night. *As* it moved me to settle the fugitives at Althalen."

"A question, is that? *Should* you have heeded Paisi in the first place?"

"Do you think *Mauryl* sent him to guide me? Was it his doing?"

"Think you so?" Emuin asked him.

"Who else might?" The impatience in him scarcely restrained his hands from clenching into fists. He wished to leap up and move, tear himself from this uncomfortable confrontation he had provoked.

But he had not sat learning of wizards for no gain. Listening and trying to answer Emuin's questions was the best course, the only course that would ever bring him an answer.

And it was so, that Mauryl, lost with Ynefel, had reached far, very far with his spells. At one time it had seemed perfectly clear that Hasufin Heltain was the cause of Emuin's fear. But Hasufin was gone now, was he not?

And yet Emuin seemed more afraid than before.

"Who indeed else would have sent the boy?" Emuin said. "Since no one but Mauryl knew the why and wherefore."

"Might Mauryl's wishes for me," he asked, "have entered into some other pattern, one of, say, someone *else's* making?"

"Troubling thought," Emuin said faintly, rapping the soup-coated spoon clear on the rim of the pot. "There are so many choices."

"You."

"Not to my knowledge. I assure you I had never besought the gods for another student."

"The enemy . . . *Hasufin.*"

"A remote chance," Emuin said, and plunged the spoon back into the pot. He swung the pot off the fire.

"But you think not."

"I think not."

"Paisi himself guided the meeting?"

"Possible, too, remoter still though it be."

Remote, yes. So he had thought. "Someone should care for the boy," Tristen said, attempting a diversion of his own, from an area *he* did not now want to discuss. "And you lacked a boy. You need a good pair of legs, and he needs a Place, or something else may indeed find him. I think I was right in that."

"A gift, now drawn into our web. What more?"

"A very little of the gift, I think."

"Has the calamity of his presence been little? His Reverence sped to Guelessar? And now this boy in my care? Doubly dangerous to be poking and prying around a wizard's pots with gifted fingers. I had trouble enough with the brothers from Anwyfar, and them scared witless. A gift is not to judge by its surface or its apparent depth. By the waters that churn around him, mark me, this boy is dangerous."

"He may be," Tristen said, "but that means he's dangerous to be wandering free, too, and moiling other waters."

"Perhaps."

"He needs a Place, does he not? Is he not more dangerous without a Place?"

"And so you lend him *this* one, gods save me. He'll go through clothes, he'll eat like a troop of the Guard, and his feet will grow. I do not cook, mind you! Nothing except my own meals."

It comforted him, that Emuin did not seem as set against Paisi as he had feared, and within the mundane complaints he heard nothing so grievous as their prior discussion. "All that he needs the Zeide has for the asking. And he can cook for you." Another shift of direction. "He's running your errands, so I think, to the market, yours as well as mine."

"I sent him after turnips yesterday."

"Turnips. Is there some flaw in Cook's turnips?"

"You're such a troublesome young man!"

"I fear I've become so," he said sadly. He envied Paisi, to do no more than run a wizard's errands, and to learn the ways of bird nests, and all such things as had passed his reach. Another boy belonged to Emuin. He did not. He had become something else, as Cefwyn had passed through Emuin's hands and become something else. A severance had occurred without his seeing it coming.

But he had learned Emuin's greater lessons: patience, and examination of himself. And what had he interrupted Emuin saying to him: something about turnips and the marketplace?

"Taking in thieves," Emuin muttered. "Conversing with exiles . . ."

"Cevulirn came north to discuss Cefwyn's affairs with me," Tristen said sharply, "and something very powerful wished to prevent him. I'm all but sure it wasn't Auld Syes who raised that storm. Tell me again and tell me true: *was it you?*"

Emuin's brows lifted in mild wonder, and Emuin did look at him eye-to-eye, his gaze for the moment as clear as glass. "No, not I. Have you another thought?"

"What do *you* seek in the market?" Tristen asked in Emuin's style: divert, feint, and under the guard.

"Much the same as your questions to the boy, thank you. Especially the old women have ears, *and* the sort of awareness you and I have. They're a valuable resource, the witches, the wisewomen of Amefel. I've used them from time to time. Now you've thought of the same resource and asked the right question.

Shall I tell you what I know?"

"Yes, sir. If you please."

"Then look about you: the people have had a rebirth of their faith. So the Bryaltines say. The old symbols appear openly in certain alleys, and people wear charms and set them in their doorways. They hang bells in the wind, so their dimmer ears can hear what we hear in it. All this affronted the good Quinalt father, and scandalized our missing sergeant, I'm sure, gods save his devout soul." This Emuin said not without sarcasm.

"I suppose I've seen it."

"You know you've seen it. You've not found it remarkable until I mention it. And in your absence, however brief, the Bryalt father turns out to have gained two nuns of his order, women formerly in the service of the Zeide, who two days ago were prophesying in the street . . . saying openly that the Sihhë have risen in Henas'amef and in Amefel. And, do you know, they prophesied the rewakening of Althalen?"

Tristen was appalled.

"Oh, and this *before* you came back to say so, perhaps on the very day you did it. So they have the Sight and have it in good measure. And on *that* news, the good father quit the town and struck out down the road in mortal offense, behind the captain and the sergeants who *also* went to Guelemara. Can you imagine the meeting at Clusyn?"

The monastery where travelers stayed.

"So you're building at Althalen," Emuin said, "nuns are in the street foretelling the rise of the Sihhë-lords and the return of the King To Come, and gods save us all . . . they saw what you were doing."

He heard. The words echoed in the air, off the walls of events past and present. He heard the hammer strokes of men at work on stone, not uncommon in the

Zeide these days; but it echoed work elsewhere, on a ruined wall; he heard the whisper of the wind at the eaves, warning of change in the weather: he heard the running footsteps of a boy on an errand, illusion only, for the boy himself, desperate and afraid of help as well as harm, was well out of the vicinity by now, seeking wood and salt, he had said.

"I have *not* resettled Althalen, not as a name. I settled a handful of fugitives there, a mere handful of desperate folk wanting shelter from the snow. There were walls to use, and it's remote from the road. Is that wicked of me?"

"And what more do buildings and walls do, young lord, what do they do more than shelter us from the weather?"

Nothing, was the quick answer; but, no, that was not so, in wizard-craft, and in his heart he knew it: buildings had wards.

And those ruins had the strongest in all of Amefel, the protection of the Lord Regent, Ninévrisë's father, whose tomb was there. He had chosen Althalen precisely because of that, and it had seemed right. Now Emuin chided him on that very matter, and the whole complexion of his decision shifted.

"They are a Place," he said. "Lines on the earth."

"So you have given Place to Elwynim at Althalen. And lo! you have subjects there, Lord Sihhë. You have subjects who are *not Amefin*, not in our king's gift, not in authority he gave you. And we have nuns telling visions in the streets. Was this wise?"

He was struck cold and silent, asking himself how things could have so turned about.

"I have," he admitted after a moment, "likewise ordered the wall restored near Modeyneth. What do you say about that?" But he already knew. He had himself rebuilt the ward there, too, consciously, in defense of

Amefel, and never thought of its other significance, as a ward the Sihhë had laid. He had thought of the protection the wards afforded the fugitives. He had not thought of the strength inhabitants gave the wards: Althalen was alive again, and of his doing.

"Thank the gods," said Emuin, "His Reverence left before he heard this news."

"I sent a message to Cefwyn from Anwyll's camp. So has Anwyll, already, once we knew Ilefínian had fallen. The messenger was to ride straight through, not even stopping here. I sent another last night, before I slept. The people that escape Tasmôrden will flee into Amefel. It's all they can do. But I can't allow the border to be overrun by troops and fugitives, stealing and slaughtering the villagers. Do justice, Cefwyn told me, and I swore I would. Is it justice to stand aside and let war come here, when I could stop it?"

"Justice is a hard word to define. Kings battle over it."

Diversion and regrouping. The ground had become untenable. "*Whose* storm was it?"

"*I* had no wish to prevent your talking to Cevulirn. I had no forewarning, and I would never quarrel with Auld Syes.—Whose was the lightning stroke that drove you from Guelessar?"

"I don't know," he confessed. "Was it a wizard? It must be a powerful wizard who could do that. Could it be Auld Syes?"

"I doubt it. Amefel is her concern, and her Place."

"Yet . . . conspiracy among the earls, the overthrow of Lord Parsynan . . . all these things were happening when the lightning came down."

"None of which His Majesty knew when he sent you. Lightning struck the Quinaltine roof, and you found yourself on the road."

"So it was not chance, not the lightning, and not Cefwyn sending me."

"It was, and it was not. Do you know so little of wizardry, young lord? No. I forget you *need* not know a damned thing about wizardry. You need not learn anything. Things Unfold to you. Might leaps to your fingertips and all nature bends when you stamp your foot."

Emuin was exaggerating, vastly so, but reminding him how little he had bent himself to Emuin's art, and how little he knew of it.

"For us mere Men," Emuin said in a surly tone, "it's chance and not chance that such things happen. Learn this: wizardry loads the dice, young lord, but they still can roll against the wall. Surely you know that much. And maybe it's a flaw in you, that you need not study, but find it all at your fingertips: gods know what you can do."

"I wish to learn, master Emuin. I *wish* to be taught. I've asked nothing more."

"Oh, you've asked far more, young lord. You've asked much, much more. But let us walk together down this path of chance and if and maybe. Let us look at the landmarks and learn to be wise. If there had been no lightning stroke and you had not come, and then Amefel had risen . . . what would have happened?"

"Calamity."

"So. But then what did happen?"

"Crissand's father and his men took the fortress. And then I took it."

"And Crissand Adiran survived, but his father did not. Was this chance, too? The rebels took the fortress. They died. Two events not necessarily benefiting the same power. Crissand escaped the slaughter. A third event. You seized Amefel. A fourth."

Not necessarily benefiting the same power.

"Lad," Emuin gazed straight at him. "Lad, are you listening to what we're saying?"

"Yes, sir."

"What have I told you?"

"That there may be two powers."

"No. That there may be more than one."

"Yes, sir," he said in utter solemnity. "I do hear."

"You are one of those powers," Emuin said. "That's always worth remembering. Don't act carelessly. Don't assume the dice have only one face. It's only by considering all the faces that you can load one of them. *That's* wizardry, young lord. That's why it means learning, difficult, farseeing learning."

The echoes in the air remained, a brazen, troubling liveliness, as if all events balanced on a point of time and might go careering off in any direction without warning.

"I can swear I didn't raise the storm or conjure Auld Syes," Tristen said, grasping at that straw.

"Then reckon at least three with the ability must be involved here," Emuin said, "and four, young sir, for *I* didn't raise them, either."

"Lady Orien?"

"Think you so, lord of Amefel?"

Emuin changed salutations and none of it was without significance. It was lessons again. It was a signal to him: he was not at this moment *young lord*.

And he gave Emuin as honest answers as he had given to Mauryl, last spring, in hope ultimately of revelations about himself such as Mauryl had given him.

"Her dragons lean over me as I write. Lady Orien broke the great Lines there, in that room in particular, when she opened it and let in Hasufin. I repaired them as I could. But I never am at ease in that place."

"Well, well," Emuin said, "and well reckoned. Now never after this say that I failed to advise you. I have advised you. Now and at last you may have heard what I say, beyond all my expectations. I have warned you, as best I can."

"And else?" Tristen asked. "Is Orien all your warning?—Or is it Hasufin?"

Emuin's charts lay scattered across the table, charts of great sweeping lines and writing that teased his eye with recognition, but that was not the fine round hand Men used nowadays. He moved one, in Emuin's silence, and made no sense of the parchment, the visible sign of studies Emuin pursued and would not divulge.

"Don't disarrange my charts, pray. Go raise walls against the law. Chastise the fool boy you've given me. I leave it to you. Leave me to my ciphering. Gods! Don't—"

He had picked up a chart, almost, and let it down again.

"Don't disarrange them. I've enough troubles."

"Does the order matter? *What* do you cipher, sir? Wherein is it wizards' business, all these writings? Do you draw Lines also across the sky and ward the stars, too?"

"None of your concern, young lord! Leave my charts, I say, and go find that wretched boy wizard you freed from a just and deserved hanging. He's probably filched three purses on his way to the kitchens."

"He's mine, at least . . . that he's in my care. And his listening in the town is for my sake. And if he helps you, claim duty of him; but he won't cease to be mine, master Emuin, unless you ask for him. Until you give me reasons, I won't change it." His converse with Emuin had skipped from question to question, all around the things he most wished to know, and grew cryptic and uneasy. "Why the stars, sir? What can you hope to find? Or to do?"

"Curiosity. A lifelong study. My diversion. All wizards have such charts."

"Mauryl did. Parchments, papers, everywhere, and

all blown about when the tower fell. I find it curious you have the same study."

"Mauryl lived centuries. The planets were a passing show to him."

"And to you, sir?"

"Damn, but we're full of questions. Question, question, question."

"So Mauryl taught me. So I learn, sir, or try to. I've been respectful and said *yes, master Emuin.* But you said I should study wizardry. You said I should look at all the faces of the dice." He understood dismissal, however, in Emuin's distress and reticence: Emuin wished him gone, so he rose and crossed the room and set his hand on the door, with a backward look at the stone, unplastered chamber, at shelves untidy and groaning under their load, and a bed at least supplied with new blankets.

More blankets were under the bed, where Paisi had tucked a pallet, perhaps; it looked to be that, or a repository of Emuin's discarded clothes.

"I'm glad you've shut the windows," he remarked in leaving, "and I'm glad you're not alone here."

"Bryaltine nuns," Emuin muttered. "The Sihhë star in the marketplace and hung on pillars, and His Reverence to Guelessar. Don't surprise Cefwyn with these things. And in your writing to Idrys, apart from Cefwyn, make a thorough job of explaining, lad. Make it very thorough. I've no doubt His Reverence will."

CHAPTER 7

⚜

The senior clerk came to the ducal apartment at Tristen's request, and proudly presented a thick set of papers, figures, great long lists of carefully penned numbers and tallies. Tristen had found a keen interest in his resources since his venture out to the river and back. He had inquired of his clerk what he had at his disposal.

But this was not the answer, at least not in a form that Unfolded to him. And asking the clerk what the sum of the accounts meant he could buy produced only confusion, a business of owed and received and entitled and the seasonal difficulty with contrary winds in distant Casmyndan, southward.

"Ciphering," Uwen said, when the clerk had gone, and added with a little laugh, "which I don't know wi'out I count on my fingers, an' for large sums I wiggle toes. So I ain't a help there. I'd best take mysel' to the horses an' the men and leave ye to your readin', which ye don't lack in that stack."

"It's coins. It all stands for coins, does it?"

"Coins, m'lord. Aye, I reckon, in a way, it does that."

"Crowns and pennies," Tristen said, and drew up that sheet of common southern paper, one of a score of papers on which long columns marched in martial order. But not of martial things. "Five hundred crowns and seventy pennies of sheep."

"'At's some few sheep," Uwen said. "An' 'at there's why Your Grace has clerks."

"I have no difficulty with the numbers," Tristen said, "only this business of pennies and pence coming from them."

"Pennies and ha'pennies and small pence," Uwen said, in that quiet, astonished mildness that attended such close, odd questions, "an' being as we're in Amefel, the king's pence an' th' old pence an' the far-thing an' ha'farthing, an' the king's reckonin' an' the old reckonin'. All in the market at the same time, in Amefel: no small wonder if ye blink at it."

"Show me," he said, pushing the papers across the desk, "if you will. *You* understand."

"Good gods, I ain't the one."

"The clerk hasn't helped. *You* show me."

Nothing had Unfolded, nothing showed any least promise of Unfolding to show him the sense in these papers and accounts, which he had asked for, and he had until the first hour after noon before he should meet with the earls and give his own report.

Uwen obediently came closer, picked up a paper, and looked at it.

"Here's fine, fair writin', but the sense of it's far above me, m'lord."

"So are farthings and half farthings above *me.*" Tristen laid his finger on a number on a paper that chanced to be in front of him, that of one fleece. "What's that to a penny? That one there."

Uwen craned sideways to look. "That 'un I can show ye."

"Here." He swept aside the papers, and found a fair unwritten one. But Uwen, disdaining the pen and the clean sheet, sat down on the other side of the table, emptied out his purse, and showed him how many coppers made a gold crown, and each five coppers a king's penny, and what was a farthing piece, worth a cup of ale, and why ha'farthings were *in* the reckoning but left out of the actual payment because there was no such coin ever minted in the history of the world.

Ha'farthings, a petty sum, did not pay the bill when he considered what the cost was to feed and clothe and house the staff, and then to fit out men-at-arms and build the ruined walls.

And Uwen professed his purse out of coins, and not even one fleece was accounted for.

"Get those in the cupboard," Tristen said, for he knew there were gold ones there, and silver, and Uwen and he made stacks and piles in order, until they accounted for a whole flock at once.

After that he could look at his list of sheep and know how much gold that was, and therefore how many of those sacks that were in the strong room deep, deep in the heart of the Zeide, where the strongest guard was mounted.

"Let us go downstairs," he said.

"M'lord," Uwen protested, "we can't be stackin' the bags in th' countin' room."

"I wish to see it," he said, "now that I understand this much."

So down they went, the two of them, and the guard that always attended him, all rattling and clumping down to the main hall and down and down the stairs that otherwise led to Emuin's tower, until they came to the strong room and the guarded door.

To him the strong-room guards, members of the Dragon Guard, deferred, and unlocked and unbarred the place. The escort as well took up station outside, and Tristen and Uwen stood amid stacks and bags of gold, and plate, and cups, and all the service that had graced Lord Heryn's table, besides the ducal crown and various jeweled bracelets and other such.

"Now, them jewels," Uwen said, "I hain't the least idea."

Tristen said nothing, for the sight of all of it seemed at last to Unfold to him a comprehension of the treasure Lord Heryn had. He had been down here once before, in his first days here. But only now, well lit and laid out as it was, he began to know the extent of it.

"M'lord?"

He drew in a deep breath, more and more troubled by what he saw.

"This is a very great lot of gold," he said.

"That it is."

"Men died for this," he said. "Very many men died for this."

"An' damn cold comfort," Uwen said, thrusting his hands into his belt and letting go a great sigh, "'cept as it buys firewood and all. An' don't ask me why gold should be worth so much, 'cept it's such as a man can carry the worth of a horse in his purse, an' damn unlikely he could carry the horse."

He scarcely heard Uwen, except the last, and he gathered up the threads of it belatedly and gave a small, shaken laugh. "That it is. But there are too many horses in this room and not enough in the stable; and too many loaves of bread here and not enough in Meiden's villages, aren't there? That's what you mean."

"I think it is, m'lord. A box like as we brought from Guelemara, we'd fill it a lot of times in this room, and that box full up with gold is enough for two hundred men and horses for half a year. That's the ciphering I know."

"Imor and Olmern sell grain for gold."

"Both do, and is likely to be jealous of each other, if ye pardon me, m'lord. Imor don't like the Olmernmen, but the Olmernmen have the boats."

Amefel could do with both grain and boats in its defense, Tristen thought, and standing in all this wealth of gold, he knew that he beheld a kind of magic in itself, to summon boats, and feed men. Gold became grain, and sheep, and well-fed villages. Parsynan had gathered taxes and put them in this room; so had Heryn, over years of rule, and aethelings before him had done it since the time of Barrakkêth and before. Cefwyn, he knew, had taken some sum of money away, so Cefwyn had said at summer's end, for the welfare of the province, and because the king's tax was due, but far more was here than the tax should ever have required, and what was anyone doing with it?

It was far in excess of what needs he even yet understood, in flocks, grain, wagons, food, and horses.

The visit to the strong room was in the morning; the afternoon belonged to the earls, Crissand, Drumman, Azant, Marmaschen, Durell, and the rest, with some who had come in from the country, all gathered downstairs in the little hall, over maps which told their own story . . . the capital of Elwynor, not far from the river, fallen now, and the loyal subjects of Her Grace prey to the rebels under Tasmôrden: red marked the disasters, red of blood.

"I've given Her Grace's men leave to cross the river," Tristen said to the earls, seated at the end of the table whereon the maps were spread, heavy books weighting their corners. A stack of books the clerks had found pertinent in the ravaged archive sat beside the maps, overwhelming in the sheer volume of what he did not know. "Captain Anwyll has orders to disarm the armed men when he finds them and assure them they may trust Amefel for protection. So we must provide that protection." By that the earls might understand he intended them move to a winter muster, but he added quickly, "The Ivanim are providing that guard of archers for the days the bridge is open, and Lord Cevulirn will send more if they find themselves pressed. So may others. He's advising all the southern provinces of the danger. What we need to do is stand ready to help the troops they may send with supplies and transport. And in some part of which we may be able to rely on boats from Olmern. Lord Cevulirn will request that, too, and Lord Sovrag is our friend."

"The Olmernmen will want pay, all the same," said Drumman.

"Let them have Heryn's gold dinnerplates," Tristen said, "if they value them. I had far rather boats full of grain and enough men to keep the border."

There were glum looks, then. He did not quite see why.

"Do you think I'm wrong?" he asked in all honesty.

"Your Grace," Azant said, "*I* will contribute."

"And I," Crissand said, a little ahead of a muttered agreement from others, men who days ago had been arguing the poverty of their people.

"Use your resources for your villages. And to help Bryn build its wall," Tristen said, for he had sent word to everyone about his promises to Bryn: Drumman was here, but his men were already moving to Bryn's aid. "I ask of you all the same thing. Amefel has a treasure-room full of Heryn Aswydd's gold. I don't know the cost of the boats and the grain, but we'll use that first, build the defenses in Bryn's lands, and supply food and shelter to the Elwynim that cross to us."

"We can't deplete the treasury entirely."

"I'm told a gold coin is a sack of grain, and I think we have more coins in the treasury than we do sacks of grain in all Amefel."

That also drew a curious stare. "How many?" was the careful distillation of the question.

"I'm sure I don't know," Tristen said, and in fact, did not know the tally. But at that, one of the younger Amefin clerks looked as if he had something behind his teeth he was afraid to let escape.

"Sir?" Tristen asked the man, seeing the look.

"Elwynim," the young clerk said, faintly, and had to clear his throat in mid-utterance. "And the tax collecting. —Which I'm not supposed to know, my lord, but master Wydnin fled across the river when the king came back from Lewen field, and he took some of the books with him. So we don't *have* the account of the treasury, not since this summer, and not even the king had an accounting. Parsynan started one. But he went away." The clerk moistened his lips. "It never was done."

"We have no accounting? But Tasmôrden does?"

There was a murmur among the lords, all of whom had conspired with Tasmôrden . . . that Tasmôrden turned out to know more than they did about what was in the Amefin treasury.

And the clerk's report made perfect sense. No few of the house servants had fled when it turned out Cefwyn had won at Lewenbrook. The archivist, who might have known more secrets than he had yet told, was now dead, murdered, in the matter of Mauryl's letters. More, if Parsynan had had a counting in progress, that was a mystery to him.

"Master clerk," he said, to his own clerk, who had come with him out of Guelessar, and the man stepped anxiously forward. "Do you have any account the lord viceroy began?"

"No, my lord. I fear not."

"So that's gone, too."

"It seems it has."

This flood of papers toward Tasmôrden was alarming: Tasmôrden knew very much of their resources, their proceedings, and Mauryl's correspondence with the Aswydds, Heryn, and those before him . . . and that contained, surely, some of Mauryl's notions about defense, perhaps about Althalen, perhaps about wizards and wizardous resources as great as the treasury. It was not alone the accounts that Cefwyn had found muddled when he arrived here, the books all out of order and in stacks on the tables and jammed into the shelves . . . it was the books of the library itself that had been disappearing to avoid Cefwyn discovering the Aswydds' fortune and their dealings with Mauryl and perhaps other wizards.

They had assumed it was Mauryl's writings that had been secreted in that wall, because that was the nature of the burned fragments . . . but those letters they had burned, he suspected now from going through the fragments, were useless to them. The question was not what they had left as chaff, but what they had taken as valuable, and how long this traffic in books and records had been going on.

And had some of those found their way to Elwynor . . . missing books of unknown nature, themselves as valuable as gold. The senior archivist was dead, and the junior fled, with what final treasure . . . and of Mauryl's writings . . . or someone else's?

The archive of correspondence had probably gone into the wall when Heryn knew Cefwyn was coming . . . and when *he* was coming the junior archivist had murdered the senior and fled with a few precious items, likely to Lord Cuthan; and Lord Cuthan, confronted with his own treason . . . fled, again, to Elwynor, leaving behind his own culling of less important, less concealable documents, for they had found certain things left behind in Cuthan's house that they were relatively sure should have been in the archive. They suspected those were part of the stolen documents . . . but they had never found the junior archivist, and while they suspected Cuthan might have gotten something past the searchers and into Elwynor, they were never entirely sure.

More and more, however, he was sure it was not just one theft, but a pattern of theft, the slow pilferage of years, and a junior archivist overwhelmed with fear, seizing the best of the concealed items, burning the rest and fleeing for fear of the whole business coming out.

"My lord," said Marmaschen, who rarely spoke. "Lord Heryn was known for asking gold for favors, besides his surcharge on the Guelen king's tax. We knew he had accumulated a great deal in the treasury, but no man but Lord Heryn's closest familiars went there. And his master of accounts. But that man fled to Elwynor."

"Very likely, too," said Drumman, "Lord Heryn sold the old king's life, and had gold for it. So I think. No Amefin will be mourning Ináreddrin, as may be, but that's likely the source of some that's there. Blood money."

"And anything Aséyneddin might have wanted to know," said Marmaschen. "That, too, Lord Heryn would have reported, if gold flowed."

"What would he do with it?" Tristen asked, and received astonished, confused stares, which he took to mean his question was foolish. "Did he buy grain?"

"He kept it," Drumman said.

"He had gold plates. Gold cups. He had boxes and boxes of it."

"My lord," said Marmaschen, fingering his beard, and in a cautious voice, "does this mean my lord will levy no war tax?"

"I see no need to," Tristen said. "When there is need, then I shall."

There was a general letting-forth of breath, as it were one body.

"And the levy of troops?" Drumman ventured. "Will we be taking the field, or does the wall answer the need? We've no great disadvantage sending men off the land in the winter, while the weather holds."

"I hope it will hold. I *wish* it to hold." He dared say so with these men. "And Bryn needs all the help all of you can send, to build the wall. The more men, the faster the stones move. And they'll need ox teams there for the heavy pulling. I've delayed the king's carts as long as I can. I can't keep them into the spring."

"The spring planting . . ." Crissand said.

"We can let the land lie a year if need be. We'll still have grain. We'll have brought it in Olmern's boats."

That brought consternation.

"Do we understand Your Grace means to supply grain to all the families in the villages and the town as well as to the men under arms? And to muster out every able man in Amefel? Is that what we face?"

"No," he said. "But to feed an army, that we may. The southern lords *will* come. Cevulirn will bring them. We won't let Tasmôrden bring his war here, and *I* won't let him have the riverside."

There were slow intakes of breath, the understanding, perhaps, that all they had discussed with Cevulirn before they had gone to the river had begun to happen.

"So we're to provide for an army," Crissand dared say, for all the rest. "And does the Guelen king know, my lord? Or to what are you leading us? Go we will, but to what are you leading us?"

The question struck *him* to silence, a long silence, gazing into Crissand's troubled face across the width of the table.

"I don't know," he said, the entire truth. "But to war with Tasmôrden, for the king's sake, and ours, and all the south . . . that, yes. There will be war."

"Lord Ivanor's ridden home without a word,"

Azant said. "And to do what, Your Grace? To bring his men?"

"And how will we determine the need for this gold and grain?" asked Marmaschen. "Who'll decide one claim against another? Shall we simply come with a list and say, Your Grace, give us grain?"

"I'll ask you the truth," Tristen said, "and you'll tell me."

One lord lifted his head instantly as if to laugh, and did not, in a very sober, very fearful silence. The silence went on and on, then, oddly, Crissand smiled, then laughed.

"Lies will find us out," Crissand said. "Will you not know the instant we lie, my lord?"

"I think I would," he admitted, though he had kept from others the truth of the gray space, and what it told him . . . he judged all men by Uwen Lewen's-son, and what made Uwen uneasy, he told no one casually. He thought, too, of Cefwyn's barons and Cefwyn's court, and how the men there were always at one another's throats. "But I'd hope none of you would lie to me."

There was again that silence.

"No," said Crissand cheerfully, "no, my lord, we shan't lie to you. And *you* won't charge Heryn's tax."

"I see no need of a tax, when we have so much gold."

"But, Your Grace," Drumman said, "this *wall* you want . . . if you will forgive me my frankness . . . if I dare say . . . my men are on their way, with every intent to obey Your Grace's order. But the Guelen king forbade our fortifications and our walled houses. He ordered them torn down. Dare we do this?"

"Aye," said Azant. "What will the king in Guelemara say? And shall *only* Bryn have defenses? We have ruined forts aplenty, from the Marhanen's order. And shall only Bryn raise a wall?"

"And will we have a Guelen army on our necks?" Lord Durell asked.

"No," Tristen said. "Cefwyn wouldn't send one. I'm his friend."

"His advisers will urge him otherwise, my lord," said Drumman. "And in no uncertain terms. Your Grace, with all goodwill, and obeying your orders, I'm uneasy in this."

"I know they'll be angry," Tristen said. "But the king doesn't like their advice, and he's far cleverer than Ryssand. He knows his best friends are in the south."

"Then gods save His Guelen Majesty," Azant said with an uneasy laugh, "and long may he reign—in Guelessar."

"Aye," said Drumman, "and leave us our Lord Sihhë."

"Our Lord Sihhë," said Marmaschen, "who spends his treasury instead of ours and bids us build walls . . . walls I will build, Your Grace. Two hundred men is the muster of my lands, three hundred if you'll feed the villages through next winter. Do that, and we'll join Drumman, and raise your wall in Bryn, and then my own."

"Three hundred from mine through winter, spring, and summer," said Lord Drumman.

"Two hundred from Meiden," Crissand said, "no trained men: shepherds . . . but we sling stones at wolves that come at our flocks. Give us some sort of armor and our maids and boys will man Bryn's wall. That we can do, and will."

There was never a doubt Crissand was in earnest, and others named numbers, a hundred from one lord, fifty from another, until the tally was more than Amefel had fielded at Lewenbrook.

"Now is the need," Tristen said. "Ilefínian's people are coming south. But so may Tasmôrden's. We have to set the signal fires, the way we did before Lewenbrook. This, until we have the Ivanim horse to defend us, and then whatever other help will come to us . . . they'll come."

"With Ilefínian fallen, and the snows coming," said Drumman, "there's likely no grain to be had in Elwynor. There can't have been a crop last year in the midlands; there's none this year: all they sowed was iron. Tasmôrden's stolen for his army whatever the poor farmers put in, his army's stolen what they could carry, and now he'll plunder the capital storehouses, none preventing him . . . whatever the siege didn't consume, if there's anything left at all. Hunger across the river is inevitable, Your Grace is right. *Grain* is what they'll want, and even innocent villagers can grow desperate enough to turn outlaw. It's not all quiet, peaceful folk who'll cross the river in winter. There'll be some bent on taking."

"We'll give them grain," Tristen said. "As much as they can carry."

Worried looks had attended Drumman's assessment; astonishment attended his answer, slight aversions of the eyes, flinching from the notion; but it seemed reasonable to him.

"And if we give it, they'll be fed, and if they're fed, maybe they'll be quiet neighbors," Drumman said. "But can we find that much grain, Your Grace? Can we get it?"

"We'll ask the Olmernmen," Tristen said, in utter sobriety. "Cevulirn is doing that."

"The king should have pressed across the river last summer," Azant muttered. "Her Grace was willing. The army was willing. And, no, he turned aside and went back to Guelessar. Now we empty our treasury to feed Elwynor?"

"A sack of grain is one gold coin," Tristen said,

"and if you put it in the ground, it's a field of grain. Isn't that so?"

"If you can get the soldiers off the ground," Azant said. "There's the matter."

"With all the starving peasants of Her Grace's land at our doorsteps," Durell said. "Save this grain we give of our own accord, and no recompense from His Guelen Majesty, as I understand. And we'll have more than hungry peasants before all's done. We'll have hungry soldiers, bands of them, with no leaders, no thought but their bellies."

That was so.

"And if there's famine," said another lord, "disease, that goes with it."

"Then there's need of medicines, too," Tristen said.

"And is our treasury enough for it?"

"The grandmothers don't ask much for their cures. But it's a good thing if we tell them, and pay them." He had understood this matter of paying folk, finally, so there was bread enough. "And if we don't have enough herbs for their powders, we'll buy them from Casmyndan, too. Sovrag's boats can bring them."

"And a good store for us, too," said Marmaschen. "No crops, no store of food untouched in Elwynor, no planting this spring, in all that kingdom. It's an immense undertaking."

"And treasury gold to pay for it, Your Grace?" asked an ealdorman of the town. "Recompense, for what we supply?"

"And a fair price," Crissand said. "The merchants know what that is. Fair price, and fair quantity. Weavers to weave: they'll need blankets and cloaks. Cobblers, dyers, wheelwrights, tanners, and smiths . . ."

"For gold?" the ealdorman asked.

"For gold," Tristen said, and added, because Crissand was right, "at the prices things are."

"My lord," said Azant, from the other side of the table. "We know we have our own to save. But I have a question, and trusting Your Grace, I'll be plain with it. The king cast out Lord Cevulirn, who by all accounts was the only honest man left in Guelemara. All fall long, he's heard only the Guelenfolk, and shown no regard at all to the blood we poured on Lewen field: he gave us Parsynan, was the thanks we had. I did think better of king Cefwyn, and I know I'm putting my head at risk, here. But he's only proved himself Marhanen, this far. Your Grace says he loves us dearly. Your Grace trusts him. Your Grace says if we commit ourselves and raise this effort, there'll be Guelenmen carrying the war into Elwynor and flying Her Grace of Elwynor's blue banner all the way. Bear in mind our love for you, my lord, but we don't so easily love the Guelen king, and we're not altogether sure the Guelenmen are going to cross the river."

He had wished the earls to speak plainly. And this *was* the truth, from men who had been prepared to join the Elwynim rebels against Cefwyn.

"My lord," Crissand had said to him while he chased those thoughts harelike through the brambles of Cefwyn's court, "my lord, we've come here to tell the truth. I said we dared, and Lord Azant's done it. So now I will."

Crissand drew forth a small, much-abused bundle of paper which he had carried close to his person, and he laid it on the table.

"My father's letters sent to Tasmôrden I don't have, though here are drafts of two of them. But all Tasmôrden's representations to him of whatsoever minor sort, they're here. I know they set forth names of some of those present, regarding those promises, and they knew I would do this. We trust my lord's forgiveness for any here that may be named; if you would be angry at them, be angry at me, first, and any punishment you set on them, set on me, first. I said I would do that. But I trust my good lord, that there'll be none."

"No," Tristen agreed.

"Ask the Bryaltine abbot about letters, too," Azant muttered, "if Your Grace wants a store of them. Aye, I've a few of my own, as damning." He drew another, neater bundle from his breast, and others laid them down.

They might, Tristen could not help thinking, account for some of the purloined archive, for there was a fair pile of them. And the Bryaltine abbot had trafficked with Tasmôrden? The Quinalt father he had known was inimical to him, but that the Bryaltines, who had sheltered Emuin's faith, might be a difficulty . . . he had not suspected.

That meant the Bryaltine abbot was, like Emuin, very good at secrets.

More than one wizard, Emuin had said.

Suddenly there seemed more than one side to Tasmôrden's scheming, and many to his own lords' duplicity with Cefwyn.

So the abbot had a glimmering of the gift, in himself, and had carried on treason and never let it be known.

"Uwen," Tristen said, "send for the abbot. Crissand. Lord Meiden." He reminded himself of pride, and courtesies by which Men set such great store. "Do you know what's in the letters?"

"Lord Heryn's dealings with the Elwynim . . . with Caswyddian," Crissand said, and so Lord Azant, red-faced, confirmed his own letters were part of it.

Then Earl Zereshadd broke his long and wary silence, and poured out a tale of Heryn's dealings. "Caswyddian sought permission of Lord Heryn to come into Amefel, to outflank the Lord Regent's forces . . . he'd already crossed the river, but he asked, to keep good relations; this while Prince Cefwyn was in Henas'amef. The Lord Regent was sending messages to the prince, and Lord Heryn intercepted every one. It was an agreement between Lord Heryn and Caswyddian to ambush the prince at Emwy."

By the prince Zereshadd meant Cefwyn before he was king. And the earls had supported Lord Heryn in his schemes . . . perhaps, in fact, all of them had conspired with various of the Elwynim pretenders, not necessarily one side, not necessarily one pretender, and perhaps even two or three of them at once, wherever reward offered itself. Deception had been the rule in Heryn's court, and Cefwyn had known he was living in constant danger. But not the extent of it.

And once started, the other lords had details to lend, perhaps matters which they had never told each other . . . in certain instances, provoking angry looks, then rueful laughter. Confessions and tale-bearing poured forth like nuts from a basket, everyone with a piece to tell, all of it with new kernels to glean, but nothing more of the greater doings of Lewenbrook than Tristen already knew: the conspiracy against the Lord Regent Uleman, which had driven Uleman into exile and at last to his grave in Amefel, had had Amefin help from beginning to end.

On their side of justice, the earls had suffered under Marhanen prohibitions and decrees. The order that had torn down the fortified manor houses was one such, and was the reason most of the earls lived in Henas'amef, in the great houses around the Zeide. The prohibition against the earls keeping above a certain number of common men-at-arms was another, which had left Amefel no standing army and no stores of arms to which anyone admitted . . . the disappearance of swords and spears after the last muster was suspicious, and the earls quietly said they would ask among their villages.

The number of men said to be bastard kin within the houses and therefore entitled to weapons turned out exaggerated . . . but these lords' houses had paid taxes for generations under the aethelings and the Sihhë and contributed to the building of Althalen and its luxury. Then came the Marhanen tax, and, worst of the lot, there had been Lord Heryn's extravagance; but they had kept quiet. Lord Heryn had been their own, their aetheling, their claim to royalty and their man accepted by the Marhanen crown.

"Heryn said," said Marmaschen, "that the tax went to the king. We see it didn't."

"What could we do?" Zereshadd asked. "There was no other lord we could turn to. So we tolerated his excesses. And gods save Your Grace, indeed, if there's as much as you say, it may save us all."

"There are other reserves," said Drumman slowly, "since we tell the truth here. More than one of us has laid by against need."

That brought an uneasy shifting in the seats.

"Truth," Crissand said. "We promised truth for truth. And hasn't our lord given us the truth?"

"This is my truth," Drumman said. "When the Marhanen king ordered the manor houses razed, records were lost; and in the losing of those records, my district preserved reserves with which we hoped one day to rebuild. This timber and stone I will give to the wall. The gold . . . I will also bring forward."

There were grudging nods among the others, as if this was far from an unknown practice.

"More might be found," said Zereshadd, and Marmaschen inclined his head with a pensive expression.

"Your Grace has allowed Bryn to fortify his north-ernmost village," Azant pointed out. Azant was also bordering on the river. "Since each has such ruins in our districts, holdings forbidden us by the Guelen king, and since we have reserves for building . . ."

He understood slowly that justice and evenhanded-ness meant allowing all such fortifications, if he had allowed them in Bryn: that was what Azant was saying . . . and there was a great silence in the hall, and an anxious look at him and at Azant, as if seeing what he might do with such resistance.

"First," he said, "defeat Tasmôrden. First let's take account of the map and fortify where there's some chance of the rebels coming across."

"We will need to leave the court and take command in our districts," said Marmaschen in a low voice. "At least at the start."

"I've very few couriers to carry messages," Tristen said, "and a scarcity even of guards, if I send Cefwyn more of his men home, as I have to this spring. I've no one, until Ivanor comes north. If I raise a levy for my own guard in the spring, men who've not exercised at arms, they're no defense. I need an *Amefin* guard."

"If each of us," said Crissand, "were to give ten men with horses to His Grace's service until Ivanor supplies the need, His Grace would have guards *and* couriers. Uwen Lewen's-son is a Guelenman, true, but a fine man, and a good captain, and any man of Meiden would be honored to have the post."

"Twice ten young men," said Drumman, "and at my own charge. With horses. And *past* the time Ivanor may arrive. I'll not have our lord served by another's men, for pride's sake, sirs. I challenge you."

"Men I'll give," Zereshadd said, "but where shall we get trained men here and trained men there, and now horses, gods save us, and men fit to ride them?

From under mushrooms? The Guelen king refused us any but our house guard."

"Send those you can," Tristen said, "and they'll learn."

"Give His Grace at least some with the skill," Crissand suggested, "and the rest, as likely as we can find. His Grace has no house of his own. Where is he to get them, if not from us?"

"Where will they lodge?" Azant asked. "The Guelens have the barracks."

The vision of a second barracks suggested a solution: a barracks might stand . . . had stood . . . Tristen drew in a breath, having suddenly a location in the South Court in mind, and wondered where they should find the stone . . . but on a second, more sober thought, simple timber would serve and make warm walls, and timber stood available on the nearest hillcrest—

If, that was, they could spare workmen from carving eagles and embellishing doors that were otherwise sound enough.

"I've workmen enough to raise a new barracks," Tristen said, "and the men you send will camp in the guardroom and the stairs and in the lower hall until there's a place, and help the workmen . . . and master Haman. We'll have our allies here by Midwinter, and all their horses." He drew a breath. "So. Let's do everything we've promised, and see that we're ready for what comes."

"His Reverence is here," Uwen said, when he had settled in his apartment to sort through the pile of the letters, and indeed he was, a shy presence at Uwen's side, a shy one in the gray space, unmasked, and honest at the moment, though he had never detected it before.

Of all priests he knew, save Emuin, who maintained

he was not a priest anyway, this was the only one such he recollected: this one had the gift, a faint one, or one secret by nature. If so, there was some strength in it.

"We were learning Tasmôrden sent to some of us," Tristen said. "Did he send to you, sir? Or has any other we might wish to know about? We've collected letters, all sorts of letters, which came from the north, and you may have some of your own."

The abbot bowed, and bowed again, white-faced. "Your Grace," he said in a faint voice, and then took several breaths before starting over. "Your Grace . . . yes."

"And what did you answer?"

"Nothing," said the abbot. "I sent no answer. And if the lord across the river should send again, I would tell Your Grace immediately, on my oath."

"Are you telling me the truth?" Tristen asked, listening in both realms, and the abbot nodded and bowed fervently.

"On my life, my lord, on my life and on my faith, I tell you the truth."

It was the truth, at least that the abbot had not betrayed him. The gift glimmered faintly, ever so faintly, full of fear, and there was no deception in the gray space.

"And have you heard from other men?" Tristen asked.

"From Earl Crissand's father," the abbot said anxiously. "From the old earl. And him I upheld. The king's viceroy I cursed," the abbot added on a little breath, "and all his men."

"Don't curse the Guelens," Tristen said mildly, "since all the Guelens we have left are mine and choose to be here, and Uwen, beside you, is Guelen. Don't wish ill at all, sir. You *can,* and I strongly wish you will not."

"*Yes,* Your Grace."

Blessings and curses alike had abounded in Efanor's little Quinalt book of devotions. But that book declared they all flowed to and from the gods.

He was not so sure they did not flow from men like this, a slight wizard, a whisper of a wizard, less even than Her Grace, but gifted with a hard, single-minded devotion and a steady purpose. He peeled through it like layers of an onion, bruising nothing, laying bare the heart.

"Go to master Emuin," Tristen said to the abbot, "immediately, and help him in any way he asks. You've helped him before. Help him now."

"My gracious lord," the abbot said, still white-faced, and bowed, and sought his leave. Uwen took him toward the door.

So there was a man in the midst of all Crissand's father had done; and by the letters he had, he knew this man had sheltered noble and common folk alike when the viceroy's justice was for hanging them.

"Who are these nuns?" he asked on a sudden recollection. "Emuin said there were nuns."

With women he had had very little to do, and nothing Unfolded to him to tell him whether that was common or not, or whether the gods, whom the Quinalt book said considered women as vessels and not as capable of acting, were quite the same for the Bryaltines. It all eluded him.

"My lord?" said the abbot.

"Are there nuns?"

"Priestesses," said the abbot in a quiet voice, utterly honestly. "As the Quinaltine never admitted. They've been with me for all my service here. But now they go in their habits, and we serve Your Grace in whatever modest way we can. Praise the gods, we do it in plain sight now."

*　　*　　*

"The Quinalt doesn't approve of priestesses," he said later to Uwen, having taken a second look in Efanor's little book, and having found what he recalled, that the Quinaltines thought women were a source of evil. But he disbelieved a great deal in that book.

"That they don't," Uwen said. "Women's fine enough by me, howsoever, an' a smile an' a wink from a lass is an even better thing, so ye might say."

"The Quinalt doesn't agree with that."

"The Quinalt ain't in charge here, an' besides, I fear I ain't that good a Quinalt."

"You used to wish to the gods. I seldom see you do it now."

"That." Uwen gave a faint laugh. "'At's a soldier's habit." Then he became sober. "I watched the dark come down at Lewenbrook, an' 'twixt us, m'lord, I ain't been a good Quinalt since."

What could he say to such a thing, when he was not sure whether Uwen regretted it or not?

That, however, was the sum of matters from the council, except the abbot's servants, the priestesses, arrived at his chambers within the hour, carrying a thick parcel of letters, all from the other side of the river, all very small, and tied up with red cord.

"Be assured," said the older nun, a plain woman robed all in gray and black, "His Reverence never did any of the things the Elwynim asked, save only to send aid to His Grace the Lord Regent."

To Ninévrisë's father, that meant, during his time in hiding. That was certainly no fault in the man: treason against Lord Heryn, as it happened, but none to the fair cause.

And the letters were not the only object of curiosity the Bryalt abbot had sent . . . and that not without conscious decision, Tristen thought, gazing at the women who had brought the letters, the elder a quiet woman, common as

any face in Henas'amef. She might have been a grandmother in the market . . . or perhaps she was.

For there was, indeed, when he probed it, a little spark
of a presence.

"Do I know you?" he asked, for the face seemed
familiar to him, and the women made a little bow like
willows in a gale.

"We served in the Zeide."

"In this room?" he asked, for suddenly *that* was the
point of familiarity . . . he recalled women gathered
together about sorcerous objects: Lady Orien and all
her company, with Hasufin's presence attempting the
breached wards.

The gaze that looked up at him, suddenly direct,
was dark and wide and terrified.

"You *were* here," he accused her.

"I served the Aswydds," came the faint response.
"But all the while I served the gods, by your leave,
lord. As does my sister. Let us go."

A lit straw, that was all the woman's wizardry was,
the sort a wisp of wind might cause to flare or extinguish altogether . . . and was not that the danger in
what Emuin called hedge-wizards . . . that they might
set a whole field alight?

"What is your name?" he asked, holding her with
his stare.

"Faiseth," she said, or that was what he thought he
heard. *Faiseth*. It seemed to echo here and there at once,
and now she knew she was observed. So did her sister.

A presence flitted past him, sought concealment in the
gray space. A hare in a burrow, the woman was, heart
beating quickly, and her sister with her. She had not
wanted this errand. The lord abbot had not wanted it
either, and the abbot commanded. So much he knew in
an instant. And the other woman . . .

—*"Pei'razen."*

The woman looked at him, stricken, addressed in the gray space as well as the world.

—*"Orien's servants."*

"The gods' servants, *your* servants, at your will, my lord."

He considered the women, and the knowledge he had, as thorough as if it had Unfolded to him. The women concealed nothing, to the walls of their souls they concealed nothing.

It was worth knowing the nature of such servants. It was worth remembering. Such as a lord could lay a ward *within* a soul, he laid one, sure and fast, so neither woman should betray the house, or him, without his attention, not in all they ever did. They were his.

And sharply a breath came in, and the younger covered her mouth with her hands as if her soul were trying to escape. The other pressed a hand to her heart.

"I've not harmed you," he said, "but you touched the wards of this room on that night, and now I've laid new ones." He abhorred what they had done, but he saw in them now a small, a wavering hope, a desire of life, of favor, of something he had to give that these woman desperately, fervently lacked and adored and sought with all their life.

"What do you wish of me?"

"Nothing, Your Grace."

"That's not so," he said. "What do you wish that I might give you?"

"To be the gods' true servant," she said, then, and that was false.

"The truth," he said, and took it, not that it was right to do, but that they sought mercy, and there was one safe way to pour it out to them. They wished to have skill, to be greater than they were. They wished to be regarded by one and all, feared, for it was fear they had understood.

"You need not," he said, "be afraid of anyone. You need never be afraid." He held out his hand, and took cold, thin fingers he could break with the pressure of his hand. He wished her *well* and wished her sister the same, and she began to tremble.

"Master Emuin would tell you," he said, "and will tell you, when you go to him, that breaking things is no help." He warmed the woman's hand in his, and reached for her sister's—so slight a pressure, her fingers, against his, as if he held one of his birds. "Don't do anything so foolish as that again. Don't curse. Don't fear anything."

He let go their hands, but now they tried, in that other place, to hold to him, as if he, after all, was what they had wanted.

"Tell the abbot I thanked him," he said. "And go to master Emuin. He'll know all you've done. Don't be afraid of him. Don't be afraid."

One and the other, they backed away, wanting his forgiveness, striving to reach into the gray space and not to let him go; but he had no wish to be their answer: he pushed them gently out into the world and shut it as it were a door.

He could not be Mauryl. He was never made to be Mauryl, or Emuin, who could teach. He delayed for a glance at their departure and said nothing to Uwen's look at him, before he added the letters to the pile.

The darkness had not even bothered to devour these sisters. It had had other prey in mind, and their understanding had never told them their danger.

Meanwhile, while the letters accumulated in lords' hands, priests had contended with curses while Hasufin prowled the wards like the wolf at the fold . . . never ask what curses the Quinalt patriarch might have laid on them all a matter of days ago, before he left; but he had felt no trace of it. The wards of the Zeide were sound.

The harm a priest could do seemed not to have touched what he guarded.

He went back to his burden of letters and confessions, his accounts and his requests, and his small stacks of coins.

By ranks and rows they stood on the desk to remind him, Uwen's lesson.

By such means he understood the simpler things that did not Unfold to him, or leap full-blown into his sight in the gray place. The lord of Amefel needed such advice, and had before him the correspondence of the Bryaltines with the enemy, the earls with the enemy, and the earls with the falsified accounts.

Now they began all to tell the truth.

Even Lady Orien's servants had told him their small truth at the last, and left running.

CHAPTER 8

Aletter from Tristen and a letter from Anwyll arrived on Cefwyn's desk in the same packet. Idrys brought them, on a cold, rainy night. Something close to ice was spattering the windows of the study. Water stood in beads on Idrys' black armor, from a recent trip outside.

"Two letters," Idrys said. "And a bit of news I fear my lord king won't like. The Amefin patriarch has just arrived at the Quinaltine, with four Guelen guardsmen, and on a lame horse."

"The *Amefin* patriarch," Cefwyn said in wonder. Nothing he could imagine could deter him from the letter he had in hand, but that did divert him a moment. "Why? Did Tristen send him?"

"With guards that haven't reported to me," Idrys said, "no. Without a message to me, no. And not wearing the Guelen red, no. Lord Tristen didn't send them. One man arrived in his proper colors, and came to his officer. The others I would call deserters."

"With the Amefin patriarch." Worse and worse news. It was not a flow of information this evening, it was a torrent becoming a flood, and by Idrys' face, he had only part of it in hand, in these letters. *Something* was going on that involved the Quinalt. And a man who had no reason to be running errands, at his age, and who was not likely to be running to higher authority on any ordinary matter.

With Tristen in charge in Amefel . . . was any matter of religion ordinary?

"Report," he said. "Master crow, don't deliver me this diced in pieces. I want to know. Report, or hie you downstairs and find out."

Idrys did not go. He loomed, a standing blackness against the dull, glistening color of the stained-glass window. Night was outside. But a little of it had gotten in with the Lord Commander, as if it were one of those shadows Tristen talked about, the cold spots his grandfather had claimed to feel on the stairs.

The world had been moderately ordered until Idrys came. Now there was no likelihood he would leave this office before dawn.

"The one man," Idrys said, "the honest man, to all appearances . . . that one pleads a sick mother. To deliver another piece of unpleasant news, the *captain* of the Guelen garrison is one that went into the Quinaltine, and my lord king will recall he was captain during your tenure, during Parsynan's . . ."

"I know the man," Cefwyn retorted. "He's a prig, a hardheaded and objectionable man. And a deserter, is it? A captain of the Guelens, a deserter."

"The man with the mother says they aren't deserters, but disguised themselves, and he professes not to know anything, except they went with Lord Tristen's permission, and met with the patriarch at Clusyn. It was, he says, the patriarch's idea to disguise themselves, but he had his captain's permission to go on, because of his mother."

"Did he come with them?"

"A very interesting point. He came just after Lord Tristen's message and Anwyll's. *These* came by the same man, Dragon Guard, from the river."

"From the *river*."

"So the man says. Lord Tristen was there. Meanwhile the patriarch took to the road—whether Lord Tristen was in Henas'amef or not at the time remains unclear. And if we believe the man with the mother, they disguised themselves and the patriarch, and came as fast as they could."

"With Tristen's permission, while he was at the river for some godsforsaken reason."

"The story is tangled, admittedly. I'd suggest, modestly, my lord king read the letters."

"You haven't."

"I was inquiring after the patriarch. First the messenger through the gates, by a quarter hour later the man with the mother, and half an hour after that, in this weather, draggled and soggy, the Amefin patriarch and the rest of the men. We'd not have known, necessarily, except the one man wearing his colors reported to his regiment first, as he should have, and the captain of the Guelens fortunately had his wits about him and sent for me." Idrys was dripping on the tiles, as happened . . . had had no cloak, by the soaking he had had, and a cold rain. Idrys had wasted no time on either end of his passage.

"Your best guess, crow. Guesses, now. Free for the making."

"I don't believe any of it. I think our man with the sick mother wants to reach her, doesn't want to entangle himself—that part of the story is true—with the business at the Quinalt. He's scared. The regimental captain had sent to know about the mother, who *was* ill, that was true; but recovered; she was at her house, knows nothing of all this, likely doesn't know her son's in the town. I've a handful of pieces with no ends that match."

"I agree. The whole pack is lying in some fashion, and Tristen didn't send them—no, he sent the man with the mother. I can guess that. He would. Stay. Let me read this."

"Read, my lord king. I've an order to pass, by your leave, maybe a report to receive, and I'll be back before you finish."

What order that was he did not ask. The deserters had better secure sanctuary at the gods' own altar before Idrys laid hands on them, Cefwyn thought to himself, for there was fire in Idrys' eye.

Ilefínian has fallen. I write this from Anwyll's camp at the river, where Cevulirn has set Ivanim archers to watch the bridges . . .

Cevulirn was with Tristen. Anwyll's camp at the river. The names rang like blessed bells, familiar and sounding of protection, safety, matters well in hand . . . the two most loyal of his lords, aware of the calamity and taking precautions.

I have set the thane of Modeyneth to be the new earl of Bryn. His name is Drusenan. His wife is Elwynim. He lives in the village.

I have found women and children fled from the fighting in Elwynor and set them in his care. Also I have ordered a wall and gate across the road there, where two hills make a natural defense. The Emwy road is warded.

Tristen broke laws. What else did he expect? Tristen appointed an unknown man to office, and he would wager there was good reason. The south was in good order—in excellent order, except he now knew his carts were farther away.

What shall I do, Tristen? was his silent appeal, which he knew Tristen would no more hear than he could understand two wizards looking at one another and nodding. I need the damn carts, Tristen. Well-done on the riverside, but my gear sits in camp, and it's the better part of a month to move those carts here.

Idrys' footsteps heralded his return. Cefwyn ceased reading and waited, as his Lord Commander came back to him.

"News?"

"I've sent a messenger to His Holiness advising him things may not be as he's told. I hear His Reverence was muddy, lame, and bruised. The report I have says he fell off his horse."

"Tristen couldn't have done it. He was at the river."

"At the river, my lord king?"

"With my carts. I know damned well that's what he's done. Go on."

"He's almost certainly here to complain of the lord of Amefel. But not even the Majesty of Ylesuin can demand entrance into the Quinaltine."

"We can demand other things."

"Shall I send for the Holy Father?"

"I want him there till he's found out something. Advise him so. Get those men with him in hand. I count that a necessity. Damn them for deserters. Damn all they say."

"And the patriarch of Amefel?"

"A knottier problem. One the Holy Father will have to solve. One he'd damned well better solve. Can you get *that* to him?"

"I'll attend to it," Idrys said, and left. His armor had just dried from the last foray out into the wretched weather. It was unlikely he would stop this time to obtain a cloak.

There were layers of command over the Guelens, the various companies jealous of their prerogatives, the Guelens, the Dragons, the Prince's Guard, all, all with officers reassigned and no little sorting out of men after his accession, Captain Gwywyn going to Efanor's guard,

Idrys becoming Lord Commander in Gwywyn's place, and no great love spent on either side of that transaction. Lord Maudyn was a civilian commander on the river, where most of the Guelens were assigned, and some of the Dragons. He hoped Idrys might lay hands on the Guelens that had come in, but there was a delicate matter of protocols involved, and it was credit to Idrys' oversight that the one man who had reported in had gained Idrys' immediate attention—averting disaster, Cefwyn thought.

And if they had any more men sifting into Guelessar from Tristen's command, well to send them immediately to the riverside, to work out their disaffections within sobering sight of the enemy shore.

Ninévrisë arrived in the doorway, robed for evening, her hair about her shoulders; he had not come to bed. She had waited, and he had no idea how long.

But it was not offense which had brought her.

"A page said there were dispatches."

"Anwyll's report," he said, knowing Ninévrisë ached for any message, any shred or scrap of news about her kin, her people, her land and her estates, such as remained of them. "It just arrived. And a letter from Tristen."

"All at once?" She folded her robes close about her and came to sit and see the letters, not knowing the other things. She read Anwyll's letter first, brief as it was, and then Tristen's, a long letter, for him.

"Cevulirn has gone there," Ninévrisë said.

"And this is all we have," Cefwyn said. "Look you. Not: *Cevulirn arrived* . . . or *Cevulirn came to me from Guelessar* or a damned scrap of information does he give! He writes worse letters than my brother!"

"He's building a wall . . ."

"A royal decree, several laws, and a treaty down at a stroke. It's the Sihhë wall he means."

"Gods bless him!" Ninévrisë exclaimed, laying a hand on her heart. "*I have made provision for those fleeing the capital since its fall; and also for armed men loyal to Her Grace who may escape. Them I will save if I can* . . . He understands! He's moved to help them. A place where my men can come." Her eyes were bright as lamps as she looked at him, and how could he say Tristen was wrong? "He *can*, do you think? He can have them come!"

"He might well," he said. He envisioned an Elwynim army, the army he had hoped would rise from the villages along Ninévrisë's route into Elwynor, but gathering in Amefel, far to the south.

Small chance the remnant of the loyal army would come east to cast themselves on Guelessar's mercy, or that of Murandys. They would go to Tristen.

And Ninévrisë's eyes were aglow with hope, for the first time since the news had come to them.

"Tasmôrden's men will loot everything they can," Ninévrisë said. "Aséyneddin had some good men, but Tasmôrden scoured the leavings of three armies. He'll be in Ilefínian till he's looted what's there, and he'll not have his army sober again until they've done their worst . . . so there'll be no pursuing anyone. They have a chance."

And failing that, there was a wall at Modeyneth, gods save them: the old Sihhë defense, for Althalen of the last High King had had no walls, only Barrakkêth's defenses, that wall that ran among the hills of Amefel. It had fallen into ruin even by the latter days of the Sihhë High Kings.

Now a band of Amefin peasants wielding picks and axes were remaking it. And was it chance that Tristen had thought of that wall?

Barrakkêth. First of the Sihhë-lords, Barrakkêth the warlord . . . whose black banners had swept every field, whose iron hand had struck down his enemies without pity.

He sat with Ninévrisë considering the letters. He sent a page for hot tea, against the chill of the dark. Rain made a cold, rattling sound against the windows.

"He might *bring* them to him," Ninévrisë said. "He might even *wish* them there, once he knows."

And could he say it was wrong, what Tristen had done? "Never say so," Cefwyn said, "even in the sodden father's hearing, but I hope he does."

The world had gone differently since his grandfather's day, when his grandfather had used wizards' help to win his war . . . much differently than the Sihhë-lord Tashânen's day, when wizard-work had exceeded siegecraft.

Once magic entered the lists, the advantage shifted incalculably.

Running feet, a boy's feet. It was not the tea that arrived, but more news in the rainy night.

"His Holiness," a page said from the door. "My lord king, Your Grace, excuse me. *His Holiness* is coming up the stairs."

In this weather?

"Bring a lap robe, mulled wine . . . Where's the damned tea, do you know?"

"No, my lord king, please you."

"Then find it! Bring me what I ordered!"

The boy fled. He had shouted at the lad. He had not meant to.

But if the Patriarch of the Quinalt had met with the patriarch of Amefel and had something to say to him, he wanted nothing out of joint. He went swiftly to the door, leaned out it to shout again. "Boy! Advise Annas! *Get me my guard!*"

"He's heard from the priests in Amefel," Ninévrisë said faintly, from her chair.

"Oh, I don't doubt he has." He returned to his seat. The page, forbidden to shout in the royal apartments, ran, steps echoing in the hall. "Don't fear. Idrys will have it all in hand. The Patriarch himself isn't to trifle with, and he's on our side, or I'll see to it Sulriggan sits on a bridge this winter."

The tea arrived at the same time the head of his bodyguard came in, Nydas, on night watch, who never excelled at soft-footed approach, and he came in a hurry. The hall had more traffic than High Street at noonday.

"My lord king."

"Tell Idrys the Patriarch's here. That's all. He'll know what this is about."

Annas had appeared behind Nydas, a head and shoulders shorter.

"Annas. The Patriarch."

"Yes, my lord king."

"Shall I stay?" Ninévrisë asked, with more prudence than he had thought of, and made him suddenly realize, gods, no, the Patriarch would not confess before a Bryaltine and a foreigner and a woman. His Holiness was bought, sealed, and paid for, but Annas and Efanor were the limit of his tolerance for such meetings: guards, pages, and priests failed to count as persons . . . Idrys not excepted, in that sense. But Ninévrisë . . . no.

"Love," he said, catching her hands. "Love, Nevris, heart of my heart—go. You'll have the entire sordid report, whatever it is, from me. But you're right. Grant me this."

She pressed his hands, nothing more, and went out in a whisper of footsteps, calling her maids and her own guard outside, and little time to spare, for a breathless page came back to report His Holiness in the corridor outside.

"And white as a ghost, Your Majesty."

"Well, gods, move chairs by the fire."

"Here?"

"Here, goose! Don't breathe like a hound at the chase, just move the chairs. *Seemly*, now! With grace, there."

Annas habitually kept a poker hot in the coals and warming bricks on the hearth, and had arranged two cups of mulled wine on a tray before the Patriarch reached the outer doors of the apartment, and had heated bricks for the Patriarch's feet on the hearth before he arrived.

The man was white as a ghost. His white hair was plastered to his face, and his shoulders were soaked. He had brought no one with him but a young lay brother, who saw His Holiness's cloak robe off, and the warm dry robe about him, and set His Holiness's feet on the warm bricks.

Annas needed do nothing more than offer the wine, of which the old man took a great swallow.

"Your Holiness," Cefwyn began, as Annas shooed the lay brother out with the pages and servant staff. "Dare I guess. The Amefin patriarch."

"Too far. He's gone much too far, Your Majesty. You *must* call him to heel."

"The Amefin patriarch?"

"The lord of Amefel, Your Majesty, I beg you don't make light of this."

"Far from it." He rested in his chair, the old man sitting wrapped in his robes, looking at death's door tonight. "The duke of Amefel wrote to me. Oddly enough, his letter *and* the patriarch arrived the same night."

"The patriarch and these soldiers waited their chance, when Lord Tristen had gone out of the town; they fled as far as Clusyn, and they were there when a messenger overtook them and went on without rest. They *chased* the messenger all the way, fearing what that message would say or request of Your Majesty— But His Reverence fell in the ditch." The wine had spread a modicum of warmth. The Patriarch took a larger breath. "His Reverence ordered the soldiers with him to ride on and overtake the messenger, but when they tried, His Reverence couldn't prevent his own horse running. His Reverence believes the horse was bewitched."

"I would laugh, Your Holiness," Cefwyn said, with a finger braced across his lips precisely to prevent that, "save the gravity of the situation. Horses follow horses. It's their nature."

"No luck accrues to anyone crossing his lordship of Amefel. Horses may follow horses, Your Majesty, but disaster follows Lord Tristen."

"Disaster? Only to his enemies. He owes us only good. We two should be quite lucky, should we not, Your Holiness?"

"Don't make light of it, if you please. What His Reverence reports is grimly serious."

Now he listened. "Say on."

"First, the people hail him Lord Sihhë . . ."

"So they did when I was there, and His Reverence knew it. That's no news. He probably *is*. What of it?"

"The appearance of it—"

"What am I to do? Come down with troops on my friend because cobblers and shopkeepers call out in the street? My enemy is across the river laying curses on me daily. I save my efforts for Tasmôrden."

"The law—"

His temper flared. He restrained it. "He's failed in some minute particular of doctrine, probably two and four times daily, not being a good Quinalt. But so does the Bryalt abbot! What of it? We both know Amefel is exempt from the ordinances, and is so by treaty and observance. If Tristen chooses to use those exemptions, he is entitled."

"Witches. Witches have appeared. Witches traffic in the marketplace, the forbidden tokens are sold without fear of rebuke . . ."

"They did that when I was there, too. Reprehensible, but hardly new, and His Reverence saw all of it. Had he news, or a history?"

"His Reverence *witnessed* witchcraft. Lord Tristen has promoted thieves to household service, has displayed the black banners, has consorted with witches, has . . ." Coughing overwhelmed the old man's vehemence. "He's conspired with Ivanor to gather an army and preferred Amefin officers over honest Guelenmen."

"It is Amefel, the black banners are my grant to him, written down in the Book of the Kingdom, and locally sanctioned by His Reverence, to boot, who's seen *them* fly before this. Cevulirn left here: I don't wonder he's paid a visit to Tristen. In fact I'm glad he has. So what sent the patriarch of Amefel breakneck to Guelemara, and what has a man I counted honorable and holy to do with deserters?"

"The captain of the Guelen garrison—"

"A deserter, with the other, who skulked away when Tristen was out of the town serving *my interests*! A deserter, sir, and with the kingdom at war. Tell me how I should deal with them? Shall I encourage every man who has a quarrel with his lord take to his heels? Every man who disagrees with his sergeant?"

"The point is—"

"The point is these men are not credible."

"But the report they have . . ." The Patriarch drew an old man's deep breath, seeming to fight for wind. "Majesty, take this seriously. In the hearing of witnesses, of the Guelen Guard, out in the country, a witch hailed him and prophesied to him. And directly after, the lord of Ivanor appeared as if magic had summoned him."

"A witch, you say?"

"Up from the roots of a great oak, that seven men couldn't span with their arms: the tree fell, the witch appeared in a great burst of snow and a wind of hell."

"I think I know the witch."

"Majesty?"

"Auld Syes. The witch of Emwy. Dead or alive's a guess. She's a harbinger of trouble."

"And Ivanor came."

"I don't wonder at that."

"After which Lord Tristen has cast down the authority of the garrison, fomented lies against the viceroy . . ."

"Tristen is a wretched liar. He knows he is. As for Parsynan, he'll be lucky if I don't hang him. That was Ryssand's choice, mind you. I never should have listened to him. Tristen was restrained in dealing with the man. Don't give me any blame for that. And don't trust him."

"Your Majesty." The tone was one of agony. "His Reverence brought men to swear to these things. He saw sorcery. His claims raise questions, Your Majesty, which I cannot counter. The orthodoxy, which *Ryssand* supports . . ."

"Ryssand."

"*Yes*, Ryssand." His Holiness was short of breath, and inhaled deeply before quaffing a great two-handed mouthful of the heated wine. Drops stained his chin, and he wiped them with a trembling hand. "But not only Ryssand. The strict doctrinists . . . have adherents in the Quinalt Council and the ministries of charity . . . and they were . . . they are . . . adamantly opposed to the appointment of the lord of Althalen and Ynefel to a province. They are doctrinally opposed to Her Grace's Bryalt faith, and they demand a sworn conversion and a Quinalt adviser at very least."

"They'll whistle to the wind for that!"

"I know. I know, Your Majesty, but . . . but . . ." Another spate of coughing, another deep draught of wine. "Forgive me. But His Reverence has documents, Bryalt prophecy. In every point, the lord of Amefel fulfills every point of them."

"The Quinaltine is promoting a Bryalt prophet?"

"Listen to me, Your Majesty! The stricter doctrinists—"

He was wrong to have baited the Holy Father. The old man was greatly agitated, having come here straight from conference with the Amefin father, which might not be the most prudent course to have taken. It was reckless—counting disaffections within the Quinaltine itself. "Sip the wine for your throat, Holiness, and give me the straight of it. I won't spread it about. The doctrinists. Is it Ryssand's priests stirring this up?"

The Holy Father shook his head and sipped the wine. He was calmer. A hectic flush had come to his white, water-glazed face, while his hair had begun to dry to a wild nimbus in the fire's warmth.

"Not Ryssand's urging. Not Ryssand alone. They *are* patrons of some of the doctrinists, but so are Nelefreissan, Murandys . . . all the north."

"I am aware."

"I am an old man. They're waiting for me to die."

"They can go on waiting."

"There's no debate with these absolutists . . . and they're not fools. There's power . . . power in their hands while they admit no truth but their own. They wish me dead."

"The king wishes you alive. I imagine even Tristen does, no matter what ill you've done him."

"I—!"

"You have the Patriarchate, Holiness. Use it! Be rid of these priests! You have the electors!"

"I have enough of the electors—but they're old, too, and divided in their minds. Here we have a displaced patriarch of a provincial shrine, whose authority was not respected, and, having these damning witnesses . . . witches, Your Majesty . . . and the people cheering the Sihhë . . ."

Idrys had arrived at the door, and at a nod, came in, apprised at least of the last the Patriarch had said. He stood, a bird of ill omen and dark news, with arms folded, rain glistening on the black leather of his shoulders.

"Well?" Cefwyn asked.

"The soldiers were legitimately discharged and have written authority to have returned," Idrys said. "The patriarch of Amefel overtook them after they'd drunk themselves half-insensible at Clusyn. He commanded their escort. When the Dragons' messenger passed them on the road, they made all haste to overtake him, but His Reverence met with a haystack and a ditch. The Dragons' messenger not unreasonably thought them bandits and rode for his life."

Ludicrous. He could imagine the scene, the descending dark, the patriarch in the mud, the courier, one of the elite regiment, in desperate flight from the patriarch of Amefel.

"I beg you take this in all seriousness," His Holiness said. "The devout fear this, among the electors, they fear us all endangered by witchcraft and wizardry, and Your Majesty must remember these are honest men, genuinely offended by these goings-on in Amefel . . . if nothing else." A cough brought another recourse to the wine cup, which must be nearing its bottom. Cefwyn had not touched his, having no wish to numb himself.

But the Patriarch clearly had no caution left tonight.

"Threats of violence," the Patriarch said, "omens. There are such, as there is magic."

"No man who stood on Lewen field denies that, Holy Father. *What* omens, and is it time we sent to Emuin? If you can't stop them . . ."

The Patriarch shook his head. "No. The Teranthines are no help, and Emuin is less, in this business. I come here . . . I come here . . . in hope of reason. Receive the Amefin patriarch, hear him patiently, realizing . . . realizing that what he says the doctrinists take as the very substance of their fears, so much so . . . some preach actions . . . actions which would aim at the lord of Amefel's life."

Idrys was not at all smiling, his dark-mustached face utterly intent on what the old man was saying.

"Buren," Idrys said, naming a name which had at least crossed his desk, a hedge-priest, a wild-eyed sort.

"Buren, Neiswyn, all these barefoot sorts." The Holy Father manifested no love for them either, and in truth, they were of long standing, going about the countryside praying over cattle and orchards and making their living off charity. They had always been at odds with the well-fed priests of the great Quinaltine. "*Ryssand's* priests support them, call them holy. *This* is what we can't counter. These are holy men!"

"Holy troublemakers."

"This Buren wanders about," said Idrys, "prophesying, speaking in vaguest terms about unholiness abroad in the land and blood on the altar. It's nothing new. He derives a living from it. He always has."

Self-made prophets not within the Quinaltine turned up, and vanished, and said things not quite blasphemy, not quite treason . . . and did so freely, since they couched it in prayers for the cleansing of the kingdom and the Quinalt.

"Your Majesty," His Holiness said in anguish, "it's reached a point of danger. There it is. This has come at a very bad time."

"Then I suggest you draw a distinction between sorcery and wizardry in your homilies, Holy Father, start now, and nudge your doctrine toward some measure of reason on the subject of magic . . . and soon."

"I dare not!"

"I suggest you dare, Holy Father. I more than suggest you dare. You have authority over His Reverence. Wield it! Modify his testimony! Be in command! The doubters and the ones who'd follow you are looking to you to know what side to take. Give them a signal, for the gods' sake!"

"I am an old man, Majesty."

"Would you be an older one? Act!"

"Yes, Your Majesty. I'll try."

"Well that you came tonight. Bravely done. Annas, see His Holiness back to the Quinaltine in good order, and dry and warm."

"Your Majesty." It required an effort for His Holiness to rise, between the wine and his exertions on the stairs. Annas assisted, while a page brought the lay brother back, insisted he keep the dry robe, found a dry cloak for him, and helped him on his way.

All the while Idrys had waited; and as the door latched, and they were alone:

"Two letters from His Grace of Amefel," Idrys said, and drew out a small, unsealed missive from his belt. "Yet another messenger chased the lot of them . . . a postscriptum, at considerable effort. I did read it."

"Is it bad?" Cefwyn asked, with a sinking of his heart.

"Only what we know," Idrys said. "The Lord Tristen realized the danger in the patriarch's flight.

He arrived home, evidently to find this, and bent a great deal of effort for his second rider to reach us before His Reverence and the guardsmen did. I find it worth remarking that he failed . . . considering his abilities."

"I can't assess his abilities," Cefwyn said, and took the letter and sat down.

Be careful of the Quinalt father who has left Amefel and gone to the Quinaltine. He did so while I was absent and Uwen had no authority to prevent him, yet I wish we had done so. He is angry with me.

Regarding the fortifications at Modeyneth and elsewhere I mean to pay those out of the Amefin treasury. Many of the earls are ready to lend help. Also the earls are willing to lend me men for an Amefin company, which I will set in order by the spring and send you the rest of the garrison at Henas'amef, as well as Anwyll.

The work on the wall seems likely to go quickly. I hope that in all these things I am doing what you will approve.

Raising an Amefin company for his guard instead of the Guelens was well within sense. The duke of Amefel had that grant of power from his hands. It was the only thing in the message that *was* clearly within Tristen's grant and honor.

"You'll note the bit about fortifications," Idrys remarked.

"My grandfather's decree to bring down their strongholds was a good idea then. It no longer is. I regretted not having them this summer."

"Will you tell that to Ryssand?"

"Damn Ryssand. Damn the Amefin patriarch." He folded the letter and tucked it into his own belt. "At least we're prepared in the south. What he's doing will turn the war north, when Tasmôrden hears it, mark me. He's being left no choice. And if he doesn't move toward him, we'll be the hammer and Amefel the anvil. Damn Ryssand twice and three times, he and Murandys will catch the arrows if Tasmôrden invades. And as for Ryssand . . . I may let my brother's marriage go forward."

"You jest."

He swung around and fixed Idrys with a direct stare. "Artisane's *husband* would inherit, were Ryssand to fall in a ditch. My brother might be duke of Ryssand *and* duke of Guelessar."

"Shall I find the ditch?" Idrys said.

"After the wedding." He found himself well out on a limb, far, far from safe ground. "But maybe not. I'm not my grandfather."

"Your grandfather died in bed, my lord king, a grace the gods did not grant your late father, who spared his enemies."

"My grandfather died fearful of ghosts, master crow."

"And does my lord king fear them?"

"There has to be a wedding, before an inheritance. I'll think of it then."

"Think now, my lord king. If not Ryssand, then these troublesome priests. The Quinalt won't fault you."

"One doesn't win by killing priests. They multiply. They become martyrs. Gods know we need none. His Reverence of Amefel will get his comeuppance, when His Holiness wakes up and uses his wits. Then Ryssand will have his, if my brother weds the Ryssandish minx. He far underestimates my brother."

"As my lord king wishes," Idrys said, "and again, as my lord king wishes. And a third time, as my king wishes."

"Plague on you! You don't approve. Say so!"

"Consider, I say, that Tristen himself would have

wished his messenger arrived timely; but he came too late. Our revenant is still fallible. Wizards failed."

"He asked a man to make up days on His Reverence. He failed. It's not portentous."

"His Reverence fell in a ditch. And alas, survived it. Failed, I say."

"He'd not wish for a death," Cefwyn said, and wondered in himself why he held his hand. He had not been so moderate once. He followed a wizard's path without a wizard's power.

He wished not to be his grandfather, that was the truth. He wished to win his battles on the field, not in some ditch.

He wished not to become the king his grandfather had been. That dark pit was always there, a defensible place, a lonely, loveless place . . . and he had been on his way there, when he had met Tristen, and met Ninévrisë. He had listened to Heryn Aswydd, adorned his gate with heads of men who might have been his best allies, had he only known how he was deceived.

Then in Tristen's company, seeing the mystery of forest leaves and the wonder in a water-polished stone, a light had come on him, a bright, bright hope, that this was the true world, all around him, truer than his darkening sight. And ever after that and forever, he hoped for himself, and whenever he thought of dark and practical deeds, why, that light distracted him toward this dream he had, and made him, perhaps, not a good or a reasonable king, but a king who wanted to be better, a king who wanted all his kingdom to enjoy their lives.

"My lord king?" Idrys prompted him, and he knew he had been woolgathering, looking toward that nonexistent but oh, so real light, dreaming, not being responsible toward his duties.

"Let's trust His Holiness," he found himself saying,

covering that soft part of his soul that could deal with Tristen and his crownless queen, and finding the reason to gloss it over, undetectable by Idrys' critical eye. "He sees his danger: it's inside the Quinalt. Let's see what he can do about it."

CHAPTER 9

The wind blew and blew in the dark of night, battering at the windows in the dark, spitting rain, not snow, wailing around the eaves and rattling shutters.

"Like a spring wind," Lusin said, "an' us not to Midwinter yet."

Tristen remembered the gray rain curtains that had swept down on darker gray towers, and knew with a vague edge of fear that at last his year was coming full circle: someone named a characteristic of the coming season and it did not Unfold to him; he recalled very keenly the look and the feeling of it at Ynefel, the crack of thunder, rain, creeping wormlike along the horn-paned window of his room.

Here, his servants went anxiously about, even Tassand casting worried looks at the besieged windows, and saying it was unnatural.

"It's only wind," Tristen said. "A true wind."

Yet he had wished fair weather on the south and all the ill to the north, on Tasmôrden's army, and if it rained here, he thought it might snow to the north.

It was still his wish, and for more of it, but he feared such tampering with nature. He thought, as the storm raged and thunder rolled above the roof, of going to master Emuin and asking. But Emuin slept, when he wondered: was snug in his blankets in the tower, ignoring the fuss in the heavens, and would not be nudged to wakefulness.

If master Emuin could sleep through the racket, he supposed it was not so harmful . . . but he could neither sleep nor ignore it.

Neither, it seemed, could Uwen, who had been down to the stables and now came back with his boots wet and his cloak dripping.

"Not natural, m'lord, for it to be so warm so late in the year. The yard's a mud puddle."

"No trouble, however."

"All's well, as I saw." Uwen slung the cloak off, and a servant took it. "It blew the lantern out, and the horses is all glad to be in. Liss don't like the thunder."

"Take a cup of ale," he said, for he knew Uwen liked it at the end of a long day, and so they shared a cup, and talked of other things, the building of a second barracks in the scant free space of the Zeide court. That would go faster in warmer weather; and so would the training of the Amefin guard, which Uwen meant to oversee.

Uwen went off to bed, then the thunder quieted, and Tristen felt the pigeons all snugged close, a sleepy feeling, somewhere near in the eaves and the stable loft. Warm, warm together, and peaceful, they felt.

And with master Emuin sleeping, and all the world quiet, the fire crackling and the spatter of rain against the windows, he found sleep still eluding him. He read . . . read philosophy, the sound of the rain comforting and peaceful. When he slept, he slept in the chair, and so Tassand found him in the small hours of the night, and threw a blanket over him.

In the morning Tassand called him to the window, that portion of clear glass amid the colored, and showed him the hills.

They all showed brown, with patches of white. The

snow had gone, bringing the land back to autumn, all in a night.

"Do you see?" he said to Uwen, as he came in for breakfast.

"Aye," Uwen said, "and a soggy mess of mud. I saw it from the stable-court steps: I weren't goin' down in the muck before breakfast. Did ye ever see such weather?" Then Uwen laughed. "O' course ye hain't. All's to find."

"Have you?"

"No. A manner o' speakin', m'lord, *ha' ye ever seen*? I ain't, not like this. The streets is runnin' torrents, an' the streams'll Flood."

Flood Unfolded to him in a dismaying instant, bridges hit hard by trees, livestock and houses swept away. He had not thought of that in his wish. He wondered how much water was bound up in the snow.

"Are the villages in danger?" he asked. "The bridges?"

"The bridges is to ask," Uwen said, "but the villages is generally set high, the countryfolk bein' no fools. Amefel's had floods afore this, an' they'll have brung up their sheep last night, I'll warrant, when they heard the rain."

He had been careless. He had cast hardship on people who trusted him, without thinking of the consequence to them. "I wish the weather may be kinder," he said.

"It *was* you," Uwen said.

"I think that it was," he confessed. "And just as much rain as fell here, I wished snow on Tasmôrden . . . not enough to prevent the people from crossing the river. Now I wish the ground may dry."

"Then if it don't happen by unnatural sort, I wager the winds'll blow," Uwen said. "An' blow for days."

And indeed by the time breakfast was done, the

wind had risen. When Tristen took the accustomed tribute of bread to the pigeons on the ledge, their feathers were ruffled, and their wings beat hard when bad manners shoved one another off the edge.

But despite the wind the morning was bright blue and clear beyond the glass, and the change in the land was a curiosity. "I may ride a turn, today," Tristen said to Uwen, who stood by to watch. "I should see how the streams run. Dys wants exercise."

"It'll be muddy," Uwen said. But all the same they laid their plans, for they had very many horses due to arrive, and before this master Haman had had men out in the snow and the frozen ground walking the fences and building weather shelters and moving hay and straw—against the belief that the winter was sure to deepen, and that what they must do by Midwinter they must do now. Now the whole effort to prepare the province waited for boats, and streams swollen with melted snow ran to the Lenúalim, on which transport of grain depended—all such things had become a worry. They had sent a message to Olmern, over-land . . . a cold and soggy messenger, last night, if he had not stopped in a village . . . that, too, his wishes had done.

He vowed more caution, and went down to a muddy yard somewhat sheepishly, not to confess the reason of the sudden turn in the weather, or the source of the rising of the wind that tugged at canvas shelters and whistled through the eaves, on this bright blue morning.

"A fine mornin'," Uwen said, seeming to take it all in stride. "Only so's we get cold for a few days yet, enough to freeze the fleas in the sheds, as I can swear ain't happened yet."

"Do they freeze?"

"Time was ye were askin' me what winter was,"

Uwen said, "an' now ye're sendin' it away. Aye, fleas do."

"I don't think it's a good idea to wish against what wants to come," Tristen said, "and master Emuin slept through it all. He calls me a fool, which is probably true. It shouldn't have rained last night. But I didn't think of rain. I thought of snow and ice melting and never thought of rain at all."

"So will we have fine weather for ridin' today?"

"I think we will," he said. "Except the wind."

The pigeons walked about in the morning, slightly damp, looking confused as they dodged among the puddles, but dodging about on very important business, always, at least to look at them.

Haman's lads, as Uwen called them, saddled Gia and Gery and the guard horses, for Lusin was coming down, with Syllan and the rest.

"It's a muddy mess down there, m'lord," Haman advised them as they waited. "And there's only piles of timbers as yet where the shelters will stand."

"We'll have a look, all the same," Tristen said. "Uwen says the streams will be up."

"The east meadow'll be under, afore all," Haman said, "but the timber's on the high end, where we're building, m'lord. There's nothing lost, I'll wager, and grass laid bare, which if it dries before the horses tramp it down, is no bad thing."

It meant less need of hay, less clearing of stables . . . perhaps no need of shelters at all for many of the horses if the weather held; but dared he do that? They were not at Midwinter yet. Had the heavens a store of snow that must fall, before all was done?

He saw he needed to face master Emuin and have his word on it, if master Emuin would tell him a thing.

He saw he needed inquire afresh about the state of the villages, and pay at his own charge any losses: fair was fair, as Uwen said, and none of the folk of Amefel had merited flooded fields.

He could not have done such a thing when he walked the parapets at Ynefel. He could not have done it before Lewen field. He was not sure when or how the gift had Unfolded in him, perhaps that very day that he and Cevulirn rode home and he foresaw the plight of the fugitives in Elwynor, harried by armed men. Pity and anger had moved him; and could he say he had thought as much as he ought before his heart swept the hills clear?

Young lord, he could hear Emuin chide him, in that tone of disapproval, *don't ask me.*

How could he ask Emuin . . . when by all he knew Emuin had no such strength in him, an old man and frail, and very likely this time to disapprove what he had done. He did not look forward to that meeting, and did not want to face Emuin with only a guess how the land had fared. He wished to see it, and assure himself by the sight of what he could see that he had not done too great a harm, that villages and the settlement at Althalen alike would have come through it undamaged.

They had no official need, however, and escaped the display of banners and all the commotion that went with them. On what had become a windy, damp morning it was no procession, only a snugly cloaked faring-forth, down the streets where shopkeepers were sweeping debris from their walks, past the small repairs of battered shutters and fallen roof slates and tattered awnings.

The day was, despite the fierce wind, warmer, and the town had gone from white to brown and unlovely. The jewelry of ice had crashed in ruin from the eaves of buildings up and down the street and lay in dull heaps. Everything was muddy water and piles of ice and dirty remaining snow, all the way to the gates. The gutters ran full, and great puddles of cold water stood in the lower town, through which the horses went with disdain.

Outside the gates and to the west lay the establishment of the stables, the pigs, the geese, the cattle, all manner of pens and sheds, and some of those pens were covered in water.

South were orchards and sheep pasture, and near the walls, the untidy small dwellings of the gooseherds and cowherds and kennels and their yards, many of which had standing water. The granaries were on a mound, and stood clear. And to the west and north and up the nearer hills, the pastures spread out. Those that master Haman claimed for the horses were, by his foresight, the best drained and finest, where the land had streams running from the hills, but no threat from rising water.

Dysarys and Cassam, his and Uwen's heavy horses, had pride of place in the stables, and when they came within sight of the stables, there they were in the first two paddocks, out to tramp about on this muddy morning. They were Cefwyn's gift, and had their own grooms from the day they were foaled: when the horses came, so the grooms came to Amefel, and there was some little ado while they turned Liss and Gery, their light horses that had been on call in the fortress stables, out to the paddocks for their turn at sunlight and room to run, and ordered the boys to brush down and saddle Gia and Petelly, their other two mounts, for the trip back up the hill.

That brushing down was no small task, for the horses out in the pens had all coated themselves in mud this morning. Well-groomed hides stood up in winter coat and caked points, and the stablehands were brushing and combing their charges in pens all along the row.

More, Lusin and the household guard, too, had sent for their second horses, and a sorry-looking lot they faced in exchange, to the stablehands' great embarrassment.

"As we didn't know ye were comin', m'lord."

"Saddle 'em. An' no mud on the gear," Uwen said gruffly, and without any grace for the weather. Haman would say much the same: horses should have been inside this morning, kept ready. "Suppose there'd been Elwynim across the river. Suppose we'd had to saddle, an' ever' man in the Guard callin' for his horse, an' them muddy as pigs! Get to it!"

Boys ran.

"They'll roll," Tristen said, seeing Gery do exactly that, turned out in the paddock. She waved her feet in the air, then rose triumphant, with a fine muddy coat.

"Horses," Uwen said in disgust, but there was little he loved better in the world than being in the stables and having his hands on a fine horse.

Dys and Cassam, however, were clean and brushed, first among all the horses, and had no more than spattered legs. They were ready to ride, to Tristen's great pleasure, and with no ado at all. The guards' were not.

"Get us some horses," Lusin protested, "with His Grace bound out and us afoot. Damn the mud."

"We'll not be far," Tristen said. "No great need. Uwen will be with me."

"M'lord," Lusin said unhappily.

"At my direct order," Tristen said. "We'll be riding just down the lane."

Lusin was not happy, but in a trice they had saddled Dys and Cassam and he and Uwen were out down the safe lane between the rows of paddocks, an unprece-

dented lack of guards, a privacy Tristen found pleasant. Dys and Cassam were in a fine, cheerful mood, for
they used the light traveling harness, not the heavy
fighting gear, and that meant it was exercise and frolic,
not work: both were tugging to have more rein as they
reached the end of the paddock lane.

"Oh, we're full o' tempers this mornin'," Uwen
said. Indeed Cass was taking Dys' excited mood,
throwing his head, working his mouth at the bit, both
horses tending to a quicker pace as they made the turn.
"Hold there, ye scoundrel."

The great feet spattered puddles far and wide as Dys
took to a quicker and quicker pace, and Cass did, and
step by step it was riders and horses in the same wild
rejection of discipline, mud flying. They made a wild
charge past fences and to the very end of the paddocks,
far, far past the lane.

"To the trees," Tristen called out, his heart cheered
by the lack of troubles they had found. The wind stung
his face and his eyes, tore at cloaks and manes, and
had a bracing edge of cold.

"We told Lusin," Uwen began, but the horses'
excitement swept them on, and it was only a little distance more. Off they went, as far as the skeletal gray
trees, and the turn there that led to the west . . . the
west, and riders on the road.

There were no pennons, no color about them; and
they were not Ivanim. Tristen drew in quickly, and Uwen
beside him, at once in sober attention, Dys and Cassam
fighting the rein now, for they had well-taught notions
what to do with strangers confronting them, and now
the high spirits were for a charge and a fight.

But the riders, three men, who looked as if they had
ridden far and slept rough, never changed their pace,
though it was sure they had seen they were not alone.

"M'lord," said Uwen, "I'd have ye ride back. At least

stand fast an' let me ride to 'em an' ask their business."

"No," Tristen said. They had their swords with them, if no shields. They never left the Zeide gates unarmed or unarmored.

"Ye got that plain cloak, m'lord, an' no color nor banner showin'."

"Let's find out their business all the same," he said, "and let them explain who they are."

They came a little farther, then, until at a stand of beeches on one side and a flooded patch across the road, they had come within hail. "I'll bespeak 'em," Uwen said, Tristen saying nothing. "Hullo, there! Ye'd be men out o' Bryn, or what?"

Then the riders did stop, on the other side of the flooded patch. "Messengers," said the foremost, and raked his hood back, showing a bearded face, and it in want of trimming and shaving. A rough sort, they all looked. "We've come to meet with the Sihhë-lord in Amefel."

"An' to whose pleasure, if it ain't his sendin'?" Uwen replied. "As it ain't! What business have ye?"

"With *him*, I say." The speech was not a common man's, not Amefin, nor like any but Her Grace's, and hearing that lordly tone, Tristen slipped his cloak back, showing the blood red of Amefel and the black Eagle beneath.

"You?" the man asked, suddenly respectful. "Your Grace?"

"Tristen," he named himself. "Duke of Amefel. Messengers from whom? Not from Bryn."

"Elwynor, Your Grace."

"My men had orders to gather in weapons." He saw a sword at a saddlebow, and for the rest there was no knowing what the men hid: armor at very least, perhaps heavier armor than his and Uwen's, but he trusted to his own skill.

Yet his remark brought no threat. Instead, the leader of the band dismounted from his weary, head-hanging horse and went to one knee in the mud at the edge of the puddle.

"They said at Althalen Your Grace had given them leave to make a settlement, and we've come to ask shelter for all the men in our company, our arms to serve Your Grace."

"Ye didn't come by the bridge on this road," Uwen said, "where His Grace has appointed ye to cross."

"No. East. East of Anas Mallorn, such as we could, where we could."

"Gettin' horses across in this weather," Uwen said in amazement. "A hard thing, that."

"A raft and rope, sir, all we had. We crossed to Bryn, but the lord in Modeyneth said we should go to Althalen, and so I sent the company there under a sergeant. But we four came to pay our courtesies and ask . . ." The officer had taken to trembling, there exposed to the cold, and the others slid down from their horses and caught him up, themselves in no better case. "To ask your lordship for relief for Elwynor," the man reprised with a fierce effort, "and to swear to your banner, because we will never swear to the likes of Tasmôrden."

"So all of us," another said. "Lord, men, and horses, numbering near sixty, of ten houses, all to your service."

"Such houses as they are now," said the third. "And our lands all cinders and ash."

They were no common soldiers, by the sound of their speech: Tristen had learned that distinction, little attention he paid to it when men were as brave as these seemed. They were noble by their actions and by their deeds, and while armed Elwynim were the very presence he had wanted to keep away from

Henas'amef, considering his duty as duke of Amefel, here were Ninévrisë's men, at war with Tasmôrden, carrying their quarrel into his borders.

But here, too, were horses near to foundering and men who had camped or ridden through the storm he had raised. He felt keen remorse for their hardship.

"There's food and shelter ahead," Tristen said, "for you and your horses."

"I'll walk, by your leave," the foremost said faintly. "I can't get up again, and my horse can do with the relief."

Indeed the man set out walking, wading knee-deep through the water, unsteady in his steps and leading his horse, and so the others walked, leading theirs.

So Tristen and Uwen rode on either side of them, escorting them all the way to the paddock lane, and the muddy track there.

"Ho!" Uwen called out as they came down the lane. "Boys for these horses, an' quick about it! See to 'em and mind them legs! These horses has come through that storm an' through flood!"

Boys appeared from sheds and shelters, and so, too, did Lusin and the rest, from the grooms' shelter, near the wall.

The bedraggled Elwynim managed to walk that far, where Aswys and other senior grooms marshaled a warm place, dry blankets, and a cup of warmed wine apiece, even fresh bread and butter . . . at which the grimy-handed visitors could only stare in exhaustion and desire, too weary even to eat more than a few bites.

But Tristen, wrapped in a warm cloak and having dry boots, as these men did not, sat by the fire and listened, with Uwen, to the account of men whose news was as they feared, that Ilefínian had gone down in looting and confusion, and that very little of Elfharyn's force had escaped the walls at all.

These men's company, losing touch with any coherent resistance, had run from east of Ilefínian to the river, and escaped with their weapons and their horses, by great resourcefulness, expecting to live like bandits in the hills of Amefel and to get a message to Ninévrisë, to learn whether they might have refuge.

"But from the new lord in Bryn we heard different things," said the foremost, whose name proved to be Aeself, a lieutenant, a nephew of Elfharyn's line. "We heard in Modeyneth about the old wall and Your Grace and Mauryl Gestaurien, and so we came to offer all we have, ourselves and our weapons and our fortunes such as they are."

All they had was very little, except weapons and exhausted horses, but not of little account was the courage and the persistence that had carried them this far, to a town that, before, had seen the heads of Elwynim messengers adorn its gates.

"Sleep," Tristen said, for he judged these men had had no rest last night. "Come to the Zeide when you have the strength, and borrow horses for the ride up. You'll show me on maps where you crossed." It was in his mind that what these men had managed, more might do, and not only Ninévrisë's men. They lacked sure knowledge of such crossings as scattered intruders knew to use.

To Uwen he said: "Find two riders to carry a message to Althalen. Tell them their men came here safely."

"Better send more grain from here," Uwen said. "Wi' horses to feed, they'll need it, and it's quicker than sendin' to Modeyneth."

"Do so," he said.

"Tents," said Uwen. "And axes and good rope; that too. 'At's a whole damn village they've become, m'lord, and now there's a company."

No longer the domain of mice and owls, Tristen

thought, and as he was taking his leave, Aeself, falling to his knees, insisted to swear, and gave his oath to him.

"Take my pledge," Aeself said, "to be your man in life and death, and gods save Elwynor."

"So with the rest of us," said Üillasan, oldest of the three, and went to his knees and took his hand and swore.

But Angin, the last and youngest, said, "To the hope of the King To Come . . . for I've seen him."

That brought sharp looks, even from Uwen.

"I'd have a care there, m'lord," Uwen said for Tristen's ear alone, "and not take that oath from him. It ain't wise, an' it ain't loyal."

"What Uwen says I regard," he said to the young man.

"All of us think it," said Aeself, "and damn us if you like, the boy's said it for good and all, my lord. You *are* our lord."

He saw the distressed looks of the Guelenmen who guarded him, and Uwen's look, and the shocked faces of the grooms, Guelen and Amefin together.

"I was Shaped, not born," he said bluntly, "and some say I'm Sihhë and some say I was Barrakkêth. That may be. But I say my name is Tristen, and while I say so, not even a wizard's wish can turn me to any other creature."

"What my lord wills," Aeself said, and so the others said, in exhausted voices, wrung thin by cold and hardship, men sinking to the last of their strength.

"Take care of them," Tristen said to the grooms, for it seemed added hardship to send them to horse-back again, and up the hill, when they were only now warm and eased of sodden armor: here in the grooms' quarters were men skilled in medicines and armed with salves and every comfort for men or horses. "Send them up the hill when they're well and able.—Are our horses ready?"

"That they are, m'lord."

"An' as for what they said and what they wished to swear," Uwen said gruffly, "an' all ye witnessed, the wine come over 'em, is all. Talk, an' ye'll have me to deal with."

"The wine came over 'em," Aswys said. "'At were the case. Isn't a man here heard aught else or remembers it, or *I'll* skin 'im, m'lord."

Heated wine might have brought out the oaths, so Tristen said to himself, and held in his heart what Uleman had said of him, and what Auld Syes had said, and now these men.

But the Elwynim might hail him king or High King or whatever else they wished: things were true in a wizard's way of speaking that were not true to ordinary Men, and the converse, as well. He had been Barrakkêth and he was not, while he was Tristen, Mauryl's heir, and that was what he chose. Sihhë-lord Barrakkêth might have been, and lord of all the lands the High Kings ruled, but he had never been king, in the sense the later lords had been.

"If it were true I was Barrakkêth," he said to Uwen and Lusin and the rest on the way back to the gates, while they were still outside the streets of the town and alone, "if that were true, still, Barrakkêth was never King. What the Elwynim think doesn't change that."

"Wine an' truth," Uwen said, riding bay Gia beside Tristen, on honest, shaggy Petelly. "They meant it wi' their hearts, an' think they've sworn. So thank the gods His Reverence *is* in Guelessar. Their lord dead, one an' the other, an' the Elwynim lookin' for their King To Come for the last sixty years, so who's to say? That old prophecy's been rattlin' about for sixty years lookin' for a likely place."

"This is not that place."

"Ye're Sihhë an' you're a lord, an' ye must say that's uncommon in Ylesuin, m'lord."

"Duke of Amefel, Cefwyn's friend, and Her Grace's. Mauryl's heir. Emuin's, someday. That's enough."

"Ye should say so often enough the Elwynim hear it," Uwen said, "beggin' pardon, m'lord, but I'd be damn careful to say so, because the Elwynim's apt to get notions."

The people who on festive days called him Lord Sihhë in the streets saw nothing unusual in his coming and going on this day, and lacking the signs of an official procession, they only paused in their business and bowed as he passed.

A handful of children ran along beside, untrustable and noisy, at which Petelly also looked askance. Such were the hazards of Henas'amef. It had assumed a beloved, homelike character, even its obstacles and hazards: he loved it, he decided, and the men in the stable threatened that love . . . threatened him as much as they helped Her Grace.

He had to make them understand that. They wanted from him what he could not give, and wanted to give him what was not his to hold . . . what he had never held. *This* was his Place in the world, his, Crissand's, the two of them, as Barrakkêth had valued Crissand's remotest kinsman, long, long ago—so he fancied, yet remembered nothing, saw nothing further Unfold. Three riders from the north could threaten his peace this winter, and ride in on the wings of storm, but he drew a deep breath and willed his land quiet, and his visitors safe, and the war far from the people he battered with rain and wind—far gentler enemies than otherwise threatened them.

Deep let the snow lie on Ilefínian, deepest there, and

give no relief to the enemy; and a blessing of wind on the south, drying the puddles, drying the fields. Let the river empty out the flood, and give easy passage to Olmern's boats, and let them come to feed the hungry and to provision the defense of Amefel: *that* was his business, and he found in all he saw that he had not done badly.

So he wished. And when he reached the citadel again, and his own apartments, he gathered up his maps, he called in Crissand, and sent also to Azant, as the lords nearest to hand.

"We have guests," he began, in the intimacy of what was, at other hours, his dining table. "We have guests in the downhill stables and others at Althalen. An Elwynim company escaped, with its weapons, and swears to our service."

What the men had wished to swear to him, and what they might have sworn in their hearts, he did not say, nor did Uwen. By now he was sure the men were sleeping, and likely to remain asleep for hours.

In all of it since his return he was aware of Paisi slipping about, and running here and there for master Emuin, and by now he was aware that master Emuin was listening to all that happened.

It seemed superfluous to mount the stairs to master Emuin's chamber, but when he had told Crissand and Azant all he knew, he took that belated course, quietly, even meekly.

"Well, well, well," Emuin said when Tristen shut the door at his back and faced him, "and what have we done today, young lord?"

"I've settled Althalen with a village and had men swear to me as the King To Come." He flung all of it out, the bald truth, and felt oddly abashed. He feared in the matter of inviting the Elwynim there was very much more than he had yet accounted of, and that he had been very much the fool Emuin called him. Done was done, yet not as widely or as publicly as might have been . . . or might yet be. He was at least fore-warned.

"Well, well." Emuin was seated at his table, charts spread far and wide and weighted with dubious small pots and a teacup. "And you say you're distressed, young lord? But are you quite surprised?"

"I wish *nothing* to Cefwyn's harm. And what shall I do?" His voice sank, so difficult was it suddenly to utter. "I find myself afraid, sir. The Elwynim are in the stable, with men who've sworn to me not to talk. But they said it, all the same. And they will say it, and the lords of the south will come here, and what will hap-pen then? This army is Cefwyn's army. Elwynor is Her Grace's, not mine."

Emuin rose from his table and turned his back, set-ting his face toward the window shutters. Paisi was out and about somewhere, for which Tristen was thankful: he could at least speak without another witness.

"Cefwyn knows," Emuin said in a voice as quiet. "So did his father, for that matter."

"Ináreddrin? About me?"

"Cefwyn wrote to him this summer saying he had found the Elwynim King To Come. Saying also he'd bound you by an oath of fealty—underhanded, since at the time you had no notion what you are, and pre-sumptuous in the king's way of thinking, his son and heir taking oaths from . . ." Emuin gave a long breath. "From the heir of the Sihhë. And directly after, Ináreddrin rode south in a fair frothing rage of suspi-cion . . . which sent him into the Aswydds' ambush, failing a little of delivering *all* the Marhanens to one battlefield. *There* was folly, if you wish an example of royal extravagance. He could have sent someone. Sending subordinates would have changed everything, a fact I've urged on Cefwyn most vehemently. And Ináreddrin died for that extravagance of passion."

He heard it all in alarm. And one thing came clear to him. "Cefwyn knew."

"Oh, no doubt."

"He knew the prophecy when he gave me Althalen."

"Oh, aye, indeed he did. For that matter, young lord, *I* thought long and hard on what he'd done. But do it he must, perhaps, one way or another, and chose the easiest course, with no blow struck."

"I'd not strike any blow at him. Ever."

"Of course not. You call him your friend. So now we may wrestle with prophecies, and wizardry. He's your friend, and therefore has avoided the worst pitfalls. He knew from the first he laid eyes on you that he saw something uncommon in you, and yet he liked you well, and he made you his friend on *my* advice. That *was* my advice to him, and it served him very well."

He was struck to the heart. "I'm glad you gave it, sir. But only on your advice?"

Emuin shook his head. "No, not only on my advice. He does love you. That's the truth of it, as you love him."

The fear was no less. "What should I do? And do not you give me a glib answer this time, sir. Should I take horse and ride back to Ynefel and face his enemies? Perhaps . . ." The thought had come back to him, as he had thought this fall, that perhaps Mauryl had set a limit to his Summoning and Shaping, and that there was no time for him beyond this year, or some night this spring. "If Mauryl's spell vanishes with some midnight this spring, that would solve it all, would it not? Will I vanish, with it? And should I?"

"I don't know," Emuin said. "As to wizardry, I see no reason the spell should end."

"I do. I see very many reasons, if Mauryl had any care for the Marhanen."

Emuin looked at him with the arch of a white brow. "Care for the Marhanen? None that *I* know."

That gave him no cheer at all. It had begun as a remarkable day, and the day came down to dark in one frightening admission after another.

"Was Mauryl their enemy? What was in those letters to the Aswydds? This is where you lived, was it not? What was in the letters?"

"Ah. A good question."

"Then answer it!"

"Mauryl used the Marhanens to bring down the Sihhë. They were not friends, but they saw the use in each other . . . as Selwyn Marhanen exempted two wizards from the Quinalt ban. I was one."

"And Mauryl the other. What of the others who helped him at Althalen?"

"Dead. Three there, others over the years. One in Elwynor."

"In Elwynor!"

"Dead, I say. An Aswydd. Taryn was his name. But if he were alive, I'd know it."

"How can you not have told me this?"

"Perhaps because it doesn't matter. Taryn Aswydd is irrelevant to you. The others—"

"The others—"

"May have relevance. The Aswydds living and dead Cefwyn exiled from this province. Dug them up, hauled them out of their tombs, and sent the whole lot over the border to hallowed ground in Guelessar. *That* for necromancy. The only one missing is Taryn, in some tomb or grave in Elwynor."

"I need your advice this time. I know you wish me

to think of things for myself, but in this, I ask you, sir, tell me most solemnly what you see."

Emuin breathed deeply. "Advice? I'll cut through all the cords at once. One stroke. As I advised Cefwyn to win your friendship, I advise you . . . win his."

"Have I not . . . his friendship?"

"Win his."

Emuin at his most obscure, most informative, and most obdurate and maddening. A dead Aswydd in Elwynor, live ones in exile in Guelessar, Elwynim down in the stable, and Emuin talked of friendship. Cefwyn had lamented that trait of obdurate silence, and cursed it, but Tristen did neither, at the moment. Curious strictures bound Emuin, he had begun to know that: to know somewhat, and not to know enough, and to know that naming a thing had power . . . that was a burden. He had let loose a wish for snow and fair weather and had almost loosed disaster, unthinking.

The narrow escape sobered him, chastened him, made him think twice how he railed on Emuin, who did very little and that after long, long thought.

"Thank you, sir."

"For what?"

"For your constancy. Your silence. Your thinking things through."

Now Emuin laughed, of sheer surprise, it seemed. "Mauryl said I was fickle as the breeze."

"As hard to catch." Now the boy Paisi was on the stairs, thumping and gasping, carrying something heavy, and their time of privacy was ended.

Win his. Win Cefwyn's friendship, of all tasks Emuin might have set him the dearest to his heart, and perhaps the thorniest. He had come here almost in despair, and now opened the door for the boy with a light heart and a consciousness that, no, he no longer was the boy, the wizard's fetch-all and carry-all. Master Emuin had set him a task he could do, and wished to do, a great task, a lord's task.

Paisi had baskets with him . . . supper, meat pies, by the delicious aroma. "Shall I fetch for you, m'lor'?" Paisi asked in dismay. "I didn't see your guards, m'lor'."

"I escaped them," Tristen said, and went his way out the door and down the steps as if his feet had wings.

Below, far down the hall, two of his exasperated guards did find him. So did importunate workmen, pleading that the doors had to be finished, and they were fine carpenters, not makers of stables.

"Yet it's stables and barracks we need," Tristen said in all patience, "so we needn't have axes at these doors again, if you please. Finish your carvings later. Make them fine when there's time. Now we need beams up, and roofs."

"Get along there," Lusin said . . . only Lusin and Tawwys had come for him. "Shame, to be pestering His Grace with plaints and preferences, gods bless!— M'lord, the Elwynim has come up the hill, or Aeself has. The others . . . master Haman's seein' to 'em, sayin' they've the look of fever an' he don't want sick men in the town."

Disease and all the ills of war, Tristen recalled the warning. Would an unscrupulous wizard unleash that against them? Any gap in their armor had to be seen to.

"Master Haman can deal with fevers," he said, "but all the same, go up and tell Emuin. He'll have something for them, to prevent it. He'll know."

"Aye, m'lord." Tawwys was up the stairs in a trice, but Lusin stayed below with him, and the two of them walked toward the stairs. "Cook's sent supper to the little hall, m'lord, an' a small table set, countin' the visitor."

"Set out the maps," he said. "Not *all* the maps, but sufficient to ask the man where he went and how he crossed, and where Tasmôrden might be, and doing what.—And I'll want a clerk, to have it all written down." The whole day had passed in one rush after another, and Lusin caught a passing servant, sending her running for the archive and the clerk.

He would write to Cefwyn with what he learned. He would *deserve* Cefwyn's friendship.

Meanwhile Uwen was coming down the stairs, and Crissand joined them from the west, in from the stable-court, with his bodyguard. Durell was close behind him.

Likely curiosity had spread through the court, until he had as well have used the great hall for his welcome to Aeself and the rest. Lords he had not summoned were finding excuses to come and obtain an invitation.

"Here, and here," Aeself said, a noble conversant with maps and charts, a commander willing, in the carrying-away of the dishes of their simple supper, to move a trembling and much-injured hand over the canvas map and show them all what he knew.

"There," he said, drawing a line by Ilefínian to note the presence of Tasmôrden's forces, and the road that led up to the border and the riverside Cefwyn defended, all but one of its bridges destroyed. "The Guelenmen move with heavy wagons," Aeself said, "and this Tasmôrden expects." He had a cough, himself, and took a sip of wine laced with one of Emuin's potions. "So Lord Elfwyn believed the reports we had. My lord is dead, now, almost beyond a doubt . . . and so all this army . . ." Aeself passed his hand over the region of the town. "The gates did not withstand him. They opened."

"Force of arms?" Tristen asked. "Or did he use other means?"

"My lord . . ." Aeself lost his voice a moment, in coughing. "I don't know. They opened at night, and if a man of ours would do it, then damn him for it, but we don't know how, otherwise, except wizardry, and that we don't discount."

"Is he known to have such help?"

"He's known for one himself, my lord."

That was not quite a surprise, counting that the claim to be a High King meant Sihhë blood, however thin.

"But sufficient for that?"

"No one knows. Some say it's all trickery, to fulfill the prophecy. Some say he hides what he does have, and sheds his soldiers' blood when he could win past without a battle, all to hide his wizardry from us. To this hour we don't know."

Either a strong wizard or not: again, no news, and Tristen had no knowledge of his own on the matter.

"We were on the outside of Ilefínian," Aeself continued, "had been, attempting to bring relief to the town, back from the north. But when we came there, we found the gates breached, the earl's men inside looting the town. We attempted to turn the tables on him, and besiege the besiegers, but he was cannier than that, and we rode into archers at the east gates. So twenty-two of us died, and the Saendal, the damned brigands, dragged two more of us down. It was no honor to us that we ran, my lord, but I looked to save something, and we'd no prospects there. There was no knowing then where the earl was. They knew where we were, they always knew, and if that was natural, he's a clever man."

"What do you think?"

"He claims the Kingship, and he claims to be Sihhë. He has to have the blood, so he has to say so, true or not. He has somewhat the look."

"Does he?" asked Crissand, and Aeself faltered.

"Not so much as m'lord does," Aeself said faintly. "Seeing him, one knows the difference, as I've *never* seen, not in my life."

"Tasmôrden's army," Tristen said, unwilling to allow that to go further. "Where?"

Aeself touched the map, the circle around Ilefínian. "Here's the most of his forces, which with the loot and the taverns, isn't likely moving. And here to the east, there's a shred of Her Grace's men under arms, that the earl hasn't gone to take yet, but the loyal army is thin, they're thin, my lord. There's force on the earl's side and force in his hands, and there's some who say he *is* what he says, and has the blood, and the magic in him, but if he has, he can't keep his men out of the wine stores. That saved us, if anything."

Tristen listened, hands braced before his lips, eyes fixed on a canvas land that became visible to him with Aeself's telling, and a fair telling it seemed to be. He had come to Emuin in fear, he had come from Emuin in hope, and now he saw the quandary laid before him . . . bad news regarding the forces at Ilefínian, bad news regarding Her Grace's loyal forces in the country, and a bad outlook for the eastern bridges where Cefwyn proposed to force a crossing, but Cefwyn had foreseen that would happen, and had good maps . . . had taken the best maps, as he knew, out of Amefel, leaving him older, less reliable ones. He had brought two good ones with him out of Guelessar, but they informed him no better about the height of hills or the difficulty of a given road.

Aeself might. Aeself, however, was all but spent, and had grown more pale and more unsteady as a fair-sized supper and the ale combined with the volley of questions. Now he looked torn between desire to be believed and the exhaustion that was near to claiming him. Tristen set a hand on Aeself's arm, and said, "Will you go back to your friends, sir? Or rest in the Zeide tonight?"

"At my lord's will. But I'd rather go to my comrades."

"Go," he said. "Tawwys will escort you down." He reached into the gray space as he said it, and gathered nothing of presence there, as he had not for these men from the time they had met.

But within that space he could do some things he could not do in the world of Men. He brought out a little of the brightness of the gray space, and encouraged the life in Aeself: he snared a little of that silvery force and lent it to Aeself, so a ring on his wounded hand flared with an inner spark—and Aeself gathered himself as if he had gotten a second wind, and looked at him with trepidation.

"My blessing on you," Tristen said. He had gathered that word with difficulty out of Efanor's little book and Uwen's anxious seeking; but now, faced with pain, he knew the use of it, and he saw the ease come on Aeself's face, and the light into his eyes.

"My lord," Aeself said, all open to him, utterly, so that what Aeself knew he was sure he knew, and it was not great. A second time he touched Aeself, this time on the hand.

"Go. Rest. Take the little basket with you."

Emuin had sent down a collection of simples during their supper, odorous little pots, wizard-blessed and potent, Tristen was well sure, salves and pungent smokes that would cure horses and men alike. And Aeself understood him, and the need for silence: Aeself saw how authority sat in this small council, and that he met as a man among men with these friendly lords, needing no kneeling or other signs of respect. M'lord he was. He made that enough.

"Go," Tristen said again. "M'lord," Aeself said, and taking the basket, took his leave.

His guests, still standing about the table and the maps, had no awareness that something had transpired in that last moment. Durell was contentedly diminishing the quantity of wine remaining.

Crissand, however, sent a thoughtful look at Aeself's back, a look not completely pleased.

"You find something amiss," Tristen said quietly, between the two of them.

"No, my lord."

He caught Crissand's eye by accident and the gray space gaped around them, not of his own will.

He was amazed. To assail him in the gray space was temerity on Crissand's part, a rash venture at meeting him in wizardry, on his own ground.

The gray place exposed hearts without mercy, and that exposure Crissand might not have realized until it was too late . . . for Crissand whipped away from him, angry and ashamed, and the gray winds swirled and darkened steadily.

—That he has sworn to me? Tristen wondered, and *would not let Crissand go or break back into the world of Men. Are you jealous? Why?*

Crissand was snared, and could not escape. And shame burned deep in Crissand's heart.

In the world, he bowed his head. "My lord," Crissand said, red-faced, and all the while Durell sipped his wine. So with Azant.

But he looked straight at Crissand, in whom, more than any other, of all the earls, he saw a love, not of what he was, but of him.

But what Crissand wanted he wanted with a great, a heartbending passion, exclusive of others. It had become a stronger and stronger one, his rebellion just now an assault of love and need, desperate, and now confounding both of them in its sudden, disastrous misdirection.

—*Have I offended you?* Tristen asked.

There was a stilling of the clouds then, a great heartbroken calm.

—*The wrong isn't in you, but in me. I'm Aswydd, doesn't that say it? The flaw is in the blood. I was not with you. For all of this, I haven't been with you, and now you have an army without us . . .*

—*You've found this place. Who told you?*

—*I followed you, my lord.*

Followed him, indeed. Friendship, love, jealousy, all had broken down the walls. And Crissand had perhaps done it before, but at distance, and learned what could set him in danger.

—*Being here is easy once you find the way,* Tristen said. *Isn't it? That's the very easiest thing. You believed me when you swore. Believe me now. Jealousy moved you.*

—*Truth,* Crissand said, downcast, then, fiercely: *But we are your people, my lord. We were first.*

He weighed that, and a sudden sureness made him shake his head.

—*For now. But there'll be a day I'll only have you for my friend. You'll sit where I do. You'll be the aetheling. So Auld Syes said. Have you forgotten that? Or didn't you hear?*

—*Never in your place, my lord!*

—*Never separate from me,* Tristen said, oddly assured and at peace in his own heart. *But not lord of Amefel. Lord of Althalen and Ynefel. Cefwyn was right, was he not?*

"My lord," Crissand said aloud, shaken, and pale of face.

"Go home," Tristen said, then, to all the company, and Crissand, too, bowed and went his way, downcast and ashamed.

He went with Uwen and his guard.

But he was with Crissand while Crissand walked the hall, and while he gathered up his guard near the doors.

He was aware when Crissand walked out and down the stable-court steps, in fearful thought.

He was aware and while he himself walked upstairs and Crissand walked, farther and farther away, across the muddy cobbles of the stable-court, seeking the West Gate, and his own house.

He left Crissand standing confused on the damp cobbles outside the gate. *"My lord?"* Crissand's guard asked him, finding his young earl lost in thought.

But Tristen did not approach him further, only left him to think his thoughts, and to reach his conclusions, inevitable as they must be.

Aetheling. Ruler of Amefel.

He went into his apartments, into the care of his staff. He suspected that, in the stir the two of them had made in the gray space with their quarrel, Emuin had been aware, and that Emuin at least did not disapprove his action—or his warning to Crissand.

He gave his cloak to Tassand, his gloves to another servant, let a third remove his belt, and set his sword in its accustomed place, by the fireside.

Illusion was the writing on one side of his sword, and *Truth* was written on the other.

And he had learned the edge was the answer.

Finding Crissand's edge was no simple matter. Crissand he feared would cause him pain, as he had caused Cefwyn pain.

They were models, one of the other. Cefwyn had doggedly followed Emuin's advice, regarding him; now he must do the same for Cefwyn—and for Crissand.

He took up his pen, dipped it in ink, wrote on clean paper what he dared not say openly, but what he hoped Cefwyn would understand obliquely . . . truth, and illusion, trusting Cefwyn again to find the useful edge.

"Ye should rest," Uwen said, straying bleary-eyed from his bedroom. The candles had burned far down. Some had gone out. It was the dead part of the night, and nothing was stirring but the wind outside and the steady battering of wind against the windows. "Ye don't sleep near enough, lad. Now what in hell are ye doin' at this hour?"

Now that Uwen said it Tristen felt the weariness of actions taken, decisions made, the small hope of things accomplished. Before him, he saw a stack of matters dealt with in a night that for many reasons, Emuin's answer and the Elwynim and the confrontation with Crissand included, had afforded him no prospect of sleep.

It was the second such night in a row . . . yet weary as he was, he had no inclination to sleep.

Uwen had gone sensibly to bed at midnight, but his face too, candlelit, stubbled with gray beard, seemed weary and fretted with responsibility and his lord's sleepless nights.

How much had Uwen watched, he asked himself.

"I nap," he said to Uwen. "Go back to your bed. Don't worry for me."

"I don't know where ye find the strength to stay awake," Uwen said with a frown, "or again, maybe I guess, an' I'd ask ye take to your bed like an ordinary lad an' rest your head if I thought ye'd regard me. I don't know whether witchery's a fair trade for hours again' a pillow, but honest sleep is afore all a good thing, m'lord, and makes the wits work better, an' I'd willingly see ye have more of it."

"I'll try. Go to bed."

He thought that Uwen would go away then. But Uwen lingered, came closer, until the same circle of two remaining candles held them both, the other sconce having failed.

"Ye recall," Uwen said quietly, "when ye was first wi' us, how ye'd learn a new thing and ye'd sleep an' sleep till the physicians was all confounded. D' ye recall that?"

"I do recall."

"And now it don't happen, m'lord, 'cept down there in hall, wi' you an' young Crissand staring back an' forth an' not a sensible word. Ye don't sleep. Ye're not helpin' yourself."

"No," he agreed. "I suppose I'm not."

"An' by me, my lord, I'd far rather the sleepin' than the not sleepin', if ye take my meanin'. So I ask ye, please. Go to bed. Take some wine if ye will. But try."

He had been all but set on a more forceful dismissal, but of all others, *Uwen* did not deserve a dismissal or a curt answer.

Indeed, differences. A change had happened in the way he met the world of new things, and the way he ordered Men here and there. What new things he encountered did not so much Unfold to him these days as turn up in the shadows of his intentions, warning him only a scant step before he must wield the knowledge. His life had acquired a sense of haste, and feeling of being a step removed from calamity. He was engaged now in battle with paper and clerks and carpenters, with Elwynim companies and grain from Olmern, with the adoration of desperate men and the jealousy of his friends.

He resented sleep.

But . . . Flesh and blood as well as spirit, Mauryl had indeed warned him, with the sharp rap of his staff on the steps. *Crack! Crack-crack!* The echoes still lived in his memory, still made him wince. Pay attention! Mauryl would tell him. Uwen had told him. Should he not heed?

"See here," Uwen said with a sidelong glance at the brazen dragons. "Will ye take *my* bed? I don't have any of them things leaning above *my* rest. I don't wonder ye don't sleep un'erneath them damn things, but rest ye must."

"I promise. I *promise*, Uwen. Go off to bed. I'll put myself to bed in a very little time."

Uwen looked doubtful, and began to leave, then turned back, feet set.

"Swear," Uwen said.

"By the gods?" he asked wryly, knowing Uwen knew where that study sat with him, in Efanor's little book.

Uwen said not a thing. But neither, now, would Uwen leave.

"I'll go to bed," Tristen said, conceding. "Go on. I'll not need Tassand."

"Tassand'll have my head if I don't call 'im," Uwen said, and went off to do that.

So difficult things now became. And now Uwen had set his teeth in the matter of his master's difficulties and would no more let go than a dog a bone.

"M'lord?"

Uwen was merciless, and insistent.

So he took himself to bed, attended by two sleepy servants, loomed over by Aswydd dragons.

Then, lying still in the dark, he found himself at the edge of exhaustion, and afraid, wanting just the little assurance things in the place were in order . . . he stretched out his awareness as thin and subtle as a waft of air to the rooms around him, touched Uwen's sleeping thoughts, and his guards' drowsy watching at the door. Gathering sleep was like pitching a tent for protection, stretching thin ropes this way and that to ground he knew was stable.

And when he extended his curiosity farther still, he was able to reach Emuin, who was distracted, and a boy, whose feet were cramped in new boots, and who kept Emuin's night hours.

He had not alarmed them or even attracted notice in his tenuous wandering. The boy poured tea and served in fear, his concentration all for the gray-haired untidy man in the tower with him, while Emuin chased the mysteries of the stars through his charts. The boy thought mostly of food and whether he dared reach for the last small cake.

It was enough: he had succeeded once at subtle approach, assured himself his household was safe and folded around him like a blanket.

He spread himself thinner and thinner on the insubstantial winds . . . was aware of all the servants and the guards throughout the Zeide, all about their own business when they were not about his; he was aware of the town, asleep but for a few who watched or worked, and one man of ill intent whose hand shook under his attention and faltered of the lock he had meant to open.

The man ran, and did not elude him, but hid shivering in the shadows, in fear of justice that might last him for days.

But fear was enough, unless he found the man twice.

He sailed away, longed to reach Crissand, but in this fey mood sent his thoughts past that house, down the street, to the gates.

He was aware even further, of men and horses outside the walls, and villages drowsing under a sifting of snow north and south of Henas'amef.

He felt the lonely camp at Althalen, and the soldiers' camp on the Lenúalim's cold and windy shores; he dreamed of wings shadowing the road, broad, blunt wings, peaceful in the night. Snow began, and fat flakes whirled and spun beneath those wings.

He had found Owl, so his dream told him. At last he had found the source of his fey restlessness, and rode Owl's thoughts, as Owl showed him all the land from high, high above.

Owl flew right across the village of Modeyneth, the guard posts, the bridges, and the river, and soared on above the land of Elwynor, to a city afflicted by siege and ravaged by fire.

There was Tasmôrden. *There* was the enemy that threatened Ninévrisë's people and Cefwyn's peace, and Owl circled above that place, finding the insubstantial Lines of the fallen town also broken and faltering in their strength.

Now he was well awake in this dream, and angry, and violating every sense of caution he had urged in Crissand.

He saw, yes, the faint glow of wizardry about Tasmôrden, not that Tasmôrden himself wielded it well, but that it was in the air of the place, and that somehow it moved there, raw and reddened and white with struggle.

There was wizardry about the town as well, ragged blue of guard and ward, Uleman's making, Tristen thought: that clear light, however fragmentary, was like Uleman's work, Ninévrisë's father. His care, his courage, all, all defended Ilefínian, but had not prevailed to hold it. The ragged red had come in on the edge of sword and axe, leapt up in the burning and smoldered in the glow of embers.

Bodies, untended and unburied, lay frozen in doorways and at shrines, under a dusting of snow that began to bring innocence back to the night.

A banner flew above the high fortress of Elwynor, and he knew that banner . . . not the black-and-white Checker and Tower of the Regent of Elwynor, no, but a black banner, a single star that was very like the black banner of Althalen.

With a crown above the star.

Was it a vision of things now, this very night, and was *that* the banner Tasmôrden claimed? If so, *dared* this man appropriate to himself the land and honor Cefwyn had given, and then set a crown on it, the emblem of a king?

Away, he wished Owl, on a thought, and Owl soared away south, bending a long, long turn, and crossed the river again far to the west, where Marna Wood shadowed the snow, and glimmered with far more potent wards.

Up, up, up and aside from the barrier, Owl's wings tilted sharply, and Owl took a dizzying plunge through buffeting winds as Owl met something and flinched.

Suddenly Tristen found the wind rushing past him and the earth rushing up.

Air turned to substance, became the bedclothes, and the frantic pounding of his heart became a leaden rhythm of recent threat.

He was still in midair, even lying on his bed. That was the way it felt. And Emuin had stopped his pen, having blotted his page. His agitated next reach overset the inkpot. He righted the pot without a second thought and held his breath at the feeling that shivered through the night.

—Tristen? Emuin asked.

—Safe, he said within the gray space.

Yet the west in the gray space shadowed dark as his dream, and the winds blew cold to the bone.

—It was a dream, sir, no more than a dream.

—Was it? Emuin asked. Hovering there within Emuin's heart was a question and a fear directed toward that shadow, for that was a deep and dark one.

But in the east, now, a second shadow grew, a niggling small one, and a faint glow of light that had no explanation.

And a third, in the north, where the black banner flew.

—There is a wizard, Tristen said, and sat up in bed, catching the covers about him against the chill. *There is someone, here, and here, and here. Do you see the glows, sir? It is more than one. One's come close . . . one's followed me . . .*

—Be careful! Emuin chided him.

But Tristen flung himself out of bed, caught the bed covering around him and trailed it to the room next, losing it as he reached the hearth and his sword that stood against the stones. He snatched up the hilt and slung the sheath off.

The silver inscribed on the blade, *Illusion*, flashed in the dim light, and the sheath clattered across the floor. Naked, sword in hand, he faced the window into the shadowed night, and saw all the town of Henas'amef flared up in Lines beyond the glowing Lines of the Zeide's walls. There were all the wards, all the magic of craftsmen and householders warding their own doors and walls: the common magic of parents and homekeepers and the pure trust of children . . . all these things Unfolded to him in that unworldly glow, block by block, house by house, outward toward the great defensive wall of Henas'amef itself, a blue bright Line often retraced and constantly tended.

Something had challenged them.

But they held. They held.

Uwen's reflection arrived in the glass, Uwen's pale skin ghostlike across that angular maze of Lines before his vision. Uwen's silver hair was loose and at odds about his balding temples; he had his sword in hand and a cloak caught about him, nothing more, nor asked the nature of the alarm . . . he had simply come, armed, to his lord's side, the two of them naked to the cold of the threatening night and the glory of the town.

"The Lines," Tristen said, "all have leapt up. Stand, stand still."

"What does 'e mean?" Other reflections arrived, night guards coming in from the doorway, servants from their quarters and the back hall.

"Nothing's gotten in," Tristen said. He was aware of all the Lines before and below and behind and above him, even with his eyes open, a net in which he stood; and then of the stairs that ran to Emuin's tower.

At that, he was aware of Emuin, who with stealth and subtlety he was only learning had been there for the last few moments. Emuin stood with him, there in the gray space, and the blue lines glowed softly, running along the edge of the steps of Emuin's tower and down and down again and along the lower hall on the opposite side, and up again, quick and live as the spark of the sun on winter ice.

"M'lord?" Uwen asked.

"Nothing has come in," Tristen said. "The place is safe."

"Aye, m'lord," Uwen said, and the guards with him said nothing at all, only looked about them uneasily.

Then, only then, Tristen set his hand on the stone of the sill and wished the whole town safe.

Only one place resisted him, and it was that discontinuity of stones in the lower hall, that change from old to new that marked the join of the old fortress to the new: from the first time he had confronted it he had known it was a weakness in the building.

And was it lack of courage, he asked himself, that he did not tonight go down and dare that black middle of the eastern hall?

Was it, instead, prudence, that he did not directly challenge what at the moment was doing no harm . . . and what had, with the whole town, resisted whatever his foolish curiosity had roused out of the dark.

He traced the one compromised windowsill, drawing the Line with his finger, and willing it sound and safe.

Then he could say, with some assurance. "I'm sure now. Go back to bed. Go back to bed, all of you. The threat is gone."

The night guards went, quietly and doubtless to talk among themselves once they reached the hall. Uwen's reflection remained, pale ghost against the dark that now filled the window.

"I dreamed of Owl," he said to Uwen. "There's wizardry abroad."

"Aye, m'lord, that I rather guessed."

It struck his fancy, Uwen's quiet humor. It touched his heart with a relief almost to tears, that Uwen still dared deal with him as friend and guide, and he would not profane that offering or examine it.

"I don't think it's a danger tonight." He turned and faced Uwen's solid presence with his own, and handed Uwen the sword he held, for he did not trust his own steadiness to sheathe it: his eyes were still bemazed by the vision of Ilefínian and of Henas'amef, and the black banner and the Lines. "Tasmôrden is flying the banner of Althalen."

"Is he?" Uwen failed to ask how he had seen that, and simply heard it for the truth. "He ain't right wise, then, is he, m'lord? You an' His Majesty will have summat to say on that score, I fancy."

"That we will," Tristen said, not without thinking of Auld Syes' birds, and the use to which he had put Althalen's ruins. Tasmôrden thought to claim back or kill those who had fled his brutal seizure of their land; and by that banner Tasmôrden thought to claim not merely the Regency but the High Kingship, the office the Sihhë-lords had last held and which Cefwyn himself did not aspire to hold.

And did he fly it defiantly above the devastation of Her Grace's capital and the murder of its citizens?

"Go to bed," he said to Uwen. "Forgive me the commotion."

"Forgive *you*, m'lord, when I persuade ye to sleep an' the whole night turns on its ear? If something's amiss out there, it certainly ain't your doin'."

"Nor mine. I know now I didn't draw the lightning stroke on the Quinalt roof. And Cefwyn had to send me here. I had to come. The Quinalt father has gone where he has to go, and Aeself and his company have all come where they have to be. Lord of Althalen and Ynefel: that's what I am."

"Spooky to think of, m'lord, an' odd as it is."

"The truth," he said, with the sudden conviction that all the world would have bent itself to achieve that one thing. He could not resist it any more than he could have resisted Mauryl's summoning.

Mauryl's handiwork? he asked himself. Had it always been? Or was it yet?

"Will ye go to bed?" Uwen asked meekly. "Or dare ye? If ye wish 't, I'll watch."

It was a draw, his concern, Uwen's. And after such debate, and thinking on it, he found himself wearier than he had thought, and after many late nights, at last very inclined to sleep, as if he had waited for this event, and now it had happened, he could let go.

"Yes," he said. "Yes. I will."

"Ye're sure."

"I am sure. Good night to you. A peaceful night."

"An' to you, m'lord." Uwen remained dubious. He wished Uwen a peaceful night, wished it with wizardly force, so that he hoped Uwen would sleep soundly and take no chances with such things as wandered the night.

He himself went back to bed—Orien's bed, Heryn's bed, he could never forget it, and the dragons loomed above him with claws outstretched and brazen wings spread.

Dreaming of Owl was better than some dreams, and better than the lack of them, for he had no imagination of the time to come, such as he understood Men had: it was his misfortune to see only time present and the recollections of his brief year thus far, but any notion of where he was going, any imagination of the year after this still appeared to him in conjectures and fragments, and he had no notion how much Men knew of their life to come.

An unwritten slate, Mauryl had called him once; and in some regards that was still so, and truths were still finding space in the blank ground.

Perilous to write on, Mauryl had said that of him, too, but many people had written their truths in his heart: Mauryl, Emuin, Cefwyn . . . Uwen, even, and Tassand, and Lusin and the rest. Crissand. Orien Aswydd, in her way. And Ninévrisë. It was why he gathered up Aman and Nedras, the gate-guards, and young Paisi, whose wizardry was a candleflame in a strong gale, and apt to go out if he ventured away from safe walls, or flare up in wizardous fire if he someday touched the right substance.

There was Cook, who had fed him, Haman, who had provided him an example of honest work and good management . . . all these men and women who had given their skills to him, now he ruled, and managed, and attempted to manage wisely and honestly.

He had stood on a hill in Guelessar not so long ago wondering what it would be to remember far back in years he did not have; and what it would be like to imagine forward from the moment of his standing on that hill.

He could not have imagined this, or ever foreseen that he would return here.

He still could not imagine with complete confidence that he would see the spring, or that the Zeide and Henas'amef would not swallow him down in its long memories.

Had not Emuin said that the Midwinter was the hinge of the year, when all things done turned again and the year began to fold back on itself? Then, if ever, did not magic have its moment, when all things swung into a new path and all things were possible?

And in mid-spring, *his* year of life would be complete. And would he have another? Despite Emuin's assurances, it was never promised him. Mauryl had called him into the world in spring and by summer he had done all that Mauryl purposed . . . had he not?

Had he not? Or was it still shaping itself, and moving through the world?

The gray space roiled gently with Emuin's contemplation of that question, and of him.

But Emuin said not a word to him of why all the wards of the town had flared at once.

INTERLUDE

Stitch and stitch, pearls and more mounds of blue and white ... since Murandys' colors, blue, the Quinalt sigil on a white field, bend or, were very like those of Ninévrisë's own house of Syrillas. None of the stitchers, inching their way pearl by pearl across plains and hills of satin, could miss the irony in that coincidence.

Least of all did Ninévrisë miss it. She dreamed at times of the more pleasant hours of her own preparation, and the candlelit glow of her wedding in the great, echoing Quinalt shrine.

Luriel of Murandys, applying cordings to a satin sleeve, maintained her delicate posture between affront to her former betrothed's wife and praise of the lordly bargain she had in her current betrothed ... wise, since the gentleman's sister, Brusanne of Panys, was seated close by her, another and prior member of their small society. Luriel professed herself utterly charmed by Rusyn of Panys ... had never, in fact, considered him as a suitor, but now that he put himself forward, why, he was fine and handsome and witty, he had become quite the young man, and she thought she might be falling in love ... an extravagance of charity, perhaps, but a brave effort.

The peaceful meetings would have been intolerable if Luriel were a fool, but she was not, thank the gods.

Nor did Ninévrisë intend to be one. If jealousy reared itself in her heart it was not because Cefwyn had ever loved this lady—in fact she was convinced that Cefwyn had never cared for Luriel at all beyond the chivalry he had for all ladies who had ever drawn *his eye. The marriage he had almost made with Luriel had been an affair of state, the same necessity Efanor now faced—and if Ninévrisë was jealous, it was jealousy that this bride of a minor noble, while she drew the inevitable darts of Bonden-on-Wyk, seemed so in command of the court . . . her court. That was a situation she had not foreseen, and one which she meant to remedy, but had not yet discovered how.*

Stitch and stitch, and tongues flew rapid as the silver needles, la! the sins of Artisane, the ambitions of Artisane, the onetime leader of the malice in the court, were now under intimate examination. The ladies smiled to Luriel's face, gossiped absent Artisane to her least flaw of taste and wit, and the barbs sped.

And believe that Artisane was the only subject of their talk? No. Ninévrisë was sure there were other topics . . . the only pillar of sober sense in the women's court being Dame Margolis, the armorer's lady, who would say the truth, and the honest truth, and tolerate none of the more wicked gossip.

Of course, it meant when Margolis was in attendance one learned less, too . . . and by now the rumor of a royal message to Ryssand had broken in various houses, with a clamor that was worth hearing . . . if not for Margolis' presence. All the court was sure this message meant negotiation and reconciliation with the king.

And that meant all alliances, some newly formed and unprecedented, were now to reconsider.

Might Ryssand return, and in some chastened new connection to the throne? Might Ryssand have found a means to come back intact, and, la! what might Artisane do, having thus affronted the Royal Consort? Would there be redemption? A nunnery, perhaps? There were shudders at that, for none of these young women fancied the contemplative life, bereft of festi-

vals and dancing . . . Quinalt that they were, there was not a one who could say what she thought by reason of her philosophy, only by rote learning of what she must avoid.

Curious, Ninévrisë thought, making small, neat stitches on her rival's hem. Curious that the soul and sense of all these Quinalt maidens' morality was not to be seen to love. La! it might be witchcraft that the king had given his bride an acorn as countryfolk did, and witchcraft and wizardry were what the Bryaltines did, oh, and did anyone mark how the Bryalt father ran his fingers round the rim of his wine cup at the feast?

Her maid had told her that yesterday, since the ladies had not remarked the maid's presence before they began to talk. In anyone else that gesture with the cup was insignificant: but in Father Benwyn's case, oh, certainly a strange Bryalt practice, warding his cup from poisons, and, la! who would poison the Bryalt father, who truly was an inoffensive sort . . . though a heretic, of course. Or nearly so.

So her maid, Fiselle, a girl of good sense, had reported to her.

So the days drew on, pearl by pearl, stitch by stitch. She smiled at Luriel every day, and saw troops and bridges to Elwynor. Every night was love, unthought and measureless, a warmth of candlelight and a lover's passionate embrace. They were mad things, she and Cefwyn. They burrowed beneath blankets and invented their own kingdom to explore. Then everything was wonderful.

But every sun came up on the world and measured it with a cold, wintry eye. She had headaches, and craved raspberries, which could not be had, and did not confess the desire, but measured herself in her mirror and wondered, desperately, to what wild chance of fate she had committed herself.

Every day her people died and still the needles flew, seeding pearls and schemes in a world of virgins and matrons. Efanor courted Artisane, Cefwyn redeemed Murandys, and rebuilt the walls of his kingdom.

I bear you no ill will, Ninévrisë had said to Luriel, early in their meeting, in their one conversation on the matter of old loves.

"Your Grace is generous," Luriel had said, "beyond all women." And then Luriel had added, in that deadly honesty that partook a little of contempt, "I could not be, were I in your place."

It warned her, then and from the start, that neither generosity nor love had made it possible for them to sit side by side. It was that they both were set on separate campaigns, both desperate, both under the weight of censure, both willing to endure any other affront to secure what they wished . . . and their wishes were not mutually exclusive. On that slender point, peace rested.

She had not retorted, *Because you cannot be generous, you are* not *in my place . . .* although that was what she thought. Luriel had stinted Cefwyn of her love, her troth, her loyalty, and Cefwyn, not being a fool, had never given her his. Cefwyn could not love this woman, and the closer he had grown to Luriel the more he had known it. Ninévrisë had thought that, too, on that occasion, and had not said it.

But she had taken that conversation for her one moment to tell some truth to Luriel of Murandys. "What I do," she had said, "I do for my husband's sake. Never mistake my tolerance for folly." And having said that, she never placed her trust in Luriel.

Stitch and stitch. In the patterns one could lose oneself. In the making of stitches, small and precise, there was no tomorrow and no yesterday, only the need to count threads and remember. The prattle of schemes *and suppositions was only idle noise. Outside, the weather spat, and drizzled, then burned bright blue and icy cold. Cravings for raspberries turned to dishes of custard, which she had had as a child, and could not well describe to the cook, though her tongue remembered the taste exquisitely. Custard after custard failed her expectation.*

"Did you hear?" Odrinian came in saying, one morning. "Someone painted the Quinalt sigil on the street outside Father Benwyn's door last night."

"Did they?" asked Bonden-on-Wyk.

"Benwyn will lay a curse on them," Odrinian said.

"If he sobers enough," said Brusanne.

Ninévrisë had said nothing in this exchange. Glances drifted toward her like moths to the forbidden fire, and hers to them. Needles stilled. There was the least hint of fear.

"He's not a wizard," Ninévrisë found herself saying. "No such thing. That's not right."

The silence lasted a moment. They never asked her what it was to be Bryaltine, and in fact she failed to practice the faith in any nightly observances. Benwyn did, nightly visiting the shrine, and having his wine flask with him . . . but most times being sober, since Idrys had lectured Benwyn very sternly.

He made fine salves, did Benwyn of Amefel. Bonden-on-Wyk used them. Her feet and hands pained her, and she swore Benwyn had given her more relief than the Quinalt with their charms and herbal baths. But Bonden-on-Wyk did not speak up on Benwyn's behalf now. Only Margolis said, "Well, painting the sigil on streets is no great respect of the Quinalt, either, is it?"

"No," said Ninévrisë, gratefully, "it is not."

Tristen had acted recklessly: Cefwyn's letters advised him so; and so did Idrys, which she hoped Tristen would heed, but one was never sure with him. News of the schism in the Quinalt frightened her. So much was fragile. Elwynor itself had become fragile, poised on the edge of starvation and dissolution. The prophecy of the King To Come might well be fulfilled in Tristen . . . she saw the signs, and for that she was also afraid . . . a selfish fear, she had thought at first; but more and more she knew that there was more than need of Guelessar that had turned Cefwyn from crossing the river last summer's end. That he might fulfill the prophecy was something they shared, and then she had been swept by doubts, one time desiring to be queen and not a stranger in Guelessar, one time asking herself dared she stand in the way of prophecy and was she so great a fool?

But now when she heard the women talk of attacks on her priest she knew another fear, for nowhere in the prophecy of the King To Come did it promise miracles or even salvation for Elwynor. The King To Come was the High King, the King at Althalen . . . and Elwynor only a province in his hands, nothing said of its safety or its fate when all was done.

She spoke for Elwynor itself. She secretly nursed a hope within her, as yet untested.

Meanwhile Efanor courted Artisane, sending her letters and gifts, and Ryssand remained unprecedentedly quiet, while she knew the Holy Father of the Quinalt pursued debates with priests Ryssand sponsored.

All these things, all these things, troubled her thoughts when her hands fell idle.

Her heart and her hopes had soared when she heard that Elwynim, her Elwynim, had found safety with Tristen, but oh, there were dangers still. Spring, spring would bring their answers; and in the meanwhile events proved that in Tristen's hands the prophecy was a dangerous thing, much as she loved him for his innocence and his devotion to Cefwyn.

Now the angers pressed in on her, angers she would have been free to satisfy if they had crossed the river this summer and engaged all of Elwynor without warning.

And at such moments she wondered if it had not been unwise ever to have entangled herself with the Bryaltines instead of the Teranthines, difficult as that had seemed. Benwyn, poor man, had no understanding of the currents that swirled about him. Angry Guelenfolk painted signs at his door. They gossiped about him.

The rare times she had ever talked with the man, it was not philosophy or religion, but herb lore out of Elwynor, and the obscure history of the shrine in Amefel. The sad truth was Benwyn well knew he was hated, and drank when he must face roomfuls of good Quinaltines.

Consequently he drank often . . . not the wisest solution, but then, if Benwyn had been wise, he would have confined his ministry to Amefel and not been the only Bryalt priest in Guelessar.

While she, if she were wise, would have bowed her head and accepted the Teranthine compromise, and never accepted this priest, near as he was to her father's observances. She saw now what a difficulty it was to force Ylesuin and Elwynor into union, and she knew that if there could not be a peaceful compromise of the Guelen clergy, Ylesuin itself might be rent apart. As might she.

"It's shameful," Ninévrisë said now, regarding this latest outrage. "It's shameful to use the Quinalt that way, and it's shameful to treat poor Benwyn that way."

For the Crown itself could not, dared not defend Benwyn too zealously. She knew how delicate a balance that was.

"Oh, dear," said Brusanne, and began that urgent search of her skirts that told of a lost needle. Others began to search, too, about her, through the mountains of fabric around her, for the needles that sewed the pearls were fine and easily lost, and tended to turn up in the folds of the work, to prick the wearer when she next tried the garment on.

"Here it is," said Margolis, and returned it to the daughter of Panys, who thrust it through the sleeve above her wrist.

"There," said Brusanne. "I'll not stab my brother's bride. I'm sure it's bad luck."

"It's bad luck to say bad luck," said Bonden-on-Wyk.

"There," said Luriel, vexed. "Will you not refrain from saying it twice, then?"

BOOK
THREE

BOOK

THREE

CHAPTER 1

Sergeant Gedd was back from Guelessar, a fortnight past all expectation and after they had all but given him up for lost. "And glad to be here, m'lord," Gedd said fervently, reporting to Tristen in the privacy of his apartments. Gedd had surely come straight up from the stables, stopping only to wash the dust from face and hands, for the fair hair about his face was wet, his beard, ordinarily carefully trimmed, had stubble about the sides, and his clothes were spattered with two colors of mud different than any in the stable yard.

In such guise, too, of dirt and disrepute, Gedd handed him a precious and very belated letter. Stripped of coverings of dirty cloth, it emerged cleanly, resplendent with red ribbon and the royal seal. "Forgive me that I'm so late. Word directly from the Lord Commander, too, m'lord, that I have in memory."

"Tell it to me," Tristen said. He laid the letter on the desk before him, as Uwen stood near his chair, silent as the brazen dragons. "What happened?"

"Respects first, m'lord, from the Lord Commander, and then this, which is weeks late: that the guardsmen who left the Amefin garrison by your leave have gone to the Quinalt for protection and so has the patriarch of Amefel. The Lord Commander says to tell Your Grace kindly give him no more such gifts. His words, my lord, as he said them, forgive me."

He could all but hear Idrys say it, and he was glad it was no sharper barb. He knew he deserved one.

But weeks late. He had no more recent news and had feared to send.

"And from His Majesty," Gedd said, "who says to tell Your Grace that the patriarch of Amefel put the Holy Father in a difficult position, and that there's trouble in the Quinaltine. Those were His Majesty's words. Trouble in the Quinaltine. He said tell Your Grace that His Reverence has friends in Ryssand."

"Was that all?"

"Yes, my lord. He gave me the letter with his own hand, and I was straight off and away."

"But late."

"Yes, my lord."

"Why?" Uwen asked, from the side and behind, and Gedd cast an anxious look in his direction.

"I had someone on my trail. I took up to the hills. But . . . Your Grace might want to hear . . . talk started about the tavern . . ."

"Tell me everything," Tristen said. "Don't hurry."

Gedd drew a breath. He was a strong man and a good soldier: it was from exhaustion, surely, that his hand shook as he raked back the damp hair. "Priests are going about the town preaching, talking against wizards and Bryaltines and generally against the war, that's one thing. There's talk among the people against Amefel and Her Grace as a bad influence on the king, and the war as costing too much, being too dangerous, and bringing honest Guelenmen among wizards and heretics. That's everywhere."

It was dire news. And unjust. Cefwyn was good. What he did was good, and they said as unkind things about him as they said about Heryn Aswydd.

"Everyone says so?" he asked.

"Say that it's safer to say that than to praise His

Majesty," the sergeant said, "on account of His Majesty's friends don't damn you to hell or look at you as would curdle milk. There's ugliness in the town, and it's got knives, m'lord."

"He's in danger."

"As I'd say, and as the Lord Commander knows, and I think His Majesty knows. But," Gedd said, "His Majesty rode against the dark at Lewen field, such as none of the layabouts complaining never had to face, and if a common man can say, m'lord, there's a king."

"He is that," Tristen said, and added, half to convince himself, "and if he knows, then he'll deal with it."

"Only so's he guards 'is back," Uwen said, "against Ryssand."

"And you were attacked?" Tristen asked.

"Not as it were attacked," Gedd said, "only there were men after me that I knew was the Lord Commander's, and then they weren't there, and these were, and they weren't his. And right or wrong I decided a late message was better than no message and went to ground. There's a nasty mood even to the villages, such as I was glad I wasn't wearing Amefin colors on the way in. Safer to be a common traveler, out of Llymaryn, says I, as I came into Guelessar: they're pious down there, left and right, and I know the brogue. And being Guelen," Gedd added, "I could get through. On the way back, I gave up being Llymarish and in the open and just hid and moved as I could . . . I let my horse go. Master Haman says he's not made it here; he might have run for his old pastures, up by Guelemara. And the one the Lord Commander's men gave me . . . no telling where he is. I walked."

"Well ye did," Uwen said, "by that account."

"The other news—" Something came to Gedd, on a

deep breath. "The other news, which may not be news, now: Murandys' daughter's to marry Panys' son, by the by. She's come back to court, and she's betrothed to Rusyn of Panys."

"Luriel?" He had heard of the lady in his days in Guelessar, and that she had been Cefwyn's almost-betrothed, and had left to something like exile.

That she had come back to court was surely no good news.

"Come on His Majesty's invitation," Gedd went on, "as had to be, of course. Her Grace met her in the face of all the court and took her amongst her women. This isn't what His Majesty told me, but it's what I heard in the town, and I heard it in more than one place, so I take it for true. And the Lord Commander isn't himself daunted, but it was his instruction to wrap the message up in rags and shove it deep in the rocks or heave it down a well if I thought I was followed. And I thought of that. But I thought I could get it through."

"Well-done in that," Uwen said, "too. —Ye were careful what ye said, yourself, I wager. Was it in Guelessar ye picked up these followers?"

"Captain, I swear to you, my tavern-going was discreet. Between talking to the Lord Commander immediately as I reached the town and being called to His Majesty the same night, in secret, in all that time I had the Lord Commander's men close by. I gave out freely that I was a courier, but I said I was from Llymaryn, and hoped I didn't meet a Llymarishman, which I didn't. After I had my meeting with His Majesty and left the Guelesfort, I had the Lord Commander's men in the street, them as I knew were his, while I nabbed my gear and my horse from the tavern where I'd left him. And I had the Lord Commander's men on the street, too, and out past the gate, where they gave me a horse besides my own that they'd brought. That was how they watched over me, and I took the warning, m'lord, and was watching my back, when one hour they were there and the next was a pair of riders coming up on me. That morning was when I saw a third show up, and I ran hard and sent my horses one way and I went to ground, right then. The rest was walking, mostly at night."

"And gettin' the better of the Lord Commander's men," Uwen said with a shake of his head. "That ain't ordinary bandits. And from the town. I'd almost say there's a man amongst 'em as ain't on the straight. That's too damn quick."

"We can't warn him," Tristen said in distress, "except by another messenger."

"I'd trust the Lord Commander to figure it. His men ain't fools, but I'd lay to it one's a scoundrel."

"I wish he may find out," Tristen said, with all intent, such that the gray space shivered.

"And you an' I'll have a talk," Uwen said to Sergeant Gedd, "an' a healthy sup of ale, an' see what little things ye might know else, if there's any ye've forgot. Besides which, ye're due the cup, and a good horse, as I'm sure His Grace will say."

"I do," Tristen said, his thoughts meanwhile ranging to Guelen hills, and ambushes, and Idrys, with Ryssand's men insinuated into every council, in among the priests, likely; and now spying on Idrys' spies.

"Thank you, Captain. My lord."

"Thank you," Tristen said fervently, and as Uwen gathered up the sergeant and showed him out, he uneasily cracked the seal with a small knife, and spread out the letter that had been so long in coming.

My dear friend, it began, which he heard as warmly as if Cefwyn had said it aloud. *The weather has held remarkably well. We are now moving supply.*

The good sergeant who carries this letter will have

*other, more common news for you. I should say that
Her Grace is well and sends you her love and her great
thanks for your rescue of her subjects, and I send also
my approval of all you have done.*

*Yet I pray you recall the Quinalt steps and the
means by which a very little thing became a great controversy. You must know that various persons returning from Amefel have spread rumors concerning the
people's regard for you, and the open display of Sihhë
symbols in the market, which I am sure is true. They
were doing it this summer. But remember that certain
men hold all that is Amefin in great fear, and the tale
of strange doings on your riding out to meet Ivanor
has reached the Quinaltine, although it is possible that
the story has grown in the telling.*

Grown and grown, Tristen thought. He was part of
the discontent among Cefwyn's subjects, and the
source of trouble with the Quinalt, and now a messenger going to the king went in fear for his life. He did
not know how to mend it.

*Her Grace takes great encouragement in your sup-
port of Elwynim women and children. I find encouragement knowing you are doing as you have always
done in defending them, and I give you all authority
you may require to secure them a safe haven.*

*There are many things I would write, but the messen-
ger is waiting.*

*We hope that Emuin is well. This cold damp always
makes his joints ache, and we hope he is keeping himself well and warm.*

This, in full knowledge of Emuin's habits with the
shutters.

*We are close now to the Midwinter and wait for
spring. You, not being Aswydd, I hold not therefore
bound by the prohibitions laid on the Aswydds. I hold
that your preparations against incursions from the*

north are in accordance with your oath to defend the
land. To this I set my seal, below, with all love and
confidence in your just use of that authority.

Cefwyn gave him liberty then to defend the helpless,
clearly aware of disaffection in his own Guelenfolk on
his account, and still adding to his authority . . . but it
was not alone Aeself and his men, but enough scattered bands to double the settlement at Althalen . . . so
Drusenan had sent word two days ago. Bands of
Elwynim loyal to the lady Regent or opposed to
Tasmôrden—they were not quite the same—had
avoided the bridge that had stood open with Guelen
and Ivanim forces on the watch, as a potential trap.
Women and children and the old and lame had come
that way as the only way they knew how to take, but
the fugitives from the lines at Ilefínian were veteran
men and wary of what seemed too easy. They had
crossed the icy waters at other points, however great
the effort; they had kept their weapons and sought
refuge with sympathetic Amefin, who had sent them to
Drusenan, and Drusenan had directed them to
Althalen—for they refused to go to the Guelen camp
and turn in their weapons to Guelenmen: Drusenan
had sent an anxious message, but the accommodation
had been peaceful, even counting two different loyalties amid the armed bands . . . their situation was so
desperate, fearing Tasmôrden and with their own lord
lost, they declined to fight each other.

Walls were up at Althalen, so Drusenan had also
said in his report, and two roofed halls stood, built of
the tumbled rubble and the still-standing ruin, one hall
for the women and children and one for the men,
dividing some households in the need for quick and
snug shelter, and flinging Ninévrisë's men in with
those who were otherwise minded. The Elwynim
doubtless wished better, but they had not yet built bet-

ter, and had to work together to have the roofs they did have.

The birth of a child in the camp, Drusenan had written, seemed to have brought men to some better sense.

But Drusenan had sent word, too, written for him, for Drusenan was better at building than at writing:

Some of Her Grace's men ask to settle a camp on the river and attack Tasmôrden from there, but I have not agreed, believing Your Grace to hold a contrary opinion. What shall I say to them?

Refuse them, he had sent back that same day, and urgently. *They will have their day, and justice done, but not yet.*

There were more men now than women in Althalen, with horses, and grain was now a matter of critical need. Cevulirn's men had ridden home after their seven days of watch at the bridge, with the lives of fifty-eight women, old men, wounded, and children saved at that crossing and now settled at Althalen; Drusenan's men at least now had the help of the Elwynim who were whole of body, who carried supply on their backs, and who hewed wood and raised their walls with little grumbling and in decent gratitude.

Gratitude flourished far better there, it seemed, than in the streets of Guelemara.

We have missed you, Cefwyn's letter said, a postscript, below the seal.

The pigeons are in deep mourning. I have taken to feeding them myself. I have become superstitious on their account.

He could scarcely imagine. Cefwyn had so many important other concerns.

The weather continues to amaze me. I think of your urging after Lewenbrook and yet I know well the hazards if we had proceeded.

Below the seal Cefwyn the king had fallen silent and at that point his friend had begun to write to him, a hasty scrawl, an outpouring of the heart after he had said everything so carefully, so discreetly. What followed was not discreet.

In some measure I trusted your urgings then and wished to go on across the river, and yet I see around me the disaffections and distrust that would have rendered all we might do ineffectual to assure a just and true peace. Talk to Emuin. I would that I could. Consult with Cevulirn. I recommend him as a friend and a wise man.

Then the handwriting changed, and grew more careful.

I add one other thing: some see in you the fulfillment of Elwynim prophecy. I have been aware of this from the start. If you are the one I think you are, no matter how dark, you have no less of my love and regard, which I hope you have in kind for me. This Emuin advised me to win for myself, and it was the wisest advice and best he ever gave me.

Cefwyn knew it all, and trusted him, and was not angry.

It was a precious letter, and Tristen sat with his hands on it as if that in itself could bridge the distance and place his hands in Cefwyn's hands. His heart beat hard, a knot stopped his throat, and he heard again the bells that had rung the hour they had parted, the wild pealing, so joyous, when there was nothing of joy for either of them in the hour, but only for their enemies.

His pigeons had sprung aloft, the banners had flown bravely on the wind, but in that hollow pealing of bronze, the warmest thing in the world had been Cefwyn's embrace, and the look Cefwyn had flung him eye-to-eye before the Quinaltine steps.

You have no less of my love, Cefwyn wrote now.

And the world became warm and safe for a heartbeat.

Win *Cefwyn's* friendship, Emuin said, but he did not take Cefwyn's reassurance to fulfill that, not entirely, not truly, in the magical sense. Emuin had given his advice, and like Mauryl's advice, it struck at the root of intentions, not at the flower.

And both root and the flower were important to him, one having to do with what one meant to do . . . and the other, most fearsome, with the outcome of it.

With all his heart he wished to write back to Cefwyn . . . but considering the message within Idrys' message, the way he had protected Gedd, and the danger Gedd had run to reach him, the exchange they had already had exposed not only the messenger but Cefwyn and Ninévrisë to danger. If their enemies did not know the content of the message, at least they knew a message had come and gone, and at such a time.

He had no news worth the risk of the bearer's life. The business with the bridge was done: in spite of Idrys' urgent message to send him no more gifts . . . he had to fear he had: all the discontent carters who had labored in one service after another, who might even as he sat here be telling their tale of Elwynim and walls and settlements at Althalen in every tavern in Guelemara.

There was nothing he could do but wish Cefwyn's people to see the truth, and to know their welfare lay more with their king who wished an honest, lasting peace, than with Ryssand, whose wishes were tangled and dark with hatred, some for Cefwyn, but far, far more of it for the Bryaltines and the Teranthines and everything southern . . . himself not least or last in that reckoning. *There* was fertile ground for hostile wizardry, or ambitious, or greedy, or any that did not scruple to use a hateful, hating man.

Ryssand's son was dead. He had a daughter for his heir . . . which the Quinaltines, ironically, would not allow, and he the greatest supporter of the strict Quinaltines. What was he to do?

Something to save himself, that would somehow twist and turn until it came out profitable to himself, that was more than likely.

And meanwhile he could get no message to Idrys to tell him there was a traitor within his ranks, no message to Cefwyn to assure him of better news from the south—not without risking a life and possibly putting a dangerous letter in the hands of Lord Ryssand.

He had now only boats to look for . . . Sovrag lord of Olmern's boats, and the grain they carried. The storm surge had gone down the Lenúalim, the river ran calmly now at its ordinary level, by the reports he had from Anwyll, and there was no reason for delay, unless Sovrag's boats had suffered—

Or unless Sovrag had doubts or fears of aiding him, considering the storm brewing in the heart of Ylesuin. Any of the lords who had awareness of the situation Gedd had reported might well think twice about joining their Midwinter feast . . . and Sovrag's grain had to be here to avoid famine.

He gave it another day and then he must send a messenger south to Olmern, a far safer direction to ask reasons; and he had to send another rider to Cevulirn to inform him of the delay in supply for the horses.

Midwinter was coming on apace, and the needs of the province were absolute. If Sovrag for some reason failed them, then they still must obtain the grain, all the same . . . if not from Sovrag, then they might appeal next to his constant enemy among the allies of Lewen field, the lord of Imor Lenúalim, dour, Quinalt Umanon.

Umanon might or might not favor their enterprise,

might or might not be keenly aware of the sentiment against him, and might or might not answer Cevulirn's invitation—and if he came, might or might not tell everything he learned to friends to the north. The plain fact was that Umanon was a Guelen, different from all the other southern lords, associated with Lewenbrook only because Cefwyn as a Guelen prince had brought him in to have the heavy cavalry Cefwyn relied on.

Now a southern call had gone out, furtive and hoping for secrecy . . . and yet they had not omitted Umanon, who had been one of them, whatever else he was.

And would he answer the call, or betray them?

A gathering of all the south was a difficult secret to keep . . . and the more difficult as the time drew closer and all the staff down to Cook and her crew assembled the makings of a great holiday.

The best news in recent days was the assembling of young men of Amefel, earnest young men . . . feckless boys, Uwen called most of them, but well-meaning, with some experienced veterans in the number. It was a good lot. But they were far from the Amefin guard that was yet to be . . . that must exist by the time the buds broke on the trees.

The Guelen Guard, at Uwen's order, had undertaken to show the men the use of the long Guelen lance and the small sword, and that the training and short tempers and stung pride failed to provoke Amefin and Guelenmen to open warfare, it was itself a wonder . . . but that was the regiment they had at hand, and that was what had to be.

The southern longbow many already knew; and perhaps half had horsemanship enough, but those were green youths on of the edge of nobility, accustomed to ride to the hunt, vying with one another to be first to the quarry—not to make an iron front against an enemy. The lads, as Uwen called them, were in great earnest for their lords' pride and their own, but there were two sent home with broken bones, and one all but died of Maudbrook's icy water on a windy day— his horse had sent him there.

But in recent days the recruits had gone out about the land, faring out toward the remote villages to parade their weapons and make known the authority that sent them.

More, even given the chance there were enemies in the land, they practiced ambushes on one another in the bitter cold and the winter-barren land, merry as otters, Uwen called them. They were noisy, determined, and since the Guelenmen teaching them had not killed them, they had necessarily improved in the lance and the sword.

Tomorrow, orders which also lay on Tristen's desk, under his hand as he read, they were to ride east to Assurnbrook, as far west as the limits of Marna Wood; they had already ridden down to Modeyneth and to Anwyll's camp, to Trys Ceyl in the south and Sagany and Emwysbrook, to Dor Elen, Anas Mallorn, and Levey, displaying the banners, answering questions, bearing news.

That was one thing he wished he could tell Cefwyn.

And, aside from the want of grain, stores had turned up, out of cellars in town, out of caves and cists in the hills: reserves of grain, preserved meat, gold and silver which the lords had held secret, and, mysteriously, too, but from different sources, a number of weapons which had not been in the armory since Lewenbrook had shown up in the hands of these young men.

"As they ain't fools," Uwen had said wryly, "an' now they know they have a lord who ain't Guelen, why, back the gear comes from under their beds."

Over all, while the news from Guelemara chilled Tristen's heart, there was reason to think the south was safer than it had been. If Tasmôrden intruded into his lands at this very hour he would meet both an armed and organized band of Elwynim veterans . . . and the otters, those small, scattered squads of an Amefin cavalry he would not expect, on horses that were increasingly fit.

And that Amefin cavalry was armed with both bow and lance, for harrying an enemy and making his foraging impossible: such were their orders—no all-out engagement, but a deliberate harrying, keeping contact with an enemy band while they sent a series of messengers with word to Henas'amef, to bring in the heavier-armed Guelens.

There was that force out and about.

Modeyneth and Anas Mallorn, which lay near the sites of likely crossings, had built stout shutters and towers for archers.

The old wall beyond Modeyneth was now, by work proceeding by day and night, man-high across the road, with a stout gate, braces, and an archer's tower. The men who built there, both of Modeyneth and other villages of Bryn, built in weather which never mired the roads, and built with the advantage of stones already cut.

Not least, Anwyll and the Dragon Guard at the river maintained close, fierce guard over sections of decking which could again be laid rapidly over the bridge frameworks, and which were stout enough to support even wheeled traffic—once his Midwinter gathering determined to secure the other bridgehead as theirs, and set up a camp inside Elwynor.

They were as near ready as he could hope . . . save only the grain to feed all these men. And the fear, now made clear in Gedd's report, that he might have taken far too much for granted, regarding the Guelen and Ryssandish fear of him and the south.

Talk to Emuin, Cefwyn had written him.

Paisi, hair disheveled, roused from the diurnal night of the shuttered tower, made tea. Emuin read Cefwyn's letter atop the clutter of charts, then nodded soberly as Tristen meanwhile relayed Gedd's report in all its alarming substance.

"Well, well," Emuin said, and bit his lip then, shaking his head. "What Cefwyn wishes me to explain when he says consult me, is the Quinalt, and its distaste for things Amefin. I think you know that."

"I know the guardsmen I sent and the patriarch all went to Cefwyn's enemies. And the drivers of the carts I sent back will talk."

"The carters you sent back will talk, and the soldiers that went without leave have talked, and the Amefin patriarch has certainly had words to say within those walls, all manner of words about the grandmothers in the market, and about me, and any other sign of wizardry. That's nothing we can prevent now."

"As for the other, sir . . . the prophecy . . ." He disliked even to think about it, but it was there, part of the letter, with Cefwyn's assurances.

"It's all one."

"It is *not* one, sir. I fear it's not. The carters will talk about the same things the patriarch complained of, charms in the market, and about the Elwynim at Althalen—"

"No small matter."

"But the greater is, Ninévrisë's father called me *young king.* Auld Syes did much the same. The Elwynim wait for a King To Come, and Tasmôrden flies the banner of the King of Althalen above Ilefínian."

"Does he?"

"Yes!"

"What will you do about it?"

I won't allow it, he almost said. But he thought then of the disparate elements he had just set forth to Emuin, and found in them subtle connections to events around him that frightened him to silence.

"Tea, sir, m'lord." Taking advantage of the silence, Paisi desperately set the tray down and poured. It was bitter cold in the tower, and Paisi's hands trembled, hands as grimy as ever they had been in the street.

"Wash," Emuin said. "Treat my potions as you treat common mud, boy, and you'll poison both of us."

"It's only pitch, sir."

"Dirt," said Emuin. "Scrub. You shouldn't sleep dirty, boy. Gods!"

"Sir," Paisi whispered, and effaced himself.

Emuin took up a teacup. "What will you do about it?" Emuin asked again.

"I don't know, sir," Tristen said, turning his own in his fingers. "I think the first is coming here and asking you what I ought to do. And I earnestly pray you answer me. This is beyond lessons. I can't take lessons any longer. What I do may harm Cefwyn."

There was long silence, long, long silence, and Emuin took a studied sip of the tea, but Tristen never looked away or touched his cup.

"So you will not let me escape this time," Emuin said.

"I *ask*, sir. I don't demand. I ask for Cefwyn's sake."

"And with all your heart."

"And with all my heart, sir."

"Do you think you *are* the King To Come? Does that Unfold to you, as some things do?"

He asked Emuin to give up his secrets—and his question to Emuin turned back at him like a sword point, direct and sharp and simple.

"No," he said from the heart. "I've no desire to be a king or the High King or any king. If I could have Cefwyn back as Prince Cefwyn and his father alive so he didn't have to work so, and all of us here at Amefel, that's what I would most wish, for everything to be what it was this summer . . . but I can't have that, and I could only do him harm if I wished it, so I don't. I won't. You say I must win Cefwyn's friendship . . . and that doesn't come of anything I've done that I can see. Everything I've done has turned his own people against him!"

"Young lord," Emuin said, "you've gained very many things, and know far more, and now you've almost become honest."

"I have never lied, sir!"

Emuin fixed him with a direct and challenging stare. "Have you not?"

"Not often. —Not lately."

"Ah. And have you often told the truth?"

"Have *you* told it yourself, sir. Forgive me, but is this not the lesson you showed me, to keep silent, to leave and not answer questions. I keep quiet the things I fear could do harm, and the things I don't understand!"

"Exactly as I do."

The anger fell, left him nothing, and still no answer.

"Is that all you learned of me?" Emuin asked. "Silence?"

"No, sir, there were very many good lessons."

"And do you not, as you say, count it good, to keep silent when speaking might work harm?"

"What harm would it have worked, for you to have stayed by me this summer? What harm would it work now, for you to tell me the dangers ahead, if I swear to take your advice?"

"Harm that I might do? Oh, much. Much, if I interfere—"

"—If you interfere with Mauryl's working. But do you say, then, sir, that you *can* interfere with Mauryl's working? Or can anyone? Are you that great a wizard?"

"Who *are* you?"

Back to wizard-questions, the quick reverse, the subtle attack, and that one went straight as a sword to the heart.

"Who *are* you?" Emuin repeated. "This time *I* require an answer."

Tristen drew a deep breath, laid his hands on the solid table surface, on the charts, the evidence and record of the heavens, for something solid to grasp . . . for very nearly he had said, defiantly, out of temper, and only to confound the old man,

I am Barrakkêth.

So close he had come, so disastrously close it chilled him.

"I am Tristen," he said calmly, lifting his head and staring straight into Emuin's measuring eyes. "I am Mauryl's Shaping. I am Cefwyn's friend and your student. I am the lord of Althalen and Ynefel. *Tristen* says all, sir, and all these other things are appurtenances."

"Not lord of Amefel?" Emuin asked with that same measuring look, and his heart beat hard.

Crissand, he thought.

Crissand, Crissand, Crissand.

"Cefwyn must grant me Amefel," he said to the wall, the wind, the fire in the hearth, not to the boy sitting silent or the wizard gazing at his back. "Cefwyn must grant me this one thing."

"Has he not? It seems to me he granted you Amefel."

"No. He made me lord of Amefel, in fealty to him. He hasn't *given* it to me. And that he must do, for his own safety."

There was a long, a very long silence.

"You know," said Emuin, "if other things have disturbed Ryssand and Murandys, this one will hardly calm their fears."

"Crissand Adiran is lord of Amefel. He is a *king,* master Emuin, he is the Aswydd that should rule, and if I set him here, on this hill, and see him crowned, I would think I had done well, and that I had done Cefwyn no disservice at all."

There was long silence, a direct stare from Emuin and Paisi's eyes as large as saucers.

"The next question. *What* are you?"

"Mauryl's Shaping, sir. Cefwyn's friend, and your student, lord of Ynefel, lord of Althalen."

"And of those folk there settled?"

"*If* they remain there."

"And this is your firm will."

"I am Mauryl's Shaping."

"What we say three times gathers force, and what *you* say three times has *uncommon* force, lord of Althalen."

"I've told you all I know, sir, and beyond, into things I hope. So what do you advise me to say? More, what to do, sir? Idrys has a liar in his service, and Cefwyn is in danger."

"If I knew that, young lord, I'd sleep of nights." Emuin moved the letter aside and moved one of his charts to the surface, a dry, stiff, and much-scraped parchment. He looked at it one way and another, and then cast it toward him, atop a stack of equally confused parchments.

"*This*, this, young lord, is as much as I do know. This is the reckoning that Mauryl himself would have seen coming, that once in sixty-two years these portents recur in the heavens, and where they occur at the Midwinter, there is the Great Year begun, that is, the time until the wandering stars hold court together and move apart again. This is the season of uncommon change . . . but this is nothing to you, I suspect." Emuin's tone took on a forlorn exasperation, much like Mauryl's when confronting his helplessness. "Nothing Unfolds. No great revelation."

"No, sir." He looked at the parchment, and considered the things Emuin said and cast it down again, unenlightened. "I don't know what you're saying. About the stars, I gather, but nothing more. I know Mauryl studied them. And you do. But I've never understood the things you find."

"Magic is an unfettered thing. *You* . . . are an unfettered thing. But wizardry, *wizardry*, young lord, is a matter of numbers . . . patterns, as nature itself is patterns, and the gathering of forces. Think you that winter happens by magic? No. Everything in nature, young lord, is a march of patterns, the chill in the air, the sleep of the trees, the waning of the summer stars and the rise of the winter ones, that in their turn will set . . ."

"These things I see, and you tell me they recur."

"Yes! So if you would work a great work of wizardry, do you see, there's no sense doing hard things, only the easy ones. Do you want a snow? Ask for it in winter! Much easier. Find patterns in nature and lay your own Lines where they go, much as you set the Lines of a great house, observing doors and windows where they want to be."

Emuin seemed to expect agreement, understanding—something.

"Yes, sir."

"But you don't! All this is frivolous to you! You

treat patterns the way a young horse treats fences, to have the fine green grass at your pleasure. And gods save us on the day you treat natural laws as that great dark stallion of yours treats stall slats, and simply kick them down."

"I trust I'm never so inconsiderate of your work, sir, as Dys of master Haman's boards."

Emuin grunted, then gave a breath of a laugh, and at last chuckled and for the first time in a long time truly did regard him kindly. "Good lad. *Good* lad. When I fear you most, you have your ways to remind me you *are* Tristen."

"I am. And shall be, sir. And never would treat your patterns carelessly. I have more understanding than my horse."

Emuin did laugh, and wiped an eye with a gnarled finger, and wiped both, then his nose. "Oh, lad. Oh, young lord. We're in great danger."

"But we are *friends*, sir, and I'm yours, as I am Cefwyn's."

"That, too, is a snare, young lord, and one I avoid very zealously: we must both look at one another without trust, *assuming* nothing, as we love one another, as we love that rascal Cefwyn. Fear friendship with me! Avoid it! Examine my actions, as I do yours, and let us save one another.—But you asked, and I answered, and let me answer, again, such as I can. Hasufin—"

"Hasufin!"

"Regarding this matter of the Great Year, I say, sixty-two years of the ordinary sort, and Hasufin Heltain, who *was* a wizard, and who bound his life to the cycle of the Great Year. Great works need great patterns. And his was the most ambitious: to use the Great Year itself would have given him more than one opportunity for a long, difficult magic, at long intervals. But there is more: there's a Year of Years, a pattern of patterns that only the longest-lived can see, let alone use. Do you guess? Hasufin is *old*, as Mauryl was *old*. And the dawn of the last Year of Years was the hour of Hasufin's first seizure of Ynefel, when he drove Mauryl Gestaurien to seek help in the north. But before it was done . . . the Sihhë came down. And *that* was the pattern of that beginning. That was what Mauryl did to Hasufin Heltain: he wrought the Sihhë-lords into Hasufin's rise, so he could never be free of them—and the Sihhë-lords, like your horse, respect no boundaries and kick down the bars. He lost. Mauryl rose . . . and the Sihhë-lords reigned."

"And fell."

"Ah, and the dawn of the last cycle, the second such time, you may well suspect, sixty-two years ago . . . was Hasufin's second rise. We are in the last of the sixty-two years of the Great Year that marks the Year of Years. The spring solstice, last spring, when Hasufin overthrew Mauryl the second time . . . Mauryl knew his peril; and chose *his* moment: the time of rebirth, *your* birth, young lord. Now that Great Year closes and a new Great Year begins the next Year of Years in the season of the deepest dark. At Midwinter the last element of the heavenly court will enter the House in which all the others stand. This movement marks the dawn, at midnight, of that new Year of Years. At Midwinter the moon stands, changeable queen that she is, at the darkest of the dark. By the time the sun rises, either the elements of the Great Year favor Hasufin . . . or something stands in opposition to him. What is, at that dawn, will be, for centuries of years as Men reckon time."

"So Mauryl never sent me to Lewenbrook. That wasn't what he wanted of me."

"Oh, it was certainly part of it. But Cefwyn opposed Hasufin. *Cefwyn* opposed him, and opposes him now, and there's that damned Elwynim prophecy of a King To Come. It's probably true, more's the pity. Uleman was a good wizard, but he talked too much, and now everyone expects there to be a new High King. It doesn't serve Cefwyn well at all . . . and by chance it doesn't help Uleman's daughter, either."

Here was truth, so much truth it was hard to know what part of it to seize and question, but he found one question salient and unavoidable.

"And is Hasufin our enemy still?" Tristen asked. "And shall I fight him again? And where?"

"I can't say," Emuin answered him with a shake of his head. "Above all, Midwinter Eve is perilous to us, and of all damned days you might have chosen to assemble the lords . . . that one you never asked me."

"I had no knowledge. Now I do. What other times shall I fear?"

"The spring solstice . . . evidently," Emuin said. "But what more may happen I don't know. *I* haven't lived through a Year of Years. You have."

"I haven't *lived*."

"As much as Hasufin. Mauryl's the only one who's lasted one in the flesh, as it were. And now is stone, in his own walls, so you say."

He shivered, not wishing to recall that day of waiting, that terrible hour, when he knew the enchantment of the faces was not the ordinary course of the world, and that there was something dreadful about Ynefel, where the Sihhë had ruled, where the Lord Barrakkêth had maintained a dreaded fortress . . . where at last only Mauryl had lived, alone, in solitary correspondence with the latter generations of Men, at Althalen, and what Men had used to call Hen Amas, and now Henas'amef.

"So Mauryl did the best he could: sent you, without warning, without guidance, without instruction . . . lord of Althalen. That you surely are. Lord of Ynefel . . . I would never dispute. That you are Tristen . . . I leave that to you, and would never say otherwise. This I do tell you: the stars point to Midwinter. The hinge of the year. The hinge of many years, this time, when all things reach an end, and a beginning, and when patterns begin for the next Year of Years. Against your years, I am a youth." Emuin reached across the table to lay his gnarled hand on his young one, a touch like Mauryl's, half-remembered, touching his very heart. "Tristen is your name. So be it. Have a sip of tea. It's grown cold, boy. Boy!"

"Sir!" said Paisi, scrambling up.

"Tea. Cakes if they've escaped your avarice."

"Avarice, sir?"

"Things don't Unfold to him," Emuin said, aside, "and, thief that he was, he has no notion what avarice is. A fine boy. A discreet boy, who has no desire to become a toad. Where are the cakes, Paisi?"

"I'll ask Cook," Paisi said, swinging the kettle over the fire and poking up the heat. "I'll be back, I'll be right back, sir. I di'n't hear a thing, I di'n't."

"Toads," Emuin said, and Paisi adjusted the kettle and fled, banging the door, or the wind did it, seeping in from the cracks in the shutters.

Quiet occupied the tower, then, only the slight whistle of the wind.

"He's no trouble, is he?" Tristen asked, hoping he had not inconvenienced master Emuin.

Emuin gathered up a handful of beads, a collection of knots and strings and feathers, beads and bits of metal. "A grandmother's spell, a protection. He came back clattering with it, a thing of moderate potency, in very fact. Do you see the Sihhë coin?"

"Yes," he said, curious, for just such a coin had banished him from Guelessar. "And you keep it?"

"The wretch gave it to me," Emuin said, "saying I

surely needed protection. And he had bought it with coin your Uwen gave him."

"There's no harm in it," Tristen said, lifting it in his fingers. "Is there, master Emuin?"

"You see nothing amiss in it, do you?"

"No, sir. I don't."

"A grandmother's spell, cast on *me*, if you please, and bought with Uwen's spare pennies, from the rise of his good fortunes." Emuin shook his head, and cast a pinch of powder into the fire. It burst in a shower of smoke, and a smell that would banish vermin. "Boys," Emuin said. "He takes greatly to the powders and smokes. They make him sure I'm a wizard."

"Yet so is he."

"And steals cakes, the wretch!" Emuin laid aside the cords and trinkets, and dusted off his hands. "When a request would obtain them, he steals."

"As you say, he is a thief. That's his trade."

"Out on it! But he must *not* curse. I fear that in him, above all else. I've told him so, in no uncertain terms."

"Accept his gift," Tristen said. "His stealth is a skill."

Emuin lifted a white brow. "That it is, in its good time." There was a riffle of touch in the gray place, an overwhelming sight of Emuin as a presence there, and the place they occupied was small and furtive in itself, their visits there few, these days, and now, after so much of shared confidences, they sat, touched and touching, only for comfort.

A little removed was a little mouse of a presence, visible, if one knew to look for it. *Paisi the Gray,* Tristen thought. *Paisi the Mouse.*

Above them the day, and before them the night and the ominous stars. He had a question and wrenched himself out of the comfort of the gray space and into the clutter of Emuin's tower, where the old man sat, far less imposing than in that other place, with tea stains on his robe and ink on his fingers.

"What were the stars when Mauryl Summoned *me*, sir? Tell me something else. Am I bound to one year? Or to this Great Year of yours?"

"Gods know what you are bound to. Or . . . being Sihhë, gods know."

A horse, running in the field. In his heart he had not known there was a boundary, a place, a fence, a limit to freedom, until Emuin and Uwen had begun to make him know the seasons, and the Year had unfolded to him, in its immutable cycles. He had viewed it with some dismay, to know such repetitions existed.

On such things Men pinned their memories. Uwen would say, in the winter of the great snow, or in the spring I was fighting in the south, and such wizardry did Men practice, fencing things in, establishing patterns as they made Lines on the earth.

"Is it wizards who made years?" he asked. Questions still came to him, though few there were he dared ask, these days.

"I believe it was," Emuin said. "For so much of the craft relies on it. Yet we have no constraint on the moon, which observes its own cycles."

"And what have *you* bound to this Year of Years? And what have *you* wrought, regarding me, sir?"

There was a small silence, and Emuin turned as furtive as Paisi, and did not look him in the eyes at once.

"I've chosen to do very little."

"Keeping an eye on me, as Uwen puts it."

"So to say. And I can't fault you, beyond your disposition to raise walls and give away provinces."

He laughed, obediently, but his heart still labored under all that Emuin had said.

"Gods know what you are," Emuin said then, "but

I know what I am, which is an old wizard who has seen the largest pattern he knows reach its end and swing round again . . . or it will do so, on Midwinter, when my young lord is holding feast with the lords of the south. Then's the hour to keep the wards tight and the fires lit. —After that, I'll breathe more easily."

"The wards." He had forgotten their strange behavior, in that way wizardry slipped past one's attention. "Do you remember that night, sir? Did you see it, the night when all the town stood in light?"

Emuin gazed at him curiously, as if struggling to recall. "Yes. That night. And I wondered was it you."

Tristen shook his head. "Not that I was aware. I thought of you, sir. Or even Paisi. It wasn't so much that something tried the wards. It was as if the town waked. As if the building did."

Something happened then in the gray space, perhaps a subtle inquiry. And a two-footed mouse skipped on the stairs, fearing shadows and sounds in a hall gone strange to his eyes.

—Get up the stairs, young fool!

Emuin was stern and protective at once, and there was a rapid running on the steps from the scullery, and a rapid passage through the lower hall, wherein there was special danger, to a boy with a tray of cakes and a pot of jam.

—I'm coming, sir. I'm coming.

So Ynefel had seemed at times to live, and what he knew now for ghosts to haunt the stairs and trip an unwary lad.

In a strange way he felt grieved not to be Paisi, with no danger apparent to him but his own wise fear of shadows and cold spots on the stairs.

Had he not learned theft himself, and stealth, and known all the nooks and crannies of the old fortress at Ynefel?

And had he not gone as oblivious of its wards and its terrible secrets?

"Silly boy." Emuin sighed. "He's learned to hear us, you can tell, and we have few secrets. Now if he only learns a bit more, and respects the wards, we'll have something in him."

The grandmother's cords and charms seemed peculiarly potent, almost a point of light in the gray space. Elsewhere in the town, an old woman had wished well, and now stopped in her weaving, and held a hand to her heart, for that wish might require a strength she had never had called. That heart all but burst with the shock, the life all but fled, before Tristen realized the outpouring of it and closed the gap with his own hand as he touched the cords of the charm.

He gathered them up, held them in both hands, and drew a bright, burning line from the Zeide to the roof of a house near the wall, and an old, old woman who had nearly died.

"Rash," said Emuin. "Rash. You've made that woman a target."

"I've given her a shield. So with all the town."

There was a clatter on the stairs, a crash and a rattle just outside the door, a rush of wind as Paisi struggled to open it, wide-eyed and sweating from his haste.

"I di'n't break the pot," said Paisi, but edged a cake back from among the rest. "This 'un fell. I'll eat it."

"Nobly offered," Emuin said. "Take two. Go, the water's long since boiled, and His Grace is patient. Don't offend him. He's terribly dangerous when offended."

"Aye," said Paisi faintly, scrambling for the cups. "Aye, an' I washed, sir! Cook made me."

CHAPTER 2

Tailors and purveyors of costly goods were having a prosperous winter . . . first the royal wedding and now the wedding of Rusyn of Panys with Luriel of Murandys.

Luriel, who had come within a vow of being queen of Ylesuin, would yield nothing to a royal bride in show or extravagance: she was absolutely determined to have a pageantry to erase all memory of her disgrace, and her expense in satin cloth might have sustained the villages of her province through a far worse winter.

Cefwyn watched the bustle and hurry with a cautious eye, wondering himself just how much show and pageantry Lord Murandys would allow, and how much Luriel dared, with a keen eye as to whether at any point it went over that fine distinction between the redemption of Luriel and an affront to his wife.

Most of all he was glad that the to-ing and fro-ing and measuring now involved another bridegroom— and yet, and yet . . . to his astonishment the piles of fabric in the old scriptorium, the Royal Consort's domain, brought down another controversy of petticoats, beginning with the fact that Luriel had chosen the traditional gown, and had not modeled herself off the fashion of the consort.

It was a decision which might have signified the bride's desire simply to avoid controversy, and to avoid a slavish flattery of her royal patron, who, among other things, had no reason to invite comparison with her lord's former lover.

But that lack of adherence to Ninévrisë's side of the petticoat controversy ended up angering *him*, curious notion. *He* was offended, when Ninévrisë refused to take offense, and he could not lay his finger on what in Luriel's choice annoyed him.

The fact was, the ladies did whisper that Luriel wished a *traditional* wedding, with all the Quinalt blessing: so the rumor reached him through Idrys, of all unlikely sources, and he was incensed, all but ready to signal his disfavor of Luriel in a public snub.

But he was not willing to bring the Majesty of Ylesuin to the issue, not ready to stamp the royal seal on a decree, gods help him, regarding ladies' petticoats. There were limits. He had fought his battles on that ground once, and Ninévrisë had, and he told himself it was done.

And just as they held back, Fiselle, Ninévrisë's maid, vain and feckless girl, unwittingly struck the telling blow in the fray, prattling on to Luriel's maid how Her Grace refrained from sweets and heavy foods to keep her lovely figure, which one of course had to have, in order to wear Her Grace's shape-revealing clothes.

A siege engine could hardly have kicked up more consternation, and as of one morning's news, two of the ladies *were* wearing Ninévrisë's single petticoats.

Then Luriel cast all hers away, down to a shift, even taking two panels from the gown.

If wishes were mangonels, bodies would lie like cordwood.

But everyone sincerely praised Luriel's form, and the single petticoats had, in a sevenday, scandalized the Quinalt.

The frivolity of women, certain priests called it, and the flaunting of immorality.

Then, on royal suggestion, His Holiness countered from the pulpit that certain priests spent too much time considering frivolity and not enough attending the needs of the people.

Seven days of shot and countershot, and, portentous surely, while the snow piled higher across the river, the wind blew steadily warm in Ylesuin until most of the hills were bare. Sorcery, some said, and blessed sigils turned up on doors, and candles burned a sweet savor to the Quinalt, the prayers of the honest faithful, while the priests fired barbs at one another in a doctrinal war that had begun in the women's court in the issue of petticoats and tradition and continued over the uncommon weather.

It made the king's court seem lately quiet by comparison, and in the absence of controversy on his own doorstep, Cefwyn found himself spending untroubled evenings at his own fireside . . . comfortable and pleasant evenings, in which he might sit in private with his own wife and dine without the constant intervention of ill tidings from the riverside or the Quinaltine.

Without, too, the clack and clatter of court proceedings, since the lords seemed weary, also, hoping only to pass the wedding without disarrangement of the arrangements that had settled a winter truce. At last they knew where they stood, at least in the middle lands. At last they knew what they must do, beyond all the furor Ryssand had kicked up—and that was to see their young men equipped for war and their lands so arranged that the fisheries and the orchards would not much suffer for the young men's absence for a season. The grain lands were exempt from the muster, and also the royal granaries would open, giving out the abundance they had stored in the good years previous.

It would be enough, all taken together.

In the meanwhile he looked forward to Luriel's marriage for very private reasons: there seemed something mildly indecent in hearing from his own wife's lips the doings of his former mistress and confidante, and while both of them could find wry humor in the situation—Luriel was a witty, wonderful young hothead, if it were someone else at whom her malice aimed—he was very ready to have an end of Luriel's crises.

She might be some sober use when she had settled in as a married lady, for as often as not her shafts of wit flew at her uncle, for now that she was marrying well, she gained a voice, and her uncle had to worry whether Luriel the featherwit had any interests beyond finery.

"She's likely gathering a fine dowry from her uncle," Ninévrisë remarked, "just from her silence. One wonders what she knows."

"Murandys has approached Panys seeking a conference," Cefwyn said, holding her close, the two of them in night robes, and the fire crackling and friendly. "But Lord Maudyn isn't guesting with him. He's staying at the river in his tent until the wedding, not even coming to the capital. Gods send me a dozen like Lord Panys."

The damned *carts* had come home, thank the gods, undamaged, not mired on the roads or lost in snowdrifts . . . with a discontent lot of carters complaining of the high-handedness of the duke of Amefel, true, but Idrys had been ready for them, this time. With no more than a day's sojourn in the town, the discontent carters had gone on to Lord Maudyn.

So the offended carters, ousted prematurely from the joys of Guelemara, surely spread rumors among the troops. But the guardsmen stationed there had the sobering sight of the river before them, and would surely find no fault in Tristen for making strong preparations in the south . . . not when they faced the eerily snowy shore of Elwynor just a wooden span away from their fair-weather side. And they would not fault a little friendly wizard-work in the distant south, when sorcery was a constantly rumored threat from across the river. Many of them were veterans, and the carters themselves might sing a different tune when the veteran guardsmen told their Midwinter tales.

Meanwhile, too, another simmering stew, the negotiations between Efanor and Corswyndam of Ryssand meandered on, and as yet Efanor signed no document. Ryssand was still aghast, perhaps, *not* having expected his proposal to be seriously considered . . . let alone accepted. More, there was the queasiness of a wedding preparation during an official mourning: Ryssand was high enough to set convention aside; Efanor certainly could . . . but by now Artisane had launched her own campaign, sure she would come back to court in all her glory.

Efanor had not broken to the lady the news that he had a fine estate wanting a lady's hand, oh, at the remote end of Guelessar.

And in genuine courtesy to Luriel's moment, they delayed the official announcement . . . but now with couriers rushing back and forth, necessarily through Murandys, Murandys ached to know what was in the messages . . . and evidently Ryssand had held Murandys, his old ally, from knowing anything.

"Do you suppose Ryssand holds Prichwarrin responsible for his son?" Ninévrisë wondered quietly.

"I've wondered, too. Prichwarrin urged it too far. It was Brugan's stupidity, no mending that, but Prichwarrin didn't take strong enough action. It wouldn't grieve me if those two fell out."

He asked Idrys, on the following day, whether there was any hint of breach.

"Murandys sends home often," Idrys said, "but I've no report he's receiving messages from Ryssand. He seems genuinely concerned, and has a worried look when anyone mentions priests. This is a man who may not know as much as we do."

"Perhaps after the wedding he'll seek Ryssand out."

"Leaving his niece unwatched, and no presence in court?" Idrys said. "No, my lord king. I very much doubt it."

His Reverence of Amefel, meanwhile, being an old man, had had a taking, a serious crisis of health—Idrys swore his innocence. But His Reverence had had a falling spell, and retired into an apartment within the Quinaltine, spending his time between his bed, his privy, and his prayers for his benighted province.

The controversy and the division was by no means healed. Efanor himself had argued vehemently with Ryssand's priest at a most uncomfortable state dinner, a mincing of doctrine and dogma at that table that Cefwyn hoped not to see repeated. There was no profit in it, none: neither Efanor nor the priest emerged converted, the damned petticoats figured in the issue, and everyone's digestion suffered.

"Silence this damned doctrinal nonsense!" Cefwyn had insisted to the Holy Father's face, utterly out of patience, and the result, the very next morning, was a hesitant, rambling homily from the Holy Father on the subject of unity in the state, a discourse that made no sense, seeming to court all sides . . . a parable of brothers and the healing of breaches and somehow off to the rights of a father to order his family and a king to order the state and a husband his wife.

"Damned useless," Cefwyn said to Idrys in his apartments after services. "Is *this* his word against that damned priest wandering the taverns? He's a father and that priest—what's his name—is some errant son? Or a wife? Fetch me Sulriggan. No, tell *Sulriggan* bring His Holiness and I'll talk to him. Good gods, can't the man come to a point, say yea or nay, not both in the same sermon?"

"And what more is my lord king, but yea and nay regarding this priest that's preaching sedition? I still advise my lord—"

"Dead priests are trouble, master crow, of a sort even you stick at, don't deny it. Now the patriarch of Amefel's taken residency in the Quinaltine, where you can't reach him, save his bad stomach."

"Unhappy man," said Idrys, long-faced. "And holy men have been known to vanish. It's a known aspect of holiness."

"For shame."

"For a long reign, my lord king. I'll be far plainer than His Holiness. *Kill this priest.*"

Cefwyn looked long and soberly at his Lord Commander, saying to himself he had just asked for the hard truth, asking himself whether he was not a fool for sticking at this one deft, swift act, that might, in fact, save other lives.

But there was, beyond his own scruples against murder, the prospect of outright disaster in any miscarriage of Idrys' proposal.

"I have observed this priest meet with those who meet with Murandys and Ryssand," Idrys said. "Often. I'm not sure there's a content beyond the offices of priests, but the fact remains: this priest has their patronage, and if messages do flow between Ryssand and Murandys to which we have no access, there is a conduit for them. The man's no dullard, no wide-eyed believer, and he has far too sleek a look for a man that sleeps in hedgerows."

"You have suspicions of Ryssand, do you? Is he playing two games?"

"Oh, of suspicions of Lord Corswyndam I have full store and several wagons over; of substance, there is only that one priest I know has his ear, and the ears of a half a score of the barefoot and hair-shirt sort, the ones who plague the streets. But what this one might sing if I laid hand to him could be valuable. If we can come at Ryssand that way, His Highness needn't marry to rein Ryssand in. If we can find a cause to shorten Ryssand by a head—gain to the whole kingdom."

It was a tempting thought. But he dared not. Would not. "I am not my grandfather. And, gods, if something went wrong—"

"Your grandfather lived to die in bed, his son with two sons and the kingdom secure. I *ask* instead of acting because I will not trample on policy. I serve my king; I beg to serve him *well*."

Idrys chided him and provoked him humorously on many things. This time there was no humor, no mask. "You're saying I'm a fool to let Ryssand live. What need to justify it, if I were my grandfather?"

"I say if Ryssand had died before this, you'd have no priest stirring up resentments in the populace. Now, lo! the priest. If my lord king fears to become his grandfather, let him remember his royal *father* failed to be rid of Heryn Aswydd, and look how that tree grew."

It was not a pleasant memory. Idrys was telling him what was the more prudent course. Profitable if Efanor could somehow convert Ryssand's interests to the Crown's interests, for Ryssand's talents and resources were formidable; but that still left him with Ryssand for company, and Ryssand's narrow doctrine to battle for all the years of his reign . . . while he hoped to settle a lasting peace with Ninévrisë's kingdom. The

Elwynim would never become Quinalt, and it was a far leap to think he could bring Ryssand away from his doctrinist allies, on that score. When he looked that far, he saw all manner of trouble.

But that was far, far downstream from where they stood.

"If I do this," he said, "we risk dividing Ylesuin. We risk years of unrest. We risk making a holy martyr, in this priest, and that is nothing we can sweep away. My grandfather, with all his faults, avoided martyrs."

"What to do is Your Majesty's concern. How, I consider is mine. But the harm grows, day by day."

"Ryssand's no easy horse to ride. There's no one I could set in that saddle *but* Lord Ryssand, precisely because he *is* a narrow, provincial doctrinist like every other man in Ryssand. I've thought about my choices. I detest the man. We're well rid of that son of his. But what do I set in his place, if not my brother, gods help him! And I'll postpone that day at least until there is a wedding."

"Disarm him of this priest."

"If not this one, there'll be another one."

"Oh, aye, my lord king, and if we down one of Tasmôrden's men, there'll be another. Shall we forbear to fight Tasmôrden?"

"You know it's not the same."

"Be rid of this one. And the next. And the next. Eventually there will be a dearth of Ryssandish priests."

"And enough anger to breed there and fester. Words deal best with words."

"Ah. Another of the Holy Father's sermons?"

He let go a breath, beaten down by the mere memory of tedium and indirection.

"Give me leave," Idrys said briskly. "And the matter is done by evening."

"And the town stirred up to a froth."

"A *lack* of a priest isn't noisy."

It was ever so tempting: his piety, such as it was, halfway argued him toward it, as the safest course for the peace, and all the lives he held in his hands. But he had Luriel's public show approaching, on which there would be crowds, tinder for a spark, and that rode his thoughts, inescapable.

"I want the town quiet. I want Luriel safely wedded and bedded and no untoward event to undo that alliance. When Murandys has Panys for a bedfellow, and *we* have Panys reporting to us . . . *then* we can consider measures."

"I fear I've not told you everything, my lord king."

Cefwyn drew a lengthy breath and sank, somewhat, against the back of his chair, Idrys black-armored and seeming by now like an implacable fixture of his office. "Sit, damn you, crow. My neck aches from looking at you. What morsel have you saved for dessert?"

"Cuthan, my lord king." Idrys reluctantly settled his black-armored body onto a frail, brocaded chair. "The priest is a straightforward matter. Lord Cuthan, I fear, is not."

"Cuthan."

"Your Majesty may remember him . . . the one Tristen exiled, that vain old scoundrel . . ."

"Out on it! I know who Cuthan is and where he was and where his cursed ancestors slept, *in* their own beds and out! I know Tristen exiled him, and I know he's in Elwynor."

"He is not in Elwynor, my lord king."

"Where, then? *Dare* I guess?"

"Ryssand?"

"Damn."

"Ryssand is honest in one thing," Idrys said, "that he bears a father's grief for a son and heir. That, marriage with His Highness or no, he will never relinquish . . . not greed, not ambition, not the promise that his line might weave itself into the Marhanens can ever erase the matter of his son."

"His one virtue and more inconvenient than his sins. Now he has Cuthan. And Parsynan. What a merry court!"

"I've not told His Highness yet. What I wonder is how he passed through all of Elwynor and its weather and all the way to Ryssand."

"A rowboat. We're not speaking of a regiment."

"Yet my lord king knows the man is old, in no robust health. How did he bear the snow, the ice, the pillaging army, if nothing else? A very hardy man, or a very lucky, if he did that alone."

"Damn. Twice damn. Tasmôrden!"

"Exactly so. I fear Cuthan may be very close to Tasmôrden. He may bear a message, or gather one."

All of a sudden the depth of Idrys' knowledge suggested a fearsomely deep involvement in Ryssand, volatile as it was, dangerous as the spying was—and fruitful as it proved.

"How did you learn this?"

"Efanor's messenger."

"*Efanor's* messenger. Crow, it's my brother's name, his reputation . . . his *safety,* for that matter—"

Idrys, rarely abashed, looked at him with a half-veiled effrontery, defense in every line. "Your Majesty, you once asked whom I served, your father, or you. And where there was a choice of loyalties, your father is in his tomb, and I have only *one* lord, as does His Highness."

"So you insinuated a spy into Ryssand, a spy wearing my brother's colors."

"Briefly."

"Do you know the furor if he were found? Efanor is honorable to a fault!"

"Very much to a fault. My lord king, but some risks are worth taking, and spies within Ryssand are hard come by."

"Wearing my brother's crest, good loving gods . . . I'd like to know where else you have them.— No! Don't tell me! I've become worse at lying than Tristen is."

"I fear you were never good at it. It's *Tristen* who's become adept in the art."

He was not certain for a moment it was no jest. But Idrys' expression advised him the matter was serious.

"You don't fault *him*," Cefwyn said. There seemed a fist still clenched about his heart. "You don't tell me he's deceived me. This is my *friend*, damn you! You've spoken against him before, and you've been wrong."

Idrys gave a rare and rueful laugh. "Lord Tristen is extremely canny about disposing my spies at distance from him. As a result, I have not a single man in Henas'amef. He's sent them all to the river, beginning with Anwyll. I have better intelligence of *Ryssand* than of His Grace of Amefel."

"And what do your spies learn, beyond his sins at Althalen and his wall-building?"

"His fortification of the province? His permissions to the witches to flourish? His countenancing of Sihhë emblems, spells and charms openly displayed in the market?" Idrys held up fingers and ticked off the points, one by one. "His banishment of Guelen Guard, his appropriation of Your Majesty's carts and drivers, his holding of Parsynan's goods in consequence—" Idrys began the tally on the left hand. "His alienation of the Amefin patriarch, his banishment of an Amefin earl old as the hills in his title . . ."

"All these things he confesses. Justify your spies, master crow. I defy you to report to me *one thing* Tristen hasn't freely owned."

"He's holding winterfeast and invited all the lords of the south to come and camp under arms, for, one suspects, some use besides a winter hunt. The preparation is for a host as many as took the field at Lewenbrook."

He forgot to breathe.

It was, on the other hand, exactly the sort of feckless doing he could always expect of Tristen—and it was not aimed at him. There was nothing of Ryssand's poison in what Tristen did. Rather it was Tristen's doing what his king could not do . . . and so secretly it had taken Idrys this long to know it.

"He's doing what I did this summer. He's gathering his allies about him, people he well likes . . . men who like *him. He's reknitting the damned southern alliance, is what he's doing* . . . and gods save him for the effort! What I can't, he does, and I wish him success. I wish him every success."

"But it will provoke just a small bit of comment among the northern barons, will it not? He's told Anwyll prepare a landing for boats bearing grain. An immense amount of grain, out of Casmyndan."

"He's importing grain? I had to show him the use of a penny this autumn, for the gods' good sake."

"Well, and made him lord of Amefel, my lord king, which I do recall counseling you was a—"

"You agreed it was a good idea."

"I agreed he would be a most uncommon lord of Amefel, and perhaps it was a safe direction for him, considering the Elwynim prophecy."

"Damn the Elwynim prophecy! If he wants to be king in Amefel, between the two of us—" He drew a deep breath, his heart still laboring from the realization of new complications in all his plans. "Between the two of us and the walls, master crow, if he would *be* High King at Althalen and rule the damn province between me and

Nevris' kingdom, I'd grant it. The *Aswydds* styled themselves aethelings."

"So does he."

"When?"

"That the first night, in the oath of Crissand of Meiden, my lord king, who is also Aswydd, may I say? And who swore to him as aetheling. And may I say that that small rumor is starting to make the rounds of the taverns? The word came out of Amefel, I daresay."

"Like Cuthan."

"Never forgetting that now troublesome man. And now Ryssand's priest knows."

"Damn this zealot priest—what *is* his name?"

"Udryn, my lord king. Chief of them, at least. And while Your Majesty has a very sensible desire to have the Lady Luriel's wedding without incident—very many rumors may begin to make the same rounds, from the same lips, from the same source. Do you still bid me refrain from this priest?"

"I want none of his crowd creating a commotion at the wedding. No. No blood. Just keep that priest out of the way. That's all I ask. If the Holy Father can't rein him in . . . see to him. Frighten him. That's the best course. And don't let him know who's done it."

Idrys accepted that thrown stone without a ripple. "Will Your Majesty still wish, then, to see His Holiness today? Or Sulriggan?"

"No. I don't need indigestion. But I'll do something, perhaps, to uphold His Holiness."

"A wedding largesse . . . that might serve."

"And on the *day* of the wedding, for the hour after. Make preparations, noisy preparations, all for the Wintertide, and a wedding feast in the square. Gods give us good weather. That will sweeten the mood in the town. Hard to make converts against a feast and free ale. Particularly if that zealot priest is too scared to show his face."

"Dancing in the square, all the merry townsfolk." No more unlikely proponent of festivities ever arranged a ball. "I'll have the Guard drawn up, martial display. They *will* be there, and the weapons will not be the parade issue. A royal decree to make merry and a proclamation from His Holiness to sanctify the wedding. Then a royal gift."

"A penny a head. No, two. Make them say, Gods bless His Holiness, and give them the pennies, as from him. Gods! To think I should be doing this to bolster the old fox."

"And your former—"

"Never say it! And for the gods' sake don't make any noise about this Udryn."

"For the gods' sake?" Idrys asked with irony. "Perhaps. Certainly for the kingdom's sake. And a greater reward you could never give His Holiness."

CHAPTER 3

The doors in Henas'amef were hung with winter garlands and the shrines in the Zeide's East Court were festooned with evergreen and berries, with every manner of garland and banner, in anticipation of Midwinter Day and the turn of the world toward spring.

For the duke of Amefel the tailor brought forth splendid clothing, red, with black eagles on the sleeves; and a warm cloak with the arms of Amefel worked on it. It was wonderful new wool, kind as an embrace in the winter wind. Tassand and the tailor had insisted, for their own pride, to see he did not go to a new year in old clothes. There was magic implicit in that choice, and he agreed with it in all its meaning.

Still the weather held fair. It was cold enough to sting faces, but not a bitter cold.

Ale flowed with particular good cheer all over town, so the staff reported, and the two youngest of Tristen's servants came back from town late, and in disgrace. The taverns were hung with lights and kept their doors open all night.

Pack-ponies went out the gates of Henas'amef heavy-laden with supplies for Anwyll, who was doomed to the watch by the river for the festive season: it was on Tristen's order they sent him a special load of ale.

Another train of mules kept continual rounds between Henas'amef and the river and between Henas'amef and the winter camp at Althalen, where more and more of Auld Syes' sparrows came. The mules brought special supplies, sweets, for the Elwynim, the same as the Amefin, hallowed Midwinter Day.

But beneath the cheer of the festal season, and despite the new clothes and the well-wishes, Tristen worried, for there was no sign yet of grain or boats. Especially in the evenings he watched the main gate from the windows where his pigeons gathered. Noting this congress of pigeons, some of the house servants said the birds were his spies, but this was never so, and his birds brought him nothing but comfort—never a hint of the passage of boats or of any other sort of transport that might bring him guests or grain.

What would be the outcome if he had made all this preparation and only Cevulirn returned?

So he wished, and he wished for days, all but in despair, and Uwen's best wishes could lend him no assurance.

But one morning that he waked after a deep, peaceful sleep, he faced the windows early and with a joyous, inexplicable confidence.

He said no more to Uwen than that he had a hope this morning; and Uwen cast an eye to the banners cracking and straining at their poles, and said with that good south wind he had the same.

For the next three days after the wind blew from the south, so strong and so constant it might even melt the snow across the river . . . so Tristen began to fear, and he sent word to Anwyll not to let down his watchfulness a moment during the holiday.

But on that wind, he believed the boats were coming. Olmern was on the wing. His pigeons flew out to the north on the third day, and returned at evening, noisy on the ledge, all accounted for, but not so hungry as he would expect.

Paisi came in the same hour, announcing that master Emuin would attend in hall the Midwinter celebrations, and begged Tassand's assistance to make his robes presentable.

There were travelers on the road as well as on the water. Tristen became convinced of it . . . distracted while Tassand complained that whatever master Emuin had spilled on his gray robe would not come out, and he must call on the tailor, who was busy with other holiday requests, and at his wits' end, and might he afford the tailor an extra coin for the effort?

Cook had more preparations now than a general contemplating battle, for an arrival Tristen assured her was coming precisely on the day.

There were the tables in the stable-court, well to the side of the stables, where staff and servants would hold their feast, in a tent set up for the purpose, with torches set up to light the premises. There was the table in the South Court that would be spread for the notables of the town, aside from those high lords and guests the great hall would accommodate.

The hams, the preserved meats, all these things laid by since fall, came out to be decorated; so did the stored apples and nuts and spices. There were partridge pies. The whole west wing smelled of baking apples and spice cakes.

Tristen bade Tassand advise the lords to expect a Midwinter Eve banquet as well as on Midwinter Day, for as he had dreamed of white-sailed boats coming to Anwyll's camp, now he dreamed of Modeyneth and Trys Ceyl, and of camps more distant, all with weather blessed with the south wind and not a hint of snow or hindrance. Emuin had foretold Midwinter Eve as full of chance, fearsome and dark, but now the prospect was of wishes fulfilled.

On the afternoon of Midwinter Eve, indeed, while the sun was still high, the bell at the town's South Gate announced arrivals—and shortly thereafter the courtyard erupted in brawling confusion, horsemen and banners of not one but *two* lords, Umanon and Sovrag, who had arrived both from the riverside and down that short northern road from the guard stations.

Their arrival was the fulfillment of a promise. Their arrival together was a marvel, and the fact that they had traveled together was a miracle. Neither lord had liked the other. Yet here they were, and Tristen stood amid the din of yapping dogs and shouting stablehands to welcome them in great relief.

There were never in Ylesuin two more opposite men . . . even a wizard's Shaping knew how very little likely they were ever to admire one another. Umanon was Guelen, Quinalt, proper and lordly, fastidious with his person, and Sovrag of Olmern was a stout old river pirate lightly glossed with nobility—king Ináreddrin having found it easier to ennoble him than to ferret him out of his river-cliff stronghold.

Umanon, having just precedence over Sovrag in any courtly encounter, hung back frowning and amazed at Sovrag swaggering ahead to meet his host with open arms and a broad grin on his red-bearded face.

"Well, well-done, lad," Sovrag declared, clapping Tristen fiercely about the shoulders. "Lord of Amefel! Gods damn, I said to myself when I had the horselord's letter that the Marhanen had a rare good sense, damn but he does!" Sovrag stood back then, ceasing his friendly battering in favor of a broad, estimating view of him. "And a far better neighbor ye'll be to us all than lord thievin' Heryn Aswydd or his sisters ever could be, an' by this beginnin', a good customer, too. I asked His Grace here"—this with a nod back to Umanon—"I said as he was supplyin' the grain, he might as well come on the river and have a look at the far shore hisself. As I might say, your grain is all safe at the landin' with that Guelen captain, who I trust'll get it moved to some right place, wherever ye wish it."

"He'll manage," Tristen said, having all confidence in Anwyll's resourcefulness.

In truth, he had expected to feel great pleasure at the sight of familiar faces, but Sovrag's assault was not within his plans, and his heart widened dangerously in the honest joy of that friendly embrace.

Yet he feared the disaffection of the silent man in the meeting. If Sovrag had never been his enemy and had never dealt coldly with him, he could not say the same for Umanon, who, being Quinalt, was least likely of all the lords to approve of a wizard's Shaping. He had somewhat doubted Umanon would come. He had thought Sovrag might go to the south for grain rather than to Imor's ample warehouses, for one thing because Umanon supplied Cefwyn, and might not have grain to spare from that army's needs—and for the other, because Umanon would never trust Sovrag.

Yet Umanon had come with the grain. And on boats, not the heavy horses that were the pride of Imor. Umanon had, therefore, a share of Lord Heryn's gold dinnerplates . . . he did hope it was a fair one.

With all that in mind he resolutely braved Umanon's icy calm and dared a warm welcome and a reach toward Umanon's hand. "Thank you for coming, sir. Thank you ever so much."

"Lord of Amefel," Umanon said, distant as ever, but pleasant, amazingly so. In fact Umanon had a far different expression toward him than he had ever had, not so much that the face changed, but that the eyes lacked hostility and the hand that met his had no coldness at all.

"Welcome. Very welcome, sir." He found he had no idea quite what to do with Umanon, or how to keep him in this good pleasure, but he had learned at Lewenbrook that this was a brave, hard-fighting lord, if a prickly and difficult one; and well-begun with him secured all the rest.

"A bold choice on His Majesty's part, your appointment," Umanon said. "I take it there are northern noses sorely out of joint."

"Very much so, I fear."

"And this moving of grain? What's the purpose here? To finish the business we left unfinished this summer?"

"Aye," said Sovrag, having followed on Tristen's heels. "Cevulirn's man had no great store of news, and your man out riverside's no better. But partridge pies was a lure good as gold, well, close on it, and here we are. There'd better be those pies. I promised me lads there'll be pies."

"There will be," Tristen said. "Cook says so. Master Haman! Take the horses!" The horses on which Sovrag and Umanon had ridden in had Imorim and Olmern emblems on their tack, no mark of Anwyll's company. And how they had gotten them upriver on boats he could not imagine. More, they were handsome, well-groomed animals, having no signs of a hard passage. He was quite amazed, and thought of large barges, as if the thought had Unfolded to him, Boats such as he had never quite imagined.

"And our answer?" Umanon asked. "Is it to Ilefínian, then?"

"Sir, before we say much, I think we should have all of us at once. But you do know Ilefínian's fallen."

"That news indeed traveled," said Umanon, and Sovrag:

"I said we'd pay for not goin' on across last summer, didn't I say it?"

"Many of us said it," said Umanon, and then, dryly: "Our grain is in this Olmernman's boats, *to* which I have tally sheets, fair written, and signed to, and in my possession."

As if the grain coming from Umanon might somehow become confused with the tally coming from Olmern's warehouses. Tristen would not have understood that possibility so long ago, but he knew it now, having dealt with Parsynan's accounts, and saw Sovrag's wicked grin.

"Enough grain for an army," Sovrag said, "twixt his warehouses an' mine."

"I've men on the way," Umanon said, "heavy horse. I took Cevulirn at his word; my escort is large."

"An' my boats," Sovrag said, "an' my men with all their war gear. Are we goin' deep into Elwynor? Is that the game? Or do we sail to the northern bridges?"

Cefwyn had found it hard to contain Sovrag's disposition to bluntness. Tristen foresaw no less difficulty. But there was no one in hearing who was not aware of this gathering of forces, even down to the stableboys busy gathering up the horses, and that Cefwyn was preparing in the north.

"The question is what Tasmôrden may do when he learns boats have come," Tristen said, "and since you've come, and we have supplies, his choices are more limited."

"I asked had you indeed taken counsel of His Majesty in our gathering," said Umanon, equally blunt, and straight back to Sovrag's question about the north. "Ivanor's messenger professed not to know that answer."

"I've not yet advised the north," Tristen said with utter candor, "and I was never sure till now whether I could gather everyone. He's given me leave to build, and to fortify, and that I've done, so Tasmôrden won't cross the river southward. But here and now, sir, *nothing* against the king's welfare, sir, ever. The northern barons have objected to my being here, they've raised accusations against Her Grace, and the last man I sent to Guelessar with a message went in fear of his life, going there and bringing back Cefwyn's message. Idrys watched over him, and even that wasn't enough. It's not safe to send. I'm not sure *Cefwyn* is safe."

That brought a worried frown to both lords.

"At dinner tonight, when the others come, then I'll tell you what I know besides," Tristen said. "I've asked you here for your advice, among other things."

"By way of advice," said Umanon, "wise to move sooner rather than later, considering the temptation of all that grain, not to mention the boats."

"Which I'll wager already ain't stayed at Anwyll's crossin', beyond the night," Sovrag said. "Is that right, Sihhë-lord?"

"He's to move it behind the Modeyneth wall. Modeyneth's to send men, to carry it on their backs if nothing else."

"Drays are coming with our heavy gear," Umanon said.

"And the boats is off south," Sovrag said, "quick as they set their cargoes ashore, and back after more grain, supposin' Marna stays passable. Hooo, such a place as that woods has become."

"Is it different?" Tristen asked.

"Unsavory," was Umanon's succinct answer. "A place I was glad to go through by day. All that passage, there was no breath of wind on the river, yet we saw the treetops bend. We heard voices in the woods, the sounds of a battle, but no sight of anyone."

"Them old trees," said Sovrag, "is sadder an' lone-lier than they ever looked in Mauryl's day. Haunted, if ever a place was."

"Even before Lewenbrook," Tristen said, "it was haunted."

He had not ventured into that part of his lands, not in the gray space and not in the world. He was sad to know that it had gone darker than his fond memories of it under Mauryl's rule . . . it had frightened him, then, too, but that had been a moderate fear, a friendly haunt to him, much as Sovrag had treated it with casual famil-iarity in all his trade with Mauryl and never professed to fear it.

But now Sovrag gave a different report—and still came. He valued Sovrag of Olmern, for the courage he had, and found new respect for Lord Umanon, who had dared it in coming with him.

"I wish them safe passage," he said. "And I've lodg-ings ready for you, west or east or south, whatever your preference of windows, since you're the first here. The west, above the kitchens, is warmest."

"The south, for the clean good wind," Sovrag said, and Umanon: "The east, for the morning sun."

He had looked to dispose these two men at opposite ends of the fortress, but if they had shared the boats and the river, there was surely no fear of quarrels breaking out among their bodyguards. They went up the stairs and down the inner hall together, asking news of Cefwyn's court, and asking what he knew, and most of all what things were coming to when the Lord Commander himself had to protect a messenger.

The halls echoed back things that had been secrets and servants paused, respectful of lordly visitors, wide-eyed at what they heard: Tristen did not miss the fact. But Sovrag had come: there would be few more secrets

in Henas'amef with him here, and certainly there was
no more secrecy for what would gather in the fields
and pastures beyond the walls.

An army was on the move, and Tasmôrden, if he
reached out to have the grain, would find that out to
his peril; but learn it soon?

Beyond a doubt he would.

It was not the last arrival of the day: for before
Sovrag's and Umanon's horses were sorted out in the
stable, the bell rang again at the town gate, reporting
more travelers in the distance, this time on the western
approach.

The banner they flew, a rider informed them, was
the Heron banner of Pelumer of Lanfarnesse; but it
was no great number of men.

They had provided for five hundred men, as Cevulirn
had said he would ask of each lord. But Pelumer at last
came riding in under the West Gate of the Zeide, lord
and men alike in modest gray and green, he came with
only his banner-bearer and eight of his house guard.

They were likely rangers, these men, riding horses,
as they did not when they fought . . . Pelumer's was a
foot contingent, far more comfortable in deep forest,
even daring Marna's edge . . . and on that thought,
Tristen did not give up hope of Pelumer.

"Welcome," he said.

"Ah," Pelumer said as he stepped down and cast a
glance to the banners in evidence, two lordly banners
flying in equal honor with the Eagle of Amefel above
the curtain wall. "Olmern and Imor."

"Your own banner to join them, sir, and be welcome, as you were in the summer."

"Good news out of Amefel, after a great deal of bad.
I've watched this business since summer in no good heart.

I was glad to hear the call. I have wagons, with the win-terage of a company of a hundred, and other men dis-posed on various byways among the villages. My rangers know the intrusions to the west, and the gathering at Althalen, not spying, I trust you'll know, but being aware you have forces there, sir, being aware is all."

A hundred men, not five. Lanfarnesse fielded few men, and despite all assurances managed never to fight in the field.

What Lanfarnesse knew *before* any battle, however, might pay for all, and though Pelumer had fallen out of the favor he had once enjoyed with Cefwyn, per-haps, Tristen thought, his heart beating more quickly—perhaps these elusive few men never belonged on a battlefield.

"At Althalen," Tristen said, "Elwynim have settled, and we supply them. But you know that, too."

"Ah," Pelumer said as if he were surprised. He turned evasive the moment anyone asked him his men's doings, and that had repeatedly angered Cefwyn, to the point their alliance was in jeopardy.

But these were not heavily armored men who fought in the Guelen way.

"Settle your men where you will, sir. At Althalen or here, or any lands between."

That did catch a glance, a second, even alarmed assessment.

"Where you will," Tristen repeated. "For their best service to us."

"I take you at your word," Pelumer said, and earnestly so. In his youth Pelumer had been first to the taking of Althalen, Tristen recalled, and forever after had the right of precedence over all the lords of Ylesuin, north or south. *Selwyn* Marhanen had valued him . . . but Ináreddrin and Cefwyn, steeped in the Guelen way of war, had ordered him.

"I need you," Tristen said from the depths of his heart. "*Welcome*, Lord Pelumer."

"Amefel," Pelumer said with uncommon warmth, and clasped his hand in both of his. "Well, well, we're here with our finery, for a feast. Where shall we lodge?"

"Olmern is south and Imor is east. The west is free, and warmest. Come, if you will. I'll bring you there."

Pelumer had wounded him once, when he had over-heard how Pelumer spoke of him, and then was friendly to his face. But Pelumer went in gray and green through a forest; he had no less skill to put on the right face with every man: so Tristen saw, and for-gave him his past offense. Pelumer learned most from men who thought Pelumer was of their opinion, and what Pelumer *did* then was the important thing.

There were only the horses, and them, Haman's lads attended; Pelumer himself took up the light saddle kit he brought, and ordered his banner set beside the others on the wall.

"Olmern reported the forest darker and sadder than ever," Tristen said, as they went up the steps together, his guard and Pelumer's easy in company and admitted to confidences. "Did you see it so?"

"Remarkable if not," Pelumer said. "It's very law-abiding, Marna's verge, at least in Crown law. The ban-dits all are dead. We've found them by ones and twos, fallen in hazards sane men would avoid. A rash of bad luck, or the like. I'll not risk my men in the heart of it. I trust it does very well by itself."

"Do you think it does well?"

"You would know that sooner than I, if it were otherwise, would you not, sir?"

"I think I would."

"Ghosts aplenty walk that woods. The old trees have their roots amongst far too many bones."

A gloomy sort of converse it was, but it lent a vision of the Pelumer who had served the first Marhanen . . . wary now, having saved his life when many another had died, and having lived long enough to be a repository of old lore, interesting tidbits—and warnings.

"We should have crossed this summer," Pelumer said. "So I told the king."

It wanted only Cevulirn. And the day went on toward dark, cloudless and still.

The lords had rested since their arrival. Now they began to ready themselves for the festivities of this day of welcoming, and servants ran to and fro with buckets of hot water for baths, buckets and towels, turning the stairs treacherous. Others mopped, lest someone slip, while still other servants laid fresh fragrant evergreen along the tables in the great hall.

The musicians warmed their instruments by the fire, sending up a disordered, somehow soothing sound. One tuned a drum.

Tristen walked the circuit of the great hall with Uwen at his heels, assuring himself that everything was in order to accommodate the guests that he did have, and trying not to worry for the one yet to come. Certainly he had no need to remind Emuin of the doings in hall. Tassand had taken Emuin his festive robe, and Paisi was in and out and among the preparations downstairs in a beatific anticipation of cakes.

Tristen himself stole a morsel from a platter, and Uwen had one, too.

"Not to spoil supper," Uwen said with a wink, "only to stave off the pangs, and make sure the ale don't land in an empty spot. All's ready. Be easy, m'lord."

The timely arrivals were, as he had heard from Lord Umanon by way of Tassand, no accident: Cevulirn had prudently appointed the day before Midwinter Eve as the day by which they all should arrive . . . and on Cevulirn's word these lords had set forces on the road and traveled ahead, themselves, trusting that there would be a camp, there would be stabling, there would be food and firewood and all such things as they needed without their transporting it over winter roads.

All these men had trusted him, and committed men to be encamped here in the uncertain weather. More, the men with them were separated from their homes during the festive season, either here with their lords or still out on the roads, and by Uwen's attentive management the earliest come had their feast: the garrison set up a tent for the lords' men the same as the festive tents for the town, and under it the garrison's cooks prepared to serve kettles of uncommonly thick stew and baskets of bread, and kegs of ale bought from every tavern.

That was to last all through the holiday, and to repeat for every contingent to arrive. It set the men in good cheer.

And just as the sun was at its last, the gate bell rang, heralding their last, most welcome visitors.

"The White Horse!" one of Haman's lads ran in to say, wide-eyed. "The Lord of Ivanor, and all his men!"

It was not all the men of Ivanor, but certainly a goodly number, bringing their tents on packhorses. They set to work making camp on last summer's site even as their lord, in a fine gray cloak, and dressed fit for a lord's hall, rode up through the town.

Cevulirn had not failed the day, after all, but had come exactly at the last of the daylight. In the dusk one of Haman's lads set the White Horse of Ivanor in its place on the wall, and in the firelight from below the creatures of the banners tricked the eye, as if they were bespelled to life.

Crissand arrived, and Drumman and Azant, all the lords who had come to the shrines and the tombs of the East Court, and now trooped in, all in modest finery—no extravagance in these days—and met the lords of the south with open arms and honest delight.

It was the best, the most wonderful sight. Tristen came to Crissand in particular, for Crissand had ridden out to his villages and made it back again, hard riding, for this night before Midwinter Eve.

"You came," Tristen said, and Crissand:

"I'd have ridden through drifts, my lord: as it was, I followed tracks on a fair road and fell in with Ivanor."

The old keep rang with voices. Outside, the several courtyards were all packed with guests and their entourages going here, going there, with horses being brought uphill and down and food being sent out.

It felt as lively as it had felt in the summer . . . but then had been days of dust and sweat. Now the nip of winter was still potent enough at night to sting cheeks of arriving guests to ruddy color.

And the smell of spices, rich meats and bread baking wafted through the gathering, while the pungent scent of juniper fought that of horses and leather and wool . . . all these things were in the air when Cevulirn, arriving last in the hall, accepted the embrace of brother lords, both Amefin and otherwise.

"We are all here," Tristen said, and felt something settling, solid as stone and almost as old, into place. He had his hands one on Cevulirn's shoulder and one on Crissand's, as he turned and faced his guests.

The gray space flared before him, a bright flash of light. *We are all here,* rang through the wizardous air and touched Emuin in his tower, and rang all the way to Assurnbrook.

CHAPTER 4

The morning of Midwinter Eve dawned pearl and pink, fit for a wedding . . . and that well-omened weather together with the event was a relief so great Cefwyn had difficulty to keep a silly cheerfulness from his face, even with the necessity of wearing the Crown and the royal regalia.

They were marrying off Luriel of Murandys. He wished to smile at everyone.

Most of all he smiled at his royal wife, likewise bedight in her regal finery, with the circlet crown of the Regent of Elwynor on her brow . . . for they had reached this day without a rift between them and in good sorts. And by his order, Ninévrisë, whose small court all attended the bride this morning, went attended not by ladies, but by the martial display of Dragon Guard, the whole power of the Crown, and a very clear statement for all witnesses both that the king held her very dear . . . and that she did not attend Luriel this morning.

It was for the lesser lights, the maids and matrons of the court, to be sure all the requisite things, the book of devotions, the sprig of broom, the small packet of salt, and the pinch of grain, found their way into the bride's possession, disposed about her person in various traditions old as time.

"I've made her gown," Ninévrisë had said with

acerbity, in deciding not to attend the bride's robing. "Her kin may see her into it."

Peace had prevailed just down to the night before, so Cefwyn had heard, when Luriel had gone into a fit of temper about her shoes, which had turned out too small, despite careful measuring. Luriel's feet hurt, and now the unfortunate shoemaker went in fear for his life and trade.

"She ate this sweet and that," Ninévrisë said, "and she would have the shoes the finest, the daintiest when she had the measure taken, oh, no, no grace given, all advice disregarded. We heard a thousand times how all her house has dainty hands, dainty feet. Now the shoes pinch. Pray, shall I pity her, or the shoemaker?"

"Mark that man, and I'll order a pair of boots," Cefwyn vowed. Ninévrisë had extended the utmost of tolerance and kindness to Luriel of Murandys, and now when she should be most grateful, the bride had thrown a tantrum about the shoes and flung scissors and a sewing basket in Ninévrisë's presence.

"Plague take Luriel," he thought, and said. But he wished honest good fortune to the bridegroom, young Rusyn, and had sent him a prayer book, a kingly gift, and traditional for a young Quinalt groom. His friends, besides, would present him a silver dagger, and a sprig of rue, the groom's other gifts. Young Panys would bathe in water brought in from Panys, without benefit of warming, and commit the first shavings of his beard, saved for this purpose, to a holy fire.

All these customs the groom bore with, and the pranks besides, which Rusyn was likely not spared: the king of Ylesuin at his wedding had had only a boot stuffed with stockings when he tried to put it on, Annas' doing, he was sure . . . but to his disappointment no one else had ventured a wedding joke, not even his brother.

Now . . .

Only have us through the day, Cefwyn prayed as they went down the stairs from the royal apartments toward the lower hall. Holiday evergreen entwined the balustrades.

Midwinter Eve for a wedding night and Midwinter Day for a first morning, the night of changes and the morning of a new year . . . omens of ending one thing and beginning another made it not an unpopular day for weddings, and sure, there were two more to follow today in the Quinaltine, notable sons and daughters within the town and the outlying villages, which the Holy Father would also perform.

Cefwyn kept Ninévrisë's hand in his as they descended into the gathering wedding party at the foot of the stairs—he smiled on the well-wishers, on Lord Maudyn, the father of the groom, and even on Prichwarrin Lord Murandys, who was trying to seem both cheerful and calm: the smile seemed entirely to unnerve him, and that was pleasant.

There was an exchange, stiffly formal, of courtesies and well-wishes, a small cup of fine wine all around, drunk standing, the cups a gift and a tradition of the midlands, Panys' lands.

Then the entire party went down the outside steps and gathered up Efanor and his guards. The Lord Commander joined them, wearing his ordinary black, even for weddings.

Outside, where the processional formed, all the lords in the Guelesfort had turned out in their winter finery, ladies in wide skirts and no few of the simpler variety, in Ninévrisë's fashion. Maidens bore juniper boughs and gave playful lashes to young gentlemen in their path, where amorous young gentlemen deliberately contrived to be: there was marriage-luck in the exchange.

Trumpets sounded thinly and a little sharp in the cold air, but the pearl and pink of the sky had given way to a bright, fair, glorious blue, and outside the iron gates of the Guelesfort and all along the way, puddles reflected that sky on scrubbed limestone pavings—at least in the aisle the guards kept safe, for the whole town had come for the festivities, the food, and the sights. Tradesmen and sweeps alike rubbed elbows—maids crowded close, to have a glimpse of the passing show. Custom had it that seeing a bride and groom was lucky . . . and this one, so far-famed a scandal of royalty and nobility, brought onlookers to a frenzy of excitement, waving kerchiefs through the grillwork and shouting out wishes of a sort to make a bride blush.

Those cheers rang off the high walls of the Quinaltine across the way, more fervent wishes than when their king had married a foreign bride: Cefwyn prayed Ninévrisë failed to make that comparison.

The quantity of ale flowing by now had something to do with it, surely—not an extravagance, yet, for they wanted no drunken truth affronting the peace. The penny largesse had found wild favor, so Annas had said, and the crowd now was in a giving mood. Cups spilling ale froth lifted high among the crowd as the royal banners swept by—the king and his consort must by law walk before all others. Then Efanor must follow; and only after the royal family came the bride and groom, who were honored for their day above all the lords of Ylesuin.

So they walked amid cheers and the press of the crowd, on the short processional course that wound along the wall of the Quinaltine and around to the right, to the center of its now pigeonless steps.

Hands reached continually past the guards. Cefwyn reached out his own right hand, and Ninévrisë her left, brushing unwashed fingertips, and this brought a great surge forward, of sick folk seeking cures, of common folk seeking luck for their ventures. So they would wish to be touched by the bride and groom, as well, for good fortune and a cure for childlessness on this auspicious day.

The Quinalt doors, too, were decked out with evergreen and berries, and as they walked up into the great shrine the place was alight with hundreds of white candles and echoing with high, pure voices. The panoply of Murandys and that of Panys were both in evidence all about, the colors of both noble houses draping the altar and the rails, and wound about the columns to which the banner-bearers customarily retreated.

Cefwyn reached his place in the first row of seats with Ninévrisë and Efanor. The trumpets continued to peal as lord after lord behind them found their way into the shrine, each one with a flourish of trumpets.

Idrys joined them, privilege of the Lord Commander to slip into the first row from the side, and without ceremony: he was within the royal party. Then came the groom's relatives, with Lord Maudyn of Panys, and the sole representatives from Murandys, Lord Prichwarrin, with young Lady Odrinian.

Above all the pageantry was the patched hole where rain no longer found an entry . . . not an elegant patch, but sufficient to winter weather: after the workers had risked life and limb, the Quinalt was dry and free of drafts, and the weather fair, even warmish for the season, making the air close, candle-scented, perfumed with warring perfumes, and the smell of incense which never quite left the place.

Cefwyn braced his knees back against the seat and stood, and stood, through all the filing-in. It was the tiresome protocol which dictated that, contrary to the custom of the court, in the Quinalt the king, who could not kneel, stood or sat, and since the nobles were still filing in and the king's back was to the company, it was therefore the duty of royalty and the high nobles to stand . . . and stand, under the heavy royal regalia. Cefwyn's eyes wandered, while he kept his face straight ahead. As the benches filled, the air grew warmer and the echoes changed from the hollow quaver of an empty vault to the soft muted stir of many bodies. One learned to judge, even counting the flourishes or watching the signal of the preceptor, that the benches were approaching full.

It was enough waiting. Cefwyn made his decision, and sat, and Ninévrisë sat, and Idrys and Efanor sat, and then the court, with a general rustling and sighing.

Cefwyn looked beside him, found that wonderful small smile and that dimple at the edge of Ninévrisë's mouth that told him she was in exceedingly fine humor even yet, anxious to be through this. Beyond her, Efanor was resolute and brooding in profile, beyond Idrys' dark-mustached visage . . . Efanor was thinking, perhaps, on Ryssand's daughter and his own prospective marriage: that was reason enough for a grim, worried countenance.

He had not told Efanor yet about Cuthan, but he had moved to make a breach with Ryssand devastating, and his displeasure clear. Once Luriel was a happy bride, with a firm footing in the friendly house of Panys, let master crow fly, not of passion, but of clearheaded policy: the infamous Marhanen temper would do very foolish things in that regard; but because there was Ninévrisë, he thought twice about everything.

Because there was Ninévrisë he did so many things more wisely this year than last . . . and he was not fearful of Ryssand's doctrinist priests: he had walked the processional with his hands touching the people's hands, unshielded, and unwilling to give up any of the tradition that brought him out among his own.

There was one less priest haranguing at tavern corners this morning. Likely no one even noticed the lack. The absence of a thing was harder to notice than its presence, and Idrys had created no stir at all. Well-done, he thought, deft and silent, and no deaths, no accusatory bodies.

Now trumpets hailed the processional of the groom. Young Rusyn marched up the aisle. Junior priests lit candles and swung censers, sending up blue-gray clouds of incense around the golden glow of the lamps. Rusyn arrived in the tail of Cefwyn's eye, resplendent in Panys' colors, and Lord Maudyn, back from the riverside where he had done faithful duty, was clearly aglow with pride.

The gathering applauded the groom as he took his place at the altar. A second sounding of trumpets, and now highborn young maidens came with lamps, so Cefwyn imagined without turning his head. The choir sang at their utmost range as Luriel of Murandys walked down the aisle.

But within the crowd a stunned silence fell, and almost Cefwyn did turn his head, asking himself what distressful thing might be going on.

Luriel arrived in the edge of his sight, and then he saw what everyone had seen, the ironic and unintended similarity in the two notable brides of the season. The heraldry of Ninévrisë's house and that of Murandys were alike blue and white, and that was the inevitable similarity: no, it was the slim gown, the lack of the cursed petticoats—so that, for a moment Cefwyn saw two Ninévrisës.

He held a firm, angry grip on the rail in front, and thanked the gods when Luriel and Rusyn joined hands, with no ill omens, no hindrance. The trumpets sounded, the priests swung censers. The rising white smoke all but obscured the altar, which was the magical moment the Holy Father would appear through the smoke, a moment of high mystery and candlelit miracle.

But the Holy Father did not come through the smoke. The moment's expectant silence began to fade in a crepitation of small movements, shifting of feet, then small laughter and whispers.

The trumpets sounded again. The censers swung furiously, maintaining the smoke.

There was still no Holy Father, and now the pause after the fanfare filled immediately with a murmur of consternation, and the bride and groom faltered, likewise uncertain.

Some laughed, but Cefwyn looked at Idrys, in the center of the row, and necessarily at Lord Panys and Lord Murandys and Efanor, all of whom had worried frowns. Idrys quickly signed to someone off among the columns, then turned to Cefwyn and excused his armored way past Ninévrisë in the narrow space between the benches and the rail, to reach him.

On the dais a figure hurried through the smoke, and Cefwyn turned his head as all the congregation gave a relieved laugh, thinking the Holy Father was late. But it was only a hurrying priest, who spied authority past the railing and came desperately off the platform toward the royal bench.

"The Holy Father," the priest gasped out, "the Holy Father . . ."

A tumult had begun, some talking aloud, some trying to hush the hindmost. The bride and groom stood staring as, from confidence and security, now bodyguards began to move quickly to their lords, crowding in from the sides.

". . . dead," the priest said. "With evil things, *evil* things around him! And the blood . . . oh, the blood—"

"Stand in your places!" Lord Maudyn shouted out, that voice accustomed to ordering soldiers in battle. "Everyone stand in his place! Let no one move! The choir may sing! *Sing!*"

Even a king might find himself jumping at that voice; and a heartbeat more Cefwyn hesitated as the priest took off into the smoke, and priests and lay brothers ran after him. Ninévrisë was by him, in whatever danger existed in the place, and where assassination had at the highest of all priests it would surely not scruple to strike down a foreign consort at the center of the storm.

Cefwyn had no true weapon but his dagger, the ceremonial sword more show than blade. Efanor was at Ninévrisë's other side, armed with somewhat better, at least; and Idrys shouted out orders to the Dragons, who had been halfway to their king when Maudyn's order had halted them in confusion.

"*Guardsmen!* Here! Now!"

"This way!" Cefwyn shouted, seeing the rush of priests and acolytes around them, men he did not trust rushing this way and that and row after row of guests behind the nobles, and the doors open to the outside.

Immediately the Dragons came around them, curtaining them from the crowd and whatever danger might come from the outside. Cefwyn drew Ninévrisë by the hand, leaving the benches, passing the rail beyond the altar with Ninévrisë close before a second, desperate thought informed him no women went past that holy boundary.

But neither should murder pass it, and behind that rail, Cefwyn well knew, was no mystery of the faith, rather a maze of robing rooms and closets and storages, apt concealment for one assassin, but not for what he more feared, a movement of the crowd itself—passions were dry tinder in the town, and in narrow halls he had the advantage, places one could hold, places Dragon Guard shields could make a wall, and did, as Idrys shouted the order, "Stand fast! Let no one through!"

That sealed off the tumult from the great shrine, and left them that of priests within, wailing and crying, themselves smeared with blood. They were near that small room, Cefwyn knew from his own investiture, where the Holy Father robed.

Idrys and Efanor stayed with them, Idrys with sword bared, Efanor cautiously keeping his hand at his belt. Priests were taking no account they jostled the royal party as they advanced or retreated, one after another straining to see, then turning away in horror at the first glance inside.

Cefwyn was driven, the same, and elbowed his way past weeping, praying priests, still with Ninévrisë's hand safely in his, and armored men pushing others aside.

His Holiness lay sprawled in his vestments, and if any blood was left in him, between the walls and his vestments, it was a wonder. Feathered cords were bound about the chair, run to the candle-sconce, back again to the chair as if some spider had done it, and the Sihhë star was painted in blood on the far wall.

"This is sorcery!" a priest breathed.

"This is *murder*," Idrys said sharply. "Stay to your praying, priest, and leave judgment of cowardly, murdering *men* to your king and the rightful authorities! Do spirits wear boots?"

Indeed, and Cefwyn saw it: there were footprints in the blood, leading out under their very feet.

"What are those cords?" a monk asked in all innocence.

Cefwyn had no need to wonder. He had seen the like holding charms in the market of Henas'amef, and dangling among the skirts of an Amefin witch, ghost, Shadow, whatever she was.

The star was for the less informed, who would not take the subtler clues the assassin had spread about like largesse.

"Dismiss the wedding party," Cefwyn said, cudgeling his shaken wits into order. "See where the tracks lead before they're trampled over! Efanor! Is Jormys here?"

"Yes," Efanor said. "He's here!"

"I appoint him to the Quinaltine for the interim and give him the Patriarch's authority, temporal and spiritual, in the gods' name!" He ran out of breath in the utterance of what was, always before, formula, and now was a weapon in his hands, the king's power to appoint and dispose. "Advise him so! Set the robes on him! Meanwhile His Holiness is dead—show some reverence and cover him!"

"Gods save us, gods save us," more than one priest kept saying, and another wailed, "It's the gods' judgment!"

"Gods' wrath on fools!" Cefwyn became aware he had clenched Ninévrisë's hand far too hard. "This is an assassin's doing! And damned unlikely any of this gaudy display is real! There's no sorcery here, it's a planned assassination, and who'd hate His Holiness but those blackguard seditionists who prate their righteousness in the street! That's the source of this!" With relief he saw Efanor appear again with his priest, Father Jormys, and seized on him, gentle, sensible Jormys signing himself in fear and distress at the horror in the room.

"Father," Cefwyn said sharply, "take charge! I set you over the Quinaltine, as of this moment."

"My lord king, I protest I am not worthy, or scholarly—"

"The king's choice!" he shouted, his voice what he used on the field. "Our choice! Only the king is anointed to make that choice, and we make it, *we* propose and dispose with the anointment of the gods on our head, and I set my seal on you as His Holiness held the office from my grandfather's hand." *Damn you* was not auspicious, and he restrained the breath on which it rode. *"Take charge, I say!"*

Outcries from the sanctuary drowned the murmur from the inner halls. Wood splintered, light wood. Priceless carved screens stood behind the rail and the altar, and it was an ominous sound.

"Get back!" a soldierly voice shouted, and then Idrys:

"Push them out!"

The Guard moved, and shrieks attended, dim, in the distance of the maze as the Guard pressed intruders back and back.

"Out of here, Your Majesty!" Idrys shouted. "Take the West Door!"

"The East!" Cefwyn contradicted his Lord Commander, fully conscious Ninévrisë was in danger in any rising, and would not leave him, not the woman who had defended her father against rebels in the hills. He felt the firm grip of her hand and took his dagger from its sheath, pressing it on her with no difficulty at all, and not a word.

Idrys had taken the order, and cleared the halls before them, all the way out into the sanctuary, where the groom's father, Lord Maudyn, had marshaled a defense that kept the guests to one side and the sanctuary, give or take a few men lying in the aisle, secured.

"Maudyn!" Cefwyn shouted out. "Dismiss the gathering out the main doors! Proceed in the ordinary order! Sound the trumpets!"

"Your Majesty will not go out there!"

"Sound the trumpets, I say!" The populace was apt to wild rumors enough. The trumpets would carry, gain attention, inform them their lords were taking action and authority still stood. A tide of the common and curious pressed at the doors, against the house guards of half a dozen lords of the realm, wild with speculation and fear, and no slinking of the king to his gates could deal with it. "By precedences, behind me! Take your places!"

But in that same moment the priests, at Jormys' ill-timed direction, bore the Patriarch's bloody body out of the sanctum and into the fore of the sanctuary, a sight that brought shrieks from no few even of the nobles, and from wild-eyed lesser priests, who shouted entreaties to the gods. Benches overturned as a score of hands handled the bloody corpse over the rail to the altar itself . . . where they disposed it atop the wedding colors on the altar, staining them with blood.

"When shall I be married?" Luriel cried, from the assembly of nobles, as if it were some personal affront, and burst into tears. Rusyn was with her, and she slapped away his comfort, even struck at her uncle Lord Murandys when he attempted to quiet her outburst.

"Your Majesty, the procession," Idrys said in utter, low-voiced calm. "Now. Your Highness, if you would be so good as to combine your guard with His Majesty's . . ."

"Go," Cefwyn said, and Idrys gave his orders, rapidly and by name, telling off the lords in their order, dispersing other men to archers stationed in secure places Idrys never yet revealed, but his couriers knew.

"Clear the doors!" Cefwyn shouted, and slowly, using pikes gripped along the shafts by several hands, the Guard and bodyguards of various lords opened a gap in the press, and progressively formed a barrier of the sort the crowd was used to at functions, pikes held crosswise, hand to hand.

Cefwyn came out into daylight, affording all the Quinaltine square the sight of a crowned head and the woman beside him. Down the steps he moved, with dispatch, as hundreds pressed against the Guard's efforts to open a corridor.

"Quickly now, Your Majesty." It was Gwywyn, commander of the Prince's Guard, who reached him, a good man, and a brave one, if obstinate, and having six strong men with shields. Gwywyn's sharp voice and the press of shields cleared a wider path along their exposure to the open square.

Then the largest Quinalt bell began to toll: the whole tower rang for weddings, feasts, and calamities, for fire, for proclamations, and for deaths—but there was none of the peal of the lighter bells that should have rung out the wedding party. The sound was only the deep-voiced Passage Bell, which tolled over all the voices, *death and doom, death and doom.* It chilled the tumult to a shocked stillness, and what might happen toward the steps was no longer in Cefwyn's command. He could make no more haste than Gwywyn's men, but the nobles behind him did not press, lords and ladies whose only armor in this passage was their unshakable dignity and the expectation that no hand would touch them, no weapon withstand their rank and their rights.

In the same way Ninévrisë moved beside him, a foreigner in their midst, her noble, unhurried bearing a bulwark to his demand for room. No battlefield had ever seemed wider than that dreadful processional ground, blindly around the corner of the Quinaltine, toward the gates of the Guelesfort, shut and secure, and, he prayed the gods, handled by some officer with more than ordinary sense, for there they could be trapped outside and crushed or those gates could open and stay open a moment too long, provoking the crowd to press in. It was hallowed ground, lordly ground: the commons ordinarily would not press them hard; but there were so many, the strength bearing against the guardsmen that of men being pushed and trampled themselves by those behind. Panic surged along beside them, ran like hounds, pushed with the force of a river in flood.

The gates opened. Cefwyn swept Ninévrisë and his brother to the side where he had immediate access to the men managing the gates, and when he recognized the very last of the procession approaching the gates, with the mob surging behind, he gave the order to shut the doors.

The gates began to swing, admitted the very last with a right to be there, and a scatter of dazed commons pushed in by the press, whom the Guard swiftly swept aside and placed under arrest.

Distraught questions abounded, as noble restraint gave way . . . Who had done it? Was it sorcery? Was it the Elwynim?

"A sword or a dagger," Cefwyn shouted over the din. "Sorcery at Lewen field left no blood! I've seen the one, and this was no sorcery, by the gods, it was not! Look inside the Quinaltine for the assassin!—Boy!" Cefwyn said, spying one of his pages near him in the press. "Fetch down my armor, to this courtyard! Now! Don't gawk! Call any servant who crosses your path, no excuses!— Captain Gwywyn, good men to see Her Grace upstairs to my chambers and stand watch outside!"

Ninévrisë was no fool, to cling to him when the whole of his kingdom shuddered to the brink of riot; he wanted every encumbrance gone and every weapon around him. But she seized his hand for one urgent warning.

"They've killed a priest. What will they stick at now?"

He stopped for the moment, struck with chagrin and guilt at once . . . for *he* had struck at a priest: no one knew but Idrys, and Idrys' men. But she accused him without knowing why the priestly authority was in ruin, and in front of the frightened, pious court, he could say nothing more than, "We'll bring things to order. Father Jormys is in the Quinalt, and whatever else, he's no common priest, and no fool." Please the gods, he thought, that Jormys is not a fool. He seized on Efanor's arm, fiercely. "Direct matters at the gate. Your guard, there. See no one passes. I'm going outside. The town needs to see its king."

"They need him *alive*," Efanor retorted fiercely, informing him this was folly; but it was the only course, folly for him or not, that might stem the riot before it swept into burning and looting and then to guardsmen dead and commons hanging. They were all safe behind an iron grill and an iron gate, but shouts and screams echoing off the walls outside informed him Idrys was in no such safety—and Cefwyn hurried, without running: a king must not run, must never run, never more than stride, he told himself all the way to the steps, where he thanked the gods a handful of guardsmen was marshaling some sort of order, sending the elderly and frail upstairs.

His pages had indeed run and, faster than he dared hope, were coming down the stairs, four of them, utterly white-faced and out of breath, with his field helmet, his sword, and the pieces of his best body armor. "Good lads! Haste!" He stripped off the ceremonial plate and chain where he stood, heedless of hazard, and by now Isin and other lords were likewise cursing confused servants and calling for their own horses and weapons for a sally out into the Quinaltine square in his support.

"Bring Danvy!" Cefwyn shouted at a page, sending

him to the stables, for a horse was a way to be seen above the heads of the crowd, and Danvy had experience in crowds and battle alike. No one expected restraint from a warhorse—and no one pushed Danvy twice.

"My lord king," his bodyguard protested his determination.

"Get your horses or walk!" He headed back down the steps, still buckling straps, surrendered his side to his pages to do the lesser buckles as stableboys began to bring their charges through, to the peril of everything in their path.

"That's tight enough," he said to the trembling page, reassured the boy with a clap on the shoulder, and gratefully took a plain guardsman's shield as the quickest available. Danvy arrived, straining at a stablehand's lead, throwing his head, already hot-blooded from the confusion around him. Cefwyn took the reins himself, set foot in the stirrup, rose up into the saddle.

The Prince's Guard, too, was getting to horse, and he moved through the press of nobles and bodyguards with Isin and Nelefreissan, of all unlikely others—northerners, Ryssand's men with their household guard, all mounted and joining him. It was not the company he would have chosen, but all but a handful of his reliable men were outside holding the square. He trusted his back to them out of necessity and ascribed their offer to honor or fear: they were in as great a danger from the drunken crowd they faced. No one was safe out there.

"Open the gates and close them hard after us!" he ordered, and guardsmen afoot used main force and the threat of pikes to press the gates outward against the stubborn few drunk enough to assail the Guelesfort gates themselves.

Free and foremost, Cefwyn rode Danvy straight at the laggard townsmen in his path, his guard a hard-riding mass at his heels as townsmen scattered from the path of the horses. Around the corner of the Quinaltine wall, into the Quinaltine square, he met little to check him; but the Quinaltine steps were beset with a crowd in the wild flux of rumor and grief, clots of confused and frightened citizens. A man ran past waving scraps of cloth soaked in red, screaming, "The Holy Father's blood! The Holy Father's blood!"

Cefwyn swore and maneuvered through the gap, laying about him with the flat of his sword, sent three men sprawling and one reeling aside who thought he could pass Danvy's guard and get at the bridle. Danvy stumbled over him, came up with an effort, steel-shod feet racketing on pavings as he drove to the foot of the Quinaltine steps.

There the Dragons and the portion of the Prince's Guard and the Guelens that had stayed to hold their pike-line were sorely pressed at the Quinalt steps. The mob wanted into the shrine: the Guard forces would not have it, and blood slicked no few faces.

"Back!" Cefwyn shouted at the crowd, striking still with the flat of his blade where it was a man's back, the edge if a man showed a weapon . . . he had no idea how many such, where the Guard was all but overwhelmed. "I am your king, damn you! Back away!"

"Silence there! Silence for His Majesty!" the cry went up from some few, amongst his personal guard, and with a screen of horses and their own bodies his bodyguard in their distinctive livery made the crowd give back.

"Silence that racket," Cefwyn said peevishly. His eyes stung. Smoke wafted at him, from across the square. "Quiet that bell! No one can have his wits with that din!"

"My lord king." Idrys had come up beside him, afoot, by Danvy's shifting hooves. "This is too great a risk."

"There's fire somewhere. What's burning?"

"The Bryalt shrine," Idrys said.

"Damn!"

There fell a sudden hush then, a sudden numbness of the air underlying the shouts, for the bell had, on a few false strokes, ceased tolling. It was as if the riot had lost its breath, and then fallen apart into individual, frightened men.

"The Holy Father was murdered," Cefwyn cried, lifting his sword high in the brief chance that silence gave him, and using the words that would catch the attention even of the drunken and the mad. "Within the Quinalt itself, a murder! A new Patriarch sits the gods' throne, His Highness Efanor's priest, Jormys, a good and saintly man, who prays you all stand aside from this lunacy! The gods do not sleep, and will avenge this blasphemy, and the blasphemy of drunken men who profane this holy precinct! Stand back, I say! Stand back and be silent!"

A handful raised their voices against him, but the majority hushed them in fearful haste; and he caught the breath of a further silence.

"Jormys, I say, is the new Patriarch, whom the council of priests will confirm. And he will ferret out the murderer, among whom I expect to find traces leading to enemies of the Crown, of the peace, and of this land!"

"Death to the Elwynim!" a drunken voice shouted, as generations of Guelenmen had shouted.

"Elwynim are across the river!" Cefwyn shouted at the limit of his breath. "It's Guelen traitors among you!" It was blood he called for and knew he did it. "Down with traitors! Gods save Ylesuin!"

"Gods save Ylesuin!" Everyone could shout that, and did, in the wildness of their fear, and kept shouting, filling up the silence so there was no more anyone

492 - C. J. CHERRYH

could say. A priest, up on the steps, raised his arms and tried to quiet them, with some success, a situation still full of hazard.

"Gods save Ylesuin indeed," Idrys said, at Danvy's shoulder. The Lord Commander was blood-spattered, a fine dew on his armor and his grim face. "Go to safety. Let your guard deal with it. They've seen you're not afraid, my lord king. It's enough."

"They'll continue to see it," Cefwyn said harshly, for now that terror had given way, anger rushed up hand in hand with it. They had threatened his kingdom. They had threatened Ninévrisë, and men in the crowd had cried against the Crown and all it stood for. He would not go back and cower in the Guelesfort, waiting for the Guard to make the streets of his capital safe for him to show his face.

Idrys could not prevent him, and the persistent sting of smoke provided a goal in the confusion: it was no small fire, and if there was a siege and a burning at the other side of the square, he meant to stop it.

But when he drew near the farside he saw it was the Bryaltine shrine afire, a black-robed corpse dangling from a rope cast to the rooftree of the Bryalt shrine. Beneath the body a pile of books smoldered, all of a library in that blackened heap.

The mob, seeking foreigners in their midst, had hanged poor Father Benwyn.

CHAPTER 5

The lords had eaten and drunk their fill on the evening of their arrival, fallen asleep and rested late, even down in the tents, and out into the town. Tristen, too, took his time rising, advised that all his guests were asleep. For days they had struggled to reach here, and now all the lords who had been at the welcoming feast in the Lesser Hall either slept late or nursed last night's folly behind drawn drapes.

Tristen himself fed his pigeons, and sat by the fire, and did the little directing he had to do. He could not persuade himself to sleep so late. He was jealous for every hour his guests were sleeping, unavailable to him, unprecedented anticipation, and his thoughts flitted and buzzed like bees.

The time felt auspicious, if any time had. His dream of the southern lords had come to life around him, and Emuin had not disapproved last night, rather had grown merry and cheerful. The lords had laughed together: Crissand got along famously with Cevulirn, and Pelumer and Umanon had sat talking with Sovrag despite old grudges.

Had ever he dreamed so much could go so well, when the stars were so chancy?

And even before the sun was a glimmering in the east the kitchens had gone into their ultimate frenzy before the feast, ovens hot, the smells of baking and roasting meat wafting everywhere about the yard . . . not a lord stirred forth except Cevulirn, down the hill to see to his horses before the sun was well up.

By noon the last stragglers had come out of their quarters, and by midafternoon, now, the smells of food were all but irresistible: Cook had prepared small loaves to fend off hunger, and that was the fare they had.

But there was good converse all the afternoon, and a small venture out to see the pastures and the camp-grounds, of which all the lords more than approved.

There was a moment, standing facing those pastures, and unheard by any but the foxes and the passing hawk, when Tristen explained the situation at Modeyneth and Althalen. It was a curious place for a conference, with the horses cropping the brown winter grass and the wind blowing a brisk, dry chill.

"It's only a village," Tristen said. "And some make a great deal of it, and some think I've fulfilled some prophecy, but that's not so, not to my thinking." He added, honestly, "But Emuin bids me be careful."

"Yet Your Grace is loyal to the king," Umanon said.

"He's my dear friend," Tristen said. "And always will be."

"So His Grace has us all to swear," said Crissand. "And has us to believe His Majesty has our good at heart."

"So he does," said Cevulirn, "and to that I swear, too. King Cefwyn's never been false to us, never forgotten Lewenbrook—he trusts us *too* much and doesn't say so: all his attention is for the ones he can't trust. But a true king, that he is."

"That's so," Tristen said. "That's very much so. He hasn't time for everyone. He has to tend the things that aren't going well."

"Ryssand," Crissand interjected.

"At the head of the list," Cevulirn said. "Gods save the king."

So they said, and so they finished their ride with the sun strongly westering, having ridden up an appetite.

Meanwhile Cook had outdone herself, and as the sky dimmed in the west, the kitchen poured forth platters of food, even enough to fill Sovrag's belly, at least in prospect.

Then the lords made themselves scarce, and buckets of water and servants were in short supply as all the guests wanted baths and attention to their dressing. There was shouting, there were harried servants pelting this way and that and out, in one instance, to a tailor shop—but no one was late downstairs, to the processional Tassand had arranged, with trumpets and banners.

They filed into the great hall in all ceremony, and all who could possibly find an invitation and a place at table were in that processional, the benches fiercely crowded at their lower stations. Emuin came—was simply there, when before that he had missed Emuin in the line.

The piper and the drummer lost no time after the fanfares, and swung into cheerful tunes, one after the other . . . for there would be dancing. Tristen loved to watch it, and was especially glad to see so many ladies at the tables, all in fine cloth and wearing jewels. He knew Crissand's mother and Durell's pretty daughter both by sight; and he recalled the two very young girls from Merishadd who put their heads together and giggled at every turn. They seemed to want his attention, but they were only children.

"Your Grace should welcome them," Tassand said close to his ear, helping him as Tassand had agreed to do. "Then ask the priests to pray."

Tristen stood up somewhat abashed and looked

around him; he had to wait for silence.

"I wanted you to come," he said when there was sufficient silence. "I need all your good advice. And I've missed you very much. I'm glad to see you. Be welcome."

There was applause to that. "Here's to the Sihhë-lord!" Sovrag roared out, that word that he hoped never to hear, but there was no restraining Sovrag at all. "Gods bless 'im, say I!"

He was supposed to invite the priests. Emuin stood up, to the rescue, splendid in his new robe. Teranthine gray he wore, and he wore the Teranthine sigil, standing forth as a cleric, tonight.

"Father," Emuin said with a wave of his hand toward the other end of the high table, where the Teranthine father and the Bryaltine abbot sat in close company. "If you'll do the honors."

"Delighted," said the Teranthine, shook back his voluminous sleeves from his forearms like a workman preparing to work, and gave a prayer so rapid and so authoritative the soldiers present all but came to attention. "Gods bless this gathering," the Teranthine concluded, passing the matter to the Bryaltine, who rose with his cup and tipped out a few drops onto the stone floor.

"Honor to the earth," the abbot said, "honor to the dead in the passing of the year; honor to the living, in the coming of the new. A Great Year passes tonight. A new one begins. Let the good that is old continue and let the rest perish. Gods save the lord of Amefel."

It pleased some: Tristen thought it should please him, but he was less certain about the matter of perishing . . . and if ever there should be a moment the gray space should come alive, on this night, with these two honest priests and Emuin, now it should . . . but it failed without the flicker of a presence, not even Emuin's closely held one.

And what should he do now? Tristen asked himself, for there was a ritual aspect to this feast, this gathering of close friends—as if Men wished to be sure where all they loved was when the world changed. And was that enough, and had they raised enough godliness in this gathering?

But just then the servants paraded out with another course, the fabled pies, so there was an end to the speeches and the gods-blessing and all speculation on the new year. There was laughter, and Midwinter Eve, that had loomed so ominous through Emuin's year, turned to high good spirits and the praise of Cook's pastries.

Midwinter Eve had been imagining, and planning, all these things . . . and now the very night assumed a solidity and a scent and a sound all around him: it progressed, and the famous pies which, baked over the last sevenday, came out steaming, in great abundance. There was course after course besides, and music and laughter. There was nothing terrible, nothing to dread. Friends were like armor about the heart, and nothing could daunt him.

Then Sovrag called out that a good Midwinter Eve wanted tale-telling, and he had heard of the business with Ryssand's son, but he wanted a full recitation for the wider hall.

A small silence fell—Sovrag was several cups past sober and meant no harm at all, but it was no good story, and Cevulirn, with that still, dignified calm that hushed all around him, refused.

"It's too recent, and I'd rather Lord Pelumer. He has a winter story."

"Which?" asked Pelumer.

"Why, when you were young, Lanfarnesse. The deer in the treetops."

That caught interest even from the drunken, and Pelumer needed no pleading. He told of the year the

Lenúalim froze so deep carts could cross it, and how the ice had lasted into spring. He told how the snow had drifted so high up the trees the deer browsed the high branches.

Then it was so cold a man carrying wood had his fingers break off, and it was so cold an ox team turned up frozen in their yoke, still standing.

Tristen thought that part very sad.

"A man could walk to Elwynor from here," Pelumer went on, "since the river was a highroad, white and smooth as glass. I saw it. I was a boy of seven years, and I walked from Lanfarnesse into Marna and back, chasing the deer and seeing what I could see. Marna was all asparkle with ice. The High King sat in Althalen, and the High King's rangers kept the woods. But no one dared kill the deer in Marna Wood. And no one went to Mauryl's tower, either.

"Yet I saw it through the trees, and knew then how far I'd come. I turned back, walking the river home, not wishing even in those days to have the sun set before I'd cleared that part of those woods. Down and down went the sun, and the ice went from bright to gray. Then I walked as fast as I could, and began to run, with the clearest notion there was something right at my shoulders. I ran and I ran and I ran, until a shadow rose up right in front of me.

"It was a King's Ranger," Pelumer concluded, to the relief of the young girls from Merishadd, who had leaned closer and closer together, and all but jumped. "And he said it was very well I never looked back, for those who did never came out again."

There were delicious shivers. But Tristen knew better, and so did Sovrag, surely, who leaned back in his chair, and began his own tale of river-faring, less eloquent than Pelumer, involving his own first trip up to Marna, with his father's crew, even then trading with Mauryl.

"We went to the old tower, right up where the water meets the stones, and the old man'd come and never bargain, but say what he'd pay. That was his habit. And me da was careful about the hour, that's so. By sundown we cleared that wood—and was raidin' the shore by Lanfarnesse after that . . ." This with a wink at Pelumer. "But we're honest men, now, an' sittin' in a warm hall, with clear water an' the wind turned out of the north this evenin'. That's the breath of the hoary old north wind, as blows the boats home. Mother South Wind, she's blowed us here, and old man North Wind, he's chasin' us home—can't ask for better. Wizard-luck, that is for us, 'specially if it blows us back with the next load."

"Wizard-luck, indeed," Emuin said somberly, from Tristen's right, next Crissand at the table. "Luck *and* wizardry."

"Was it you?" Sovrag asked—respecting the cloth and the wizard, as it seemed, for there was a caution in Sovrag whenever he spoke to Emuin. "Uncommon lack o' snow, there is."

"It is, isn't it?" Emuin said, not the admission Sovrag courted, and it left Sovrag with not a thing to say on that subject. Tristen took quick note of the tactic, seeing it turned on someone other than him.

But Sovrag was rarely without something to say. "An' no ice in the river, master wizard, not this year. Boats, boats can run free an' *bad* luck to Tasmôrden, say I! Here's to wizard-luck an' Ilefínian—an' to hell with that blackguard Tasmôrden!"

"So 't is!" Uwen said, from Tristen's left. "But there's tomorrow for that." It was a valiant effort for a shy man to speak out and stem the flood of war talk— but his effort failed, for Lord Durell was drunk enough to propose they should make a foray against the enemy immediately.

"Deck the bridge at the Guelen camp and have the blackguard's head within the week!" Durell cried, lifting his cup. "To hell with 'im!"

"I doubt it will be so easy," Cevulirn said.

And Crissand, who was no more drunk than Cevulirn, which was to say, not at all, said, "On any cold, clear morning, with a will, we're ready."

"Damn Tasmôrden," said Lord Azant, and Drumman: "Long live Lord Tristen!"

Then Emuin, who had had more than one cup himself, and who had blunted Sovrag's first foray, lifted a hand. "Inappropriate for me to curse," Emuin said. "And His Majesty has demanded patience of us. And no talk of war tonight."

There was a muttering at that.

"Which," Emuin said above the protest, "the stars declare is wise! There would be no good outcome of a venture planned this side of midnight. Say no more of it!"

"And after?" Sovrag asked,

"Tonight is not for war," Tristen said, for Emuin's warning had struck a certain chill into him, and he foresaw that very soon they would be saying things he had as lief not have laid before every visitor to the hall tonight . . . the Teranthine father was there, and the Bryalt abbot, with the two nuns, the thanes and squires of villages, and the ealdormen, not mentioning their wives, and the guards and servants besides. Any one of them might spread news that might not serve them . . . whether it reached Ilefínian—or Guelessar and the north.

But he looked at all his guests, his friends— Crissand, Cevulirn, Sovrag and Pelumer and Umanon, Merishadd and Azant and the earls, and he saw around him, willing and earnest, all the power of the south, all on the verge of motion.

He saw the ladies, all in their finery, and the meal ended. But not the evening.

It was Midwinter Eve, the night the heavens shifted . . . and he felt an equal disturbance in the gray place, between one deep breath and the next, as all the hall hung momentarily silent, awaiting the next move.

"Play," he said to the piper, ending all discussion. "Move the tables back."

Servants hurried to obey, and in high good cheer. For a moment thereafter everyone was disarranged and the squeal of wood on stone and the laughter of well-sated guests alike underlay the music.

The shriek seemed to go on, shooting through stone, into the earth, wounding the ear.

Hinge of the year, Emuin had said, hinge of the Great Year and the Year of Years. Shriek by shriek, tables and benches moved, the arrangement of things undone, set aside, drawn back to clear the floor. It was so common a sound. But the gray space roiled of a sudden, and the very air turned to liquid silver.

Lewenbrook itself was a heartbeat away. So was Ynefel. There was suddenly so much chance and harm flying in the wind that Tristen found no quick counter to its malice.

And when the moving of tables was done, and before the couples took the floor:

"I wish our happiness and the king's," he said, standing, lifting high the cup he held. And wish he did, with all his might. *"I wish happiness for all of us, when the world is turning round and the new year is coming!"*

"And happiness to you, sir," said Pelumer, lifting his cup, and so did they all. "To all our lands, happiness and good outcome."

"And happiness to the king in Guelessar," Crissand cried in that moment of warm extravagance, not base flattery, but the outpouring of a generous heart. "Happiness to him for sending us our lord! *Gods bless His Guelen Majesty!*"

"The Guelen king's health!" said Merishadd, and Azant lifted his cup, and all the rest in a body as Azant added, "And our lord's!"

"Hear him," said Pelumer. "Health to our host, Lord Tristen! Long may he prosper in Amefel."

"Long may we all prosper!" said Umanon.

Tristen drew a breath, feeling steadier, as if in such a great number of good wishes from those he counted friends the dark of midnight had passed and the currents of the new year had begun to find a direction.

How could one do better for a beginning, he thought, than in wishing one another well?

How could he have any more profound a shift in the currents than for Amefin lords and southerners to drink the health of the Guelen king? He could wish—and so could Crissand, who had set wizardry behind that generosity.

The piper played, and a handful of the younger folk moved to the floor, eager to dance.

But one lady in attendance came from the shadows by a column, all in gray and gold, a wisp of a woman gray of hair and hung about with cords and stones and charms.

The incipient dance paused. Guards moved, and hesitated in doubt. Emuin stood forward, but not far, and the priests rallied uncertainly to Emuin as the woman came.

But only Uwen set himself directly in her path, as the music died.

The woman's gown seemed old fabric and strange, like cobwebs over lace, like gold cloth dimmed by dust. The ornaments that she wore were perhaps costly, perhaps not. She was neither old nor young, and she made a low and graceful bow, sinking into her gold-touched skirts and rising from them like gray smoke from embers. It seemed a music played, but none that the pipers made, a gentle, eldritch air like the stirring of broken glass.

With a nod and a quizzical look, the woman held out her hand, invitation to the dance. And still Uwen barred the way.

But on a breath and accepting a challenge, Tristen moved past him, reached out, took dry, cool fingers, moved in stately paces, turned as the woman turned, all to that strange, distant music.

Within the murmur of consternation the piper took up a wavering tune, the same that filled the air, and the drummer found the hum and thump of a rhythm different than the tune they had played, haunting, majestic measures.

It was Auld Syes, whose eyes sparkled and whose whole bearing held the dignity of a queen.

"Lady," Tristen said, when the measures brought them close, eye-to-eye, and her gaze was dark and deep. "Welcome."

But while the musicians played on Auld Syes stopped the dance and stood, breathless and aglow.

"Lord," she said then, and made another deep bow, rising again to face him. "Lord of Althalen, of Meliseriedd, of Ynefel! High King and lord of all the middle lands! Beware your enemy!"

"I am no king!" he said doggedly. But Auld Syes backed away from him bowing yet a third time. The candles blew sideways, threatening darkness, and a small shadow skipped around Auld Syes and him alike, then nipped after a tray of honeycakes at the side of the room. A sudden whirlwind ran the circuit of the room, blowing up skirts. The guests cried out in alarm, but the whirlwind ran toward the doors with a laughter like harp strings, a wind spinning and turning and dancing with a mad, fey lightness.

For a moment in the gray space, pipes sounded, and a woman ran lightly over a ghostly meadow of gray almost green, a child chasing in her footsteps.

Auld Syes had left the hall, and as she did the massive doors of the hall burst open, and the doors of the inner hall all at once banged wide with echoes down the corridor outside, one after another.

Winds swept through, riffling all the candles, then snuffing them, every one, leaving all there in utter dark.

A smell of evergreen attended.

"Light!" Emuin cried furiously, over the cries from the guests. "Gods bless! *Give us light!*"

Men were blind in the darkness, blind and afraid, and still the wind blew. Yet it needed nothing but the wish to see, to draw the gray, bright light out of that place and touch the candles with it, and Tristen did that, obedient to Emuin's wish to lend light. His wish lit the hall not with the warm golden glow those candles should bear, but the icy silver of the gray place, every candle aglow, but casting little light abroad. The candle-sconces all became islands of scant luminance, and the hall outside the open doors appeared as a place of darkness similarly lit, every candle in the hall aglow but doing little good.

The guests were cast into strange, small groups in that pale gray light.

Lord Umanon and Lord Cevulirn both had found their swords.

Of Auld Syes there was no sight nor sound.

Beware your enemy, Auld Syes had said, but if there was an enemy he had to fear, it was not the darkness.

But suddenly something reached through his source of light, through the gray space itself, and threat streamed like poison through the light he had gathered and set atop the candles.

That was not the enemy, either. It remained out of his reach. He sent challenge back through the gray: he was in a Place, had his feet set, and would fight for these lives if it came.

"Lord!" a man cried from the open doors, and in starkest urgency: "*Lord! The hall! The light, in the hall!*"

The way Auld Syes had trod here had not sealed itself. When the man cried that, all the gray space bid fair to spill in upon them—not baneful in itself, but a cascade too much, too swift, too terrible a knowledge, from every candle in the hall. He steadied it back.

And neither was that the source of the danger, for danger had followed Auld Syes like a hound on a scent. It sought a Place in the fortress; and now he felt the widening of a rift—a breach in the wards at that place he had never trusted.

It was from that place the poison came, from that place the lights were threatened; and from out of that gulf the wind buffeted them. It was that spot in the hall, that one most haunted place.

"Uwen!" Tristen cried as he began to run toward the doors of the great hall, for no other man would he have as a shieldman, and no man else in the world would he trust to beware the Edge.

In the next instant a hand caught his sleeve, and stayed him long enough for a sword hilt to find his hand. A buffet on his shoulder sent him on.

"Go, lad!" he heard Uwen say, so run he did. He was the defense Uwen had, the defense any Man of his guests had, and he plunged into the corridor where conditions were the same: the candles there streamed the same silvery gray toward him, spots of light in a dark where Shadows ran, dark small streamers along all the mortar.

He flung up his hand, called the wards all to life, threatening all that broke the Pattern of the stones, the ancient masonwork.

At his summoning, a blue glow intruded into the gray sheen of the candles, and a glow ran along the base of the walls, up over doorways . . . every Line of the old fortress glowed, walls and doorways made firm and real. Shadows that flowed moved along those Lines, obedient, until they began to race toward that Place, that foreignness in the hall.

Beyond a doubt he knew Auld Syes herself was in danger, as if a thread of her being had come through this doorway, and now, retreating, stretched thinner and thinner within.

He was aware of the great mass of the ancient stone around him, and of the presence of friends at his back: he reached the old mews, that most haunted place, the place where the wards were least firm—and in and out of which the winds rushed.

He settled a tighter grip on the borrowed sword, felt with a sweep of his left arm for Uwen's presence where Uwen would always stand. He was there. He felt Cevulirn and Crissand likewise near him, wizardous and detectable in the gray space, more than the others. Emuin, too, was there, reaching toward him a strong and determined power, in an attempt to hold the wards . . .

But the blue light grew, source of the winds that battered and buffeted them.

There, there within the old structure, the Lines were almost overwhelmed, and there if dark could glow, this did. Shortly before the struggle at Lewenbrook, he had stared into a vacancy and faced the rousing of countless ghostly wings.

So the rift began to grow, and grow, and he knew what he would face.

"There it is," he said. "Where it always was. It's open. —Emuin? Do you see?"

"I see it," Emuin said, and others crowded near.

"Stay here," he said. "Uwen. Stay here. Keep the others safe."

"No, my lord," Uwen's voice said flatly, at his very shoulder, "Lord Crissand's close behind ye; but he ain't your shieldman an' I am, beggin' his pardon, an' lord Cevulirn's. I'm wi' ye, so go on."

"Bear a light!" Crissand called out, and the answer came back, "There is none!"

"Then find one!" Umanon cried angrily. So yet another of the lords had followed him. "Gods bless, man, find one!"

No light would serve, not here, and he needed all his strength. The light he had lent the candles everywhere in the hall he gave up, so that the dark came down in the mortal world and overwhelmed the corridor in which they stood. Men cried out in alarm. But the blue of the Lines and the blue of that Place shone the brighter in the darkness, guiding him forward.

He could not say he walked. He held the sword half-forgotten in his hand, and it seemed now instead of the solid stone of the wall, a slatted, airy structure through which blue light streamed. That was the old mews as they had been. He advanced, knowing Uwen's presence at his side one moment and then gone abruptly as he walked beyond the solid stone of the existing wall and the Place within the walls opened wide.

Blue light softened to something near moonlight, just enough to see by, sifting through rafters and broken beams of a ruined gable end.

Perches stretched along either wall of this place, and above him wings stirred and whispered. To his first impression it was the sound of his pigeons, and safe, but in the next blink of an eye the wings that spread and bated about him were nothing so innocent. Cries came to his ears, birds of prey, hawks in great numbers, and the scream of wood on stone and the shriek of the birds and the shriek of the wind were one and the same.

The hawks pent here, scores of them, were ghosts out of a Place and a Time all but forgotten, and if they were tame at all, were tame to hands long dead.

Yet had Auld Syes gone this way?

Was it after all a doorway, that broken gable, a breach in the Lines that Were, admitting him to Lines that Had Been?

He saw before him a Place within a Place, and a Door that had never quite closed, perhaps on purpose.

There was the entry, there, in the heart of the moving wings and the haze of the streaming light that cast a glow on pale, black-barred feathers, on mad, wild eyes and open beaks that seemed to shriek forth the sound of winter storm.

The semblance of snow flew then, a battering storm half-obscuring the light, and when it ceased . . .

When it ceased it was not the old mews about him now, but the loft, *his* loft this spring in Ynefel, and the fluttering wings were only his feckless, faithful pigeons on their rafters.

He had come home. Mauryl would be below, at work at his table, elbow-deep in his charts of stars and movements of the planets, all of which pointed to this night.

He was in his loft again, and the blue glow of moonlight brightened to sky, and latest dusk, and his birds were coming home, arriving by ones and twos, stirring up dust and old feathers.

He had no names for them, had never thought they needed names, no more than the aged mice who dwelt in the wall of the downstairs hall, near Mauryl's table. But oh! he knew them, and welcomed them, and for a moment the place opened wide to him, in utter innocence and happiness. He flung wide his arms and turned to see the familiar pattern of sky and broken boards . . . no need to ward such places, Mauryl said, for they were only holes. The Lines of Ynefel had stood firm despite those gaps, and Mauryl had remade the wards every evening—

—warding his window for him, too, at the foot of the first bed he remembered: his little horn-paned window, beneath which the first sinister crack had come into the wall. The rain had written patterns on it. He had, never knowing what he did or undid.

He stopped turning and stood still, heart skipping a beat as he recalled that widening, dreadful seam. He was sure now beyond all question that the ruin that had brought Mauryl down had begun there, proceeded there, worked there until there was no way for the wards to hold. Hasufin in his assault on Mauryl's tower had come to that window and pried and pried at the stones, trying his young dreams, stirring up the shadows that were all too frequent there.

He had been the weakness in Mauryl's defense: he, his dreams, his curiosity, his tracing random, foolish patterns on the window, amid Mauryl's wards.

His room was below him. His bed. The stairs that led down, led there, to that room with the window.

And he knew at the same time he was in the old mews at Henas'amef, in the Zeide, near the new great hall.

He still remembered how he had come here. It was so easy here to forget his very life, to lose the thread that bound him to Uwen, and Emuin, and all the rest. He kept firm hold of that memory, clenched it like a guiding thread—he knew the way . . . no, not *back*, back was too little a word. He knew the way *home*, and his home was no longer here, was not this loft, this hour, this dim evening last spring.

He knew at any moment a youth might come up the stairs. That youth would bring a candle and a book, the Book, which at that time had been a mystery to him, but was not so now.

Nor were the secrets in that book secrets any longer. He knew why he had felt vague fears of presence when he lived at Ynefel, so now he knew what at least one ghostly presence was.

And if he knew when he had been afraid, he might predict, perhaps, the sites and times of his visitations to Ynefel; and by that, he might come here again.

He stood very still. The boy hid in nameless terror of Mauryl's steps on the stairs, and feared the voices, oh, the voices, as all the imprisoned faces in the stone walls cried together.

Any moment Mauryl would come through that door, and confront him, the dearest sight and the most dreadful in all the world.

And dared they meet? Dared they, he and Mauryl, cross life and death and stand face-to-face, time present, time never to come?

Dared he? Dared they? Was it folly, or would Mauryl even see him if he tried?

His very breath seemed to stick between the bellows strokes of his chest, the hammerblows of his heart.

But he was not done with the loft. To go back undefeated, still master of this place, he must not run from it in fear: he must find what it wanted *tonight*, in Henas'amef.

There was a terror here besides Mauryl. And to find it he must face the blank wall at the end of *his* loft . . . which was not the end at all.

That wall secluded the true Shadow which ruled the heights of Ynefel, a perch surrounded by detritus of his depredation.

Owl lived there.

And one day a boy in Ynefel had found the way to Owl . . . and now the man came back, seeking what he had feared in that hour.

He looked through the broken boards, saw Owl on his perch, and Owl turned on him a furious glance.

Then wind rushed through the loft, a dreadful wind, and the place changed. Light streamed and spun through the broken beams and ruined wall, and ghostly wings stirred about him, hunters seeking prey, seeking *him*, so it seemed, and denying him any gain here. The old mews reshaped themselves around him, drawing him back and back, but Ynefel was still just beyond, still with danger in it.

"M'lord!" Uwen shouted.

And in the pale heart of the light, at the very end of the old mews, he saw a great blunt-winged shape flying, flying, striving to reach him in the world of Men. Owl was coming, desperately beating through that storm of light and wind.

He lifted his hand the rest of the way, offering a place for Owl's feet, and called out to him, "Owl!" which was all the name Owl had. The blued light caught the great orbs of Owl's eyes, whose centers drank in all light, whose intent seemed some prey beyond him.

Perverse bird. Owl was never biddable. He would miss him, fly astray, Tristen thought.

But at the very last Owl reached him and checked his speed, blunt wings rowing in the wind . . . lowered with a buffet of air, and feather-skirted feet clamped hard on his hand.

Owl sat safely then, no great weight, despite his size, but a weight, all the same. Abruptly Owl's head swiveled completely around, golden eyes regarding him sharply, in what seemed profound amazement at one instant, and secret knowledge in another.

"Owl," Tristen said, resettling his grip on the borrowed sword to nudge Owl's feathers with a finger. Owl struck with his beak—closing on nothing, for Tristen was quicker.

"Where now?" he asked Owl, unoffended. "Where must I go?"

But Owl gave him no answer, only hunched down, no glowing apparition of an owl, now, but a lump of untidy feathers and a turned shoulder, as obstinate in presence as he had been in illusion.

"M'lord," Uwen said, right beside him.

The wind had fallen away. The perches all around him were vacant. The light quieted to a soft and dimming glow.

Of a sudden he was aware of the Place diminishing around him, and of his way back diminishing as well. He swung around, saw Emuin and Uwen too close to him for safety.

Then he was in a hallway under a few faint candles. Crissand and Cevulirn were waiting. Umanon and Sovrag and Pelumer all had weapons drawn. Even the waif Paisi was there, his eyes wide as saucers.

"M'lord," Uwen said then, as if to call him back to himself, to life, and his friends.

"I was at Ynefel," he said. He had never intended other than honesty with the lords, and knew he would trouble them with that advisement, but honesty he would hew to. "Owl came to me. I don't know why."

"What meaning to it?" Sovrag asked. "D' ye know?"

"No. I don't." He was cold from his sojourn in the gray space, and now very weary. He saw they were troubled. Emuin watched, with what feeling, whether approval or disapproval, Emuin did not impart to him, not even in the gray space. Crissand gazed at him as if he had found a strange creature in their midst, a strange creature, fearsome, and dreadful. Cevulirn regarded him with doubt. Only Uwen was still by him unchanged, undaunted, faithful as the stone underfoot, standing here before an ordinary wall, before candles which had turned out to be lighted after all.

What might he do, but what he had done? The wards had stood fast. Nothing had gotten in.

He turned, he walked, still holding Owl, toward the only refuge of comfortable light that beckoned him, and that was the great hall.

He was aware of his allies following him. He met the shocked whispers and stares of frightened guests as he walked back into his hall. The young girls who had been so full of chatter were silent, now, holding close to their mother. Men stood in stark, stiff groups, watching, asking themselves, surely, to what they were sworn.

Owl launched himself suddenly and flew ahead of him on silent wings, rising to alight high up on a cornice, above the oak-leaf frieze.

Tristen wished the comfort of a table, a cup of ale—most of all a laugh to dispel fear. But even Sovrag failed him in that, and the tables were drawn back for the dancing, so there was no place to dispose his trembling limbs but the dais and the chair of state. So he climbed up and sat, necessarily facing the solemn gathering of lords, whose looks toward him were unanswered questions.

Where did he find an answer for them?

To his dismay Owl chose that time to swoop down and settle on the finial near his hand, regarding first him with that mad, impassioned stare, then swiveling his head to cast his mad stare at all the hall, daunting those who had waited.

Some backed away. But Uwen, Emuin, and the

lords of the south stood fast, and Crissand—Crissand of all of them—came closer, pale of face, but daring the moment and the silent question.

"He's only an owl," Tristen said, desperately. He teased Owl's breast feathers as he would those of his tame pigeons, to make light of him, and Owl gave him a look of furious indignation: never at ease, never at peace, was Owl. "He was at Ynefel, and guided me through Marna Wood, and generally he minds his own business." A further assay of the soft feathers won a nip at his fingers, a sharp strike that failed to draw blood.

Dared he forget that Auld Syes had been here, and that now there was Owl? So many things seemed ordinary to him, that did not seem so to Men. The lords had seen Owl before, on Lewen field . . . but that was hardly reassurance.

"Uwen," he said. And Uwen stepped up to the low dais at once and without question, while he continued, helplessly, to look out at the assembly.

"Is there any threat, any harm to the halls or the town?"

"None as I see, m'lord," Uwen said, in that reasonable, plain voice that brought quiet to horses and men alike. "Gi' or take the old lady an' the owl."

There was laughter, then, an anxious, brief and loud laughter.

Tristen laughed softly, too, and afforded Owl the side of his hand to sit on. Owl's talons this time drew blood, but that was negligible. He was rescued by the laughter, grateful to tears for the presence of friends who he now believed would not turn their shoulders to him and whisper behind their hands.

"Owl's not altogether an ordinary bird," he said in the difficult silence that followed, and drew another, uncertain laugh. "He goes and comes where he likes, and I suppose at the moment he likes to be here, but he may just as well decide to live in the woods. I think it bodes well, his coming."

As if Owl heard, he took off toward the cornice again, and sat up there, staring balefully at all below him.

"There," Tristen said. He wondered, distracted thought—if Owl was a Shadow, did Owl need to eat? The loft had shown he did. The servants should leave at least one door open . . . to a fierce winter draft and the hazard of his pigeons, he was sure. He dreaded that prospect, and saw the lords' lingering disquiet. "He's only an owl," he said, "no matter how he comes and goes."

"Lord Tristen is no different than he was," Emuin said then, speaking up. "And be assured, he wishes well to all of you."

It was in some part strange to be talked about in his hearing, much as Cefwyn and Idrys and Emuin had used to discuss him as if he were a chair or a table, when he had first arrived in Cefwyn's hands.

Now he heard Emuin assuring his friends he would do no harm to them—and was it so? Whatever Owl was or meant, he was no natural bird, and did an ordinary lord keep a Shadow for a guest? He had his few, his faithful; but he saw all the faith, all the trust he had built with other Men near to falling in shards and pieces.

"Dance," he said, "and drink."

"'At's right," Uwen said loudly. "Fill the cups, there, and bring the sweets, and you harpers set to, somethin' quick, wi' the drummers!"

The drums rattled into a light cadence, Owl glared from the cornice, and the piper found his wind.

Then as Uwen came close, so Sovrag joined them, and Umanon, Azant, and others of the earls . . . not shunning him, but seeking his presence.

"What's the meanin' on 't?" Sovrag asked. "Lights goin' out and strange old women comin' into hall . . . were she a ghost?"

"Change," said Emuin. "Change is in the stars, change is in the wind, and safer to ride it than to be ridden down."

And meanwhile the gray space roiled and swirled, alive not only to the two of them, but to other presences, however faint and far.

Close at hand he felt the preternatural awareness of lords such as Crissand, in whom the wizard-gift burned, in Cevulirn, in whom it shone like a candle-flame, and in more than one of the others in the general company.

—*Do you know? Tristen asked Emuin. Were you aware there were so many with the gift?*

—*This is the south, Emuin said, as if that answered all. And you are lord of it. Be wise. Bare no more secrets to these men, for your own sake. And Cefwyn's.*

Owl, on his perch, turned his back to the sounds. Men and women uncertainly took hands and danced.

Emuin, in his gray court robes, stood silent and composed himself until he made not even a ripple in the gray place.

Are you angry? Tristen wondered. He found he was, and he did not know at what, except the fear he had just passed.

And that fear perched, a little ball of feathers, up on a cornice in the hall.

Come here, he wished the bird peevishly, expecting no obedience. But to his surprise Owl flew down and, instead of perching, flew out the doors of the hall, out into the corridors.

Half the matter was solved, at least. The guards opened doors to let various folk come and go, and Owl would take care of himself.

CHAPTER 6

The smell of burning might be only the fire in the fireplace, but Cefwyn's memory could not purge itself of the unholy reek that had hung over the square.

Fire had not spread from the shrine to the wooden porches nearby, which some cited as a miracle; but it was no miracle that the rioters, driven from the square, had slipped out into the town to make mischief.

All through the night the several Guard companies had alternately stood guard and chased drunken looters, until exhausted men, a tavern owner, and short tempers had clashed bloodily at Market and Hobnail Alley just before the hallowed dawn.

It was Midwinter Day.

A new year began, and the streets stood at last in numb, universal quiet, the convulsion spent . . . so Idrys had reported, blood-spattered and smeared with soot when last they had spoken to each other.

Toward midnight they had admitted an orderly line of mourners through the shrine, the Holy Father decently robed and the shrine aglow with hundreds of candles and echoing with choral music. Passions sank, in that solemn, dignified sight, and Efanor's suggestion of a second penny to every man, woman, and child who passed the altar had brought whole streets out, with wives and children, outnumbering the ruffians and bringing a more sober, decent crowd to the heart of the town. The line had gone on till dawn . . . was still going, at the last he heard, and some likely in line three times, but the royal coffers would disburse it, as cheaper than burned buildings.

But at the dawn he had heeded his guard's strong requests to take himself out of the dangerous outer streets, and go back to the safe center and up to his apartment, to lie on his bed if not to sleep. "The kingdom needs a live king with his wits about him," Idrys had said, when they had dealt with a roving, armed band of thieves. "Go. Hunting brigands is my work."

So he had come back, under escort, and found Ninévrisë had never gone to her own apartments. She had taken charge of his pages, taken his desk, sat all night directing the servant staff's oversight of the threatened Guelesfort and the care of the town's wounded—rendering judgment, too, where Annas found her advice useful, with her primary aid a handful of exhausted, frightened pages. The Tower of Elwynor, Annas had called her gratefully, referring to the arms of her house; and that was the way she had stood through the storm, the center to which all messages could come and where all news could be found.

She slept, exhausted, once she had him by her, resting against his side.

"Where is Luriel?" he finally thought to ask her, at one waking. "Is she still in her apartments?"

"She came back," Ninévrisë said. "Her gown is the worse for wear, so Fiselle says."

"Panys' son was with the Guard, the last I saw him. A good man." His fingers strayed across Ninévrisë's shoulder, finding her arm as prone to tremors as his own, utter weariness, no more. Then the enormity of it all, and memory of the Holy Father's last visit, when he had been so afraid, came back to him. "I never expected it, Nevris. The old man warned me. He tried to warn me. I didn't think they'd dare anything like this."

"Poor Benwyn." Her voice was hoarse, unlike herself. "He had nothing to do with sorcery, or magic . . . he never threatened the Holy Father. He had nothing to do with it."

Benwyn had nothing to do with it, but someone had taken pains to paint the murder with an Amefin look.

And who would know so well what Amefin charms looked like, but one who had been there?

And was that not the Amefin patriarch . . . but suspect the man of murder, and him shut in his quarters, a sick man?

He doubted it. He much doubted it.

And yet they urgently needed a suspect, a place to point the blame, something, *anything* to distract the commons from Benwyn . . . Benwyn's connection with Ninévrisë. The mob that had risen had gone for Benwyn because he was Amefin . . . one of their own, but not Guelen. And because he was the foreign consort's priest.

"The soldiers that came back with the Amefin father," he said. "They're familiar enough with Amefin charms, and the Bryalt." He held her close, his thoughts scurrying through the underbrush of lordly ambitions and guilty secrets like so many frightened hares. "But would they dare, on their own? And why? Emuin would say . . . Emuin would say if a thing is common, you don't see it. And what's common under the Quinaltine roof?"

"Another priest?" Ninévrisë asked. "That zealot priest?"

"Udryn. *Udryn*, the name is. Idrys removed him somewhere—at least—he's *been* removed somewhere, dropped in the country somewhere remote. Scare him, the notion was. But a priest could reach the robing room without notice. A priest could gain entry. We thought this Udryn was the primary danger. But who would dare attack the Holy Father?"

"Ryssand?"

"Not directly. Not directly. But a zealot could do this, he well could. Jormys himself is in danger. He's in a mail shirt at the moment . . . Efanor gave it to him and told him wear it constantly. But Father Jormys will eat and sleep in the Quinaltine, where our guards can't go. And meanwhile we can't point the finger at the zealots or Ryssand without better proof than one of them being in the Quinaltine where they have every right to be. We can put one of them out. We can drop Udryn and whoever else we catch down a well. But how many are there? Who are they? We know the ones that have argued in public, but how do we find what a man thinks?"

"The priests might know."

"We have no authority except to appoint. We can't arrest, we can't charge, we can't investigate. The priests have to do it."

"They aren't all murderers, and they know each other. Make the murderer ashamed to face them. Make him guilty."

He had taken it as his part, man and king, to console her fears, even to lie to her, to see her have rest. He drew back a little, remembering that the warm, sweet presence was the Regent of Elwynor, Uleman's daughter, priestly and canny as ever her father was . . . and it was clear good sense she was offering him.

"They've passed out cloths with the Holy Father's blood—anything that touched him. The people stand for hours to see him. He's half a damn saint—forgive me." He had been with soldiers all night, and under attack.

"The people need one. Don't they?"

"But who killed him, but another priest, *Ryssand's*

priest, and if I had Ryssand's signed confession with his seal on it I couldn't use it. I *need* Ryssand, until I can marry Efanor to his daughter, gods save me. There's still a murderer in the Quinaltine, and Benwyn's still dead, and there's still the Amefin charms, real or not. For your sake and for Tristen's we can't have that."

"What can we do?"

"Accuse a murderer . . . accuse Tasmôrden, who's the likeliest the people know."

"An Elwynim. And will *that* make me safe?"

"It's a better direction than any other. It's all we can do. Say it was sorcery and Tasmôrden suborned it. If you can't damn a man for what you know he's done, damn him anyway. It was a spy. An assassin slipping in from outside, concealed by sorcery, moved by sorcery."

"And my people, innocent people, are taking refuge in Amefel, inside Ylesuin, where they have such charms. Where will *that* go?"

"We can't let it turn to Amefel. We can't let people ever take the notion. It was sorcery, and it was Tasmôrden, from straight across the river. Gods know we've bodies to spare: sixteen dead and one burned beyond recognition. We'll say first we caught the assassin. We have him in chains. We dole out the news day by day and keep the people in expectation. Then we display the remains. Sorcery killed him in his cell." He felt no pride in what he was saying, or planning. He liked far less making her party to it . . . but it was her advice that had prompted him. "Where will the people's anger light then, but where we need it to nest?"

"The murderer will know," Ninévrisë whispered. "And what will he think?"

"He'll tell Ryssand and Ryssand will know. And Ryssand will share our secret, only Ryssand and the murderer . . . and one day Idrys will see justice is done. It may not be tomorrow. But it will happen. Efanor's Jormys is in office now—the Quinalt council has to confirm, but the Holy Father had enough votes to rule there, and they hate the zealots. We'll banish sorcery. We'll make saints of Benwyn *and* the Holy Father."

"Sorcery isn't remote from us," Ninévrisë said faintly, leaning her head against him. "And it might, after all, be true, this lie. Send to Emuin. He should know this."

"We can't send a letter like that. No. There's far too much risk. Our couriers have had narrow escapes." He forgot, at times, that Ninévrisë had wizardry of her own. And now it worried him. "*Was* Benwyn a wizard?"

She shook her head, a motion against his heart. "Not a shred of one."

"*Are* there wizards?"

"There's Emuin. There's Tristen, if one counts him."

"I'd count him."

"He's—"

"Not a wizard." He understood the exception. "But there are others."

"One hears them. One feels them."

"Do you think what we plan might not *be* a lie?"

"I don't know," she said faintly. "At first I thought so, but now I don't know."

Ryssand would expect blame for the Holy Father's death. He had immediately to send a message to reassure Ryssand of that notion, dangle favor before him to keep him from the desperation that would drive the scoundrel to protect himself. Desperate, Ryssand could bring the kingdom down.

It was a dangerous course they steered, but it was one that would keep the north united. In the Holy Father he had lost a valuable ally. In Jormys, loyal to Efanor, he had another.

Yet he must send condolences to Sulriggan, the late Patriarch's cousin, and keep that lord tied to him, assured of his continued favor even with the Patriarch dead. That man could be useful.

Luriel's marriage had to go forward, early. Young Rusyn might become a hero of the defense of the Quinaltine. He had deserved it. His father certainly had. A reward of lands would shore up Panys' wounded dignity: he cared not a jot about Murandys, though he supposed he must.

Something rattled like claws against the window.

Rain, he thought it first, but saw no drops on the glass.

It kept up, and kept up.

It was sleet coming down.

CHAPTER 7

To Tristen's distress the weather turned . . . natural weather for winter, so everyone said as the sleet came, and then the snow. Owl must have found some nook out of the wind, or was hunting mice: the pigeons came fearlessly to the window for bread, and the servants mopped and swept continually in the halls against the traffic that came and went.

But it was not Tristen's wish that the weather turn, and he found something ominous in the worsening storm. Wagons with tents and other gear were on the road in the storm that first froze the roads—that was a help—and then began to ice them, and that was no help at all.

Umanon's few wagons arrived out of a blinding white, to set up camp in ground beginning to freeze.

"One can't hold off nature forever," Emuin said with a shake of his head, when Tristen went to his tower to consult. "I've not seen such a spell, and I suppose it's simply given us all the snow at once."

"I'm havin' men pound in pegs now," Uwen informed him when, wrapped in his heaviest cloak, he visited the camps outside the walls, "there bein' little difference in the tents, an' if there is, they'll rig somethin' clever. If this goes on, they'll just be damned thankful the pegs is drove in before the ground freezes. Granted they can find 'em. We're settin' markers, and hope the rest on 'em's quick arrivin'. I figure they'll press on into the night to get here."

"I wish," Tristen said, "but my wishes aren't all that's had effect, or the snow wouldn't fall yet."

The lords prowled the hall and the stables and hoped for their tents and supplies, concerned, clearly, while Emuin sat in his tower hoping in vain for a sight of the sky and the stars at night.

And just at sundown, the storm gave up to a general, an eerie quiet.

More riders came in, Ivanim, cold men and cold horses, glad of a great bonfire Uwen had ordered set up for a beacon in the night, to guide men to the town. Cevulirn went down to meet the newcomers, who were his, but the heavy horsemen of Imor with all their gear and remounts were still out in the storm. Sovrag went down to help. Umanon and Pelumer simply fretted, near the town lords gathered in the great hall. It was their men still to come, still out in the storm.

The fact was that contrary to all Pelumer's intentions the handful of Lanfarnessemen who should have come after their lord were late: Lanfarnesse was late again, and now it was their lord who worried and paced beside Umanon, until, past midnight, the two lords decided to go down to the bonfire, and called for heavy cloaks.

"I'll go with you, sir," Tristen said, having no more easy rest than Umanon, thinking that if he were outside the walls and away from the clamor of a living town, he might hear less noisy things, out across the land.

Crissand, too, who kept them company among the local nobles, said he would go, or even send out his household men searching for the missing.

"My men know the road," Pelumer said—temerity to suggest that the rangers of Lanfarnesse could not find Henas'amef. "They're delayed, is all. My folk don't press the weather if they see a hazard in it.

"They may well have stopped for the night," Pelumer added as they rode down through the town, cloaked and gloved and wrapped up snugly. The wind was gathering force again after sunset. Any surface exposed quickly turned white on the side facing the gale, and all of them were half-white by the time they passed the gate.

"Bridges won't support the heavy wagons," Umanon said, "and my men will have to ford at several places. That means a camp to dry out, with the wind like this. But if they're close, they'll press on, no matter the hour."

The place outside the walls had blossomed with tents over recent days, and most of the horses were moved out to shelter in the places provided for them, with warm, dry straw, so they were comfortable.

And there, just as they came down, came a last weary number of carts, in from the road.

"They're here!" Umanon said, knowing his own, and vastly relieved: indeed, the men were riding not the light horses they used for travel, but the heavy horses, whose great strength had brought them in.

So they were safe, and so the men from the garrison and the Amefin guard fell on the wagons to get the frozen canvas spread in proper places, and to get wood for warmth.

More, the tavern near the gate had prepared a hot meal on a standing order, and men went through the gates and out again, all on the town's hospitality, fed and fed well, with no need to rely on their own resources on this bitter cold night.

Everything was taking shape despite the snow, and men called to winter camp were surprised and relieved at the comfort they did have.

"We have everything in order," Cevulirn came to Tristen to say. "I'll spend the night with my men, and in good comfort, too. We've things to talk about, my lieutenant and I."

It was not all that easy. Men struggled with stiff canvas, stiffened ropes to unpack the wagons. Umanon's men elected to move the teams and to leave the wagons standing where they were until morning, and that proved a wise expedient, for the wind was increasing, carrying snow so thick it was difficult to keep the torches lit.

The bonfire alone shone through the veiling snow, a light grown wan and strange in the opening of the heavens.

Nature let loose, Tristen said to himself, hugging his cloak to him and wondering if indeed they would have all the snow they had been due. Gusts buffeted him, carried away a tent from cursing men, who simply let it go and caught it when it fetched up against another tent.

Things went well, but not without struggle. He rode Petelly disconsolately along the aisle, hooded against the fall, and told himself he should give up worrying and take Petelly up to his warm stable, having done all he could do, and the Imorim having come in.

He could do most by wishing for the weather to improve. He might prevail. He had done it once.

Yet he had not heard the Imorim until the last. He had failed with the weather.

Was that the way the new year and the Year of Years was setting the pattern, and had things gone as well as he had hoped on Midwinter Eve?

When he thought that, the gray space worried him with a sense of something amiss, nothing he could catch, only a trace, like a scent the wind might bring one moment and carry away the next. It was none of the men here, nothing like Cevulirn.

He was in the last aisle of Pelumer's camp, and about to enter Cevulirn's, when the notion came to him that someone was in the storm, strayed men, perhaps . . . perhaps some of Pelumer's men, or stragglers after the Imorim.

Then something brushed his shoulder and made him start, until it happened a second time and he knew it had been Owl.

"What do *you* want?" he asked the uncooperative bird. He suddenly realized that he was alone: his guards had helped at the wagons, and somehow now they and he had separated in the driving snow.

Now of a sudden Owl brushed past him and wheeled away, off toward a troubling sense of presence in the storm. *Follow. Follow me.*

In the world of Men that track led simply down the road, as it bore toward Levey. It was a road he knew, in the heart of his province, and it was the road down which Umanon's men would come. There might be stragglers.

But stragglers that Owl cared for?

He turned Petelly's head and followed.

No one knew he had gone. Uwen was at work in the farthest camp, and Crissand had gone to assist Cevulirn, and by now the snow came down so thick the surviving torches were faint, blurred stars, the bonfire a hazy sun.

Owl brushed his arm on another pass and raked right past Petelly's mane, startling the horse to a heart-stopping skip under him, a skid on a snowy ditchside, right off the road.

Yet here, remote from all the lives that occupied his attention in the camps, remote from the town and wrapped in snow-laden gusts and storm, he discovered a clear wisp of a presence, not one life, but two, or maybe three.

What was more, now at least one or two sought *him,* aware of him, and desperate, trying to come toward him. If they were Umanon's men, at least one had wizard-gift.

He rode Petelly up onto the road again and in that direction, still bearing toward Levey. Owl flew generally ahead of him, appearing at times out of a veil of snow, and gone as quickly, always in that direction. *Follow. Follow. Don't delay.*

By now, he thought, there might be a general search for him, and Uwen would be upset with Lusin and his guards, who would blame themselves for his straying.

But Owl was persuasive, and miraculous things had happened on this road, on which the old oak lay overthrown, and Auld Syes had met him.

It could not be Auld Syes using the gray space. It was a fearsome thought, for something about her and her daughter he had always been reluctant to challenge there.

Yet he went on. If danger was here, it was not the sort Uwen or Lusin could face, nor Crissand with a dozen men-at-arms behind him, and the presence he felt was faint and weary and fading, as if at any moment it would go out and leave him no guide at all in this snow-choked night.

"Hallo!" he called out, and searched the gray space, as well, trying to learn its nature.

But fainter and fainter the presence grew, no longer moving toward him. Whether the travelers had a horse, or whether they went afoot he had not been sure, but he often could tell whether creatures lived and moved in a place, a fox, a hare, a horse, or a man: he had no such sense tonight, only of himself and Petelly—not even of Owl. Such as a wish would help, he wished them to stay alive and not to sink down and become lost in the snow, for things were chancier and chancier, and he no longer trusted the gray space to tell him . . . only Owl, only Owl, moving against the obstinacy of the storm that did not want him to reach these lives. The weather fought him—had broken free of his will, poured snow and sleet and bitter ice, and now he fought it, and Owl fought it, and brave Petelly lowered his head and plodded as best he could, shaken by the gusts, wishing continually to turn back.

Came the third and the fourth hill, and a cold so great Petelly stumbled to his knees and he had to get off before Petelly could rise again. He stood with his arms about Petelly's ice-coated neck, wishing him health, wishing not to have harmed him by this mad venture, and Petelly all at once gave a great sigh and brought his head up, as if he had taken a second wind.

Mount he did not, however, for Petelly's sake. He led him, the reins wrapped securely in gloved fingers too stiff with ice to feel what they held, and he walked, and walked, until he saw a something like a rock in the middle of the road, a lump that should not be there.

He reached it, and prodded it, and it Unfolded into a cloaked, exhausted woman, and another, in her arms.

"Lord!" she breathed, and clung to him as he helped her up. "My sister . . . my sister. Help us."

Even in the dark and the driving snow he knew that voice and that shadowed face, knew it from his earliest meetings in the world of Men. Lady Orien clasped his arms in entreaty, the thick snow gathering apace to the side of her hooded cloak and her face, and he bent to help her fallen sister, who lay huddled in the snow, limp and difficult to rouse. "Come now," he said, and laid his hands on Lady Tarien, and wished her to wake.

But he did not wish alone. Orien lent her efforts, laid her hands on his, and the gray space shivered around them. Then the limpness became shivering, and Tarien half waked.

"They burned the nunnery," Orien said between chattering teeth, the snow battering their faces. "They would have killed us. We had no choice but flee. And my sister, my sister . . . we couldn't walk any farther."

"We'll put her on my horse," he said, and gathered Tarien up to her feet, feeling the thickness of her body as he held her. It was not at all the lithe, lissome Tarien he knew.

"She's with child," Orien said as he half carried her. "Be careful of her."

He stopped, looked at her, dismayed at what he heard, dismayed that Owl had betrayed him, and led him here, to this unwelcome presence. Yet what could he do but leave them to die here, and nowhere had he learned to be that heartless.

Half-fainting, Tarien tried to grasp the saddle leather herself. He lifted her as high as he could, and willed Petelly to stand still while with some difficulty and Orien's help with Tarien's skirts and cloak he managed to settle Tarien upright on Petelly's back.

"He'll warm you," he said, and settled the cloak over her and Petelly together, about her legs. He reached up, caught its edges, and closed her half-senseless fingers on it. "Keep hold of it. It's not far to Henas'amef, and the wind will be at our backs, now. It's not that far to shelter."

"We were nearly there," Orien said.

And Owl had led him.

Orien faltered in the high snow, her boots snow-caked and inadequate, but Petelly had enough to do with one. They walked, and Tarien rode. Orien leaned against him at times, seeking to shore up her strength through wizardry as she must have done for more than one night on this road—not a good heart, but brave, and now failing. With trepidation he lent her what she must have to walk, not at all pleased with the rescue, and strengthened that much, she began to speak in broken phrases of fire and sword, of their walking day and night.

"Where was this?" he asked, and learned from Orien's labored speech of an attack on Teranthine nuns, of the two of them hunted through the night as the nunnery burned.

"We had a horse," Orien said. "But he ran last night. The snow came, and the weather grew worse and worse—we slept in a farmer's haystack, and never found the house. We walked, and walked . . . and then we heard you, where we had all but given up."

Winter had raged from the time they must have left their exile. It had chased them with a vengeance.

But the storm wind had seemed to lessen from the very moment he had found them in the snow, as if wizardry or outraged nature had spent its strength and now gave up the battle. The clouds broke and scudded past until, under a heaven as black and calm as the land was white, they topped that last hill before the town.

There the night showed them stars on the earth, the watch fires of camps around the snow-besieged walls of Henas'amef.

"An army?" Orien asked in dismay. "An army, about my town?"

"My army," Tristen said in that moment's pause, and added: "My town. My province."

He began to walk again, leading Petelly, with Orien at his side.

Owl flew ahead of them, on broad, silent wings.

LEXICON

Concordance for the Fortress Books

YLESUIN

AMEFEL—*southern province; banner: black Eagle on red field*

Royalty / Lords
  Aswydd Household
    Heryn Aswydd—Duke of Amefel, the aetheling
      His twin sisters:
        Orien Aswydd—Duchess of Amefel
        Tarien Aswydd—secondborn
          Thewydd—Heryn Aswydd's man
  Tristen's Household
    Tristen—Marshal of Althalen, Lord Warden of
      Ynefel
    Uwen—Lewen's-son, Tristen's man, sergeant of
      Cefwyn's Dragon Guard, captain of Tristen's
      guard
  Tristen's Guard
    Lusin—Captain of Tristen's bodyguard
    Syllan—one of Tristen's guards
    Aran—one of Tristen's guards
    Tawwys—one of Tristen's guards
    Aswys—groom
      Cassam, Cass—Uwen's warhorse, bow-nosed,
      blue roan gelding
      Dys, Dysarys—Tristen's warhorse, black, full
      brother to Aryny and Kanwy

Gery—Tristen's light horse, red mare
Gia—Uwen's light horse, bay mare
Liss—Uwen's horse, chestnut mare
Petelly—Tristen's cross-country horse, a bay of no
   breeding

Amefin Earls and Their Households

Edwyll Adiran—earl of Meiden, remotely related to
   Aswydds; banner: gold Sun
Crissand Adiran—son of and successor to Edwyll
Azant—lord of Dor Elen province, which borders the
   orchard district
   A daughter: widowed twice, once when married
      only seven days
Brestandin—Amefin earl
Cedrig—elderly Amefin earl living in retirement,
   owner of room Tristen lodges in, then where
   Ninévrisë lodges in Henas'amef
Civas—Amefin earl
Cuthan—earl of Bryn, distant relative of Aswydds
Drumman—lord of Barardden, youngest of earls
   except for Crissand; his elder sister is Edwyll's
   wife, Crissand's mother
Drusallyn—elderly lord, married local gentry in
   Amefel
Drusenan—earl of Bryn, successor to Cuthan; wife:
   Ÿnesyne, an Elwynim
Durell—Amefin earl
Edracht—Amefin earl
Esrydd—Amefin earl
Lund—Amefin earl
Marmaschen—Amefin earl
Moridedd—Amefin earl
Murras—Amefin earl
Prushan—Amefin earl
Purell—Amefin earl
Taras—earl of Bru Marden

Zereshadd—Amefin earl

Other Persons

Clergy / Clerics

Cadell—Bryaltine abbot in Henas'amef
Faiseth—Bryaltine nun
Emuin Udaman—wizard/tutor/priest, Teranthine, tutored Cefwyn and Efanor
Del'rezan—Bryaltine nun
Pachyll—priest, Teranthine patriarch in Henas'amef

Military

Cossun—armorer
Ennyn—Guelen Guard second in command
Gedd—sergeant in Tristen's guard
    Aman—gate-guard
    Nedras—gate-guard
    Ness—gate-guard
    Selmwy—cousin of Ness at town gate
Wynedd—Guelen Guard commander

Minor Officials

Tassand—started as Cefwyn's servant, now Tristen's chief of household
Haman—stablemaster at Henas'amef

Local Gentry

Ardwys—thane of Sagany, leader of the peasant contingent from Sagany and Pacewys

Miscellaneous

Auld Syes—witch, in Emwy village, near Althalen
Paisi—street urchin
Seddiwy—Shadow, Auld Syes' child
Wydnin—former junior archivist

Titles, Places, et cetra

Aetheling—title, used instead of king in Amefel; royal in their province
Althalen—old Sihhë capital, where last of Sihhë died,

now Tristen's, in ruins. Banner: argent Star and Tower on black field

Amefin—of Amefel province

Anas Mallorn—Amefin village, on riverside

Ardenbrook—brook after Maudbrook on way to Henas'amef

Arreyburn—camping spot of Emuin on the way back to Henas'amef from retreat

Averyne crossing—crossing to Guelessar from Amefel on the way out of Henas'amef

Arys—district/town, Arys Emwy, Emwy village: destroyed when Ináreddrin was killed; district contains Althalen and Lewen field

Arys bridge—bridge near Emwy to west, where Elwynim rebels could enter Amefel

Arys district—near Henas'amef, contains villages of Emwy and Malitarin

Asfiad—old name for Aswyth

Asmaddion—place in the province

Assurn Ford—river border of the province

Assurnbrook—river

Aswydd, Aswydds—surname, Heryn's house, also Orien's, Tarien's; there is Sihhë blood in this line

Aswyddim—of the Aswydds

Aswyth—a village

Athel—Amefin district bordering Meiden's land

Baraddan—Drumman's district, contains orchards

Bru Mardan—Taras district

Bryn—Cuthan's estate

Ceyl, Trys—Trys Ceyl—Amefin village south of Henas'amef

Dor Elen—Anzant's district, orchard district

Drun, Trys Drun—next to Trys Ceyl, village south of Henas'amef

ealdorman, ealdormen—council of Henas'amef

Edlinnadd—old name for Ellinan

Ellinan—a village

Emwy—village/district, see: Arys, Arys Emwy, Emwy village

Emwysbrook—brook near Emwy

Forest of Amefel—near Althalen

Grayfrock, grayrobe—nickname for Emuin

Hawwyvale—village

Hen Amas—old name for Henas'amef

Henas'amef—capital of the province

Kathseide—old name of Zeide, fortress in Henas'amef

Levey—Amefin village, part orchard, part pasturage for flocks

Lewen—brook giving its name to area of battle

Lewen field, Lewen plain—near Althalen, battlefield where Hasufin was destroyed

Lewenbrook—brook

Lewenford—area of battle, see Lewen field

Lewenside—area of battle, see Lewen field

Lysalin—Amefin village

Maldy village—Amefin village with crossing to Elwynor

Malitarin—Amefin village two hours from Henas'amef

Mallorn, Anas, Anas Mallorn—Amefin village on riverside

Margreis—ruined village, haunt of outlaws, near Emwy

Marna, Marna Wood—haunted forest

Marshal of Althalen—Tristen's title, bestowed by Cefwyn

Massitbrook—camping spot on way to Lewen field for Cefwyn and troops

Master grayrobe, grayfrock—nickname, refers to

Emuin, wizard/tutor/priest, Teranthine
Maudbrook—on the way to Henas'amef
Maudbrook Bridge—bridge on the way to
    Henas'amef
Meiden—sheep district; banner: blue with gold Sun
Pacewys—Amefin village, sent troops to Lewen field,
    commanded by Lord Ardwys, thane of Sagany
Padys Spring—one hour south of Henas'amef, once
    called Bathurys
Ragisar—Amefin village
Raven's Knob—past Emwy on way to Lewen field,
    Lewenbrook near Althalen
Sagany—Amefin village on way to Althalen and
    Lewen field, sent troop to Lewen field
    commanded by Lord Ardwys, thane of Sagany
Sagany Road—on way to Althalen and Lewen field
Tas Aden—town in Meiden
Trys, Trys Ceyl—Amefin town near Trys Drun
Zeide—shortened name for Kathseide fortress in
    Henas'amef

CARYS—northern province

GUELESSAR—north-central province;
banner: quartered, gold Dragon on red,
gold Quinalt sigil on black

Royalty
Selwyn Marhanen—Cefwyn's grandfather, king of
    Ylesuin; banner: gold Dragon on red
Ináreddrin Marhanen—king of Ylesuin, father of
    Cefwyn and Efanor
Cefwyn Marhanen—third king of the Marhanen

dynasty, brother of Efanor

Idrys—Lord Commander of the Dragon Guard

Annas—Cefwyn's chief of household in both Amefel and Guelessar. Later Lord Chamberlain

Lasien—senior page at Henas'amef

Efanor Marhanen—His Royal Highness, Duke of Guelessar, Prince of Ylesuin

Gwywyn—soldier, Ináreddrin's captain at Althalen, made captain of Efanor's guard at Guelemara

Royal Household

Alwy—Ninévrisë's maid and one of Cefwyn's former lovers

Brysaulin—Lord Chancellor after Cefwyn is crowned

Cressen—Lady, one of Cefwyn's former lovers

Fisylle—Lady, one of Cefwyn's former lovers

Trallynde—Lady, one of Cefwyn's former lovers

Parsynan—Guelen gentry, Cefwyn's viceroy at Amefel until Tristen's appointment as lord of Amefel

Horses

Aryny—heavy, warhorse, full sister to Dys and Kanwy

Danvy—Cefwyn's light horse

Drugyn—Idrys' warhorse, black stablemate of Cass, Kanwy, and Dys

Kanwy—Cefwyn's warhorse, black

Synanna—blaze-faced black, usually Efanor's horse

Clergy/Clerics

Patriarch—priest, absolute head of Quinalt sect

Jormys—Quinaltine priest, serves Efanor

Benwyn—Bryalt sect, assigned as Ninévrisë's priest

Buren—Quinaltine doctrinist

Neiswyn—doctrinist among the Quinaltines
Udryn—Quinaltine doctrinist

Military
Anwyll—captain of the guard, assigned to Amefel
under Uwen
Kerdin Qwyll's-son—Kerdin, second-in-command
under Idrys, captain of Guelen Guard, died at
Lewen field
Essan—captain of Guelen Guard in Guelessar
Andas—soldier, eleven years in Dragon Guard,
Andas' son, Tristen's banner-bearer, was killed
at Lewen field
Brogi—soldier
Brys—soldier, in Anwyll's company
Cossell—soldier in Anwyll's company
Hawith—soldier, killed at Emwy, one of Cefwyn's
men
Jeony—soldier, killed at Emwy
Lefhwyn—soldier, rode with Cefwyn at Emwy
Nydas—soldier, rode with Cefwyn at Emwy
Pelanny—soldier, Guelen scout, presumed dead or
taken by Aseynéddin at Lewen field
Peygan—armorer for Cefwyn at Henas'amef, old
friend of Uwen's, married to Margolis
Pryas—king Cefwyn's messenger

Minor Officials / Household
Margolis—wife of Peygan the armorer. One of
Ninévrisë's ladies
Mesinis—slightly deaf clerk
Tamurin—Cefwyn's accountant

Other Persons
Rosyn—Cefwyn's tailor in both Henas'amef and
Guelemara

Places, Titles, et cetera

Amynys—river, old boundary of Guelemara

An's-ford—town, on road between Guelemara and Henas'amef

Anwyfar—Teranthine retreat near Arreyburn

Blue Hall—place, in Guelemara, in palace

Clusyn, Clusyn monastery—Quinaltine religious house in Guelessar

Cressitbrook—town near Guelemara

Crown Wall—Guelenfort's official limit

Dary—Guelen village at first ring road outside Guelemara

Drysham—Guelen village

Dury—Guelen village

Guelen—of Guelessar

Guelenfolk—people of Guelessar

Guelenish—of Guelessar

Guelenmen—people of Guelessar

Guelesfort—citadel in Guelemara

Guelemara—capital of Guelessar; banner: red with gold Castle

His Highness—Efanor

Holy Father, His Holiness—title, highest Patriarch in Quinalt sect

Lyn—soldier, messenger sent from Tristen to Idrys with Ryssand's treasonous letter

Marhanen—surname, Cefwyn's house banner: gold Dragon. Surname of Cefwyn, Selwyn, Efanor, Ináreddrin

Master crow, raven—nickname, refers to Idrys

Red Chronicle—Marhanen history book

"The Merry Lass from Eldermay"—country song played at Cefwyn's harvesttide festival

Wys—any of a series of villages

Wys-on-Cressit—a village in Ylesuin

Wys-on-Wyetlan—Guelen village

IMOR—*southern province;*
banner: Wheel

Ruler
Umanon—lord of Imor Lenúalim, Quinaltine

Places, Titles, et cetera
Hedyrin—river south of Imor
Imorim—of Imor

ISIN—*northern province*

IVANOR—*southern province;*
banner: white Horse

Ruler
Cevulirn—lord of Ivanor, southern baron,
    Teranthine
Geisleyn—Cevulirn's man, captain of light horse,
    from Toj Embrel, Ivanim
Erion Netha—friend of Cevulirn, Lord of Tas
    Arin in Ivanor, wounded at Lewen field

Places, Titles, et cetera
Crysin—horse breed of Ivanim
Embrel, Toj—Toj Embrel, Cevulirn's summer palace
Ivanim—of Ivanor
Ivor—district
Ivorim—of Ivor
Tas Arin—town
Toj Embrel—Toj Embrel, Cevulirn's summer palace

LANFARNESSE—southern province;
banner: Heron

Ruler
Pelumer—duke of Lanfarnesse
Feleyn, Feleyn's—a Lanfarnesseman

Places, Titles, et cetera
Lanfarnesseman—people of Lanfarnesse

LLYMARIN—central province;
banner: Red Rose on green background

Ruler
Sulriggan—lord of Llymarin, cousin to the Quinaltine Patriarch
Edwyn—nephew of Sulriggan, attends Efanor

Places, Titles, et cetera
Llymarish—of Llymarin

MARISAL—southern province;
banner: gold Sheaf with bend and crescent

Ruler
Sarmysar—duke of Marisal; personal banner: Lily

MARISYN—southern province;
banner: blue Field and blazing Sun

MURANDYS—*northern province;*
banner: blue Field, bend or, and white below
with Quinalt sigil

The Nobles
> Prichwarrin—duke of Murandys,
>> Cleisynde—Lord Prichwarrin of Murandys' niece
>> Luriel—Cefwyn's most recent lover, niece of Duke
>> Prichwarrin of Murandys
>> Odrinian—younger sister of Luriel, Duke
>> Prichwarrin of Murandys' niece

Other Persons
> Romynd—Quinalt patriarch of Murandys

Places, Titles, et cetera
> Aslaney—capital of Murandys

NELEFREISSAN—*northern province;*
banner: pale azure with white Circle

Places, Titles, et cetera
> Nelefreimen—men of Nelefreíssan

OLMERN—*southern province;*
banner: black Wolf

Ruler
> Sovrag—lord of Olmern (rivermen), in Olmernhome
>> Brigoth—Lieutenant of Sovrag of Olmern
>> Denyn—Cefwyn's door guard, Olmern youth,
>> Kei's-son

Places, Titles, et cetera
> Capayneth—Olmern village, traded with Mauryl

Olmernhome—Sovrag's capital
Olmernman—person of Sovrag's province

OSANAN—*eastern province*

Ruler
Mordam—duke of Osanan

PALYS—*north-central province*

Places, Titles, et cetera
Wys-in-Palys-under-Grostan—a village

PANYS—*northern province*

Ruler
Maudyn—lord of Panys, commander of Cefwyn's
forces on the riverside
Rusyn, Lord Maudyn's second son

Other Persons
Uta Uta's-son—squire of Magan village

Places, Titles, et cetera
Magan—village

RYSSAND—*northern province;*
banner: blood red with Fist and Sword

Ruler
Corsywndam—lord of Ryssand

Brugan—Corsywndam of Ryssand's son and heir
Artisane—Corsywndam of Ryssand's daughter,
one of Ninévrisë's ladies-in-waiting

Places, Titles, et cetera

Ryssandish—of Ryssand; also, an ethnic group
distinct from the Guelens, but closely tied to
them

SUMAS—*eastern province*

TEYMERYN—*northeastern province*

URSAMIN—*northeastern province*

ELWYNOR

The Regency

Uleman Syrillas—Regent of Elwynor, father of
Ninévrisë
Ninévrisë Syrillas—daughter of Uleman

Lesser Nobles

Aeself—lieutenant of loyal force
Angin—companion of Aeself, q.v.
Elfharyn—Elwynim lord, loyal to Ninévrisë, holding
throne and regency for her
Haurydd—Ninévrisë's man, earl of High Saissond
Palisan—one of Ninévrisë's men

Tasien—earl of Cassissan, Uleman's man, captain of his army, related to Ninévrisë through her mother

Ysdan—Ninévrisë's man, earl of Ormadzaran

Aseynéddin—rebel earl of Elwynor, enemy of Ninévrisë, died at Lewen field; banner: Griffin

Caswyddian—rebel Elwynim lord, earl of Lower Saissond, enemy of Ninévrisë, killed by Shadows at Althalen

Tasmôrden—Elwynim rebel lord, enemy of Ninévrisë

Üillasan—companion of Aeself

Places, Titles, et cetera

Ansym—bridge, at border of Elwynor

Ashiym—place in Elwynor, seven towers, old Sihhë connections, one tower destroyed

Banner of Elwynor—black-and-white Checker with gold Tower, quartered with blue

Casissan—Tasien's earldom

Criess—village near Ilefínian

Elwynim—of the kingdom of Elwynor

Her Grace—title for Ninévrisë

High Saissond—Elwynim province, Haurydd's home

Ilefínian—capital of Elwynor

Lower Saisonnd—lord Caswyddian's province

Melseriedd—old name for kingdom of Elwynor, prior to Regency

Nithen—district and hamlet near Ilefínian

Ormadzaran—Ysdan's earldom

Saendel—bandits who served Aseynéddin at Lewen field

Syrillas—surname, Uleman Syrillas, regent of Elwynor, Ninévrisë Syrillas

Syrim—bridge at border of Elwynor

GALASIEN

Persons

    Hasufin Heltain—wizard, possibly a prince of
        Galasien, enemy of Mauryl

    Mauryl Gestaurien—wizard, Galasieni

Places, Titles, et cetera

    Galasieni—a lost race

    Kingsbane—nickname of Mauryl

    Kingmaker—nickname of Mauryl

    Nineteen Gods—the unnamed hidden gods wor
        shiped by wizards

    Silver Tower—at Ynefel, Mauryl's symbol, then
        Tristen's: black banner with silver Tower and
        Star

    Ynefel—Mauryl's tower: silver Tower

OTHER LANDS

    Arachim—northern tribe

    Chomaggari—southern barbarians

    Casmyndan, Casmyndanim—far southern tribe on
        the coast

    Lyra—a hill tribe

    Lyrdish—belonging to Lyra

SIHHË / SIHHË CONNECTIONS

Persons

Barrakkêth—one of five Sihhë-lords

Elfwyn—last Sihhë king, a halfling

Harosyn—Sihhë king

Sadyurnan—Sihhë king (ancient) in Hen Amas

Sarynan—Sihhë king

Ashyel—Sihhë halfling, son of Barrakkêth

Tashânen—Sihhë halfling, engineer and strategist, wrote *The Art of War*

Aswyn—Sihhë halfing, youngest brother of Elfwyn, thought stillborn, body inhabited by Hasufin

Places, Titles, et cetera

Arachis—old name, Sihhë connections

Aryceillan—old name, (possibly old tribe with Sihhë connections)

Deathmaker—nickname for Barrakkêth

Hafsandyr—mountains in north, original home of Sihhë

Kingbreaker—nickname for Barrakkêth

Sihhë, Sihhë's—lost race. Five Sihhë came down from north to rule in Ylesuin and Elwynor

OTHER

Bryalt—religious sect of Ylesuin, mostly Amefin

Bryaltine—of the Bryalts' faith

Bryssandin—horse breed, used in breeding Crysin horses

Far Sassury—proverb: "the back of beyond"

Five Gods—the unnamed gods worshiped by the people of Ylesuin

Ilenéluin—mountain range

Jorysal—a place, an old name in histories

Lenúalim—a river, major border between Elwynor and Ylesuin

Manystys Aldun—philosopher, wrote tome on oceans

Marchlanders—refers to the southern lords and their armies, excluding Amefel

Merhas—truth, carved on one side of Tristen's sword

Quinalt—a strict religious sect

Quinaltine—of the Quinalt

Shadow Hills—area north of Ryssand

Shaping—a creature or person called into being and shaped into flesh by a wizard

Spestinan—horse breed

Stellyrhas—illusion, carved on one side of Tristen's sword

Teranthine—moderate religious sect